A Gathering of Eagles

A Novel of Rome and Parthia

LEWIS F. McINTYRE

Copyright © 2023 by Lewis F. McIntyre
Cover artwork by Fiona Jayde Media

All rights reserved. No part of this book may be reproduced or transmitted in any form or by any means, electronic or mechanical, including photocopying, recording, or by any information storage and retrieval system, without permission from the Publisher

>   Lew & Karen McIntyre, Authors, LLC
>   11891 Knollcrest Ln
>   La Plata, MD 20646

Library of Congress Control Number: 2023916336
Lewis F. McIntyre, La Plata, MARYLAND

Tags: Ancient History, Ancient Warfare, Rome, China, Parthia, Mesopotamia, Christianity, Judaism, Silk Road
ISBN-13: 978-1733143295

DEDICATION AND ACKNOWLEDGMENTS

This book is dedicated to my wife Karen, who has steadfastly supported this effort for twenty years. She has been tireless as a source for new ideas, a fearless editor and critic, without whom this book would never have been completed.

I wish to acknowledge the many people who helped me through this long effort, my very professional editor Hildie Block, my cover designer Fiona Jayde, and Gary Knight, George Galdorisi, Cap Parlier, Allan Rypka and Bill Coyne.

Table of Contents

CHAPTER 1: THE FUNERAL 2
CHAPTER 2: THE WEDDING 6
CHAPTER 3: HOMECOMING SURPRISE 13
CHAPTER 4: THE KILLING SPOTS 16
CHAPTER 5: A PLAN FOR WAR 24
CHAPTER 6: SON OF THE FATHER 31
CHAPTER 7: A FOUL PLAN 34
CHAPTER 8: A BAND OF RAGAMUFFINS 42
CHAPTER 9: A SMUGGLER'S STASH 46
CHAPTER 10: THE CARAVANSERY AT TURFAM 50
CHAPTER 11: OUTCASTS REJECTED 55
CHAPTER 12: INTERVENTION 59
CHAPTER 13: OUTCASTS ACCEPTED 63
CHAPTER 14: CONSPIRACIES 68
CHAPTER 15: TALK OF WAR, TALK OF PEACE 74
CHAPTER 16: TENGRI'S SIGN 78
CHAPTER 17: TENGRI'S PATH 81
CHAPTER 18: A COMMON LANGUAGE 86
CHAPTER 19: A CHILD IS BORN 91
CHAPTER 20: A FATHER AND HIS SON 96
CHAPTER 21: A DEATH IN THE FAMILY 101
CHAPTER 22: ALEXANDRIA-THE-FARTHEST 106
CHAPTER 23: JUST ANOTHER DEAD SLAVE 112
CHAPTER 24: NEW LOVERS 120
CHAPTER 25: THE GHOST COHORT 124
CHAPTER 26: A SUSPECT CAUGHT 126
CHAPTER 27: AN OPERATION GONE WRONG 132
CHAPTER 28: A KING DEPOSED 134
CHAPTER 29: GALOSGA'S STORY 137
CHAPTER 30: CAPTURED 140
CHAPTER 31: A VISITOR IN THE NIGHT 144
CHAPTER 32: THE EMPEROR'S RIGHT-HAND MAN 146
CHAPTER 33: THE PALACE AT ECBATANA 148
CHAPTER 34: UNACCUSTOMED LUXURY 153
CHAPTER 35: PREPARING TO MEET THE SHAH 156
CHAPTER 36: A MEETING IN ATHENS 158
CHAPTER 37: A GRAIN OF SAND FOUND 164
CHAPTER 38: THE CAPRICORN REBORN 166
CHAPTER 39: WAITING IN AQUILEIA 170
CHAPTER 40: TRAJAN IN ANTIOCH 172
CHAPTER 41: KEEPING ONE'S HEAD 177
CHAPTER 42: THE HORSE RACE 180
CHAPTER 43: A PLAN FOR REVENGE 187
CHAPTER 44: A WALK IN THE GARDEN 190
CHAPTER 45: THE ROAD TO CTESIPHON 192

CHAPTER 46:	THE FOLLOWERS	195
CHAPTER 47:	AN OFFER DECLINED	198
CHAPTER 48:	THE WAR BEGINS	200
CHAPTER 49:	THE PALACE AT CTESIPHON	204
CHAPTER 50:	A SECRET WORD	209
CHAPTER 51:	THE SPARRING MATCH	211
CHAPTER 52:	A BLOODLESS VICTORY	214
CHAPTER 53:	A SOLDIER REBORN	220
CHAPTER 54:	FRIENDS IN HIGH PLACES	226
CHAPTER 55:	A SNAKE IN THE HOUSE	229
CHAPTER 56:	A CROWN IN THE DIRT	233
CHAPTER 57:	BATTLE ORDERS	239
CHAPTER 58:	FRIENDS IN PRISON	244
CHAPTER 59:	AMBUSHED	248
CHAPTER 60:	THE PALACE AND THE PALM TREE	251
CHAPTER 61:	A NEW SPY	255
CHAPTER 62:	PLANNING THE SEIGE	257
CHAPTER 63:	MAKING ENDS MEET	259
CHAPTER 64:	THE NORTHERN ROUTE	263
CHAPTER 65:	IN ROMAN HANDS	265
CHAPTER 66:	REUNION	270
CHAPTER 67:	A NEW SET OF CARDS TO PLAY	275
HAPTER 68:	THE WINTER CAMPAIGN	277
CHAPTER 69:	A LIFE-LONG FRIEND	282
CHAPTER 70:	AWAKENING TO CONFUSION	288
CHAPTER 71:	AWAKENING TO A NIGHTMARE	291
CHAPTER 72:	UNDER DURESS	294
CHAPTER 73:	BAD NEWS	299
CHAPTER 74:	FROM ONE HAND TO ANOTHER	303
CHAPTER 75:	CAUSE FOR WAR	305
CHAPTER 76:	ANOTHER SNAKE RETURNS	307
CHAPTER 77:	SLAVES AND YET NOT SLAVES	311
CHAPTER 78:	MARCHING OFF TO WAR	313
CHAPTER 79:	A PAIR OF PLAYING CARDS	317
CHAPTER 80:	INFLEXIBLE PLAYING CARDS	321
CHAPTER 81:	AN AGENT NAMED TAURUS	326
CHAPTER 82:	LEGIONS ON THE ROLL	330
CHAPTER 83:	A GATHERING OF FRIENDS	336
CHAPTER 84:	A DIFFERENT KIND OF WAR	341
CHAPTER 85:	A DEAD BENEFACTOR	347
CHAPTER 86:	UNRAVELING THE SCROLLS	350
CHAPTER 87:	WORD FROM TAURUS	353
CHAPTER 88:	INSURRECTION	357
CHAPTER 89:	DISTRACTION	361
CHAPTER 90:	ESCAPE	363
CHAPTER 91:	THE ONLY WAY OUT	368
CHAPTER 92:	ON THE ROAD	371

CHAPTER 93: PLAYING CARDS LOST 375
CHAPTER 94: DURA EUROPOS 377
CHAPTER 95: REUNITED 381
CHAPTER 96: TOGETHER AGAIN 384
CHAPTER 97: GARRISON UNDONE 389
CHAPTER 98: BETRAYAL 394
CHAPTER 99: RESCUE TOO LATE 398
CHAPTER 100: JUST IN TIME 401
CHAPTER 101: RELUCTANT LEADER 405
CHAPTER 102: A PLAN FORMS 409
CHAPTER 103: PLAN FOR REVENGE 412
CHAPTER 104: REVENGE TAKEN 414
CHAPTER 105: A CITY RETAKEN 417
CHAPTER 106: INSURRECTION SPREADS 419
CHAPTER 107: UPRISING 424
CHAPTER 108: COHORT ON THE MOVE 427
CHAPTER 109: RENEWING FRIENDSHIPS 430
CHAPTER 110: THE EARTH MOVES 433
CHAPTER 111: AFTERMATH 437
CHAPTER 112: ARRIVAL 441
CHAPTER 113: THE POINT OF THE SPEAR 447
CHAPTER 114: REINFORCEMENTS 452
CHAPTER 115: TENDING THE WOUNDED 456
CHAPTER 116: A GRAND GATHERING 458
CHAPTER 117: A CITY IN RECOVERY 462
CHAPTER 118: SEDUCTION 466
CHAPTER 119: MISCALCULATION 470
CHAPTER 120: CROSSING THE TIGRIS 472
CHAPTER 121: THE RATPACK RETURNS 476
CHAPTER 122: AWARDS 480
CHAPTER 123: A DECISION TO GO HOME 484
CHAPTER 124: BARBARIANS IN THE PALACE 486
CHAPTER 125: NIGHT TALK 492
CHAPTER 126: FIRST TIME TO SEA 494
CHAPTER 127: THE FINAL PUSH 499
CHAPTER 128: EVACUATION 502
CHAPTER 129: LANDFALL IN ITALY 505
CHAPTER 130: A MOST SERIOUS UPRISING 510
CHAPTER 131: AN UNRESISTING FOE 514
CHAPTER 132: TRAJAN AND THE PRINCESS 525
CHAPTER 133: ALEXANDRIA BURNING 529
CHAPTER 134: RETURN TO AQUILEIA 532
CHAPTER 135: TRAJAN'S VICTORY TOUR 534
CHAPTER 136: HADRIAN'S ALARM 538
CHAPTER 137: TRAJAN AT CHARAX 541
CHAPTER 138: TRAJAN TO HATRA 545
CHAPTER 139: TRAJAN ILL, HEADING HOME 547

CHAPTER 140: DEATH AND SUCCESSION CRISIS 549
CHAPTER 141: THE IMPERIAL FUNERAL 551
CHAPTER 142: LEAVING WITHOUT FAREWELL 553
CHAPTER 143: ADOPTION 557
CHAPTER 144: A WINTER WIND 562
CHAPTER 145: DEATH OF A SON 567
CHAPTER 146: ONE STAYS BEHIND 569
CHAPTER 147: AN UNWANTED SURPRISE 572
CHAPTER 148: THE NEW PRINCEPS 576
CHAPTER 149: HOME AT LAST 580

Roman-Parthian Borders @110AD, Legionary Force Deployments

CHAPTER 1:

THE FUNERAL

Liqian, China: October 111AD

The townspeople shoved smoky torches into the stacked wood, which quickly caught with a snapping crackle. From a safe distance, the spectators watched the fire build, holding their robes about them against the chill fall morning as the grey smoke was torn to tatters by the wind. With a roar, the fire blossomed, fed by the wind, reaching the bundle on top. Smoke began to percolate through the linen-wrapped bundle as it caught. Then the fire concealed its business, reducing that object to a barely perceived dark shape inside a torrent of flames.

Mei grasped Marcus' hand as he watched the ceremony impassively. A thick cloud of black smoke, dipping and swirling in the wind, indicated the flames were doing their duty, consuming the package. There was the pungent smell of cooking meat in the air.

By late afternoon, it was done, and the pyre began to collapse into itself in a shower of scattering sparks. The townspeople had gradually turned away one by one, to return to their homes and shops, their duty to one of their own completed. Marcus and Mei remained, alone now, with just a few fire tenders remaining to ensure that the flames did not spread out of control on this windy October day.

After a few hours, the embers had cooled enough that Marcus could collect his mother's ashes, putting them into a vase. How was it that someone so vital, such an important part of his life, could be reduced to a few handfuls of ash and lumps of charred bone? He savored each handful as he put them into the urn to preserve them. What was it they said? *Non fui, non sum, non curo* … I was not, I am not, I no longer care. No, she had very much existed, and cared, and for him would exist in his life forever. And somewhere, somehow, she still cared.

His hands, now black with ash, and with more than a few blisters from hot coals, scoured up one last handful, then sealed the urn, Vera's new home.

The fire tenders, assisting him, stood silently around. One of the men put his hand on Marcus' shoulder, soiling his toga a bit. "She was a good woman," he said in *han-yu*.

Marcus nodded. "She was. She will be missed." He turned abruptly to head home, holding Mei's hands. *Can't they at least speak Latin at a Roman funeral?*

They reached their home after a half-hour's walk, set back among the pines on a steep hill. They entered in, and Marcus set the urn gently on the table, then took a seat in the rocker, the rocker that had been his father's, and now was his. The house was strangely silent, brooding, dark. He sat quietly, rocking, thinking. *Ave, pater, you two are together again,* he said under his breath, hoping his father's *manes* spirit might answer, or perhaps his mother's. But there was just silence.

Mei busied herself quietly about the cooking stove. After a while, she brought herself to ask a question. "Would you like something to eat? Some wine, perhaps?" In *han-yu*. Mei had never mastered Latin well enough to be comfortable with more than few phrases.

"Some wine, please."

She brought a ceramic goblet to him, and left him alone, silent in his thoughts in the darkness.

After several hours, Marcus stirred himself from the rocker to set about lighting the fire, as the room had become quite chill. As he did so, Mei came out of the bedroom wrapped in a heavy robe.

"I thought you would never do that," she said, smiling shyly.

"It was getting cold," he said, rubbing his hands together as the flames caught, radiating heat into the room. But he did not smile.

"It was good she did not suffer," said Mei, struggling to engage him in conversation.

"Dying in one's sleep is good."

"She lived a full life, and she was full of joy that you were back in her life, and that your sister is well."

Marcus' black mood was resisting all efforts by Mei to cheer him. "At least Marcia was, the last we heard. More than a year ago."

"And we had news of our new niece."

Marcus' resistance gave way under Mei's persistence, and he managed a small smile. "Yes, we did. Little Aena. As close as she could get to Hina in Latin."

Marcus' solitary brooding lasted the full nine days of the *novendialis* mourning period. Mei allowed him his solitary times, bringing him wine and food when asked, politely asking questions as necessary. But she was puzzled. To be sure, Marcus and his mother had been close, but death came almost as a relief after the past few months. She had grown increasingly frail and forgetful, then came the morning when she woke up, unable to move or speak. They had spent the last several weeks tending for her, feeding her, combing her hair… and when the morning came and she no longer needed that, there was a sense of relief. That powerful woman, such a force, such a cause for joy in their lives, was finally at rest. So why was Marcus still mourning so?

At the end of the mourning period, Marcus took down the white banner over the door, and Mei and Marcus, bundled against the chill fall weather, interred the urn in the family grave in the fields outside of town, next to Marcus' father Marius. They returned to the house, and Mei, released from mourning, felt obligated to determine the reason for her husband's almost morbid silence. As he reached for the door to enter, she put her hand softly on his. "Let us sit on the porch, I think the snow will start soon."

Marcus grunted, taking a seat on the hand-hewn wooden bench, half a tree trunk split lengthwise. Mei sat next to him, waiting, hoping he would break his silence. Should she ask? No, he should speak when he is ready.

The first flakes of snow began to fly, the chill wind from the northern steppes swirling the last brown leaves of autumn to mingle with them. "It will be cold tonight," she said.

"It will." Then more introspective silence as he studied his hands.

"Si Nuo, enough!" Mei turned toward him, using his Hanaean name, 'Western Bull'. "The mourning period is over. Or are you to mourn the rest of your life?"

To her great relief, he smiled. "No, Mei, but I am concerned what to do with the rest of my life. To be sure, I will miss my mother, but that was not what occupied my thoughts."

"And what is that?" She snuggled closer, hoping to draw some warmth from his body, maybe even a physical response.

"Life here is not what I expected ten years ago. I have done my duty, I have cared for my mother. She is gone now, and I am free. But free to do what?"

"You could continue with the school. I thought you wanted to do that."

"Liqian is not the same as when I grew up. Then, there were still many families that wanted to preserve our *romanitas*, our language and our customs, to set ourselves apart from our neighbors. There is no interest in that now. There will be no school. And nothing to hold me here."

"Where would we go?"

"It is chill. Let's go inside."

He slammed the door behind him against the cold, and put another log onto the fireplace stoking it until it caught. He then lifted a tile from the floor and drew out a leather bag, black with age. It clinked metallically as he set it on the floor.

"I still have the gift from Ibrahim. We can go where we want."

"And where is that?" Mei asked, seating herself on the floor next to him.

"I would like to go west, to see Rome again, to find Marcia and Antonius and our nieces and nephews. But it will be a long, hard trip. It was hard the first time, with a large, well-armed group."

Mei sat in silence, pondering her reply, listening to the hiss of the fire, the patter of the snow outside. It might be a heavy storm, come early.

"Si Nuo, if that is what you want, then we should do it."

"Your friends are here."

"You are my best friend. If you wish to go, then let us depart."

"The house? And all that is in it?" Marcus surprised himself, trying to talk her out of her unexpected agreement.

"Frontinus' son will be married soon. We could make it a gift to him."

"We could. And it would keep it in our group of friends. But it will be a hard trip."

"Never, with you by my side." She twined her fingers in his, smiling, hoping to elicit a physical response.

She succeeded. Marcus put his hand on the back of her neck and kissed her long and softly. She explored his body, finding the response she sought.

An hour later, their passions sated, they lay in a bundle on their heavy coats which served as a temporary bed by the fire. Marcus caressed her bare shoulder, smiling. "I marvel each time we make love, Mei. That which I thought was taken from me forever, you gave back to me. I thank you each time for making me whole again."

"You were never not whole, Si Nuo. You are the most complete man I have ever known." Her fingers explored his scar. "Those did not make you a man." She smiled, giggled playfully and turned to tap his head. "That is your manhood, silly western bull!"

Marcus turned toward her, kissing her again, his mouth melting onto hers. It might be a long night. Outside, the wind rose. It was indeed going to be an early storm.

CHAPTER 2:

THE WEDDING

Liqian, China: April 112AD

The wedding feast of Frontinus' son Bolin with Chunhua, both resplendent in their black silk wedding robes trimmed in red, was a lavish Hanaean affair. The banquet tables, laden with fish, symbolizing plenty, were arrayed outside Bolin's new home, Marcus' old one. The spring weather cooperated, a brilliant warm day with flowers exploding all around, the cherry trees in white bloom, nearly all of Liqian in attendance.

Marcus and Frontinus evaded the crowd of well-wishers to chat quietly and drink the red wine that had made Liqian famous.

"Thank you so much for the house, Marcus," said Frontinus, addressing him in Latin. "A fine old house. Been in the Lucian family for generations."

"It goes back to the Settlement, when we first arrived here. The original Marcus Lucius built it when he married, so it has been here as long as we have. And will be here a lot longer."

"Bolin will care for it very well. We will be sorry to see you two go. Are you really going all the way to Rome?"

"Unless something stops us!" smiled Marcus. "I am looking forward to seeing the City again, and hopefully finding Marcia and Antonius. They went to a place called Aquileia, she said, a week's journey north of Rome. Their letters stopped coming last year, but I wrote her after *mater* died, to tell her we were coming."

"Amazing how your letters covered such a vast distance to find their destination. So, more traveling till you get there!" Frontinus refilled Marcus' cup from a white ceramic bottle. "Liqian may forget its *romanitas*, but it will never forget how to make good red wine. Drink up! To Bolin and Chunhua, may they give me many grandsons!"

"To your grandsons... and granddaughters, too, Frontinus. A man needs women around him to keep him honest."

"So, when are you leaving?"

"We wanted to stay for this, but everything else is ready. There is a caravan coming in tomorrow or the day after, some outriders just checked in. We will go with them as far as Turfam, then on from there. I don't know how to get 70 what cities, but the caravans all go out of there. Westbound is all I know."

Mei came up to join them, to stand quietly by Marcus' side. "So, Mei, Latin was never your favorite language. Are you looking forward to your new home?" asked Frontinus.

"I look forward to the adventure. I must speak better Latin, all Marcus lets me speak now, grammar very confusing me, still." She smiled shyly. "I have never been away from Liqian in my whole life."

"Your Latin is much improved, Mei. You speak very well. May *Fortuna* smile on you both." Frontinus levered himself onto a mostly empty table and addressed the crowd in a stentorian voice, switching to *han-yu*. "Guests, we have a second reason to celebrate today! As most of you know, my life-long friend, almost like a brother to me, Si Nuo, is leaving very soon with his wife Mei, for the far west, to return to the land of the *Da Qin*. Let us toast to the safe journey of Si Nuo and Mei."

The caravan arrived with a clangor of bells, creaking wagons, shouting men, nickering horses, braying goats, and the silent, implacable, smelly camels, pulling to a halt in the broad field next to the main road, the Hexi corridor from Chang'an running northwest to Turfam. The caravans always stopped overnight at the tiny village of Liqian, to purchase its claim to fame, the most delightful red wine in all of China, the only red wine in China. Four to six amphorae of wine, well-padded in fleece panniers, could be loaded on a single camel, or stacked in boxes in a wagon. And of course, the caravanners could purchase the hand-held sized bottles for quick consumption. The townspeople laid out their local crafts, clothing and tools for trade or barter, in exchange for far-away goods from inner China: bolts of silk, rice wine, artwork, and intricate tools. The arrival was always festive, and the night ended with a huge bonfire with much singing and drinking, some of the caravanners hoping to steal off into the darkness with one of the cute country girls.

Marcus wandered down to the organized chaos, and accosted one of the rough, bearded caravanners. "I am looking for the caravan master," he asked in *han-yu*, but got an annoyed, puzzled look in return. He finally located a man with Chinese features, with a long drooping mustache, and repeated his question. The man answered in a Shaanxi dialect. "*Sartpaw* there. Abmatak his name." He pointed out a burly man, with a wild black beard and cold blue eyes, wearing brown felt riding gear.

"Thank you. Where are you from?"

"Chang'an." He smiled. "My first trip."

"Does Abmatak speak *han-yu*?"

"A little."

"Thanks again." Marcus smiled and turned to seek out the caravan master.

Abmatak was studying some local articles when Marcus came up to him. "You are Abmatak, the *sartpaw*?"

Abmatak seemed annoyed at being bothered. He nodded, saying nothing.

"My wife and I want to go to Turfam."

Abmatak grunted, and took a sip of wine from his bottle, then spat, sizing him up. "Long trip, lots of work."

"Whatever you need."

"Women always problem."

"I will take care of her."

"Rough people on road. You good fighter?"

"Yes," answered Marcus. He was being a bit deceptive. Before leaving Liqian the first time, he had learned a little swordsmanship from his father. But then came that change in his life, and swords were forbidden to men of his ilk, though they were trained in Hanaean defensive fighting with hands and feet. Ten years ago, he had been trained by Antonius, so at one time he was as good as good can be, without ever having experienced a fight to the death. He had sparred regularly with Frontinus in Liqian over the years, and spent months preparing himself for this trip, practicing sword work on a post in the backyard, a suspended leather sack filled with sand, and an occasional goat or pig carcass. He was fit for his age, so yes, he was as good as he could be, without being an active fighter.

"You may have to be. One silver coin for you, two for the woman."

"The going rate is one for two people. I will give you two, no more."

"Two then, and you both work loading and unloading. Bring own food."

Marcus extended his hand to the surly caravan master to close the unsavory deal. It hung in the air for several seconds in the empty air separating them. Then Abmatak took his hand reluctantly to close the deal. "Load up tomorrow at first light, both. Be ready or we leave, you catch up if you can."

"We will be there. Thank you." He spun on his heel and left. *I expect trouble on this trip. I am glad I taught Mei the rudiments of knife-fighting. But if we kill one of his men, what then? On the road, he is lord and master.*

The rest of the day was hurried preparations at Frontinus' home where they had been staying, readying the animals, packing goods and food into the small sturdy one-horse wagon. One would drive, the other would ride, two relief horses tethered to the wagon. Frontinus contributed a long iron pry bar, two spare wheels and a clanking canvas bag, filled with iron tools, hammers, chisels and the like. "You may need these if the wagon breaks," he said, laying the sack, pry bar and wheels into the wagon bed.

"Thanks!" Marcus rearranged the spares in cargo bed. "I don't much care for the caravan master. I think there might be trouble."

"So don't take this one. There will be others in a few weeks, all summer long."

"No, I don't want to put this off any longer. The weather won't be in our favor later, turning hot as an oven."

"Can you handle any trouble?"

"I don't have a choice, Frontinus. I intend to try."

"Be careful, Marcus. Take care of Mei. Can I help with anything else?"

Marcus chuckled. "As a matter of fact, you can!"

The two set to work, packing and re-packing until sunset, then continuing by lamplight until all looked in roadworthy order, secured so heavy items would not shift and upset the balance, things most often needed on top. Mei busied about the kitchen, preparing two months' worth of non-perishable foods, dried meats and bread, filling leather sacks with water and wine. They then trundled the wagon down to the caravan's encampment for a few hours' sleep.

Long before the first shades of dawn's gray streaked the night sky, the camp began to bustle, with the bells of animals and shouts of men. Mei and Marcus struggled out of their wagon where they had slept, wrapped in a nondescript blanket, and tried to orient themselves, to find Abmatak for their morning instructions.

A group of men loading two camels stopped them. The bigger one growled something that sounded like *"Gher ersid."* He motioned to his companion, who tossed two heavy sacks in their direction. Marcus caught his, but Mei stumbled under the unexpected heavy load. *"Gamban kirid!"* the man cursed, his breath foul in the morning air. Marcus turned to help Mei, but the big man, obviously in charge of the group, struck him hard across the shoulders. *"Gamban kirid!"* he repeated, pointing to an unladen camel.

"It is all right, Marcus, I can manage," she said, wheezing slightly under the load. Marcus glowered back at the overseer, choosing to say nothing. The man would probably not have understood, anyway.

Another man of the group, a stocky bearded man with rotten teeth, picked up the game. As Mei loaded a sack, each the weight of a small child, onto a recumbent camel, he would throw another at her, with increasing force, until one knocked her down. Marcus put his arm firmly on the man's shoulder and said "No!" in a tone that was sure to cross the language barrier. As Marcus turned his back to help Mei to her feet, the man grabbed Marcus and spun him back around to face him, jabbering in his guttural language.

He is testing me. Well, let us see the test. He appears to be a brawler. Let him brawl with this. Marcus' left leg flew in a swift arc, catching the man by his side. No sooner had Marcus' left leg regained its footing, then his right leg scissor-kicked his assailant with considerable force in the gut, knocking him backward onto the ground, to the considerable amusement of the man's companions, laughing and hooting at him in derision. The man struggled to his feet, red in the face with anger, and rushed Marcus without much thought. Marcus had already shifted his stance to present his side to the man, left arm extended, his right arm cocked by his ear. As the man closed with Marcus, he encountered several light blows, almost slaps, from Marcus' left hand, distracting him so that he never saw Marcus' powerful right cross until it exploded onto his nose with a crunch.

Antonius would proud of that one! He is out of the fight, for several minutes at least. Marcus however retained his stance, while the man sat on the ground, groaning and holding his bloody nose, maybe broken, certainly painful.

The noise of the fight, and the hoots and laughs of the men, had attracted the *sartpaw*, who spoke tersely with the overseer, who pointed in turn to Marcus, Mei and the man on the ground. Abmatak spat angry words at the troublemaker, who struggled to his feet, apparently chastened, now holding a bloody rag to his nose.

Abmatak then approached Marcus. "I see they already put you to work," he said. "Good! Many camels and wagons left." In the dim light, Marcus could make out at least ten more camels being led up, and a large wagon trundling in, towed by two oxen. Abmatak left without saying anything more, but Marcus could have sworn there was flicker of a grin on the *sartpaw*'s face

Marcus turned to Mei. "Are you all right?"

"I am fine," she answered. "I have worked in fields at harvest time harder than this." She smiled as she swept a damp strand of black hair out of her face. "*Laboremus!* Let's work."

"Not bad!" said Marcus, returning her smile, as he hefted her another of the heavy bags. "Load the cart, it's lower than those damned camels."

The fight seemed to have cleared the air, and they worked without further harassment. Marcus thought the overseer's name might be Yanak, as whenever someone yelled that word, he would turn to face the man and answer something unintelligible. Yanak eyed him and Mei, but left them alone, as the first streaks of dawn appeared. The troublemaker worked on, his face bound in a rag, but he seemed to have no interest in further confrontation.

By the time the sun was over the horizon, five hundred camels, donkeys and wagons had been loaded. A horn sounded, and the caravan lurched away to the northwest, Marcus and Mei somewhere in the middle in their wagon. Frontinus and a few other townspeople had come down to see them off, and Marcus gave them a final wave. He suddenly did not want to leave Liqian, but it was too late for that.

Breakfast was a little water and bread, something the caravanners called *nan*, flat, round and durable. They plodded on through the day, eating more *nan* in midday without stopping. About two hours before dark, the caravan ground to a halt in a sheltered area by the road, circled the wagons, and began the long process of unloading the animals and putting them to forage. Marcus sought out Yanak's group, as the fight seemed to have established some respect for him with those people. He and Mei turned to, even managing some laughs as they playfully tossed the heavy sacks a bit harder. The man with the rag across his face wasn't smiling, however.

After the last animal was unloaded, Marcus went up to Yanak, called him by name, and extended his own, "Marcus," he said, relieved when Yanak returned the grip firmly. "We'll be here tomorrow morning," he said in *han-yu*, knowing that Yanak wouldn't understand. But Yanak babbled something incomprehensible and smiled, exposing yellow teeth underneath a bushy mustache.

They returned to their wagon for a meal, to find the *sartpaw* waiting for them. His gut tightened with anxiety. *I wonder what is up? Something about the fight?*

"You join me by campfire tonight, please," said Abmatak in his halting *han-yu*. "You and wife."

"Certainly ... now?"

"Please."

Abmatak turned without waiting for a reply. They followed him a few dozen yards to his large wagon, covered with a felt shelter over circular rings. Some people were already gathered around a fire, someone cooking a stew in a big iron pot. The caravan leader motioned to a log. "Here, you sit. Wife no cook tonight." At last, he smiled, and Marcus felt more at ease. They sat, and Abmalak continued. "First day good?"

"Hard work, but yes, good," answered Marcus.

"Men who work caravan tough men, they like tough men. You tough man. Where you learn to fight like that? Soldier?"

Someone brought them each a bowl of stew, filled with rice and big chunks of meat. Abmatak speared one of the chunks with his dagger and put in his mouth, chewing while eyeing Marcus intently.

"No. Years ago I traveled with the Hanaean government to the west, as I spoke a language they needed. It was a dangerous trip, so they taught me to fight Hanaean style. More traveling later with soldiers, I learned a rougher style."

"Which you use this morning?" asked Abmatak, his eyes twinkling as he chewed on the meat.

"Both. I am sorry I hurt him. Is he all right?"

Abmatak, laughed, a big rumbling laugh, and dismissed Marcus' concern with a wave of his hand. "He be fine, just shame. More talk than fight." He speared another chunk and continued. "You good travelers. Many travelers no want to work. Hard work, many animals, load and unload every day. We test to see who works, who ... how you say? ... want to sit on ass and watch. In a day or two, they turn around and go back where they come from. You, I think you go all the way to Turfam with us, you and wife. Her name?"

"Mei," answered Marcus. Mei smiled shyly.

"Why go to Turfam?"

Marcus paused. *Should I tell him everything? No... he may think we are worth robbing.* "We are going west to find a place to teach ... uh...the western languages that I know. Perhaps Kashgar."

"Hmm." Abmatak turned his attention to the rest of his stew, and Marcus and Mei began to eat theirs.

"When you get to Turfam, Jamshid runs all our caravans. He get you to Kashgar."

"That's good. Thank you! Perhaps we will not fight anyone on the next leg," Marcus chuckled, and the caravan master smiled.

They had passed their first day's test.

CHAPTER 3:

HOMECOMING SURPRISE

Aquileia, Northern Italy: April 112AD

Marcia lolled in the sun by the atrium's pool, trying to read some poetry, though her Greek was not up to it today. She set aside the scroll to watch her children play. Little Colloscius was playing with a little wooden cart with a horse and rolling wheels. He moved it around the paving stones, occasionally rearing the horse skyward and making horsey sounds. His younger sister playfully tormented their dog, tugging gently at his ears. Somewhere a fly buzzed. Marcia grasped the amulet of *Bona Dea*, hanging on a leather thong around her neck. *You know it's not the Greek, Mother. And you know why I am afraid. Help me.*

One of the servants came out carrying a tray of sweetmeats, and tumblers of juice. "Marcia, it is time for lunch. I brought you and the children some."

"Thank you, Desdemona. It is so beautiful today, I almost forgot about the time."

"It is time for you to take care of yourself." She smiled, and went back to the kitchen, through a door under the portico. To the horror of their neighbors, she and her husband insisted that the servants call them by their first names. Her husband Antonius was the only one who called her *domina*, the lady of the house. Which is as it should be. She also had insisted on nursing her own children, rather than purchasing a wet nurse, and playing with her children, rather than relegating them to servants' care. Nevertheless, the servants were always eager to entertain the children when Marcia's duties required her to be elsewhere.

Marcia gathered up her children. "Come, Colloscius, Aena, it's time for lunch. Look what Desdemona brought us!"

The two children made eager squeals of delight, jumping up and down with glee.

Marcia was smiling inwardly, greatly contented, when there was a commotion outside, a carriage coming to the front door, hails from the servants. Marcia stood to go see what was going on when Antonius burst through the door into the atrium. He crossed the distance between them in the space of one breath, put his arms around her and lifted her up, feet off the ground, to give her a long passionate kiss, his thick black beard tickling her chin.

"I take it you are glad to be home, Antonius," she said with a flustered smile. "It is a good thing all my lovers decided to stay home today."

"And I left all mine in Alexandria, *domina!* But none as beautiful as you."

Antonius set her gently down among the children clinging to his legs, crying "Papa, Papa!" Antonius bent down to attend to them, fishing out a pouch from under his cloak. "And Papa brought you something from Egypt," he said, eyes, bright. He fished out a bronze soldier and handed it to Colloscius. "That's for you, if you have been a good boy and the man of the house while I was gone."

"Thank you, Papa! Is it like you were?"

"Yes, it is." He fished in the leather sack again and drew out a cloth doll of an Egyptian princess, with wide eyes and bare midriff. "And this one is for you, Aena."

Aena fingered the doll. "She boo'ful"

"Like you, princess." The children, distracted from their returning father by the unexpected presents, fell momentarily silent while they fondled their gifts. Antonius stood to face Marcia.

"How are you? Did all go well while I was gone?"

"Very well. We had three more enroll in the language classes, and they have been coming several times a week. One, I think, would like to be one of my lovers, so I am glad you are back," she said, delivering a playful punch to his mid-section.

"I am sure you can handle him, *domina.*"

"Oh, yes, and you left something behind."

"What was that? Nothing important, I hope?"

"I think rather important. You left it behind the night before you left," she said, putting her finger to the side of her cheek. "Or was it the night before that?" She smiled shyly and rubbed her ever-so-slightly distended tummy. "The midwife dangled a needle over my belly and she tells me it is a boy. She claims to be right half the time, too."

Antonius, stepped back, flabbergasted. "Really? Again already, amazing… I don't know what to say. Are you feeling all right?"

"A little sick in the morning, just an upset stomach. Not as bad as with Aena… with her, I almost couldn't eat for the first few months without throwing up."

"I remember… and I was worried I might lose you. Here, sit down," he said, taking her arm and steering her to a stone bench.

"I am fine, but I will humor you." She sat down, rearranging her white *stola*. Neither wanted to remember how very difficult that last delivery had been. After a long pause, she changed the subject. "So how was Alexandria?"

"Beautiful as ever. The people at the Library couldn't find out enough about our trip. They wanted to know every town, even the distances, the terrain, the weather. What languages they spoke, what clothes they wore, the animals. Everything. I wish I had kept a little journal ... and oh, yes, the Bull and Dove is still there!"

"That dive?"

"Yes, and still a dive. Had to go there to toast Ibrahim's memory. And they still serve rotgut wine."

"To be sure, from what you told me." She turned to the kitchen. "Desdemona!"

"Yes, Marcia?"

"Could you get one of the servants to watch the children, please?"

Desdemona dried her hands on an apron about her waist and gave her a big smile. "Of course, Marcia. Leda, please come and watch little Coloscius and Aena."

Marcia intertwined her arm about Antonius' waist and leaned her head on his shoulder. "Come, Antonius. It's been a long trip and I think you need some time in bed, and I am not so far along that I can't make it interesting for you."

In their chambers, they lay in the half light, savoring the aftermath of the intense lovemaking, Antonius' arm around Marcia, who snuggled into his shoulder. "I wasn't expecting that today," she murmured.

"I have been expecting it all week, since we landed in Ostia." He kissed her gently, then patted her tummy. "Is he.... Is it... moving yet?"

"Not yet. He's only three months old. And never mind what the old crone says, I knew it was a boy, your son. Don't ask me how, I know it's a boy. We need to find some way to force 'Ibrahim' into Latin. What do you think of that as a name?"

"Abaramus? I'll think on that. Too close to 'we might have' for a name." He paused for a long time, then turned to her. "Are you afraid?"

"When I missed my courses after you left, I was terrified. I almost died having Aena, I thought at one time we were both dead. And now I am thirty, getting too old to be having children. But no, not now, I'm not afraid. If I die, I will die happy, knowing I had ten of the best years of my life with the best man in the world." She grabbed his beard and pulled him to her to kiss him.

"Arrgh, don't start something yer can't finish, *domina*."

"I can finish it, if you can start it," she giggled.

CHAPTER 4:

THE KILLING SPOTS

Dzungarian Gates, China: April 112AD

Galosga rolled onto his side beside his sleeping wife. He swallowed in the darkness, feeling the tell-tale scratchiness of his throat, and now the heat of fever. It was time.

His movement awakened Hina, who stretched and yawned, her red hair scattered on the pillow.
"Mmmh," she muttered, pulling the blanket about her shoulders. "Are you awake, Galosga?"

"I am." He nestled spoon-fashioned against her, her buttocks warm against his stomach, and reached his hand across her firm stomach. *Should I tell her?* He could not withhold it from her any longer. "*Huldaji*... the sickness is upon me. I must go to the sickness yurts outside the encampment today."

Hina turned abruptly under the blankets to face him, her full breasts against his hairless bronze chest. "No!" She reached up to touch his forehead, hot with fever. She knew.

He felt her sigh and put arm around her. "I must go before the spots appear. If I wait, then you and the children will have to come with me. And we will all die."

"No, Galosga, you will not go alone. If you are to die, then I will die with you, in your arms." She returned his hug, her battle-hardened muscles holding him firmly against her.

"The children... Andanyu and Marasa, little Adhela. No. You must stay for them."

"Narna will wet-nurse Adhela, as she has in the past. And she and Nedyu will raise them as their own when we die. Or send them to die with us, if the spots come on them also."

They lay together in the darkness, saying nothing, thinking about the horror that was upon them, her head nestled on his shoulder.

"Galosga, my beloved, the man who fell into my life to heal it, I love you. My sister Marcia told me long ago that love meant being willing to die for the one you loved, and if you are to die, I will be at your side to follow you. There is no other place for me." She kissed him wetly, pulling him to her. "I want to make love to you, while we still can." He grasped her body, naked as she usually slept, and pressed into her wetness, feeling her body quiver with pleasure. She hissed in delight as he entered her, the two moving together with increasing intensity, until they both exploded in an ecstasy of pleasure, then lay there, savoring the residual motions of their bodies, Hina watching the low-banked firelight reflecting off the red and blue *shangyrak* centerpiece covering the smoke-hole in the middle of the roof. Afterward, they slept, as the sun was not yet up.

It was like any other day when they awoke an hour later. They fumbled for their clothes, Galosga adding more dung to the fire and blowing on it stir it into life, Hina going about unwrapping Adhela's swaddling to change it for fresh wear, waking the twins, and enlisting their help in preparing the morning meals. It was a day like any other that they had spent in this yurt for the past eight years. But it was to be their last.

Hina took the children over to the yurt adjacent to them, scratching on the yurt's leather door. Narna opened it. "Good morning! I didn't expect you."

"I did not expect to be here." She turned to the twins. "Go find your friends. Momma must talk." The twins scampered off to join their friends on the far side of the yurt.

"You look very concerned. What is going on?"

Hina shuffled restless little Adhela in her arms. "Galosga has the spotted sickness. He does not yet have the spots, so the children do not have to follow him when he goes today to the sickness yurts. But I am going with him. I cannot let him die alone, and I cannot live without him. I want you to take my children, Narna, and raise them as your own." She handed Narna a bag of silver coins. "This is for you and for them."

"Oh." Narna sat down in a folding chair by the fire. "Oh, the spotted killer. Will it never end?"

"Tengri alone knows that. Thank you." She handed Narna little Adhela, squealing with delight at the prospect of new hugs. She then called the nine-year-old twins back, a boy and a girl, both copper-skinned and raven-haired like their father. "Mamma and Dada must go away for a while. You stay with Aunt Narna and be good, do what she tells you, do all your chores."

"Where are you going, Mamma? Why can't we go?" asked Andanyu.

"A long way off."

"When are you coming back?"

Hina could not bring herself to say never. She just shook her head from side to side. The children looked disappointed, but brightened when she scooped them up in her arms for hugs and kisses. "Goodbye, Andanyu and Marasa. Momma will be watching you!"

She left the yurt, her eyes burning fiercely with the tears she did not shed freely.

Back in their own yurt, she went about methodically packing, as if for a hunting trip: water, *naan* bread, cheese, yogurt, cooking gear, *kumis* fermented mare's milk, and blankets, into two stout backpacks. They then doused the dung fire for the last time, and set out for the sickness yurts.

Even before they reached the ten or so yurts clustered a mile outside the perimeter of the encampment, they smelled them… a smell of death and human offal. And heard them from fifty yards off, a symphony of moans, hacking coughs and mad rantings. Hina's heart sank at the thought of entering this foul place. They went from yurt to yurt, each as foul as the last, dead bodies inside amongst the dying, the smell of rotting flesh, excrement and urine. Few had any fires going, despite the freezing weather. Eyes looked hopefully on them, but they moved on. Finally, at near the last of the low cylindrical felt tents, they found a familiar face, huddled in despair at the far end from the door.

"Hadyu!" exclaimed Hina, shifting her pack off her shoulders to the ground. "Not you, too!"

Hadyu struggled to his feet. "It appears that Tengri has called me. I have a fever, but no spots yet."

"The same," said Galosga.

"And you, you are sick?"

"Not yet. I came to die with my mate."

"That is fitting. You were inseparable in life, you know." He managed a smile.

"But I am not going to die in this filth!" She grabbed the leg of one of the bodies that appeared to have been dead for several days, its mouth gaping open in a soundless scream. "Are you strong enough to help get some of these bodies out of here?"

"I used to be your second-in-command, remember? Of course, I am strong enough."

The three hauled the five corpses unceremoniously out to a place in the field fifty yards away. "No time for a proper sky burial, but at least they will rest with their eyes on the sky. Hopefully the buzzards will get to them before the wolves. Let's go tend the living," said Hina

Back in the yurt, they examined those still alive, giving each a much-needed drink of water, and a bit of the bread that Hina had brought for themselves. Two were raving incoherently, unaware of the three tending to them, their foreheads like a hot stove, pustules yellow and foul-smelling. The three coherent ones were Altan and Bataar, the girl was Gan, spots speckling their faces but not yet gone to pus. "Thank you," rasped Gan, through parched lips. "It has been days since we had water." Galosga looked intently at the fouled blankets. Traveling years before, the foreigner Antonius had impressed on him the important of cleanliness in preventing sickness. The residents had been fouling themselves where they lay. "Hadyu, start a fire outside. We need to wash these blankets, and dry them before they get cold enough to freeze."

Hina started a small dung fire inside, warmed some water, and began washing the private parts of the survivors. She shared their three blankets among the sick, then sat down to wait for the others to dry, hanging on makeshift lines outside, whipped by the strong *buran* wind from the north.

"Well, it still stinks in here, but it is not as bad," said Hina. "No wonder so many die out here."

"Everyone is afraid to tend them. If their pus gets on you, then you get the sickness also."

"Well, we will make their last days less unpleasant. I wish we could do something with the other yurts," said Galosga. "There's just not enough of us, not enough supplies."

The next day, Galosga and Hadyu showed spots. One of the sicker ones died, carried out join the others in the field, and Altan, Bataar and Gan began to rave. Late on the third day, both Hadyu and Galosga began to rave, their fever like a blacksmith's forge. Hina held Galosga's hot body against hers, as he trembled in feverish chills. She heard him call his pet name for her, *huldaji*, 'mountain lion' in his foreign tongue, and a few other words she knew. At last, she could release her tears, crying choking sobs against his powerful chest, now marked with pus-filled spots. "Damn you, Galosga, damn you! You taught me to cry." She pummeled his chest, but he seemed unaware, just continuing to murmur in his own language. "I haven't even gotten sick yet. What if you die and I don't? I can't live without you!" For the first time in a long time, she felt fear.

Somehow, amid the cacophony of moans and cries, Hina fell asleep. She awoke with a start in the chill predawn to a silent yurt. She was sure Galosga had passed in the night, and she pressed her cheek against his now-cool chest. Then she felt it rise imperceptibly, heard the sibilance of his breath. She turned to Hadyu by his side. He, too, was sleeping, his fever broken. Altan and Gan, too, had survived, though Bataar and the other, whose name she had never known, were stiff and cold. And she was still unaffected.

After several days, the shamans came out to inspect the sickness yurts. They brought with them a pockmarked boy who had survived the disease, leaving him permanently scarred, his face cratered with 'the Mark of Tengri.' The shamans stood off at a safe distance, while the boy inspected each of the yurts. The five survivors sat on logs in the meager sunlight before their yurt, their pustules now scabbing over. Hina, unscarred, stood up to challenge the shamans. "Are you afraid to come in here to see the work of your hands? Get in here before I come to drag you in."

Hina was big woman, nearly as tall as most men, with arms powerful from years with sword and bow. The shamans, unused to anything but deferential respect, walked in cautiously. "Perhaps if you did not force these poor souls to live their last days in filth, more might live. Out of eight in this yurt, five live, four with the Mark of Tengri. Had we come earlier, perhaps the other three might have lived," she said.

"It is better that a few die, rather than the many," said one of the shamans defensively.

"You are not doing a very good job of protecting the many." She tossed her reddish-brown hair, her eyes flaring green. "The newly-sick are arriving faster than we can carry out the corpses of the dead, so with your tender mercy, the Huyan clan will be no more very soon." Hands on her hips, she glared at the shamans. "Here is what you are to do."

Hina was no stranger to giving orders to men, for she had commanded her own *zuun* of a hundred warriors before motherhood intervened, and she had remained a valuable advisor to the *shanyu* Bei. "I have about forty people to care for. You will bring out skins of water, food, *naan*, goat, butter, cheese and yogurt, clean blankets, cooking pots, everything that forty healthy people would need for a week. Send them out with those who have the Mark of Tengri on them, for they do not get the disease again. And bring wood poles for proper sky burial platforms for the dead, about fifty so far. They deserve better than to be left to the steppe wolves. Those with the Mark will remain here to help us tend the sick. We will remain here until the dying stops. Now go, carry out your tasks!" She turned peremptorily for her yurt, leaving the shamans, unused to getting orders, discussing her tasks amongst themselves.

The dying abated, but the last to be touched was the household of the *shanyu*. Hina, having heard of this, went into the encampment unbidden, to see the stricken ruler. As she walked through the encampment, people gave way before her in awe, for the story of her work in the sickness yurts, and her bold orders to the shaman that no one dared to question, had spread from yurt to yurt. For the first time in a year, people began to hope that the spotted killer might leave them. She came to the *shanyu's* tents, nodded to his guards armed with pikes, who snapped erect at her approach, and she entered into the luxurious yurt. *Shan-yu* Bei, although spotted, continued to sit on his throne of power, wrapped in furs against the chill that always accompanied the fever. He coughed that hacking cough that marked the final stage of the disease.

"Welcome, Hina. Once again, you have done what few have ever done, you avoided the spotted killer, though you lived among its victims. You are one of Tengri's special children."

"You honor me, sir, but I have done nothing to deserve this honor."

"You have saved the Huyan clan from certain death. Though perhaps not me." He turned his head as choking coughs wracked his body. Catching his breath as they faded away, he resumed. "My entire household, wives, children, servants, all have the disease. For the safety of the Huyan clan, I must remove myself to the sickness encampments. I fear the disease lingers in my yurt, so it too must go with me."

"I will send the Marked Ones over to assist you in moving to the sick encampment. Can I do anything else for you?"

"Continuing doing what you are doing. And…" he stopped to cough harshly again, bringing up something nasty into a rag he held. "Go to the Han. They are our hated enemies, but among them are many wise shamans, who can cure many things. Perhaps one knows how to drive out the spotted killer."

"Yes, sir." She paused, not used to offering praise or gratitude to those in power. "I thank you for being a wise and courageous *shanyu* to our clan. And I thank you for accepting me into your clan as a homeless waif, for allowing me to become one of your warriors."

"You have repaid my decision a hundredfold, Your mentor Mayu would be proud of you. Now let us do what we have to do." He lapsed back into coughing.

Despite all efforts, the *shanyu* and all his heirs died not long after moving into the sickness encampment, leaving no clear line of succession. Civil war seemed likely if the factions vying for leadership did not find an agreeable candidate. Some factions wanted to return east to their ancestral homeland north of the Yellow River, others to go further west onto the grassy plains beyond the Dzungarian Gates, still others to attack the clans that had put this spell upon them.

It was a noisy clan meeting, with angry voices, and on several occasions, drawn swords, thus far quickly restrained. Hina raised her voice above the roar, her battleground tenor silencing the contentious yurt. "Enough! You have but two enemies here, only two! One is the sickness that is killing us. The other is your ambition, all of you, that will kill the rest of us. We need to confer, quietly, to agree on a leader who will unite us."

The dung fire in the pit in the center of the yurt hissed. After several seconds, "How about you, Hina?" asked Hadyu. "You have commanded a *zuun* of a hundred men, something no other woman has done. You could unite us. You, alone of all of us, you have not stepped forward the fill Bei's place."

Hina believed there were evil spirits, spirits that put temptation before humans, temptations so strong that if seized upon would destroy them. Everything she had done had led to this moment, to be *shanyu*, to be the leader of the clan. She had the strength, she had the ability. But that was her temptation, her own ambition for ultimate power. She knew she could resist it now, but later she might not, and that temptation would destroy her and the Huyan clan. She saw it as clearly as if Tengri had shown her a vision. "I decline," she said at last. The gathering audibly gasped. "I will carry out my last charge from the *shanyu*, his dying wish, that I go to Turfam and seek out an Hanaean cure for the sickness. Pick a candidate amongst yourselves." She turned abruptly and left the yurt, listening to the turmoil resume behind her. *What have I done? Why?*

Two weeks later, a small party of Xiongnu reached the area around Urumqi, a man, a woman, two children and an infant, riding on horseback leading a camel laden with their folded yurt, framing poles lashed alongside, and three spare horses laden with baggage. Galosga was the first to notice something amiss, reining his mare to a halt and raising his hand. "Wait. Silence." Hina, the infant Adhela asleep in his carrier across her breast, and Andanyu and Marasa, halted theirs, waiting in disciplined silence for Galosga to explain. "I heard something, riders, coming hard behind, I think. The wind is up now, I can't hear it." The *buran* wind picked up, moaning along the dusty arid plain between the snowy mountain peaks.

Hina listened, turning her horse to look behind. "There! A cloud of dust a mile back. You have good ears, Galosga."

She unslung the infant from around her neck. "Marasa! Come, take your brother." She handed the girl the carrier with the sleeping baby inside, drew the bow from the shield behind her back and strung it in the saddle, pulling a handful of arrows from the quiver slung on the saddle's pommel. Galosga did likewise.

Galosga motioned to his son. "Andanyu, protect your brother and sister. Take them and our animals into that draw over there, the other side of the tree. Stay out of sight." The seven-year-old strung his bow, then drew a short sword from a sheath on the saddle. "If it comes to fighting, you two remember all that we taught you. Marasa, shelter Adhela out of sight before you engage if you must fight. But until then, stay out of sight, the best fight is the one not fought." He then wheeled his mount to follow Hina, who was looking for a concealed spot to survey the interlopers.

Side by side, they watched the riders coming on. Bandits? Some hostile clan? But as the riders got closer, they recognized the distinctive hawk feather standard of the Huyan clan. Still, this might not be friendly. Fighting had already broken out between the factions when they left, leaving many dead.

Another few hundred yards, and they could make out the now-pocked face of Hadyu. He raised his hand, and the riders pulled to stop, their horses snorting and blowing in a cloud of dust. He turned in their direction. "Hina, Galosga! Can you hear me?"

She nodded her acquiescence, and Galosga rode up over the rise to expose himself. "Hadyu! That is some hard riding."

"We have been tracking you for days, we hoped it was you."

"Do you bring news?"

"Yes, can I join you?"

Hina urged her mount over the rise, beckoning to him to come on. He did so, the other riders behind him, and pulled up alongside the two.

"So why are you trying so hard to catch us? Is there news of the clan, a new *shanyu*, perhaps?" asked Hina, putting her arrows back in the quiver.

"There is news, but not good. The sickness broke out with a vengeance after you left, and the competing factions all blamed each other. The civil war killed those the sickness did not take. There are just a handful of survivors. The Huyan clan... it is no more." He looked down, to hide the tears in his eyes.

"When you offered to make me *shanyu*, in a brief flash, it was what Tengri showed me, that the clan's time was up. Narna and Nedyu? Their children?"

Hadyu shook his head.

Her eyes now also burned with tears. Another clan, gone, lost forever, just as the clan of her birth had disappeared in a cloud of black smoke, torn by the wind over the grasslands of the steppes so many thousands of miles away. Memories of her mother and father, her brothers, memories she thought she had forgotten, merged with memories of Narna and Nedyu, who had taught her the skills of being a mother, her long-dead lover Mayu ... and the friends, now dead, that she had held so long at a distance. "Where are you going?"

"We are going to try to go back to our old homeland. Can we ride with you to Turfam?"

"We would be honored."

CHAPTER 5:

A PLAN FOR WAR

Antioch, Roman Province of Syria: May 112AD

Gaius Aetius Lucullus, his senior tribune Marcus Cornelius Trebonius, and the other legion commanders were escorted by silent servants into the palatial conference hall of the Syrian governor's praetorium in Antioch. Gaius' escort led him to the table in the middle room with the other commanders. His seat was marked with a small brass marker indicating *Leg II Trai*, his legion's identifier, a blank sheet of papyrus, writing instruments and ink. The other sixteen seats were similarly outfitted, identifying each legion in attendance.

Gaius was not surprised to see the commanders or senior tribunes of the seven eastern legions from Cappadocia, Syria and the newly formed province of Arabia. Rome's primary threat was Parthia, and these front-line forces were to hold the line against any Parthian attack until reserves could be summoned from further west. The legions of Moesia at the mouth of the Danube were the first defense-in-depth reserves for the eastern front, so it also made sense for them to be here.

But Gaius' *Legio II Traiana*, Trajan's own legion, was among several legions still actively involved in pacification after the hard-fought Dacian war, and the Pannonian legions were back-up to their effort there. And the *XXII Primigenia?* What was the legate of the 'Lucky Capricorns' doing so far from the Rhine? In all, half of all Rome's legions were represented in this room by either their *legati* or a senior tribune.

There were no windows in the room, brilliantly illuminated by sconces and candelabra from the ceiling. The servants distributed wine and food, then quietly left, closing the doors behind them. Dour soldiers secured the doors behind them with heavy beams, then resumed their positions at parade rest, legs spread, lances at an angle.

Gaius studied the huge hanging tapestry, a wall map of Europe and Asia Minor, Roman areas woven in red, from Britannia as far east as the Parthian eastern capital of Ecbatana, from Germany in the north to the deserts south of Cyrene and Carthage. Parthian territory to the east was in green. In the center of the room was another map on the table, apparently a relief map for detailed planning of a campaign. Gaius could see mountains formed from lumps of clay, but little else.

The uncharacteristically-bearded governor, stocky, trim and fit, clad in military uniform and purple cloak, strode confidently into the room from a side entrance, guards snapping to attention and rendering a salute across their chest at his entrance, then returning to parade rest. The governor wasted no time in welcoming the men in his booming voice. "Welcome to my Praesidium! I am Publius Aelius Hadrian. Thank you for taking the time to join me here, ostensibly to welcome me as the newly-appointed governor of Syria, who is taking stock of the seven legions at my disposal, and many more that are not mine. As you will find out shortly, there are other, more serious reasons for my summoning you that have nothing to do with my vanity." Chuckles of polite approval rippled among the audience.

"First some introductions. I believe you all know each other, at least by reputation, and most I believe know me, or know of me. I most recently commanded the Second Minervan in the Dacian Wars, and served in three other legions as tribune. For a senior governor, I have spent a fair amount of time under the eagles, and met most of you on our way up in the Dacian wars. Let me introduce the outsiders. Please stand as I call your legions. First the Moesian legions, *I Italica, V Macedonica,* and *XI Claudia,* our immediate reserves in any war with Parthia."

The commanders rose as their legions were called.

"Next, we have the legates of the Dacian legions, *II Traiana, I Adiutrix, XIII Gemina,* and *XXX Ulpia Victrix,* taking time from the pacification of that new province. Finally, we have tribunes representing some more distant legions from the west. Please stand as I call your legions: *II Adiutrix, XV*

Apollinaris, VII Claudia, XII Primigenia." Gaius rose, as did the other commanders. They nodded to their counterparts, then reseated themselves.

"As you can tell, this is no minor gathering of military leadership. A note to security... what I am to tell you is not to leave this room, not even to the men of your legions when you return. Tell them it was a boring social call on a governor with too high an opinion of himself." Relaxed now, the legates and tribunes allowed themselves a laugh.

Hadrian continued. "The *Princeps* Trajan deputed me to Syria as governor, to bring my military background to focus on preparing for the largest military operation Rome has ever undertaken. Greater than Pompey's campaigns, greater than Caesar's Gallic campaign, greater than Claudius' conquest of Britain. That operation is to be the conquest of Mesopotamia ... and maybe beyond. We await only a pretext, which we expect will come soon in ever-troublesome Armenia. When that pretext comes, we intend to have a plan in place that the enemy will never expect."

A hushed silence fell on the generals and tribunes. Hadrian paused to let the dramatic moment sink in. "Know this for certain, this will be the greatest campaign ever undertaken by Rome, and the price of failure will be immense. And we have never succeeded against this enemy." He faced his generals before the wall map. "For two centuries, since the time of Sulla, we have defended Asia Minor against the Parthian threat. Time and again, we have forestalled their advances into Armenia on the Caspian Sea, from whence they could launch massive attacks on Cappadocia and Syria with little notice, advancing into Greece as they did centuries ago. Or into Judea and then south to Egypt." He paused for effect. "We all know the threat they pose to our narrow foothold on Asia Minor. It is time for us to be the threat to them and let them defend their territory against us!"

Legionary abbreviations pinned to the tapestry map marked the locations of all the legions of the Roman Army. Hadrian pointed to the seven legions facing Parthia directly, three in Syria, two to their west in Cappadocia, and one each in Judea and Arabia. "These seven legions can hold the line against any Parthian thrust north toward Armenia, or west toward the Mediterranean, while we move reinforcements from Europe. But they are not enough to mount an offensive. With surprise, we might initially succeed, but ultimately we would put forty thousand men at risk for no gain."

"I propose a bolder plan." He stepped to the left, indicating the red thumb-shaped Dacian salient north of the mouth of the Danube. "Four legions, Trajan's new *II Traiana* and *XXX Ulpia Victrix*, along with *I Adiutrix* and *XIII Gemina*, led the war against Dacia and are still stationed there. I think you would all agree, we don't need four full legions there for pacification six years after that war. South of the Danube, the Moesian and Pannonian legions now face no threat with Dacia reduced. And along the Rhine in Germany, the Lucky Capricorns of the *XXII Primigenia* have nothing to do except drink German beer and chase German *madchen*, as they did when I was there." The generals chuckled at the joke. The Dacian War had solved a lot of problems along the Danube.

"I propose we begin making preparations to move some of these legions, or cohort-sized *vexillatio* detachments, to the Parthian front. I would like us to launch an offensive against Parthia with a force of seventy-five to a hundred thousand men. "Lusius," he said, addressing the dusky general Lusius Quietus, who, true to his name, had stood silently by the governor's side, "Your Berber cavalry, which played such a key role in the Dacian campaign, will once again be the *Princeps'* mobile strike force. So, gentlemen, unless there are questions, I propose you spend the next several days during this beautiful Syrian spring to determine which legions and *vexillationes* to commit to this effort, and when they can be in place. I don't need to remind you that security is utmost. Do not discuss this outside of this room. If the Parthians get wind of this, no matter how many legions we commit, we shall meet a reception that will make short work of our troops." Hadrian turned to depart abruptly, his purple cloak swirling about him.

With the governor gone, Gaius Lucullus and the other legion commanders circled about the planning map on the table in the center of the room. Ten feet on a side, it accommodated all seventeen commanders, with their staff tribunes, clustered around it without crowding.

Gaius' tribune, Marcus Cornelius Trebonius, eyed the intricate planning map on the table, covering Cappadocia, Asia Minor, and Mesopotamia to the Zagros mountains, from the Black and Caspian Seas in the north to the Red Sea below its northern fork. "That is a magnificent piece of work, Gaius. Ports, roads, deserts, hills and mountains of clay, rivers… even bridges. It is all there," he said, quietly so as to not disturb the other commanders and tribunes also admiring the work. Tiny legionary symbols of bronze were placed at their current locations, and smaller symbols identified *vexillationes* detached from their parent legion.

"It is only as good as it is accurate, Marcus Cornelius," said Gaius through a smile. "You and I have had experience with maps before."

"Have we not!"

"But this should be good enough for us to figure out how many of each legion to take, how to get them and their supplies to wherever it is they need to be." Gaius picked up the bronze marker for his legion, its abbreviation *II Trai* over a shield marked with a stylized Hercules, their emblem. He turned it in his hands to admire the metallic artwork.

One of his fellow commanders stepped in beside Gaius. The commander was also holding a bronze legionary marker emblazoned with a miniature Neptune under *X Fret*. "These markers are nice work. Gaius Aetius, I believe you served under my older brother Lucius, some years back in the *XII Fulminata*."

"Then you would be Tiberius Julius Maximus, of course. Yes, that I did, and a model commander he was. The Twelfth Thunderbolt was a good legion under him. You are commanding the Tenth?" Gaius asked, indicating the marking Tiberius was holding.

"Yes, the *X Fretensis*, the Legion of the Straits. Tiberius is fine for me, we are fellow commanders."

"And plain Gaius for me also. I have always hated using the name of my *gens* Aetius. It just seems pretentious."

"To be sure. My brother always thought it one of your strengths, that you never took yourself too seriously. But now you have the *cognomen* Sirica as well?"

"You can blame that on the Senate. They awarded me with the title 'Silky' after a very long trip to that strange land of the Hanaeans ten years ago."

"Hmm, I heard about that trip. So will you be committing *II Triana* to whatever we are cooking up for Parthia?"

"Actually, I have directives from the Dacian governor, Gaius Nigrinus, to hold the Dacian legions in reserve, especially the garrison legions *II Traiana* and *XXX Ulpia* in-country. All of the legions that took part in that war have people who know the languages, which locals to trust and which bear watching. Their centurions know every hill, valley, and cow path in Dacia. We have spent several years turning that trouble spot into a promising province, and we don't want to commit our legions to another campaign, just to have Dacia fall apart in our rear. I don't think the *Princeps* would appreciate that."

"So what can you commit?"

"Ah, Tiberius, I don't give away my bargaining position before the game begins." Gaius clapped his fellow commander on the back and returned to study the map.

The legion commanders or their representatives, sequestered in the room for a week, had all argued vociferously for their units to be included at full strength in this historical campaign, something not seen since the time of Alexander the Great. All except Gaius Aetius Lucullus.

"You are not serious, Gaius Aetius! You would withhold the Dacian legions from this campaign? That is insane! Including those raised by Trajan, bearing his own name, *Traiana* and *Ulpia*, to sit it out in Dacia? That war is over!" Gaius Claudius Severus, governor of Arabia and commander of the *III Cyrenaica*, made no attempt to veil his contempt for his fellow legate.

Gaius was unmoved. "Gaius Claudius, if I were to lead with my ambition, I would put myself forward as the ideal choice to lead the invasion. But I have instructions from the governor to not leave our hard-won victory in Dacia smoldering, to light off a firestorm in our rear when we least need it. His recommendation, and mine as well, is to detach the least experienced *I*

Adiutrix for the campaign, but to keep *II Traiana* and the other Dacian legions in place, each contributing a cohort of five hundred men to support the Parthian campaign. If Hadrian orders otherwise, of course, I will carry those orders out without hesitation. But that remains my recommendation."

Gaius Claudius shook his head. "That's very noble, but you are a fool. No matter." He turned to the other commanders. "Put down *I Adiutrix*, and cohort *vexillationes* from the other five. Brutus, do you have the final allocations?"

"We do, sir."

"Fine, Summon Publius Aelius Hadrian and let's lay out the order of battle before him."

The final disposition lay on the map board. They all rose as Hadrian entered the room to hear their plan.

"At ease, at ease," said the governor. "Do we have a plan?"

"Yes, Your Excellency," said Severus. "Before you on the board is our final recommended disposition and staging. We use all seven legions in Asia Minor, *III Gallica, III Cyrenaica, IV Scythica, VI Ferrata, X Fretensis, XII Fulminata,* and *XVI Flavia Firma*. These will remain in their current billets, so as to not tip our hand to the Parthians."Severus glowered at Gaius Lucullus. "On the recommendation of the Dacian governor, conveyed by the senior *legatus* from Dacia, Gaius Lucullus, the three Dacian legions, *XIII Gemina, II Traiana Fortis, XXX Ulpia Victrix*, with *V Macedonica* in reserve, will remain in place to support pacification, but each will contribute a single cohort. We will relocate *I Adiutrix* to the staging area in Cappadocia here, along with *XV Apollinaris* from Pannonia and *XXII Primigenia* from the Rhine. This gives us a legionary strength of sixty-five thousand men, plus twenty thousand horse of Berber cavalry under Lusius Quietus, for a total of eighty-five thousand. We will of course, have other local auxiliary forces as well. The exact number of those will depend on political climate at the time. A respectable force, perhaps the most powerful one Rome has ever fielded."

"A good force indeed! I particularly like the idea of maintaining the Dacian occupation at strength. How about moving our forces?" Severus cast a sidelong glance at Lucullus, who gave no indication of smugness.

"Security, as you said, must be paramount, Your Excellency. We intend to openly relocate *I Adiutrix* to Cappadocia, justified by post-war realignment. Not close enough to the Parthian border to raise their hackles, close enough to be another reserve in case of trouble. The Parthians will see that as a defensive measure, no more."

He paused to consult his notes on a wax tablet. "*XV Apollinaris* and *XXII Primigenia* are more of a problem. The Parthians would notice their arrival, for sure, as staging for war. We propose moving them a cohort at a time to Cappadocia. Five hundred men on the move is not unusual, six thousand raises a lot of attention. To make the cohort even less conspicuous, as they transit another legion's area, they will use the symbols and colors of that legion, rather than their own. The two Cappadocian legions, *XII Fulminata* and *XVI Flavia Firma*, along with *I Adiutrix* when it gets there, will disperse cohort formations into the countryside and keep them constantly on the move. When *XV Apollinaris* and *XXII Primigenia* cohorts trickle in, they will use the colors of those three legions, pair up with their counterparts, and stay mobile. This will look, to Parthian spies, like that shell game with beans under shuffled cups. Unless they are very good at counting cohorts on the move, all looking alike, they are not likely to notice that we just slipped in twenty-five new ones. They probably will not even notice that we are drawing down the European legions." He paused for the Syrian governor's response.

After a long pause, Hadrian studied the board. "Interesting. I think that will work. What about your opening gambit?"

"We expect some sort of provocation by Ctesiphon in Armenia. With that as pretext, we propose to take Armenia using the seven eastern legions. Lusius Quietus' cavalry will then strike out across the Araxes River with twenty thousand horse, ostensibly to extend the boundary of Armenia southward along the Caspian Sea. The Parthians will resist this, but will see it as a defensive measure on our part, making Armenia more defensible. With the eastern flank secure, elements of those legions will advance along the Tigris River, following Alexander the Great's route, while the European legions advance along the Euphrates to form a pincer around the capital Ctesiphon, where the two rivers come closest together. This is more of a concept, Your Excellency, and the details will change over time. But we believe we can launch a surprise blow with overwhelming force." The Praetorian Guardsman at Hadrian's shoulder hastily completed scribbling notes he had been taking throughout the presentation.

"You all have done well," said Hadrian. "I have one change to make. Herrenius Saturninus, *legatus* of the *XII Fulminata,* is in failing health which prevented him from attending this meeting. Gaius Lucullus, you have made the excellent point that *II Traiana* is essential to the Dacian pacification effort, but you, sir, are not. I want like you to relieve Saturninus as *legatus* of your old legion, the Twelfth Thunderbolt."

Gaius stood to attention, slapped his arm across his chest. "I would be honored, Your Excellency." Once again, he was going to war.

CHAPTER 6:

SON OF THE FATHER

Melitene, Cappadocia: June 112AD

The spacious centurions' tent for the Fifth Cohort, *Leg XII Ful*, contained a worn wooden desk, some folding campaign chairs, frames on which hung the two occupants' uniforms and gear, and two cots. An oil lamp hung from the overhead crossbar, unlit as the sunlight penetrating the canvas gave the interior a yellow glow.  The flap was open when the young tribune approached the entrance. He stood there momentarily. "Centurion? A word with you, please."

The centurion put down his documents and stood respectfully. He studied the young man intently, sizing him up. Old for a tribune on his first assignment, about twenty, maybe older. The narrow purple *angusticlavia* strip identified him as of the equestrian order, and his uniform was well-made but plain, not ostentatious, no gold or silver jewelry as decorations for awards not yet earned. The centurion knew him immediately, though they had never before met: the short-cropped but still unruly curly black hair, intense eyes, square jaw, broad shoulders tapering to narrow hips. Yes, this was the father's son, indeed. The centurion rose. "Sir, of course, please come in. I am Centurion Samuel Elisarius."

"I am Secundus Aetius Lucullus, to be your cohort's tribune." He extended his hand, and they shook in legionary fashion. He took a chair before the desk and indicated that the centurion should likewise be seated.

"I wanted to meet you, ask you some questions."

"Sir, beggin' your pardon, I am just the *optio*, second in command, and new to that. Silvanus Vegetius, he's the centurion in command, out today with the *quaestor* supply officer to requisition things." *Thoughtful of the tribune to come here. Other young pups would have just sent someone to summon me.*

"Oh. I am sorry. I guess I will return tomorrow."

"I knew your father, sir," the centurion said hurriedly, uncomfortably aware that he had just dismissed the young man.

The tribune halted his effort to stand, and turned again to face the centurion. A smile lit his face, showing his fine white teeth. "You were in Dacia with him?"

"Before that, even. I was with him and his centurion halfway around the world from here, in the land of the Hanae. Quite the adventures we had. Your father is a good man. We wouldn't have gotten out of there alive, but for him."

"Amazing. I never tired hearing of that trip. Every time he came home, he would share those stories with me. I don't remember a Samuel, though."

"He knew me then as Shmuel, the Jewish rebel. I had a checkered past, before I joined the army."

"Ah, yes, that's the name I remember. How did you come to be in the army, unusual for a Jew, if you don't mind?"

"Not at all. I was sort of Antonius' *optio* and we did a lot of fighting on that trip. We got back, I got my citizenship, and a pardon for all my past crimes and stuff. I went back to my family in Galilee. I'd been gone for five years, they didn't know if I was dead or alive that whole time. My father had passed on, and I think my mother was hangin' on, just to see if I might come home. She died shortly after I got back. So ... fightin' was all I knew, I wanted to learn Latin, which I hardly spoke at all then, and as a citizen, I could join, so I did. I rose fair fast, makin' centurion in ten years, but I had all that experience behind me, made it easy. And you, you are a bit old for a tribune. Twenty?"

"Twenty-one. I turned seventeen when the Dacian wars broke out again. I wanted to sign on then, but my father, he was in the thick of it with the *II Trai*. He wanted me to stay home and be ready to be *paterfamilias* head of household if anything happened to him. Now that things have quieted down, it was time." He paused to collect his thoughts. "I wasn't here to discuss cohort matters, so I might as well ask you now, rather than wait for Centurion Vegetius to come back. What do you expect to see from a young tribune? You have done and seen everything, and it is all new to me."

Insightful and intense, this young man is going to go far with that attitude. "Well, that is a very good question, a very good question. Let me be givin' you a good answer to that one... first, you need to be competent. You don't hafta pretend to know all there is to know about soldierin', strategy, tactics, 'cause you don't, but you got to be willing to learn, and try to be the best you can at what you do know. All right?"

Secundus nodded, and Samuel continued. "Second, you gotta have courage. Not just on the battlefield, though you'll probably shit and piss yourself your first big fight ... I did. That's all right, as long as you keep on going. But the real important courage is to be honest, stand up for your troops, always do the hard thing, never go linin' your pocket with the supply money, never let anyone else do it either. And the third ... care for your men.

If they're cold and wet an' hungry, you go be cold an' wet an' hungry with 'em. If they're sleepin' on the ground, that's where you sleep. Your father ... he said he always wrote a letter to the families of men who died under him. Antonius, his centurion, said the men all knew that, and loved him for it. So, that's it. And by the way, you look just like your father."

"Thank you, centurion. That means a lot to me. I always wanted to serve under him but he wouldn't have it."

"That's a good idea, it's hard to have two people close to each other in the same unit. An' by the way, come back tomorrow an' talk to Silvanus. Have that same conversation with him."

Back at the centurions' mess tent, Samuel was not surprised to find them serving pork again. Not that it made any difference anymore, and he had not been strictly adherent to anything for most of his life. *Maybe those Christians got it right, just don't eat anything sacrificed to idols.* He was carving off a slice, when someone clapped him firmly on the shoulder.

"Hey, Jew-boy, you been keeping that circumcised prick of yours up to no good?"

Samuel grinned at the outwardly offensive greeting and responded in kind. "Aw, you idol-worshipin' fucker of whores, an' father of most of 'em to boot! What the hell you doin' back so soon, Silvanus? I didn't expect you till tomorrow."

"Got everything we needed in one day. That never happens. Enjoy being in charge for a bit?"

"Like you left me anything to do. I did get to meet the young tribune, Secundus Aetius Lucullus. Happens I knew his dad, Gaius Lucullus, ten years back. He looks like he'll do well, wants to come talk to you about some shit tomorrow."

"Gaius Lucullus his father? An' you know him, no shit? Haven't you heard?"

"Heard what?"

"The *librarii* clerks just got the letter from Antioch. Lucullus has just been posted here, to relieve the Old Man Saturninus before he dies. Shit, we got the new Old Man's son!"

CHAPTER 7:

A FOUL PLAN

Enroute Liqian to Turfam, China: June 112AD

The new relationship with Abmatak improved Marcus' relations with the other caravanners. They had tested him and not found him wanting. All except Kirmog, who resented being bested in a fight, and then being the object of jokes from his fellows. His resentment smoldered, but he did not want to challenge Marcus openly,
given the newcomer's relationship with the sartpaw.

Sitting late around the fire, having drunk many sacks of white *kumis*, fermented mare's milk, with his three friends, Kirmog threw out his idea. "The Han bastard and his woman must have a lot of money."

"Why do you think that?" asked Skag, spitting into the fire.

"I heard from someone around Abmatak's group that he wants to go to Kashgar. That is a helluva long way to go, just to set up a new life."

"They don't look like they have much."

"Smart travelers don't, not if they want to keep it. But they got it."

"Forget about robbing them, Kirmog, that's crazy. Abmatak would put our heads on stakes, after he finished flogging us almost to death, if we fucked with paying travelers ... not to mention his new friends," said Sigo, taking another swig of *kumis* from his small leather sack.

"Not if he doesn't know about it, he won't." Kirmog picked at his teeth with his dagger, dislodging a piece of meat from one of his rotten teeth, then also spitting into the fire. Everyone fell silent, waiting to hear what he had in mind, but he just downed another bowl of *kumis* and belched.

"What do you have in mind, Kirmog?" asked Lado.

"I want to disgrace the slant, make him look like he left the caravan and ran off."

"What are you going to do, just ask him to leave?" mocked Skag, his hand on his big black beard.

"At the point of a sword, yes. Take him and his woman out in the desert, have some fun with her, kill him. Keep her if she's not too much trouble. We can always use a good fuck once in a while, and someone to cook for us. Kill her, if she gets to be a problem."

"Too risky. If they put up a fuss, that's it for us."

"Two of us take the bitch when she's alone, gag her and drive their wagon out a couple of miles behind us. She'll be easy to handle, she's just a slant. The rest of us offer to help her man find her, follow tracks like, you know. When we join you, then we threaten the woman to find out where his stash is, and kill him. Abmatak will think she ran off, he followed, and they decided not go on."

"The *sartpaw* is not stupid. We'll be missing too, and he knows you hate the slant's guts. He'll come looking for us."

"We keep going back the way we came. We can get far enough back that he won't be able to find us in a day or two, and the caravan is moving on. If he doesn't find us the first day, there'll be fifty miles between us on the second. He won't put the caravan at risk for two strangers and us three."

"Yeah, but we better not ever be seen in Turfam again," said Lado. "Him and Jamshid have long memories."

"I don't ever intend to go there again. You know, Chang'an was a pretty nice city. I could enjoy living around slants, if I had a lot of money. Think on it, boys, we have a couple of days. I want to be three or four days outside of Zhangye before I make my moves. And remember, if any of you are not in with me, keep your fuckin' mouth shut. I'm going to get some sleep, first light comes too early." Kirmog lay down on the ground next to the fire, wrapped himself in his ragged wool blanket, and was soon snoring. The others sat up, thinking about what he said, but did no talking.

The caravan wound through the Painted Hills of Zhangye, a multicolored tapestry of mountains striped in reds, brilliant yellows and blues, vermillions and greens. Seated alongside Marcus on their sheltered wagon, Mei took his hand in hers. "This is so beautiful, Si Nuo. You don't mind if I speak this in *han-yu,* my poor Latin is not up to describe this. Like the gods draped a tapestry on the mountains. So brilliant!"

"It is, Frontinus and I used to come up here to hunt when we were boys. I haven't seen these hills since."

They rode on in silence, Marcus occasionally clucking the horses on. Cooking pots rattled in the bed as the wagon lurched in the rutted road. At one point, Kirmog rode up beside them. Marcus tensed, but Kirmog smiled, tipped his brimmed hat, and smiled at them "I am sorry, I was rude to strangers. Forgive me, please."

Marcus returned the smile and answered haltingly. He was rapidly learning Sogdian, the language they spoke, enough like the Persian that he had learned many years ago on his travels. "All well, Kirmog... *Ne*, not angry. Forgiving."

Kirmog smiled again, revealing the blackened stumps of his teeth behind his bushy beard, and tipped his hat. "Good day!" He whistled up his roan horse, wheeled and rode off in a cloud of yellow dust.

"I am surprised. It looks like that trouble is over," he said to Mei.

"I do not trust him." She kept her eyes firmly on the road ahead.

"Perhaps the *sartpaw* set him straight."

"Perhaps. Perhaps not."

A few days out of Zhangye, one of Kirmog's friends rode up to Marcus' wagon during a water break for the animals at a small river a few hours before sundown. "The s*artpaw* needs to see you, right now. He is at the rear of the caravan."

Marcus nodded. "Take care of the animals, Mei, I'll be back shortly." He headed off at a walk.

Mei busied herself with the horses and mules, then sat in the wagon, waiting for Marcus' return. After about an hour, the rider returned, babbling something in his language. She didn't understand a word, and just shook her head, indicating confusion. The man spoke slowly, using Marcus' *han-yu* name, Si Nuo. He gestured, indicating she should take the wagon and follow him.

She shook her head in the negative. *I do not trust these people. I don't know where he is taking me.* She reached down to scratch her leg, discretely loosening the thong on her dagger in its calf sheath.

The man shouted and gesticulated. Mei wasn't going anywhere, so the man grabbed the lead horse by the bridle and struck off, Mei helplessly holding on, screaming for him to stop. Caravanners looked up at the site, but shrugged and did nothing, assuming it was some sort of argument between a man and a woman.

After about ten minutes, the man pulled the snorting team to a halt well behind the caravan, near a scrub tree by which stood another of Kirmog's friends. The two of them lifted Mei, kicking and screaming, bodily off the wagon seat. As they did so, one of them discovered her calf sheath as she attempted to kick at them. One held her foot, while the other slid the dagger out of its sheath. They passed the weapon back and forth between them, laughing, amused at her anger.

"Let me go! Abmatak will hear of this!" The men looked at her, laughing and talking among each other. She caught Abmatak's name and Si Nuo's, but nothing else. One produced a coil of rope and bound her hands behind her, then put a filthy rag in her mouth for a gag and laid her back in the wagon. *I was right not to trust them, but it matters not... they have me. What do they want?*

The two men stood off a way, quietly conversing, sharing a skin of wine. *Waiting for someone. Kirmog? What have they done to Si Nuo? Just watch and listen, look for an opportunity.* She wrestled with the ropes binding her wrists, but they were expertly tied, and she was unable to undo the knots.

In the rear of the idled caravan, Marcus walked about, searching vainly for Abmatak. No one had seen the *sartpaw*, he was normally at the head. There was some confusion, sounds of a wagon driven hard, shouts and the neighing of horses. Probably a runaway. He was about to go back to his wagon, when Kirmog rode up. "Trouble with your wife's wagon. Come, ride with me." He put out his hand and lifted Marcus into the saddle in front of him. After a minute, Marcus realized they were not headed back to where their wagon had been. "Where are we going?" he asked.

"Back. Your wife's horses ran away."

"She is all right?"

"I don't know. They said to bring you."

They had ridden for about a mile when they caught sight of the wagon, upright, apparently undamaged, the horses idly tossing their heads at flies, no signs of distress. Kirmog's friends Sigo, Skag, and Lado stood around idly, but Mei was nowhere in sight. Marcus slid off, followed by Kirmog.

"Where is she?" asked Marcus.

"Inside the wagon with your treasure. Tell us where you hid it and we'll let her go."

"Treasure? I have no treasure!" His halting Sogdian did not allow for profanity or fancy expressions of anger, but his face showed it all.

"You're not going to Kashgar with empty pockets, Slant," sneered Kirmog. "And don't reach for your blade, I've had mine out since we left the caravan." He turned to his friends. "Get her out, boys. Did you search the wagon?"

"Yes, but there wasn't anything of value in there," answered Lado, shrugging. "Just the usual shit." He turned and with Sigo helping, they dragged Mei from the bed of the wagon and dropped her rudely on the ground with a thump.

Marcus started toward her Kirmog restrained him. He held out his hand. "Give me your blade."

Marcus withdrew his dagger and reluctantly handed it to Kirmog, hilt first.

"Now both of you know where the treasure is. It's a question of who talks first." He turned to his friends again. "Take off the bitch's gag. Let's cut on her slant husband first, starting with the parts she likes the most. Skag, grab his arms behind, and Sido, you help."

The two of them pinioned Marcus from behind, while to Marcus' horror, Kirmog slid down his riding breeches and unwound his loin cloth.

"What have we here?" he said in amazement. "Someone beat us to them. His balls are already gone! You're of those slant-eyed eunuch bitches, aren't you? I bet you've had more men than your bitch over there. Well, they forgot your cock, so I guess we'll settle for that." He pulled the tip of Marcus' penis up, positioning his knife, when Mei, sobbing, screamed and began babbling in *han-yu*.

"No, No, No! Don't hurt him! I'll show you whatever you want."

"What's she saying, Slant?" said Kirmog, releasing Marcus' organ and lowering the knife.

Marcus' heart was hammering in fear and shame, but he collected his thoughts. "She'll show you where the treasure is. It's in the wagon under a false bottom." He switched to *han-yu*. "Mei, give them our traveling money. That's what they want."

Mei nodded, still sobbing.

"Let her up, Lado. There's a false bottom, she'll show you."

With Mei's direction, Lado found a stick to push through a hole underneath the bed, to push up the false floor. He removed the panel, pulling out a sack the size of a large melon, and looked inside. "It doesn't seem to have anything in it but some grey shit." He pulled out a large block of beeswax. "Beeswax, but it sure is heavy." Lado worked the wax with his knife, until he was able to extract a silver coin. Mei continued sobbing, holding onto the wagon bed.

"Well, looks like we got what we came for, almost. We were going to kill you, but now looks like maybe we can just remove a few things here and there, and have you as a bed partner, too," said Kirmog, eying Marcus' penis again.

Marcus was reliving the horror of that night twenty years ago, when he had ceased to be a whole man. And the shame ... no whole man had ever seen his scars, no man knew what had been done to him, so long ago. He braced for the pain, tears pouring from his eyes.

Then a clatter of horses rode up, Abmatak with ten men. He and five men dismounted, swords drawn, while the other five notched arrows, taking aim at Kirmog's party. Abmatak strode up to Kirmog, knocked the knife from his hand and hit him full on the mouth with a powerful blow, knocking him to the ground amidst a spray of blood and shattered teeth. The *sartpaw* turned to the men holding Marcus and roared, "Release him! Now!"

Trembling, they did so and stood back. Lado put the sack and beeswax treasure back in the wagon and likewise stepped back from Mei.

Marcus hastily pulled up his trousers, trying to conceal his shame.

"I am truly sorry, Si Nuo," said Abmatak in *han-yu*. "Did he hurt either of you?"

Marcus shook his head, squeezing his eyes shut in a vain attempt to stop the tears that were running down his cheeks. They had not yet hurt him physically, but what they had done to his soul was far worse. Mei ran to him, clinging to him, soothing him like a distressed child.

Abmatak spoke to Kirmog's gang. "You have dishonored us. We don't steal and assault those who have put their faith in us. This is the last day of your miserable lives, and it will be a long one! Tie them up, and drag them back to camp behind the horses."

He turned again to Marcus. "Can you ride? Do you need help?"

Marcus shook his head, helping Mei onto the wagon. He stepped up and took the reins. His heart refused to stop pounding.

The men were quickly bound, then tethered behind four of the horses. The riders clucked their mounts into movement, as did Marcus. The riders kept it slow at first, the men struggling to keep pace. But the pace kept quickening, until Lado stumbled and went facedown onto the rough trail, his body kicking up dust as he writhed to avoid rocks and obstacles. Then Kirmog went down. Soon all four were plowing up the road behind the horses.

"All right, boys, first one to the camp gets a silver coin!" The horses broke into a gallop, the four men bouncing along behind.

Marcus kept pace in the wagon, but the men's torment did nothing to ease his own. Mei reached her arm through his and said nothing.

Back at the camp, the *sartpaw* called a meeting of all the caravanners, his men holding up the bloody, battered bodies of the miscreants, their clothes in tatters

"We all know the rules. We don't steal from each other, we don't steal the valuables we carry, and we never steal from those who have put their faith in us to travel safely with us. Is that not so?" said Abmatak, in a loud voice that carried over the assembly, Marcus and Mei by his side.

There was a murmur of approval from the crowd.

"These men not only stole from two of our traveling companions, they were preparing to assault and kill these two people standing here, betraying that sacred trust." He turned to Kirmog. "Do you have anything to say for what you did?"

Kirmog's torn and bloody lips could barely form the words. He mumbled something incoherent and shook his head.

"You have broken that sacred trust, and you will pay for that with your heads, after you are flogged." Abmatak indicated the wheels of Marcus' wagon. "Tie them. Kirmog will be the last. I want the perpetrator of this outrage to see his men suffer, the better to anticipate his own."

The flogging began, one man at a time, fifty lashes with a heavy leather bullwhip, each stroke landing with a loud snap that drew blood and tore away flesh. At the end, the quivering mass of tattered bleeding flesh was unbound and thrown to the ground, crying and pawing the dirt futilely. Kirmog was pale and shaking when he at last was bound and tied for the beating.

Kirmog joined his companions on the ground, his flogging done, but not for long. The men were dragged away, as they could no longer walk, to the execution block, a simple stump. The executioner placed one man's head on the block, hoisted his axe to descend on the exposed neck, and the head flew off in a shower of blood. One, two, three times, Kirmog's allies went to their death. When it came Kirmog's turn, the executioner pulled his stroke at the last minute, partially severing the neck but not killing the man instantly. Kirmog's face distorted in a horrible scream, but no sound came forth. His body shook in violent convulsions for several seconds. Then Abmatak nodded, and the executioner completed the act.

"Take these animals out to the fields as food for the wolves. They don't deserve a burial."

The crowd dissipated. Abmatak turned to Marcus and Mei. "You would do me a great honor if you would join me at my fire, at least for a few moments."

Marcus nodded.

At Abmatak's fire, they were the only ones. The *sartpaw* pulled from his purse two silver coins. "I cannot charge you for passage with us after what happened to you. He pulled out a gold one as well. "Here is a small payment besides for your suffering. Please accept my apologies, those men shamed me."

Marcus nodded dully and accepted the coins. *Had Abmatak seen my shame? Did he know that I am not a whole man? I had been unable to protect myself, much less Mei.*

"I will understand if you choose not to eat. Our justice on the trail is harsh, to make sure that none take advantage of opportunities. But some *kumis*, at least, please." He filled a bowl with the white liquid from a leather sack and offered it Marcus, then prepared another for Mei.

Marcus accepted the bowl, took a sip to savor the sweet almond flavor and its alcoholic warmth, then downed it in a single gulp. He handed the bowl back for more.

Abmatak smiled and poured him another. "Finish that one, and I have a skin of Turfam wine for you. I believe this would be a good night to drink, to forget all that happened today. I don't want to know what they were planning to do to you, but it appears I arrived just in time. They had made such a commotion stealing your wagon that the whole caravan knew what was happening. You are all right, they didn't hurt you?" Abmatak's eye's showed real concern.

"We thank you for what you did today, Abmatak," said Mei, speaking for the silent Marcus in a voice barely perceptible. She too was shaken to her core.

"You are most welcome, and more for you also," said Abmatak, refilling her bowl.

The next morning, despite a splitting headache. Marcus was up at first light to help load the animals.

CHAPTER 8:

A BAND OF RAGAMUFFINS

Petra, Roman Province of Arabia Petraea: July 112AD

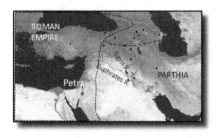

The man chased the ragged little boy through the back alleys of the pink sandstone buildings of Petra. The lad had propositioned him for sexual favors in exchange for money, a common enough practice among street urchins to supplement begging and thieving, but when he offered to take to him to Jacobus' home, the boy ran off. Street urchins were like rats, nimble, evasive and attuned to every hiding place, but Vergilius had tracked them down before, wise to their tricks.

He had pointedly shaken his head in disgust and ostentatiously gave up the chase, walking off slowly, knowing that boy was following his every move. When he got to the intersection, he doubled back through alleys to come up behind the boy, who was watching the street intently from behind a rock.

The boy never knew Vergilius was on him until he felt himself seized in the man's strong arms. "Gotcha, ya little bastard! Gotcha! We're taking you to someone who will really like you." He tucked the kicking, screaming boy under his left arm and headed off down the street. No one paid him and his unusual parcel a second glance. After all, it was Petra, and the urchins were a nuisance the locals called 'mosquito boys.'

Vergilius strode down the Siq, the road through the narrow canyon by the same name guarding the approaches to Petra, leading to his friend's place near the new Roman amphitheater. Like most everything else here, this home too was of soft pink sandstone blocks. He rang the bell hanging by the door. "Jacobus, I have a present for you."

"So you do, so you do," said Jacobus, stroking his gray-flecked pointed black beard, his eyes bright with anticipation. Vergilius was always struck by Jacobus' weasel-like appearance, due to his short, thin stature, narrow features and piercing black eyes. "Come in and close the door, so he can't escape and lead you on another chase."

Vergilius set the boy down on the floor. Clothed in just a loincloth, he might have been anywhere from four to eight years old, probably the latter, his dusky and dirty body stunted by years of infrequent meals and sleeping outside in the cold desert night. There was nowhere to run, so he stood trembling, black eyes defiant and terrified at the same time, under a mop of stringy, unkempt black hair. He smelled.

Jacobus tucked up his white robe and crouched down to the boy, talking softly to him in Nabataean, as one would a timid alley cat. "There, there. My name is Yakov. What is yours?"

The boy hesitated. "Stick."

"Stick? That's an unusual name. Do you have any other names?"

"Stick. That's my name."

Yakov smiled. "How did you come by that name?"

"I'm always Stick. Never had no other name."

"Well, Stick, I bet you are hungry. When was the last time you had a good meal?"

"A piece of bread this morning. I found it in the garbage. It was this big." The boy held his small hands to indicate something perhaps two inches across.

"Well, that's a pretty good find. You know, I used to run these same streets when I was your age, so I know that's a big find. We were going to have some stew, hot meat, would you like to have some?"

The boy's eyes grew wide with excitement. "Yes! You give me dinner for a blow job?"

"No, that's not why Vergilius brought you here. I used to be a little street kid like you, until someone gave me a new life, and now I am trying to return the favor."

Jacobus clapped, and a servant girl brought a tray with a steaming bowl of stew, bread and cool juice, and set it down on the floor by the boy.

"Thank you, Miranda." He nodded in the girl's direction. She smiled and bowed, ever so imperceptibly. Jacobus turned to Stick. "Be careful you don't burn yourself, it's hot."

Stick ignored the spoon and put his face into the bowl, eating like a dog. He lifted his smiling face up, covered with stew broth. Jacobus took a towel and washed his face. "Easy, Stick. Let's try the spoon, shall we?" He put the spoon in the boy's hand and guided it to the bowl, then to the boy's mouth. At the last minute, the boy jerked the spoon, overturning its contents onto his lap. "Let's just let the table manners go for another lesson, Stick. Eat it however you like."

Stick returned to lapping the stew noisily like a dog. He then tore the bread into chunks, devouring them. Finally, he drained the glass of juice in a single swallow.

"I hope you don't get sick, eating so much so fast."

Stick gave a contented belch.

"So, do you remember your mother and father, Stick, and how you came to be on the streets?"

"Never had no mother and father. Always been on the streets. I guess I was born there."

"I don't remember mine, either. I never knew who they were." *When I came back, I dreamed of finding them here. Maybe I did, but we would never have recognized each other. Or maybe they died, or maybe moved on, maybe, maybe ...* "I used to steal purses. Do you do that?"

"I'm good at it, but the big boys don't let me keep any money." said Stick, licking food off his hand.

"So was I, and they didn't let me keep any either. One day I picked a man's purse, and he came after me like Vergilius did you, and carried me off screaming and kicking. When he found out I had no family, he took me off the streets and raised me like his own son. The adventures we had together!"

"So you want me to be your son?"

"If you will have me. I have a room full of my new sons that you can meet. We all get along, nobody beats anybody up, everyone gets plenty to eat. And you get to sleep inside under blankets. You won't miss your old pack, will you?"

Stick shrugged. "Maybe a few. The little kids. I tried to take care of them so the big boys didn't beat 'em up or make 'em do stuff."

"So, let's set you up for the night." He clapped his hand and the servant girl reappeared from the shadows. "Miranda, would you take Stick here and give him a bath, then take him in to meet the other boys? Set him up a place to sleep."

"With pleasure, sir." She smiled and squatted down to Stick's level. "I'm going to help you take a bath, little man, because I think you haven't had one for a very long time. Maybe never. Come with me." She took his hand and led him off.

"This is truly God's work you do here, Jacobus."

"Thanks, Vergilius. Caesar's work as well. The Romans appreciate my getting the 'mosquito boys' off the streets."

"I see you took down your fish symbol from the door."

"Yes, the new Roman governor Claudius Severus and some of his people paid me a visit a few weeks ago, and I had just enough notice to take it down and put it out of sight, now that we are officially a Roman province. I didn't want to give the good governor a reason to think anything but good thoughts of me, though his informants no doubt would have seen it up earlier if they checked the place out. He apparently did think well of our work, because the occasion was to give me a small bag of gold *aurei* to take care of the children, enough to feed them for the rest of the year. He said getting them off the streets was good for business."

"I heard he has a 'live and let live' approach to Christians, as does *Princeps* Trajan."

"He does, but others don't. I just don't think it's wise to fly a red flag outside."

The next morning dawned hot and sunny, as did every morning in Petra. The ten boys, ages ranging from four to nearly adult, trooped down for breakfast, all except for one. Miranda went off to look for Stick, and finding his blanket warm but empty, went back to the table. "Boys, have you seen Stick, the new boy?"

They all shook their heads, had heard nothing, seen nothing. She took the bad news to Jacobus. "I am sorry to hear that. I guess he figured he would take the free meal, and go back to the streets," he said.

"How could he have gotten out? Everything is closed up."

"They are like little rats, able to squeeze through the smallest space to make their escape. Maybe he will return someday, or Vergilius will find him again. He'll survive, he's gotten this far." But Jacobus sighed. He had liked the little Stick.

A few hours later, there was a knock on the door, so soft that Jacobus almost didn't hear it. He opened the door to find Stick, holding the hand of a diminutive little girl with ragged blonde hair in tangles.

Jacobus squatted down, mussing her hair. She was still sucking her thumb, she was that young. Three? "What's your name, little one?"

She twisted shyly, then answered, still sucking her thumb, "Mouth"

"Well, Mouse, we haven't had a little girl here with us. Stick, was this one of the ones you wanted to take care of?"

Stick nodded. "Um hm. Can you give her nice food like you gave me?"

"Sure, come in." He closed the door behind them, then clapped his hands. "Miranda, come here, please. Stick is back, and he brought a friend."

CHAPTER 9:

A SMUGGLER'S STASH

Enroute to Turfam, China: July 112AD

The next month passed uneventfully. Which was good, because Marcus could not have handled more events. His shame at the hands of Kirmog and his men, their mockery of him, these were the things he had dreaded for the past twenty years of his life. Their gruesome deaths did not assuage his fear. Had anyone seen his shame? Did they tell anyone what they saw? As each caravanner looked at him, to speak or just in passing, he averted his eyes, fearful that he might catch a hint of their knowledge.

The evenings with Abmatak were the high point of the day. The *sartpaw* was eager to improve his command of the Hanaean language, for he often made the run to Chang'an, and hated having to deal with translators, never believing they gave honest translations. And Marcus could find a word in Parthian or his rapidly improving Sogdian to help explain an Hanaean word or phrase.

For his part, Marcus was grateful for the rescue and the swift justice. If anyone had seen his scar, it should have been Abmatak. But if he had, he gave no hint, asked no questions. Marcus could relax with him, with Mei by his side.

"So, Si Nuo, how did a man from China come by these many languages? I've known people on the caravans that use these languages every day, and they don't speak as well as you. You must have done some traveling?"

Marcus took a sip of wine from the sack. "Yes, indeed I did. You have heard of the *Da Qin?*"

"Kind of a mythical people far to the West, we call them *Romi*, I have heard of them, even seen a few *Romi* merchants in Samarkand once."

"Not a myth. I have been there."

"Been to ... Rome?"

"To be sure. I am *Da Qin* by ancestry. That is why I have blue eyes and my Latin name Marcus. Some *Da Qin* soldiers were captured and ended up settling in Gansu more than a century ago. They passed their language on, so their descendants grew up speaking both Latin and *han-yu*. When the Han Court sought to send a mission to Rome twenty years ago, they took me and my sister Marcia from our town of Liqian to the court to prepare us as translators. We went to Rome by land, through the cities of Khojand, Bukhara, and Samarkand. The *Da Qin* emperor sent a return mission to the Han court, and my sister and I went back by sea with some of our companions from Liqian."

"An impressive trip, no wonder you picked up so many languages. Where is your sister now?"

"She married one of the *Da Qin* in Liqian, with our family there. They went on to Rome with the rest of the *Da Qin*. I stayed behind to care for my mother. But now she has passed away, and I want to return to Rome, perhaps to find Marcia and her husband."

Abmatak slapped his leg and laughed. "You have a sense of adventure like no other, Si Nuo. Or should I call you Marcus? Around the world and back again, and now you want to go again. Here, this is going to be a two-skin night. Have some more wine and tell me more."

Marcus basked in the sense of acceptance, even admiration. He needed that for healing. Mei grasped his hand quietly, as she always did, letting him know she was there and cared.

The next morning Marcus awoke with a desert-dry mouth, a splitting headache, and a stomach that rebelled at the thought of food. Though Abmatak had excused him from the morning loadout, he rinsed his mouth with water, then went to help load the animals and wagon, hoisting the bags, some the weight of a large man, onto camels, donkeys, and wagons. By the time the sun was over the horizon, the baggage had been loaded, the animals hitched to the wagons, time for him to rig his own wagon. By the time Abmatak's horn blew its 'move out' message, Marcus was ready to go. Mei took the reins from his hands with a smile and pressed gently on his shoulder. "Go lay down, Marcus. I will drive. You drank too much wine last night."

Marcus acquiesced, noting that Mei had used all the correct tenses and cases. Her Latin was improving.

Over the next several weeks, Marcus' mood improved, as the events outside Zhangye faded in their immediacy. But something in him resisted letting go. He periodically awoke in the middle of the night screaming, having dreamed of seeing a leering Kirmog holding his bleeding severed member before his face. Trembling, he would cuddle against Mei. But sleep would not return on those tortured nights.

They reached the Hanaean customs station at Dunhuang, outside the fort that marked the boundaries of Chinese control. Marcus, with his fluency in *han-yu*, assisted with the blue-robed customs officials, standing beside the *sartpaw* and translating between them. They were exceedingly thorough, carefully checking off names of the men who had entered several months ago, with those exiting. "They want to know what happened to Kirmog and his men, Abmatak."

"Tell them they were killed in a terrible accident… that their wagon went over a cliff on a steep mountain pass."

The customs men bought the explanation. They then went to inspect the wagons, in particular making sure that no one smuggled out the precious silkworms, to sell to some nation wanting to break the Chinese monopoly on silk. The penalty for that was death, and the customs officials had the authority to carry out that sentence immediately. As they came to his wagon, Marcus remembered with horror that he had not undone the false bottom. *Will they find it? And then what?*

Find it they did, and Marcus watched, trying to betray no emotion, his heart thudding, as they lifted the panel amid cries of discovery. They grabbed the sack and dumped out the block of beeswax. The head customs official turned to Marcus, his face dark with anger. "Whose wagon is this?"

Marcus bowed respectfully. "It is mine," answered Marcus, as impassively as possible.

"What is hidden inside the beeswax?"

"Our life savings. We are going to Kashgar to begin a new life. As it is a lot of money, I sealed it in beeswax to keep it from making noise, and built the false bottom to hide it. Your men are admirably thorough, Dian Xi. It did not take long for them to find it. Would you like to inspect the coinage?"

Dian Xi grunted and nodded his head ever so slightly. Marcus produced his knife, carefully showing them what he was going to do. He cut out a few of the coins, and handed one to the customs agent. He scrutinized the coin. "It is not Hanaean. Where did you get it?"

Marcus switched to perfect Hanaean court language, rather than the rough Gansu peasant dialect he had been speaking. "They are *Da Qin* coins. They were given to me by a party of *Da Qin*, representing their emperor before the Sun of Heaven. I was their official translator, before the Son of Heaven. I escorted them out of the Middle Kingdom, continuing to act as their translator. This was their gratitude for my service."

The court language had the intended effect. Dian Xi straightened up and bowed respectfully, placing his fists together before him. "Forgive my impertinence, Your Excellency. Your speech and dress did not betray your high station."

"Please, there is no offense. When one is traveling with a lot of wealth among strangers it is wise not to appear to be wealthy, if one wishes to keep it. Please, take the coin I gave you as a souvenir. There are many more in that block of worthless-looking beeswax. Continue your inspection as you see fit."

"Your Excellency, I believe we are done. I will have my men restore your conveyance to its proper order. I regret any inconvenience. "

"There can be no inconvenience from a servant of the Son of Heaven doing his assigned task with great diligence. Please, I insist you complete your inspection of my wagon first. I, too, am but a humble servant of the Son of Heaven."

"As you order, Your Excellency." Dian Xi bowed yet again, then ordered his men to continue. After a perfunctory inspection they replaced his stash and reassembled the false bottom. This time, all five saluted Marcus, their fists together before their bowed heads. "We are complete, Your Excellency," said Dian Xi, handing Marcus a bamboo strip with black Hanaean characters on it. "Here is your caravan's clearance. The caravan master is free to proceed."

"Thank you. I shall send word to the Court of your great diligence." Marcus gave a barely perceptible nod in return.

As the men quickly left, Marcus handed Abmatak his clearance. "This certifies that you are good. Should we run into any more customs stations, just show them this."

"What the hell did you just do?" asked Abmatak in Sogdian, "I thought they were going to execute you on the spot for smuggling, then they acted like you were some prince. And suddenly I couldn't understand what you two were saying."

"Well, in a way I was. I let them know that I had translated for the *Da Qin* party before Emperor He himself, and explained that those were *Da Qin* coins given to me by them in gratitude for my service. In the high court language, not country bumpkin talk.'

"Well, that was a neat false bottom you had there, and the coins in beeswax... an old smuggler's trick."

"I learned that from a pirate, so I guess he must have done some smuggling in his time."

"You keep strange company, Marcus."

"That I do, Abmatak, that I do."

CHAPTER 10:

THE CARAVANSERY AT TURFAM

Turfam, China: July 112AD

After the animals were unloaded and put to pasture, Abmatak assembled the caravanners before they made camp and disappeared for the night. He addressed them in a loud voice carrying over the crowd, holding aloft a handful of ribbons of various colors. "The riders from the caravansary were here today and gave us the ribbons to use. We will be arriving in Turfam in two or three days. You must tag your loads by destination." He held up a white ribbon. "White is for goods destined for Turfam." Then holding up a ribbon of each color, "Yellow is for Kashgar and everything west, red is for Hotan and everything south, black is for Urumqi and north into Mongolia. You will attach a ribbon to each animal, harness, wagon and load going to these places. Don't put one on your personal baggage, unless you don't want to see it again. Take it with you, label everything else. The crew will be on us like locusts, and they will put away the labeled stuff under lock and key. Jamshid, the master of caravans, is the only one who can open up the storage to help you look for something you mislabeled, and he won't be happy with you if he has to do that. The stuff we bring in will be going out with another caravan, so pay attention. If you don't know what color to use, see me. Questions?"

"What about stops in between like Aksu?" someone queried.

"Mark it for Kashgar. We won't be breaking up the load at Aksu."

There was a murmur of understanding, no more questions, and with a wave of his hand, the *sartpaw* dismissed the group their camps. He handed Marcus a handful of yellow ribbons. "See you at my fire when you are done. Let me know if you need more."

Marcus nodded, accepting the ribbons and headed off.

He and Mei returned an hour or so later, taking a seat by the fire, in what had become an almost nightly occurrence. "Well, Abmatak, we certainly have enjoyed these nightly chats. They have helped make the weeks pass swiftly. I thank you for all you did for us, and in gratitude, I have a special gift." Marcus drew two white ceramic bottles, with Hanaean characters on one side, and on the other, the six-teated Roman wolf, underneath the letters 'SPQR'. "I told you my ancestors were Roman soldiers. When they got to Liqian a hundred and fifty years ago, there was no grape wine to be had in all of China. They got some grape shoots from a passing caravan, set up a vineyard, and began making wine. It made our little village famous, the caravans regularly stop there just to buy our wine. This one is for you," he said, handing the bottle to Abmatak. "Mei and I will share this one."

Abmatak studied the little bottle. "You are right, all the *sartpaws* say to stop there, and we have picked up several large amphorae for sale in Chang'an. It is very popular there, gets a good price. But I've never drunk any, just sold it." He worked the wax seal off with his knife and took a sip. "Ah, I see why they like it so much. That is very good. Warms my soul ... So how did Roman soldiers wind up in China?"

Marcus likewise opened his and took a sip. "They were defeated in a disastrous battle with the Parthians more than a century ago. A general from the east admired their courage, felt they were worth more to him alive than dead, and got the Parthian king to release them to him. They wound up after several years in Liqian as border guards. Liqian was a frontier town, and also a place where the Chinese resettled all sorts of captives. So today you have all sorts of people living there, some Chinese in appearance like me, some blonde-haired people called the Yuezhi, some Mongols, Xiongnu... everything in between."

"Mei is Roman, too?"

"No, Mei is all Chinese. My 'Red Gem,' the meaning of her name."

They drank quietly for a minute, the fire crackling.

"I have a question, Abmatak. Our traveling money in its smuggler's stash... should we tag it for storage, or keep it with us?"

"It's yours to do with as you see fit, but if I were you, I'd tag it and let it be put in storage. It will be under lock and key, and if anyone were to get caught stealing baggage, they would lose their right hand. In your room, on the other hand ..." He left the thought unfinished. "I'll introduce you to Jamshid, He'll set you up the rest of the way to Kashgar. You will like him, he is a good person ... for a Tocharian." He chuckled.

"Will I be able to talk to him?"

"He speaks better *han-yu* than I do. By the way, thank you for the time spent in this language. I feel much better at it than when we started. That was why I kept inviting you to my fire ... language lesson." He took a swig of the Liqian wine, then looked at the bottle in disgust. "It's empty. You don't have another, do you?"

Marcus reached in a sack and pulled out another. "I didn't think two would be enough for us."

"Anyway, Jamshid and his crews speak mostly Bactrian. It's almost the same as Sogdian, which you speak pretty well now. Bactrian sounds funny, some of the words are different, but you'll pick it up fast. The Bactrians used to run all the caravans, but when we Sogdians started moving in as newcomers, we got the leftover routes, all in China, and we made a fortune there! We run all the caravansaries around Chang'an."

In two days, after an arduous two months of travel, the caravan reached the city of Turfam. The city was situated on a high plateau separating two rivers, giving it the Hanaean name of *Jiaohe,* 'River Junction.' Below the city on either side of the plateau, for miles on either side until the desert challenged the greenery to a halt, was a broad expanse of green fields, vineyards, fruit trees planted in orderly rows, and one enormous caravansary on the flat plain.

The townspeople flocked to see the caravan's arrival miles before it got to the building. The arrival of a caravan was an opportunity for the townspeople to sell or barter their local crafts and produce, to purchase some hard-to-come-by goods from far-away places, and to catch up with news from a world that was otherwise far, far away.

Marcus and Mei watched the caravansary emerge from the distance, a giant octagonal structure of stone, huge wooden doors on each side, one of which was swung open. "That building is two stories high, Mei. And maybe two hundred feet across, more like a fort."

"It certainly is big. And the townspeople. There must be hundreds lining the roads, Marcus." The crowd was waving and cheering, as if in celebration. Fathers carried children on their shoulders, the tykes waving excitedly at the animals, the heavily-laden camels with their slumping gait, the horses, the mules, the oxen.

"Looks like they are glad to see us. Probably want to sell us something. Or steal something."

"Marcus, don't be rude." She elbowed him in the ribs with a smile.

In their wagon bed, yellow silk ribbons fluttered in the breeze.

As they reached the open doors, high enough for a man on camelback and wide enough for a big wagon, they were met by boys of perhaps ten or twelve in age, who expertly took the animals in tow. Abmatak was right; as they entered the compound, hollow inside like a fort, the boys were on the wagon like locusts, some unharnessing the mules and stowing the harness, leading the animals out to pasturage outside the opposite gate. Others loaded bags their own weight into large wheelbarrows, checked the ribbons and wheeled them off to storage rooms marked with flags of the same color. In a half an hour, all five hundred animals of the caravan were grazing contentedly in the fenced paddock, and the last of the storage walls slammed shut, locked to secure goods, all bound to the same destinations.

Marcus and Mei looked around. Between the big storage rooms at each gate, the inside walls were lined with offices, shops, bars, brothels, baths, eateries of various kinds, with the pleasant smells of baking bread and roasting meat filling the air. In the center of the compound the locals had set up markets, dozens of merchants and farmers selling their wares from under multicolored awnings.

Abmatak strolled up to them. "I warned you it would be efficient."

"It was. Each of those storerooms have goods for a particular destination?"

"Yes, and not just our goods, but anything else that might have come in, or local produce going out. Let's go see Jamshid." He led them off to one of the offices, entering without knocking.

"Jamshid!" he called out in Bactrian, and a man in his mid-fifties looked up from his desk. He was stocky, swarthy with streaks of gray in his dark hair and a bushy beard, in his forties, wearing a long light-colored shirt over trousers of beige felt. His complexion was fair, but it was obvious from its leathery texture that he had not spent most of his life inside at some desk.

"Abmatak! You Sogdian grave robber, welcome back!" He gave the man a big hug and kissed him on both cheeks. "Who are your friends?"

"Your next pair of travelers. They speak better *han-yu* than Sogdian, and they are hearing Bactrian for the first time." He switched to *han-yu*. "This is Si Nuo and his wife Mei. They want to go to Kashgar."

Jamshid walked over and took Marcus' hand in a firm grip, then looked intently into his eyes. "Have we met, Si Nuo? Even your name seems familiar."

"I think not, Jamshid. I have never been here before."

"The eyes, the blue eyes. I have only seen one other Hanaean with blue eyes, and that was many years ago. A woman she was, a very remarkable woman, traveling with some *Da Qin* going back west."

Marcus' heart thudded for joy. "About ten years ago? Was her name Si Huar?"

"Something like that, yes, I think that was. Married to a big *Da Qin* soldier."

"Antonius!" said Marcus, his face lighting with joy. "That was my sister!"

"Well, if you are her brother, the trip to Kashgar is on me. She fought off a bandit raid almost single-handedly, my security guard said she fought like Xiongnu. She was the talk of all the caravans for years to come. What takes you to Kashgar?"

Marcus had always been evasive about his final destination, because that might reveal his resources, resources definitely worth stealing. But if Jamshid knew Marcia and Aulus' party, he would know that Rome, too, was his final destination. "Kashgar, then on to Rome, however one gets there."

"We can take good care of you and your beautiful woman, Mei is your name?"

Mei smiled sweetly and bowed ever so slight. "That is correct... *Ja-Shi?*" as she tried to get her Hanaean tongue around the foreign consonants of his name.

Jamshid turned to Marcus. "Please, do me the honor of joining me for dinner tonight. That Sogdian scoundrel can show you how to find my house, and if he takes his muddy shoes off, he can join us also." He gave a wink in the direction of Abmatak.

CHAPTER 11:

OUTCASTS REJECTED

Turfam, China: July 112AD

Hina's group reached the outskirts of Turfam after a journey that depleted their supplies, leaving them nothing to eat but milk drained from the udders of their mares and camels. In the past, Hina had been here to trade several times with the clan on its annual migration south, and the reception at the caravansary was always welcoming, but she had never been in the city. Few Xiongnu had, finding the walls and narrow streets confining, a sense of danger at every blind turn and alley. Hina's group set up their camp about a mile out from the octagonal stone building, by a stream for water and bathing. Having slaked their thirst, they gleefully shed their clothes and stepped into the icy cold mountain stream to wash the grit and sweat accumulated on the dusty two-week journey.

Hina dried off and put on a clean set of felts, tossing the traveling clothes in the water.

"It would be a good time to eat, if we had anything," she announced. "Galosga, you and the men take care of Adhela, I think he would rather nap now. I'll take Andanyu and Marasa up to the caravansary and see if I can find something to eat. I have a bit of money."

She walked the distance with the twins, but as she got close, she sensed something wrong. Instead of the welcoming smiles they had always encountered, there were scowls, people spat on the ground in their direction. This did not feel right, but she ignored it.

When she got to the open gate, someone stood in front of her and told her she couldn't go in. Hina muscled him aside with disdain and entered the caravansary, where food stands and displays of goods were set up in the courtyard.

"Look, mother! Apples!" said Marasa, indicating a stand stacked with big yellow apples, a rare treat back in Dzungaria.

"Let's see if we can get some."

The merchant, a fat little bearded toad of a man, his belly protruding through his white vest, was anything but friendly. At first, he ignored her, his brow beetled in an angry scowl, but she insisted. "Apples. I buy, have money," she said haltingly.

While Hina was negotiating, Marasa picked up one of the treats up and took a bite out of it. The man exploded loudly. "Thieving Xiongers! Your brat stole one of my apples!"

Hina felt her face flush red with anger, her hand going automatically to her dagger. On the steppes, honor was all, and the penalty for an insult could be death. But not here. They did not understand honor in cities. She knew that if she drew the blade, men would come to take her away.

"Thieves! All of you, look! Thieving Xiongers come to rob us blind!"

"I not steal, I pay!" She opened her pouch and dumped several silver coins into her palm. "I pay! How much?"

The toady merchant looked greedily at her coins. "These are very expensive apples, Xionger. Three silvers."

Her hand trembled. She only had five silver coins in all. If apples cost that much, how would they live?

Then there was a familiar voice from long ago, a voice she never thought she would hear again, calling her by name in *han-yu*. "Hina, what is the problem? Can I help?"

She turned just enough to see a face from her distant past, Marcus, her sister Marcia's brother. But no time for reminiscing. "My daughter picked up one of his apples and took a bite."

He gently closed her fingers over the coins. "Put these away, I'll handle him." He spoke so fast that she could follow just a few words. "greedy bastard…three coppers." The merchant looked angrily at him and called him a 'slant,' and insisted on three silvers. Then Marcus mentioned a name, Jamshid, and the merchant's demeanor changed. Still scowling, he held out his hand, and Marcus put three coppers in his palm, then deftly took one back, picked up an apple and took a bite. "Good, but not that good," she understood him to say.

The merchant continued his tirade, "Xionger stink… drive buyers away." Marcus continued talking quietly but firmly to him, "…back tomorrow," she caught. He then ignored the rest of the glowering merchant's grumblings, turning his back to him to face Hina. She noticed the smiling, round-faced Hanaean woman by his side. "Marcus, thank you."

"No problem. This is my wife Mei. Mei, this Hina."

Mei bowed slightly and smiled. "I have heard so much about you! It is a pleasure to meet you, Hina."

"And these are my twins, Andanyu and Marasa. Ten years old, almost adults. I promised Marcia when we parted that I would name our children after them."

"Andanyu, Marasa, you bring honor to your family."

"We are honored to be part of our family," responded Andanyu, in very fluent Gansu *han-yu*. Xiongnu children grew up so quickly, Marcus knew from a year of traveling with them, so he treated them as the adults their mother said they were, as the full-sized daggers at their waists demanded; he was sure they did not wear those weapons for show. In size and musculature, they looked like Hina, but their hair was silky black, eyes piercing brown, and their skin coppery.

"These have to be Galosga's children."

Hina managed a smile. "He is in our camp about a mile away, with our youngest, Adhela. We have a small group."

Marcus gave her a wry grin. "Let's go, Hina. I think I need to explain some things to you about money, and get you some smaller coins. And help you buy whatever you need."

In short order, they bought yogurt, cheeses, fruit, and a goat, already prepared for cooking, all purchased by Marcus. All of the merchants were obviously hostile toward her and the children, but none gave an outburst as the first had. "I told the first that you were a friend of Jamshid. He runs this caravansary, the word spread fast."

They went off to one of the eateries for snacks and some of the local wine. "So what brings you to Turfam?" he asked.

"Nothing good, I am afraid."

"What is going on?"

"The Huyan clan, my friends, they are all gone." She choked back a sob, but could not stop a tear trickling down her cheek. Trembling, she fought to regain control, producing a weak smile. *Honor, honor is all!* "Sickness, then infighting. I could have been the *shanyu* when Bei died of the red spots, but … I turned it down. The infighting that finished them off… that is my fault, I could have prevented that, maybe prevented the sickness from spreading, but I didn't. And I don't know why I didn't."

"So, what are you going to do?"

"I don't know. I came here to find an Hanaean doctor, one who might know a cure or a treatment for the disease, but there is no one left to heal." She took a sip of her wine. "But what are you doing here, Marcus?" she asked, easily getting her tongue around his Latin name.

"Mei and I are going back to the land of the *Da Qin*. We hope to find Marcia and Antonius. She had a boy, Colloscius, and a girl Aena, named after you and Galosga, as close as she could get in Latin!"

Hina smiled, truly pleased at that. "That is so far away. How do you know these things?"

"We exchanged a few letters, two or three, but then they stopped several years ago. I hope they are all right."

"Letters? Oh, yes, the paper that talks. I would love to see my sister and Antonius again."

"She would be glad to see you."

Marcus reached into his pouch and pulled out some copper and bronze coins. "Silver coins, that is a lot of money, you could have bought four or five goats with the three silvers you offered that man, for one stinking apple. Don't bring silver coins out here, you'll get cheated like that bastard tried to do earlier, or someone will steal them. They'll probably overcharge you for these little ones, too, but it won't be so bad. Where are you staying?"

"In a yurt, north of town by a stream. We are the only ones there."

"We have to see Jamshid, the man who runs this caravansary, in a few hours. I will talk to him about you, he can make sure the merchants treat you fairly. I will see you mid-morning tomorrow. Mei will show you how to use the coins."

"Thank you, Marcus. It didn't used to be like this, but things have changed."

"Maybe we can set them right again."

CHAPTER 12:

INTERVENTION

Turfam, China: July 112AD

A few hours later, Abmatak, with Marcus and Mei, rode their horses across the grassy plain, and up the steep road clinging to the southern cliff-side of the plateau, to the city gates through the wall circling the city on the top of the plateau. Guards lolling with their spears waved all comers through, and the horses clattered onto the city streets. Jamshid's home was a white two-story adobe building on the perimeter road next to the wall, with hitching posts in front. After tethering their horses, they lifted a brass striker to announce their arrival. The door creaked open, held by a wizened old servant in a full-length white robe, a ring of snow-white hair around his pate, and a closely trimmed white beard. "Welcome," he said in a faint voice. "You are Marcus and Mei."

"We are."

"Follow me." He led them into a luxurious sitting room, decorated with fine Hanaean silk tapestries on the wall, and elaborately designed multicolored carpets. Greek-style sculptures and bronze statues were strategically placed to catch the eye, small oiled-filled ceramic bowls illuminating them with yellow flickering light, filling the room with a sweet scent. Jamshid and another man rose from the brown leather sofa to greet them, joined by a dark-haired woman wearing a long white silk shirt and loose-fitting blue trousers, of the style they called here *salwar kamis*.

"Welcome to my humble home, Marcus. This is Farhad, who will be your *sartpaw* to Kashgar. And my wife Aramo, who unfortunately does not speak *han-yu*."

"You are truly beautiful, Aramo," Marcus said in his best Sogdian, hoping she would understand, bowing in the Hanaean style to her, "and the house as well."

"You are most kind," Aramo said, smiling, and nodding a bit. "I will leave you men to talk about caravans, I will go up on the roof to supervise the servants preparing our dinner."

"My wife will accompany you and assist in any way she can. She speaks a little Sogdian, though not much." The two women exchanged greetings and left the room by the stairs leading up to the second floor.

Marcus turned to Farhad, extending his hand, as was customary among these people. Farhad took his in a firm grip. "I am pleased to meet you," he said.

Jamshid beckoned to black leather chairs facing the sofa. "Please sit. My father Alisher built this house, and he collected most of the decoration. He passed away, sadly, several years ago, so I inherited the operation and the house as well. And Zvarto, his most faithful servant," he said, smiling toward to the elderly doorkeeper, who nodded in return. "He will bring us some wine. Tell me how you came to stay in the Han lands."

"Here, we have something special for you." Marcus reached inside his red silk robe to extract the white bottle of Liqian wine and handed it to Zvarto. "Marcia and I were born in Liqian, before being taken by the Han court as translators. When we passed through there with the Xiongnu on our way back, we found our mother was still alive after ten years. That seemed like the perfect time for a grand wedding for Marcia and Antonius, and afterwards I wanted to stay to take care of Mother. And I married Mei," said Marcus.

"Yes, Marcia told me about that."

"Well, we were the fifth generation of Roman descendants, and few of us when we were young wanted to learn the language and customs of a land we would never see, just because some long-dead ancestor came from there. Now no one does. So, when my mother died, I decided to return to Rome, to see if I could find Marcia."

"I know some letters passed through here for Liqian, two or three, with big fancy *Da Qin* seals. My father always emphasized how important it was to get them to Liqian, as they came from one of the Romans who was very high up in their government. But they stopped coming. I haven't seen one in several years," said Jamshid.

"That would have been Aulus. He arranged for us to use his seal, so that it would get to him quickly, if it got to Roman territory, and he would send them on to Marcia. It worked for a while. The last I heard, she and Antonius were in some place called Aquileia, and she had two children, a boy and a girl. But then, like you said, the letters stopped. I hope all is well with them."

"Word from the westernmost caravans is that there is some tension on the western border of Parthia, maybe a war looming with Rome." The servant returned with a tray of brass wine goblets and the bottle. "Thank you, Zvarto," said Jamshid, taking a goblet. He sniffed its fragrance, then took a sip. "Very nice! Your ancestors taught you to make good wine."

"From a grape vine from Shiraz in Parthia, we grow it outside of Liqian. It's the only reason the caravans stop there, it is such a small village. So, what happened while my sister traveled with you?"

Jamshid continued reminiscing. "So, Marcia was quite the young woman on that trip to Kashgar. All of the Romans wanted to ride security for the caravan, including her. I don't think her man approved of that much! Farhad ran the security for me then, and they did everything they could to discourage her."

Farhad laughed. "My boys really did not want a woman riding with them. But when we tried them out, she took no shit, she almost took my hand off with her sword when I drew mine on her to see what she was made of! I took her as my partner, because I didn't want someone else getting stuck with her. We ran her ass with extra shifts to make her quit, and Aulus too, because we thought he was too old. I don't think either of them got much sleep for six weeks, but neither gave an inch. Finally, Marcia and I had a set-to with some bandits, about ten, just the two of us. I was going to send her back for help while I stood them off, but she had her own battle plan. She rode off screaming like a Xiongnu before I could figure out what she was doing, and killed a bunch. The rest turned tail and ran, she was that good. She earned her place with us after that, so we got her shit-faced drunk in Kashgar to celebrate. She drank as well as she could fight. And told some of the most outrageous stories! The one about the Xiongnu 'wrong hole' still makes the rounds among the boys on that run. Your sister was quite a woman!"

"Sounds like that was a real adventure. How far is it to Kashgar?"

"About seven hundred miles, six weeks or so, depending on the weather. We should be there in early fall, before the first snows."

"Interesting. What is involved in riding security?"

"Not to be outdone by your sister?" laughed Farhad. "Are you any good with sword and bow?"

"I'll probably never be as good as Marcia, after what Hina taught her, and I have never had to use my sword in anger. But we all got to be pretty good ten years ago, and I started practicing months before I left Liqian to get my skills back. And the bow... I do a lot of hunting. So, yes."

"Hina, now that is a name I haven't heard for many years. Yes, I recall she had something to do with teaching your sister her fighting skills. The Greeks would call her some sort of an Amazon. You knew her well, I guess?" asked Jamshid.

"We got to know each other quite well. And in fact, she is camped right now outside of the caravansary, which brings me to my next topic. When we last here, the town seemed to welcome the Xiongnu like they did any caravan. Today, they were insulting, trying to cheat Hina. What is going on?"

"I would like to meet her," replied Jamshid, smiling. "As for the Xiongnu, beginning last year, they began showing up here, not with their clan but in groups of five or so. They would beg, steal, or try to intimidate the townsfolk into giving them food and other things. Not at all like the Xiongnu of old."

"There is some kind of sickness up north. Hina's clan was all but wiped out, and she and her little group may be all that's left of her clan. All the clans are suffering up north."

"So that explains it. I guess they're coming south to get away from the plague, trying to get whatever they can. So, what happened to Hina today?"

"She had her two children with her, wandering the food stands, looking for something to eat, I guess. Her little girl picked up an apple and took a bite out of it, and the merchant got really angry. Hina was trying to pay for it with some silver coins, she had no idea of the value of those things, and the merchant was going to take them, calling them ugly names to boot, when I intervened. I handled the merchant. In fact, I told him she was a friend of yours, so he backed off, and the rest were sullen but left her alone. I did the buying for her, and Mei is going to show her how to buy things tomorrow. You know, the only thing the Xiongnu use silver coins for on the steppes is to melt them down to make jewelry!"

"Good. Point the merchant out to me, and I will let him know that if he does that again, I'll cut his hand off for stealing. So Hina has children now? I wonder who settled her down?"

"She has a boy and a girl, twins about ten, and a third small one I haven't seen yet. Galosga was in our party, but he went off with her, so you probably never met him. Strange person, very unusual appearance. They were very close when I was with them, they often slept in our yurt."

"Interesting. Can you bring her and her companions up here tomorrow? In the meanwhile, let's go up on the roof for dinner."

CHAPTER 13:

OUTCASTS ACCEPTED

Turfam, China: July 112AD

Marcus and Mei reached Hina's camp a little after breakfast, just a single yurt with ten horses, hobbled and grazing. Marcus scratched on her door. Hina opened the flap, a one-year old sucking greedily at her breast. "Good morning, Hina. I found some *kumis*, though I suspect the local variety is not up to Xiongnu standards." He handed her a large leather bag, its liquid contents sloshing inside.

"Thank you, Marcus. Please, come in. Galosga, he is here!"

Galosga unwound his tall sturdy frame from a sitting position around the dung fire in the center of the yurt, and four other men rose as well. Andanyu and Marasu studied them silently.

A smile illuminated Galosga's pockmarked face, a feature he shared with the other men. He embraced Marcus, kissing him on both cheeks, Xiongnu fashion.

"You look good, Galosga ... except for your face. What happened to you?"

"The mark of Tengri, what we call this scar left behind by the sickness on those who don't die from it."

"So, some don't die from it? You got it and recovered?"

"Yes, and some don't even get it. Hina tended me and Hadyu in the sickness yurt, covered with our pus, but never got it. So, introductions here. This is our friend and traveling companion of long ago, Marcus. And this is Hadyu, formerly her second in her *arban*, and Arnu, Tenyu, and Pedyu." The men nodded as they were introduced. "And this is little Adhela, getting his morning meal from his mother."

"And this is my wife, Mei. We brought some *kumis*, for Hina said your supplies were low. We are bound to you by a thousand debts of honor, you will not be wanting for anything."

"Thank you, especially for the *kumis*. We finished our last several days ago." Galosga uncorked the leather sack and took a sip, savoring the almond taste of the mildly alcoholic white drink, and passed it around.

"I talked to Jamshid, and he explained what happened yesterday. Apparently, your plague has driven many Xiongnu to leave their clans in small groups, but they come here causing a lot of trouble. He is going to talk to the merchants, and explain that you are to be treated hospitably. And we are going to teach you how to use money."

"Yes, we usually barter, like my people did in my homeland." Galosga had not lost his deep booming laugh over the years. "I have something, you have something, we swap. Except now we have nothing to swap."

"We'll take care of you, Galosga. All of you."

After acquaintances and small talk, Mei took Hina off to the markets. "So, you really know nothing about money?" she asked, as they hiked up the trail to the big building.

"Some of my people do… did. They did all the buying and selling, when it was necessary. I wasn't one of them. The rest of us, we just bartered, like Galosga said."

"Well, coins are what we use instead of bartering. If I have something, it's worth so many of some kind of coins. If someone wants what I have, they can give me those coins. Then I can use those coins to buy something else."

"I understand, but so many different coins. I offered some silver coins yesterday for an apple, and he looked really interested."

Mei laughed. "He was! Because you could have bought his whole stand, and the one on either side of him, for the three silver coins you offered. Silver and gold are very valuable coins and should only be used for big things. People will steal them from you, they are so valuable." She produced a large number of coins, threaded through their square empty centers, to form a long string. "There are a thousand of these *wu zhu* copper coins, which can be traded for one silver *taeli* coin. Let me see your silver coin." Hina handed it to her. "Interesting, this is a *Da Qin* silver coin, a *denarius* like Marcus has. But I guess about the same as an Hanaean *tael*. Where did you get it?"

"From the *Da Qin*, the man Ibrahim gave me a bag of them when Galosga decided to leave with me. He said it was his wedding gift."

"It is very valuable, keep them safe and out of sight. You won't be needing silver coins." She showed Hina how the string was divided up into ten groups. "You can break up the string into these, which will do for most of your day-to-day things."

The conversation went on into what different things cost, and how to negotiate. And inside the marketplace, Hina took the lead, with Mei advising. At the end, with a week's supply of goods in a wheelbarrow, Hina approached her nemesis of yesterday at the fruit stand. The man was not happy to see her, but concealed his displeasure this time.

"I hear my people come here, cause trouble, steal from you. I am Hina, leader of my people, and their actions shame me. I am sorry for what they did."

The man reacted with surprise. "Why, no... they were not you. And I am sorry for treating you like one of them. I shamed your friend, Jamshid."

"They are Xiongnu, they shamed all of us. Though they fled bad things." She produced the cash string and cut off one of the hundred-coin segments. "Here, if they come again, give my people what they need. They come here with nothing."

The man finally smiled, showing brown and twisted teeth. He picked up an apple and handed it to her. "Thank you. Here, for your little girl."

"Thank you. Thank you very much," she said, adding the apple to the stack on the rickety barrow. "Good day, sir."

"Good day to you ... Hina"

Later that day Hina's group, led by Marcus and Mei, rode up to Jamshid's house in the city, Adhela in his breast-board carrier. When they got to the gate at the top of the long ramp, the guard dropped his lance to bar their way. Marcus growled in his most authoritarian tone, "Guests of Jamshid." The guard looked questioningly at the fierce warriors, women and children, then lifted his lance to wave them through.

The narrow winding streets, alleys and building towering over them two or three stories high, intimidated the Xiongnu, attuned to fearing an ambush in such tight quarters. On reaching Jamshid's house, Marcus and Mei tethered their horses, while the Xiongnu hobbled theirs.

Jamshid welcomed them in, and immediately led them to the open roof. "I have entertained Xiongnu before, and I know you people prefer the open spaces of the roof." The view was panoramic in all directions, the grassland, Hina's yurt like a white mushroom on the far side of the caravansary. Far to the southwest, a faint yellow glare marked the beginnings of the Taklamakan Desert, while the Flaming Mountains and the snow-clad Tien Shan range dominated the east and north. Somewhere, a steppe eagle wheeled overhead, screeching its shrill cry.

There were blankets on the floor, on which the Xiongnu chose to sit cross-legged, while Jamshid, Marcus and Mei chose the wooden chairs. On the other side of the roof patio, servants slowly turned a whole goat roasting over a low-banked fire, occasional spatters of grease dropping onto the coals to emit fragrant smoke.

"Hina, welcome to my humble home. You are truly a legend, and I am honored to have you in my home." Servants brought around trays with sacks of *kumis* and flagons of wine and glasses.

"I am honored to be here. And thank you for talking to the townspeople here. I found the merchant with whom I had trouble, and apologized for any troubles my people might have caused him in the past. I gave him some Hanaean coins and asked him to take care of any others who might pass through, as they steal because they have nothing."

"Was he courteous?"

"He gave me an apple for Marasa."

"I talked to him, and to all, about what is going on up north. They all agreed they will try to help them as best they can, if they come through." He took a sip of wine. "So how bad was it?"

"It was horrible. The disease has been with us for several years, it made us sick, and left some scars, but rarely killed. Then something changed. This year, it came with a killing fever. The *shanyu* tried to separate those with the sickness into yurts outside the encampment, but it did little good. And the conditions inside those yurts! When Galosga got the illness, we went out before he showed the spots, so our children would not have to go with us, but I came to take care of him. Conditions inside were awful. Corpses in there, flies buzzing around them, some gone for several days. Those still alive were lying in their own filth and hadn't had water for days. Hadyu was in there ahead of us with the disease, and we cleaned the others up as best we could. I think because we kept the sick clean and well-watered, we only lost two out of seven in our yurt. But I never got the sickness. Hadyu, what happened after I left?"

"Well, what you said, but with the *shanyu* dead from the disease, the people stopped going to the sickness yurts, they stayed in their homes, and the sickness leaped from yurt to yurt like flames. There was a handful, like Hina, that never got the spots, and some like us who got it and recovered, but the survivors started forming factions, blaming people for putting curses on them, burning out their yurts, then attacking other clans. Though by this time, all of the clans near us had it as bad as we did. In the end, most of the animals were slaughtered or had wandered off, there was no way to go on living there. Arnu, Tenyu, Pedyu and I headed off with what we could put together for supplies, hoping to catch up with Hina and Galosga, who were going to Turfam to find a cure or treatment."

"What are you going to do next?" asked Jamshid, concern in his voice.

"I don't know, sir. Whatever Hina and Galosga decide to do. But the Xiongnu way of life, for us it is over."

"Hmm, I may have something for you. Our caravans ride with mounted security, to fight off bandits wanting to steal our rich cargo. Some of Farhad's boys are Xiongnu. Do you get along with the Xubu clan?"

"I would get along with a demon if he spoke Xiongnu!" answered Hadyu, then glanced at Hina for approval. Arnu, Tenyu, and Pedyu stared at the ground, saying nothing.

"We are riding to Kashgar, leaving next week with Marcus and Mei. You are welcome to ride with us, as my guests."

"We will consider this," answered Hina. "It will take us far from our traditional homelands and way of life. But maybe that will be a good thing."

"Fine. Now answer me one more thing, Hina, how did you become such a famous warrior in the first place?"

Hina extended her goblet. "That will require more wine!"

So, her story began, the loss of her village twenty years earlier that had left her an angry waif, homeless and clanless, wanting not a home, but a sword, and the chance to kill the hated Han. Her first kill, her first time with a man, her beloved Mayu, her terrible loss. Her decade of isolation when she single-handedly became the fiercest warrior, man or woman.

"I had, by then, risen to command an *arban* of ten men, something no woman had done in a long time. But the clan felt I was 'a bow strung too taut,' likely to snap unexpectedly. I allowed myself to feel nothing, no friends, not among the women, who feared me, nor among the men. Ten years ago, a strange traveling party of *Da Qin* on the run from the vengeance of the Han court came to our encampment, Marcia and her brother Marcus, the big Antonius, and Galosga." She cast a smile in his direction, "Ever the biggest and kindest. I allowed my boys one night a week to spend time with their families, and I spent one night with my new *Da Qin* family in their yurt. Marcia wanted to learn how to fight, though she was just a slip of a girl, to never again be defenseless, so I took her and taught her as I would a Xiongnu. I worked her so hard, for a time she came to hate me, and hate what I taught her. Whatever I demanded, however, she rose to meet, and then went a bit beyond! At some point, since neither of us had sisters, we agreed to be so to each other, and I was honored to be her sister in her wedding in Liqian." She paused and considered. *The story of Wang Ming? No, not yet, she was sworn to secrecy on that.* "Galosga comes from a place far away, a place to which he had given up all hope of return. He surprised me, telling me that he wanted to join my clan, as they lived much like his people. I tried to talk him out of it." A servant came by and refilled her empty goblet.

"We decided to put it in Tengri's hands that night, to show me the way to go. And there they are, twins, Marasa and Andanyu, named for Marcia and Antonius, the way Tengri wanted us to follow."

"A beautiful story, Hina," said Jamshid. "What is that amulet around your neck?"

"Galosga gave this on our first time together." She took the amulet off her neck, an arrowhead carefully worked out of grayish black stone, attached to a leather thong. "It is what they use in his homeland instead of iron or bronze."

Jamshid examined it. "Farmers and miners find things like this sometime, tilling their fields. There are legends about them, but I have never known anyone to actually use one."

CHAPTER 14:

CONSPIRACIES

Ctesiphon, Parthia: July 112AD

Seen through the still, sheer curtains of the high, wide windows of the Parthian palace, heat waves shimmered above the Tigris River as Ctesiphon baked under the dry heat of the July afternoon sun. The *shamal* winds from the north would soon bring relief with sand-laden gusts, but they had not yet begun. The city stagnated in the oppressive heat, to be relieved only by the longed-for sunset.

Cyrus Mithridates, the brother to King Osroës, sat at his highly polished wooden desk by the window, wearing a loose-fitting light green silk robe, studying scrolls while two slaves stirred the air above him with brilliantly-colored ostrich-feather fans. Sanatruces entered the room, his military boots clicking across the white marble floor, his red-plumed helmet under his arm. "Father!" he announced simply.

"Sanatruces! Sit, please," he said, beckoning to a woven chair in front of the desk. He clapped his hand, and another servant, wearing just a white linen kilt, materialized. "Lemon juice. With ice." The servant nodded and departed soundlessly.

Sanatruces took the seat, leaning forward a bit. Sanatruces was in his thirties, and despite their age difference, looked remarkably like his father, both with long aquiline noses set between piercing grey eyes, under thick black eyebrows. While Mithridates' black hair and beard was meticulously coiled and coifed, oiled and dyed to an iridescent shine that hid any sign of gray, Sanatruces' beard was bushy, unoiled and cut short in the military manner. "Have the protocol people prepared you adequately for your presentation tomorrow before Osroës?"

"They have. Though one is never prepared for the first presentation before the king, even if he is your uncle."

"Especially if he is your uncle, and my brother. You are presenting to him as the *Shahanshah* king of kings before his full council, so do not show any familiarity. If he ignores it, the council won't, and that may create enemies needlessly, for all three of us. But you will do well."

The servant returned with two Egyptian glasses filled with water and clinking ice, their exteriors beaded with condensation.

"Ice from the Zagros Mountains. I wish we were up there hunting elk and wild boar, and not down here in this furnace."

Sanatruces took a sip, savoring the coolness. "That would be nice. At least you are not in this uniform. The Romans call our uniforms *clibanarii*, 'bread-ovens', and I think they are right, I am well-baked."

"So, tell me about your presentation. The protocol people told you how to present it, tell me what you are going to present. I have been advising this king, and Pacorus before him, for many years, so I can give you some guidance."

"Yes, father. Well, since this is my first intelligence presentation, I thought I would keep it simple. I intend to lead with the boring stuff first, to get it out of the way quickly, then bring up the more important stuff at the end, with plenty of time for questions. So, we'll start with the Roman forces. As of the last two months, there have been no important changes in the seven eastern legions facing us. They are going into the summertime exercise period, what they do every year, deploying in the field for extended periods. There are no movements of forces into or out of the area, nothing close to our borders or to Armenia."

"Good."

"Politics. Dacia is quiet now, the Romans are consolidating it as a new province under the governor Nigrinus after their big victory, and a lot of settlers are moving into the new land. They have had four legions tied up there since Decebalus was overthrown, but there doesn't seem to be any serious resistance. I expect to see some troops redeploying south of the Danube, perhaps soon. Trajan remains extremely popular because of the war. It netted the treasury two hundred and fifty tons of Dacian gold, worth two and a half billion of their *sesterces*."

"Good, next."

"In Armenia, Axidares is becoming far too independent, in my opinion. He is allowing Roman legions free transit across his territory to their client states in Albania and Iberia along the Caspian Sea and Colchis along the Black Sea. He is supposed to be a buffer state between us and Rome, not their highway to our heartland."

"I will have to remember that phrase...what did you say, 'a buffer state, not a highway to our heartland?'" He took a sip of the cold lemon juice. "Osroës was not happy to inherit that mess from Pacorus. When Pacorus was *Shahanshah,* King of Kings, he allowed his son Axidares far too much latitude in running Armenia, and Axidares was far too accommodating to Rome, maybe even in their pay. For a time, the Romans were even building a garrison at Baku!" He leaned forward and lowered his voice, lest a servant might overhear him. "This is not for discussion outside the two of us, but my brother has been seriously considering rectifying that situation, even though we are bound by treaty with Rome to have a mutually agreeable king there. He is considering putting a more reliable king on the Armenian throne, with or without Roman approval, treaty be damned… so what is next?"

"Syria, and this is where it gets interesting. The new governor of Syria, Publius Aelius Hadrian, is what the Romans call a *vir militaris*, a military man, tribune in three legions, and command of one, from here to the Danube. He is Trajan's cousin, married to Trajan's great niece, and is reputed to be his favored successor."

"That's a powerful figure, indeed."

"The first thing he did on arriving in Syria was to call all his *legati* to a meeting in Antioch for a week."

"As he probably should. They are his defense against us, he wants to know his commanders, what they see as strengths and weaknesses, what he sees as strengths and weaknesses in them."

"And those from Cappadocia, Judea and their new province of Arabia Nabataea…"

"Coordinated regional defense. Go on."

"And legates and tribunes from Moesia, Pannonia, all six Dacian legions, and several German legions along the Rhine."

"That does get interesting … a week, you say?"

"A week. More than a month on the road to get there from *Germania Superior*, even using the fastest stages, for a one-week visit. And another month back."

"You have my attention. Anything else?"

"Immediately after the meeting, the commander of one of the Dacian legions was transferred to take command of the *XII Fulminata*, himself a real *vir militaris*. He had distinguished himself quite well in that war."

"Who is he?"

"One Gaius Aetius Lucullus."

"By all the gods and demons, I know that man! From my time as envoy in the Hanaean court! He was the right-hand man of the head of their delegation, but he kept a very low profile. Said little, but I felt that nothing missed his eye. So now he is here on our border?"

"Well, after he leaves the Dacian border, but like you said, it is part of their regional defense. Or the core of their offense."

Mithridates sat quietly, fingering his beard, contemplating what his son had told him. "Well, we will wait to see them start to move their forces before I present what you just told me to my brother. If you present partial or incorrect information to the *Shahanshah* before his council, some may force him to take action prematurely. Nevertheless, you are presenting to me a very plausible, though circumstantial, case that something is afoot. That is far too many legions to target anything other than us, but no pieces have yet been moved on the board. Perhaps my brother's best move might be to expedite replacing Axidares in Armenia, present them a crisis there that will deny them freedom of movement. That may cool their ambitions a bit, maybe even make them change their minds. I will discuss that with him myself, one on one. And we might want to cool things down with Vologases in the east, so we don't have to fight a two-front war. Anything else?"

"That brings up my next subject, Vologases is…"

Mithridates held up a finger to interrupt. "You will be followed by Zacharias the Jew. He has so many agents embedded in Vologases' hierarchy that he probably not only knows which wife the bastard slept with last night, but how many times he fucked her. And he is jealous of his turf. Publicly defer to him, acknowledge his supremacy on that, something like 'my colleague Zacharias will cover the doings of the pretender Vologases in far greater detail than I could … "

Sanatruces smiled and gave him a wink. "Court politics?"

"Court politics. What is next?"

"The most interesting part of all. You remember that two years ago, you ordered me to intercept all correspondence bearing Roman official seals crossing our border?"

Mithridates nodded.

"It took a while to get around to reading them all, with only a few really good Latin readers, and a lot of correspondence to go through." He paused to sort out some scrolls, putting them on the desk before his father, seals opened, rerolled with thread. "Most appeared to be commercial or personal in nature, letters to caravansaries on our side requesting certain products, inquiring about prices. We suspected some of them might also be communications with Roman agents operating here, so I put our code breakers and cipher experts on them."

"Any insights?"

"None. Most believe that if these are secret communications, these are codes, almost impossible to break without the code book. For example, 'I want a hundred bolts of red silk for fifty *denarii*' might mean 'Kill King Osroës on the fifth of April'. But without the codebook, you can't know that."

"Go on."

"Then there are these." Sanatruces handed another set of letters, rolled in tubes and each bearing a red wax seal, carefully detached from one side to remain intact, to his father, who examined them carefully.

"The seal of Aulus Aemilius Galba! My nemesis in the Hanaean court ten years ago! To whom is he writing?"

"The delivery instructions are on the side, in ink."

Mithridates scrutinized the scroll, fine-quality papyrus indeed, no sign of the ink bleeding through to the backside, expensive stuff. On the side were instructions in Latin: *trade ad Marcum Lucium, Lisiana in Ganasienses,* again the same in Greek, then in Chinese. All the same: 'Deliver to Marcus Lucius, Liqian in Gansu.' Mithridates' hands shook as he slipped off the thread and opened the scroll, reading the text, his lips moving with the unfamiliar Latin. When he was finished, he sighed. "What a reunion you have brought me! First, Gaius Lucullus, now all the rest of that Roman party I hoped never to hear of again, Galba and Lucullus' foul-mouthed centurion Antonius, and their translators Marcus and Marcia." He chuckled, rereading the letter. "So, Marcia married Antonius after all. I tried very hard to get her consort Wang Ming to see what was going on between those two, to get them executed for her infidelity and discredit their whole delegation, but Galba had to play on Roman honor and defend her, they all got sentenced to death. I thought that was the end of it, but they escaped somehow. Liqian, Liqian. Yes, that is where the Han next caught up with them, Marcus' and Marcia's hometown, but by then Emperor He had a change of heart and pardoned them. And Wang Ming went with the Emperor's party carrying the word of their pardon, expecting to return with her, but he never came back. I always suspected he ran into Antonius there."

"You never told me that story, father," said Sanatruces. "Sounds like a colorful one."

"It was indeed … this is about the most expensive papyrus you can buy, maybe of the grade the Romans called Augustan, a silver *denarius,* at least, per page. To exchange this family chit-chat under an official Roman seal halfway around the world? 'I wanted you to know that I am pregnant again… I hope all is well… Antonius loves teaching.' Drivel not worth the ink, much less this expensive papyrus!" He admired the expensive papyrus paper from a distance, stroking his carefully coiffed beard. "What happens when these leave Roman territory?"

"Some can go by personal messenger. Others, like the Chinese ones, go by caravan. I talked to several caravanners, and correspondence is important to their work also. Mostly orders ahead for things, requests for information, and of course, personal correspondence. The caravansaries try to pass them on as best they can, until they get close to the destination, preferably on a caravan route. It's not completely reliable, but they tell me that if it gets to a caravan, it will probably get to its destination, even if it's in China."

"I am afraid to ask, but do you have anything else for me, son?"

"Well, this was two-way communications, because 'Marcus' responded, using the same seal. They are more of the same family chit chat, though on cheap Hanaean rice paper instead. When he stopped getting letters, he sent several more inquiries, then this." He handed his father the last letter, unrolled.

"Hmm. Looks like we don't have to go to China to find Marcus, he is coming here. Very interesting. Marcus was highly connected in the Han court. When he left, he was working for the head eunuch, Lady Deng's head of household. And now she holds the reins of power as Empress, as the new Emperor An is very weak, a child. I don't think this is family chit-chat, but Trajan's direct communication to the Han court, with Marcia and Marcus as intermediary encoders."

"I think you are right… but as you cautioned me, circumstantial."

"I think you have found something potentially huge. If they could bring China into the war, even as harassment, we could be in a very difficult position, a bone torn between two big dogs. But this is too circumstantial for presentation now. Tell Osroës that you have intercepted all official Roman correspondence on this side, and are carefully examining them for evidence of covert communications. Leave it at that."

Sanatruces nodded, and took another sip of the lemon juice.

Mithridates scrutinized the first letter again. "Where is Aquileia?"

"At the top of the Adriatic Gulf, a few hundred miles from Rome."

"Can you get some agents up there? We need to renew our acquaintance with his sister and her husband, also. And find out where Galba sleeps when he is not causing me trouble."

CHAPTER 15:

TALK OF WAR, TALK OF PEACE

Rome: July 112AD

Titus Flavius Petronius, Aulus' long-time Senate colleague, political ally and close personal friend, always enjoyed visiting the Senator's house on the Aventine Hill, opposite the imperial palace on the Palatine, the *Circus Maximus* in the *Vallis Murcia* between them. The house was divided into two spacious halves, each with its own atrium. The business side of the house consisted of Aulus' office, a library, a room big enough to hold several dozen people, and guest rooms on the second floor. The family side was for personal use, *triclinium* dining area, rooms for socializing, his wife Livia's office and reading room, and upstairs bedrooms. A wing for the kitchen, latrines, storage areas, and upstairs slaves' quarters divided the two. The door keeper escorted Titus into Aulus' rather spartan office on the business side, where green marble columns contrasted tastefully against the yellow walls, sheer lime green curtains filtering the light from the window opening onto the atrium. The floor held a mosaic depicting a huge conch shell surrounded by various sea creatures, real and mythical. Intricate ship models, complete down to every detail of rigging, lined the walls. The Senator, clad in a white tunic with a purple senatorial border and sleeves filigreed in gold and silver, stood up behind his desk and extended his hand to Titus. "Welcome, welcome, Titus! Always a pleasure to have you visit. Take off your toga and sit, please. Some wine? Watered, I believe?"

"Watered, please. It's early," Titus doffed his toga, hanging it on a wooden peg on the wall, and in his tunic took a seat in front of the highly polished teak desk. Aulus sat back down, the morning breeze through the window stirring the silk drapes. He clapped his hands and a servant girl appeared in a fine linen frock. "Chloë, wine for our guest, please, watered, and neat for me."

She smiled and nodded. "Certainly, sir."

"What did you think of the Old Man's speech today?" asked Titus.

"Trajan didn't say enough to put the factions at rest. Peace and war, war and peace! Sorry to see the factions break out again. It's been nice the past ten years, with everyone in agreement and working together."

"You knew that wasn't going to last. It's his age. Trajan's coming up on sixty, and everyone is maneuvering to place their favorite candidate in line to succeed him."

"Good luck to them on that! My money is on Nigrinus or Hadrian, each the center of the war and peace factions. But Trajan has been very coy, he hasn't adopted anyone to send a clear signal."

"He likes to keep everyone guessing. But what do you think the chances are for a war?"

"The most I see is some confrontation over Armenia again."

"Again! I can't understand why that backwater keeps becoming a problem for us."

"Come here, take a look at my most prized possession, and I will show you why this keeps happening." He stood up and led Titus to the world map behind his desk. "The King of Bactria had the original made from both Hanaean and Alexandrian sources, creating a map that is accurate both in the east and west. He gave it to me as a gift for Trajan, who had a copy made for me. I updated that copy with sailors' maps for Africa and the Indian Ocean and colored in our different provinces and clients. It is probably the most accurate map in the world, more accurate than the Old Man's, even." He chuckled, "This is the only map where I can show my whole journey, my one claim to fame."

Aulus located Armenia. "Here is our problem child. The treaty says that neither Rome nor Persia can station troops there, and we must jointly agree on the King. But here," he said, indicating Caucasian Iberia and Albania on the Caspian Sea, north of Armenia, "these are client kingdoms of ours that we have promised to protect against the Sarmatians, Alans, and a host of wild nomads north of them, waiting to raid, loot and kill thousands. The province of Colchis is well-protected from the north by the Caucasus Mountains. We could send troops from Cappadocia to Iberia and Albania through Colchis, but they would have to go through the Likh Mountains to reach them, through restricted passes ideal for ambushes. The only way we can protect our client states is through Armenia."

The two returned to their seats. "The whole treaty issue rotates around the phrase 'troops stationed'. We don't consider troops in transit to be 'stationed' in Armenia, and with a little bit of gold," Aulus said with a wink, "we have convinced King Axidares to agree with us. The Parthians don't like it much, because they would like to have those client states for themselves. But then, we would be the ones bitching about troops in transit. This comes up every couple of years, maybe a little show of force that never comes to combat. Nothing is going to happen."

"But why, then, did he put Hadrian in charge of Syria? That is the most military muscle he has."

"To be sure, and it is a good bargaining chip with Parthia. And grooming Hadrian for the purple, I think. But word is, Hadrian leans toward the peace faction. Unlike most of the other 'warriors', he has extensive military experience, he knows what war is. There's not going to be one."

"That is good to hear." Titus paused, looking at the ship models, and continued. "So which faction are you with, peace or war?"

"Neither, because in the end, there's not going to be a war."

"The war faction is willing to start one, using Armenia as an excuse. Their argument is that we dawdled for decades over Dacia, launching ineffective slaps against Decebalus that got him to the bargaining table to make agreements that he quickly ignored. An all-out effort with six legions solved the problem in less than a year. He is gone, and the treasury is two and half billion sesterces richer with his gold. Unusual that, for a barbarian king. The war faction argues that we would get ten times that much treasure from Parthia, and guarantee peace on our eastern border for centuries."

"Oh, yes, and imitate Alexander the Great. I've heard their arguments, too, Titus. I try not to snooze during my colleagues' speeches. The difference is that Parthia is not some petty barbarian kingdom. They know how to field big armies like we do, they have fought us to a standstill every time we fought them, and their huge treasury the war faction wants can finance a very long war. Don't mistake me as leaning toward the peace faction, just because I think that there will be no war. The peace faction would sacrifice everything, endure any insult from Parthia, just to avoid a war with them. They would abandon our clients in the Caucasus to appease Parthia. So, no, not them either. But in the end, cooler heads will prevail and there will be no war."

"I hope you are right, Aulus. Myself, I am not sure, nor am I sure what side I would be on. I think the war side, for the reasons you gave, to not abandon our clients. But reluctantly. Very reluctantly."

"War is always hell on earth. Too many in the Senate have never experienced it, have no idea how horrible it is."

The servant girl brought in a silver tray with two green Egyptian glass goblets, and some small pastries. She gave each their wine. "Some pastries, sirs?"

"Thank you, no, Chloë. It is too close to lunch for me," said Aulus, patting his firm, flat stomach.

"Did you know your colleagues are beginning to joke about your being too skinny to be a senator?" said, Titus, taking one.

"I wasn't aware there was a girth requirement for the Senate, but to judge from our colleagues' bellies, there may very well be. Ten years ago, I lived hard on the road for several years, and when I came back, I felt better than I ever did in my life. I still keep up with the army regime that my cousin Gaius taught me, and I intend to stay like this as long as I can. And you have trimmed yourself down quite a bit from what you once were."

"Thank you, I think it was your example."

Aulus' wife Livia entered the room, red hair over green eyes in full-length green stola. "Titus, it is good to see you again. Will you join Aulus and me for lunch in the atrium?"

"I would be delighted, Livia."

CHAPTER 16:

TENGRI'S SIGN

Turfam, China: July 112AD

Well after dark, the moonless sky above the fields ablaze with stars, the men retired to the yurt, leaving Mei and Hina by the campfire, now flickering low. "Why don't you go to bed also, Mei?" asked Hina, adding another small log to the fire. "I will sit up for a while."

"Because you are troubled. I will be here if you need anything."

"Thank you." The log caught, casting a little light on Hina's face. Mei caught the glitter of moisture in her eyes, but chose to say nothing, clasping her knees to her chest. Hina went back to studying the sky intently.

A brilliant shooting star flared, multiple shades of blue, green and bright white, then broke into fading sparks. "I think Tengri has given his sign of approval in that *ala-shan*... I do not know the *han-yu* word."

"Shooting star," volunteered Mei.

"It was going west, my direction. Tengri has a plan for me there, so I must go, though I would rather stay here, even if I were to die."

"Tengri is one of your gods?"

"Tengri is the one God, the God of the Sky. Twice before, he gave my life direction. Now again He is telling me to do something I have never done before. And, Mei, this time, I am afraid."

"You are with friends. What is it Tengri wants you to do?"

"I don't know, but He says I must go west with you, far from my green steppes, far from my people. Somewhere out there, I will learn what it is."

"Didn't Galosga come from far away, to be with you?"

Mei noticed that for the first time, a faint smile crossed Hina's lips. "Galosga, my man who fell down into my life. That is what his name means, you know, 'he who fell.' Perhaps Tengri will lead us back to his homeland, and it will be my turn to be the stranger in his land." She fingered the arrowhead amulet around her neck, twisting it, watching the firelight reflect off the worked stone. "Many years ago, when we were traveling with the *Da Qin*, he was just keeping my bedroll warm at night with me, having children was out of the question, that would have changed my life as a warrior. When we got to Turfam, he announced that he was joining the clan. At first, I was horrified and angry at having him a permanent part of my life. But I could not give him to another woman. It was a week before my bleeding, when I would never usually take him, so I asked Tengri to send me a sign. I would take him that night, and if Tengri approved, He would make me pregnant, and we would make a life together as mates. If not, I would find him another woman." She chuckled to herself, working a stick in her hands. "That was the night the twins came to be. Tengri showed me which way to go, and I followed. Tonight, He is showing me again which way to go. You know, I never told anyone this, not even my sister Marcia, though she knows a bit. Hmm … you are married to the brother of my sister, so I guess you and I are sisters-in-law."

"Indeed, we are. That is a beautiful story, Hina. This new life, I will help you all I can. It is going to be new to me also. I guess Marcus will be teaching you and Galosga Latin as well as me."

"And Andanyu and Marasa. Will we be able to find them, Marcia and Antonius?"

"I don't know. Marcus thinks he knows where they were a few years ago, and we have a year or more to go."

"At least traveling with the caravan, that will be like being on a migration. Mei, you never saw anything so beautiful, the whole clan on the move, hundreds of wagons, thousands of animals, rolling through the wind-whipped grass. I shall miss that."

"You said Tengri shaped your life twice before. What was the other?"

Hina paused. "I don't want to offend you, my new friend, but you are Han. You will hear things your people did to mine that were not good, why the Xiongnu hate the Han."

"That is all right. Tell me the story."

"There was a battle, many years ago, when I was about twelve, the battle of Ilkh Bayan. After that battle, the Han went from encampment to encampment, slaughtering hundreds of thousands of my people. My clan's turn came, and I was the only survivor, a child. My father told me to run away on foot so I would be hidden by the grass. My last view of my home was from several miles away, black smoke rising to the skies, the screams … it was horrible. I wandered aimlessly for days until I found the Huyan clan. The *shanyu* offered me a family, but I insisted on becoming a fighter. All I wanted to do was to kill Han. I became a fighter, a good one, and I took my first lover, the man commanding my unit. We made love every chance we could, even on patrols, dangerously irresponsible, and during one, we were overrun by five Han. I escaped but he was caught and tortured. At the end, there was nothing I could do but put him out of his misery. I killed him with an arrow as he smiled at me, then I killed the other five Han."

"How old were you?"

"Just fourteen. But woman enough to fight. I carried that story, untold inside me for years, becoming bitter and angry, feeling his death was my fault, my secret shame. My dead lover Mayu came to me in a dream, the night the *Da Qin* joined us. He told me I must tell someone, or I would die. So, I told Galosga the next day, and we have been lovers ever since. Mayu said he approved of him in that dream. That was first time Tengri gave me a direction for my life. And now, He is doing it again."

Again, Mei noticed her smile. She could feel Hina's heart begin to thaw. "That is also a beautiful story, Hina."

"Well, it is late, and I am riding with the dawn patrol when we get underway tomorrow. I think we should join our menfolk in the yurt." She turned to take hold of Mei's shoulders, facing her. "Thank you for listening. I have Tengri's sign, so now I will need your help."

CHAPTER 17:

TENGRI'S PATH

Caravan Enroute Turfam to Kashgar, China: August 112AD

Hina shared Tengri's sign with Galosga and her children the next day, and of course they agreed that they should go, Galosga seeming very enthusiastic about the new adventure.

She then assembled Hadyu, Pedyu, Arnu and Tenyu. "As you all know, I have struggled to determine what I should do, now that I am clanless," she addressed them. "Up until now, I believed, as you all do, that we should return to the steppes to seek out another clan and begin again. But here in Turfam, I received not one, but two signs, that my life should take a very different path. The first was meeting Marcus, the brother to my *Da Qin* sister. He is enroute to the *Da Qin* city to rejoin her. Last night, I prayed to Tengri for a sign as to what I should do ... continue my life as a Xiongnu, or go with my brother to join my sister, whom I believed I would never see again. As I prayed, a brilliant *ala-shan* shooting star lit up the night sky, heading west.

"This was Tengri's sign in answer to my prayer, but it need not be your sign. You may continue with me, but that will mean abandoning your life as a Xiongnu, learning new languages, living among people whose customs you do not know. And Marcus, who has made that trip before, tells me that the journey will be long and hard, longer by far than our longest migration to Dzungaria. So, you may choose to accompany me, or go back to the steppes with my understanding. I will give the four of you a moment to decide." She turned her back on them and stepped away to let them talk among themselves. Whatever decision they made, she did not want to influence it by her presence.

After a few minutes, Hadyu summoned her back. "We have made our decision," he said simply. Hina said nothing as she rejoined the group of men.

Pedyu was the first to speak. "You are the greatest warrior the Huyan clan has ever produced, and our formidable leader. You have close ties to these new people, and know their customs and languages. But we are

Xiongnu, and we choose to remain so and return to our steppe lands to find another clan. We wish you the best on your journey, knowing that you go with Tengri's blessing."

"I thank you, Padyu, and thank all of you for your many years of faithful service. I shall pray that you find a good clan, a new home and new families. But I shall miss you all, and especially you, Hadyu, my ever faithful second in command," she said, her eyes burning with emotion.

"I am coming with you, Hina," said Hadyu in a husky voice. "That was their decision, not mine. I have followed you through hell up to now, and will follow you on this new hellish journey, no matter where it leads."

Hina's emotions got the best of her, and despite her best efforts, she felt a tear trickle down her cheek. "Hadyu, are you sure? It will be a whole new life for you."

"With you I will stand in Tengri's shadow." He raised his fist upright in salute.

"I am honored by your decisions, both of them. Padyu, Arnu and Tenyu, go with Tengri, as will Hadyu and I. We will all feast together one last time tonight to celebrate our new lives."

Heartened by Tengri's sign, Hadyu was ready to ride with Hina's family, Marcus and Mei, to whatever new world the Sky God had in mind for them. Would the Sky God have power where they were going? He must, else why would He send them there?

Hadyu met with the security patrols, along with Marcus, Hina, and Galosga, each pairing up with a Sogdian partner. Though they were subordinate to their partner, they would still be riding as a Xiongnu ought to ride, with characteristic wildness and freedom. Each would do a day patrol while the caravan was on the move, a night patrol around the encamped caravan the next night, then a day off, repeating until they reached the security of the next caravansary. Mei agreed to care for Adhela while they were on patrol.

The night before departure, all was ready, the wagon packed, Padyu and his companions ready for departure, awaiting only the yurt and essentials to be loaded after sunrise. The eight, with Marcus and Mei, gathered in the yurt for a light evening meal, with little Adhela toddling around, exploring.

"More *kumis,* Hina?" asked Arnu, proffering her the leather sack.

"No, thank you. It will be an early rise for Galosga and me, and I do not want to be hung over on my first day. Feel free to make a night of it, the three of you."

"We would rather be riding with you, mother," said Andanyu.

"Perhaps, but not today. This is not our clan, and we do not know their traditions. It is very important that you both help Aunt Mei with the wagon tomorrow. Right now, I would like father Galosga to tell us about the strange world to which we will be going."

Marasa and Andanyu turned to face their father, subdued smiles on their faces, though they had heard these stories many times. But never in their dreams had they ever thought they might actually see the places he had been. Now that they were on their way to them, the stories were no longer make-believe.

"In my home, we didn't live in yurts, but in houses made of logs. But they were not much bigger than yurts. We stayed in a place called a *gaduwuh'i*, a village. But it was smaller than our encampments here, not nearly as many people."

The young ones' faces lit up. They loved the way he sprinkled the strange words of his native language in amongst the stories.

Galosga continued, speaking as much with his hands as with his words. "So, one day on the seashore, I see this big boat, a really big boat, with masts like giant trees, just a little offshore. Men on the beach waved for me to come. I couldn't talk to them, but they pointed to the big boat, and then to their little boat, and I got in. On the big boat, they set me to pulling on ropes, the sails fell down and filled like giant wings, and the big boat began to move. We went out to sea, far out to sea, until the land fell out of sight. Night fell, and the stars began to come out."

"What is the sea like?" asked Marasa.

"The sea is like the steppes, only it is water instead of grass, blue instead of green, and like the steppe, it just goes on forever until it meets the sky. Just like the wind ripples the grass, the wind makes the sea ripple, but sometime the ripples turn into mountains of water."

The young ones nodded, and Galosga continued. "I tried to tell them I needed to go home, but we couldn't understand each other, and they got very angry. Day after day, we rode the sea, rolling back and forth, and after many weeks, I came to my first city. I didn't know so many people could live in one place. The houses were made of stone, not logs, so big you could put my house inside one and not even fill it up. And there were horses there, pulling carts, or men riding them. I had never seen a horse, we didn't have them in my home."

"How did you get along without horses, father?"

Galosga smiled. "We walked a lot, Andanyu. And carried everything on our backs. Horses are one of the things of this world that I have come to love." He took a sip of *kumis*. "We went from city to city by that big boat, like a caravan does. They traded me off, in a city called Carthage, to a new ship, and there I met my first friend in this world, a man named Shmuel. He taught me how to speak in his language, and finally I could talk to someone. Then we came to the finest city of them all, a city so fine it terrified me. Alexandria, it was called." His spread wide to emphasize its size. "From miles away, we could see the lighthouse, towering over the city as high as a mountain. The city was all white stone, as white as a summer cloud. And the people, so many it looked like an anthill, all going somewhere carrying something. Alexandria had hundreds of ships, all bigger than ours. We went down a very big river on a boat there, a long way from Alexandria, until we found our new ship, bigger even than the ones in Alexandria. It was on that ship that I met your uncle Marcus, and Antonius and Marcia for whom you are named. We had many adventures together."

"Where was Aunt Mei?"

"I wasn't in Marcus' life yet, Marasa, I was still back in Liqian." Her broad faced beamed with a smile. She, too, liked the story. "I have not been to any city like that, either. It will be new to me, also."

"Enough stories now. We have important business left for tonight. Marcus is going to teach you Latin, the language they speak where we are going, so you won't be like I was, stuck in a strange world and not able to talk to anyone. And he is going to teach you how to put the magic signs on paper that will make it talk. We are all going to learn with you, Hina and I, and Hadyu."

Adhela interrupted the talk, toddling up to the dung fire and poking at the embers with his bare hand. Mei gasped, but Hina just looked on impassively. He predictably found a hot ember, cried "Ow!" and put his fist in his mouth. He looked plaintively to Hina for sympathy, but none came. "You have done that before, Adhela, and now you have burned yourself again."

Mei looked at her quizzically, and Hina continued to Mei. "That is how Xiongnu young ones learn. The steppes are very harsh, and you must be wise at an early age. He will not forget this again."

"But he is a child."

Hina smiled. "Mei. we don't have a word for 'child' in Xiongnu. A *narai* is an infant, one who can't yet walk. But Adhela walks, so now he is a *zaalu*, a young one, the same as the twins. Next year when he is two, he will learn to ride. Childhood is a luxury we cannot afford on the steppes. At twelve, they will be fully grown, ready to accept the responsibilities of the clan." Suddenly she choked with emotion "I am sorry ... the clan is no more. But we will raise them as Xiongnu, despite that."

"We are the clan. We may be small, but we are the clan, Hina," said Hadyu.

"You are right." She sighed, and the low firelight made the tears in her eyes glisten, tears that came with increasing frequency these days, to her great frustration. "Now, Marcus, on with the language lesson."

Hina prided herself on her ability to wake up well before dawn. She savored the warmth of Galosga's body against hers one last time, then shook him gently. "It is time." She rolled out of the bedroll, naked, and went outside to relieve herself. She returned to stir the fire back to a feeble glow and gently wake Adhela to nurse him from her breasts, achingly full of milk. That complete, she put him on her shoulder, patting him until she got a loud wet burp. Full of milk, he promptly went back to sleep, and Hina put him back on his little bedroll. By now, everyone else was stirring, and she, too, began to dress in gear laid out the night before, easily found in the dark. Black felt riding pants over her cold thighs, boots. She looked at Mei. "When he wakes again, please feed him some mare's milk and yogurt. He can feast off me again this evening."

Hina pulled on her beige riding shirt, tight fitting so that in a fight, there was nothing for someone to grab, nothing to distract her by flapping loose or getting tangled. She did up her hair and donned her tall black conical hat, feeling very much the warrior, and slinging her shield, with sword and bow crossed behind it, onto her back. She was ready. She joined Galosga and Hadyu, ready to ride.

Her Sogdian partner Warnu greeted her. The first gray of dawn had just begun to appear in the east, but a half-moon hung over the grassland, illuminating the still-sleeping caravan in its encampment almost like day, casting shadows here and there. "Good morning. At least we have a moon. Won't be anything to see this close to Turfam, but you will get to know how we do this. We'll just ride out ahead at a canter, no need to waste the horses, cast back and forth. Keep me in sight, and at sunrise, I'll signal you to join up. Let's ride."

And they were off. The rhythmic motion of the horse between her legs, her body rocking to the stallion's gentle rhythm, was almost sensual, but she kept her eyes alert for any movement. On Warnu's signal they rejoined, and he blew his horn. Other horns echoed the call, and Farhad's bass horn responded. From several miles back they heard the susurrations of hundreds of animals beginning to move, clanging bells, barking dogs. They were on their way.

Hina turned her face westward. *Take me where you will, Tengri.*

CHAPTER 18:

A COMMON LANGUAGE

Turfam to Kashgar, September 112AD

The caravan settled into the organized chaos of camping for the night, unloading animals noisily protesting the rigors of the day, people erecting tents and yurts, the daily evening ritual after several weeks on the road. The sweet smell of wood and dung fires began to fill the air as the sun settled below the snow-capped, rugged peaks of the Tien Shan Mountains far in the distance. A white-bearded man, beturbaned and wearing a multi-colored cloak of reds, greens, blues and many other smaller threads, buffeted by the crowds as he tried to make his way, suddenly stopped, listening intently to a group speaking. He listened again, then turned toward them. "Excuse me, I had not expected to hear Latin spoken at all this far east, much less as well as you speak it." The man smiled at Marcus, interrupting his conversation with Mei, Hina and Galosga.

"I thank you. And you are?" asked Marcus, eying the man. Obviously rich, probably a merchant. His Latin was accented, but Marcus had no familiarity with regional accents.

"I am sorry, I am Nathaniel of Hormirzdad, in Parthia. I didn't mean to be rude. You speak like a native, but … you can't be," he said, eyeing the slant of Marcus' eyes, the tawny skin and straight black hair. "You look Hanaean."

Marcus relaxed a bit. "Both are true. I am Hanaean, but of Roman ancestry, my eyes give that away. I am also a native Latin speaker, as well."

"Indeed. And your friends?"

"My wife Mei. She is Hanaean, and my friends Hina and Galosga, Xiongnu from north of China."

"*Libens sum,* I am pleased to meet you, Nathaniel," Mei intoned with a slight nod of her head, a broad smile at her chance to speak Latin with a stranger.

"*Etiam, et Hina et … Galosga?*" replied Nathaniel, struggling with the unfamiliar syllables.

"*Etiam, libens sum!* I, too, am pleased to meet you," said Hina, somewhat unsure of using her new language on a stranger.

"There are Xiongnu riding with us. Are you with them?"

"We ride with them," answered Galosga.

"I wonder why I have not met you sooner," said Nathaniel

"We are usually up before dawn, riding security, and not back until after the evening encampment. Or sleeping all day, so we can ride around the camp all night."

"Interesting. So where are you going, Marcus?"

"We are going west. Hence the language lessons for my wife and friends. I am pleased that they speak so well after just a few months. It is one thing to speak well with one's tutor, but quite another to talk to a stranger. So where are you bound, Nathaniel of Hormirzad?"

"I am returning to my home, by way of Ecbatana. I am on a mission by Parthia to better understand lands east of Khojand."

"Did you get to Chang'an?"

"No, we turned around at Turfam. Language problems. I did not want to enter Hanaean territory without a translator, someone who knew the customs."

"You speak Sogdian, I am sure. There are many people in Turfam who speak both Sogdian and Hanaean quite well."

"Alas, I am lazy. I can only barely get by with Sogdian. Not well enough to translate into another language. And anyway, at Turfam, I had been gone from home already a year and a half."

"That long?"

"We spent a long time in Samarkand, Bukhara and Khojand. You will be going there?"

"I believe so. You are on an official mission?"

"Of sorts. At least, they gave me a lot of money to make my way. How far was I from China?"

"Not far, about a month or two past Turfam, you would have entered at Dunhuang."

"Too bad. If you were going the other way, you would have made a good translator." The elderly man smiled. "Perhaps you can tell me of your country? Have you seen much of it?"

"I was in Luoyang for several years."

"I can see we will have much to talk about!"

"But not today, Nathaniel. We will be posting the night patrol shortly. Perhaps tomorrow on our day off?"

"Yes, for sure."

"And you can tell us of Bukhara and the other cities on our way. And Parthia. Pleased to meet you." They shook, and Nathaniel left.

"He is interesting," said Mei.

"Interesting ... and interested. Perhaps too interested. He is Parthian, so don't trust him too much. Goes for all of you. They are the enemy of all

Romans. All right, let's ride," Marcus said, swinging himself onto his black mare.

The next evening, the sun had not yet set and Marcus' group had not even gotten their campfire going before Nathaniel showed up. Marcus was intrigued that he had located their camp so quickly, among the several hundred other campsites amidst the evening encampment. *Perhaps he speaks better Sogdian than he lets on?*

"Welcome back, Nathaniel. Will you join us for our spare evening meal?"

"Why, thank you."

"Please, sit here, while we get the fire going and pitch the yurt."

"No, please, let me help." Nathaniel crouched by the prepared but unlit fire, pulled a cow's horn from his cloak, and fished out a coal with a small tong from the damp moss inside the horn. He put it in the tinder and blew on it till it flared, adding twigs and dried grass, then dung, until a good, pungent blaze was going. He then helped erect the yurt, holding the felt while poles were added to stiffen the structure.

"Thank you! I guess you have earned your dinner, Nathaniel." Hina, Galosga and Hadyu went to get the night baggage from the wagon to put in the yurt. Marcus handed him a leather sack of *kumis*. "Here, drink!"

Nathaniel sniffed the contents and took a mouthful of the white liquid. "Mmm. Tastes like almonds. What is it?"

"Fermented mare's milk. A Xiongnu drink. Easily made on the road, nourishing, good for relaxing. Or more than relaxing, if you drink too much."

Nathaniel looked quizzical, but took another sip, less tentatively this time. "Yes, it is good."

"So how did you find us so quickly? I thought you said you didn't speak much Sogdian."

"Enough to get by. And you are well known. I just asked for the Hanaeans traveling with the Amazon woman."

Marcus chuckled at Nathaniel's dry humor. "Yes, I guess we are unusual. Hina gets quite the attention." He fixed a steady gaze on the man. "Nathaniel, an unusual name, it doesn't seem to be Parthian, I think"

"Not Parthian, Jewish. It means 'Gift of God' in Hebrew. I and my family fled to Parthia when the Romans burned the Temple."

"When was that?" Marcus had, of course, heard the story from another Jew, a traveling companion of years past, but he was volunteering nothing.

"When I was a young man. Some of my hot-headed countrymen decided to throw Rome out of our homeland Judea. We had some initial success, defeated one of their armies, but the Romans simply came back with four more. The Temple, the center of our religion, was looted, burned and destroyed, my people scattered. My family and I escaped to Parthia. They gave us refuge, and I set myself up as a merchant, selling the beautiful carpets they make there. So how did you come to speak Latin?"

"My ancestors were Roman soldiers, defeated by the Parthians, and eventually resettled in China. Like your people, scattered, but they kept their language and their Roman-ness, their *romanitas*."

"How do you come to be traveling so far from your home?" Nathaniel smiled behind his beard, and took another swig of *kumis*, apparently enjoying the unlikely beverage.

"Our ancestors settled there a century and a half ago, and no one wants to remember the old language or the customs anymore. Mei and I have no children, and I came by some money, so, well, we just wanted to go to see the land our ancestors came from."

"You have some fierce bodyguards." He nodded toward Hina, with Adhela at her breast, and Andanyu and Marasa, who had settled in beside Marcus, listening seriously.

"Old friends who had a tragedy. Their people were wiped out by sickness. Hina believed she had a sign from heaven that they should follow us. But tell us about those cities you mentioned yesterday, and Parthia."

"First you will come to Osh, after a steep mountain climb that will take most of a month, if the snows don't come early. After that, the road opens out onto a wide flat grassland valley, the Ferghana, hundreds of miles long between two mountain ranges, famous for their horses. At the western end is Khojand, a beautiful blend of Greek and local architecture, marvelous temples. And bazaars! Every corner you turn there will be another bazaar, selling rugs, silks, clothing, gems and jewelry, weapons. Every bazaar specializes in one of those items and there will be thousands in each, haggling in their own language. Beautiful! Do you speak Greek?"

"I am sorry, very little. But Greek? So far east?"

"The people there claim it was founded by Alexander the Great as *Alexandria Eschate*, Alexandria the Farthest, and they are proud of their Greek heritage. Though Alexander 'founded' it on the Sogdian city of Khojand. This is where your Sogdian companions on this caravan come from. If you can talk to them, you can talk to the merchants ... or anyone else there, for that matter. And anywhere for the next many months, until you come to Parthia."

Marcus nodded saying nothing. He was not looking forward to Parthia.

"In another week, you will come to the next city, Samarkand. There is no place in that city that is not green and pleasant. Even the mountains are green with trees, in every home are gardens, cisterns and flowing water. And, again, the bazaars!" Nathaniel took another swig of *kumis* and Marcus noted that the bag was nearly empty. Could the Jew be getting a bit tipsy?

"Finally, in another week, you will be in Bukhara in the land of lakes by the Oxus River. And more bazaars. I am sorry, I did not know that this was alcoholic. I seem to be a bit drunk."

"Here, have some more," said Hina, offering him another sack.

"I shouldn't, but ..." He took some more. "How'd you get to be a fighting Amazon?"

"You mean a fighting woman? When I turned twelve, I wanted to kill Han rather than get married and have babies."

"Greeks have legendary women fighters they call Amazon, but you're real." He laid back by the fire and was soon snoring.

"Well, I guess we'll find out about Parthia another day," said Marcus, fetching a blanket to toss over Nathaniel. "But at least I have an idea what lies ahead for the next few months."

CHAPTER 19:

A CHILD IS BORN

Aquileia, October 112AD

Antonius sat in the atrium on the edge of the *impluvium* rain-catcher on this warm fall morning, staring at the as-yet-uneaten breakfast Desdemona had brought him an hour before.

It had indeed been a difficult pregnancy for Marcia. Morning sickness began two months in, and lasted for three months, far longer than the other two carries, then the bleeding and spotting, the swollen ankles. She was afraid she would lose the child, and he was afraid he would lose his *domina*. For his first forty years, he had been blind, but for the last ten, his *domina* had taught him to see. He smiled, thinking about how she had come by that pet name, first a respectful title to a woman he thought was of high status, representing the Hanaean emperor as a translator. Afterward, it had become a joke between them, eliciting her laughter as he elevated her status above what it was, a virtual slave to an unworthy master. And when they became lovers, a term of endearment, his *domina*, his lady, the center of his world.

So, this morning, well before daybreak, as Marcia shifted her weight to relieve the ache in her back in bed, her water broke with a gush, saturating the bedding, herself, and Antonius sleeping beside her. Desdemona, ever prepared, answered the call bell already armed with fresh linens and a wide, loose gown for Marcia, turning the sleeping room into the birthing room with silent efficiency, lowering the ceiling oil lamp closer to the bed. She arranged for the servants to keep Colloscius and Aena in the day room at the end of the spacious house on the far side of the house, far from any noise that might upset them.

Antonius sent a runner to fetch the midwife Maria, who arrived with her servant girl just in time for Marcia's first serious labor pain, a bit after sunrise. After about an hour she emerged, asking for the runner to bring Demaratos.

"The doctor? Why? Is there some problem?"

"No, but at her age, complications can happen. Thirty-two is far too old for bearing children. Demaratos can do things I cannot, and I would rather have him here now, than have to send for him later."

The doctor arrived a bit later, and went straightaway into the birthing room, drawing the curtain behind him. Antonius sat morosely waiting, listening to the moans, the undercurrents of conversation, feeling helpless. And fearful, not an emotion with which he dealt well.

There was a bit of commotion at the door, and the doorman escorted in Gnaeus Decimus Septimus, portly senator and the senior student at the Academy, in full toga for the occasion.

"Gnaeus Decimus, I am glad to see you, but I can hold no classes or discussions today, my wife is giving birth," pleaded Antonius.

"Nonsense, Antonius, that is why I am here, to keep you company. Your runner alerted me that this was happening."

"What? That rascal, I gave him no such orders, sir!"

"I don't think he needed any. You looked like you needed company when I came in. Here, let's open this bottle of wine I brought, and keep your mind off what is going on in there. She'll be fine." Desdemona appeared out of nowhere to take the ceramic flask from his hands for opening and returned with two brass goblets. The Senator lifted his in salute. "To her health, and to the health of the newest Aristides"

Antonius tasted the wine. This was just what he needed.

Another commotion at the front of the house, and the doorman showed in Paulinus, his old army companion and veteran of many marches around the Danube, as well as Titus and Faustus, his drinking companions summoned by the runner, all bringing more wine. Antonius would have to see that Desdemona watered his well; he did not want to be drunk for the great occasion. Then the doorman brought in yet more, Marcia's close friends Adelia and Cassandra, and their husbands Silvanus and Brutus, with gifts and sweetmeats but mercifully no more wine. The runner had done well. They spent the morning laughing and joking, doing much to lift Antonius' spirits. *Hell, she's tougher'n my hickory stick. She'll do fine, she always does.*

Morning wore on into afternoon, and Desdemona continued to circulate with trays of food and drink for the guests. The sun slipped below the walls, casting the atrium into shadow, and still the moans and occasional screams continued to emanate from the birthing room. The crowd had long turned somber, attempting to comfort Antonius, who had once again become increasingly fretful. The women assured him that eight hours was not unduly long for labor. But it was not the length, rather the intensity of the occasional screams that concerned him; he knew, through two previous births, that Marcia was exceedingly stoic. By sunset, all but Paulinus and the Senator had excused themselves.

After a particularly intense outcry, Antonius had had enough. "I'm going in there," he announced to his two remaining friends, marching forcefully toward the entryway, pulling aside the green linen curtain. He entered, blinking as his eyes adjusted to the candlelight. Marcia lay on the bed, knees up, while Maria and her servant hovered between her widespread legs, illuminated by the ceiling oil lamp, lowered for better light. There was a pile of bloody rags in a bowl below them. Demaratos looked on from the far end of the bed.

The midwife noticed his entry and spoke to him over her shoulder. "Get out! You don't need to be seeing any of this that is going on!"

Antonius reverted to his uncultured Latin acquired during years of soldiering. "Arrgh, I helped her make that damned baby, I damn sure kin help her get it out!" He made his way to the head of the bed, opposite Demaratos on the other side of Marcia. The midwife scowled at him, continuing her work between Marcia's legs.

"No need for you to be in here," said Demaratos quietly. "There is nothing for you to do."

"There's plenty fer me ter be doin' here, sir!" He touched Marcia's cheek with his hand tenderly and smiled at her. "How're yer doin', *domina*? Havin' a rough go?"

Marcia smiled. "A bit. But we're fine. I am glad you are here." She took his hand and pressed it to her sweat-soaked cheek.

"Demaratos, can yer hand me one of those rags soaking in that bowl of clean water over there, please?" The doctor did so, and Antonius used his other hand to wipe down her face.

"Ah, that is so cooling. Squeeze a few drops on my tongue." She opened her mouth and savored each drop. "Give me some water, please."

"Antonius, we don't give women in labor water. It might make them throw up."

"Damned foolishness. She's sweated out all the water she started with a long time ago. Get it and be done with it!"

Demaratos glowered but obeyed, sullenly returning to hand Antonius the goblet. He held it to her lips and she drank, slowly but thirstily."

"Thank you, love. Oh! Here comes another one. Antonius, hold my hand!" She squeezed shut her eyes and pursed her lips as her whole body went into the contraction, her back arching forward off the pillow, her exposed thighs quivering.

Putting one hand around behind her back for support, clenching her hand with his other, he watched in awe at the power of the contraction, as Marcia cried out a sustained groan of intense effort. "Keep breathin', breathe easy, makes the pain better," he said. It was an old soldier's trick, hopefully good for women in labor also.

She gasped in between spasms. "Easy fer yer ter say, fucker!" She had long ago mastered Antonius' soldier's Latin and could match him profanity for profanity whenever she wanted.

The contraction died away as fast as it had come, and she lay back, gasping for breath. "That was a good one! Whew!"

Maria tossed another bloody rag into the bowl. Antonius was concerned about the blood, but nobody else seemed to be, so he looked away and said nothing, still holding her hand tightly. Maria and her servant girl huddled between Marcia's open legs, intensely absorbed. "I think you are getting close," the midwife said finally, peering over Marcia's swollen abdomen.

"That's good to know." Marcia smiled, unconvinced.

"The next time, I want you to push hard. It may hurt, the baby's head is going to tear you down there, but don't let up."

Marcia nodded. Antonius wiped her forehead, and gave her a few more drops of water, waiting for the next contraction. It didn't take long in coming. Once again, her shoulders came off the bed, her face screwed up in effort, Antonius bracing her. "Ow, ow! I am feeling that! The burning!"

"Don't let up, just push, *domina!* Yer can do it!"

The midwives busily wiped her bottom, tossing the bloodiest rag yet into the bowl, while Marcia strained with all her might. The midwife cried out. "The head, the head! It is going to come out on the next push!" The contraction ebbed away for a minute, then returned with a vengeance. This time, Marcia screamed, but suddenly there was a flurry of activity at the end of the bed, and Demaratos went down to take a look, holding a lamp for additional light.

"Get it, get it, here it is!" said the midwife. There was a gurgling sound, then a high wailing cry. "It's a boy, Marcia, it is a boy, and it is healthy!"

Marcia lay back, smiling and panting. "We did it, Antonius, you and me, we did it!" She was beaming with happiness, her blue eyes bright under their epicanthal folds. "We did it!" She looked over her abdomen, rapidly deflating after the passage of the child, at the midwife and her servant. "Hurry, I want to hold him. Please!"

"Just a second, dearie, we are cutting the cord and cleaning him up a bit, and you need to pass the rest. Make one more little push, there, that's a good girl, it's out now."

Antonius had no idea what was going on, but the three of them were studying something intently.

"I think we have it all," Demaratos pronounced. The women tossed something that looked like a hunk of bloody liver, with a long green tube attached to it, into the bowl with the waste rags.

The servant girl brought up the little red-faced baby, wrapped in a white blanket, his little wrinkled face seeming enraged at having been taken from the warm tender place he had been living, to be cast into the chill outer world.

He flailed his little fists spasmodically, making angry, choking cries as the girl handed him to Marcia, who took him and held him before her exposed breast.

She caressed him, murmuring nonsense to him until he began to nurse noisily, intensely concentrating on filling his belly with the first meal of his new life. "He looks like you, Antonius, all serious, ready to fight the world. Little Androcles, glorious little warrior."

Antonius touched the baby's head, smiling, as Paulinus and the Senator came into the birthing room to see the new arrival.

CHAPTER 20:

A FATHER AND HIS SON

Melitene, October 112AD

The four-wheeled wagon, drawn by four white horses, its stiff black cover emblazoned with the lightning bolt symbol of the *XII Ful*, pulled into the legionary field camp a few hours after sunrise. The wagon was escorted by thirteen cavalrymen on dark horses. Their circular *clipeus* shields were  slung on their backs, bouncing to the rhythm of their horses' canter. They received crisp salutes from the guards at the entry point of the *Via Principalis* thoroughfare transecting the camp. The cavalcade pulled up to the *praetorium* tent of the commanding *legatus,* halting in a cloud of yellow road dust. The guard on duty stepped up to the wagon, opening the side panel to assist the occupant to exit, saluting as he did so.

The new *legatus*, in uniform but without his helmet, stepped down, and acknowledged the salute with a nod. The commander was tall, square-jawed, with short-cropped curly black hair going gray around the temples, his muscular body molded by years of hard living under the eagles. He turned to the guard. "At ease. Is *legatus* Herrenius Saturninus in?" he asked.

The man looked a bit saddened. "Your Excellency, the *legatus* just died. The second in command, Tribune Sergius Celsus Severianus, awaits your presence in the *praetorium*, along with the Prefect of the Camps Marius Callaeus."

"I am sorry to hear of his passage, soldier. I heard many good things about your commander."

The young soldier escorted him in. The tribune, clad in just a tunic with the purple stripe denoting his position as second in command, rose to meet him, along with the Prefect of the Camps. "*Vale, legatus* Gaius Aetius Lucullus! We have been expecting you. Unfortunately, Herrenius Saturninus suddenly worsened, and he passed away two days ago." The tribune was young, perhaps not yet thirty, a shock of blond hair. The prefect at his side was much older, a retired centurion, still looking the part, grim and serious, though long since gone gray. The young man stepped from behind the desk, followed by the prefect. "Please, sir, your seat. Some of the troops will bring in your baggage from the wagon."

The *legatus* took his seat behind the desk, indicating that the two should likewise sit opposite him. "I am sorry to hear about Herrenius. I was hoping for a face-to-face turnover with him. I never met him, but he had a good reputation throughout the region. Has the funeral been conducted yet?"

"We have held that off for your arrival, sir, but it will have to be in the next day or two. Everything is in readiness, but we knew you would want to conduct the services."

"Thank you, that is good. When would you be ready to assemble the men for the ceremony?"

"As early as tomorrow morning, sir, if that is all right with you," the prefect answered in a raspy voice. "Unfortunately, bodies do not keep well in the heat."

"Tomorrow will be excellent. Have someone go over the particulars of the service with me after dinner."

The prefect scribbled a note on the wax tablet.

"Now, Sergius Celsus, bring me up to date on the state of my old legion. Remember, I am much more interested in the things not quite right, not the things that are as they should be."

"To be sure, sir. We are nearly at full strength, about a hundred men short due to illnesses, retirements, so forth. Ten deserters, unfortunately. The troops are a bit on the green side, the veterans are working them hard. We spent most of the summer in the field, forced marches, camps built each night, as close to war as you can get without shedding blood."

"We plan to do some cold-weather work in the winter, about two months in December and January," volunteered the prefect. "Digging for a camp when the ground is hard is a lot harder than in the soft summer muck."

"How is the cavalry?"

"At strength, four squadrons of ten men each, about a hundred horses. I'd like more spare mounts, of course."

The turnover continued for about an hour, covering their engineering and artillery, local politics and issues, supplies, the humdrum things essential to the life of the legion. At last Gaius concluded the meeting. "Thank you for your efforts, gentlemen. Since we will have the troops turned out for the funeral tomorrow, I would like to hold an inspection after the ceremony. Battle gear, not parade crap. And with that out of the way, I think I will bathe and refresh myself after a long trip."

The funeral pyre had been prepared in a field outside the camp. The legion, numbering over five thousand men, was mustered in sixty orderly squares, six deep, their tribunes and centurions to the front by their *signifier* standard-bearers. Two squadrons of horsemen flanked either side of the men, their *vexilla* flags snapping in the wind. A platform had been erected before them for the new *legatus* and his staff, adjacent to the pyre, on which rested Saturninus' body, wrapped in white linen. Legionaries stood by the base, torches in hand. A priest rose next to the legate, shrouded in white wool. He raised the white woolen shawl covering his head to observe the skies with rheumy eyes, raised impossibly thin arms to declare the auspices good, then seated himself.

Gaius addressed the crowd. "Herrenius Saturninus was a good general, though he fought no great battles. He kept you prepared for one, and that is the main and most thankless task of any general. Let us send him on his way with the honor he so greatly deserves. Light the pyre!"

The torchbearers carefully torched the prepared piles of logs and timber, coated liberally with naptha to accelerate the blaze. The fire leaped to life, snapping and swirling in the breeze, then caught with a roar that engulfed the timber pile, smoke black against the sky as the troops looked on.

The fire burned for a half-hour, before settling down to smoldering, glowing coals. Gaius Lucullus nodded to the prefect, who roared loud enough to be heard by all the men. "Make ready for inspection!"

Gaius started with the senior First Cohort, with its tribune and Paulus Herrerius, the 'first lance' *primus pilus* of the legion, going down each of the sixth centuries of each cohort, inspecting the men, chatting with some. He repeated this with each cohort, but when he came to the Fifth Cohort, he was taken aback to see his son standing as tribune. He knew Secundus had decided to follow the eagles, headed for his first posting, from letters Camilla had written him posted from Byzantium. But she had only mentioned that he would be in Cappadocia, not a specific place or legion. To the young man's credit, Gaius noted that he kept his eyes rigidly fixed in front, betraying no recognition of his father. The centurion and his *optio* behind him as well kept their eyes to the front, emotionless. But there was something familiar about the *optio*.

He directed his attention to his son. "Tribune, *tues vires integres sunt?* Are your men ready?"

"Yes, sir, *integres sunt*. They are ready," the young man answered, his eyes never wavering.

Damn, he looks good as a soldier! "Let's start with the last century first," said Gaius with a hint of a smile. "The centurions always stash the bad apples to the rear." He marched off down the side of centuries, trailed by the tribune flanked by the two centurions.

Gaius went by the first rank, looking each soldier up and down. Well-equipped, iron brightly burnished, no rust, leather well-oiled. Well-shaven, clean, looking muscular and lean, the way soldiers should look. He came up on a young lad, who might be just sixteen, the greenest of the green. Though he struggled to contain himself, his nervousness showed up in his darting gray eyes, his hands flinching around the shaft of his lance. "Soldier, what is your name?" Gaius asked.

"Titus, sir, Titus Flavius."

"And where are you from?"

"Pannonia. Aquincum by the Danube, sir."

"Beautiful area, good hunting on the hills overlooking the river. Did you do any hunting there?"

"Boar and elk, sir. Boars with spears, elk with bow." The lad smiled, but kept his eyes front. His nervousness seemed to abate.

"That's good. Hunters make good soldiers, and you look like you will be one."

Finishing the with the last man, Gaius turned back to the front. The tribune and centurions took their places in front of the men. "Your men look good, Tribune. Your centurions have done a good job with them. Who are your centurions?"

"Silvanus Vegetius, and his *optio* Samuel Elisarius."

Gaius felt like a thunderbolt had struck him. Samuel Elisarius? The Latinized form of Shmuel bin Eliazar? It couldn't be him, not a centurion. He switched to his rusty Aramaic learned years back, on a bet. "Shmuel, I wouldst not have recognized thee, without thy beard."

"Nor I thee, sir. Good to see thee again, thy Aramaic hath not gotten any better." No hint of a smile, but a twinkle in his eye.

"We shall have a talk sometime." Gaius saw no need to hide his smile, switching back to Latin. "In my quarters, please, after the troops are dismissed. The three of you, not more than an hour."

The inspection was finished well before noon, and the tribune and his two centurions made their way to the praetorium.

"I wonder what this is about?" mused Vegetius.

"Whatever it is, I am sure it has something to do with me," answered Secundus, nodding in return to the salute from the sentry at the tent entrance. The three entered, saluted and stood at attention. "Tribune Gaius Aetius Secundus Lucullus, as ordered, sir!"

The legate rose from his desk and offered them chairs he had made ready in advance. "Seats, gentlemen. You may remove your helmets." He scrutinized his son closely, then turned his attention on Vegetius. "Are you two aware of our relationship?"

"We are, sir."

"That is good. Son, and this will be the last you hear me call you that for a long time, your being attached here surprised me. I confess I hadn't had time to check the rolls yet, and certainly did not expect to see you in the *XII Ful*. Let me congratulate you, Tribune, for remaining admirably stoic."

"I am sorry. I sent you and Mother … your wife, sir … a letter informing her of my posting, but you must not have received mine, or her response."

"No matter. We both understand why I did not want us both in the same legion. You can't be seen as having any advantage as my son, and many will think you do anyway, and hold it against you. I would transfer you out, but Hadrian has frozen transfers without cause. So, we have to make this work. You are Tribune Lucullus, Tribune of the Fifth Cohort, and if I have to order you to certain death, I will do so. Do you understand?"

"I do, sir. I certainly never expected you back in your old unit, as that rarely happens, which was why I chose this one."

"Fate intervenes. Well, since this is our last father-son moment for a long time to come," he clapped his hands and a servant appeared with wine and goblets. "Wine for the leadership of the Fifth."

The servant handed each a goblet, and Gaius raised his in a toast. "To our new relationship as legate and tribune." The other three raised theirs. "To good relationships," offered Samuel.

"To good relationships." Everyone took a sip, then Gaius continued. "And that brings me to you, Samuel. You are almost an unexpected find as my son. At least I knew he was in the army, but you? And a centurion, yet."

"Long story, I'll make it short, sir. After I got my citizenship, it just seemed a natural thing to do, fightin' bein' what I had done best. I trained under the best with Antonius, so I rose fast. Speaking of Antonius, are you in touch with him?"

"I am. He and Marcia are well, running a little academy of languages and philosophy in Aquileia. Just had his third child, a boy, in their last letter. He is absolutely the happiest man alive."

"With a wife like Marcia, he should be. He was so rough-cut, kind of unexpected, him to be running an academy now."

"Antonius is a man of many sides and hidden depths."

Vegetius stirred in his seat. "Sir, may I ask a question about operations?"

"By all means."

"A lot of strange things going on, like your transfer back, a freeze on other transfers, More training than usual. Is there something in the wind?"

Gaius pondered his answer. The guidance had been clear, not a word to the troops, or Ctesiphon would know about it before breakfast. "Nothing that I know of, and I would be the first to know." He said with a smile on his lips that hid the pain in his heart. Never before had he lied to his men about anything, and he had enforced that same honesty from them. "Just an overall tightening up. Just train the troops hard. Well, I have a staff meeting in an hour or so, so I must dismiss you." The three rose, re-donning their helmets. "One last thing … Vegetius, Samuel, take care you show your new tribune the ropes. And you, Tribune, take care of your men."

"Yes, sir," the three responded in unison.

CHAPTER 21:

A DEATH IN THE FAMILY

Rome: October 112AD

Aulus examined the completed copy of his last speech. "That is excellent, Diodorus, nice work!" he said. "Perfect, ready for posting in the Forum on the *Acta Dialis* bulletin board. You have exquisite handwriting."

"Thank you, *dominus*. Uh, your lordship ... may I be excused? I would like to go visit Trajan's Market to see if I can find a gift for someone." Diodorus shifted uneasily from foot to foot, a slight lad with a map of brownish-blonde hair.

"Certainly. Tell Ennius that you have my permission. Be back for dinner, however. He tells me that he is fixing something special for you servants tonight." A smiled played around the edges of Aulus' mouth. "A gift, eh. For Chloë, I presume?" His eyes twinkled under his graying eyebrows.

Diodorus did not answer, but his blush betrayed his answer.

Aulus pulled a pouch of coins from his tunic and fished out several *denarii*. The boy's eyes brightened. "Here, get her something nice," he said, handing the boy the coins.

"Yes, *dominus!* Is it that obvious?"

"There are few secrets in the Galba *familia*. Go, enjoy yourself, and don't miss Ennius' nice meal tonight."

Diodorus exited Aulus' home on the Aventine Hill. It was a beautiful fall day, he was in love, his master was happy with him and he was free for the afternoon. He whistled a tune as he walked along, a bounce in his step, turning onto the *Clivus Publicius* to descend the Aventine. As he passed the Temple of Ceres, he noticed a lad about his own age in a red tunic, lounging under one of the plane trees. As he approached, the boy straightened up and hailed him "Hello! Aren't you Galba's servant Diodorus?"

"Yes, I am. Who ..."

Someone hit him from behind on the head, a solid blow that made lights flash in front of his eyes. Momentarily dazed, he was unable to resist as the person behind him bound his hands, gagged him, and put a rough hemp sack over him. He felt himself thrown into the back of something. A wagon, for it started off, clattering down the street. Then all went black.

Sunset glowered red over the smoky air of Rome. Ennius knocked at the doorway to Aulus' study. "*Dominus?* A minute of your time, sir?"

"Certainly, Ennius. My head steward can have much more than a minute, if he wants. What is it?"

"It's Diodorus, *dominus*. He hasn't come back from downtown yet. I have held dinner as long as I could, but I am concerned. He is very meticulous about being on time."

"He is very meticulous about everything. He went to Trajan's Market to buy a gift for someone," giving Ennius a big wink and eliciting a smile. "He is probably looking for just the right gift for that special person, whoever SHE might be."

"Whoever, to be sure. I will start dinner and save some for him. If it is cold, well, he is in love, he won't notice."

"To be sure."

After breakfast the next morning, Aulus sent for Ennius. "Would you send Diodorus up here, please? I have some correspondence for him to work his magic on. He did get back last night, didn't he?"

"No, sir, he did not. I was just coming to see you. I am very concerned. The streets aren't safe after dark, not even up here on the Aventine."

"He said he was going to Trajan's Market. Send some of the boys along and send a bodyguard with them. Andromachus, if he is available."

"Right away, *dominus.*"

Aulus put on his toga, brushing off Ennius' attempts to assist. "Never mind that, I can dress myself. You go off and get that search party going for Diodorus. I am going off to see the prefect of the *Vigiles* and see if we can get them to do some police work for us, maybe some of their informers. I, too, am concerned."

An hour later, Aulus and his partner Lucius Parvus came to the headquarters office of the *vigiles* in the *Basilica Julia* in the Forum. "I want to see the Prefect, please," Aulus asked a minor functionary examining one of many wax tablets littering his desk.

"Do you have an appointment?" The surly clerk did not even bother to look up from his work.

"Do you have any funding for next year?" Aulus growled, his face dark. "Tell him Senator Aulus Aemilius Galba requests his presence immediately."

The functionary stood up soundlessly and went to a back office, returning with the prefect. The prefect's tunic bore the narrow purple stripe of an equestrian.

"Senator, what an honor!" He said, extending his hand. "I am Gnaius Petronius."

Aulus returned the grip, and nodded to Lucius. "And this is my right-hand man, Lucius Parvus. It's not honor that brings me here, it is bad business. One of my slaves is missing, and we believe he may have been the victim of some crime."

"Come back into my office, Senator. We'll be more comfortable discussing this in private."

The prefect's office was dark and windowless. A few lamps cast fitful, flickering light over the pile of scrolls and tablets on his battered wooden desk, its surface scarred by years of hard use and no care. "Please sit." He offered the two a pair of folding chairs and seated himself, picking up a wax tablet to take notes. "Slaves go missing all the time, Senator. Most of them just run away and are never seen again. Has he had any discipline problems?"

"None. Quite the contrary. He is among my best servants."

"Name?"

"Diodorus."

"When did he go missing?"

"I gave him the afternoon off yesterday to go shopping at the new market on the Quirinal Hill. He was to be back for dinner, as my steward was fixing a nice dinner for my boys and girls. But he didn't come back, not last night, not this morning. I have some of my boys out trying to find him now, with a bodyguard, just in case."

"How old?"

"About twenty. Good looking Greek lad, blondish hair, spare frame."

"Greek, huh? Does he like boys or men? He may have just found a friend."

"I don't think so. He is actually quite smitten with one of my serving girls. In fact, he was going out to get a gift for her."

"Well, someone may have taken a liking to him, whether he was inclined or not, and now he just doesn't want to come home and face everyone. Happens, you know. Carrying any money for that gift?"

"A couple of *denarii*."

"Enough to be worth robbing. When did you acquire him?"

"About three years ago. My old personal secretary, my freedman still living with us, died, so I bought Diodorus as his replacement. Highly recommended, highly educated, flawlessly fluent in Greek and Latin, exquisite handwriting."

"Hmm. This changes things a bit. Your personal secretary? For personal business, or Senate business?"

"Both. And I also run a fleet of ships out of Alexandria and Myos Hormos."

"I thought I recognized your name, Senator. 'Galba and the New Argonauts!' You were quite the hit a few years ago." For the first time, Petronius smiled, revealing well-set teeth.

"Yes, Lucius Parvus and I put that expedition together."

"Well, back to the matter. He is your personal secretary, involved in your Senate business, your shipping business, and all your personal matters. Did you keep anything from him?"

"Not really. Do you think someone is trying to get something from him?"

"Happens, Senator. Well, I'll take this case, but I can't promise any results. Missing people are hard to find in Rome, unless their bodies float to the surface of the Tiber and they get tangled in the weeds along the shore. Anything else you can tell me?"

The senator shook his head negatively.

"Well, let me know right away if he shows up so I can call off my men." He escorted Aulus and Lucius to the front of the office and out the door.

Aulus' boys turned up nothing. None of the shopkeepers in the market recalled anyone matching Diodorus' description. They returned about sunset, glum and empty-handed. All had liked the studious but happy-go-lucky lad.

Livia and Aulus were in the front atrium, talking with twelve-year old Pontus when the doorman led in Petronius, flanked by two *vigiles*.

Aulus rose. "You found him!"

Petronius was somber. "We did. I am sorry. Can you ... come out and identify him?"

Diodous lay in the back of the *vigiles'* wagon, covered by a sheet showing signs of mud and blood. Petronius exposed his face, battered and bruised, one eye swollen shut, bloody lips. Aulus gasped.

"It's worse, I am sorry." Petronius pulled back to show his torso, mutilated by ragged, torn flesh. "Death probably came to him as a blessing. Someone tortured him to death."

Aulus pulled away from the wagon, bent over and vomited. He straightened back up and wiped his mouth with the back of his hand, spitting to clear his mouth. "I am sorry," he said, his eyes brimming with tears. By now, Ennius and Lucius had joined him. Livia held back, not caring to see death up close. "Who would do such a thing?"

"Do you have any enemies? That person wanted something very badly. Some information?"

"There is nothing in my life that I wouldn't have up on the *Acta Dialis*, though some things I'd rather not."

"We need to play this worst case. The killer thinks that what you know, the lad knew, and it was worth his knowing what it was. And it's easier to pry information out of a slave than from a senator. But now he may come for you. Consider yourself in serious danger. How many bodyguards do you have?"

"Five, all ex-gladiators, supervised by a retired centurion."

"Don't go out without at least two of them, and post continuous watches in your house all day and all night. Whoever it is may come for you next, or for someone else in your *familia.*"

"Yes, sir, and thank you." Aulus said, extending his hand. Petronius took it in a firm sympathetic grip, and he and his group stood off a bit. Aulus looked at the forlorn body in the wagon, then turned to his head steward. "Ennius," he said, his voice breaking, "Diodorus is to have a very fine funeral, and we will lay his ashes in our family tomb on the Appian Way. See to it." He put his hands on the edge of the wagon bed, then turned toward his lifelong friend and freedman. "Lucius, prepare his manumission, we will lay him away as a free man."

CHAPTER 22:

ALEXANDRIA-THE-FARTHEST

Khojand, November 112AD

Marcus' party had arrived in Kashgar in late September, just in time to take the last caravan northbound across the Irkeshtam pass to Osh before the snows shut that route down for the winter season. Cold and treacherous was the passage, but mercifully brief, winding along the Alay Valley for a few days, then across the rugged passes of the Pamirs for several more, before beginning the descent to Osh, with warmer weather and breathable air. They arrived in Osh in late October, continuing on to Khojand in mid-November through the Ferghana Valley.

The green of the Ferghana Valley grassland, the heartland of Sogdiana, was so intense that it almost hurt the eyes. The valley lay like a flat carpet of grass spread between the Tien Shan Mountains to the north and the Pamirs to the south. Ferghana was well-watered by the Pearl River in the north, in Persian the *Yakhsha Arta*, approximated in Greek as the Jaxartes. The plain's temperate climate supported a host of cities, each a major hub for trade, Osh, Kokand, Khojand and many smaller ones, each separated by just a day or two of easy travel. And here and there vast herds of horses grazed, occasionally rounded up in organized stampedes, their hoofs echoing like a rumble of thunder.

The city of Khojand, situated by the Tien Shan foothills to the north, beside a small lake formed by an earthen dam on the Jaxartes, lived up to Nathaniel's enthusiastic descriptions. Canals distributed plentiful water from the lake to the city and surrounding fields. The architecture of *Alexandria Eschate*, Alexandria-the-Farthest, Khojand's Greek name, would have done tribute to any city in the Aegean, with white marbled temples and porticos around the central *agora* marketplace.

Here Marcus decided to take a month-long layover, purchasing rooms for all at a comfortable inn by the lakeside.

Hina's Xiongnu party was adapting very well to their new life, though missing the wild freedom of their old ways. Now speaking quite passable Sogdian, as well as Latin, and with a better understanding of the culture common to all city-dwellers, the Xiongnu comfortably negotiated the markets of the various cities, bargaining for goods in coin or barter.

Hina needed a replacement for her faithful but tired beige stallion Eagle. She found a corral outside of town where men were breaking horses to saddle. She dropped the reins to the ground, and Eagle stayed put as though tethered, as he had been trained.

She watched the goings-on through the timbers. One man was trying fiercely to get the attention of a tall, sleek black stallion with curses and whips from his quirt. What he got instead was an enraged horse, rearing, bucking and kicking at him. At last, the man got a halter on the horse's head, getting it into the animal's foaming mouth without losing any fingers. Hina watched with amusement as the man eventually got a rope around the animal's middle. This was going to get very interesting when he attempted to get on the animal's back.

Hina stood with one foot on the rail. The horse circled, dancing around the man, whinnying and stirring up a thick cloud of dust, as the would-be rider tried to get a grip to climb onto the stallion's back. He rushed his move, prematurely throwing his leg over and trying to pull himself upright. The first buck caught him only halfway to the vertical. The animal arched its back and leapt into the air, tossing the poorly-seated man rudely onto the ground, to roll rapidly away to escape the flaying hooves. Getting upright, he ran toward the men, now convulsed with laughter. "He's a devil! If I can't ride him, no one can. Good for nothing but stud!"

The men then noticed Hina by the fence. One of them called out to her. "What the fuck are you laughing at, bitch? You think you can ride this devil? He just threw the best horse-breaker in Khojand."

"There's not a horse been foaled I can't ride."

"You want to try?" He took the quirt from the disgruntled rider, approached her, extending it to her.

"Oh, I won't need that. But if I ride him, he is mine."

"Seems safe enough of a bet. No quirt? Sure?"

Hina bent under the corral timber to enter in. "No. I won't need that. But all of you, you spooked him. Back away to the far side, and please keep quiet."

The men slowly did as she said, muttering among themselves as they went.

Hina reached into the pouch of her felt vest to draw out an apple. She approached the stallion, stopping about ten feet away to hold out the fruit. "Here, fellow. I bet you like apples. They are hard to come by this time of year."

The horse's nostrils flared as he caught the scent of the treat. But he pawed the ground, pitching his head and snorting. "No, you have to come to me if you want it. When you are ready."

The gentle chit-chat continued for several minutes, the horse gradually getting closer and closer, eyeing her for any threat. Finally, he took a chance and nuzzled the apple in her hand, devouring it in one juicy crunch. But Hina got a loose grip on his halter, and soon stroked his nose. "There now, that is like silk. You have a beautiful nose." The animal fretted nervously, but did not pull back to break free, or attempt to bite or attack her.

"That's all right, just get to know me. I won't hurt you. Now I am going to touch that rope around your waist, but I am not going to mount you yet. Just let me touch it."

The horse flinched, its sides visibly shivering, but he allowed her touch, allowed her to stroke his sides.

After about half an hour, Hina thought the animal was ready, and she flowed effortlessly onto his back, getting the predictable response. The horse bucked, swapped ends, did everything he could possibly do to dislodge this foreign presence from his back. Hina anticipated the horse's every move, one hand high in the air, continuing to talk calmly to him, her thighs clamped firmly around his sweating flanks. The dust rose in a yellow cloud, fetid with the smell of manure.

Suddenly the horse gave up the fight, settling down to walk over to the water trough to quench his thirst. The men started to approach them, but Hina shook her head. "Not yet. He's not ready for you. Stay where you are."

His thirst slaked, Hina introduced him to the basics, soon having him walk nervously around the corral, almost with a bit of a prance as he passed close to the men for the first time.

"Open the corral gates. I want to take him out for a gallop."

"No way we're going to lose our horse. He'll throw you and take off."

"You've already lost him, remember our bet? See that fence, fellow?" she said, pointing to the distant end of the corral. "You think we can jump that? Let's go! Hiyaa!" She flicked the halter and the horse responded with a burst of speed that took it well over the fence to land at a gallop, disappearing down the road in a cloud, his hooves clattering.

After about fifteen minutes, Hina returned, this time to the corral gate. "You want to open it this time? I tired him out, and I don't think he's ready for more jumping. And I'll need a brush. Time he learned about grooming."

The men opened the gate, she dismounted as smoothly as she had mounted him before, patted his sweating sides, and led him docilely to the watering trough, where he drank noisily. One of the men handed her a brush, and she began grooming him, eliciting shivers of delight at her touch.

One of the men approached them, causing the horse to roll his eyes and turn toward him.

"Easy, talk softly, he doesn't like you men too much."

"Where the hell did you learn to ride like that, woman? Chaxren is our best breaker, and that devil threw him like a child's doll."

She smiled. "He doesn't break many stallions. And this one is a hard-headed one. Stallions are like men. They'll do everything you want them to do, as long as they think it's their idea." She smiled.

"Well, thanks anyway for breaking him for us. We thought he'd be only good for stud."

"I didn't break him. And anyway, by our bet, he is mine." She stroked his muzzle, eliciting a whicker.

"You're not taking him. He is worth a lot of money, the Han pay up to a hundred *drachmae* for one of these horses."

"That much for one that can't be ridden?"

"Well, maybe half, if no one can break him."

"But I rode him, without breaking him. You should not have made the bet."

"Bets with a woman don't count for much."

She put her hand on her dagger, not in a threatening manner, but to let him know that she perhaps could do more than ride. "Do you want to make another bet that you will also surely lose?"

The man studied her eyes, probing for a sign of weakness. Hina gave him none. At last, he shook his head in the negative. "Just testing, to see if you were serious."

She allowed a small smile to return to her face, not to gloat, but to let the man know the confrontation was over, if he wished it to be. "What is your name? Mine is Hina."

The man scratched his beard. "I am Bhurz. Where are you from, Hina?"

"The steppe lands north of China."

"Oh, and is that your horse over there, the small beige? A steppe pony?"

"He is, and a stallion."

"No wonder you get along well with such horses. I have been interested in getting a steppe pony. They have a reputation for sturdiness and endurance, not as fast as these, but hardy. They are hard to come by here. How old?"

"Four. Eagle has been ridden hard, and I actually came here, hoping to trade him. We have traveled almost continuously for eight months, he has earned his time at stud. Would you like to trade this unrideable devil for a tired but rideable stallion?" She smiled again, pleased at the turn of conversation.

"Let's take a look. No injuries?"

"None."

After a few minutes of inspection, the deal was sealed with a handshake, after which Hina threw in a silver coin for a larger saddle and harness. "Come on, Devil. They have given you the appropriate name." She mounted up and headed out, passing by the gaggle of men, pulling the reins just in time to keep Devil from biting Chaxren.

Nathaniel found his Parthian handler in his well-appointed white stone house beside the lake to the east of town. The house sat at the end of a long, paved walkway lined with trees, now barren with the autumn weather, and punctuated with bronze statues in the center. A servant led him to Spandarates, seated by a large fishpond, shaded by a tall evergreen in a garden overlooking the lakeside. He was feeding the fish, large orange carp, crumbs of bread which they devoured hungrily, when the servant presented Nathaniel.

Spandarates rose and greeted the Jew effusively. "Nathaniel, Nathaniel! So long you were gone! Please be seated," he said, indicating a wicker chair by the small table. He turned toward the servant. "Wine for my friend, please."

Nathaniel seated himself, wrapping his cloak around him against the chill. "A long trip. Two years. I am glad to be back."

"Anything interesting to report?" The servant brought each a glass of ruby-red wine.

"Not really." Nathaniel went on for about a half an hour, relating mostly inconsequential details of trading goods, local rivalries, the movement of the Sogdians deeper into Hanaean territory. "In short, nothing much," he concluded.

"Nothing much, but such details can be important." Spandarates picked up a scroll. "Here, this is something interesting that just arrived from Mithridates in Ctesiphon a few days ago. He appears to be looking for a particular individual." He unrolled the scroll, reading, following his finger, until he came to the relevant part. "An Hanaean eunuch, he says, who speaks fluent Latin, and his Latin name is Marcus. His Hanaean name is She Noe, or something like that. Odd that he would be looking for someone with such specifics."

Odd indeed. But I didn't know he was a eunuch. "A eunuch? How would I tell someone was a eunuch? I mean, without inspecting?" Nathaniel was not a gifted liar. Getting caught in a lie now might cost his head, for Mithridates certainly didn't not want to just send his greetings to this eunuch. But over the past several months Marcus and his odd group had become his friends, and he did not want to throw them to the wolves.

"I don't know, I guess a high-pitched voice, feminine manner."

"Oh, no, no one like that that, not at all. I did hear in Kashgar, that there was a eunuch going to Bactria, I think Bagram. Might that be the one of interest?"

"A long shot. I don't know what he is looking for, but I will mention that, see what comes."

Nathaniel shared several more cups of wine, then excused himself, passing up the opportunity to spend the night at the palatial residence. There were not many Latin speakers in Khojand, but just one would be enough to tip the balance.

Nathaniel stopped at the inn where Marcus had ensconced his party, finding him and Mei in their room. "Marcus, I have urgent news."

"Come in, what is it?"

"I just spoke with my Parthian contact here, to give him my report on my travels. He said something very disturbing. It seems Mithridates, the head of Parthian intelligence in Ctesiphon, is looking for you in particular. Who in the hell are you that Parthian intelligence cares about you? I lied, said I hadn't seen you, and that could get me killed."

"Mithridates? First name Cyrus?"

"The same, and brother to King Osroës. He is looking for an Hanaean eunuch by your name, and he knows your Hanaean name also. And that you speak fluent Latin. Though you aren't a eunuch, are you? Tell me he is just looking for a long-lost friend."

"Si Nuo is my Hanaean name. Something like that, right?"

"Yes, something like that. He said 'She Noe'. How do you know each other?"

"About ten years ago, he was the Parthian envoy to Luoyang, the Hanaean capital. I was in the court, and we had some contact. But we were not close. There was that incident with the Roman envoy, I told you of that, and I think he was involved with that. But why he would be interested in me personally, now after ten years? And him the head of Parthian intelligence? There must be some mistake."

"Do me a favor, please, you and none of your party speak any Latin, anywhere, anytime. Sogdian or Hanaean all right, but no Latin. And use a different name. Please. To keep my head on my shoulders, because I lied to protect you."

"Thank you, Nathaniel, and we won't let you down."

CHAPTER 23:

JUST ANOTHER DEAD SLAVE

Aquileia, December 112AD

The wind chased wisps of gray clouds in the overcast sky, promising rain. The man wrapped his heavy brown cloak about him against the winter chill and settled into the undergrowth overlooking the villa below. Out of his leather pouch, he pulled out his vellum sketch pad and some charcoal pencils. The man had a good view of the villa half-mile off, the road leading up to it, the outbuildings, and even a partial view into the building itself. This would be good for a start. He made a few confident strokes for the first outline on the sketch pad.

As the work progressed, his rendition emerged on the beige sketch pad. He sketched in the outline of the building, two abutted hollow squares forming two atria, four low watch towers on each corner. He completed the tile roofs over each side of the squares with short choppy strokes. He squinted, trying to discern the details of what he could see of the second floor of the first atrium; his eyes weren't as good as they used to be, and the light was bad. There appeared to be a portico, with five or six doors on the two visible sides. Quick horizontal strokes and six little vertical ones, good enough. He penciled in the chimney over the middle of the building, smoke curling from it. The first floor of the division was probably the kitchen, baths and latrines. A side door, probably a servants' entrance, surrounded by plentiful stacks of stacked wood, barrels and a cellar door, rounded out the sketch. That door would be locked from the inside at night, and probably unguarded. Why waste a night watchman on a locked door?

He sketched in the surroundings, the main road, a tree-lined carriage way to the entrance door on the left side, a perimeter road around the side of the building past the servants' door, to the back side. There might be another door back there. One side was used for the academy, and the other for the residence. But which was which? There were no people moving about. He'd figure that out later. He drew in some of the shrubbery, just fuzzy balls, perhaps every ten feet along the perimeter, then the corral, barn and stable behind it for the animals. Clear grass for about a hundred yards around the building, then the surrounding trees.

The man looked at his work. For a quick sketch, it was remarkably artistic, catching the texture of the walls, even some cracks, all sketched out in light, confident strokes.

Behind him, a twig snapped. The man set down his sketch pad very quietly and turned his head slowly around, making no sound or sudden movement, in case he hadn't been seen.

"Sonny, artists prefer to sketch on sunny days in nice weather. What're ye doin' up here in these woods?" The speaker was a lean old white-haired man, slender and wrinkled.

"As you said, sketching. I prefer gray light. It adds to the mood. You are?"

"Janus. May I see?"

The man stood and handed Janus the sketch.

"Hmm, very nice. A lot of detail here," said Janus

"Thank you. Are you from around here?"

"You could say so," Janus said with smile. "I am the doorman for that building. It is Antonius Aristides' home and academy."

"What a fine coincidence," said the man. "Which side is the academy?"

"The left side, facing the main road."

"Nice, so they don't disturb the residence, of course. Do you come up here often?"

"My afternoon walk, just by myself. What did you say your name was? Oof!"

The wind went out of Janus' lungs as the man stabbed him in the left side, between the third and fourth ribs. Janus breathed his last with questioning eyes as the man retrieved his sketch. He then lowered the body gently to ground, hoping that Janus had been alone as he had claimed. He put the sketch back in the pouch, pulled Janus' body into the nearby bushes, then crawled into the underbrush beside it.

After fifteen minutes, there were no sounds of others, no cries for Janus. He had indeed been alone. The man dragged the body deeper into the woods. There was no proper pathway up to this location, just a little-used animal path. While the old man claimed this to be his afternoon walk, he might have lied. Had the old man caught a glimpse of him and followed him up here? Or was this just a crazy coincidence? No matter, he would have to leave the body to the foxes and vultures, as he had nothing with which to bury him. It would be dark soon, and no one was likely to find him tonight, a good half mile from the villa. Maybe not even tomorrow.

Desdemona set the servants to lighting the lamps throughout the house, as it was near sunset on a gray, cloudy day. The fire in the hypocaust below made the floors feel warm, but the air was chill and damp.

Janus still had not shown up for work. "Maria, would please check Janus' room? He may still be napping and he has door duty tonight."

"He went for his walk, Desdemona. I haven't seen him come back yet, but I may have missed him."

She bustled off to check his room. Desdemona went to the residence to let Antonius and Marcia know that dinner would be ready whenever they were. She found Marcia nursing little Androcles in her sitting room, Antonius sitting with her. "Dinner is ready, Marcia."

"Thank, you, Desdemona. Is everything ready for Aulus Aemilius' visit tomorrow?"

"Indeed. We have a very special feast for him, roast pheasant and venison."

"Good choice. He likes our country-style meals."

Maria entered the sitting room, interrupting the conversation. "Excuse me, Desdemona, Marcia. Janus is not back from his walk. We searched the whole house; he is not here."

Antonius grumped. "Probably turned his ankle up there in the damned woods. He should slow it down a bit, he is seventy now. Have Brutus take his door duty, and get Alaric to bring me some torches and some servants. We'll go up and find him before he freezes to death. Damned fool!"

Antonius, Alaric and several of the menservants fanned out into the hills, after blowing horns and calling loudly from the watchtowers to see if they could elicit a response. Antonius had a general idea where Janus might have gone, as he had accompanied the man on several of his excursions. The man was sprightly for his age. Antonius would have liked more light for tracking, but he thought he found indications of the direction where Janus had gone. However, after about three hours, it seemed futile. There were no responses to horns or calls, and they themselves were stumbling in the dark.

Antonius shook his head in despair. "I hate to say it, lads, but I think we need to call it a night. These winter woods are dry as tinder, and if we drop one of these torches when the next one of us falls on his ass, the whole thing could go up. Let's get started tomorrow at first light, and hopefully, he's found someplace to hole up that's not too cold."

Everyone murmured in agreement, though if asked, they would have stayed out all night. The old doorman was popular with his fellow servants.

The next morning, the buzzards made it easy to find Janus, a cluster of them wheeling over his final resting place. Alaric found him first, buzzards worrying the old man's concealed body. "Got him, Antonius, over here by the big oak!"

Antonius shooed off the obnoxious birds and helped haul the body out into the light, the cause of death obvious. Antonius bent down to study it.

"Looks like murder to me, but why? I don't think he even put up much of a fight, no bruises. And he never carried any money, so why robbery? Let's rig a litter and get him out of here."

They had just gotten the body back to the villa when Aulus Aemilius' carriage rolled up. He didn't wait for the coachman, but opened the door himself and hopped out, coming to embrace Antonius in a big bear hug. "My good Antonius. How good to see you again! How is little Androcles?" He released Antonius, sensing something amiss. "What's wrong?"

"We just found one of the servants up on that hill there, murdered. Stabbed in the heart. I am going to send Alaric down to Aquileia to get someone from the urban cohort up here to look into it."

"You don't say? I had one of mine murdered in a very mysterious way a few months ago. Tortured to death, as though they wanted to some information. My personal secretary."

"This was our doorkeeper. He liked to take long walks off the trails into the woods, and somebody stabbed him in the heart."

"Was he tortured?"

"No, didn't even seem to put a fight, taken completely by surprise. Sorry, this is going to put a damper on our festive occasion."

"No matter, the coincidence seems odd, first mine, now yours? Do we have enemies?"

"None for me," Antonius laughed. "But you senators, I don't know about that." He turned toward Alaric. "Get him into the barn, and then go into town and let the prefect know what went down here. Don't let his lads put you off talking to him, talk to him directly, use my name if you have to."

"Yes, sir!"

Turning back to Aulus, Antonius said, "Let's get you inside and out of the cold, so we can introduce you to little Androcles."

Aulus spent the afternoon playing with Colloscius and his horse cart, and Aena with her Egyptian doll, cavorting on the floor as though he himself was five, while Antonius and Marcia looked on smiling, offering suggestions, and occasional juice and cookies. Androcles, after a sleepy introduction, hugs and a change of swaddling, went back to sleep in his little cradle, waking up once in a while to nurse.

In mid-afternoon, a clatter of hooves outside announced the arrival of cavalry who dismounted, entered into the house, swords drawn, leading Alaric in chains. A young tribune, perhaps twenty, approached Antonius, and without introducing himself, announced "You must assemble all your slaves here at once. Bring me a list of their names so I can verify there is no one missing. We are taking them to the praetorium for questioning." Marcia gasped, and swept up the children to another room.

Antonius sauntered up to the young man and adjusted his helmet, which sat a bit askew on the officer's head. "Yer'll be a-wantin' ter tell me what's goin' on first, youngster. I sent Alaric to town to fetch the prefect regardin' a murder of one of my slaves, an' yer back wantin' ter haul 'em in fer questioning. I suppose under duress, right?"

"That is standard procedure for investigating murders in the household, and don't touch my helmet again!"

"I'll touch yer helmet again if I want, young pup, an' rip it off your head and shove it up yer arse! Yer'll get respectful with me real fast, or I'll embarrass the shit out of you in front of your men."

Aulus intervened, trying to cool the deteriorating situation. "Tribune, I am Senator Aulus Aemilius Galba. I, too, find your tone offensive. Unless you want to find yourself accounting to the *Princeps* personally for your conduct in this man's home, I suggest you either sheathe your swords, or prepare to use them." He casually took Antonius' old *gladius* from its hook on the wall, drawing it slowly with a menacing hiss. "Are you prepared to kill a senator in the execution of your duties?" He held the sword at ready, in a manner that clearly communicated that he knew how to use it.

Antonius scanned the men. A few of them in the back snickered. He had sized the lad up properly. The young man hesitated, obviously uncertain, his sword trembling.

Aulus' voice changed from conciliatory to battlefield, as he leveled the sword at the young officer's breastbone. "Sheathe your sword now, tribune, or take me on!"

The officer sheathed his weapon with a snap. "The prefect will hear of this! You have insulted a tribune of the urban cohort."

"I am sure we will pay dearly for that misdemeanor, boy. Order your men to sheathe theirs as well, and release Antonius' slave. There is no need to come into a citizen's home with drawn swords with no provocation."

The tribune gave the order. Alaric came over to take his place besides Antonius, who decided to let Aulus continue to speak for them, as he was making headway. He nodded in the senator's direction.

"Now, welcome to the house and academy of Antonius Aristides, equestrian citizen and retired *primus pilus* of the Twelfth Lightning Bolt, with so many *phalerae* for valor I can't remember, and I doubt he can either. You and your men stand easy, introduce yourself, and state your business."

"I am Appius Tatianus Gallus, tribune of the urban cohort, acting on behalf of the prefect. We are here to collect your slaves for questioning with regards to a reported murder of one of their own."

"The prefect gave you that order?"

"He is out of town. I acted on my own authority."

Antonius' face grew red. "Yer'll flog me before yer touch a hair on the heads of my *familia*, lad."

Aulus interjected again. "What do you know of what happened, Tribune Appius?"

"What that slave told me, that there was a murder of another slave, that no one outside the house had reason to kill him. He said he was killed in the woods up on the hill, that no one else knew he went up there. So, it had to be one of your slaves. Murders like that, some other slave always did it, for a debt, for jealousy, for a slave girl."

"The murder victim was seventy years old, hardly a likely candidate for any of those motives. I just had one of my servants killed under mysterious circumstances six months ago, tortured to death, and no one from the Roman *vigiles* even suggested that my other servants be tortured to confess. So, the procedure is not standard, as you say."

"You are a senator, sir."

"I am a citizen, Tribune Appius, the same as equestrian citizen Antonius. The same rules apply to him as to me, or at least we say they should."

"I am concerned that if there is an uprising in one household, that it could easily spread to others."

Antonius' anger was fading. The soldiers were relaxed now, quietly talking back and forth, a few chuckles here and there. "Tribune Appius," he said, adopting the polite address that Aulus had been using, "there won't be an uprising because we treat our servants decently here. Would you like to see the body as part of your investigation? We will be happy to give you all the information we have on the incident. Aulus tells me that there may be a connection between this incident and the one in Rome, so his testimony might be relevant, also."

The young tribune smiled for the first time since entering the house, relieved that the unexpected angry opposition to his presence was abating. "You don't speak at all like you did before."

Antonius smiled for the first time also. "Depends on the circumstance, lad, depends on the circumstance. Now let's get on with this investigation."

They spent the rest of the afternoon examining the body, then retracing the route up the hill as best they could. Whatever marks Janus had left behind had been pretty much obliterated by their own, the night before and in the morning. They found what they thought to be the actual crime scene, a pool of blood a few dozen yards from where the body was found.

One of the soldiers found something interesting. "Look at these, charcoal pencils! I recognize them 'cuz I do sketches and have a set just like 'em. This Janus guy an artist or somethin'?"

"Not that I know of," answered Antonius. "Alaric, does Janus have a new hobby?"

"No, Antonius, I never heard of him doing any drawing."

Antonius looked out at the villa from where they stood. A good view of the building. Could someone have been sketching the building, someone willing to kill to keep it secret? This was a conversation to have with Aulus over wine after dinner.

"All right, Tribune Appius, we are losing light, so I think we should make our way down to the villa. Since you're not going to be flogging my slaves, they may let you and your men take some pheasant and venison along to eat on the road."

The soldiers departed well before sundown, and Aulus joined Antonius and Marcia. A couch had been provided for Aulus to eat reclining, but Antonius and Marcia had never adopted that style, preferring to eat from a chair off a table opposite Aulus. The events of the past twenty-four hours put a damper on their spirits. Alaric entered ahead of the waiters. "*Dominus*, I want to thank you on behalf of all the *servi* and *servae* here for defending us today. You have truly earned our deepest respect and gratitude."

"Alaric, plain Antonius is fine, as you well know, but thank you. No, you are all my *familia* here, and if any of you need flogging, I'll take care of that meself"

"Aye, and you would no doubt do fine job of it, sir. Seriously, we do thank you."

"No problem, now hurry on with that feast. That tribune made me miss my lunch and I am starving."

The servants brought in the repast, and the three began to eat.

"Delicious, truly delicious. Makes me realize how overdone some of our meals are in Rome. Simply too heavy, too many spices and sauces. Just plain well-cooked food is far better."

"We killed both the deer and the pheasant here. I got the deer, a nice buck, and Alaric got the pheasant. He has an eye for taking a bird on the wing, far better than I. I usually just waste a lot of arrows on them," said Antonius.

"Aulus, you mentioned you had an incident at your household," interjected Marcia.

"I did. Though a bit more sinister than yours. My personal secretary, privy to my most personal and professional dealings, was apparently tortured to death. I feel that someone wanted information from him, information about me."

"Mine is a bit sinister, too. There's the charcoal. Not taking notes, stylus on a wax tablet. Someone drawing something, maybe my villa. But why?" asked Antonius.

"The connection is between you and I, Antonius. But what?" asked Aulus.

They ate in silence a bit. Then Aulus changed the subject, as there was no pursuing that line any longer. "I think I have found out why you are no longer hearing from your brother Marcus, Marcia."

"Why is that?" she asked, gnawing carefully on a pheasant leg.

"The Parthians sealed off their borders to all Roman correspondence more than a year ago."

CHAPTER 24:

NEW LOVERS

Petra, Roman Province of Arabia Petraea: January 113AD

Jacobus answered the knock on his door, with Stick by his side, and Mouse peering up from between his legs at the bearded man at the entrance. Clad in a brilliant blue robe over a white ankle-length *kethoneth* linen tunic, a checkered *keffiyah* on his head held in place by a band of interwoven thick gold and silver-colored cords fronted by a square leather phylactery, the man gave the impression of high status in the Jewish community.

Jacobus welcomed him in Aramaic. "Aharon, welcome to my humble abode, my good friend. Come in from the hot sun."

Aharon smiled, exposing healthy teeth, stained with age. "Thank you. Thou art well, Yakov?" he asked, entering the room with a flourish of his robe.

"I am well. Please, seat thyself." A small fountain in the anteroom gave off a cooling mist that abated the heat. Miranda was waiting with wine, well-watered, and handed each a decorated ceramic cup. Stick and Mouse took seats quietly on the floor, attentive but reserved. "What brings thee here?"

"A gift from thy friend Shmuel, of the legion in Cappadocia, and correspondence for you from him." Aharon produced a fist-sized leather pouch from his robe and a sealed wax tablet, handing them to Jacobus, "He is apparently a wealthy man. A hundred silver coins for thee, and his letter."

"Not wealthy. He collects from the men under him. He explains what I do with these children, and reminds his men that some of these may be their own offspring. Which is possibly true. And he gives them a day off the watchbill for each *sestercius* they give." Jacobus unsealed the wax tablet, scrutinizing its wooden leaves. "Interesting. Shmuel says that an old friend from days gone by has taken command of his legion, and the man's son is his tribune. Interesting!"

"Shmuel has risen high in the Roman army. My friend Manasseh is curious how a Jew could do so. It seems blasphemous to him."

"I really don't know the story myself, Aharon. We stayed in touch after our trip, and he promised to help us out here with the home. But he never told me why he joined. He was very close to another in our party, who was a senior centurion. Perhaps that is why."

"Manasseh wonders what he would do if he were ordered to attack rebelling Jews."

"You don't have something like that in mind, do you?" Yakov asked, an eyebrow cocked quizzically.

"Of course not. One such lesson sufficed. But there will come a day, and another Cyrus, who will smite the Romans with all his power to return us to Jerusalem, to build anew our Temple. God wills it, and Rome has no power over Him."

Yakov smiled, resisting the opportunity to engage in a religious sparring match with Aharon. "Perhaps. Who is Manasseh to you?"

"He is a mutual friend of Shmuel and me, in Cappadocia. Shmuel knew him from his youth twenty years ago, and he is my business partner of long standing. When Shmuel was looking for ways to get money to you, he sought out Manasseh. Since we regularly exchange large sums of money by letters of credit, it was easy. And that is how I came to be your patron, of sorts."

"Well! I always wondered how the money got from him to me."

"It doesn't really. Money on the move seldom makes it to its destination."

"What sort of business do you do with Manasseh?"

"Various sorts. The nature of our business, we find it best not to discuss."

"To be sure." Jacobus doubted that all that business was legal, but no matter, that was a problem for the authorities, not him.

Mouse began hitting at Stick, who responded in kind. Jacobus summoned Miranda. "These two are getting restless. Would you take them to the room with the other children?"

"Certainly. Come along, you two, I have juice and snacks for you." They took off bouncing and giggling, while she followed behind, her fine white veil billowing behind her dark hair.

"How many children do you have here?" asked Aharon.

"We have about ten, plus Mouse. She is our only girl, and the youngest."

"It must cost a lot to provide for them."

"It is my calling."

After a few pleasantries, Aharon made his exit, and Jacobus sat by the fountain, enjoying the cooling mist, and pondering the man. He did not trust Aharon. There was something about the man that triggered alerts in his head, warning him to be cautious. And after a life spent mostly outside the law of

Rome, his sensitivity to his instincts had been honed to fine precision, and it had seldom let him down. But Aharon was his only conduit back to Samuel for the support his old friend has been so willing to provide. Aharon most certainly took a cut of whatever Samuel sent him, and he may have other reasons for wishing to keep the conduit open, but for now he was convenient.

Miranda brought him a glass of wine, unwatered this time. "You do not like the man," she said. It was not a question.

"You are perceptive. I do not, but for now, we must use each other." Jacobus' eyes ranged over her attractive figure, inside a modest blue *stola*, with a long white veil over her black tresses. He was often tempted to touch her, but did not. "Please, sit with me."

Miranda took a seat beside him. They often just sat quietly, saying nothing to each other, an odd affinity between master and slave. He had purchased her five years ago, a twenty-year old Egyptian girl, to serve as surrogate mother for his children. She ran the household with pleasant efficiency.

Miranda broke the silence. "What you do here is good, *dominus*." Her Egyptian accent gave her Latin a bit of a musical lilt.

"Thank you. I am returning what was given me."

"Yes," she said, with a delicate laugh like the tinkling of a fine little bell. "You have told me the story many times."

"I have no idea what might have become of me, had Ibrahim not taken me from that life. Most of the boys I knew died early, of disease or at someone's hand."

"And you have been good to me, as well."

"You have been a model mother to the boys, and a big sister to the older ones." He paused. "Do you miss not having children of your own? If I am not being intrusive?"

There was that laugh again. "You are not, and yes, I do. But there is not a suitable man in my life to be their father, so I make do with the ones I have."

"If you would like a companion, I could buy one for you. Someone of your choice."

Underneath her dark eyebrows and knitted brow, her eyes flashed angrily. "A slave buying her own slave with whom to mate? I don't think so!"

"I am sorry, I did not mean it that way, Miranda. Perhaps I should not have said it."

Her angry frown dissipated. "I am satisfied to have you in my life, as my *dominus*. I have come to love you for who you are and what you do."

Jacobus cleared his throat at the uncomfortable turn the conversation had taken. He had thought many times of taking her as a lover but had always put those thoughts out of his mind. While he could take her as his slave, in any manner or time he so chose, he felt that Miranda deserved better than that. She had that effect on him.

She waited a moment, but getting no response, continued. "There is not a woman in your life." Again, not a question.

"No, there is not. My life with my father did not allow that. And now, I just have not sought one out."

"I would like to be the woman in your life, *dominus*." She reached across to take his hand in hers. Her touch was soft, cool.

Jacobus' heart was hammering. "I ... I would like that, Miranda, but you must call me Jacobus, please."

She smiled shyly, again with that bell-like laugh. "I would be honored to do so, Jacobus." She stood and led him by the hand to his sleeping quarters.

CHAPTER 25:

THE GHOST COHORT

Melitene, January 113AD

Paulus Herrierius scratched his bushy hair. "Beggin' your pardon, sir, but what the hell are we supposed to do with this new cohort?"

"Fit them in as best you can, Centurion," answered Gaius Lucullus, heading up the meeting with the legion's tribunes.

"Fit them in? As the eleventh cohort?"

"Spread their six centuries out among our sixty, same shield emblems. Make sure their battle gear matches ours. Unless someone counts them, they won't stand out."

Secundus Lucullus carried the word back to Samuel, the newly-promoted centurion of the Fifth Cohort, to fit one of the new cohort's centuries into the Fifth's six.

"If I can ask why?" pleaded Samuel.

"You can. I did, and I didn't get any answers, either," said Secundus with a wry smile, so like his father. "The legate said they were a *vexillatio* from the *XII Primigenia*, sent here from Mogunciacum in Germany as reinforcements."

"Reinforcements from a six months' march away? Reinforcements for what? Everything is quiet here."

"I understand they took river transport down the Rhine and Danube, so probably a lot less marching. I will be honest with you, something is afoot, but I don't know what it is, and the legate is not talking. No one else knows anything, either"

Not even his father, the legate? The kid is handling this well. "I'll go fit 'em in as best I can, like you said, sir. Sure wish I knew what was going on, sounds bigger than I like."

"So it does, but keep the rumors down. The legate was firm on that score."

Samuel Elisarius met with Vitus Faustus, the centurion of the wayward cohort from the Lucky Capricorns, standing easy outside the perimeter of the fort. "Welcome to the outpost of Melitene, Vitus. Seems you've come a long way to do not much of anything."

"I hope so, Samuel. The men have been keyed up sharp over this trek, and no one is telling us anything."

"It's been boring regular here, as well. Just the usual drills during the fall, and now winter quarters, keeping the gear up to speed and takin' it easy for a few months. I am supposed to 'fit you in as best I can,' my orders to the letter. I don't have space for five hundred of your men, so I am going to have to spread you out among my centuries' quarters, double-bunking. I can't keep you together. And you have to use our emblems and battle gear. I'll go over our routines, signals an' shit, after you get quartered. Tomorrow?'"

"Do the best you can. And that is nothing new, on the way down here, we switched standards every time we crossed into another legion's area of responsibility. No one was supposed to know we were on the move."

"Just you? Or did the other cohorts move out like that also?"

"Actually, we are the last. The whole damned lot of the Lucky Capricorns just up and moved out from Mogunciacum, a cohort at a time, beginning last year."

"No shit, the whole legion moved out?"

"The whole legion."

"All here?"

"That's the hell of it, we don't know. Probably here in the east, but where, I don't know. I barely know where we are, after four months of riverboats down the Rhine and Danube, a lot of forced night marches in between."

"I can see why your men are keyed up. Keyin' me up, myself. Something big is coming, but I wish they'd let us know what it is. Well, let's get your men inside the fort and settled in. I guess you are now the Ghost Cohort of the Twelfth Lightning Bolt, for whatever reason the higher-ups sent you here."

CHAPTER 26:

A SUSPECT CAUGHT

Rome & Aquileia, February 113AD

Aulus led Antonius into the center pool, next to a brass brazier lit with a flickering fire, putting out generous heat to ward off the winter chill. "Always good to see you, Antonius. What brings you to Rome, traveling through the mountains in winter? Come in, sit by the fire in the atrium."

"Thanks," said Antonius, warming his hands by the flame. "I had business in Rome for my academy, and thought I'd stop by to compare notes on our investigations."

"I wish I had something to share with you. The *vigiles* came up with nothing. Petronius suspects our two cases are connected, but he can't see how or why."

"No names, no suspects?"

"None. He suspects that whoever killed Diodorus knew who he was, what he looked like, and what he did for me, but it is all speculation right now. How about you?"

"Not much better, Aulus," said Antonius, accepting a hot spiced wine from a servant, who then gave one to Aulus and quietly left. "The urban cohort came up short, but one of me drinkin' mates said someone a bit strange was asking about me at one of the *tabernae* we frequent. Said he was an old army buddy of mine but wouldn't say anything specific. That raised my friend's hackles, an' he wouldn't tell him anything specific either. Just that my place was west of town, in the foothills."

"Interesting. Did he give his name?"

"He did, Modorus, he said it was, an eastern, foreign-sounding name. An' he was swarthy, dark-haired, with an eastern accent to match his name. Also, my friend thought he might be from around here, the Transtiberian district. Just the way he talked, and because a lot of easterners live there, Jews and Syrians. My friend used to live here and knows the different dialects around the City."

"Interesting. And a lot of thugs live there too, so there may indeed be a connection. I'll pass that name on to Petronius and see what he can come up with."

Just then, Livia swept into the atrium, a dark green woolen shawl around her light-blue *stola* to keep off the chill. She was accompanied by Aulus' son, Pontus Servilius, a gangly but well-built teenager, wearing a red woolen cloak. Antonius rose to greet them.

Livia greeted him with a hug and a peck on both cheeks. "Welcome, Antonius. My, that beard of yours is scratchy. And a hint of gray! We don't see you and Marcia often enough. Is she in town? Please, sit back down," She gestured to the edge of the pond where they had been sitting.

"Nah, she's up in Aquileia. Little Androcles is too young for traveling yet, and we don't usually both leave the academy. Somebody has to run the place."

"Aulus said he is very cute."

"So he is, a big eater, Marcia says."

"She nurses him herself?" Livia asked, with a hint of disgust.

"She has nursed all three herself. Wouldn't have anyone else do that for her." He slapped his chest and laughed. "She says that's what these things are for, not just for decoration."

"So, you are down here about the murder?"

Antonius glanced at Aulus, seeking confirmation to speak before the young Pontus. Aulus nodded, so Antonius went on. "We have a name, maybe an easterner from Transtiberia. Maybe. Not much else to go on, and that is a guess. But enough of that gruesomeness. Pontus, you are growing into a handsome young man. How are your studies?"

"Going well, I guess. I think I like the oratory better than the astronomy and geometry, but *pater* says I need all of them."

Antonius stayed overnight at the villa, and he and Aulus went down to visit Gnaius Petronius at the *vigiles* station the next day.

"Modorus? That's an odd name, but oddly familiar, also."

He went out of his office and addressed one of the clerks. "Valens. Do you recall an incident across the Tiber last year involving someone named Modorus?"

"That I do, sir," he said, rummaging through a pigeon-holed file of scrolls. "Right here, around March last year. Beat someone near to death over a gambling debt. Funny, the guy didn't want to file a complaint."

"Yeah, that's the one. If the guy is a real heavy, his victim didn't want to interest him in finishing the job. Happens."

"So a local thug?" asked Antonius.

"Could be. Rome is full of gangs. When the sun goes down, they crawl out from under their rocks, a law to themselves. You think he was in Aquileia?"

"Maybe, somebody by that name, an easterner from Transtiberia," said Antonius

"Sir, our Modorus is from Armenia," volunteered Valens.

"Armenia. Interesting. What ties you two to Armenia?" asked Gnaius.

"Other than briefly passing through there on our way back a few years ago, nothing. We thought you might tell us," said Aulus with a chuckle.

Three hundred and fifty miles to the north, the lights dimmed in Antonius' academy on the outskirts of Aquileia. Marcia finished nursing Androcles, burped him and laid him into his cradle. Alaric rapped on the door to announce that all was well. She banked the fire, shedding her clothes and donning a nightshift, her dagger in its sheath on a lanyard around her neck. Next to the bed was her sword, a light one made for a woman, given to her by another woman many years ago. With Antonius gone, and the events of the last month still fresh, she was not going to depend on someone else to defend her.

She went to sleep, but after several hours, she awoke, her heart pounding. She took a deep breath to quiet herself, listening intently. Hearing nothing, she decided that it had been a dream, then suddenly she heard just the slightest of sounds, someone moving outside, down in the atrium. She listened some more and heard it a second time. She silently slid from the bed, buckled the sword around her waist, and went out the door, locking it behind her to protect the infant. She edged along the shadows of the second-floor walkway, dimly lit by single lamps on each side. She stayed tight-pressed against the wall, creeping to Alaric's room in the slaves' quarters. She knocked quietly on the door, hoping he was a light sleeper. "Alaric," she said in a hoarse whisper. "Intruder."

Muffled movement inside indicated that Alaric was not a sound sleeper. The door creaked open, and his bulky body exited, also armed with a sword.

As softly as she could, she whispered to him. "An intruder in the atrium. I heard him, haven't seen him. The infant is locked inside my room."

"You go, I'll take care of this."

"No, I am coming with you. I will defend my children." Just then a shadow of movement in the atrium caught her eye. She pointed wordlessly to the far wall below them, then raised a single finger to indicate one person. She pointed to the far staircase for Alaric to go down that way, while she would take the one on this side. Alaric nodded and moved off silent as a cat.

Marcia took a moment to breathe deeply, to quiet her nerves. She was not afraid, she had killed before, and the excitement of combat tingled in her veins. But she must not be overconfident now. *Treat this as your first fight with Wang Ming.* She drew her sword as quietly as she could, though the rasp seemed preternaturally loud in the silence.

She crept down the stairs. The first floor was also dimly lamplit, but she avoided looking at the lights to avoid dazzling her eyes, instead scanning the blackness, continuously shifting her gaze, until she caught the intruder. She was suddenly aware of her flimsy shift, easily grabbed to pull her off balance, too light in color for her to stay hidden long. No matter. The fight is on.

She waited until she saw Alaric exit the stairs, his motions indicating that he too saw the intruder. She waited until the intruder seemed to register her presence, her white shift reflecting the lamplight.

"Ho, missy, you're up late," he said, drawing his sword with a hiss.

"Just taking a walk. Would you like to dance with me?" she said, raising her sword, shimmering silver in the lamplight.

"Wouldn't be an even match."

"No, it won't be." And with two fast strides she was on him. They parried for a few strokes, Alaric, unseen, watching from behind the man, ready to kill if the intruder got the edge on Marcia. He had trained with Marcia, and knew that wasn't likely to happen.

Marcia invited a lunge at her midsection, which the man took and which she deftly sidestepped, leaving his sword arm extended. Marcia brought her blade down, feeling the blade bite through meat and tendons, then grind against bone. This fight was over. The man's sword clattered uselessly to the atrium pavement. The man cried out, his hand over his wound, now gushing blood.

"You don't dance very well," Marcia said, the tip of her blade at his throat, not taking her eyes off him. "Alaric, thank you for the backup, and for letting me finish the fight. Tie him up, then we can ask some questions, like how he got in here."

"Please, I'm bleeding to death," the man groaned, as Alaric twisted his wounded arm behind him to tie his wrists together.

"Then you had better answer quickly, before you die," answered Alaric, in his guttural German accent.

By now several servants had gathered in the atrium, having heard the clanging of steel. One tossed a rag to Alaric who wrapped it around the man's bleeding forearm, jerking it tight in a knot.

"There, that'll do for now. Now, my lady asked you a question. How did you get in here?"

"Ladder over there, up onto the roof, then inside." The would-be thief gestured to the far side wall.

"You hurt any of the servants getting in?"

"No, you were the first I saw. Please, my arm!"

"Be glad you still have one," said Marcia, wiping his blood from her sword. "What's your name?"

"Modorus. Please, my arm, it hurts."

"That's the name Antonius' friend said was asking about him. Are you an artist, Modorus?"

"Just simple sketches, why?"

"Alaric, put him in the cellar with the cheeses. Maybe the rats will eat him before the urban cohort gets here. He is the one who killed Janus."

A runner went out at dawn to summon the urban cohort. The prefect, Brutus Agrippa, arrived with the young tribune Appius Gallus and a few men about mid-morning. Modorus was dragged out of the cellar for questioning.

Brutus examined the man's arm. "You won't be using this for much ever again. Nice work, Alaric."

"Not my work, hers" he said with a smile, nodding toward Marcia.

The prefect raised his eyebrows. "He outweighs you by half."

"But he was only half as fast," answered Marcia.

The prefect turned to the prisoner while Appius took notes on a wax tablet. "What were you doing here last night?"

"Just lookin' for shit to steal," said Modorus, cradling his crippled arm, still bleeding through the makeshift rag bandage.

"What kind of 'shit'?"

"Jewelry, coins, you know ... shit!"

"I don't believe you, and if I don't get any answers I can believe, you're not going to get that arm tended. Have you ever seen a badly inflamed arm, one that turns black and stinks? It's usually the last thing a man smells before he dies."

"I was stealing shit, that's all."

"You were willing to kill the *domina* of the household doing it. You could be crucified for that."

"She called me out!"

"She lives here. Who hired you?"

Modorus was silent, sullenly staring at the floor.

Brutus grabbed man's chin, forcing Modorus to look into his eyes just inches from his own. "Who hired you? Have you ever seen a crucifixion, Modorus? They go on for days. The birds will pluck your eyes out."

"I don't know his name. Back in Rome."

"You don't know his name? You just travel hundreds of miles up here to rob a house, because a stranger asked you?" Brutus shook his head skeptically. He turned toward Appius. "Have the men round up some heavy timber and nails and rope. No need to wait for a court for this scum."

"Aye, sir!" The tribune scuttled off.

"No, wait, I don't know his name! That's the way it's done."

"So you were to rob any house, or this specific house?"

"This house." Modorus was crying now, in real fear of what was to come.

"For 'shit'? Or something more specific?"

"For papers, letters, correspondence."

"Why?"

"He didn't say."

"Hmm. Now we're getting somewhere. Did you kill their doorman Janus? An old white-haired gentleman, two months ago"

"Yes, he caught me sketching the house. Please ... please, don't crucify me! Just take my head and be done with it."

"We'll do neither for now. You're going back to Rome on another case there."

Appius returned. "The men are throwing together a cross, sir."

"Change of plans, Appius. Have our medic clean up his arm and throw some stitches on it. He's going to Rome to answer some more questions."

CHAPTER 27:

AN OPERATION GONE WRONG

Rome, February, 113AD

The Parthian envoy Ariobarzanes was not pleased, to say the least. He stood on the esplanade, his fists clenched on the marble railing, looking out over the smoke-pocked city of Rome beyond the garden, scowling. "This was incompetence, Vistaspa, incompetence! Your ham-handed agent has to leave the City at once, and I mean by sunset, and take ship somewhere far from here. He will be gone by tomorrow, and you will be leaving with him." He tossed his blue silk robe in a flurry for emphasis.

"Yes, Your Excellency," said Vistaspa, his eyes fixed on the floor between them. "I apologize for his choice of operator."

"Apologize? That thug completely compromised our two targets. And now I have to apologize to Mithridates for having compromised them. Do you have anything I might say to him about that?" He turned to face Vistaspa, glowering, his stiffly coiled beard quivering as he clenched his jaw.

Vistaspa said nothing.

"Your agent's thug is with the *vigiles* now in here in Rome. They have linked him to both murders. How long before they pry the name of your agent from him? And he will link them to us. Which is why your incompetent agent must leave. Now!"

"The operator is in custody?" asked Vistaspa, shocked.

"Why do I know more about your operators than you do? He raided the second target's residence and was caught red-handed. The two targets know each other very well, and they connected the two strange deaths, though hundreds of miles apart. So, they sent him here to Rome."

"The operator doesn't know the agent's name. The agent never gives that out to his operators." stammered Vistaspa

"The thug had contact information, perhaps the agent's false name, and some way to get in touch to get paid. And Petronius will unravel that thread. He has a reputation in the City for thoroughness. Which you and your agent lack. In fact, I am going to reconsider. You are leaving with your agent tonight, not tomorrow. I can't have you getting sucked into this mess."

"But my family! And I'll need time to raise money."

"Come into my office." Ariobarzanes turned on his heels, his robe flying in his wake. He came to his desk, slid open a drawer, and withdrew a sack. He tossed it to Vistaspa, who caught it in mid-air. "There are five-hundred *denarii* in it. If you need more, bill Ctesiphon for it, if they'll pay you. Kiss your wife and children as you leave, but leave."

"I can't just leave like that."

Ariobarzanes' face turned black with anger. "You are not the only man here who can hire muscle at short notice. If you are still in the City by sunrise, I will see to it that your body will not be found. Now go! I must write that letter to Mithridates explaining your stupidity."

As Ariobarzanes had anticipated, it did not take long for Modorus to talk, but with Vistaspa and his agent gone, the trail quickly went cold. It took three agonizing days for Modorus to die on the cross, on the execution hill outside the City on the Appian Way.

CHAPTER 28:

A KING DEPOSED

Artaxata, Armenia: June 113 AD

King Axidares was entertaining the Roman delegation in the airy throne room of his oaken palace in the highlands of Armenia, window shutters open to the mountain air of the cool summer. "Your generosity is noted, Valens Virgilius. Rest assured, Roman legions shall continue to enjoy rights of free transit as required to support your clients to the north against the Sarmatians. But I am puzzled, you seem to have no movements planned this year."

"That is correct, Your Excellency. We anticipate no threats from the north this year," replied Valens Virgilius Thrasius. His white toga bore the broad stripe of a senator, and his portly body give hint of a life of self-indulgence. "But no matter. We are paying for right of passage, should a threat emerge, and if none emerges, the gold is yours to keep."

"We thank you for your generosity. But my people will miss the legions this year. Your soldiers spend well on their transits."

"To be sure. But ..."

Valens' response was interrupted by a squad of Parthian soldiers with coiffed black beards, blue-clad with mail overlays, carrying spears. They entered the throne room, shoving the king's bodyguards out of the way.

The king challenged them in Parthian. "What is the meaning of this outrage? We are in the midst of diplomatic discussions. Out with you, out, now!" As he turned in their direction, he turned pale, noticing one of his bodyguards lying in a pool of blood at the doorway.

The leader of the Parthian soldiers responded harshly. "You will be conducting no more 'diplomatic discussions' with Romans, traitor! King Osroës has ordered you relieved due to your infidelity."

"Relieved? He can't do that. I am King of Armenia."

A tall figure entered the room clad in black trousers and a long blue shirt. "Not any more, brother. My father has decided that I am better fit to rule this critical borderland than you."

"Parthamasiris! The king risks war by putting you on the throne. I am approved by Rome, in accordance with the treaty."

"And well paid by Rome as well, brother." Parthamasiris switched to Latin. "You, gentlemen, are dismissed. As envoys, you have safe passage back to Cappadocia, if you don't take too long. Parthian armies have control of the major roads." He nodded toward the door, and Valens and his party quickly exited.

Parthamasiris switched back to Parthian. "Seize him!" Two soldiers mounted the podium, roughly turning the former king around to bind his wrists behind him and remove the diadem from his head.

Having secured the prisoner, they handed the diadem to Parthamasiris, who put it on his head. "It fits well, brother," he said to Axidares, who glared angrily back at him.

A month later, Valens Virgilius Thrasius and his party were in Antioch, briefing Publius Aelius Hadrian, the Syrian governor, on the untoward events in the Armenian capital five hundred miles to the east.

"So that's it, Publius Aelius. An outrage! They burst into the throne room, killing several of Axidares' bodyguards. Deposed him on the spot, tied him up and led him off like a common criminal. Parthamasiris put the diadem on his head right there and took the throne. The Parthians had a wagon outside with some of our clothes in the back, but they took all our correspondence from the inn where we were staying. And the rest of our goods, took them, too!"

Hadrian stoked his carefully-styled short beard, deep in thought. "Well, this is a clear violation of the treaty between Ctesiphon and Rome. They propose a king from the royal family, Rome approves him, that's the treaty. They appear to have just annexed Armenia. What do you know of Parthamasiris?"

"He is the brother to Axidares, both sons of Osroës' predecessor Pacorus, the last king. And he lost no time reminding Axidares of that."

"They have set some big wheels in motion, but we have been expecting this treachery, and we have some big wheels of our own that we need to set in motion also. Valens, you and your men have done good service, at some risk to your lives. Take your time to enjoy the good things of beautiful Antioch and relax. I need to dismiss you now, unfortunately, for I must compose a letter to the *Princeps,* advising him of this dire situation."

That afternoon, Hadrian completed two letters, the first to Trajan:

Ave, Princeps

I hope that all is well with you, and that your family is in good health.

I fear I bring bad tidings from the borderlands. It seems that King Osroës has annexed Armenia, deposing Axidares, the rightful king, seated with the approval of Rome in accordance with our treaty. Axidares has always allowed our legions free transit to the Caspian littoral to support our client states of Iberia and Albania. I doubt that the illegitimate successor, Parthamasiris son of Pacorus, will allow such transits. This puts our clients at great risk of invasion from the north of the Caucasus by the barbarians.

You and I discussed this eventuality two years ago when you assigned me to this post, and we have assembled the necessary military force to put at your disposal as you see fit, ready to carry out your orders. I will address this matter to King Osroës as your personal representative, and attempt to reverse his ill-considered actions.

Personally, all is well. Vibia Sabina is in good health and sends her love to you and her great-aunt Pompeia Plotina Augusta.

Publius Aelius Hadrianus
The Ides of July,
856 AUD

The second, to the King Osroës, was blunter, delivered curtly to the Parthian envoy without ceremony.

To the King of all Parthian Kings, Greetings.

It has come to my attention that solders purporting to be acting on your orders deposed Axidares, the rightful king of Armenia, affirmed by our mutual treaty, killing several of his bodyguards and threatening and abusing our envoys. These soldiers imposed Parthamasiris on the throne in violation of our mutual treaty that has kept the peace for fifty years.

I demand that you reverse this illegal action. If you have issues with Axidares, we stand ready to discuss an alternate kingship. However, Parthamasiris will never be acceptable to us, because of actions already taken by him at your behest. Bear in mind that the Senate and the People of Rome have always viewed Armenia as strategically vital to our interests in the East, and shall take such actions necessary to enforce our mutual treaty.

Be in good health.
Pub. A. Hadrianus,
Governor of Roman Syria representing
Imperator Caesar Nerva Trajanus
Princeps by the Senate and the People of Rome.

The last letter was dispatched to King Osroës, and copy of it and the letter to Trajan were enciphered for delivery by fast post to Rome.

CHAPTER 29:

GALOSGA'S STORY

Enroute Khojand to Margiana, April 113AD

The sun had set on the desert, allowing the caravan to depart the caravansary on its southwestern side. The caravan would cross the desert between Amul and Margiana at night to avoid the desert heat. The lush greenery of the Oxus River banks had long since faded to intermittent clumps of grayish green sagebrush dotting the beige sands, stretching to the flat horizon in the far distance under the full moon. Here and there, the swiftly moving dark shape of some night creature disturbed the silent tableau under the preternaturally bright stars and the brilliant waterfall of the Milky Way, frozen in a silent explosion.

Galosga, off-duty for the night, rode beside Nathaniel, his scruffy, stocky steppe pony in contrast to Nathaniel's sleek black, fine-lined mare. Hina and Mei rode nearby, talking among themselves.

"Thy Aramaic hast improved considerably over the past few months. It amazeth me, Galosga, that a man from the far eastern steppes should even have heard of the language, much less speak it so well," said Nathaniel, swaying in his saddle to the rhythm of the horse's slow working trot.

"When I first heard thee speaking to others, I could understand but a few words, I had not used it for so long. But thy lessons and our conversations have helped greatly" said Galosga, evading the praise. "I am not from the east. Quite the contrary, I am from the far, far west, and Aramaic was the first language I learned in this world, before coming to the steppe lands."

"Thou speakest of this world as though thou were from up there," said Nathaniel, pointing to the heavens above.

"Sometimes I wonder if it might be so. My old world was far different from this." He slapped the neck of his pony gently. "We didn't have these. I had never seen one until I arrived here. And riding such an animal ... unthinkable. We had deer, elk, bison, but all wild."

"So how didst thou come to be here … in this world?"

Galosga related his story, the story he had told many times, of his kidnapping and being pressed into service as a deckhand, his arrival in a new world of cities and animals he had never seen. He had been treated as a deaf-mute slave by people speaking a language he did not understand, communicating with him by gestures, curses and blows, until a fellow-deckhand Shmuel taught him some Aramaic.

"In Alexandria, which made all the other cities I had seen seem like my old village, Shmuel heard of ships taking crews for a cruise to the distant east, with very good pay. He and I signed on, to a ship called the *Europa*. It was there I met Marcus, a member of that party. We ended up in the land of the Han. Our group went back west by land, and enroute I met my wife Hina. Her clan might seem primitive to thee, but they were a people with whom I could be comfortable. I shall miss them."

He went on to talk of the plague that wiped out most of the clan, left him scarred, and resulted in their unexpected reunion with Marcus and his wife in Turfam. He spoke of their decision to follow them west in Marcus' quest to reunite with his sister, who had become so close to Hina during their brief time together ten years ago.

"They joked about adopting each other as sisters, they were that close. So Hina prayed to our Sky God, and got a sign from him in the heavens that she should lead our band west with them, to rejoin her sister Marcia."

"I don't think that I have met a man in the entire world to match thee and thy travels. And the languages! Aramaic, Hanaean, Sogdian … "

Galosga interrupted with his deep laugh. "And Xiongnu! I had to be able to speak to my wife! And learning Latin, until we were forced to be silent in that tongue."

"Well, for a person in a strange land, thou hast done very well. Didst thy people in thy homeland have a name for themselves?"

"In our language, we called ourselves the *Ani-Unwiyah,* but that just means 'The People'. And our country, as thou wouldst call it, was just the Land of the People."

"Well, thy talent for language may come to be useful. Dost thou read and write in any of them?"

"I am learning to read and write Latin. Marcus showed me the shapes of the letters and their sounds. It is new to me, but I can make out simple words now."

"Interesting. Couldst thou learn two such writings at once?"

"I could try."

"Aramaic is written with a similar script but more flowing, and right to left. Wouldst thou like to try? We will encounter it more and more as we move west."

"I would like to do that."

"You may become the most valuable man in our little group."

CHAPTER 30:

CAPTURED

Margiana, May 113AD

The caravan rolled to a halt at the Parthian checkpoint on the northeast corner of Margiana. Margiana was the entry point into the Parthian kingdom, and each westbound caravan checked in there for an inventory of goods enroute for tariffs, and people as well, for those individuals of interest to Ctesiphon and Ecbatana. The caravan halted in the heat of the day, animals pawing the ground while handlers watered them, waiting for the go-ahead for the caravan to continue. Parthian inspectors, accompanied by soldiers, went from animal to animal, asking questions in Sogdian, taking notes. Marcus waited nervously for their turn to come, flanked by Mei and Hina on the wagon with the children, spare animals in tow. Galosga with the other Xiongnu and Nathaniel sat on their mounts. Galosga was to answer for them, with Nathaniel backing him up.

One of the bored Parthian officials, clad in a black vest over white shirt and trousers, walked up to them, backed by an equally bored soldier in chain mail, lance in hand. "Who speaks for you?" he asked in Sogdian.

"I do," answered Galosga.

"How many people?"

"Six, plus three children."

"Names?"

"I am Galosga and our guide Nathaniel. This is my wife Hina, our children Andanyu, Marasa, and Adhela, and my friend Hadyu. The Hanaeans are Bolin and Chunhua," he said, using Marcus' and Mei's new aliases.

"What trade goods are you carrying?"

"Personal goods only. We are travelers, bound for Margiana."

"Money?"

"Fifteen silvers. Do you wish to inspect our gear?"

"No need. You can go."

"Thank you." He raised his arm and brought it down, indicating to the group that they could proceed. As the group passed, the Parthian official said *"Gratias tibi, Marce."* "Thank you, Marcus," in Latin.

Marcus turned to him involuntarily and began to say *"Nihil est,"* before realizing he had been trapped by a very old trick. The soldier grabbed

Marcus's reins and pulled his horse to a halt, giving a whistle to call several more soldiers to help take him from his mount. Marcus called out to the group in Hanaean. "Do nothing! I can talk my way out of this. Galosga, come with me as my translator."

Galosga dismounted, handing the reins to Hina in the cart, and followed the soldiers leading Marcus off. The soldier blocked his way with his spear.

"He doesn't speak anything but Hanaean," said Galosga. "You will need me to translate for him, please."

The soldier grunted, but lifted his spear to let Galosga join Marcus, leading the two to a nearby green tent, open on three sides. Inside at a table sat an officer who conveyed a sense of authority. The soldier introduced himself to the officer in Parthian, and Galosga took great pains not to reveal that he was following the conversation, though with some difficulty. Apparently, Marcus matched the description of someone they sought, an Hanaean who spoke Latin, as Nathaniel had warned them, though Galosga was unsure how they might have known this.

The soldier turned to Marcus and face close to his, spat the words "*Quid es? Who are you?*" through his black stiff beard. Marcus did an admirable job of conveying confusion and non-comprehension, responding in a babble of Hanaean, shaking his head negatively.

Finally, the soldier turned back to Galosga. "You are his translator?" he asked in Sogdian.

"I am," answered Galosga. "Why do you want this man?"

"I will ask the questions. What is his name?"

"His name is Bolin. He is Hanaean, on a mission to see the western world."

"Just answer the question. How does he come to speak Latin?"

"He does not."

"He responded to our soldier's query in Latin."

Galosga remembered the events that led to Marcus' capture, though they had happened quickly. He did not remember the soldier's query, or Marcus' response, and his Latin was not that good. "I do not know of such a language, nor did I hear Bolin say anything unusual."

"The soldier thanked him by name, and he answered *nihil est*, you are welcome."

Galosga retorted, "What he said was 'What did you say?' in Hanaean."

The soldier turned back to the officer and related what Galosga had told him. The officer shook his head no, and the soldier returned. "We are taking him to our commander in Margiana. He can evaluate your story. You may accompany him if you wish."

"I will come with him. May I get our mounts?"

"I will accompany you."

The two went back to where the caravan lay waiting, held up in the desert heat by the problem. Galosga addressed the group in Hanaean, speaking rapidly against the chance that the soldier might know some. "They are taking our friend Bolin into custody, thinking he speaks a language he does not. Continue on with the caravan. We are being taken to Margiana for more questions. I will try to talk my way out of it."

Hina translated for Nathaniel, who then spoke up. "Let me come with you, Galosga. I can help, I know these people."

Galosga conveyed the request to the soldier, who nodded.

"It's all right, you can come." Galosga mounted his horse, taking Marcus' in tow. He turned to Hina and spoke in Xiongnu. "Leave the young ones with Mei. Follow us, steppe-style, but do not interfere. This is a time for words, not war."

Hina nodded, but her green eyes flashed, conveying her preference for action.

Galosga clucked his horse into a walk and Nathaniel followed, led by the soldier to the tent, where five more soldiers had assembled. Together, they rode off to the town, crossing a bridge over a wide river through a city of low mud and stone structures, streets shaded by pine and silvery-green olive trees, to a mud-walled fort on the southern side. Galosga made no move to look behind, but he knew that somewhere back there, Hina and Hadyu would be following them, on horse or on foot. Nathaniel and he exchanged no words, as everything they might say to each other might be heard and understood by their escorts.

At the gate, the troop hailed a sentry on the parapet, and the massive wood gate swung open with a groan. Inside, the buildings were a jumble of mud-walled buildings, open workshops and food preparation areas, corrals for horses and food animals, and wood-framed structures of various sorts, the air foul with the smell of human and animal waste. Soldiers, presumably, though few wore any sort of uniform or carried weapons, meandered about, some carrying loads or pushing wheelbarrows. A sense of disorder pervaded the fort, compared with the caravansaries and cities that he had seen in his travels, obviously an outpost far removed from the center, wherever the center was.

The soldiers rode up to a large two-story building, dismounted and handed their reins to waiting soldiers. Nathaniel, Galosga and Marcus/Bolin did likewise, entering the building surrounded by their escorts. Inside the heat was stifling, and the open windows and doors admitted not a breath of air. A fly settled on Galosga's arm, biting painfully before he slapped it to oblivion, leaving a bloodstain from its last undigested meal on his skin.

They entered a room at the far end, where a man in shimmering green and silver silks, black coiled beard, and a low conical embroidered red cap, sat studying some scrolls when they entered. He looked up, and the lead soldier spoke in Parthian, so fast that Galosga could not follow, though Nathaniel seemed to do so.

The senior officer got up and confronted Marcus, speaking a rapid Latin. Marcus betrayed no comprehension, responding in equally rapid Hanaean.

"Sir, he does not speak Latin," protested Nathaniel.

"What does he speak?" asked the irritated commander.

"I am his translator," volunteered Galosga. "He speaks Hanaean."

"What's he doing here?"

"He is on a mission to explore the west for his people."

"Likely, that. Thousands of miles, not knowing the language. Who would do that?"

"Sir, he is Hanaean. Who knows what they might do?"

"Well, I am taking him into custody and sending him to Ecbatana and King Vologases' court. Let them decide what to do with him. He may not be the one they seek, but that will be their decision, not mine. You two are free to go."

"Sir, I would like to accompany Bolin as his translator. Nathaniel can return, to inform the rest of our party of these events."

"Fine, he may go. You stay."

Nathaniel rode rapidly back to where the caravan had been stopped, but found only Mei in the wagon with little Adhela in a breast-board carrier, with Marasa and Andanyu sitting beside her, looking serious far beyond their eleven years. Nathaniel dismounted, unsaddled his brown mare, and tethered her with the other spare mounts behind the wagon. He swung into the wagon seat beside Mei.

Mei's dusty face was streaked with tears recently shed. "What happened to him? Where is Si Nuo?" she asked, using his Hanaean name.

"They are taking Marcus to the King's palace in Ecbatana. Galosga is going with him."

"What will happen to him?"

"The commander accepted his story but would not make the decision for the King. So, I think things will go well. Hina and Hadyu will follow him to Ecbatana. We need to catch up with the caravan."

"No! I cannot leave Marcus behind. We must go with them."

"We can't follow them and we can't help them. Hina will make sure he and Galosga are all right. We must stay with the caravan and take care of the little ones for Hina. When did the caravan leave?"

"About an hour ago."

"So not too far ahead. Let's roll." He tsk'ed the horses into a brisk trot, and the wagon swayed and lurched along the rutted road.

CHAPTER 31:

A VISITOR IN THE NIGHT

Enroute to Ecbatana, July 113AD

Galosga pricked his ears at the sound. It came again, the *prrt* of the little steppe bird. Not too dissimilar to other bird calls here in the desert, but different enough for him to recognize it. He glanced at the soldiers huddled about their campfire thirty yards away, talking, some already nodding in sleep. He acknowledged the call with his own *prrt*, then became aware of a soft slithering sound through the sagebrush vegetation to his left.

Hina's face looked at him from behind a bush. She was prone, crawling on her stomach through the sand slowly, almost soundlessly. She stopped a short distance from him and Marcus, waiting. He acknowledged her unspoken question and touched Marcus' arm, finger to his lips indicating silence. Galosga nodded affirmatively to Hina, and she continued her snake slither till she was hunched upright beside them at their low-banked fire. She handed him two daggers, sheathed. "I thought you could use these."

He accepted the daggers and handed one to Marcus. "It took you long enough, *huldaji*," he whispered in Hanaean, using his pet name for her. "I thought you might have forgotten about me and gone your own way."

The firelight showed the smile on her face. "I am not yet ready to unmate with you just yet. You are treated well?"

"Very well. The soldiers are friendly enough. Though we started this trek with nothing, they have seen that we did not want for supplies."

"Hadyu is a hundred yards off. We can take them by surprise and kill them all to free you."

Marcus interjected softly. "No. We are not quite prisoners, though we can't leave. They are taking us to the king in Ecbatana. If we were in danger, they would have taken our weapons, and they haven't. But if you kill the soldiers of the king on a royal mission, we will all be outlaws, and our lives not worth a pile of horse dung."

"I can rescue you here. I can't rescue you from the king's palace in ... wherever they are taking you."

"Marcus is right, *huldaji*. Just stay with us as you have done, at a safe distance, no more than one rider at a time, close enough to see us and be seen, but not be noticed by the troops. We are safe. But please, stay long enough to share some wine." He produced a leather sack from his pile of belongings and passed it to her.

"They are treating you well," she said, taking a sip.

"As I said, not quite prisoners."

She suddenly grabbed him with an urgent hug and kissed him passionately. Finally relinquishing his lips but not the embrace, she said, "I did not know what I would find here. If you and Marcus were not here, or were bound like slaves, I would have killed them all. I thought ... I was afraid ... that I had lost my man who fell into my life, and taught me how to cry again." A tear trickled down her cheek.

Galosga wrapped his arms around her, stroking her softly. "Like you, I am hard to kill."

"It is well, then." Hina released him and slithered, snakelike, through the sand and bushes, back to whence she came.

CHAPTER 32:

THE EMPEROR'S RIGHT-HAND MAN

Rome, July 113AD

The *Princeps* was seated at his desk, tastefully laminated with tortoise shell that reflected the sunlight from its polished black and orange surface. "Aulus Aemilius, welcome, welcome, my new Jason," said Trajan expansively, using Aulus' public nickname from his expedition of ten years' past. Aulus accepted the invitation, seating himself on the beige, well-padded couch along the wall, an intricate mosaic on the floor in shades of black and white separating them. "Thank you, Your Excellency. I hope all is well with you and Pompeia Plotina."

"All is well, though I terribly miss my sister, Marciana. Her death was an untimely passage, and unexpected. It reminded me how short the thread of life can be."

Servants brought refreshments, wine and sweetmeats, then silently left, closing the door behind them.

"You have heard of the events in Armenia, I am sure," said Trajan.

"The deposition of Axidares, yes. We were all surprised at their actions."

"Truly. We expected King Osroës to propose another king, negotiate with us in accordance with the treaty, and we would jointly impose the new king. Deposing Axidares by force was not expected. Not at all. And it almost certainly means war."

"I had been convinced that this was nothing more than testing, but you are right, to depose the jointly-agreed-upon king is not just a violation of our treaty, but a complete abrogation."

"Which brings me to why I summoned you here, Aulus," said Trajan, his hands together on the desk. "My place is in the East, to lead the campaign. I would like you by my side as my trusted advisor."

"Why, of course, Your Excellency, but why me? I have no familiarity with Asia Minor. I have done no business dealings there. Surely there are people far more qualified than I."

"Your modesty becomes you. First and foremost, you are the most straightforward among the Conscript Fathers in the Senate. You have not a sycophantic bone in your body. If I am about to make a mistake, you will have no fear of so telling me. Secondly, you speak, I understand, rather fluent

Bactrian, some Aramaic from your sea-faring days, and a little Parthian beside. And you can handle yourself in a fight."

"Well, I speak precious little Parthian, beyond being able to ask directions and simple things like that."

"That's more than almost anyone on my staff here can do, though I am sure Hadrian has trusted translators on his. I hope he does, I haven't asked. But it is your sense of people that I need. In particular, this could become a massive military campaign, on a par with that of Alexander the Great. I need someone to keep my hubris in check, and you may be the only one able to do that. And of course, you will be able to renew your friendship with Gaius Lucullus. He is back, now commanding the Twelfth Thunderbolt, his old legion."

"So he said in a letter to me. Along with his son, Gaius Secundus, and another member of the Argonauts whom you never met, one of my former deckhands, Samuel. He is now centurion of the Fifth Cohort of the Thunderbolt. It seems that the Fates are once again drawing us together. So when do you want me to leave?"

"Soon. Very soon."

CHAPTER 33:

THE PALACE AT ECBATANA

Ecbatana, July 113AD

The first thing Galosga noticed about Ecbatana from miles away were the walls. The outermost one was gleaming white and several miles across, the second wall within that but higher, was black, then three more, red, blue, and orange, each overtopping the last. The last two

were finished with silver and gold, glistening in the sun, dominating the horizon in gigantic layers. Behind the city lay a stretch of rugged mountains to the south and west, towering above the plain, some incongruously snow-capped, despite the blistering heat along the road. The soldiers said that the highest was Mount Harvand, perhaps ten miles south of the city.

The guards with Marcus and Galsoga cleared each of the seven gates to reach the palace, a tall white building, a replica of the surrounding walls, five floors like a layer cake, painted white, black, red, blue and orange, with an intricate roof, silver on the bottom, gold above. The royal stables were on the right. The lead soldier, Arshak, led them up to it. Attendants came to take the horses and lead them in for a much-needed rest, as the group had covered over a thousand miles the past month. Throughout that month, single riders had passed them, some going their direction, some the opposite. Each time, the harsh, barking call of the steppe eagle echoed in the distance. The soldiers had never noticed, but Galosga had. And, every few nights, Hina would join him and Marcus at their campfire, to check on them. The soldiers never noticed her furtive comings and goings.

Arshak led them into the palace, and up to the fourth floor by way of blue-lined marble steps. Fountains in the center of each floor cast a cooling mist. Arshak located a servant who led them to an office, nicely appointed with green plants about a desk, at which was seated a grey haired, bearded man in a white Greek tunic. Arshak and he exchanged some words, in Parthian, Galosga supposed. He caught words here and there that he recognized, but the meaning escaped him.

Finally, Arshak turned toward him. "Well, Galosga, I thank you and your friend for being such good traveling companions. My job is done here. This is Philippus, he will handle you from here out. We are off to a bath, then a fine meal in the Royal Guard's mess. They will feed us far better than our outpost back in Margiana. Good luck to you!"

"And good luck to you, Arshak. Thank you for your care of us."

Arshak left, and Philippus gestured Marcus and Galosga to a black leather couch, separated from his desk by an elegant woven rug in yellows, blues, blacks and reds. "Please be seated. I am King Volagases' secretary, and I keep informed of all things of interest to him, such as you two. Your friend, you say, speaks no Latin, or any other language of this area?"

Galosga grunted, giving a sense of affirmation without actually saying the words. There might come a time when undoing a more overt lie could be difficult. "Why would the King believe that any Hanaean would speak Latin, and have a Latin name?"

Philippus laughed. "That is the question we are asking ourselves here in this court. This demand came not from this court, but from the usurper Osroës and his brother Mithridates in Ctesiphon. It was unusual enough to attract our attention, to see why they might be so interested in such an unlikely personage."

"I am sorry, Ctesiphon and Osroës are just names to me."

"As well they might be, since you are from the far eastern regions, despite your excellent command of Aramaic. Parthia has traditionally had two capitals, this eastern one in the mountains for the summer when Ctesiphon is beastly hot, and that western one for the winter when this one can be quite cold and sometimes snow-bound. King Volagases is the legitimate *Shahanshah*, king of all Parthian kings, and brother to the late King Pacorus II, but Osroës seized power in the west five years ago, and bases his illegitimate rule in Ctesiphon. That hot-headed upstart is precipitating a war with Rome, and we suspect that he has some interest in China, since his brother Mithridates was envoy to China some ten years back. We would like to know what that interest might be, since we lie between the two."

Marcus gave a cough. "You will forgive me for having dissembled," he said.

Galosga put his hand on Marcus' arm, but he shook it off. "Philippus, I am the man that Mithridates seeks, and he seeks me specifically because he knows me. Though why he should have an interest in me now, that is beyond me."

"Well, my good Marcus, you do speak something besides Hanaean! I wish to commend you, because I was almost certainly ready to recommend you be released. How did you come to know Mithridates?"

"I and my sister, and several others from my village, are descendants of Roman soldiers captured at Carrhae, and ultimately resettled in China as mercenaries. We kept our language and customs for generations, and twenty years ago, when Emperor He began planning a mission to Rome, we were assigned to the man heading that mission as translators."

"You were part of the Gan Ying expedition?"

"I was, and my sister."

"But you're alive. King Pacorus had that party ambushed before they could reach Margiana, returning to China. They were wiped out to a man."

Marcus was silent for minute, his face dark. Then he said, "They were my friends, some of them fellow villagers that I had grown up with. I did not know that."

"I am sorry, King Pacorus was adamant that there should be no contact between Rome and China. You, I take it, did not come back with them."

"I did not. Emperor Trajan dispatched his own mission under Senator Galba. My sister and I, three other translators, and one Hanaean official, traveled back by sea to China. Mithridates was in the court when I arrived. We believe he sabotaged our relationship with Emperor He."

"So now it fits! You come now from the Hanaean court?"

"I have not been with the court for many years. After our mission was sabotaged, we escaped, aided by my friend Galosga, and made our way back to my home village. My sister married one of the Romans there, and continued on to Rome with them. I remained to care for my mother, until she died last year. Then I decided to try to rejoin my sister, who lives north of Rome. Hence I am here."

"Not representing the court?"

"Just representing myself."

"How did you know where your sister lives? Have you been in contact somehow?"

"Senator Galba gave me his official seal to use. We submitted a letter via a passing caravan, then on reaching Roman territory, the letter went by official post to his office, and he forwarded it to Marcia. And the reverse for her. It worked well, hearing from her once a year or so, until a few years ago when they stopped coming."

"What you say makes so many of Mithridates' actions clear. Three years ago, he began intercepting all Roman correspondence for fear that it might be coded communications. I am going to arrange for you to repeat this explanation to the King of Kings. The servants will take you to baths and provide you fresh clothes while I meet with him."

Two white-clad servants appeared, silently leading them downstairs to a red-walled room on the first floor which held a large pool. Servant girls came to strip their clothes from them, but Marcus declined, turning away to lift his dirty traveling robes over his head and shed his pants himself, stepping into the warm water, his back to them. Galosga was by no means as shy, allowing the girls to undress him. His firm bronze body elicited some covert stares from them, though his pock-marked face left something to be desired. He too lowered himself into the warm pool. The girls brought bowls with scented balls of colored soaps to help lather away a month's worth of traveling grime.

Cleaned, refreshed and redressed, the servants led them back upstairs to Philippus' office, then offered them sweetmeats from a silver platter and chilled water from a silver jug, beaded with condensation.

After about an hour, Philippus returned. "The King of Kings will see you now. As soon as you enter, prostrate yourself, head down on the floor, and say *'Shahanshah.'* He will tell you when to rise. He will speak only Parthian, so I will translate for you. Come."

He led them up to the top floor, open and colonnaded on all sides, with just a single golden throne, flanked by large silver floor lamps flickering in the breeze, in the center of the bluish-black marble floor. As Philippus entered, he prostrated himself, joined by Marcus and Galosga, making the required intonation. The king responded in a surprisingly high-pitched voice, and Philippus indicated they should rise.

King Volagases sat on the throne, wearing a black robe heavily filigreed with gold and silver, a gold diadem half-crown binding his shiny black hair. He was bearded, the hairs so intricately coiled that it seemed a solid black shiny mass, not a strand out of place. His hands rested, unmoving, on his thighs.

Philippus exchanged words with the king, then turned to Marcus. "Relate your story to the *Shananshah* as you told me, beginning with your ancestors from Carrhae."

Marcus did so, with an occasional pause for Philippus to translate, or to interject a question to direct his story. While this went on Galosga studied the king discretely. The man was slender, but Galosga surmised that underneath that bulky robe, he was probably very wiry, definitely not frail. His face was sharp, with grey eyes glittering and bright, the only part of him that moved as he flicked his gaze between the two speakers, occasionally coming to rest on Galosga.

At the conclusion of Marcus' narrative, the king spoke, and Philippus translated. "The *Shahanshah* believes your lives may be in danger if you continue to Ctesiphon. You are to remain here in the palace as his guests, until he can determine if you can safely continue."

Marcus answered. "Tell him we thank him for his hospitality. But tell him also that Galosga's wife and traveling companions are nearby, and that his children are with my wife and another traveling companion in a caravan that should arrive here shortly."

Philippus nodded, spoke with the king, and answered. "They may all stay with you here in the palace. You will all be free to come and go as you please throughout Ecbatana, keeping the palace guard informed of your intentions, but you may not leave the outermost gate of the city without his permission. I will see to locating your family and friends. Do you have any more questions?"

Marcus shook his head.

"Then prostrate yourself as you did before, then rise to back out facing the king."

Downstairs in Philippus' office, another bearded man was waiting for them. The king's secretary clapped his hands and servants produced pitchers of wine, distributing silver goblets to the four.

"You did well, Marcus," Philippus said, taking a sip from his goblet. "Very well indeed. It looks like you may be our guests for some time, though I know you would rather be on your way to your sister. That will happen, I assure you. Let me introduce my right-hand man, Zacharias. He will show you to your quarters and see to it that you want for nothing."

CHAPTER 34:

UNACCUSTOMED LUXURY

Ecbatana, July 113AD

The harsh rasping call of the steppe eagle echoed from somewhere among the trees surrounding Ecbatana, perhaps five hundred yards away. The call was in answer to Galosga's own call, from the parapet thirty feet above the main gate to the city. "That's her. She'll be here in a few minutes," he said to Arshak standing next to him.

"I heard that call several times while we were traveling," the soldier said.

"She and her friends were following us. As long as I replied with that call at night, all was well."

"What would you have done if things were not well?"

Softly, so that the sound would not carry, he gave a higher-pitched chirping call. "That is the steppe eagle's alarm call. You would most likely have been dead within the hour."

"I never saw them."

"You saw them every day, sometimes going our way, sometimes the other, sometimes crossing our path, always a single rider, too far away to recognize. We are nomads. We know how to be invisible."

Hina appeared on the dusty yellow road leading to the gate, clad in her felt shirt and black riding pants, a shield on her back carrying bow and sword crossed behind her. Her red hair was done up in a knot, topped by a tall conical felt hat. She was riding the tall, sleek black Devil, a quiver holding a dozen or more long arrows slung on his right side. Behind her rode Hadyu and some companions he had enlisted from the caravan, similarly clad and armed. Arshak barked some commands to the gate guards, and massive doors opened with a groan to admit the riders in the pavilion, while Arshak and Galosga clambered down the stone stairs.

Hina slid fluidly off Devil, and dropped his reins to the ground, tethering him. The other four dismounted as well. She greeted Galosga with an embrace. "You are well?" she said, in Xiongnu for privacy.

"I am well, *huldaji*."

Arshak approached the magnificent Devil, who backed away, snorting and rolling his eyes, pawing the ground.

"No closer, he does not like strange men." Hina commanded, approaching the horse to stroke his sweaty neck to calm him, fishing a treat from her pocket.

Galosga began the introductions. "Hina, this is Arshak, my escort from Margiana. My wife Hina."

Arshak hesitated a moment, unsure how to greet the powerfully-built yet extraordinarily beautiful woman a full half-head taller than him. He extended his hand as he would to a man, and she took it in a firm grip.

Hina introduced her companions. "This is Hadyu, my second-in-command, and others from the caravan." They acknowledged Arshak with nods, warily regarding him.

Galosga said, "We will be staying here for a time. It is dangerous for us to continue. Marcus has discovered the strange reason why he is of such intense interest, and the King here has taken us under his protection. You will find the accommodation here much different from what we are accustomed. Let's mount back up and go to the palace." A soldier handed him and Arshak the reins to their horses.

At the palace stables, Hina took care of Devil herself, warning the stable hands of his bad disposition. "Bring him treats, and he will eventually come to accept you. But always be careful around him."

Their quarters were on the third floor, one room for each. Hina started at seeing herself in the big polished bronze mirror that hung on one wall of her room with Galosga. "What witchcraft captures my soul?" she said, stepping aside so it did not capture her reflection.

"It is called a mirror. It is just metal, polished to reflect light, so you can see yourself, but reversed. Step into it, look, and raise your right hand." She did, and her image seemed to raise her left.

She giggled uncharacteristically. "Is that what I look like?"

"Yes, and you are truly beautiful, *huldaji*." He pulled her shirt over her head, showing her the reflection of her well-nippled breasts in the mirror. He took her in his arms and kissed her long and hard, stroking her back as she pressed into him.

A few weeks later, the caravan pulled in. Galosga got special permission to leave the city gates for the caravansary to find Mei, Nathaniel and the children. It did not take him long. They were camped, seated around a fire, when Galosga rode up and dismounted. Marasa and Andanyu greeted him with Xiongnu reserve, while little Adhela ran to grab him by his leg.

"Mei, Nathaniel. You had a good trip, I hope."

Mei was uncharacteristically stern-faced, and just nodded. "Marcus is well?" she asked, without her usual smile.

"We are all well. Guests of the king, in fact."

"Why did Marcus not come for me?"

"He is under this king's protection. The western king has some interest in him, and Marcus may be in danger. He cannot leave the city."

"He is the king's prisoner."

"He is the king's guest, while the king determines what the western king's intentions are."

"He is a prisoner, then, and if this king tires of him, then he will hand him over to the other one."

"Hina is in the palace also and waiting eagerly for our children. We are all safe."

Mei concentrated, her brow furrowed. Finally, she came to a decision, helped by little Adhela.

"I want go see mama," the two-year-old said, in childish Xiongnu with an odd mixture of Sogdian and Aramaic that he had picked up riding the past two months with Nathaniel and Mei. Andanyu and Marasa looked on, silently but seriously, looking more like young adults. They both nodded affirmatively.

"I cannot keep your children from you and Hina. But I am going with you."

"As am I," said Nathaniel with benevolent smile,

They rode into the palace for a joyful reunion.

CHAPTER 35:

PREPARING TO MEET THE SHAH

Ctesiphon, August 113AD

The August heat of Ctesiphon overwhelmed the marble coolness of the palace. Mithridates, clad in an ankle-length loose-fitting silk robe, and Sanatruces, clad in a long white silk shirt and trousers, watched the heat shimmering in the distance over the gardens separating them from the Tigris, fine pearls of sweat on their foreheads.

"That is quite an honor, son, that you have been chosen to represent the *Shahanshah* before the Roman despot Trajan at Athens. My heart swells with pride," said Mithridates.

"Thank you, father, though I am not sure I am up to the task," answered Sanatruces.

"You will do fine. And their negotiating position is weak. Your latest presentation showed no change in the Roman eastern forces over the past year. Just the same seven legions, doing what they do every summer, training. Enough to defend, not enough to invade."

"They have enough to intervene in Armenia."

"They have, and they could succeed there for a time. For a time, before we overwhelm them. Seven legions are what they brought to bear at Carrhae. Should they repeat that catastrophe, that will leave us with the preponderance of force to invade and conquer their undefended provinces of Syria, Judea, and their new province of Petra. We would then be poised to seize the big prizes of Alexandria and Cappadocia. Trajan can offer you nothing but bluff, because he lacks the forces to back up any threat he may make. And he will make those threats. You, son, remain firm and ignore them as so much wind."

"Thank you, father, that is reassuring."

"Your position is simple. Axidares has left his post, out of favor, and Parthamasiris is king in the interim. We simply ask Trajan to confirm the king in accordance with the treaty, for eternal peace between our two peoples, and so forth, and so forth. Do not let him deflect you from that position. Now, do you know who are emerging as his advisors?"

"Father, that is very helpful. It was my intent to follow that plan, but it is good to hear it from your mouth. As to his advisors, his lead in Rome appears to be your friend, Senator Aulus Aemilius Galba."

"I am not surprised. You will find him long on Roman honor. Were you able to penetrate the communications between Trajan and the Empress Dowager passing under his seal?"

"Alas, Father, that was a miserable failure. Our envoy to Rome, Ariobarzanes, had an agent attempt to penetrate his residence, along with another in north Italy, someone you know up there …"

"Yes, Antonius Aristides and his wife Marcia. Go on."

"Unfortunately, Ariobarzanes' agent hired someone long on muscle, but short on brains. He was caught, crucified, and our envoy just got his agent out of the City before he could be detained, questioned and linked to our envoy, and to us. There was murder involved, so both residences and personalities are compromised and off limits. I am sorry."

"Not your fault, son. But unfortunate nevertheless."

"That leaves one more link in that communications chain, the Hanaean end, someone named Marcus. We have reason to be believe, because of his intercepted letters, that he may be heading west. So, we are trying to locate him enroute. But that is like trying to find a particular grain of sand on a beach, and we have no resources east of Khojand."

"Well, that grain of sand is unique, an Hanaean who speaks Latin."

"True, and that is what we seek."

"Well, good luck to you in your efforts. You have done exceedingly well, and will do exceedingly well with Trajan in Athens. Be sure to enjoy that beautiful city while you are there."

CHAPTER 36:

A MEETING IN ATHENS

Athens, October 113AD

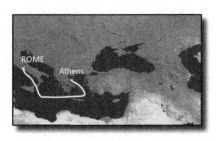

Trajan's body was wrapped in the sheets next to the sleeping Pompeia. *"Princeps,* it is time," said the servant, gently shaking him awake.

The emperor stretched, scratched, and untangled himself from the sheets to stand erect, his flat-bellied muscular body in the lamplight showing little sign of his sixty years, though his close-cropped brown hair was flecked with gray. He stretched, twisting his torso back and forth several times to relieve the stiffness of morning. "Thank you, Achilles," he said. "Hand me my tunic."

The night servants had laid out the morning garb while he had slept. Achilles selected the purple tunic with a gold geometric pattern at the sleeves and hem and a white loin cloth, and handed them to him. Trajan dressed himself, as was his wont, slipping the tunic over his head. Achilles handed him the boots, which he put on.

"Fine, thank you." He picked up a fine green Egyptian glass from the nightstand, poured himself a glass of water, swished it around his mouth, spat it into the bowl to clear his mouth, then poured another to drink.

Pompeia rolled over in her sleep, grumbling. "Go back to sleep, my dear," he said, then turned to Achilles. "Let's get some breakfast."

The dining hall of the governor's praetorium was lit by the flickering amber glow of dozens of lamps and sconces, for it was well before daybreak. The governor of the Greek province of Achaea, Titus Speratus, with several members of his staff, were seated with Aulus Galba at a marble table, a basket of assorted fruits in the middle. Against the wall, a narrow banquet table held stacks of Greek pancakes called *tagenites,* cold cuts, bowls of olives and cheeses. Attractive young male servants stood ready against the wall, clad in identical white Greek tunics that left the left shoulder bare.

"Good morning, gentlemen. I see you are bright and alert this morning despite last night's festivities." Trajan seated himself opposite Aulus and the governor. Servants detached themselves from the wall to bring each a glass of hot mulled wine. The steam lingered in the chill pre-dawn air above Trajan's purple glass.

"My usual," he said, and the servant departed to return with a bowl of porridge. The other servants brought *tagenites* with small jars of honey and cheeses for the pancakes.

"Enjoy yourself. I prefer simple army fare at this time of morning," said Trajan. "Would you pass the honey, please?"

Aulus offered him his jar, and Trajan poured a dollop on his porridge, then picked up his silver spoon. After a few bites, the *Princeps* turned toward the governor. "Our guests have arrived?"

"They have, Your Excellency, late yesterday afternoon. They are lodged in the luxurious inn on the other side of the *agora* from here. As a measure of hospitality, we paid their lodgings in advance."

"That was kind of you, Titus. Who is leading the group?"

"Sanatruces. He is the nephew of King Osroës, and well acquainted with both Axidares and Parthamasiris, the contending kings of Armenia. Military background, cavalry soldier, the equivalent of a senior tribune or *decurion* squadron commander in our army."

"Impolite of them not to reveal their delegation until their arrival. But you have made up for lost time."

"Governor Hadrian has supplied all the regional governors and military commanders with information on significant Parthian officials and their kin relationships. It's really just one big family squabble on their side of the border, so it is important to know who is related to whom. If they show up unexpected, we still have background on them from Hadrian's files."

"Publius Hadrian is doing a fine job managing this crisis," said Trajan. He leaned back in his chair, hands clasped behind his head. "Has a time been set for our meeting today?"

"No, Your Excellency, we defer to you for that."

"Thank you. What is the hottest time of day here?"

"Midafternoon. Though it's October, so not as brutal as July."

"Good. I want to start at the sixth hour, at the base of the statue of Athena on the Acropolis, next to the Parthenon. Just a curule chair for me, everyone else standing. Them, too. And don't deliver them the details of the meeting until noon."

"Yes, Your Excellency." One of Speratus' aides took notes on a wax tablet.

Aulus smiled and winked. "Is there a plan here, Your Excellency?"

"There is indeed, my good Aulus Aemilius. Our friends will have a long, steep walk up to the Acropolis in the heat of the day, about a mile from their residence, and be in a hurry to get there. We, on the other hand, will be enjoying the morning inside the cool interior of the Parthenon, observing that magnificent building and its marvelous art and statuary. I suspect they will arrive sweating and breathing hard, and further intimidated by that thirty-foot statue. It should get the negotiations off on the right foot. Not that there will be any negotiations, other than that Parthamasiris must step down and Axidares be restored, until some mutually agreeable monarch be appointed."

"And if they don't agree?" asked Aulus.

"They understand the consequences."

Servants cleared away the breakfast remnants. "Meet at the portico of the *praetorium* in an hour," Trajan commanded. "We shall walk to the Acropolis and watch the day break over Athens from there."

They met as arranged, and with a small troop of soldiers, walked unobtrusively across the new Roman *agora* to the Acropolis, the rugged granite hill seemingly erupting from the center of Athens. They followed the wide Panathenaic Way to the steep marble steps leading up to the Propylaean Gates at the top. Torches yet flickered to mark their way, as the sky was just beginning to lighten in the east.

Inside the gates, the thirty-foot statue of *Athena Promachos*, Athena-Who-Fights-on-the-Front-Lines, caught the first rays of the rising sun, glinting off her golden upraised sword. By the chest-high marble base, tunic-clad servants, dwarfed by the statue, were preparing the meeting place, some sweeping the marble pavement, and others, as directed, setting up just the single ivory curule chair for the *Princeps*.

"Well, it doesn't seem like the set-up will take long," said Trajan, turning to the governor. "Titus, you may dismiss our soldiers. They may adjourn to wherever they choose, or join us at ease, if they wish, inside the Parthenon."

Titus spoke quietly with the tribune in charge of the detail, and the soldiers, to a man, decided to remain with the emperor, joining his party as they stepped up to the pavilion of the massive temple. Trajan led the group to the east-facing end to watch the sun come up over Mount Hymettus. And it was an impressive sunrise, casting its reddish-tinted light the length of the Parthenon.

Trajan and his entourage spent the morning viewing the magnificent statuary, paintings and friezes inside the cool interior of the Parthenon, talking with the priests and caretakers about the five-hundred-year history of Parthenon and other temples on the rocky mount. The Acropolis had been closed to visitors in preparation for the meeting, so there were no interruptions or unwanted onlookers.

After a light lunch, Trajan changed into his dress military uniform for the day, a cream-colored leather cuirass decorated with gold and silver ornamentation, red *pteryges* cloth strips with decorative brass weights at the end, forming a segmented kilt over his purple tunic, and a purple cloak fringed with gold thread. A cream-colored helmet with gold edging and a purple horse-hair crest rounded out the imperial kit. Everyone else donned white wool togas with wide purple senatorial borders.

Chairs had been arranged inside the Parthenon overlooking the meeting place to its left. The group awaited word of the arrival of the Parthian envoy, seated, chatting amiably. A runner soon brought word that they had approached the bottom of the stairs leading up to the Propylaean Gate.

"Gentlemen, it is time," said Trajan, rising. "Let's go be ready to greet our Parthian friends." He led the way down the steps to the base of the statue of war-like Athena, painted in life-like brilliant colors, her face fierce and intimidating, befitting her depiction as a warrior goddess.

Trajan was seated rigidly erect on his backless ivory curule chair when the Parthians arrived. He was flanked by Aulus and Governor Speratus with his aides, twenty soldiers behind them in parade uniform against the base of the statue. As expected, the Parthians were breathing hard.

Sanatruces was clad in a long iridescent green silk shirt, elegantly filigreed in a variety of colors, slightly sweat-stained, over black trousers, his short military-cut beard tightly coiled, as was his black hair under a decorative white and gold turban. He led his party, similarly dressed, to stand before Trajan and halted.

"*Ave*, Great Trajan, *Imperator* by the Senate and People of Rome! King Osroës sends his greetings, and his wish for peace always between our two great nations. I, his humble representative, am Sanatruces, son of Mithridates," he said in a lightly accented Latin, finishing with a respectful bow.

"Welcome, Sanatruces, please convey to your uncle the great Osroës, the King of All Parthian Kings, that I, too, wish him good health, and eternal peace between our peoples. I look forward to hearing your proposals to enhance that peace."

Sanatruces nodded. "As you know, our mutual relations with Armenia on our borders are governed by the Treaty of Rhandeia between your Emperor Nero and King Vologases I that has kept the peace for a half-century. We come to ask your approval of our nominee for the new kingship of Armenia, Parthamasiris."

Trajan smiled slightly. "And what happened to the sitting king Axidares, previously installed by mutual treaty between us?"

"The former king has fallen out of favor with King Osroës."

"Again, what happened to him?"

Sanatruces paused, considering his response. "He has returned to Ctesiphon."

"And who rules Armenia in his absence?"

"Parthamasiris has taken the role as interim king, pending your final approval."

"Interesting. I heard nothing of this from the good King Osroës. Perhaps he simply forgot to tell me?"

"He honored me with the responsibility to inform you of this development."

"Perhaps a little advance notice of the palace coup before it happened, and I might have been far less concerned. As you know, Armenia is a border area of strategic interest to both our peoples, and the deposing of our agreed-upon king with no explanation ahead of time has alarmed us, caused us to question the value of our mutual treaty, if one side can simply abrogate it as they choose."

"There was no time to inform you in advance. I convey King Osroës' apologies for his failing to be able to do so."

"And what was the event that drove the removal of King Axidares with such urgency?"

"King Osroës had become dissatisfied with his actions in Armenia."

"We follow events in Armenia as closely as do you. There was no unrest, no rebellion, no threat of barbarian invasion. Had King Osroës simply conveyed to us his dissatisfaction with his nephew Axidares, we would have concurred in his removal, and assisted, if asked."

"No matter. It is now done, and the manner in which it was done cannot be undone. Now for the sake of peace, we ask you approve of Parthamasiris as the new king, and conduct the ceremony of placing the diadem on his head."

"No." This single word of rejection hung in the air, surrounded by the ensuing shocked silence from the Parthian.

For nearly a minute of consideration, Sanatruces looked deeply into Trajan's unblinking eyes just ten feet away, seeking some hint of uncertainty, some hesitation. Finding none, he said, "And what do you propose, *Princeps*, that does not involve war between our two most powerful armies?"

"I propose restoring the *status quo ante*. Restore King Axidares to his rightful throne. If the King of all Parthian Kings has issues with Axidares' kingship, we may consult with each other and identify a suitable replacement. As Parthamasiris is now a rebel and a usurper, he cannot be a suitable replacement. He is unacceptable to us now and shall be for as long as he lives."

"And that is unacceptable to King Osroës. Do you seriously intend war with Parthia over this issue?"

"If Parthia chooses war by abrogating our mutual treaty of peace, we stand ready to wage war with the full might of the Roman Army."

Sanatruces was again silent for a minute. "Is that your final answer?"

"That is my final answer. Gentlemen, this meeting is ended. My soldiers will escort you back to your ship at Piraeus, after a brief stop at your quarters to collect your belongings. Good day!" Trajan stood and led his party back to the Parthenon, leaving the soldiers with Sanatruces' befuddled party.

CHAPTER 37:

A GRAIN OF SAND FOUND

Ctesiphon, December 113

Sanatruces and Mithridates met in the latter's spacious office. "You did well, son. Trajan is bluffing. He has no more forces than his ancestors had at Carrhae, and they will meet the same fate if he were to attack us, and he knows it."

"Still, I felt it was a horrible waste, six weeks there and back for a meeting that did not last ten minutes. And not even time to visit the city. He ordered us out to our ships immediately after the meeting. He simply dismissed all our proposals."

"He will change his mind when he reaches Antioch and sees what forces he has to bring to bear, and what he is up against. You did well, and I am proud of you. And at least the fall weather is a vast improvement over the heat when you left." They watched lateen-rigged dhows, sails white against the blue Tigris, flittering about the water in the distance beyond the palm trees that shaded the beautiful green gardens surrounding the palace. Ctesiphon was truly pleasant in October.

"Who were his advisors at the meeting?" asked Mithridates.

"The governor of what the Romans now call Achaea, Greece before they overran it. A fellow named Titus Speratus, and some of his staff, taking notes for him. And your friend Aulus Galba."

"Aulus! Really? No one else?"

"That was it, father. No one else."

"Well, that is truly interesting. I would have certainly expected Hadrian and his entourage. Just Aulus... that is very interesting, given what you learned about his covert communication between Rome and China."

"And there has been a new development in that lead, Father. Our grain of sand named Marcus has turned up in the custody of Vologases in Ecbatana."

"In his custody? What are his intentions?"

"Our man in Vologases' court, Zacharias, indicated that Vologases is keeping him more as a house guest under protective custody, rather than as a prisoner. He is free to go about the city, but cannot exit the gates. He is living in the palace with some wild eastern nomads that appear to be his bodyguards. One of them, he says, is an Amazon woman warrior."

"Have you had any communications with Vologases directly on this?"

"No, that seemed imprudent. He understands that this Marcus has value to us, but he does not know why, and I don't intend to help him find out. Zacharias is working on a way to get him out of Ecbatana, but that will take time and considerable caution. He is, after all, a guest of the usurper king. Zacharias is too valuable an asset to waste, even over Marcus."

CHAPTER 38:

THE CAPRICORN REBORN

Melitene, December 113

Gaius Lucullus wrapped the loneliness of command about himself like a cloak in his office off the *praetorium* anteroom, warming his hands at a brazier. The December chill challenged him, as well as the chill of fear. The letter from Hadrian was clear: the Parthians had rejected Trajan's last best offer to settle on a new Armenian king other than the usurper Parthamasiris, in accord with the treaty. Accordingly, the eastern legions were to prepare for an Armenian campaign in the spring. He studied a fine leather multi-colored map on the wall, showing hints of terrain, troop locations on pieces of papyrus pinned to it. The reinforcing western legions, their cohorts embedded among the seven eastern forces, were to emerge from hiding, all of them converging on the northernmost fort of Satala near the Black Sea to join up with *XVI Flavia*. Their headquarters staffs, which had spent the year with Hadrian in Antioch, would join them there. The Parthians should certainly be surprised to see three new legions suddenly appear, as if from nowhere, if the ruse had been successful.

Gaius Lucullus had spent the last eighteen months studying the Parthian campaigns, beginning with the disaster at Carrhae, when the Romans lost thirty thousand men and ten thousand captured. For this he had Roman military records, plus the newly-published *Lives* by Plutarch, which gave a good rendition of the disaster. In addition, Marcia Lucia, his old friend Antonius' wife, had shared first-hand accounts passed down from generation to generation from her ancestors, the survivors of Carrhae who resettled in China. They all told the same story, Crassus' overconfidence and underestimation of the Parthians, his mistrust of a true ally who could have supported him, and his misplaced trust in another who intentionally led him into that hell.

Gaius had fought well against the Dacians, leading the *II Traiana* from victory to victory. But the Dacians were mountain fighters, not professional soldiers. Good at ambushes, not good at fighting in the line. In the end, they had melted before the disciplined legions of Rome, and Trajan made few mistakes.

The Parthian army was a different matter, the equal of Rome in every way, but at the same time totally different. They relied on a combination of heavily-armored cavalry, *catafracti*, and light horse archers. The first one plodding but seemingly unstoppable, the latter fast and nimble, able to inflict death at a distance, beyond the range of Roman missiles. The *catafracti* required the legion to open up to evade the charging horses, to attack the mounts rather than the armored man riding it. But the horse archers required the legion to bunch together, to form the *testudo* turtle defense, shields locked together, to defend against the showers of arrows they unleashed. And the Parthians used their two forces in coordination, eventually weakening and destroying the Roman infantry legion, ill-used to cavalry attack.

And thoughts of his son came unbidden. By mutual agreement, he never met alone with him, and neither acknowledged the other as father and son. Secundus was just another tribune that Gaius could order into certain death. But Gaius wondered if, in fact, he could ever do that. He was glad that his old friend Samuel had taken his son under his wing, to prepare the young tribune as only a centurion can, and hopefully guide him through the battles to come.

It was time. The last of the tribunes and their senior centurions had entered the anteroom of the *praetorium* and were huddled about the braziers casting welcome heat and flickering light against the winter chill. He noted Secundus there with Samuel, along with Tribune Virgilius Varro and his centurion Vitus Faustus, of the Lucky Capricorns' *vexillatio*. The two were talking animatedly. He looked at the script of his speech and decided to leave it on his desk. He would talk to them from the heart. Perhaps a formal speech to all the troops tomorrow, but today he would improvise.

Gaius stood, straightened his uniform and nodded to Paulus Herrerius, the *primus pilus*, the senior centurion of the legion, to call the twenty-two men to order. "Stand by for the *legatus!*" the man bawled out in a commanding battlefield voice, as Gaius exited his office to address them.

"Stand easy, gentlemen. For the past year, you all have been aware that something is afoot, and have been cautioned not to speculate, or discuss various things with the locals. I want to commend you on your leadership and the discipline of your men, as no word of some of our more unusual events, such as the embedding of the *vexillatio* cohort from the Twenty-Second, has leaked out into the population. We just received some important information from Governor Publius Hadrian that we have impending operations against the Parthians. The Twenty-Second *vexillatio* is to detach by the end of this week, resume their own insignia and standards, and proceed at best haste to Satala. There they will rejoin their other cohorts and stand up again as the Lucky Capricorns of the *XXII Primigenia*, alongside the *XV Apollinaris* emerging from the shadows where we have kept them hidden. The *Princeps* no longer wishes to conceal his intent from the Parthians.

"The Parthians have violated our treaty and annexed Armenia. The *Princeps* held his last negotiations with the enemy two months ago in Athens, and our plan for peace was rejected. Our mission is to seize that region from their foul hands. The *Princeps* is enroute to Antioch with twenty-thousand Berber cavalry from Dacia. From there he will lead the seven eastern legions and western reinforcements, over eighty-thousand men, north to Satala. This force, the largest Rome has ever assembled, will launch eastward to recover Armenia under his leadership, probably in the spring. The Twelfth Lightning Bolt's immediate task is to prepare men and logistics for at least a year-long campaign, five hundred miles beyond the border of Rome, against everything the Parthians will throw at us. Are there any questions?"

There was a buzz of comments from the assembled leadership, but no questions.

"Very well, then. Again, well done on keeping our build-up for this operation concealed from the enemy. We will call an assembly of the whole legion tomorrow at noon to tell the men directly, but you may feel free to discuss this now with the other centurions and tribunes." Gaius Lucullus turned and left, the *primus pilus* in tow.

The centurions Samuel Elisarius and Vitus Faustus, and their tribunes Gaius Secundus and Virgilius Varro accompanied each other to the barracks of the Fifth Cohort, the four having formed a close personal friendship over the year the Lucky Capricorn's cohort had been embedded in the Twelfth. Stripping off their hooded winter *paenulae* coats, they settled into the tribune's office around the fireplace.

"I don't know about you centurions, but I think this calls for a bottle of Falernian," said Secundus, producing a flask and four ceramic cups. He worked the waxed stopper out with his dagger and poured everyone a drink without waiting for their response."

"Thank you, sir," said Samuel, taking a proffered cup for a sip of the powerful wine. "Well above the kind of wine I usually drink, but not every day we get to go to war."

"And going to war we are, it seems," said Virgilius Varro. "The higher-ups did a good job of keeping this secret. Whatever we asked, it always came back, 'just an exercise'. An exercise, moving five thousand men two thousand miles, just to see if they could do it."

Gaius Secundus weighed in. "And a big war. By the time we get fleshed out with auxiliaries, we will have over a hundred thousand men. But we will be covering a lot of territory. Like the *legatus* said, five hundred miles beyond the border. Probably more. We will be on our own."

"This is beyond what I know," said Vitus. "I spent me time chasing barbarian Germans on the other side of the Rhine. Good fighters, but not real armies. What I have learned about the Parthians at Carrhae, they are good, damned good. And they use mounted archers in a way that is hard to counter."

"I learned a lot about that campaign from my father," said Secundus, referring to the *legatus* in that role for the first time. "The trick is to stay mobile. And be careful whom you trust. Assume everyone east of the Euphrates is a liar."

"Well said, tribune," said Samuel. "These are good insights, but we are going into Armenia, not Mesopotamia."

"We shall see, Samuel, we shall see. I suspect this war will take its own direction."

CHAPTER 39:

WAITING IN AQUILEIA

Aquileia, December 113

Marcia rejoined Antonius by the brazier in the atrium, the flames tossed by the eddies stirred up by the fierce northeast Bora wind blowing overhead. She wrapped her woolen shawl around her against the chill. "The children are in bed, love," she said, taking her seat beside him and accepting the proffered wine glass. "Thank you. Have you heard from Aulus?"

"Nothing other than that he was going to Athens. Close-mouthed about what's going on, as he should be," said Antonius."

"I am surprised you didn't go with him."

"I think I could've gone, if I wished. Be nice to see Gaius again. But I have things here to take care of, an' I didn't like what went on last year with Janus, and Modorus sniffin' around the house. Aulus never asked me, and I didn't volunteer."

"It's been a year since Modorus was here."

"An' I don't like it any better than I did then. Somethin' connecting us and Aulus, and somethin' enough fer him ter come back fer a second visit."

"I wonder what it could have been?" Marcia looked at him with a smile in the lamplight. "Yer revertin' to yer soldier Latin, *carus meus*. Yer must be concerned."

"Sorry. I talk like that when people are tryin' ter kill me. An' maybe you an' the children. Whatever it was, enough ter kill two people and break into our villa. Nothin' like this ever happened to either of us before." He shook his head slowly. "The *vigiles* got nothin' worthwhile out of the culprit back in Rome, just a name for the person who hired him an' where to find him. But a dead end, false name and no trace of him. Someone interested in us both, but who and why? An' fer the tenth time, yer did a good job bringin' him up short." He slapped his big arm playfully across her back, feeling the dagger in its sheath between her shoulder blades. "Always ready, *domina*, aren't you?"

"Like Hina taught me. And you. And at least ten times you've said that, love. Thanks again, but he was sloppy. Didn't think fighting a woman was going to be difficult."

"He learned better."

"You know, with Aulus hauling off with Trajan for the east, do you think that could be the connection? The trouble in Armenia?"

"Aulus didn't think Armenia was all that important, just the Parthians pushing to see what they can get away with. And why would the Parthians care about us? Aulus, yes, he has all kinds of business interests, Senate business, close to Trajan, things that might interest them. But us? Running a little language academy up here in north Italy for a handful of people who want to learn Hanaean and Bactrian? What do we have that is worth anything to the Parthians? Makes no sense," said Antonius, reverting to his more thoughtful Latin.

The two sat silently, drinking their wine, watching the fire die off to embers.

"I hope all is well with Marcus. We haven't heard from him for several years. I last wrote him about little Androcles, last year."

"I hope so, too. He will write again."

"Well, the fire is about out, and it is getting to be a cold night. Reminds me of a jailcell, far away. I think we can find a better spot to get warm." She gave him a long soft kiss, took his hand, and led him upstairs.

CHAPTER 40:

TRAJAN IN ANTIOCH

Antioch, December 113AD

On a cool December morning, Trajan arrived at the governor's *praetorium*, part of the palace complex in Antioch, with his wife Pompeia Plotina, and Aulus Galba with some note-taking assistants. He was greeted in the marble foyer of the *praetorium* by Publius Hadrian and his wife Vibia Sabina, Pompeia's grand-niece, with dozens of servants waiting in the background.

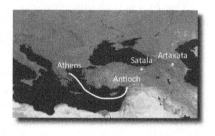

"You had a good trip from Athens?" Hadrian inquired, signaling his servants to remove Trajan's purple toga.

"I did, Publius. Beautiful sailing, despite the late season, and a fine riverboat from Seleucia Pieria. The Orontes is a beautiful river."

"It is, indeed. And Lady Plotina, you are beautiful, as ever," said Hadrian, turning his bearded smile toward the *Princeps'* wife.

"It's good to see you again, Aunt Pompeia," added Hadrian's wife Vibia Sabina, taking the older woman's hand in her own. "Welcome to Antioch."

Other servants hustled out to the imperial carriage to unload baggage onto wheeled carts, for distribution to the reserved rooms.

"The servants will show you to your rooms. Shall we meet for lunch? After that, we can adjourn to our planning room. I will review our forces and recommendations for whatever campaign you wish to wage."

"To be sure." Trajan took Hadrian's hand in a firm military handshake, hand to wrist. "And this is Aulus Aemilius Galba, my most trusted advisor, and one of only two people that I can trust to tell me when I am making a mistake. You, dear cousin, are the other."

Hadrian turned to face Aulus, his fine teeth white behind his carefully trimmed bronze beard. "Yes, the famous 'Jason and his new Argonauts'. I am pleased to meet you. Your trip to the land of the Han is truly the stuff of legend. And you made another less eventful trip there, I understand?"

"I am pleased to meet you, Publius Aelius. The second trip was mercifully less eventful, no death sentences! The Emperor He-Di and I got along quite well the second time, and it was quite informative."

"A topic for discussion at lunch, then," said Hadrian. "I would like to hear about your trips first-hand."

Lunch was served on a patio with a fine view of the River Orontes, dividing the palace complex from Antioch proper, spanned by five multi-arched stone bridges connecting the island to the eastern part of the city. The city receded beyond the river in an orderly grid of white buildings to the foot of Mount Silpius to the south, the city walls snaking up its slopes to a gray fortress sitting on the top like a grim cap. The morning chill had given way to warm sunshine.

Aulus held Hadrian in rapt attention as he recounted his well-rehearsed story of the double hijacking of the two ships *Asia* and *Europa*, their recovery and an unlikely alliance formed with one of the pirates. "The man who saved the day for us is my cousin and one of your commanders, Gaius Aetius Lucullus, of *Legio XII Fulminata*."

"Ah, yes, the Twelfth Lightning Bolt. And he is on his second tour with that unit, commanding it this time. He cut quite a fine reputation for himself in the Dacian War with the *II Traiana*," said Hadrian. The three were nursing fruit juice, rather than wine, for clear heads for the discussions to come. "So please, continue."

"As you might expect," said Aulus, "It was Parthian intrigue in the court that cost us that first mission. Their envoy was one Cyrus Mithridates."

Hadrian paused, thinking, his finger pressed against his cheek. "Did you say Cyrus Mithridates was the envoy to the Han then?"

"I did."

"And you met him?"

"I got to know him better than I would have preferred."

"You will get to know him well again, then. He is the brother to King Osroës, and by most reports, next in line for the throne."

"Really? I never expected our paths to cross again."

"I am sorry, I interrupted your story. What did he do?"

"He tried to get our translator condemned for adultery with Gaius' centurion."

Hadrian laughed heartily. "That's a crime there? Rome would have to kill off half the Senators if that were made a capital offense! Were they guilty?"

"It was, of course false, though if either had any sense, they should have been guilty. I never saw such a pair more in love than they, and Marcia and Antonius eventually married while we were on the run. Anyway, I could not choose to put our lives above hers and defended her against the emperor in his own court. By the way, the Han emperor spoke excellent Latin."

Trajan added to the conversation. "And writes it quite well, also, or has someone write it for him. He and I exchanged several letters before he died."

Aulus noticed that Vibia Sabina, though smiling at the appropriate moments, sometimes with a charming laugh like a tinkling little bell, seemed to keep her distance from her husband. They had been married for over ten years, but no children. Hadrian had a reputation of preferring boys to women, perhaps even over his own wife.

A servant came up to whisper something in Hadrian's ear. "Well, it seems your presentation is ready, I hate to interrupt this story, dear Aulus, but we must adjourn to the planning room to give the *Princeps* time to study our work. Let's adjourn and leave the women to enjoy the sunlight," said Hadrian, rising to lead them away. "Ladies, excuse us."

Hadrian led the emperor and his entourage to a door guarded by a soldier who snapped erect, saluting expressionlessly as Hadrian opened the door with a large key. Inside, two others, waiting in the lamplight, rose to greet Trajan. "*Ave, Imperator*," they intoned simultaneously.

Hadrian introduced the two. "Please meet some of my significant people here, Claudius Severus, governor of the new province of Arabia Petraea. He, as you know, oversaw the construction of the *Via Traiana Nova* linking the Red Sea to Syrian road networks. The road will significantly shorten our logistics line, and he has an enormous knowledge of Parthian politics."

Claudius was fortyish, close-cropped black hair going gray at the temples, short of stature but wiry, not given to the plumpness of soft living. "I am honored to present to you, Your Excellency.

Trajan acknowledged Claudius with a nod, and Hadrian turned toward the second. "This is Lusius Quietus, our cavalry commander, who demonstrated to you that mobile force's utility in the Dacian War. He will demonstrate how to use that force to neutralize that cavalry that is the backbone of the Parthian Army."

Lusius Quietus was tall, brown-skinned with short wiry hair, his tunic revealing powerfully-muscled biceps. He similarly acknowledged the introduction.

The men stood behind a large ten-foot table with an intricate multicolored map showing rivers and seas in blue, roads, terrain, forests and deserts, from the eastern Mediterranean to the Caspian Sea, north to the Black Sea and south to the Red Sea and Persian Gulf. Several lamps hanging from the ceiling fully illuminated the display. Scrolls in cubbyholes contained written information and notes.

"Good to see both of you again," said Trajan to Claudius and Lusius.

"Before you, Your Excellency, is our field of battle," said Hadrian, dropping the familiar address he had used at lunch with his cousin. "Several years ago, I had this map made from our best and most accurate resources, to plan this campaign. While our campaign is focused on Armenia, it may expand to cover this whole area, depending on what Parthia does. And I don't expect to repeat Marcus Licinius Crassus' mistake of getting lost in the desert, depending on foreigners to give him directions to the war," he said. He was referring the disaster at Carrhae a century and half before, when Rome had lost thirty thousand men to the Parthians. "My commanders will at least know where they are."

Positioned on the map were twelve bronze emblems of each of the legions, arrayed from just south of Antioch nearly to the Black Sea.

Hadrian continued, indicating the legions just south of Trapezus on the south coast of the Black Sea. "Here at Satala, garrisoned by the *XVI Flavia*, we have reconstituted the *1 Adiutrix* from Pannonia and the *XXII Primigenia*, all the way from Lower Germany. We concealed their trek of thousands of miles by moving them by cohorts, then distributing their men among our seven legions. A few months ago, on your orders, we stood them back up and redeployed their men here, at the northern end of the spear."

He pointed to the area of Antioch, where the rising east coat of the Mediterranean peaked like the tip of a shoe, before turning west to follow the underbelly of Cappadocia and Anatolia. "The two southernmost legions, the *III Cyrenaica* at Bostra and the *X Fretensis* from Jerusalem, have been redeployed to positions between *III Gallica* and *VI Scythica*. Besides these legions, we have six detached cohorts from various legions in Dacia and Moesia on the Danube, and regional auxiliary cohorts from the various provinces and client states volunteering to serve in this campaign. And we have Lusius Quietus, whose cavalry will certainly not be quiet. I will let him tell you his plan."

"Good afternoon, Your Excellency." His deep voice had a liquid quality to it, enhanced by his Berber West African accent. "My twenty thousand men and horses are concentrated in the middle of the staging area here," he said, indicating a point midway between the Mediterranean and the Black Sea. "When the force marches, we will take advantage of our speed and mobility to take the van, here in the north, while a second group strikes east into Armenia. We will be your eyes and ears of any danger, especially if Parthia chooses to respond in force to defend their ill-gotten gains in Artaxata." He indicated a small flag denoting the capital of Armenia, between the Black and Caspian Sea. "The Parthian cavalry has always defeated Roman infantry, by their heavily-armored *catafracti* and their light cavalry archers. The *catafracti* are an almost unstoppable juggernaut, but slow and unwieldy. Their horse archers, however, dart in from a swirling mass outside the range of your missiles, launch the volleys of arrows, then dart out of range again. Defending against their armor requires your troops to disperse, to allow the juggernaut to pass through your lines, while the horse archers require you to concentrate, to shelter under your shields against the rain of arrows.

"We have enough armor to take on the *catafracti* and enough speed to take on the horse archers. Without them, the Parthian infantry is an ill-trained, ill-led band of conscripts that will scatter at the sight of a Roman sword."

Lusius stepped back from the table, standing straight as a lance.

Hadrian continued his presentation. "On your order, sir, we will pick up the legions outside Antioch, march north to Satala picking up the rest of the forces as we go. You will have sixty-five thousand men on the march there, with Lusius Quietus' twenty-thousand cavalry already well on their way into Armenia. From Satala, we will turn east for Artaxata. And we have one more trick." He reached under the table and picked up an oblong object with a handle on it, like a racket used in the gymnasiums at the bath houses to play various ballgames. a mesh inside the oblong portions, and a low shoe in the middle. "The Armenian army's strategy in response to invasion is to retreat to the highlands in the central part of the country for the winter and launch lightning raids on the invader in his winter quarters in the lowlands. With this device on their feet instead of boots, they can walk easily on snows up to six feet deep. I have had ten thousand of these constructed, and with them on their feet, it will be our legions raiding them in their own mountain fastness."

CHAPTER 41:

KEEPING ONE'S HEAD

Ctesiphon, January 114AD

Mithridates stood before his brother, the *Shahanshah* Osroës, his eyes downcast in shame and foreboding. Others had been executed for such shortcomings. Was it his time now to die?

The king was seated on his gilded ivory throne, clad in a dark blue, gold-filigreed robe, his gold and silver diadem on his head, almost like a halo. Seated to his left were his advisors; to his right, his *spahbods,* generals of his army. The cushions on the throne and chairs, the draperies on the walls, even the columns were in a dark blue matching the king's raiment. Mithridates studied the carpet, also dark blue with a complex pattern of animals, people and geometric patterns in silver and gold woven into it. Dark blue had always been his brother's favorite color.

"Let me understand this. The Roman army has more than doubled in size since you briefed me last month, and these are not all auxiliary provincial forces."

"Yes, Your Majesty. At least two new legions have set up camp in Satala alongside the *XVI Flavia* in the fort there, the *XXII Primigenia* from Lower Germany on the Rhine, and the *I Adiutrix* from Pannonia on the Danube. Twenty thousand horsemen under Lusius Quietus have arrived from Dacia, and cohort-sized detachments from six other legions, all in independent camps with the other seven legions. And the two southern legions have left their forts in Bostra and Jerusalem, deploying to mobile field camps near Antioch. I regret we saw no indications of the movement of such a formidable force."

"Has the Roman army grown wings then, or flown on the backs of birds to arrive so suddenly?" his brother asked sarcastically.

"Your Majesty, the responsibility is mine and mine alone. I failed to detect this movement, and my life is forfeit, if you so wish." *At this moment, I want only to spare my son Sanatruces.*

The king laughed. "My headsman would probably dent his fine ax on your stiff neck, Cyrus, my dear brother. I will give the Romans credit for an incredible ruse, however they did it, rather than take your life. Any chance this could be deception? Untrained locals dressed up as a faraway legion?"

For the first time, Mithridates felt like he might see another day. His brother called him by his first name only in the family scene, never, as now, among his advisors. He considered his answer. "Our observers have questioned several of the soldiers, and they seem to be authentic. We have a handful of observers in the far west, but it may be months yet before they can confirm that these legions are no longer there."

"Our main challenge is what they will do now, what they may do in the future, and how we may best counter them. Ataradates, my senior *Spahbod* and commander-in-chief of all my armies, what is your counsel?"

Ataradates, on the king's right, leaned forward and spoke. "I believe they will march some or all of these forces into Armenia to contest the kingship there. But such a massive force far exceeds what is needed to seize Armenia. I expect them to drive south along the Tigris and Euphrates Rivers to attack Mesopotamia and Ctesiphon itself. We should send word to your rival Vologases in Ecbatana. He should feel as threatened by this as you. He could provide us at least twenty thousand heavy and light horsemen, enough to offset their cavalry."

An advisor to the king's left waited for a pause, then interjected. "Your Majesty, King Vologases feels that he should remain neutral in any war between you and Rome, letting Trajan do the dirty work of unseating you. However, a force of such size could move east against him, if Trajan were successful."

The advisors and the military *spahbods* argued back and forth for fifteen minutes, proposing various options of confronting the massive force. Finally, the king turned toward his brother who had stood silently by throughout the hubbub. "Brother, what do you advise? You are the master of my intelligence."

"There is only one general who consistently and decisively defeated the Romans, and that was the Carthaginian general Hannibal three centuries ago. The Romans cannot resist chasing an enemy in retreat. Therefore, Hannibal always put his weakest forces in the center, the strongest on the flanks, concealed as best as possible. When the center gave, the Romans pursued, and the flanks closed around them and smashed them. Every time. It was not until Hannibal was recalled to Carthage that the Romans were able to defeat him there at Zama, using his own tactics against him. I propose we not resist this overwhelming force but present a weak center like Hannibal to trade space, which we have in abundance, for time, which we need. Let them have Armenia, and if they invade our homeland, let Ataradates' forces melt eastward into the Zagros mountains to the east. Trajan's overwhelming force will not be so overwhelming when it is spread from Armenia to Charax on the Persian Gulf, from the western desert to the Zagros Mountains. It will be individual legions holding isolated cities with hostile populations, easily defeated in detail. Trajan will be forced to withdraw in humiliation, or lose them all, one at a time."

Ataradates considered this. "What about Ctesiphon? Do we not defend Ctesiphon?"

"Let them have it. In a few months we will have it back, and it won't take long to wash the Roman stink off our city."

After the tumultuous meeting, a smiling Mithridates met his son Sanatruces, waiting in concern outside the throne room. "Relax, my son, it looks like we will both keep our heads."

CHAPTER 42:

THE HORSE RACE

Ecbatana, March 114AD

With a major war imminent in the west, it was out of the question that Marcus' group should continue on to Ctesiphon. They were forced to endure the luxuries of palace life for some time to come, until the western crisis was resolved. Even Hina began to adapt to the high lifestyle, finally shedding her felts and linens for high quality silk robes and *salwars*. Marcus' group often took the evening meal with Philippus, and on rare occasions with King Vologases, both for social pleasantries and for news of the events in Parthia. Of particular interest was the impending war between Rome and Osroës over Armenia, a war in which King Vologases intended to remain firmly neutral.

"We have tens of thousands of heavy and light cavalry that we could put at Osroës' disposal," Philippus said over after-dinner wine. "But why? A victorious Osroës, no longer held in check by Rome to his west, will look eastward toward a final settlement with us, a settlement that will not be to our liking. So, let him fight a war with what he has, depleting his men and horses in another indecisive war against Rome which neither can win. And, speaking of horses, the King is sponsoring a horse race this upcoming holiday of the *Nowruz* New Year at the hippodrome by the seventh ring of the city. You should come, our horses have a fine reputation."

Hina, clad in an emerald green silk set of trousers and long embroidered shirt called a *salwar kamis*, smiled over her wine. "As do our steppe ponies in my homeland." Marasa and Andanyu, likewise in their loose-fitting *salwars*, sat beside her and Galosga, participating in silent observation, learning the ways of their new world.

"Perhaps, but your horses are far from home, and far past their prime for racing. They seem sturdy, to be sure, to have traveled so far, but race, not likely."

"My mount is not a steppe pony, a yearling very much in his prime for racing. How might I enter?"

Philippus cleared his throat. "They will not accept women in this race. The list of riders must be approved by King Vologases."

Galosga quietly gripped her thigh under the table, attempting to steer her away from a confrontation, but making little headway.

"Are you afraid that a woman might beat your men?" She asked, with a smile on her lips, but iron in her voice.

"That cannot happen. No woman can outride a man. And, as I said, the list must be approved by King Vologases. But you are welcome to come watch."

The dinner conversation dissolved into small talk, with Mei intervening to redirect the discussion to the significance of *Nowruz*, falling on the spring equinox.

"This holiday, which means 'New Light', was established by Zoroaster, who taught us to worship wisdom. We, in turn, taught this to the Greeks," Philippus intoned. "The night before this sacred day of equal light and darkness, we extinguish all fires and sweep the hearths. The priests of *Ahura Mazda*, the Lord of Wisdom, will light a bonfire at the hippodrome before daybreak the morning of the race. They light candles from that bonfire and distribute them to the observers in the stands, who take them home to light their new hearths. The stands will be as bright as day with tens of thousands of candles. We will celebrate the break of day, then the races will begin."

After a bit more small talk, everyone retired to their quarters. Hina retrieved Adhela from the servants, put him to bed, and sent the twins off to their room.

"I am riding, you know," she said to Galosga, slipping her green *salwar* over her head, the flint arrowhead swaying between her breasts on a thong around her neck.

"Green goes well with your hair, *huldaji*."

"You are trying to misdirect me," she said, pulling his red *salwar* off in turn over his head.

"To ride in the race with them you must make them play your game. I have learned from many peoples, different rules, different games. You must learn their game, but do not play it. But yes, you and Devil will ride, no one can stop you and no one can beat you."

He took her in his arms and snuffed out the oil lamp.

Everyone in Ecbatana stayed awake the night before *Nowruz*, feasting and drinking in the darkened city. Even the palace was dark. The skies were ablaze with stars unhindered by the city's normal brilliance.

But Hina was neither celebrating, feasting nor drinking. She had a bowl of mare's milk, mixed with blood, and a sack of *kumis*, retiring shortly after sundown. She rose a few hours after midnight and went to the stables to tend to Devil. He greeted her with a cheerful nicker, swishing his tail in the dark. She fetched him an apple from the pocket of her Xiongnu riding felts which he eagerly took from her hands, devouring it with a crunch. "Well, Devil, let us show them how you can run." She donned her conical riding hat over her tightly done-up hair bun, tying it tightly beneath her chin.

She saddled him up in the blackness and led him out. Fortunately, the moon was full, its brilliance accentuated by the total darkness of the city, like a night on the lightless steppes back home. *Home? I have no home now, except where Galosga and I and our children find ourselves. That is our home now.*

She mounted and trotted slowly through the six gates to the seventh ring around the city. The hippodrome was to the left of the road, its facing wall two hundred and fifty paces in length almost spanning the distance between the inner and outer walls. She dismounted, noting other riders entering the large door in the center, and led Devil in with the other participants. The audience was already entering on foot in the darkness by doors along the side. Although it was several hours before daybreak, there was a buzz of activity, as thousands of spectators had arrived to take their seats early. Latecomers might observe the ceremonies and the race standing, and the doors were closed after the arrival of the royal entourage.

There was a line of fifteen horses with their riders and tenders ahead of her, and a man checking arrivals on the track. An odor of freshly turned sand and manure made the air pungent. Finally, her turn came. *Make them play your game.* Galosga's words came back to her. She had not discussed this with him.

"We only had fifteen riders," said the attendant. "Who are you?"

"I am Hina of the Xiongnu, riding Devil." She used her deepest voice. In the darkness, he might not realize she was a woman but a beardless man, one problem out of the way.

"You weren't on the list."

"I am a late addition, at the request of Philippus, secretary to the *Shahanshah*."

"He said nothing to me about this. The list has been closed for several days."

"He will be upset if I don't ride. He has a large bet on me, several hundred silver coins."

"I will add you, but I will speak to him about this. This is highly irregular."

"I am sorry. The palace has been very busy with preparations for *Nowruz*, and he is involved in all of it. It must have slipped his mind."

"Well, go on. I hope I can remember you and your horse's name. I can't write anything in this blackness."

She took her place with the other horses and their riders by the starting point, marked by chalk in the dust at the turn facing the royal pavilion, where the king and his advisors would sit, where Hina's entourage would sit as guests of the palace. The center of the track was a long island, fifty paces wide, and on either side of the surrounding track rose the stands, row upon row, not yet half-full in the moonlight. The bonfire was assembled and ready for lighting on the island, white-clad priests making final preparation in the dark.

She stood off from the other riders, hoping to avoid her ruse being discovered, but one black-bearded rider, in yellow tunic with a red silk bandana about his neck, quoit in his hand, came up to her. "I recognize you. You are with the foreign guests of the *Shahanshah,* the woman they call Hina."

Hina took a deep breath to conceal her discomfort. "I am," she said simply.

"A fine horse, too. I will enjoy beating you both today." He smiled in the moonlight, tapping the palm of his left hand with the tip of his quoit.

"We shall see."

He left to rejoin his comrades, and Hina let out a silent sigh.

She knew the rules. Each lap was about a quarter mile, and there would be six laps. On the island by the finish line were six flagpoles, and as each lap was completed by the lead horse, a flag would be raised: red, yellow, green, blue, purple and white. The winning horse would break into a walk at the finish, and complete a circuit to cool down, the winner taking the cheers of the crowd, then stop before the king to take his – her! – award from the king.

The stands suddenly began to fill, and the royal entourage filed in to take their seats in the darkness just before dawn. There was a blare of trumpets, and announcers on the royal end of the island called the horsemen to attention before the king. Hina mounted, her mouth suddenly dry. She took a swig of water from the leather sack slung around her shoulder. Devil was stepping nervously, not sure what was going on, but knowing that, with Hina, it was sure to be fun.

The king stood and addressed the crowd, callers repeating his words to carry throughout the stadium is a disconcerting kind of echo. "My people, this morning we celebrate our most holy of days, *Nowruz,* the Day of New Light and renewal, the beginning of a new year, when the forces of Light and Dark are in balance. May Ahura Mazda, the God of Wisdom and Light, shine upon us, and drive the forces of darkness into the shadows!" With that, the priests began lighting the fire in the traditional way, with flint and steel, showering sparks into tinder laced with naphtha. A dozen points of light appeared around the stack of wood, which then erupted with a roar, its blaze casting flickering shadows around the stadium. Acolytes came up to the fire with buckets of candles, lighting one, then hopped down off the island to run up to the stadium, distributing candles to the spectators to light from theirs. An acolyte handed Hina and each of the riders a candle lit from the sacred fire, and they began a slow parade around the track. By the time they completed the circuit and returned to the chalk-marked starting line on the royal end, the stadium was ablaze with lights from the fire and the candles. They stood silently, waiting, as the first sliver of sun rose over the horizon. When the sun was high enough over the eastern wall to chase the shadows from the length of the track, a trumpet blew. The announcer called out, "Riders, prepare!".

That return leg will be difficult, with the morning sun full in my eyes. Watch for collisions there. Referees led the horses to their starting positions and cleared the track. After a tense minute, the trumpet blew again and the horses were off in a cloud of dust and clods.

Let them wear their horses out. I will stay in the backfield, move up to midfield after three laps, and take the lead in the last two laps. She galloped comfortably along, Devil holding easily but reluctantly with perhaps ten horsemen in front. The horsemen rounded the far turn into blazing sunlight, and something happened in the crowded pack in front of her, some sort of a collision, horses down in jumbles of legs and riders and dust, screams of pain, braying from the animals, as the thundering riders behind sought to avoid disaster themselves. As Hina roared by, she noted one bloody rider lying still. She kept the pace, but with just seven ahead now as she rounded the royal turn, the red flag snapping in the morning breeze to mark the end of the first lap. The rider in the yellow tunic was in the lead, his red bandana streaming behind him.

A rider from behind came alongside, challenging her, but she urged Devil on and he quickly opened the gap, moving up to fifth. As they rounded the far turn of the second lap, Hina saw someone challenge Red Bandana for first. Red Bandana shouldered the challenger's horse roughly, and Hina watched in horror as he struck it with his quoit to further confuse it. The horse stumbled and the challenger went down, taking down the rider behind him as well. Hina was determined to beat that arrogant poff. But not yet. Let him clear the field for her. She was third rounding the royal turn, and fought off another challenger. Once again, Red Bandana attempted to throw another challenger; with the field less crowded, the man evaded him, but did not take the lead, losing his momentum and falling behind Hina instead.

Hina rode well behind Red Bandana by a full length for the next several laps. Red Bandana's horse was good, but Devil was pacing him easily with plenty in reserve. The rest of the field had fallen behind them by several lengths when she passed the royal turn, the purple flag streaming. She would make her final play on the next and final lap, keeping clear of Red Bandana's quoit.

The white flag flew up and she was aware of the roar of the crowd as though from a great distance, but she was concentrating on just the horse in front of her. She stood in the stirrups and put her face close to his neck, the hairs of his mane full in her face. "Go, Devil, let it all out, you go, boy!"

Devil responded with the surge of speed that he had held in reserve, his head by the black lead horse's sweat-streaked rump when Red Bandana turned to see his challenger. He quoited his mare to a surge that Devil easily matched and exceeded, pulling abreast of him. Hina could see the man's sneer out of the corner of her eye, and the tell-tale flick of the reins betraying his intent to turn into her. She kept the distance open, evading him as they rounded the last turn. He awkwardly jerked his horse to the right to close the distance again, this time the quoit landing on Hina's thigh with a stinging but ineffective slap. Devil pulled ahead as Red Bandana's horse lost momentum after failing to unmount Hina. He was out of range now, falling behind, as Hina thundered across the finish line two full lengths ahead of him, to the tumultuous roar of the crowd. Hina let Devil continue his run, slowing gradually, completing his victory lap at the royal turn in a prancing walk, his head tossing. "Good boy, Devil, good boy! I knew you were the best horse."

She stopped in front of the king, and after a blare of trumpets to still the crowd, the announcer called out the winner as Hina riding Falcon. *Well, at least he remembered my name, if not Devil's.* Aides came out to give her a silver medallion on a blue silk ribbon, inscribed with a horse and the inscrutable Aramaic script of the Parthians. She put it on her neck, slapped Devil's sweat-drenched neck, and continued another slow walk around the track, acknowledging the screaming crowd. *Yes Galosga, different people have different rules. But Red Bandana is going to learn my rules.*

Back at the royal turn, she dismounted, and the other riders came up to congratulate her, except for Red Bandana who hung back, an angry look darkening his face. She took their accolades politely, but then quietly walked up to the scowling Red Bandana. She said nothing but grabbed the quoit from his surprised, unresisting hand and slapped him across the face with it, raising an angry red weal. She followed that with a powerful right, full in his face, catching him on the nose with a crunch and knocking him back to the ground. She held up his quoit and snapped it in two, flinging the pieces to him. The other riders cheered, as did the stadium, knowing full well how much he deserved that beating, taking place in full view of the royal pavilion.

"If I ever see you quoit another man's horse, I will quoit your ass to a bloody mess. Do you understand me?" She said in an even voice, letting it rise for the first time in the morning to a feminine pitch. The others might as well know that he had just been beaten by a woman.

Red Bandana stirred angrily, as if to rise and continue the fight.

"Do you want to stand, so I can knock you down again?" she asked, her hands on her hips, green eyes flashing.

Red Bandana chose to stay down, putting his hand to his bleeding nose. "I will see you in hell, commoner bitch. I am Farnavantes, the King's nephew."

Not too far off, one of the injured horses whinnied, its foreleg bent at a horrible angle, as attendants proceeded to slit its throat and stain the dirt with its blood. Next to the horse lay two still bodies, covered in bloody white cloths.

"He also saw you kill that horse, and two people, in your sorry attempt to win," she said, spitting out the words. *Well, I guess I will see what their rules are for this.* She led Devil off to the stalls inside the island, watered him, groomed him, then went up to join her group in the royal pavilion, for whatever was to come.

CHAPTER 43:

A PLAN FOR REVENGE

Ecbatana, April 114AD

If Farnavantes expected the King to avenge the injustice he had suffered at the hands of Hina, he was severely rebuffed. In the privacy of the King's family quarters, his father, the King's brother-in-law, expressed his outrage at a common barbarian striking a member of the royal family before the entire city, a family member who might someday be their next king. He demanded that she be put to death and her party expelled from the palace.

The King's response was brutally direct and to the point. "If you had spent your time raising your son to be a man, he would not have been beaten so badly and so easily by a woman, after cheating and injuring and killing others to win a race. I assure you, brother of my wife, that I will not put one of my guests to death for performing an act of simple justice. However, I will put this lout of yours to death, if he entertains any thought of someday becoming *Shahanshah*." Farnavantes, standing beside his father in the King's family quarters, went pale with fear, for King Vologases had not risen to his position by idle threats.

The king peremptorily dismissed them.

Farnavantes spent the next several weeks, as was his usual pastime, clad in lower class clothes, drinking and whoring with his companions among the common stews in the outer ring of the city. Farnavantes was sulking and bitter. His companions, fellow aristocrats likewise given to a soft lifestyle, sympathized with him, but were rapidly growing tired of his unending complaints.

"You know what the king told me, in front of my father? That he would put me to death!" He complained loudly, bring his mug of barley beer down on a table with a thud, spilling half of it. "I would do anything to get back at that barbarian bitch, but she's under his protection, her and her band of Hanaeans!" He swallowed the remnants of his beer and loudly demanded another.

His noisy complaint caught the ears of a stranger, clad in the desert garb of western Parthia. The man waited until, one by one, the man's friends took their leave, leaving Farnavantes alone.

"Your friends seem to have left. May I join you and get you another beer?"

"Sure, my friends are worthless. You from the west?" Farnavantes' voice was slurred from too many beers already. He forgot to affect the lower-class accent he had been using, reverting to the precise speech of the aristocracy.

"Ctesiphon, by the Tigris. I am here to do some trading. My name is Bozan."

"Farnavantes. What do you trade?"

"Many things. Often just information. Yourself?"

"Mostly this. Drink, get rowdy, fuck whores. And race horses."

"If I may be so rude as to ask, what did a commoner like you do to attract the attention of King Vologases? You said he personally threatened you?"

Farnavantes exploded in drunken anger. "I am not a fuckin' comm'ner!" he yelled, attracting the attention of too many of the clientele. "I am his fuckin' nephew! An' yes he did, right in the palace in front of me and my father."

"So, you are not what you seem?" asked Bozan softly, trying to quiet the young man before he attracted attention of the worst sort.

Farnavantes tugged at his rough and tattered dark wool tunic. "No, I am not. But sometimes I am more comfortable here than in the palace. Commoners know how to live."

"Yes, indeed they often do. So, what happened?"

Farnavantes related the story of the race, though in his version he was simply defending himself against other horsemen charging him. "I was sorry some got killed, and others hurt, but horseracing is a dangerous sport. Anyway, she publicly beat me up after the race." He took a sip of beer, slopping some on his beard.

"She? A woman beat you up?"

"Not just any woman. As big as a man and as strong. If I didn't know her from the palace, I would have thought she was a man, the other riders and even the checker thought she was."

"A barbarian living in the palace? With her friends?"

"King's protection. Apparently, the usurper king in Ctesiphon wants them for some reason."

"Well, from Ctesiphon's point of view, King Vologases is the usurper, but no matter. People who dabble in royal politics often lose their heads. Tell me about her and her friends." *This is getting interesting indeed. Someone in the palace with access to the one named Marcus, someone with a grievance against Vologases.*

"Like I said, she is tall and strong, red hair and green eyes. Actually, kind of pretty when she wants to be. Her husband is as big as she is, bronze skin, pock-marked, no beard. Her kids, and two Hanaeans, with slanted eyes. Odd, one has a Latin name, Marcus, the other is his wife, a woman, kind of quiet."

Bozan considered his options. He could make his play now, or wait until he had more confidence in Farnavantes. He shrewdly assessed that Farnavantes was what he seemed to be, not a palace agent. He decided to go for it.

"I have some connections in Ctesiphon. The one called Marcus is the one that King Osroës is interested in. There could be a handsome reward for whoever delivers him, and a place with some respect in the western palace, something you don't have here."

"They can't go past the outer gate. As much as they are guests, they are also prisoners." Farnavantes' head was beginning to droop. Soon he would be asleep, snoring on the beer-drenched table, to be dragged out with the other drunks to sleep it off on the streets in their own vomit. He wasn't going to remember much of anything tomorrow. Bozan pulled a wax tablet from his pocket, scrawled a note on it, "Meet me here tomorrow night about dinner time. Here at the Oxtail Inn." He put it in Farnavantes' pocket to make sure it got there.

CHAPTER 44:

A WALK IN THE GARDEN

Ecbatana, April 114AD

Marcus enjoyed his early morning walks in the garden outside the palace on the inner ring of the city. It was exquisitely tended, with dozens of kinds of flowers, some he knew, most he did not, scenting the air with their beautiful blossoms. There was a variety of trees, both fruit and simple decorative types, evergreens trimmed into exotic shapes. Bees hummed, birds sang ... it was a marvelous morning.

Marcus had left Mei to sleep in, as she had not felt well this morning. He wandered from plant to plant, marveling at the care taken of them by the gardeners. Off in the distance, four gardeners in dark tunics and black trousers hoed, pruned, weeded, and watered, the never-ending work to keep this garden beautiful, fit for a king as it were. Marcus went over to chat with them, as he knew most of them, but these were strangers. "Good morning," he said.

They responded courteously, but not in a way that encouraged further discussion. Marcus watched them work for a while, then spoke up again. "You are new here, aren't you?" He hoped his colloquial Aramaic might spark conversation. After all, commoners did not speak with royalty, and to them, he was royalty.

One grunted, not looking up from his hoeing. "Yes," was all he said.

Odd, the regular gardeners had all been quite friendly, once they knew I took an interest in what they did. Marcus stood by for a while, feeling uncomfortable, then turned away to let them go about their work.

Something hit the back of his head with incredible force. Marcus saw a huge flash in his head, then blackness.

Mei stretched and yawned. Light was streaming through the window, a breeze ruffling the sheer white curtain. It was uncharacteristically late for her to be rising, but a headache, now gone, had caused her to skip her morning walk with Marcus. She reached for him, finding nothing. Feeling very indolent, she closed her eyes and was soon again sound asleep.

An hour later, she awoke again, with still no sign of Marcus. Concerned, she cast off the covers, hurriedly dressed, and went out in the garden. Marcus was not there.

She found just two gardeners, not the four men she knew from their morning walks. Her inquiries, however, got little response. After what seemed to her to be feigned lack of understanding, they finally denied having seen him, and went back to work.

Concerned, she sought out Hina. "Marcus went out to the garden this morning, but he is not back, and none of the gardeners have seen him. Hina, I am worried," she said.

"Why don't we see Zacharias? That man seems to know everything that goes on here," suggested Hina. "You take charge and ask the questions, he is your husband." Mei truly envied Hina's wild self-confidence, and she had tried hard to be more like her. It felt good to be making the decisions, though they were as yet small ones.

They came to Zacharias' office and Mei knocked. Zacharias, a tall thin man with a white beard still showing threads of black, a large nose and long curly white hair under a skullcap, welcomed them in. "Please, ladies, come in, be seated. What can I do for you this morning?"

Mei led the way in and they took seats. "My husband Marcus is missing this morning. He went out to the garden a bit after daybreak and has not come back."

"It is a big garden, Mei, perhaps he found something of interest out there. Or found a bench to take a nap. I am sure he will be back by lunch."

"I went out to look for him and couldn't find him. The gardeners haven't seen him."

"Perhaps the library. He is trying hard to learn to read Parthian and Aramaic."

"Perhaps. But I am concerned that something has happened to him. Something, someone from Ctesiphon."

"Rest assured, ladies, this palace is impenetrable. He will be back by lunch. If you don't mind, I must read some more boring palace business. Let me know if he is not back by then." He turned to the scrolls on his desk, intending them to take the hint.

Discouraged, Mei took his hint and left. They were heading down the corridor, having not yet said a word to each other, when the head gardener brushed by them. He burst into Zacharias' office and bellowed in outrage. "I gave my gardeners a few hours off this morning. When they came in, their tools were scattered about, some sloppy make-work done. It ruined some carefully tended grass, done by strangers that came in their stead and then left! What the hell is going on, sir?" he demanded.

Mei grimaced, not waiting to hear Zacharias' response. "Let's get the others," she said.

CHAPTER 45:

THE ROAD TO CTESIPHON

Ecbatana to Ctesiphon, April 114AD

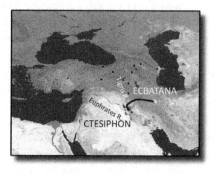

Marcus awoke slowly, swimming upward from blackness to semi-consciousness, then slipping back to blackness, to again repeat the struggle to consciousness, until finally he remained awake. He immediately regretted that effort, as his head flashed with a horrible throbbing pain that seemed to reverberate with each heartbeat. His mouth was dry, bound by some sort of gag. His hands and feet were tied, and any effort to move caused a rough rope around his throat to tighten, restricting his breathing, so struggling was out of the question. He opened his eyes but saw only veiled light coming in through the fabric of a sack that contained him. He smelled the sweet scent of hay, mixed with the acrid smell of the hemp sack. He wondered what it had contained before holding him.

He was lying on what appeared to be the rough bed of a wagon, swaying bumpily along a road. His left arm under him was numb, but he could not shift his weight to relieve it due to the strictures around his throat. He lay still and listened.

Two people were talking up front on the wagon. Parthian, but not saying much of anything about him, or why they had absconded with him, or where they were taking him. Marcus knew where they were taking him, to Ctesiphon and King Osroës, but why did the King feel he was so important?

With nothing else to do, he thought. *This had something to do with Mithridates. Mithridates knows me but why would he think me so important? The last Mithridates knew of me was ten years ago, when Marcia and I, and our Roman companions, escaped from jail in the Han palace, outlaws with a price on our heads. And I was not important in the court before that, just another eunuch, a translator for the Romans. And yet Mithridates knew I was coming. Marcus Lucius Quintus, also known as Si Nuo.*

The answer that had evaded him for a year suddenly flashed in his head. *The letters! The letters I exchanged with Marcia over the years, the letters that had stopped coming some years ago, my last letter... telling her I was coming west! Mithridates had been reading those letters, it was the only way he could have known what he knew, but why?*

Marcus listened for a while, then went back to sleep, gaining respite from the throbbing headache. He awoke from time to time, but by now, his mouth was fiercely dry from the gag. Unable to move or swallow, his head hammering, sleep on the lurching wagon floor was the only option.

The sudden cessation of movement awakened him. For a moment, he feared he had gone blind, for he could see nothing but blackness. Then the flickering light of a torch penetrated the hemp sack. The men, apparently just two, were exchanging words while getting the animals out of the traces, fed and watered. Were they going to leave him, tied up like so much garbage? Marcus' stomach reminded him that he had not eaten since last night, but that was followed by a wave of nausea.

"Well, let's see how our passenger is doing," said one. "I poked him a few times during the day to make sure he was alive." There was the rustling sound of hay being moved, then the sack was lifted off him. Hands worked the gag's knot until it mercifully left his mouth.

"We're going to untie you. You won't be going anywhere until the circulation gets back," said the man with a full black beard and blue eyes. The knots fell away from his wrists and ankles, the choke rope slipping off his chaffed neck. "We want to get you where you are going alive. We don't get paid if you are dead."

The other one, with wispy brown hairs scattered here and there on his cheeks, poured some water into Marcus' parched mouth. "Easy, now, you don't want to puke it all back up. We'll give you some more in a bit."

The circulation returned to Marcus' arms and legs with vengeance, thousands of pins and needles tingling in agony. The two men ignored his discomfort but offered him some more water.

"We're going to make a deal with you. Marcus, is that your name?" said the black-bearded man

Marcus nodded, trying to hold the leather water bag to his mouth with numb hands.

"Pretty uncomfortable riding like that. And when we get down out of these mountains to the desert, it will be blazing hot. You'll die back there, and then we don't get paid. So, if you behave yourself, and don't scream at passersby and try to run off, you can ride in the back, untied. Deal?"

Marcus nodded.

"I am Boss, and this is Horse with the waterbag. We are going to be traveling together for a while, so you might as well have names to call us.

Let's take a look at your noggin, one of those gardeners whacked you a good one." Horse held the torch while the Boss inspected the wound, pouring a little water on the tangled mass of black hair and crusty dried blood. "Nice goose egg there, Marcus. Keep that rag on it for a while. Want something to eat?"

Marcus considered the thought of food. Finally, he croaked, "A little bread."

They gave him some more water and a piece of bread, then tossed him a laborer's long linen shirt and trousers, appropriately soiled and long unwashed. "That'll fit in better than the silks you're wearing. Change and we'll wrap them up for you, give them back to you when we get where you are going."

"Ctesiphon," rasped Marcus.

"Maybe," said Boss. "Or maybe not."

The pins and needles left his arms and legs after half an hour, but Marcus had no desire to sit around the campfire and exchange chit-chat with his too-courteous captors. They gave him a blanket and he rolled himself up in it, falling quickly asleep.

The following morning, they were on the road before daybreak, the two mules setting a steady pace. Enough stars showed for Marcus to determine they were heading west, maybe southwest. Marcus swayed to the wagon's rhythm in the bed, sitting on the hay, rather than under it as before. The wagon was making good time, the men stopping only to water the horses and relieve themselves, following the well-worn rutted road through a green valley alongside a rushing mountain river through the arid mountains they called Zagros. They continued until after dark, then made camp outside a small town they called Sahneh. The men stayed up but Marcus again retired early, the better to follow their unsuspecting conversations.

Shortly after midnight, with the men still awake, talking and drinking, a rider came up to them and dismounted, slipping the saddle and baggage from his horse.

"About time you caught up with us, Farnavantes. We thought you was going to keep us up all night."

CHAPTER 46:

THE FOLLOWERS

Ecbatana to Ctesiphon, April 114AD

Mei assembled Nathaniel, Hina, and Galosga in her room in the palace. Marasa and Andana, with Adhela toddling in tow, entered unbidden to participate in the decisions.

"We must leave at once," Mei said, her heart pounding. Never before having been a decisive woman, it seemed that all of the events of the past year had been to prepare her for this moment. She accepted the challenge.

There was a moment of silence, then Hina spoke up. "We are best to wait until morning. There will be only a few hours before sunset, and they are perhaps a thirty or more miles ahead of us. They will likely camp early tonight to rest their horses, so we lose a day, but not many more miles. And if we wait till morning, it gives us a few hours more for Marcus to show up, if in fact he is still in the city."

"How are we going to find them?" asked Mei, scanning the group.

"The gardeners you met, the strangers... what did they look like?" asked Hina.

Mei closed her eyes, trying to recollect the morning meeting. "A tall one, with a black beard, bad teeth. A short one, brown beard... or was it black, too? And two more, scruffy ones, I didn't get a good look at them"

Nathaniel chuckled. "That describes half the men here in Ecbatana. Would you recognize them you saw them again?"

"I don't know. Everyone here, all the men, they all look alike."

"I don't think we are going to identify them. We could ride right past them, and unless Marcus is in plain sight, we would never know.

Nathaniel cleared his throat. "We are not likely to find him on the road. Our best plan is to take advantage of what we know, where they are going, to Ctesiphon, and arrive there before they do."

Hina nodded. "There are many travelers on that road, a major highway, and if we stop every traveler to search for Marcus, we will be mistaken for highwaymen and make ourselves very conspicuous, To Ctesiphon, Mei, I agree."

Galosga added his opinion. "He knows some of our signals, Hina, he learned them from me on the way here. We can make those signals as we pass travelers or caravans. If he hears them, and can answer, he will."

"Nathaniel, you know the palace and the city. Can we get out the gate?"

"I think we are here on our honor not to leave. The gate guards, I don't think they will recognize us."

"And when we get to Ctesiphon?"

Nathaniel cleared his throat, fearing they might think he had betrayed them with the next revelation, but it had to be said. "I have not shared this with you before, but I know Mithridates, the man seeking Marcus. Quite well. In fact, I am in his pay, though I left for the distant east long before he began seeking Marcus, for whatever reason that may be. And Marcus knows him. I owe Mithridates a report, so yes, I can get into the palace, though it is not likely that I can get you in."

Mei's eyes flashed in her round face. "Did you betray my husband?" she spat out, distrust and anger in her voice.

"I had many opportunities to do so. But I warned you instead, so no, Mei, I did not, and I would not. Trust me."

Galosga, standing by Hina's side, spoke up. "We must prepare to travel very light tomorrow, take what you need for a week of travel, just one change of clothes, *naan* bread and water. Leave everything else behind. Oh, yes, and take weapons, but don't display them going through the gate tomorrow. Hide them in your bedrolls."

Marasa broke the youngsters' silence. "We will be riding with you. Fighting with you, if that comes." Andanyu nodded in agreement with her.

Galosga smiled. "Yes, you are, you are both of age for that. Make us proud, but don't take foolish chances. And we will all takes turns with Adhela."

"Thank you," said Mei. "We should leave at first light, meet in the stables. And make no noise or talk about what we are doing. This palace has ears."

The following morning, the outermost gates opened at sunrise, and as Nathaniel had forecast, there was no impediment to their departure. They simply trotted out the gate, amidst the mass of people leaving the city on foot, on horseback or by wagon.

And there were people on the road. Caravans, with hundreds of animals and people, plodding slowly. Small groups of five or six riders, clustered together, some with armed escorts. Single wagons, single riders, some on foot.

Mei's group could not resist scrutinizing the travelers, but elicited only resentful glares, guards putting hands on swords, family wagons fearfully clutching their children against the wild nomads eyeing them closely. Off in the distance, Galosga made the harsh call of the steppe eagle, but got no response.

The next morning, they rode hard, leaving travelers in the dust, past the monumental inscriptions of past glories on Mount Behistun, down through to the foothills of the Zagros Mountains, sometimes through fertile, well-watered farmland, sometimes arid bush country, picking up the Diyalah river, following its winding route through towns and cities of many names, to the Tigris.

After a week of hard riding in the hot dry days and cool nights, they pulled up by the brilliant white walls of Ctesiphon, and its sister city of Seleucia, on the opposite bank of the Tigris, the road lined with palm trees.

CHAPTER 47:

AN OFFER DECLINED

Melitene, April 114AD

The fort was a bustle of preparations, animals and wagons being loaded, inventories checked, amid curses and commands of soldiers. Security was high, but the lank Jewish merchant always seemed to know the right passwords to enter the fort. Samuel wondered if the man's true business might be that of a spy; he certainly was an embezzler. He had long regretted having employed Mannaseh as his money conduit to his friend Yakov in Petra. At first it seemed simple, a friend from his wild youth as a bandit and would-be rebel in Galilee, now risen to respectability as a merchant, as Samuel had risen as a soldier of Rome. But each meeting left Samuel feeling used toward some end.

Fortunately, this was to be their last transaction, as they would be soon on the march north. The hawk-faced Jew stood attentively at the door, awaiting entrance. "Comest thou in," said Samuel curtly in Aramaic, without rising. A worn leather pouch of thirty silver *denarii* sat on his desk; Samuel's soldiers had been generous this time, and he knew from correspondence with Yakov that the orphanage would be lucky to see twenty-five of the coins.

Mannaseh entered, smiling broadly behind his scraggly salt-and-pepper beard, and took a seat, uninvited. And uninvited, picked up the pouch, weighing its contents. "Thou hast done well, Shmuel."

"Thou hast done well entering the fort unescorted," said Samuel without smiling, taking the pouch from Mannaseh's hand.

"Thy passwords are well-known in Melitene. Thy security fools no one except thyselves. Art thy soldiers preparing to depart?"

"A summer training exercise, that is all. But we will be out for a while, I shall have no further need of thy services for a while." He handed the pouch back to Mannaseh. "Seest thou that more reaches its destination than the last time. Twenty percent is far higher than the fee we agreed upon."

"Fees vary with the risks, Shmuel," said Manasseh, his smile never fading. "But I shall do my best. War is coming and the risks are great."

"So some say."

"You know the story of Cyrus the Great, who returned our people to the Promised Land and rebuilt the Temple."

"Of course."

"We, you and I, would be wise to be on the winning side of what is to come. There will be a Jewish army that will need someone to lead it."

"Good luck, I hope you find someone capable."

"I think I have." Mannaseh's smile vanished like a lamp blown out, and he fixed Samuel with an intense gaze. "Someone who knows all the ways of Roman fighting."

Samuel was torn by both anger and fear, anger that this conniving rat was inviting him to treason, to betray the trust and responsibility that had been placed on him, fear that the bastard might try to blackmail him into his plans if he refused. He snatched the pouch back. "On second thought, we shall not need thy services. Thou may take thy leave and depart."

"May the God of Abraham and Isaac smile upon thee, Shmuel bin Eliazar. Thou art still of the Chosen People."

"*Exite!* Get out!" Samuel said in Latin, pointing to the door, his face grim. "Or I will have you escorted out and banned from the fort!"

CHAPTER 48:

THE WAR BEGINS

Melitene, April 114AD

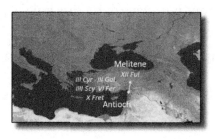

Gaius Lucullus, his hands braced on the fort's parapet, stared off in the distance toward the low mountains in the southwest. Even ten miles away, fifty thousand men and their animals raise a huge cloud of dust. If he held his breath, he thought he could almost hear them, a very distant rumble or buzz that rose and fell, but never died away. In about two hours, perhaps by the middle of the afternoon, he judged, they would arrive.

Gaius walked over to the northern parapet to observe his engineers. There, they had laid out five camps in neat rows on the other side of the road from the fort, the road over which they would soon be arriving. The ditches around each camp had been dug, the earthen walls erected, streets laid out, awaiting the arrival of the five legions with their tents and palisades. Behind the Roman army camps, several more acres had been cleared to accommodate the auxiliary forces. They would lay out their own camps, each in their own styles.

Secundus and his centurion Samuel, were observing the work on the far end of the northern wall. Gaius joined them, a rare personal moment with his son and junior tribune, eliciting salutes from the two surprised soldiers.

"At ease, stand easy, men. I was just observing our engineers. They have done a fine job preparing camps for our visitors."

"Aye, they have, sir," answered Samuel. "And I am hoping, paying attention to the sanitation. That is hell of a lot of men coming."

"Fifty thousand, plus almost as many animals. I gave them specific directions to that," said Gaius with a smile. "We don't need the whole lot, them and us, down with the shits because of sloppy latrines, now do we?"

"Certainly not, sir," answered Secundus. "And where will the *Princeps* be staying?"

"Well, to be honest, wherever he wants to stay. I made arrangements for quarters for him in the praetorium, but if he holds to form, he will be staying in the field with one of the legions. Well, Tribune Secundus, and Samuel, I must take your leave. I have some business to attend to before lunch. Would you be so kind as to inform all the other tribunes that I would like them formed up in about two hours on the road below, to greet the *Princeps* when he arrives with his legions? With their senior centurions."

Secundus saluted smartly, hand across his chest. "Aye, sir! Will do!"

Two hours later, the legionary officers formed up in the pleasant spring afternoon, Gaius Lucullus and his staff at their head. The faint murmur of men on the move had long since ceased being faint, the repetitive pounding of thousands of pairs of feet marching in rhythm, multiple competing marching songs, each different in words but with the same rhythm, the rattling of gear like hundreds of tambourines, punctuated occasionally by a braying trumpet signaling some shift in position. And, at the head of the vast army, strode Trajan, his staff personnel arrayed behind him, all in military field gear, helmeted in the heat, plain steel and bronze and leather.

As Trajan approached within thirty feet of the waiting officers of the Twelfth Thunderbolt, he raised his right hand, a circular horn behind him blew the staccato halt command, echoed back down the line from legion to legion, each repeating the call. Like a single body, fifty thousand men came to halt within just a handful of paces.

Gaius Lucullus saluted the *Princeps*. Then from his tribunes behind him, and from the men of the Twelfth lining the parapet above them, came the cry "*Ave Imperator!* Hail Emperor!" Repeated over and over, the cry of five thousand throats thundered across the valley in which the fort was situated, generating echoes from the surrounding hills which added to the sound.

Trajan accepted the accolade, then extended his hands palms down, lowering them to indicate that the tumult should end. When the last cheering soldier's voice fell silent, Trajan loosened the red *focale* rag around his neck that obviously had done its job quite well, stained dark with sweat. Trajan used it wipe the beaded perspiration from his forehead. He was taut and well-muscled. He smiled at Gaius. "*Legatus* Lucullus, thank you for such an enthusiastic welcome from the Thunderbolt. And thank you for the camps you set up for us. That will be a welcome break for the men this afternoon."

"You are most welcome, Your Excellency. We have requisitioned more provisions, should you be running low."

"That, too, will be most appreciated. I will be staying with the Sixth Ironclad's commander tonight. I don't want to keep our men waiting in the sun after a brisk twenty-mile march, so we'll be off to pitch our tents. Would you be so kind as to join us about sunset for our evening meal? And your tribunes are welcome as well. The Ironclad's centurions would like to host your centurions in their mess, as well."

"We shall see you there, Your Excellency!" Gaius gave a barked command and as one, the men behind him wheeled out of the way of the legion facing them, clearing the path to the legions' prepared encampments.

It took over an hour for all the men, horses and supply wagons to pass.

Late in the afternoon, the sun still well above the horizon, Gaius approached the command tent of the Sixth Ironclad, accompanied by Secundus and four other off-duty tribunes. Tiberius Maximus, commanding the *X Fretensis* Tenth Straits legion, and some of the other legion commanders were awaiting them outside the tent, accompanied by their own small entourages.

"*Ave*, Tiberius, it is good to see you again," hailed Gaius.

"And you, Gaius. We were planning on entering together. We are waiting for the commander of the Third Gallic, so he is not embarrassed to be the latecomer at the *Princeps'* dinner."

"Let me introduce my tribunes. This is my most junior, Gaius Secundus Lucullus … and my son. He goes by Secundus only, to avoid confusion."

"Your son? I am honored," said Tiberius, extending his hand.

"It is I who am honored, sir," said Secundus, accepting the firm grip.

"I served under Tiberius' brother Julius fifteen years back, when he was commanding the Thunderbolt," said Gaius to his son.

The introduction of the other tribunes was interrupted by the arrival of the commander of the Third Gallic legion. Tiberius took charge of the group. "Looks like we have our quorum. Shall we go in, gentlemen?" He led the group to the tent entrance, guarded by two soldiers at rest with their lances canted. They snapped erect, eyes front, saluted, and the party entered. Trajan was seated at a long table with Bruttius Praesens, the commander of the Ironclad, Aulus Galba in military gear, and several other officers and toga-clad officials. The commanders marched in unison to the table and saluted. "*Ave, Imperator,*" they hailed him as their commander-in-chief.

"At ease, at ease, gentlemen, and be seated, please."

Gaius took a seat opposite his old friend Aulus. "It has indeed been a long time, Aulus. I haven't seen you since the end of the Dacian war a few years ago. What, have you accepted a commission now so late in life?"

Aulus smiled. He was wearing a musculated leather corselet, which set off his trim figure well. "I chose to march with Trajan's company from Antioch, and togas are not good marching gear."

"You haven't walked like that since we were getting out of the land of the Han! That is two hundred and fifty miles at least."

"I came back from that trip feeling better than I ever had in my life, and I continue to live like that, as best I can. Most of the other civilians chose to ride in wagons with the baggage train. I enjoyed the marching. But it is hard to keep up with Trajan and the troops. They set a good pace."

Gaius smiled. "I remember that first day, your feet were blistered on the first ten miles."

"I see your son is in your legion," said Aulus, turning his attention to Secundus.

"Pleased to see you again, Aulus Aemilius," said Secundus.

The pleasantries were interrupted by soldiers bringing jugs of wine. When these were distributed, Trajan stood up to address the group. "Gentlemen, I have here a letter, which is relevant to why we are all gathered together. It is from the would-be king of Armenia, the pretender Parthamasiris." He enrolled a scroll to read aloud:

"To Marcus Ulpius Trajan, King of all the Romans, greetings.

I take pleasure to greet you as an equal, and to assure you that our long-standing treaty between our two kingdoms over the rulership of Armenia remains intact and honored by my father, Osroës, King of all Parthian kings. As you well know, the treaty does not forbid us to remove a king should we become dissatisfied with him. We have done so, and my father has honored me by naming me to be the successor to Axidares. I call on you to honor this treaty by presenting to me the Armenian diadem, on my arrival in your presence.

I know you do not seek war with my father over this trivial matter. I look forward to your prompt response.

Parthamasiris,
King of all Armenia.
By the will of Osroës, King of all Parthian kings."

Trajan fell silent, his cold blue eyes roaming from face to silent face, each shocked by the peremptory tone of the letter. He spoke in a voice initially soft, almost a whisper. "Our young pretender does not seem to know that Rome has no king." He ended with a thunderous outburst. "And that the would-be King of Armenia, who is not yet acknowledged with the diadem, is in no ways equal to the *Princeps*, who represents not himself, but the Senate and People of Rome!"

"This letter deserves an appropriate response." Trajan ripped the scroll in two. He turned to a parchment map on the tent wall behind the table. "That response will be to obtain the surrender of the nearest Armenian city, Arsamosata, a hundred miles east of here. Gaius Aetius, I appreciate the hospitality you have shown in setting up our fine encampments, but I fear we won't be staying long. We will decamp at first light for Arsamosata and our first victory."

CHAPTER 49:

THE PALACE AT CTESIPHON

Ctesiphon, April 114AD

Nathaniel had splurged, spending almost all the last of the generous silver cash advance given him three years before by Mithridates. No matter, he would be paid the remainder, or be put to death, probably slowly, by Mithridates' order. Either way, money was not to be a long-term problem. He had put Mei, Hina and the Xiongnu up in a nice inn by the side of a lake lined with palm trees and bought them and himself some fine clothes. In particular, his was a green-silk gown, filigreed with trees, flowers and birds, with white cuffs and a maroon belt, attire appropriate to wear for a meeting with the king's brother. He announced that he himself would be staying at another inn nearby, so he would not appear too closely connected with Marcus' traveling companions. "We must have no contact," he said. "Mithridates has eyes and ears everywhere."

"Then how are we to communicate?" asked Mei.

Marasa spoke up, offering a solution. "Andanyu and I can be your go-betweens. We speak Sogdian well enough to get by, and no one notices people our age. We are invisible."

"That sounds like a good solution. Hina, do you agree?"

"They are of age. That is their choice, and a good one."

Nathaniel went to his own residence with the twins, and prepared to meet Mithridates. He fastened his phylacteries to his arm and head, saying a devout prayer that He Who Must Not be Named would smile on his efforts and protect him from harm. He donned his *kippah* skullcap and wrapped his black and white prayer shawl around himself over the rather extravagant robe, and headed off to the palace at the center of the city, after cautioning the twins to not remain in his residence if he was not back by tomorrow morning.

Ctesiphon was a beautiful, bustling city, as befitted the capital of Eastern Parthia, situated on a bend of the Tigris. The wide streets were lined with palms, and teemed with mules, camels and wagons laden with goods going from one place to another. From the Tigris River, seagulls flew overhead in graceful arcs, squawking noisily. It might be the last day of his life, so it was good that it was a beautiful day. He had in his pocket a three-year-old letter certifying his right to enter the palace, which he presented it to a sleepy-looking young guard with barely a wisp of a beard, in exchange for a bored nod. He entered into the interior coolness. The door opened into a wide marble assembly room, in the center of which a fountain bubbled, sending jets of cooling water high in dancing arcs. People in all kinds of garb, from simple tunics to robes which made his look shabby, moved silently about, or clustered in small groups talking animatedly but quietly. High windows admitted the sunlight, augmented by carefully-placed oil lamps here and there.

Nathaniel knew the way to Mithridates' office, on the third floor, where his brother Osroës held court as king. Or he hoped that's where it still was; he had been gone three years. As luck would have it, he recognized Mithridates' gatekeeper, attending to some scrolls on his desk. Nathaniel walked up and cleared his throat politely. "Kophasates, I believe?"

The man looked up, a very plump man with a black stringy beard, plain white linen robe. "And you are?"

"Nathaniel. I am on business for Mithridates." He handed the gatekeeper the letter of reference.

"Ah, yes, you are the Jew he sent to scout out the East a few years ago. Nathaniel, it says here."

"That is I. I owe Mithridates a report on my mission, at his convenience."

"To be sure, but you may be in for a wait. There's a bit of a war on, and he has his hands full."

"I had heard there were rumbles on the border with Rome."

"More than rumbles. Wait here." Kophasates got up and waddled into the adjoining room, closing the oak-paneled door behind him.

To Nathaniel's surprise, Kophasates emerged in just a few minutes. "He is anxious to meet with you now. What you have may be as important as anything his generals have to say."

Nathaniel raised his eyebrows, pulling a scroll, his journal for the trip, from his pocket.

Inside the room, an alabaster table stood by a window overlooking a veranda and the river in the distance, light pouring in, illuminating the scrolls and maps that covered it. Nathaniel recognized Sanatruces, dressed as a general, and two other generals.

Mithridates greeted him effusively. "Nathaniel, Nathaniel, my good friend. You have come at the perfect time. What you have to tell us is of the utmost importance. You know my son Sanatruces, and this is his son, my grandson, Vagharsh, my two leading young generals, and Ataradates, the senior *spahbod*, commander-in-chief of all my brother's armies. Sit, have some wine, and tell us of your adventures."

Nathaniel sat and began to talk about the highlights of his journey. He honestly couldn't think why any of this was of sufficient importance to interrupt a war-planning conference, but he continued, answering questions as they were asked.

After half an hour, he finished. "And that is my report, Your Excellency, though I regret to say I saw nothing that I thought was of any importance on my trip. Squabbling petty kingdoms, trade rivalries, caravans cheating caravans, minor raids by bandits, equally minor ones against them, nothing of any significance."

"But that is excellent news, Nathaniel. No Han military forces on the move toward the west? In fact, you say they have pulled back from the Tarim Basin?"

"More than twenty years ago. It seemed they had reached the limit of their ability to govern from their capital. They gave that area back to locals to rule, like our client kings, and now the Sogdians seem to be establishing themselves as the powers-that-be north of the Taklamakan. But they are traders, not fighters."

"As I said, excellent news. I did not tell you this when I sent you off, lest I taint your observations with my premonitions, but I feared, based on events in Luoyang when I was there ten years ago, that an alliance might emerge between the Han and the Romans that would squeeze us in the middle quite sorely. What you tell me is that has not yet happened, and now, with war looming between us and Rome, will not happen in time to affect the outcome." He reached into his desk and pulled out a hefty sack of clinking coins. "Ten pounds of silver, fair trade for three years out of your life, Nathaniel. You are welcome to stay and listen in our discussions, you are in my trust."

Nathaniel accepted the sack and nodded, indicating that the presentation should continue.

Sanatruces spoke first. "As I said, Trajan left Antioch early in the month, picking up legions as he went. He has just left Melitene with the Twelfth Thunderbolt, heading for Satala on the Black Sea, where he will pick up the Fifteenth, Twenty-Second and the First legions waiting for him there, giving him a total of nine legions. Also waiting in Satala is a Berber cavalry commander, famous from his war with Dacia, with twenty thousand desert horsemen. And a lot of auxiliaries, but they buzz around the legions like flies. We can't count which are staying to control their local areas, and which are joining in against us. My guess is we are looking at eighty to one hundred thousand men. And I expect something dramatic, very soon."

"Any indications what?" asked Mithridates.

"No, but my gut tells it will be dramatic and soon."

"How did he respond to Parthamasiris' letter?"

"I have a copy, and he couldn't have done a better job of insulting Trajan than if he had tried. Spies tell us Trajan tore it up and threw it in the fire."

There was a commotion by the door and everyone turned to see a tall, well-dressed Parthian, eastern by beard and garb, dragging in three scruffy bound men. Two were lower class by dress and demeanor, cursing profusely at their captor, struggling against their bonds. The third was Oriental in visage, dazed, bruised and bleeding, barely conscious.

"I hate to interrupt you, sir," said the intruder in the high sibilant tones of the Parthian eastern upper class. "I believe you wanted this man, by name Marcus. I found him in the company of these two, who were trying to get him around Ctesiphon to Roman territory."

One of the bound men, the one with a thick black beard, struggled against his bonds, irate, eyes wide with hate. "You lying bag of rotting bones, you hired us to capture him for you! Son of a whore!" The man spit.

Mithridates ignored the outburst, focusing on the aristocratic Parthian. "And you are?"

"Farnavantes, the nephew of King Vologases of Ecbatana."

"I'll cut your balls off, you worthless, lying sack of shit!" Blackbeard shouted, loud enough to be heard down the halls of the royal floor, interrupting the exchange with Mithridates.

Mithridates lost his patience with Blackbeard, fixing him with a cold glare. "You there, stinking commoner! Another outburst like that, and I will have your tongues cut out. Both of you. We may have our differences between the King of Kings and the eastern pretender, but royalty is royalty."

The other man, with a scraggly brown beard, was not near so bold as Blackbeard. His eyes rolled in fright, his forehead beaded with the sweat of fear.

Blackbeard suddenly looked chastened, falling silent. His companion seemed to sigh in relief.

Farnavantes continued coolly, "As I said, these two were aiding this man Marcus to escape. You may wish to consider imprisoning them."

Mithridates pulled on a gold velvet cord, ringing a bell. Two guards came in, swords drawn. "Take these two to the place where they can ponder their sins," indicating Blackbeard and Scruffy, as Nathaniel had mentally catalogued these two unnamed vagabonds.

Nathaniel did not know Farnavantes, had never met him personally, but knew he was the man that Hina had publicly humiliated and emasculated before the crowd in the Ecbatana hippodrome. His stomach went tight with a sense of dread. Would Farnavantes recognize him? Would Marcus react to the sight of him, betraying him with his recognition?

"How do I know this man is Marcus?" asked Mithridates.

"I understand he and his traveling companions were staying with King Vologases at the palace. The King had taken him in, to keep him from your grasp."

"You may be royalty, and nephew to the pretender in the East, but if you call him that title again, I will cut your tongue out, along with those of your commoner friends."

The cool certainty of that sent chills of dread up Nathaniel's spine. He knew Mithridates to be a very ruthless individual, not one to be crossed.

Farnavantes swallowed hard, and said nothing.

"So, this Marcus, if this is who he is, he just walked off and left the palace? To go where?" Mithridates continued.

Nathaniel felt that Mithridates did not appear to trust Farnavantes, perhaps having given more credence to Blackbeard's outbursts than he had let on.

"I don't know, Your Excellency," said Farnavantes. "I presume he was trying to get to the Roman border."

"What happened to him?" asked Mithridates.

"He is from the distant east, and I don't think he traveled well in the desert."

"Get him some water. He would have traveled better if you had given him some along the way."

Farnavantes looked around for a servant, and finding none, decided he should do that menial task himself. A bronze pitcher, beaded with perspiration, sat on a table by the window, arrayed by goblets. He filled one up, and held it to the bound Marcus' parched lips. Marcus drank thirstily, but then his eyes rolled back and he slumped to the floor.

Mithridates pulled the bell cord again and a guard stepped in. "Summon a physician for this man," said Mithridates, indicating Marcus on the floor. "It is very important that this man not die, as we have important questions for him. Then escort this Farnavantes to a room appropriate to his rank. But he is not to leave that room unescorted."

Nathaniel let out a deep breath, grateful to be unrecognized. "Your Excellency, may I be excused? I believe I have nothing further to add, and perhaps should not be privy to your military planning."

"To be sure, Nathaniel. I am sorry for the rude interruption. You may go, and thank you for a long and arduous trip."

CHAPTER 50:

A SECRET WORD

Ctesiphon, April 114AD

Nathaniel hastened back to the inn and led the twins to a stone bench in the park by the lake, well removed from casual listeners. He dispatched them to summon Mei and the rest of the party. As they arrived an hour later, a large fish broke the water with a splash, sending ripples across the smooth blue surface.

Mei led of the conversation. "You have word of Marcus." She fixed him with a steady gaze, her Hanaean eyes intent.

"I do. His kidnappers did not handle him well. He was beaten and not cared for on the trip, but he looks like he will recover. Mithridates has him in custody but has arranged for Marcus to get a doctor's attention."

"Who were his captors?" Mei asked, her body visibly relaxing as she received the good news.

"Here is where it gets interesting." He eyed Hina with a smile. "Your friend Farnavantes brought him in, along with a couple of thugs. I believe he arranged Marcus' kidnapping, then double-crossed his helpers, claiming they were trying to get him past Ctesiphon."

"Charming individual," said Hina, spitting in disgust.

"I don't think Mithridates likes him much better. The thugs, the ones I believe actually did the dirty work for Farnavantes, accused him of lying in front of Mithridates. I think he believed them, though he had them locked up. Farnavantes is confined to his quarters, but detained nonetheless."

"What does this man ... Mithridates? ... want with my man?" asked Mei, trying to get her tongue around the foreign Parthian syllables.

"That he didn't say, and I was not in a position to ask, as he must not know that I was the one helping Marcus evade his net. He must not even know that I know Marcus."

"So, what are your plans, Nathaniel?" asked Hina.

"Right now, I have a free pass to come and go to see Mithridates, by appointment of course. I hope that I can actually avoid seeing Marcus, because if he recognizes me in front of Mithridates, I am a dead man."

"If he is there, say '*anjing*.' It means 'be quiet' in *han-yu*," said Mei.

"*Anjin,*" said Nathaniel, repeating the word. "*Anjin.* Wasn't Mithridates in Luoyang? I thought he spoke Hanaean," said Nathaniel

"*Anjĭng.* Mithridates speaks palace *han-yu*. He won't understand it the way we say it in Liqian."

"*Anjĭng,*" he repeated, capturing the different tone of the slightly different word. 'Good, I hope I get to speak first."

CHAPTER 51:

THE SPARRING MATCH

April 114AD, The Palace at Ctesiphon

Mithridates greeted his 'guest' effusively. "Good morning, Marcus! I am glad to see you looking so much better. The doctors said you will make a fine recovery. Please, let's go outside on the veranda, it is a beautiful day." He motioned Marcus through multi-colored silk curtains billowing in the breeze through a large doorway onto the veranda, overlooking the Tigris glistening in the morning sun a mile away. He directed Marcus to a red velvet sofa and called for a servant to bring refreshments and wine.

Seated facing each other, Marcus grunted his thanks, but waited for Mithridates to open the dialogue. Questions he had many, but he would wait to see what Mithridates had to say before he chose the ones to ask.

"First, let me offer you my most profound apologies for the way in which your captors delivered you to me. My instructions to my soldiers were to have you escorted here safely. Apparently, some brigands learned of these instructions and thought to earn a reward for kidnapping and delivering you to me. They will pay for their crimes."

"Actually, sir, the two ruffians, I only know of them as Horse and Boss, treated me fairly well. Please spare their lives on my account. It was not until Farnavantes caught up with us, that he had them manhandle me, tie me up and leave me buried in the back of the wagon without food or water for several days."

"Interesting. Were they working with Farnavantes?"

"Yes, they talked about that. They were supposed to split the reward."

"Do you know him?"

"I know of him. One of my traveling companions bested him in a horse race, though he tried to cause her horse to fall, and afterward, before the whole hippodrome and the royal entourage in Ecbatana, she knocked him down. Turned out he was the king's nephew."

"Interesting. She must be quite a woman. And nothing happened to her?"

"No. It seems he is not the king's favorite nephew."

"Very interesting, but I will honor your request and spare their two lives for your sake ... Horse and Boss? As to Farnavantes, I shall see what use I might make of him. He seems untrustworthy."

"He is." The servant brought sweetcakes, dates and wine.

"Enjoy the dates, Marcus. You will not find better dates anywhere in the world than these from Ctesiphon."

Marcus took a bite of the sweet dark fruit. It was indeed a pleasure to taste, sweet and dusky, almost a disappointment to eventually swallow. But there were many more on the glistening ceramic plate. He washed the last of them down with a sip of red wine.

"This is very interesting, *Kore-shi*," said Marcus, using the Hanaean form of Mithridates' first name of Cyrus, the name by which Marcus had known Mithridates a decade ago in the Hanaean palace of Luoyang. "Very interesting, but I would like to know how you knew I was coming, and why you so urgently wanted to see me."

"That is a fair question, *Si Nuo*," answered Mithridates, using in turn Marcus' Hanaean name, meaning 'Western Bull'. "I am pleased to see that your Parthian has improved so much. Our times together in Luoyang were very pleasant, until that unpleasant interlude with your sister."

"That 'unpleasant interlude' nearly got us executed, along with our Roman friends. But back to my question: why did you want me brought here?"

Mithridates smiled. "You are so much more assertive now. Well, as a matter of security, we attempt to intercept and read all Latin and Greek correspondence passing across our borders with Rome. There has been a war looming, which has these past few weeks come to pass, so you understand that we must protect ourselves from spies. Only the most interesting ones are brought to my attention, and your correspondence with your sister *Si Huar* under the official seal of Aulus Galba, certainly qualified as interesting." He paused to sip some wine.

"Her Latin name is Marcia."

"As this seemed to deal only with family matters, yours and hers, I directed they be sent on, to you and to her, but I could not resist the temptation to watch you correspond over such a vast distance. I hope you will forgive my intruding in your lives."

"I stopped receiving letters from her several years ago."

"So you said in your letters. I do not know what might have become of them. Caravan communications is always a difficult thing, and the Sogdians handle things differently than the Bactrians did a few years ago. When I heard you were coming west, I felt honor-bound to offer you my protection, since you are not a whole man, and likely to be set upon by travelers."

Marcus could not hide the flush of anger that rose to his face. "I need no man's protection! If that is your sole concern, you may release me into my own most capable hands, to find my wife and traveling companions."

"Please, Marcus, I am most sorry. You have grown more assertive than I remember. You have a wife? That is unexpected … given your condition. Would you like to see her?"

Marcus suppressed his anger and humiliation at Mithridates. "Yes, I would like that very much. Her name is Mei, she is Hanaean."

"I will see if I can locate her. It may take some time."

"The last I knew, she was at the palace at Ecbatana." Marcus paused, wondering if he had just exposed Mei to danger in his haste to see her. He changed the subject. "Do you have copies of my sister's letters?"

"Of course, I do not. They were strictly family matters, not worth recording."

Marcus considered what Mithridates had said. The man was lying through his teeth, and any answers to any other questions were likely to be false as well. Nevertheless, he had verified that the letters were the source of Mithridates' interest, as he had suspected. But what was it in the letters that Mithridates saw, beyond family matters?

Marcus touched the white linen wrapping the goose egg on the back of his head. "I am sorry. My head has begun to throb terribly, and my doctor advised me to rest. May I be excused?"

CHAPTER 52:

A BLOODLESS VICTORY

Arsamosata, April 114AD

Trajan's six legions did not linger long in the carefully laid-out camps that the Twelfth had constructed for them. They were up long before dawn, called from their slumber by the trumpet calls to break camp, which meant dismantling all the Twelfth's work, tearing down the newly-erected earthen walls to fill in the surrounding ditches excavated yesterday, leaving nothing for a potential foe to use as a fortification. The last to pack up were the supply wagons with food and cooking gear for each century, allowing the men to enjoy a breakfast as the sun's disk cleared the horizon. The Twelfth's fort was not abandoned, a skeleton force would maintain it in their absence along with local auxiliaries, but the bulk of the Twelfth was on the march. Before the sun was two disks above the horizon, the trumpets blew the call *ad agmine,* ordering the soldiers to form up in marching order before the Twelfth's fortress. Trajan climbed onto the fort's parapet to address the men; the commanders of each of the seven legions arrayed before him, and those of the auxiliaries formed up behind them, stood to repeat Trajan's words to their men, repeated down the line like echoes, because no one voice could reach such a multitude.

"Men of the Eastern Forces! Never before has such a multitude been gathered under the Eagles, to work as a single force to enforce the laws of Rome, the laws of the Senate and the People of Rome. I call on all of you, all of us, to do our duty to make our efforts victorious and honorable. Let us free Armenia from the clutches of the Parthian tyrants, to bring them into the fold of civilized nations, our world of freedom, our legacy to the generations that follow us."

He stood on the parapet, hearing his words echoed in front of him, then to his left and right. Four times his words were repeated, before all the legions and auxiliaries had heard his words, the last repetition audible but indistinguishable. It was a beautiful crisp spring day, and somewhere in the distance came the shrill scream of an eagle, already at the hunt so early in the morning. An omen, and a good one. Trajan's rough red soldier's cloak snapped in the breeze behind him. "The eagle in the sky has voiced the approval of Jupiter on our endeavor. Let us renew our soldier's oath before this great undertaking." He paused, then raised his right hand to make his own modified version of the *sacramentum*: "I, Marcus Ulpius Traianus, a soldier in the service of Rome, do swear allegiance to the Senate and the People of Rome and promise that I shall faithfully lead the soldiers placed in my trust against the enemies of Rome, wherever and whoever they be, and that I will not desert the standards nor in any way break the laws of the Roman people. But if I break my loyalty thus given to the people of Rome or violate the oath that I have thus accepted, let my life be forfeit to Jupiter Best and Greatest."

There was a susurration, as fifty thousand voices repeated the soldier's version of that oath, pledging their loyalty to their individual legions and to him, touched that the *princeps* had bound himself to them by that same oath. When the last murmur died away, Trajan raised his hand in a stiff salute: "To Victory!"

This elicited a roar from the massed ranks as they spontaneously erupted in cheers of *"Ave Imperator! Ave Caesar!* Hail, Commander-in-Chief, Hail, Caesar!"

The cheers went on for several minutes before Trajan made a downward motion with his hands, indicating that it was time to end. As the cheers died down, Trajan gave the order for the trumpet call to follow the standards, again echoed from legion to legion, as the Twelfth stepped off in the van, leading the way through their familiar area of operations, followed by the Sixth Ironclad, the Fourth Scythians, the Second Gallic, the Third Cyrenaican, and the Tenth Straits Legions, each picking up their own marching songs.

The Twelfth led them across the new stone arched bridge they had built twenty-five miles away. The bridge spanned the narrows of the Euphrates, 'narrow' here being almost a thousand feet, requiring fifteen arches. The far side was Armenian territory, the smooth Roman road on the other side quickly becoming a memory, the Armenian one a muddy, rutted mess clotted with horse and oxen droppings. No matter, the men had marched in worse.

As commander of the Twelfth in the van, Gaius had inherited the companionship of Trajan and his entourage. Which, on the march, meant just Trajan and Aulus, two equally tireless sixty-year-olds who marched like they were in their twenties; the rest of Trajan's entourage rode in wagons with the rear guard. And it was a delightful opportunity to renew his acquaintance with Aulus. The two had not had many opportunities to meet face-to-face in the decade since their last great adventure together.

"Strange, it seems like the country is deserted," commented Aulus to Gaius. "Houses, farms, some animals, no people."

"It's not deserted. They're in the woods or hills, no doubt watching us from a safe distance. Once we crossed that bridge, we became invaders. They took no chances, they took their families and what they could gather, and headed for safety." Gaius turned to the camp prefect, a grizzled veteran, Marius Callaeus. "Which reminds me, Marius, have our centurions put out skirmishers around the camp tonight. Make sure the foraging parties go in full battle gear. We're in hostile country now."

The Twelfth's engineers had gone ahead on horseback to scout out a suitable area for an encampment, which the legions reached after eight hours of marching. They set to work digging fortifications, setting palisades, tending to their mules, posting watches, and only then pitching their tents and preparing their meals. The scent of ten thousand or more campfires wafted into the evening sky. It was going to be an early night for all, for tomorrow would be a repetition of today.

Trajan timed his arrival at Arsamosata at daybreak on the fourth day after fording the Murat River, a major tributary to the Euphrates. A night march followed, traveling dark without torches. When dawn broke, Arsamosata found itself in the coils of a giant serpent, six legions encamped on the three landward sides. The Murat River to its south was clogged with dozens of Roman boats carrying hundreds of men.

The Twelfth had chosen the main road north out of Arsamosata as their camp, blocking any access to the main gate of the city. Trajan's entourage caught up with the Twelfth to pitch Trajan's regal purple imperial tent just out of bowshot from even the most capable archer on the city walls. The four gold eagles on each corner and the huge SPQR on the center pole glittered in the morning sun, and the alternating red and white entrance panels fluttered in the morning breeze.

About every hundred yards or so, *carroballistae* bolt throwers, torsion crossbows with eight-foot arms were deployed on wagons, each accompanied by a second wagon loaded with hundreds of bolts and kegs of pitch for incendiaries. The artillerymen were carefully sighting their weapons in on their assigned targets on the walls. Between each artillery piece was encamped a century of eighty men to protect these high-value weapons.

It was at one of these deployed artillery sites that Samuel Elisarius and Secundus Lucullus were conducting inspections. Samuel and Secundus clambered onto the wagon to take a look at the deadly machine, sitting hornet-like on its wooden tripod pedestal, and the two men responsible for it.

"Here, sir, here's a couple of things to check." Samuel pointed to the bundle of twisted ropes, a foot in diameter, that would be further twisted as the weapon was armed. "Here you want to make sure that there aren't any strands of rope working loose, check and tug everything to make sure it's all tight, nothing loose. And these brass fittings, wiggle them. Sometimes the wood works loose around them, sometimes the nails are coming out. And check for cracks in the wood along this frame, and make sure the track hasn't worn rough. Anything wrong with it, take it out of service right away. These are powerful machines. I saw one come apart in Dacia while it was being fired, took one guy's head completely off, the other's arm." He turned to the two soldiers responsible for the weapon, "All right, Gallus, Camillus, you done good assembling that and taking care of it."

Secundus turned to the two soldiers. One was blue-eyed, with light brown, almost blond hair, a bit long; the other was swarthy, black-haired. "Where are you two from?"

"About sixty miles outside Londinium in Britain, sir, on the river Cam, farming village," said Camillus, smiling that someone so important as a tribune would notice him.

"Alexandria in Egypt, sir," said Gallus. "I get ribbed a lot for a name that means 'chicken'."

"Ribbing is good for you, builds character," smiled Secundus.

"Is the commander really your dad, sir?" asked Gallus.

"Not so anyone would notice. I am just another very junior tribune to him right now, with a lot to learn," Secundus said with a smile.

Just then the signal tower to their right began receiving a message, one soldier periodically raising one or two flags, the other taking notes in a tablet. Then they turned to face the next signal tower in the chain to their left, and commencing a flurry of a left and right flag signals, relaying the message they had just received. After a few minutes, they jumped down to seek out Samuel and Secundus, saluting as they ran up to them. "Signal from the Twelfth, riders from the gate on a flag of truce."

"Looks like inspection time is over," Samuel said to Secundus. "Let's get back to the century, sir, and make sure we're ready for whatever may come. Camillus, Gallus, stand a tight watch. This may be a truce … or a ruse."

The three men, unarmed, rode up to the imperial tent. They were greeted by soldiers who insisted that they be patted down for hidden weapons before admitting them into the presence of Trajan. Trajan was seated on an ivory curule chair in his dress uniform, cream-colored corselet, white tunic with a wide purple border. Next to him, on a low round white table, sat his helmet, likewise enameled cream with a purple plume. Next to it sat his dress sword, gleaming black leather scabbard, studded with gold and silver fittings, and a carved ivory hilt. Gaius Lucullus, Aulus Galba, and the camp prefect Marius Callaeus stood beside him, all armed, and behind him were twelve soldiers as bodyguards, also armed, selected for size and fierce-looking disposition.

"What can I do for you gentlemen?" asked Trajan politely.

"King Abogares would like to meet with you, Your Excellency" said one of the men, in a heavily accented but very fluent Latin.

"I would be most honored to do so. In fact, I was thinking of sending a delegation to invite him for dinner this evening, but you have beaten me to it. I am sure my poor camp fare is far less exotic than what he has in the palace, but I brought a very good chef who can do wonders with it."

The speaker, apparently the leader of the group, perhaps the translator, nodded, and the three spoke back and forth in Armenian. Then the leader faced Trajan again. "We will convey the invitation, Your Excellency. What time and where?"

"At sundown, here. We have a big table, so he can bring companions if he chooses."

The three conferred again, then the leader responded. "We will signal you his response, a white flag above the gate for yes, red for no."

"Very well, thank you. You may go." And they left.

The answer came back quickly, a white flag, and a few minutes before sundown, a small door in the main gate opened to allow fifteen horsemen to ride out, all armed, the king riding under a fluttering blue and gold banner. As they pulled to a halt by the imperial tent, Marius Callaeus approached the King, who was riding next to the one who had led the earlier parley. "I am sorry, you Highness, but I must request that you turn over your weapons to my soldiers. They will return them to you on your departure."

The other man translated for the king, and he nodded, unsheathed his sword, and handed it to Marius, who in turn gave it to a soldier beside him. The king gave an order, and the men in company with him likewise unsheathed their swords and handed them over to soldiers who came up receive them. Dismounting, they went inside.

A long table had been set up inside, with candles at each place. A brazier flickered giving off warmth against the night chill, and strategically-placed oil lamps provided a warm illumination. Behind the table Trajan's bodyguards still glowered, officially at ease, but not really.

Trajan and Aulus stood at the center of the far side of the table, flanked by Gaius Lucullus, Bruttius Praesens of the Sixth, Tiberius Maximus of the Tenth, Claudius Severus of the Third Cyrenaican, Gaius Calvinus of the Third Gallic, and Aelius Verecundinus of the Fourth Scythian Legions on either side of him. The king was ushered to a chair opposite Trajan and his men took their places beside him, the translator adjacent to him.

Soldiers in white tunics brought out trays, one a whole pig, one a large fish, and one a goose, then trays of vegetables and fruits and nuts and breads, butter and the ubiquitous *garum* fish sauce. Wine goblets, gold for the king and Trajan, ornately carved silver for everyone else, were quickly filled by soldiers from silver jugs.

Trajan clapped his hands and smiled. "Please, let us be seated and eat. We can discuss business better on a full stomach!"

After translation, the king and his companions sat down. It was a good meal, with light conversation about nothing of any significance, the weather in Armenia, the beautiful countryside, nothing too involved for the translators. Apparently, only the three visitors from the afternoon spoke Latin.

Finally, as the soldiers cleared away the last of the plates and refilled everyone's goblets, Trajan announced that it was time for the business at hand.

King Abogares responded through his translator. "If I may be so bold, what is your intention here, Your Excellency?"

"My intention is simply to affirm your obeisance to the King of Armenia, and that you, like him, honor the treaty between Parthia and Rome concerning your state's independence. That is all."

There was a flurry of talk in Armenian. Gaius thought the name Parthamasiris came up several times, but wasn't sure.

"Of course, we are in obeisance to the King of Armenia," answered the king, sidestepping the touchy question of which king that might be.

"And in honor of the treaty?" asked Trajan. "I hope this will not be a long-drawn-out negotiation, as I have to join up with three more legions in Satala, and my twenty-thousand horsemen, in a few days. If our negotiations cannot be concluded quickly, I must send word to have them join me here instead."

Gaius watched the king go pale as Trajan's words were conveyed to him. He was just a local potentate, not involved in military matters. There were more soldiers encamped outside Arsamosata than there were men, women, and children inside, and Trajan had just indicated that could practically double that number in just a week. The king had just ten thousand troops, more police force than soldiery. Trajan was obliquely threatening a siege that the king was totally unprepared to endure.

More Armenian back and forth, some making angry remonstrations. Then the King waved them to silence, a bit angrily, it seemed. "Of course, in honor of the treaty, and in obeisance to the rightful king, Axidares, though he is regretfully indisposed at the moment in Ctesiphon," he said. "Thank you for your hospitality, and the fine meal. Please let me know if there is anything I can do to make your stay here enjoyable."

"I thank you, and we promise to be of no burden to you"

The next morning, Trajan and his fifty thousand men vanished as quickly as they had arrived, to join up with the *XXII Primigenia* Lucky Capricorns, the *XV Flavia Firma* Steadfast Flavians, and *II Adiutrix* Second Rescuers, enroute to Satala

CHAPTER 53:

A SOLDIER REBORN

Aquileia to Satala, April 114AD

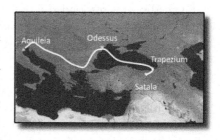

It was a beautiful spring day in Aquileia, the air filled with the perfume of new flowers, green buds on trees, the warmth welcome after chill, gray winter. There were no guests at the Academy, so Marcia put the children under the watchful care of the servants to play in the atrium, while she and Antonius retired to their rooms on the second floor for a midday nap. Which did not involve any napping.

Afterwards, still damp from their lovemaking, the two lay on the bed, Antonius on his back, Marcia on her side, her small leg over his massive thigh, toying with the tangled hair on his chest.

"You know, there are some gray ones in there now," she said, giggling, pulling one to its full length and removing it abruptly, making Antonius jerk. "Do you know what today is, *carus meus?*"

This was always a dangerous question, especially when Antonius did not know the answer. Not her birthday, nor the children's and they were married in October, so he answered cautiously, "Tuesday, *domina?*"

"No, silly, try again." She grabbed another gray strand on his chest to uncoil and pluck out, but Antonius removed her hand gently.

"Umm, the first day of April?"

"You are getting close. Thirteen years ago, you and I made love for the very first time."

"Ah, yes. In a stinking Hanaean jail cell, waiting to be executed, with your brother, Aulus, and Gaius Lucullus keeping lookout for us so we didn't attract the guards. Very romantic."

"It was, and the three of them, I think, figured out that we should be lovers, long before we understood it that night."

"As I recall, it was your idea."

"It was, and we got straw from the floor in places where there should not be straw! It was the most wonderful night in my life."

They lay together in silence, then Antonius propped himself up on his elbows. "Speaking of Aulus and Gaius, I got letters from both. Aulus is east, traveling with Trajan, and Gaius is back with the Thunderbolt, campaigning."

"The Thunderbolt? Your old legion?"

"The same, with his son as tribune, and guess who his son's centurion is now?" Her Hanaean eyes crinkled in an unspoken question, and Antonius continued without waiting for her to ask. "Shmuel, no less, going by Samuel Elisarius now, but one and the same."

"What coincidences the gods create for us!"

"Ter be sure. An' here, gittin' ready fer a big campaign, his camp prefect has took bad sick."

"He asked you to come, and you're thinking about it."

"Not asked, wished I could, I guess, but how did yer know."

"Because yer started talking like a soldier agin! An' yer do want ter go," she said, mimicking the fractured Latin of the common soldier as she had learned long ago. "Soldiering is for young men, *carus meus*. You haven't been under the eagles for over ten years. And besides, he'll have someone in place long before you get there."

"I'm not that old, *domina,* and camp prefect isn't the same, they are picked from retired senior centurions. Administrative stuff, logistics, making sure the legion has what it needs. But you're right, he'd have someone else in place before I got there. I turned that job down when we got back years ago an' left that life behind me. Besides, we have people trying to raid our home."

"That was a year and a half ago, and if you remember, you were out when it happened, and I took care of that bandit myself. There's been no more trouble, not at Aulus' home in Rome, nor here."

"*Domina,* I can't tell if you're arguing with me, or trying to talk me into taking Gaius up on something he hasn't even asked me to do." He paused to lay back down, hands behind his head, staring at the ceiling and a big fly buzzing in the dimness. "Bandits or no, I don't want your having to run our academy alone."

"No, I don't want you to go, and I am scared to death that if you do, you may not come back." She nuzzled into his shoulder. "But you never left that life behind you. You can't, it's part of who you are. And who knows what the gods have in store for us? You could stay here and get run over tomorrow by a runaway cart in the market."

"You're right, a part of me wants to be in that. Whatever is cookin' up in the east is goin' ter be big, maybe the biggest ever. Camp prefect is important. Let me check out with the local urban cohort here, if they can get me a pass on the *cursus publicus,* an' how long it might take.*"* He rolled over, took her in her arms, and rolled back so she was straddling him. "We need to talk about me getting' old, *domina,*" he said, kissing her wetly on the mouth.

Antonius met with Brutus Agrippa, the head of the urban cohort for Aquileia, the following day. Brutus studied Gaius' letter. "Not much of a request."

"I don't think he expected me to come, but I will take it as an order if you will," answered Antonius.

"We are playing fast and loose with what constitutes an order, but with that Armenian storm blowing up in the east, everyone else is, too. Can you ride hard?"

"Hard enough."

"You'll be changing horses about every twenty miles, Antonius, if you can handle the pace, at a *mansio* inn. Show them the pass, turn your animal in, then keep going. If you are good and your butt can handle it, you can cover a hundred, hundred and fifty miles a day. But don't skip the horse change, you'll wear them out. The *Princeps* is in Satala, near Trapezus on the Black Sea. The *cursus* is getting mail and supplies to the legions there in about ten days to two weeks, people in three weeks to a month. Even from a backwater like Aquileia. You will be shipping some stuff, too, I suppose?"

"Me old soldier's kit. One campaign chest."

"Sounds like you're back to talkin' like a soldier again, Antonius. Bring your kit by, we will send it ahead by ship, it will be waiting for you when you get to Satala. Don't put anything in it you can't replace, ships sink." Brutus drew a scroll out from under his desk, wrote out the pass, sealed it with hot wax and his signet ring, and handed it to Antonius' waiting hand. "Don't lose this, or you will have to walk. Good luck!"

Antonius and Marcia spent several days settling things for his departure. As each day went by, Antonius felt, uncharacteristically, less sure about his decision. Had Marcia expressed any reservations, or even the children, Antonius might have changed his mind. But Marcia did not, Colloscius, at seven, looked forward to being 'in charge' in his father's absence, and Aena at five, didn't fully understand how long it might be. So, in the chill, dark pre-dawn on the fourth day, Marcia rode down with him on the wagon to the *mansio* for his departure.

He held her to him, kissing her delicately.

"You be careful, *carus meus*, you're not twenty anymore either. As I am sure the ride will remind you."

"You take care also, *domina*. Any fighting, let Alaric do it. He's good, and a lot bigger."

With that, he picked up his backpack and panniers to sling over his shoulder, and went into the candle-lit *mansio*, without looking back. The night clerk took a look at his pass, inspected the seal and signature. "Horses in the paddock out back, each branded with a diff'rent number. Pick one, tether it out, then come back an' sign fer it."

Antonius chose the first of many horses, a dappled gray mare, reading the number 'AQ XXI' branded on its rump by torchlight. He returned to sign for it, the clerk wishing him a good trip. Antonius picked up his traveling gear, saddled up the mare, loaded on the pannier, and swung into the saddle. *Damn, I sure do miss the stirrups the Chinese used. Funny, no one has figured that out here.*

He whistled the mare up to a brisk trot. "Let's go, Twenty-One, lots of miles to go."

By mid-morning, they had reached the next *mansio*, traded horses and set off again. After four more trades, Antonius reached the Dalmatian border at sunset. The next day, Antonius realized that he was indeed not twenty any longer, deciding to keep to just four trades at least until his butt and legs grew accustomed again to rhythmic up-and-down of the trotting horse. Fourteen days of riding, at least, lay ahead.

Actually, it turned out to be half that. A week's riding took him to one of the *mansiones* on the Thracian border with Moesia. They recommended he detour north to the major naval station of Odessus south of the mouth of Danube, running regular shuttle ships back and forth with Trapezus, three days' sailing time, time for Antonius' rump to repair itself.

It was the first week in May when Antonius showed up at the praetorium tent of the Twelfth Thunderbolt, in proper field kit, took a salute from the soldier guarding the entrance, and entered silently into the command tent, lit by lamps though still daylight.

Gaius Lucullus, his back turned, was studying a desk overflowing with maps with several centurions and tribunes. "If that's lunch, just set it on my desk. We're quite busy."

"I ain't yer god-cursed servant, *legatus*. Just came by ter say hello ter me old Hanaean runnin' mate."

Gaius stood straight up, knocking one of the scrolls to the ground with a clatter and turned around, his face broadening into a big grin. "Antonius, you old bastard, and in full and proper kit. What the hell are you doing here?"

"Yer said yer might be needin' a *praefectus castrorum*, so here I am, if yer still be wantin' me."

Gaius covered the tarp on the ground separating them and seized his old friend in a big bear hug. "I got your letter saying you were on your way just a few days ago. I told you not to even think about making such a long trip, but I guess you and that letter passed on the road."

"I guess. How is your *praefectus*?"

"Not good, Marius Callaeus got sick with a cough very suddenly, now coughing up blood. The doctors think he may not last long," said Gaius, very quietly so the others might not hear the bad news. "Too weak to work, and definitely not ready for the campaign."

Gaius then turned to the others. "Gentlemen, it seems we have a new camp prefect, and just in time. Let me introduce a veteran of many wars and my long-time friend, Antonius Aristides."

Antonius wasted no time visiting Marius Callaeus. He found him in his own tent across the *Via Prinicipalis*, the main road bisecting the camp, opposite the commander's *praetorium*. He was gasping for breath in the dimly lit tent, attended by a Greek physician and two army *medici*, young soldiers.

"May I talk to him?" Antonius asked the doctor.

"You may. But please keep it short, he is very tired," the doctor answered, signaling the two soldiers that they should leave.

Antonius came up to the bedside. Marius was suddenly seized with a violent coughing spasm that wracked his rugged frame. The gray-faced man dabbed at his lips with a white cloth, trying in vain to hide the bloodstains.

"I am sorry, Marius. If this isn't a good time ..." Antonius began.

Marius coughed again, more of a clearing of his congested chest, then wheezed out an answer. "As good as any. Wait too long, and I might be on the other side of the Styx." He managed a faint grin. "You are Antonius, the one Lucullus said might arrive to relieve me?"

"I am. How are you?"

"Dying, they tell me. Well, they don't tell me, but I know I am dying. I am sure not going to war, dead or alive. I am afraid I can't give you much of a pass-down, but Lucius Severus, my clerk, he's young and can ..." His body was seized with another hacking spasm, but he continued after it passed away, bringing up yet more blood. "... Lucius is young, but he knows the inventories as well as me. You can trust him."

"I will, Marius. May I ask how you came to be sick?"

"You may. I was fit as a pack mule one day, got a cough, then a fever, then I started bringing up blood. The doctors say it can go fast or slow." He gagged, coughing. "I hope fast."

"Look, I won't keep you up, get some sleep. Can I get anything for you? Wine? Water?"

"Some water, please. And dancing girls, if you have any." His eyes twinkled, but they looked ancient in his gray face.

Antonius smiled, slapped Marius' once-strong shoulder, and took his leave.

Antonius found Lucius Severus in the former prefect's office, going over records. He seemed to be as competent as Marius had said, a young soldier with perhaps five years' service. Antonius spent days going over the scrolls that tabulated the location and quantity of all the hardware and supplies that a legion carried in its supply train, from horseshoes to arrowheads, prefabricated parts for siege engines, catapults, bridges and boats neatly organized in wagons, the boxes labeled with letters of the alphabet and Roman numerals, so the containers and wagons could be matched with the inventory scrolls. And wagon after wagon of beans, wine, even barrels of fresh water. Antonius inspected each one, prying open crates at random to verify their contents against the list.

Finally, they came to the last entry on the list, five wagons loaded with fifteen thousand *'jan dashiki'*. "What the hell are these, Lucius... *jan dashiki?* Some sort of foreign word?"

"Armenian, I think. These are the last items added, right before Marius took sick. But he handled it."

"Let's take a look."

They found the wagons at the back of the train, covered by canvas tarpaulins. Antonius tugged a tarpaulin free of the ropes holding it in place. Looking inside, he saw thousands of wooden frames about three feet long, an inch or so thick, jam-packed side by side. He tugged out one of the frames, an elliptical end woven in a crisscross pattern of sinew, the other end something that looked like a handle. "This looks like one of them rackets in the baths used to play ball games! *Jan dashiki,* that's what these are? We going to play games with 'em or fight 'em?" he said, taking a playful swing at an imaginary ball.

Lucius suppressed a laugh. "Sir, but I remember now, Marius said they're Armenian snowshoes. For fighting in the winter, Marius said. Our secret weapon."

"What do yer do with 'em?"

"He didn't say."

Nor did Marius ever say, for he died the next day.

CHAPTER 54:

FRIENDS IN HIGH PLACES

Ctesiphon, May 114AD

Mei's heart was thudding in her breast as she approached the fierce bearded guards at the palace entrance, their armor over green robes, with a dark blue cloak fastened by a silver broach at the collar. Standing on either side of the door with erect lances, they turned to face each other as she approached and crossed their lances before the finely carved wooden portal. One turned his head toward her. "Step forward and state your business," he rasped unpleasantly.

Mei swallowed hard. She took the letter Nathaniel had given her and presented it to the questioning soldier. "I ... I have a pass. From Cyrus Mithridates." Nathaniel had coached her carefully on the correct pronunciation of the harsh name, *Kurush Mehrdat*, so guttural sounding in Parthian.

Without moving his lance, the soldier accepted it with his left hand and scrutinized the fine writing. He looked it up and down several times, while Mei stood silent, dreading that he would not accept it, worse, might even accost her for some crime.

Finally, he looked at the other soldier and barked a command. The lances snapped erect to their sides, the massive door groaned and opened inward from unseen hands, and the two soldiers turned away from each other to face outward. "You may enter," he said curtly, returning the pass to her.

"Thank you," she said softly, as she walked into the palace.

Mei was surprised that she was admitted to the palace so easily, with the letter Nathaniel had given her, signed by Mithridates, inviting her to the palace to visit her husband. Never in her life had she ever heard of palace protocol, let alone expected to be meeting alone with the brother of a king. She wished Nathaniel could come with her, but he insisted she go alone, lest somehow the dangerous mistruth of his association with Marcus be discovered.

She remembered the directions Nathaniel had given her, across the interior pavilion to the white marble stairs at the far end, to the third floor, to the right and away from the gilded entrance to King Osroës' throne room, three doors down. She prayed she had not lost count. In the room, a portly man with a stringy beard was tending to scrolls scattered on his finely polished wooden desk. "Kophasates?" she asked. Hopefully, that would be him.

"It is I. And you, you are Mei, Marcus' wife?"

Mei breathed a sigh of relief. "I am she," she answered, daring a shy smile for the first time that day.

"Please, follow me, Mithridates is expecting you."

He ushered her through the fine wooden door. Mithridates was seated on purple and red velvet cushions on a throne-like chair. "Your Excellency, Mei is here to see you."

Mithridates rose graciously to greet her, taking her by the hand and ushering her to a waiting chair. "Mei, we are so glad you were able to find your way here. Please sit." He turned toward Kophasates. "Please summon Marcus, he is long overdue for a reunion with his wife."

He then returned to his chair. "I must apologize for the rough treatment your husband received in coming here. Those responsible will be held accountable. Would you like some dates and sweetmeats?"

Mei nodded, and a servant produced a silver tray.

"So how did you come to know that he would be here?"

Mei gave her carefully rehearsed answer. "Your Excellency, as we neared the border, we learned that he was being sought. And, as you are the only person who would know him in all of Parthia, it had to be you. When we reached Margiana, King Vologases took us under his protection, so he said, from you."

"I know, and he is king only in his own eyes. But go on."

"So, when Marcus went missing, Nathaniel, who was also paying a social call at the palace, he kindly offered to assist, assuming Marcus would be taken to you, because of your previous relationship in Luoyang."

"Very astute, Mei. He was brought here rather roughly by one Farnavantes of Ecbatana. What do you know of Farnavantes?"

"Nothing, other than he was bested in a horse race by one of our traveling companions."

"You companion is the woman? The one who bested him?"

"She is. She is of the Xiongnu nomads, born to ride horses." Mei offered him a shy smile; Mithridates returned it.

"I know of them from my time in Luoyang. They are fierce warriors."

Just then Marcus entered the room, unbound, followed by a guard. "Mei!" You are here!"

Mei rose, then she and Marcus both looked toward Mithridates, who just smiled. "You have not seen each other for some time."

The two rushed into each other's embrace, then Mei examined the scabs on his face. "You were hurt."

"A little. Nothing serious."

Mithridates cleared his throat. "I believe you would both like some time to catch up with each other. Mei, you may join him in his quarters, then both of you be back here by mid-afternoon."

About two hours later, Kophasates ushered them both back in. Mithridates greeted them with his ever-present smile. "I hope you two enjoyed your time together. I will make arrangements for you to visit him on occasion, Mei. Unfortunately, with war with Rome breaking out, we cannot allow you to stay here, nor can we allow him to leave, for his protection. Roman spies are everywhere, and we have reason to believe that they seek you, Marcus, for information you may have on the Han court. You will remain our guest here, for your own safety."

"I have high-placed friends in Rome and am a citizen. I have nothing to fear from Rome."

"Alas, Marcus, you don't know Rome, except as a myth in your mind. Your high-placed friends, such as Aulus Galba, do not remain high-placed when they fall out of favor."

"Has something happened to him?" asked Marcus.

"He has fallen out of favor, with all that entails. I am your only high-placed friend now."

CHAPTER 55:

A SNAKE IN THE HOUSE

Petra, May 114AD

As the relationship between Jacobus and Miranda deepened, he learned of talents he never suspected she had. He had known she could read, but he had not known she could also write, in a beautiful miniscule script that was a pleasure to read, or properly abbreviated block capitals, so unlike his scrawls, barely legible even to himself. She took over the record keeping and correspondence for their little shelter, and then displayed her other organizational skill, an ability to quickly and accurately add columns of figures on an abacus. Jacobus had never been quite sure what money they had to operate, though they seemed always to have something more than what they needed. In neat columns on a scroll of cheap Egyptian papyrus, she was able to tally what money they had received from whom, when, how much they spent and on what, what they borrowed and what was owed. In short, she knew exactly how much they had at any time, and where to get more.

It didn't take long for Jacobus to prepare her manumission papers, for he wanted her next decision to be a free one. She wrote up the documents in her readable print, and he took them down to the magnificent city hall, carved into the pink sandstone of a steep cliff. He presented her with the signed copies of her freedom on his return, and then offered her that decision that she was now free to accept or reject: to marry him. She accepted, and they were wed shortly after by the caretaker of his little Christian community.

She was going over the books, scrutinizing the sums. "Jacobus, we aren't taking in what we have been getting from the merchants. Do any of them say why?"

"No, but I think it is the talk of war. They are either hoarding their money, or spending it all now to buy things while they are available and cheap. Not much left for orphans, I guess. And with Governor Severus off to the front, his officials won't make his usual generous payments to us on their own authority. We were apparently his own private project," said Jacobus.

"I think we are going to have to economize a bit. But I am wondering, if there is war, should we be buying food now, things that will keep, like smoked meats and grain? Will food be short?"

"I don't know, dear. This is my first war, too," he said, nuzzling the fine hairs on the back of her neck that indicated his interest was no longer on the books. Her giggle indicated she might be losing interest in the books also.

However, the boy Stick interrupted Jacobus' seduction of his wife with an announcement at the door. "Father, there is a man to see you, Aharon."

Jacobus sighed, stood and rearranged his tunic. "Thank you, Stick. I'll be right down." He turned to his wife, smiling with amusement. "Later, Miranda. I won't be long."

She stood and joined him "I'll come with you. This may involve money. But later, yes, certainly."

Stick, an eight-year-old boy, tall, poised and mature for his years, clad in a spotless white tunic, led them to the anteroom and announced their arrival. "Aharon, sir, my mother and father to see you." Without waiting for an answer, he turned and left.

"Jacobus! It is good to see you again. And congratulations, I heard you had taken your slave to mate," said the Jewish merchant, his eyes bright with interest as he examined Miranda's body under her clothing.

Hiding his irritation, Jacobus answered politely. "Miranda is neither my slave nor my mate, Aharon, but a free woman and my wife. And my partner."

"Oh, my apologies, then, Jacobus."

"So, you are here with word from Shmuel?"

"I am, but not good news for you, I fear. His legion left Melitene for the north, for the war with Parthia. I am afraid you will not be hearing from him for a long while, if ever."

"Why? What do you expect will happen to him?" Jacobus was caught by the abrupt finality of Aharon's comment.

"Rome has done poorly against the Parthians. Send your wife out, I want to talk some serious things with you."

"She stays. If you can't say it in front of her, I don't need to hear it from you." Jacobus crossed his arms across his chest defensively. He did not like Aharon and did not like dealing with him. Perhaps if Aharon was no longer to be the funnel for Shmuel's contributions to the orphanage, then he could be free of this importuning individual.

"Suit yourself. I see you have much to learn about being married. May we sit, or shall I say what I have to say standing?"

Jacobus almost offered him a seat, but having had this man insult both his wife and himself in the first few minutes, decided against it. "Standing is fine. Miranda and I have things that need attending."

"Very well then. You Christians read the old books, as well as the books of your Christ, do you not?"

"We do."

"Our prophet of old, Ezra, told how Cyrus of Persia freed our people from captivity, returned us to our homeland, and gave us money to rebuild our temple, the one the accursed Romans destroyed four decades ago. You know of Ezra's story?" Aharon's lips curled with great disgust behind his gray-flecked beard as he spat the word 'Romans'.

Jacobus nodded. He did not like where this was going.

Aharon continued. "Osroës of Parthia will do to the Romans what his ancestor Cyrus did to the Babylonians, and return us to our homeland to rebuild our Temple yet again. We intend to be on the winning side of this war." He paused to let this sink in. "You Christians should be no friends of Rome, either. Didn't their emperor Nero set you people alight on poles to illuminate the streets of Rome at night? Did he not murder your prophets Peter and Paul and thousands of others?"

"That was a very long time ago, before I was born. The Romans no longer bother us, if we do not bother them. Governor Severus supported our work generously, and he knew that I am a Christian."

"And that can change with a change of governor, a change of emperor. Join with us. We worship the same God, the only God, and if you wish to dally with that Christ of yours, that is no concern to us. And I can see to it that your orphanage does not suffer for lack of resources during this war."

Jacobus stiffened, and Miranda edged closer to him.

"And speaking treason with you against Rome can bring that change to pass much sooner. I think you should leave, Aharon, and it would be better if you did not return."

"I will leave, but I warn you, your little wretches will soon be on the street again, stealing and whoring for their next meal!" Aharon swirled his rich iridescent green robe about his white tunic as he abruptly turned to leave. "You will regret this impudence," he barked, without turning his head, slamming the open door behind him.

"Should you have ordered him out like that?" asked Miranda, staring at the closed door. "He will be a powerful enemy."

"And we have powerful friends, starting with Governor Severus. What he proposed was treason and might not have been what it seemed."

"How so?"

"We Christians have enemies among the Jews, maybe more so than the Romans. He could have been setting a trap, to bait me into agreeing to treason. Then he could blackmail me into doing whatever he wanted."

"He certainly seems devious enough."

"Like a snake, and with a bad reputation. I am glad I kept you in the room for something like that, as a witness." He nudged her. "And as a free person, you can't be tortured to corroborate your testimony."

Miranda gasped.

"Sorry, I should not joke about that. A few months ago, they could have done that."

"You're not going to turn him in?"

"Not unless I have a reason. I learned from my father Ibrahim how to deal with snakes, and the first step is to get them out of the house. Then crush their heads."

CHAPTER 56:

A CROWN IN THE DIRT

Elegeia, June 114AD

Aulus' brow was beaded with sweat in the noonday sun. "Unbelievable, Your Excellency. Parthamasiris is two hours late," he said. He was wrapped in a heavy woolen toga, standing next to the *Princeps,* shifting his weight restlessly from foot to foot.

The *Princeps* Trajan was seated on a backless ivory curule chair on a white wooden dais, wrapped in an even more cumbersome purple toga, a gold oak leaf diadem on his head, and a gold serpentine staff in his hand. He, too, was beginning to sweat profusely, along with Gaius Lucullus, Antonius, Bruttius Praesans commanding the Sixth Ironclad, and various regional governors, advisers and servants ranged on the dais. On the grass before the dais, twenty-four lictors in white tunics held up twenty-four *fasces,* ceremonial axes bound with purple ribbon. They, too, were beginning to sweat.

And behind them, the men of the Twelfth Thunderbolt and Sixth Ironclad, ten thousand men strong, were arrayed at attention, as they had been for three hours.

"Unbelievable it is, and more. Two hours late, for a meeting he scheduled in such earnestness. It had to be today, he said." He turned to a servant behind him, a fresh-faced boy of nineteen or so. "Macro, be a good lad, and check with the lookouts for any sign of Parthamasiris' approach. If he is coming, have the servants bring cool water and towels to wipe down our entourage."

The lad acknowledged the order and set out at a brisk walk for the watchtower by the camp's main entryway.

Trajan turned to the two legion commanders. "Have your men stand easy, sit if they wish."

The two commanders sent servants to pass the word to their legions, and quickly cries of '*Ad laxare,* rest easy', echoed across the fields before them.

There was an audible rush as ten thousand men suddenly relaxed, sat, or began talking among themselves.

There was almost a sense of disappointment on the dais when young Macro returned with ten of his fellow servants, each with a tray containing silver pitchers and goblets. Macro mounted the stage to personally hand Trajan his goblet. "There is a dust trail, the guards say it is a few miles out, Your Excellency."

Trajan accepted the goblet and drained it in two swallows. Macro patted his brow with a cool damp towel. "Thank you, Macro. I was hoping you would come back with no sign of him, but it looks like we have an hour to refresh ourselves anyway. Gentlemen, let us adjourn to the shade of my command tent. Gaius and Cornelius, you may dismiss your men, but they should be ready to be in formation within five minutes."

The lictors started to march off formally, two by two, but Trajan called them to a halt. "No need for ceremony, gentlemen. We are in an army camp. You may store the *fasces* in my tent and join us there for my hospitality."

Parthamasiris and his entourage arrived in the late afternoon. Trajan and his company were once again seated or standing on the dais, awaiting his arrival. The lictors were perfectly positioned before the *Princeps,* the two legions arrayed in full dress, banners snapping in the June breeze. Parthamasiris was in traveling clothes, sweating and dusty, as were his entourage. Gaius Lucullus met them at the entrance to the camp in his dress armor.

They exchanged greetings, then Parthamasiris posed a question in his accented but presentable Latin. "Where might I and my companions bathe and freshen ourselves? It has been a hard ride."

Gaius smiled slightly, indicating the vast army in formation before the emperor, all waiting Parthamasiris. "We have been waiting for your arrival since noon, which by your letter was the time for us to meet. Three hours ago. It would seem that if you wished to 'freshen up', you might have arrived a bit earlier, rather than later. You will have to attend as you are."

Parthamasiris translated in Parthian for his companions, who did not appear to be happy attending a meeting with the emperor of Rome dressed as they were.

"If that is to be, that is how it shall be," the would-be king answered Gaius, handing his sweat-streaked black mare off to a waiting soldier. "Wait, before you lead her off." He fumbled in a leather pannier and withdrew a silver diadem, putting it on his head. "This at least makes up for my unkempt appearance," he said with a smile showing his fine white teeth behind his forked and coiled black beard. Gaius did not acknowledge the humor, leading him off to stand before the dais.

"*Ave, Imperator!*" He greeted Trajan with a flourish, then descended to his knees, removing his diadem and putting it on the grass before him, then putting his head to the ground.

Trajan waved off the obeisance. "Rise, please, no need for such formalities, Parthamasiris. That is not our way. Where is King Axidares? I hope he is well."

Parthamasiris stood, leaving the diadem on the ground at his feet. "My brother has been deposed, as we have communicated to you. It is the wish of King Osroës that I be confirmed as the new king in accordance with our mutual treaty."

"Since we approved your cousin Axidares as the king of Armenia in accordance with our mutual treaty with Parthia, it follows that we should also approve his removal. We were not consulted. What was the reason for your father removing him from office?"

"He was dissatisfied with the performance of Axidares, that is all. It is his royal prerogative to remove people from positions to which he appointed them."

"But it is not his royal prerogative to remove those that we have confirmed in office."

"I do not believe that our mutual treaty, affirmed half a century ago between your Emperor Nero and our king Vologases I, states that."

"You have a copy of that treaty, do you not?"

"I regret I do not." Parthamasiris was perspiring heavily, but not from the heat.

"No matter, I do, the original, signed the *Princeps* Nero. While it does not specifically so state, it follows logically that those we approve in office require our approval for their removal. Is that not logical?"

Parthamasiris glanced at the diadem on the grass, where he had left it, untouched and unmentioned, then back at Trajan. "As you said, Your Excellency, it does not specifically so state that your approval is required."

A faint smile flickered on the Emperor's thin lips. "But my approval is required for you to be placed on the throne, is it not? In accordance with the treaty?"

"In accordance with the treaty, yes."

"But you have already presumed my approval in wearing the diadem and acting as King of Armenia, have you not?"

"Of necessity, Your Excellency, I was acting King, pending your approval."

"Had the removal of Axidares been coordinated with me, we would not be in this bind, now, would we? I would have approved his removal, if the reasons were good, and I would have approved you, and there would be no awkward transition when you would be 'acting' as king without authority."

Parthamasiris swallowed hard. "Perhaps it would have been better had the King of Kings followed that course. But we meant no insult to Rome in our actions. Surely, your approval of my position is just a formality, certainly not worth a war between our two peoples. And if you do not approve of me, my father would be willing to submit another for your confirmation."

"Unfortunately, young man, what King Osroës has done cannot be undone. He has violated the treaty, and put our client states to the north on the Caspian Sea at risk. Since he has chosen to violate the treaty, we have no alternative but to annex Armenia as a Roman province, putting an end to this farce."

"But ... but that means war!"

"So it does, young man, so it does. But rest assured, you will be escorted from this camp by a century of my soldiers to the capital Artaxata. There you may make arrangements to turn the government over to the governor whom I shall appoint. I wish you well, and please give my regards to your noble father, King Osroës, *Shahanshah* of the Parthian people."

Parthamasiris bent to pick up the diadem, but Trajan shook his head. "Leave it be. It has served its purpose. We will take care of it."

A whisper ran through the army, as those in earshot relayed the conversation they had just heard. Then the army erupted in cheers as ten thousand throats hailed Trajan as emperor. Parthamasiris, red-faced, his eyes tearing at the humiliation, turned away with no courtesy. A squadron of thirty horsemen detached from behind the Thunderbolt's formation, led by Secundus Lucullus and his centurion Samuel Elisarius, riding forward to escort the former king from the camp with his party.

Three days later, the cavalry squadron escorting Parthamasiris and his party had covered one hundred and fifty miles, following the Araxes River along the southern flanks of the snow-capped Armenian Highlands. They made their final camp at the mouth of a broad, well-watered plain, at the far end of which was Artaxata, the capital of Armenia and their destination, which their guide and translator said was just thirty more miles distant.

It had not been a pleasant trip, their charge Parthamasiris alternately surly and morose. His retinue spoke no Latin and camped well away from the Roman soldiers, with their own fires. Among that lot were ten bodyguards, all openly hostile and occasionally threatening, but mostly for show, being outnumbered three to one.

That last night of escort, Elisarius observed the Parthian prince, obviously and loudly drunk, taking a piss in the direction of his Roman escorts, glaring defiantly at them in the firelight, then retiring to his tent early.

The next morning, Secundus and Samuel were up well before dawn, their men busily preparing a quick meal, then securing the tents and making ready for travel. A few of the prince's men were stirring, obviously in no hurry, and there was no sign of Parthamasiris.

"Looks like last night was hard on their former king," said Samuel. "Must have a helluva hangover."

"Well, hangover or no, he needs to get moving. I want to deliver him to the capital by noon, and be well away from there by sundown," answered Secundus. "In fact, I am not averse to riding after dark for a spell tonight. The more distance between me and his people, the better I like it."

The centurion nodded in agreement. "Right, sir. And maybe not head back the way we came in. Wouldn't take too many to cut us to pieces."

Secundus summoned the translator. "Gor, go talk to Parthamasiris' bodyguards. He needs to be up and moving now."

Gor nodded and headed off. The bodyguards were hostile as usual, but finally one went in and came out immediately swearing vehemently, gesticulating at the tent. The others went in to look. One of the bodyguards began to beat up Gor.

"Get our men. We can't lose Gor," said Secundus, loosening his sword.

They closed on the fracas as the bodyguard began kicking at the translator, now prostrate and bloody on the ground. "Enough!" ordered Secundus, drawing his sword. As he did so, thirty more swords hissed from their scabbards behind him. "Let him up!"

While the men did not speak Latin, they understood swords quite well. The bodyguard backed up. Gor struggled to his feet and staggered back to Secundus' side.

"Can you speak? Can you tell me what just happened?" asked Secundus.

"He, Parthamasiris, he's dead. Knife in his belly."

"Tell them we were charged with protecting him, that we did not kill him."

Gor translated through bloody lips, but they were obviously not believing him.

Secundus whispered to Samuel, "We have a serious problem. Any chance that someone could have gotten inside the camp?"

"We were more concerned that no one got out, but no, no way. The bastard either offed himself, or one of them did it. Probably that one, the one complaining loudest."

"Makes sense. I don't want to have to fight our way out of this mess, makes us look more guilty than we already do, but be ready for anything."

The shouting continued and one of the men threw something at Gor's feet. He brought the bloody dagger to Secundus. "A Roman army blade, sir, pulled from his stomach."

Secundus loosened his dagger and held it aloft. "Samuel, have every man do likewise. If there is anyone missing their dagger ...' He left the threat unstated.

Behind them, thirty daggers glinted in the sunlight. Secundus sighed in relief. "Gor, tell them that Roman army daggers are easy to come by, and all my men have theirs. We did not kill Parthamasiris, and if anyone had come up missing theirs, I would have turned him over to them."

More exchanges followed, but the anger was muting to a low rumble.

"Tell them we apologize for failing to protect their ... their king. Call him that, in death he deserves the title. Ask them if we can offer an assistance in preparing his body for an honorable burial."

Gor translated, but had no need to translate the angry refusal.

"Very well, then. Tell them we shall be leaving, as our continued presence does no good."

That seemed to catch the group off guard, and without waiting for their reply, he gave the command, "Mount up, draw swords, and off at a gallop, two abreast!"

CHAPTER 57:

BATTLE ORDERS

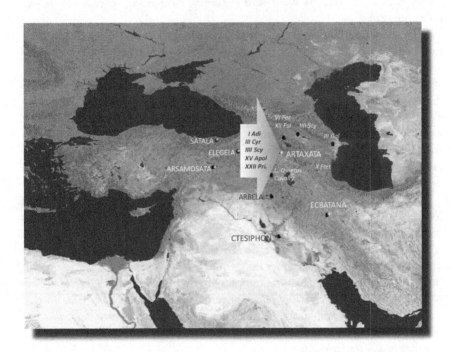

Elegeia, June 114AD

Trajan awoke, as was his wont, in the pre-dawn darkness. He stretched in the narrow lightly padded soldier's cot, feeling bones and joints popping that did not used to pop. *Admit it, you are, if not yet old, at least no longer young.*

He lay for a few minutes, attentive to the night sounds of the camp, soldiers speaking softly, a distant whinny from a horse, and somewhere, a dog barking, some century's mascot, no doubt. Then he got up, slipped a tunic over his nakedness, and lit a taper from the night-candle on his desk, to spark brighter flames in oil lamps around his sleeping quarters. As shadows fled to flicker in the corners of the tent, he relieved himself in the night pot and swigged a cup of water left overnight on his worn desk, spitting half of it into the night pot to take the morning foulness from his mouth. He shaved his graying morning stubble with a fine steel stiletto, watching his handiwork in the bronze mirror.

Satisfied he was awake, he sat at his desk before the blank papyrus sheet he had left purposely before going to bed last night, along with ink and a stylus. He studied the fine crisscrossed pattern of overlaid fibers that made up the premium cream-colored paper, golden in the lamp's glow.

If there was to be a way to avoid war, the death of Parthamasiris, at whoever's hand, ended any chance for that. So now I must prepare my commanders, refine our plans, and take the initiative.

Trajan wrote just single words, to focus his thoughts on the individual points he must make at the commanders' war council which would convene after the first watch was posted following breakfast. He had considered staying up to complete it last night, but it was already well after midnight; he did his best work, it seemed, by letting his mind mull over the problem while sleeping, then capture it, as he was doing, before the sun came up. The first word was *celeritas*, speed, paramount to victory, to exploit the advantage his forces had in overwhelming force, and the delayed Parthian response. *We must take all of Armenia before retiring to winter quarters, and those winter quarters will be in Artaxata, the capital.*

The next word was *cura*, care and prudence. *They must be aware at all times that the Parthians, however long they delay, can mount their own overwhelming force and deal us a devasting blow, especially after our legions are scattered to garrison various parts of Armenia, flushed with the hubris of an easy victory. I don't like to pre-plan defeat, but we must allow for rapid escape in an unexpected direction if necessary… but where?* He pressed his fists hard against his temples. *Somewhere unexpected… north! We can go north to Iberia, a friendly client state, then west to Colchis and the Black Sea.*

He then wrote *nix*, snow. *We can't stop fighting because of snow, no matter how heavy. The Ironclads and the Thunderbolts will have to master those snowshoes we acquired. They can handle the highlands.*

On and on he went, until he had twenty or so single points to present to his commanders, solicit their discussion, and then come to some final decisions. He was just sprinkling some sand on the paper to dry the ink when his orderly scratched at the canvas flap that served as a door to his quarters. "Good morning, Your Excellency. You are up, I see. Would you like some breakfast?"

"I would indeed, young man. Some porridge, please, and warm fruit juice."

"At once, sir."

After breakfast, Trajan donned his battle gear, the leather and unpretentious iron highly polished and oiled, but bearing various dents and scars of its many years of use in battle. Aside from a purple tunic, helmet plume and cloak, he was indistinguishable from any other legion commander.

He seated himself in a plain canvas campaign chair in the spacious meeting area of his tent, in front of the large leather map hung on the interior wall, separating his living quarters from the meeting area. He surveyed the area; dozens of leather campaign chairs similar to his were positioned to accommodate his sixteen commanders and their staffs in groups of three or four. As he was reviewing his notes, Gaius Lucullus of the Twelfth entered, with his *primus pilus* centurion and a grizzled veteran, his new prefect of camps, no doubt. "Good morning, Gaius. I am pleased to see you are the first to arrive this morning."

"Good morning to you, Your Excellency." He saluted crisply, his arm across his leather corselet, and waited for the *Princeps* to acknowledge it with a nod. "You have done us the honor the past few days of allowing us to host you and your entourage, so it is easy to be early. My *praetorium* is less than a hundred yards away. May I introduce my First Lance, Paulus Herrerius?" Paulus, too, saluted, then Gaius continued. "And you have met my new prefect, Antonius Aristides, though you may not remember him."

"Antonius, yes! And your beautiful new wife, Marcia. The same name as my mother. How is she, and what in the hell are you doing under the eagles again? You must be almost as old as I am."

"She is doing well, Your Excellency, and more beautiful with every year. Caring for our school and children in Aquileia. As for the eagles, Gaius needed help, so here I am. If I may say, though, you have remarkable memory. That was ten years ago, and just a few hours of your time."

The *Princeps* laughed, his eyes wrinkling at the corners in glee. "It is hard to forget Jason's new argonauts. You all were quite the talk of Rome for months. You have aged well."

"Thank you, Your Excellency,"

The reunion was interrupted by the arrival of the rest of the legion commanders and their entourage, and Lusius Quietus, the cavalry commander. All were seated well before the morning bugle signaled the changing of the watch.

Trajan stood. "Good morning, gentlemen. The events of the last few days, the unfortunate death of Parthamasiris at the hands of Armenian partisans, has made war between Rome and Parthia inevitable. Usurper of the Armenian throne he may be, but he was also the nephew of King Osroës who will avenge his death, as would we all in similar circumstances. It is my intent then to seize the initiative and take Armenia without allowing him time to deploy his considerable forces. It is my intent to lay out my general intentions and allow you to fill in the details as necessary. I am, for now, not *Princeps* of Rome, but *Imperator*, your commander-in-chief, and as such, I demand that you question any and all parts of my plan if you see potential flaws. I desire impertinent victory, not obeisant defeat. Is that understood?"

A murmur of assent ran through the room.

"I intend to exploit the mobility of Lusius Quietus' cavalry to bring the war quickly to our foe. Lusius and his twenty thousand Berber horsemen will proceed to the area south of Lake Van and operate as required to draw out and defeat any cavalry the Armenians may bring to bear." He pointed to the large, stylized lake on the wall map. "In past battles, their cavalry has been a challenge to our lighter forces. Lusius' Berbers will negate that advantage."

Lusius stood, and when acknowledged, spoke. "Sir, we will also be in a position to guard against any Parthian approaches, from Arbela in Mesopotamia, or from Ecbatana in Parthia. We will engage, defeat or delay them, and alert you of the threat in any case. The mountains will work to our advantage, as our force can appear out of nowhere from a mountain gorge."

"Very well, Lusius. You have always been one of my most astute tacticians." Trajan pointed to the map where jagged inverted vees represented mountains northeast of Artaxata, and another large lake. "Traditionally, the Armenians retreat from the invaders to highlands in the Lesser Caucasus Mountains. Difficult for invaders to access, with many opportunities for ambush, they become impassable to all except Armenians because of heavy snows. However, this time, not to us."

Trajan picked up a racket-like snowshoe and a pair of poles. "These are what give the Armenians mobility in the winter. Wearing these on their feet, they can traverse snow higher than a man's head without sinking in, hunt for winter game for food, and emerge in the lowlands at will to strike the unsuspecting invader. They can then retreat to the highlands without fear of pursuit. They have been doing this for a thousand years and they are good at it, wading into the mountain snowbanks for fun when there is no invader to fight. Bruttius Praesans and Gaius Lucullus, you have been given enough of these snowshoes and poles to equip all of the men of your two legions with these, plus spares. Your task is to proceed to Lake Sevan here, and begin learning how to use these in the autumn snow. By October, I expect you to deny the remnants of the Armenian armies their traditional sanctuary in the highlands. You, and not they, shall rule the snows this winter."

Trajan then indicated the curve of the Caspian Sea, the bordering land colored yellow. "The Parthians have complete control of the Caspian Sea. They can launch hundreds of ships to land tens of thousands of troops at any place along the Iberian coast, to join up and attack us from the rear with little warning. To that end, I am detaching Tiberius Maximus' Tenth Straits and Erucius Clarus' Third Gallic legions to operate along the coastline on the Iberian Plain north of the Lesser Caucasus, to oppose any such landing. And, since any battle plan may fail, our exit, if necessary, shall be north to Iberia, our loyal client state, then to the Black Sea by way of Colchis. Hopefully, we shall not need this."

He then pointed at Artaxata. "The remaining five legions shall operate under Claudius Severus, our newest governor of Armenia. You shall take

Artaxata and make it your new capital. A lot of the Roman Treasury went into rebuilding it thirty years ago, so do not raze it again. It is supposed to be quite beautiful, and I hope to visit you there to formally install you as governor."

Trajan addressed the audience as a whole. "Are there any questions?" There were none. "That is it, then. Good luck, gentlemen, and see my staff for any details."

CHAPTER 58:

FRIENDS IN PRISON

Ctesiphon, July 114AD

Sanatruces entered his father's office without knocking, without any announcement. He simply wrapped his green robe around him in a swirl of iridescence, and took a seat before the desk. Mithridates looked up, surprised at the interruption. "News?" he said, simply.

"News. And not good. The Romans have murdered Parthamasiris, and annexed Armenia. They appointed Claudius Severus, the former governor of their new province of Petraea, as the new governor, and are marching on Artaxata now, if they haven't already taken it."

"Definitely not good news. Have you informed the *Shahanshah* of this development?"

"Not yet, father. I wanted your guidance."

"Good. My brother will be furious to hear of this. He loved his son. They really murdered him? How?"

"He came to meet them, to plead his case before Trajan. Trajan turned him down, insulted him, and sent him back to Artaxata to make arrangements for his departure, with a military escort. Along the way, they murdered him."

Mithridates tapped his fingertips together, pondering this momentous event. "A hundred thousand men, nine full legions, some from Europe, plus auxiliaries from all over. Berber cavalry from the coast of Africa along the Great Western Ocean! They don't need a hundred thousand men to subdue Armenia. They intend to subdue us. Any word on the usurper Vologases? Does he know of this, and does he share our concern?"

"He does, Father, according Zacharias' latest report, and no, he does not see the Romans as a threat to his rebellion. Maybe even a positive development, keeping us occupied. Of interest to you, last month he met with a Han delegation from China. Ostensibly, about trade and security along the land routes to Asia."

"Or about a Han army to strike us in the back when the Romans attack us." He turned toward the open door. "Kophasates!" he bellowed.

"Sir," answered his secretary from the outer room.

"Fetch me Marcus from his quarters, immediately."

"At once, sir."

***

Marcus was enjoying the sweet aftermath of lovemaking with Mei, dreamily savoring the warmth of her body, when there was a hammering at the door and soldiers burst in, swords drawn. Mei gasped in horror, and Marcus shielded her body with his, sheets around their nakedness.

A soldier, evidently the man in charge, gestured toward her with his sword. "You get dressed, whore, and get out. You are done here!"

Mei, flushing redly, reached for her clothes, trying to put them on underneath the sheet.

"Just stand up and throw something on. Carry the rest with you. We don't have all day. And you, Marcus, dress quickly!"

Marcus tried to hide himself as he slipped out of bed, but no avail. The soldiers caught sight of his scarred crotch and began to giggle among themselves. "A gelding, he's a gelding!" said one.

"A gelding, still trying to be a stallion," said the other, with a guffaw.

"Keep it down," said the leader. They forced Mei out into the hallway, wearing just a shift, her other clothes in a bundle in her hand. Marcus, in a tunic, they marched off to Mithridates' office, leaving her to dress in the hall, to the amusement of those passing through.

They ushered him roughly into Mithridates' inner chamber, bypassing Kophasates. The leader pushed him in front of the desk, then fell back to stand at attention. "As ordered, sir." The leader dipped his sword in salute.

"As you were, soldier. Thank you, you are dismissed to the outer chamber. Close the door behind you, please." Mithridates waved his hand, and the soldiers left.

He turned toward Marcus. "Playtime is over, Marcus. Or should I call you *Si Nuo*, 'Western Bull'. An odd name for one of your kind," he said, with a sneer of disgust. "I want to know what you know about Rome and the Han Court, all of it, and I want to know it now. I have been very patient with you, but time has run out. The meaning of the letters you exchanged with Rome under Galba's seal, the same Galba who is now the senior advisor to Trajan as he prepares to invade our country. How many Han soldiers did you arrange to support him?"

"Is that what you think? I told you, they were all family matters, sent under the good graces of Aulus ... Senator Galba ... who lent us his seal so we could stay in touch."

Mithridates reached into his desk and withdrew ten scrolls, his with the yellowish rice paper, Marcia's the fine, brilliant white Augustan papyrus she used.

"You lied! You said you sent these on!"

"I lie as often as is necessary. Now decode each one of these and tell me what they really said."

"I told you, there is no hidden meaning in these scrolls. They mean exactly what they say!"

Mithridates slammed the desk with his palm. "Guards!" he said, loud enough to be heard behind the thick closed door. "Guards, in here at once!"

The leader entered, followed by his two men. "Take this scum to the prison, where he can see if the darkness and rats can jog his memory."

They manhandled Marcus out of the office as roughly as they had brought him in and with a soldier holding onto each arm, marched him down the hall, down the marble stairs, around the first-floor pavilion to a plain wooden door well-hidden from view. The head man produced a key, unlocked it, and they led Marcus down a dark, rough-cut stairway, perhaps two floors down. A handful of sconces cast a flickering light that left dancing shadows on the wall. They came up to a barred cell, already holding two ragged, scruffy individuals. The head man produced another key, unlocked the cell and threw Marcus inside, to land hard on the straw-strewn floor. Wordlessly, they relocked the cell and left.

The two occupants remained where they had been seated, leaning up against the wall. "Welcome to hell, whoever you are," said the black-bearded one. "The pot's over there by the corner, if you need it. It stinks, they don't change it very often. I am Boss, and this is Horse," he said, indicating the other individual, with a finer beard that might be lighter in color. Marcus wasn't sure, in the dim light, his eyes not yet adjusted to the darkness.

"Boss, and Horse… the ones who brought me here?"

"Hey, the world is very small. Yes, we did, I think… but I don't recall your name. Something Roman?"

"Marcus. Yes, it is a very small world."

Mei returned to the inn where they stayed, her clothes in disarray. Hina was the first to find her in the courtyard. "Mei! What happened?"

Mei embraced her, burying her face in Hina's shoulder. In between choking sobs, she managed to get out, "Marcus! Marcus, they … they took him away. Soldiers!"

Hina held her, comforting her as best she could. "Took him? Where?"

Mei released her, and tried to regain control of herself, taking a deep breath and wiping her eyes with the sleeve of her shift. "I need to sit down," she said, seating herself on a stone bench. "I don't know. We were visiting. The soldiers burst in, called me a whore, ordered me out and took him off. I don't know where, or why."

Hina stayed close beside her as they entered the inn, making their way to their room on the second floor. Hina had only been close to one woman in her life, Marcus' sister Marcia, now her sister, neither having one of their own. But she was also beginning to feel very close to Mei, who often on the one hand seemed helpless, but on the other hand often showed an iron inner core. She would help her rescue Marcus … somehow.

Fortunately, everyone was in, except for Hadyu, out to see the sights of Ctesiphon. Marasa and Andanyu were caring for Adhela, but as Xiongnu adults, room was made for them as equals. "Please, we must all meet and discuss this. Something has happened to Marcus at the palace, we don't know what, but we have to find a way to rescue him," opened Hina. "He was taken by soldiers somewhere."

Nathaniel was the first to speak. "Mei, I presume you witnessed this. Had he given any indications of problems?"

"No, none at all. He met with Mithridates every few days, mostly to play a board game," answered Mei.

"The rumor is that an invasion by Rome is imminent, everyone is on edge. I suspect that has something to do with it. He had a lot of freedom to come and go before. They may have decided he was now a risk with his Roman connections," said Nathaniel.

"Do you suppose they may have put him in a jail somewhere? And if so, where?" asked Hina.

"That is a possibility. There is a jail in the palace, the entrance oddly on the pavilion, unguarded. Probably locked. No one is going to try to tear down a door on the pavilion," said Nathaniel.

"Does it have an outside entrance?" asked Hadyu.

"Probably, as a way to get the nasty things that go with prisons in and out. But I don't know. Given where the inside door is, I would guess on the south side. But it will be either guarded or locked."

"Perhaps I can try to find it," volunteered Galosga.

"Perhaps, but let's not rush. Just getting you inside the walls around the palace is no small task," said Nathaniel.

"For you, perhaps. You do things the way they are supposed to be done. I do them how they have to be done. Excuse me, I have preparations to make. I will let you know where that door is soon," said Galosga.

CHAPTER 59:

AMBUSHED

West of Artaxata, July 114AD

There are a thousand sounds that go with a legion on the march. First, the tramp of twelve thousand boots, the syncopated rhythms of sixty centuries counting cadence, each slightly out of sequence with the others; *sin, sin, sin, ta dex*… in the mutilated Latin of the soldiers on the march … 'left, left, left, your right'. The jingle of thousands of pieces of metal armor, horse snaffles, the rumble of wagons, the neighing and whinnying of horses. And occasionally, bawdy marching songs, to make the miles go faster. The Twelfth had started out vociferously, but as the cool morning gave way to a hot forenoon, the voices fell silent. The troops sweated on, mile after mile in enduring silence, marching along the dusty dirt road parallel to the Araxes River, alternately through rolling hills or fertile farming plains, in the distance the gray cliff of the Caucasus, still snow-capped in July, *sin, sin, sin, ta dex*. The farmers, seemingly unthreatened by the disciplined Roman troops, smiled and waved to them in passing. Just another long march, the Twelfth Thunderbolt following the Sixth Ironclads by a few miles.

At the head of the column rode the *legatus* Gaius Lucullus, his prefect Antonius Aristides and his *primus pilus* 'first lance' Paulus Herrerius. The scouts had just reported that the next several miles would be rough terrain, the Araxes River spilling down through a rough, rocky pass.

"Ambush country, if'n yer askin' me, sir…" growled Antonius, swaying on his horse. He elicited a smile from Gaius.

"Good to have you back under the eagles, talking like a soldier again, Antonius," said Gaius.

"He's right, though," said Paulus. "Good place to jump us, if they are going to. Unless you object, sir, I am ordering shields unshouldered till we get through this pass."

"Make it so, Paulus, and put some extra skirmishers on our flanks. And bunch up our supply wagons so they don't get cut off. Also bring the *carroballistae* in close if we need artillery. I wish I knew where the cavalry is. Out scouting around somewhere, I hope not too far."

Paulus gave the order, bugles blew, men shouted, men obeyed. And grumbled. It was much more comfortable to march with the big rectangular shield slung across one's shoulder, than marching holding it at the ready with the left hand. The *carroballistae,* on wagons, were armed and conspicuously training back and forth while on the move, looking for targets.

The wide and silent Araxes suddenly began to gurgle, then became a babbling white-water torrent to their left, as the grade steepened.

A sound like an angry hornet buzzed between Antonius and Gaius, but it was no hornet. It was the sound of an arrow from an unseen archer, a sound familiar to them from dozens of past campaigns. The air was soon full of its lethal companions on high arching trajectories, seeking soldiers to kill. One horse reared, neighing, spilling its rider, another man fell from his horse, clutching his shoulder.

Gaius reacted swiftly. "Arrows! *Testudo!*" More shouted commands and bugles, and shields slammed down, interlocked from side to side, more shields from behind slid over those in front to form a roof, like the giant tortoise shell whose name the formation bore. Gaius and the other horsemen scanned the skies, hoping to stop inbound arrows with their smaller circular shields. There was no sign of the archers, but still the flights of arrows came, massed volleys arching high, unaimed, from hidden shooters, hoping to kill by quantity rather than by accuracy, an occasional shout or groan marking the spot where one found its mark. Somewhere in the rear, smoke rose from their supply train.

"Bad position here, Paulus. They have us fixed, and if they have something heavier than archers, we are in for a fight. And our cavalry is out scouting, but obviously missed this one."

"Not meanin' ter intrude, sir but why not split our *testudo* ter form an open square, an' get some of our boys out from under shelter ter be firin' back? No reason fer us ter take all the arrows."

"Sounds like a plan. Paulus?"

"I am satisfied." He turned and gave the order and the sixty centuries reformed coming into the new formation with a loud thump as six thousand shields each hit the ground with a near simultaneous thump. Within a minute, archers had slipped from beneath the *testudo* to shelter within its walls to launch counter-volleys. Now, hundreds of slender goose-quilled Roman shafts answered back, seeking their tormentors behind the cliff.

Paulus surveyed the situation. "Good idea, Antonius. I am going to bring up the artillery and put some plunging bolts behind those cliffs. Can't see what we are shooting at, but they can't either."

"Oh, yes, they can, Paulus. Look, up on that peak over there." Someone on that peak was directing fire for the people behind him, using a flag to point direction. "Get your best archer on that man and take him down. And have everyone look for others. We are spread out more than a mile, there must be more."

In a moment after the word was passed, the target staggered, then fell headlong off the cliff to certain death. The enemy's volume of arrows slackened, but then around the east and west ends of the hill on their right came the thunder of hooves, as the Armenian cavalry charged what they hoped was a weakened enemy.

The Twelfth wasn't weakened. The enemy's charge brought them nearly broadside to the *carroballistae,* close enough for aimed shots, shots that passed completely through riders, carrying them off their horse for dozens of yards. Some bolts passed through one horse with enough power left to kill another behind it. When the remnants of the cavalry van reached the legion, Gaius, Paulus and Antonius were ready, their long cavalry *spatha* swords drawn. One man recognized Gaius as the leader and charged, but Antonius rammed him with his horse, deflecting his charge, then swung viciously with a right-hand swipe of his *spatha* that nearly decapitated the man. The body fell from his horse, Antonius' horse snuffling in excitement, a true battle-mare. He found another rider to engage as the fever of battle took him over, then another, and yet another. At some distance on, he shook off the heat of battle, returning to stay with Paulus and Gaius in mutual defense. He found them, but by now the battle was over, the horsemen withdrawing, the Roman cavalry, having finally found the battle, now in hot pursuit.

"Sorry, sir, I should not have gone off ter fight, an' leave you two alone. I'm not a young pup anymore," he said, breathing heavy, covered with blood, none of it his own.

"You could have fooled me, Antonius," said Paulus with a big smile. "How many you kill?"

"I don't know, I lost count, just one big jumble. Five, I think."

"Good fighting."

"Good fighting to both of you," said Gaius, also with a smile. "Let's get a tally on injuries and deaths and damage. Then let's get out of this ambush terrain. It flattens out into farming country about a mile ahead. I think we will take an early camp tonight."

CHAPTER 60:

THE PALACE AND THE PALM TREE

Ctesiphon, August, 114AD

A single date palm grew alongside the wall in the garden outside the south wall of the palace, unusual in that date palms were usually cultivated in clusters. This one appeared to be wild, or perhaps once planted, then the rest of the grove forgotten. No matter. Its fifty-foot height, a good thirty feet higher than the wall, would provide a clear view of the south wall of the palace.

Galosga had scouted the area for several days and nights, observing the comings and goings of people, especially cultivators who might notice a man perched among the palm tree's leafy fronds. There were none. The tree seemed to grow alone, untouched by humans. So, well before sunrise, here he was at the base of the tree, clad in black, with a black wrap for his face, a light pack with plenty of water for the heat of the August day, and pouches of nuts, in case the dates were not producing. He grabbed the trunk. The protrusions from the trunk made convenient stepping points, and he wrapped a rope around his waist and the tree ... just in case. It would be a long fall if he lost his grip.

Galosga had climbed many long, straight pine trees in his youth, to no purpose, just to show his mates that he could climb higher and faster than they. He had not forgotten how, and this tree did not have the disgusting sticky pine sap. His legs wrapped firmly along the trunk, he could just toss the rope a bit further up the tree, then step up until level with it, repeat. The heavy felt trousers kept most of the friction of the bark from his skin, though they were neither good color nor weight for the coming hot day. No matter.

It did not take Galosga long to reach the palm fronds at the top, adjust the rope and rig himself a bit of a seat. And yes, the dates were in prolific production. He grabbed several of the deliciously sweet fruits for breakfast, then a few more. So sweet!

As the sun came up, he found he had a clear view of the palace inside the walls. There were three doors along the ground wall, left, center, right, neatly symmetrical. He waited.

Mule-drawn wagons pulled up by the left door, the door opened, and people in tunics emerged to help unload the wagons. Mostly crates, but some pigs and cows as well, skinned and slung on poles. Probably the palace kitchen, preparing for the day's royal repast. At the same time, the door on the right opened and someone emerged to discard the contents of a bowl on the ground. The prison? Could be. Or just someone discarding a night pot.

The wagons left, and troops came from the middle door, fell into formation, and received their daily orders. Definitely the palace security.

Galosga remained in the tree throughout the day, savoring the plentiful sweet dates, washing them down with water from his leather sack, the nuts in his pack untouched. He caught sight of Hina on the ground, waiting, prepared to deal with anyone who might see him. He waved to indicate that all was well. More comings and goings from the left and center doors, nothing from the right. Galosga decided that must be the prison door, but was it locked? Probably.

Well after sundown, when darkness had settled on the park, Galosga shinnied down the tree. Hina slipped from the shadows to join him. "What did you find?"

"I suspect I found the prison door. One more day, then we will make our attempt." He handed her a pouch, the nuts emptied out in favor of dates. "For waiting so patiently for me," he smiled.

The next day confirmed the previous day's observation. The right door was opened to discard the night waste about the same time as the wagons arrived to provision the kitchens, then never again reopened throughout the day.

"Tomorrow is the day, for better or worse," Galosga told Hina after shinnying down the tree. "Let's tell the others."

Back at the inn, they assembled the group. "We leave tomorrow. Hina and I are going over the wall, free Marcus, and hopefully get out. If we don't make it out by the first hour after sunrise, leave without us, we won't be seeing you again. We will be going on horseback to travel fast, so what you can't take, leave here. Marasa, you and Andanyu ride with Hadyu as our guard if we have to fight our way out. Mei, you and Nathaniel take care of Adhela."

There were no questions. They had talked about this for several days.

Around midnight, Hina and Galosga, both in all-black felts, approached the south wall of the palace, Galosga with a grappling hook on a rope, Hina with a ladder. He had noted in his two days in the tree that, although there was a parapet along the south wall, no one had been patrolling. He hoped there would be no patrols tonight. He spun the grappling hook on the rope with increasing speed, then let it fly in the dark. It went over the wall, as best as Galosga could tell in the dark. It landed somewhere with a thunk. He tugged but met no resistance, then it caught something and held, hopefully well enough to support his weight. He grabbed the rope with both hands, then put one foot, then the other, on the wall, walking himself up. He reached the rim just as his shoulders were beginning to burn with the effort. He threw a leg over the wall, settling onto the parapet.

He gave a signal to Hina, and she pushed the ladder up against the wall. Galosga grasped it and hefted it over, bracing it on the inside wall. No telling what sort of shape Marcus might be in. Maybe not able to climb a rope.

Another signal, and Hina walked herself up the wall on the rope, joining Galosga on the parapet, two shadows in the darkness. Galosga re-secured the rope around a bar on the parapet, tossing it down the inside wall, in case someone found and removed the ladder. But they saved their shoulders from further abuse by the rope, taking the ladder down into the darkened park.

Galosga led Hina to some bushes he had seen near the rightmost door, and the two hid themselves there, waiting. Galosga could smell the rich tang of her sweat, which he found most arousing. No matter, time for that later.

Shortly after sunrise, the man emerged from the prison door, passed the bushes to dump his pot, and Galosga and Hina slipped silently into the prison unseen behind him. Crouching, they searched for corners in the darkness, lit by a single torch on the far wall. The place stank. By the torchlight, they could make out a barred cell. Hopefully, Marcus would be in it; if not, this whole effort would be in vain.

The man came back in, closing and barring the door, and shoved the bowl, clattering, through a small opening at the bottom of the cell. "You three quit shitting so much, or I'll make you eat it. We don't feed you enough for all that."

"Good morning to you, too." Marcus, unmistakably Marcus!

The man grumbled, hung something back up on the wall opposite the cell, and left, shutting the door behind him. There was a thud, as something heavy fell into place on the other side.

They waited, but there were no sounds, other than eating sounds, scraping of spoons on bowls, as the prisoners ate their meager morning rations. There did not seem to be anyone else in the room. Galosga slithered on his belly, silent as a serpent, up to the cell, unnoticed by the prisoners. "And good morning to you, too, Marcus. Enjoying your breakfast?"

Marcus was so surprised he dropped the bowl, shattering it. "Galosga!"

"It is I. Ready to go for a ride?"

"Yes, and my friends, if possible. Boss and Horse."

"We have spare horses. How often do they check on you?"

"Not until evening, when they bring us more gruel to eat."

"Good, we have half a days' head start. Keys?"

"There on the wall."

Galosga quickly unlocked the rickety lock. "The morning guard will be forming up outside soon. Let's wait for them to go back in, then make our way over the wall."

"Right. You know, this is my second jailbreak. The last time, we went as Buddhist monks, heads shaved."

"I know. I was there."

Hina emerged from the darkness, and together they huddled by the door, listening for the sound of the morning formation and the supply wagons. At last, the formation dismissed, and the last wagon rumbled off, one mule complaining loudly.

Another few minutes. "I think this is it," said Galosga. He opened the door a crack, and the outside was empty. "Move fast, but stay under cover. There is a ladder, I hope, by the wall on your right."

Hopping from shrub to shrub, the five made their way to the wall, Marcus up the ladder first, followed by Horse and Boss, then Hina and Galosga. On the parapet, Galosga pulled the ladder up and put it down the other side, untied the grappling hook rope and tossed it to the ground. Not far off, their group waited for them by the date palm.

There was no time for celebrating their reunion; Marcus and Mei just smiled at each other as he slid into his waiting saddle. "You two," said Galosga to Marcus' cellmates, "Ride our spares bareback, we have no extra saddles." Then to Hadyu, "I think we have a half-day head start. Let's not waste it."

They whistled up their horses to a fast trot, Galosga still carrying the ladder and Hina the grappling hook. They would dispose of them some way down the road, in the Tigris.

"Where are we going?" asked Marcus.

"Follow the Tigris north. Hopefully, we will find the Roman army in a few hundred miles," said Nathaniel.

CHAPTER 61:

A NEW SPY

Ctesiphon, August, 114AD

Mithridates was not one given to profanity. But the word of Marcus' escape from prison evoked a torrent of words he seldom used, directed at the hapless officer responsible for the prison. "His friends just walked in, released him, and then walked back out? Is that a prison you are running, or a gods-cursed inn? Where in the fucking hell were the guards?"

"We ... we didn't think they needed continuous guarding. No one has ever broken out of our jail before," stammered Orontes, the prison head.

"Well, now you have not one, but three on the run. What in the hell are you doing to track them down?"

"We have alerted all outposts and checkpoints to the west, and we have patrols actively searching all roads that direction," Orontes answered.

Mithridates was fuming, well aware that this was not Marcus' first jailbreak. Many years before, he and his Roman companions had similarly escaped a Chinese prison, and though three of them were extremely conspicuous Westerners with little grasp of Chinese, had successfully evaded capture for months. Now, the situation was reversed; Marcus and Mei were of unusual Oriental appearance, likely to attract attention. Yet Mithridates knew they would not. "Why west?" he asked.

Orontes took a deep breath. "They want to get out of our territory as fast as possible. It is just one hundred and fifty miles to the Roman border. Three or four days of hard riding. Any other direction, it is just too long, too uncertain."

"To the north, toward Armenia?"

"More than twice as far, and going into an uncertain situation, the Roman invasion in progress."

Mithridates drummed his fingers on his desk, considering what Orontes had said. There was no point going on about the jailbreak, it was done and over. The problem at hand was to either find Marcus, or find an alternative to breaking the Roman coded letters.

"Very well, find them, and find them quickly. Dismissed!"

Orontes bowed very deeply and left, not turning his back to Mithridates. As he exited, Sanatruces came in through a side entrance to his father's office.

"Amusing, indeed. Father, I had no idea that you swear like a common soldier."

"Did you overhear the conversation?"

"I did, and I suspect most of the people on this floor did as well, at least your part. Seems our prisons are not too hard to break into," Sanatruces said, as he seated himself on the sofa opposite his father's desk.

"There will be hell to pay for the lack of security. We don't have any idea what happened, but it is obvious that their companions broke in and set them free. What is amazing is that we have learned that besides his wife, he had a good-sized entourage that appears to have included Nathaniel. And that Jew will pay with his head when we find him, he has been double-dealing me all along. But we may not find them, and any chance of decoding the Roman connection to the Han is lost." He sank his head in his hands.

"Perhaps not, Father, there is still the Italian connections."

"Not much of a chance of that. Ariobarzanes' thug thoroughly compromised both last year."

"Ariobarzanes has a new agent."

"Another thug? I hope this one is at least as intelligent as a flea."

"Not a thug, he's aristocracy, of their Senate."

"Really?"

"Really, father. He won't have to break in, they will invite him."

CHAPTER 62:

PLANNING THE SEIGE

Arsamosata, July 114AD

The legion commanders one by one entered the *Princeps'* purple-roofed praetorium, anchored by ropes brilliantly white in the sunlight, the lightning-bolt banner of the Twelfth snapping in the breeze next to the banner of the six-teated wolf who suckled Romulus and Remus, Trajan's personal insignia. Inside the tent, their eyes adjusting to the yellowish inside light, they saw the massive model of the acropolis of the capital of Armenia, Artaxata. The acropolis rose two feet off the floor, encircled by two walls, and on the top of which were two colonnaded temples and a complex of buildings. The legion commanders took their seats, Gaius Lucullus flanked by Paulus Herrerius and Antonius. When all were seated, Trajan strode in wearing his plain battle gear with a purple cape, flanked by Claudius Severus and Aulus.

"Seats, gentlemen. As you can see, Artaxata will not be as easy a conquest as Arsamosata. That city was lightly defended and ill-prepared for a siege. Here at Artaxata, between the outer and inner wall are at least five thousand men, equipped with heavy catapults and *ballistae*. The city at the top of the acropolis has springs within the walls, so water will not be a problem, and we expect that they will have adequate stockpiles of food and weapons. They have, I presume, anticipated our arrival. While we outnumber them, defenders always have the advantage.

"We know from defectors and sympathetic locals that the five thousand men between the inner and the outer walls are Parthians, not Armenians. It seems that the Armenian leadership in the acropolis is not of one mind to support them, now that Parthamasiris is dead. So, our targets are the Parthians defending the city, not the city itself. I want twenty-five siege towers with heavy catapults and *ballistae*, to make the lives of those five thousand defenders difficult when we arrive next week. My desire is to win this battle between the walls, leaving the high city untouched. But I will take Artaxata, no matter the cost. Study the model, pick your dispositions and targets among yourselves, and present your plan to me in two hours." He turned abruptly and left, his purple cape swirling behind him.

Gaius Lucullus stood with Bruttius Praesens. They would have little to do with planning this siege, as they were tasked to go around Artaxata to the highlands, and then to the Caspian coast. But they and their entourage observed the planning with interest, offering occasional small suggestions. The outer wall was a good two hundred feet above the surrounding plain, and the inner another hundred above that. Time would not permit building earthen ramps to match the walls, so the artillery on the siege engines would have to fire blind in high arcs over the walls. Unaimed, the *ballistae* bolts would still cause considerable damage, and incendiary pots of naphtha fired from the catapults would not require any aiming at all. Reducing the defending force around the hilltop did not appear difficult, and the legions allocated among themselves areas of responsibility around the city.

"An amazin' model he's built himself, sir," said Antonius, admiring the exquisite detail of the buildings, the trees. Even miniature *catapulta*. "Why so much detail?"

"This is for the triumphal parade when he gets back to Rome. The capital of Armenia, Artaxata, the first of many models of cities to be taken," answered Gauis.

"First? What was Arsamosata?"

"Too insignificant, too easy. Artaxata will be the one for the people of Rome to admire," answered Herrierius.

"If we take it," answered Antonius. "We need to be warm and dry inside those walls before October, or we'll be spending our winter in the cold."

Gaius clapped his prefect across the back with a solid but friendly blow that made Antonius' armor jingle. "I suspect the Old Man has a plan for this. And anyway, we and the Sixth will be spending the winter in much colder weather in the highlands. Make sure you have plenty of dry socks, Antonius."

CHAPTER 63:

MAKING ENDS MEET

Petra, July 114AD

The throng of people surged along the narrow dark tunnel-like street of Siq, threading through the steep overhanging sandstone cliffs to the center of Petra, past the imposing temple-like colonnaded city hall, carved from the soft rock. The July heat was impressive, and all were intent on getting to a destination outside of the glaring sun, paying little attention to their surroundings.

The little boy, wearing just a white loincloth on his nut-brown body, fell in behind an elderly gentleman. The man was dressed lightly in a long white tunic, out of deference to the heat, but his silk turban and rings and other jewelry spoke of wealth. The little boy diffidently followed him, attracting no attention to himself, stalking his prey.

It did not take long for the boy to determine where the man carried his purse, an elaborate filigreed sack on his left side, suspended on a strap crossing over his right shoulder. Carelessly, the man was carrying it outside his clothing, an easy target.

The boy waited patiently until the crowd thinned, the nearest person fifty or more paces away. The boy dropped back, drew a very small knife from his loincloth, then began running, calling out to a non-existent companion: "Layla! Layla, wait for me, I am coming!"

He ran into the man and went down in a tumble, deftly snipping the purse's straps. He snagged the purse, unseen, and slipped it into his loin cloth behind his back. "Oh, sir, I am so sorry! I was trying to keep up with my friend and ran into you. I hope I didn't hurt you!"

The man beamed beatifically through his white beard, tousling the lad's well-kept black hair. "No worry, my boy. You can't hurt an old man like me. Are you all right?"

"Yes sir, I am fine. I skinned my knee a bit, but mom will take care of it."

"All right, you run along now, but be careful of other people."

"Yes, sir, I will." The boy headed off at a run, calling after his non-existent companions to wait for him, then darting into a side alley. He stopped, catching his breath, while making sure he had not been followed.

He pulled the purse out and examined its contents, a gold *aureus* and ten silver *denarii*. The boy did not have a head for such money, but he knew it was a lot, enough that Jacobus and Miranda could keep their house running for a long time. He slipped the purse back into his loincloth and headed off for his sandstone house by the Roman amphitheater.

Inside, the stone kept the interior cool against the day. He sought out Jacobus, who was seated reading a scroll in a wicker chair.

"Father, I know that you and mother have been worried about money."

"Times have been difficult, but we get by. Why are you concerned, Stick? We aren't going to throw you all back out on the street. God will provide, He always has."

Stick pulled the ornate purse from his behind. "Then Father, God must have provided us this then." He put the clinking purse in Jacobus' hand and stepped back with a proud grin.

Jacobus looked inside, giving a low whistle. There was enough money there to keep the orphanage going for months. "Where did you get this, Stick?" he asked, strongly suspecting he would not want to hear the answer.

"A man gave it to me."

"Men do not give away gifts like this to strange little boys." He examined the freshly cut ends of the straps. "You know what we have taught you about always telling the truth. Do you want to give me another answer?"

The boy shifted sheepishly from foot to foot, his gaze fixed on the tile floor. "I … I stole it from him, but only because you needed it."

"We don't need anything badly enough to take something from another. We took you away from that life on the street, and we will not let you go back to it."

Miranda had slipped silently into the room, observing. "Stick, you must help us find that man and return it to him. Do you remember what he looked like?"

"I guess so, white robe, white beard, silk turban." He was described about half the elderly men in Petra, but it was a start.

"Let's go back to where you stole it."

The three went back down the Siq. They did not have to go far before they found three uniformed *vigiles* of the urban cohort standing about that same man, who was vociferously describing the outrage that had just happened to him.

Jacobus' heart fell. If this went badly, it could get serious for little Stick, very serious. But if he failed to return the purse, the *vigiles* would eventually find Stick and then it would be serious for all. "Is that the man, Stick?"

The boy nodded.

"Let's go give him his purse back."

As they approached the group, the man saw Stick and pointed. "That's him! That's the rascal that stole my purse."

"It is, and he has come to return it to you, its contents intact," said Jacobus.

Stick handed the purse to the man, who looked inside, quickly determining that it was in fact intact. "Well, thank you ... I guess."

"Is it all there?" asked the senior of the *vigiles*.

"It is. I guess I have no further need for your services, since nothing has been stolen." The three *vigiles* nodded and left to go about their duties. The old man turned to Jacobus. "You must be the only man in Petra that would turn down that much money. What is your name?"

"Jacobus. This is my wife Miranda, and our would-be thief is Stick."

"Well, Stick, I am Benjamin." The old man extended his weather-worn hand to Stick. "I must say you are an excellent thief, for I did not know what you had done until the strap for my purse slipped off my shoulder and fell at my feet. I hope you are not planning to do that for a living, apparently your mother and father don't approve of that."

"No, sir, I am sorry, sir."

"Why did you do that? That is so much money, a little boy like you could not possibly spend it."

"Our home ... "

Jacobus intervened. "We aren't really his mother and father. We rescue street urchins like Stick and raise them as our own. With the war on, it's been hard to make ends meet, but we get by. He thought he was helping."

"Really? How many do you have? "

"Eleven boys and a girl. Five of the older boys have taken jobs but still live with us, and give us half their pay. It helps. Governor Severus was very fond of what we do, and I have a friend in one of the Roman legions who encouraged his men to support us. But they are both off to the war, and the merchants are all minding the cash, hoarding goods in case they get scarce."

"To be sure. Could I see your home?"

"Certainly, come have wine with us. Our house is near the amphitheater."

They set off at a brisk walk, and by the time they reached the orphanage, Jacobus had filled the man in on his own life as a street urchin, and how they had set up the orphanage almost ten years ago.

Back inside the cool sandstone, they toured the building, introducing Benjamin to some of the boys, and to Mouse, whom Stick considered his little sister. The two men seated themselves while Miranda returned with watered white wine and dates.

"This is a good thing you do, Jacobus. The rest of us just brush them away like mosquitoes, never thinking at all what their life must be like."

"What I remember, it was pretty horrible. And for many, their lives are short."

The man jiggled his purse, making the coins clink. "It seems this purse is ruined, with the straps cut." He passed it Jacobus. "Why don't you take it? I have another at home just like it."

CHAPTER 64:

THE NORTHERN ROUTE

Mosila, September 114AD

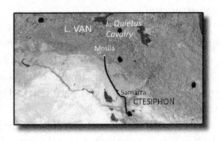

The city of Mosila shimmered in the baking sun along the steaming Tigris River, the end of the travelers' two-hundred-and-fifty-mile trek through heat they had not imagined could exist on earth. They had traveled at night to avoid the worst, but the night brought its own torments: gnats and mosquitoes swirling around them in a buzzing mist, zinging in all too frequently for a taste of fresh blood. The travelers were covered with bumps, some bloody from scratching.

They had considered, and discarded, the safer course of striking out through the desert to avoid the heavily traveled road along the river. Without knowing the lay of the land, where to find water, even how to find one's way by day or by night through the featureless terrain, that path was a certain death sentence.

They had had a moment of panic at the end of the second day near Samarra, when they were overtaken by a cavalry patrol, unable to leave the road for cover. But the patrol clattered by, their lances erect, paying no more attention to them than they did to the hundreds of other travelers enduring the heat on foot, on horseback or on wagons. For whatever reason, they were not being pursued. Several more patrols over the next few days confirmed that they were, for whatever reason, non-entities to the Parthians.

At Samarra, they ventured the risk of renting a room at an inn, an opportunity to bathe, eat, and for Marcus and Mei, and Hina, Galosga and Adhela, to sleep in the two comfortable beds. Nathaniel, Hadyu and the others got the floor. The inn had no accommodations for that many guests, and finding one that did would dangerously advertise wealth in a town they did not know.

Nathaniel went to the market in the morning and found some herbs to repel biting insects, and others that would heal their swollen welts. Marcus' prison companions Horse and Boss parted company to go their own way, deeply grateful for the rescue. The rest, as refreshed as possible in the oppressive heat, set out again on the way north, through Tikrit and too many other small towns to name. The herbs seemed to help. When they arrived at the outskirts of Mosila a week later their skins were deeply tanned but smooth, the welts faded away.

Nathaniel urged his bay alongside Hina, who was scanning the good-sized city straddling the Tigris. "We are out of Parthian territory now. This is Adiabene territory, a Parthian ally, but not under direct control of Ctesiphon. Pretty independent, actually. I think we can relax a bit."

"I will relax when I am somewhere that has nothing to do with Parthia," she answered.

Nathaniel smiled. "We are almost in Armenia. According to merchants' gossip, the Romans are operating around Lake Van, about three days north of here. And a huge force of Romans has besieged the capital Artaxata."

"That sounds like better company." Hina stuttered in broken Latin, misplacing several of the accents. Hopefully, it would be her last new language.

"That sounds like better company," he repeated slowly, correcting her mispronunciations. "But you have made good progress in Latin."

"Wonder why the Parthians are not pursuing us?"

"I think they expected us to go west, the shortest route to Roman territory in Syria, not north. If Mithridates ever figured that out, we already had several days head start, and our trail was cold. Let's go to town." He clicked up his mount to a canter, and Hina followed.

They made their way along the riverbank, Marcus and Mei with Adhela swaying in the wagon as it lurched and twisted in the ruts, spare horses in tow, everyone else on horseback.

The guard at the gate seemed to pay no attention to the throng of people coming and going through the gate in the mud wall, into and out of Mosila. Inside, the city was well-watered and green with many fountains that seemed to cool the heat. Nathaniel found an inn, two rooms, one for himself and Hadyu for a change. The journey was almost over.

CHAPTER 65:

IN ROMAN HANDS

Lake Van, September 114AD

Lusius Quietus' dark brown eyes peered from his hawk-like visage, scrutinizing the bedraggled party of travelers: An Oriental man and woman, inexplicably speaking Latin, a red-headed Amazon of a woman, a pock-marked, bronze-skinned man, head shaven, and a Jew. And a pubescent boy and girl, both in warrior garb, and a toddler. Everyone except the toddler had shields but empty scabbards, swords and daggers removed by Quietus' soldiers. All were wearing well-worn traveling clothes that had not been washed in a while. A motley crew indeed.

Outside, a string of horses nudged for position at the morning feed, neighing and jostling each other.

He wrapped his red cloak around himself against the chill September morning and rose from his backless camp chair in his command tent. "That is all, Aksil. You may go," he said, nodding the direction of the doorway. Turning back to the group, he looked them up and down, as though they were soldiers at some sort of inspection. The Jew looked down nervously, but the rest returned his gaze steadily, even the young ones. "Who speaks for this group?"

"I do, sir," answered the Oriental man. His black hair was cut short in the Roman fashion, and he had inexplicably blue eyes behind narrow slits, contrasting with his olive skin.

"You speak excellent Latin. Your name?"

"Marcus Quintus Lucius, sir"

"Roman enough name. How did you come by that?"

"I was born with it, and with all respect, my citizenship was affirmed by the hand of the *Princeps* fifteen years ago. The descendant of a citizen is himself a citizen."

"Very well. Tell me why you came here."

"I and my party were seeking to reach Roman territory. I was set upon and captured by Cyrus Mithridates, and briefly imprisoned in the palace in Ctesiphon. My friends here freed me."

"Cyrus Mithridates. Is that the brother of King Osroës?"

"None other."

"Why was he interested in you?"

"He believed my sister and I were exchanging some sort of coded communications with the court of China."

"Were you?"

"Absolutely not, sir. We were using the seal of one Senator Galba, with his permission, to keep in touch. I stayed behind in Han China on Senator Galba's expedition fifteen years ago, while he, my sister and the rest returned to Rome. My sister and I corresponded for much of that time, but Mithridates began intercepting those letters, and confiscated them. One of my reasons for returning to Rome was to find what had become of Marcia."

"Senator Galba? Aulus Aemilius Galba?"

"That is correct, sir."

"And who are these others?"

"Mei is my wife. Hina and Galosga are companions from that expedition fifteen years, Marasa, Andanyu and little Adhela are their children, and Hadyu is from their clan. Nathaniel is a traveler who joined us in Sogdiana."

"Well, that is an incredible journey. Aulus Aemilius is just a few days north of here with the *Princeps* at the siege of Artaxata. We will see if he can attest to the veracity of your story."

Marcus released control of his emotions, and smiled widely, his eyes bright. "I cannot believe my good fortune! I look forward to seeing him again."

"Your eagerness indicates you are probably telling the truth, however unlikely that truth appears to be." A small smile flickered briefly over Quietus' stern visage, and he clapped his hands. Aksil re-entered the tent, stood at attention and nodded respectfully. "See that these are taken to the baths and freshened up. Find them some fresh clothing. I would like them to join me for dinner this evening, so have Idir prepare an appropriate table for this large group."

"Sir!" Aksil brought his right arm across his chest with a thud.

"Thank you, sir," said Marcus. "May I ask your name?"

"My name is Lusius Quietus, commanding the *Princeps'* cavalry forces."

The trumpets were making the sunset change-of-watch call when Marcus' party returned to the commander's tent. They were all fresh, the men in white tunics, the women in white ankle-length *stolae*.

The guard at the entrance barred their way with his lance, but Marcus identified himself, and the swarthy soldier returned the lance to the vertical and admitted them, his eyes firmly fixed straight ahead. Inside, a long table took up most of the width of the command tent, laden with exotic food. Quietus, seated in the middle with his aide Aksil, rose to greet them. Marcus introduced each in turn: Mei, Hina, Galosga, Marasa, Andanyu, Adhela, Hadyu, and finally, Nathaniel. Quietus gripped each man's wrist in the military handshake, but just held the fingertips of the women. Mei accepted that, but Hina and Marasa, after accepting the gentle touch, continued on to their own military handshake.

The table was laden with roast goat, vegetables, dates and beakers of wine. Standing next Quietus were four men, all similar in appearance to him: swarthy, sharp-nosed with curly brown hair and well-shaped beards. All wore bright blue robes, chain mail over their chests.

"These are my generals, Izil, Meddur, Usaden and Warmaksen, each commanding five thousand horse." Quietus did not attempt to Latinize the names, but pronounced them in the guttural tones of his native language. "Now, seats, please. Your wine is poured and chilled with ice from the mountains. Marcus, please tell me what you know of Mithridates."

"Certainly, sir. I first met him in China twenty years ago. He was the Parthian envoy to the Han court when our expedition set out to Rome, and was still there when we returned with Senator Galba. The Senator's mission was to establish a relationship between Rome and the Han court, a direct dialogue. Senator Galba believed that Mithridates sabotaged our mission with false accusations, discrediting us and nearly getting us killed. I was extremely surprised, as we neared the Parthian border on this trip, to find he was looking for me by name."

"So, this is not your first trip west."

"It is my second. The first was from the Han Court to Rome, under Gan Ying, whose expedition perished by Parthian treachery on their way home overland. We and a few others were given to the Romans to serve as translators on their return mission by sea, or we would be dead also."

"You are indeed well-traveled, Marcus. And Mithridates is then treacherous?"

"As a snake. I think he feared our letters served as some sort of communication between the *Princeps* and the Han court."

"Could China possibly ally with Rome against Parthia?"

"The distances are vast. But the Chinese have put armies as far west as Sogdiana, so it is not impossible. Parthia is divided now, with a rival king Vologases in the east at Ecbatana. Vologases is more likely to seek that alliance, as they have closer contact with the Han, though indirect through merchants," volunteered Nathaniel.

"Interesting. It seems you have a lot of intelligence for Aulus Aemilius and the *Princeps*. Well, let us enjoy this good food, and the leave the follies of war and intrigue for another time." He drew his saber, longer and more curved than a Roman *spatha* cavalry sword, and carved slices from the goat meat on the platter, leaving the guests to select their preference.

Everyone set into the tasty meat, Adhela on Hina's lap. After a few minutes, Hina spoke up. "You have many beautiful horses here, Lusius Quietus."

"They are Berber horses from our homeland. Desert animals, hardy and fast."

"Your homeland is where?"

"Thousands of miles to the west of here in the far deserts by the Atlas Mountains by the Great Ocean. We grew up on horses."

"As did we."

"And your homeland is in China also?"

"No, we were in Mongolia now. We used to live in the grasslands north of China. Like you, my people grow up on horseback. Adhela is riding now, but with careful watching." She jostled the three-year old playfully in her lap, as he ate with his fingers.

Lusius smiled, lighting up his face. "Not yet ready to gallop?"

"Not yet."

"We are having a race tomorrow. Would you care to participate?"

"Yes. My last race, someone tried to cheat, but I still won."

"This is a cavalry outfit. There will be no cheating, because there are no rules. Good luck."

They established the time and place, then everyone returned to small talk. Lusius Quietus' cavalry force, twenty thousand strong, was far larger than anything the Romans had ever fielded. It was organized Berber-style, in groups of five thousand, divided and subdivided into smaller groups, down to squadrons of ten lancers. They were fast and undefeatable, and Quietus loved talking about them.

It turned out that there were in fact two rules. One is that all had to begin along the line of departure, awaiting the trumpet call, the other was that all should end up at a river five miles distant. In between, there were indeed no rules, though deliberate injuries to men and horses were discouraged. And it was not a race, but a cavalry charge, riders in leather corselets and helmets, shields on their left arms, swords in their right. Hina found the wooden terrain difficult for a headlong gallop, strewn with boulders, thorny bushes, logs, gulleys, and low-hanging branches that threatened to strip her from Devil. It was wholly unlike the grasslands of home or the deserts they had just traversed. However, her saddle had stirrups and theirs did not, giving her a bit of an advantage. She was much older than Quietus' riders, all twenty years old or younger, with the invincibility of youth. Hina had shed her youthful sense of invincibility long ago, replacing it with mature wisdom, or so she had thought. But she was not sure now, as she and Devil struggled to keep pace with the rampaging horde of young riders on their gray and dun Berber horses.

When she reached the river after ten minutes of all-out galloping, there were dozens of riders already there awaiting her arrival. Both she and Devil were drenched with sweat, his sides heaving. The horse trotted up to the riverside without direction and drank deeply, while Hina re-slung her sword and shield. Lusius Quietus was waiting. When Devil had quenched his thirst, Quietus walked up. "Well done, Hina. You finished in the top hundred."

"Thank you, Lusius. I was disappointed that I did not do better."

"Don't be. This was not a race for fun. This was a wing of cavalry, and I put each wing through this test every few weeks. This was your first time, but not theirs. Rest your horse, and join us this evening again for dinner. I will dispatch you all to Artaxata to the *Princeps* Trajan and Aulus Aemilius tomorrow."

CHAPTER 66:

REUNION

Artaxata, September 114AD

A squadron of thirty horsemen accompanied Marcus and his companions to Artaxata, following a fairly decent road. Only the commanding decurion spoke any Latin. They skirted the wastelands around the conical peaks of two volcanoes that the centurion identified as Agri Dagi. In the distance, black smoke arose, marking the siege of Artaxata on the other side of the Aras River.

At the river, a pontoon bridge spanned the flood, guarded by Roman soldiers. Challenges were exchanged, and they were allowed to pass, with an escort to direct them to the *Princeps'* praetorium. The citadel of Artaxata loomed a mile distant, on a huge gray outcropping of stone several hundred feet high, a half-mile or more in length. The acropolis on top was crowned by a brilliant white colonnaded temple, encircled between two concentric walls.

The orderly white tents of at least three legions could be seen on this side of the city, and every minute or so, a fireball climbed into the sky in a high arc from a catapult to land between the two walls, where several fires burned fiercely. Occasionally, the defenders fired back, occasionally starting small fires in the Roman ranks. Despite the ferocity of the siege, it was strangely silent, the muted noise of the engines, thousands of voices talking, the neighing of horses. The birds seemed undisturbed by all the human violence, wheeling above the fray, calling one to another.

Their escort led them to the praetorium trimmed with purple, Trajan's she-wolf banner fluttering above it in the morning breeze. He cleared them into the tent with the passes prepared under Lusius Quietus' seal, and they entered in. It was large enough to hold easily a hundred people, and against the walls were tables covered with maps and scrolls. In the center was a detailed model of the city outside. Two people, one a senior officer in uniform, the other wearing a plain leather corselet over a white tunic with a broad purple stripe, were quietly discussing the positioning of miniature catapults about the model. Braziers kept the morning chill at bay, and oil lamps provided illumination in addition to the yellowish light filtered through the tent fabric.

Marcus recognized Aulus as one of the men around the city model. Aulus in turn looked up to see who the new people were, and immediately recognized Marcus. He dropped his scroll and ran to embrace him.

"Marcus, Marcus Lucius Quintus, it can't be you! How are you here?"

"It has been a long trip," Aulus," Marcus answered, momentarily at a loss for words. "My sister Marcia, she is ... she is well, is she not? And Antonius?"

"Very well indeed, Marcus. But worried, as she has not heard from you in a very long time."

"Nor I from her, which is why I am here. You remember Hina and Galosga?"

Aulus looked at his companions. "I certainly do, but I never thought I would see you again, either."

The man with whom Aulus had been conversing wandered over, curious about who these strangers might be. Aulus turned to him. "Claudius, these are my companions from the expedition ten years ago. We left Marcus in the land of the Hanaeans, and Hina and Galosga at Turfam, thousands of miles from here. I never expected to see any of them again. Marcus, this is Claudius Severus, *legatus* of the Third Cyrenaican legion, commanding the siege of Artaxata."

Claudius smiled and nodded. "It seems you have an important reunion to attend to, Aulus. You go ahead, I'll take care of the siege." He shook everyone's hand in turn, then went back to studying the model.

"Please, let us go to my tent. We have so much to say," said Aulus.

Aulus' tent was immediately next to the imperial praesidium, a smaller, more modest affair, the overhanging roof peak edged in senatorial purple. A few servants scurried around inside, along with Lucius Parvus, his assistant. "Lucius, look who we have here! Marcus Lucius, from our Hanaean expedition."

"Marcus? I don't think I remember him."

"Oh, right, you wouldn't. He was on *Europa*, and we were on *Asia*, so you would not have known him very well at all. Please have the servants round up more chairs, this is such a large group!" Lucius clapped his hands, and servants arranged chairs in an impromptu circular group around the Senator. Aulus took his proffered seat, then beaming, turned back to Marcus, motioning all to sit. "And who are the rest of your friends?" asked Aulus, as the servants began pouring wine for all.

"My wife, Mei, the quietest of the lot."

Hina smiled. "Quiet only when Marcus is around her and safe. She is a tigress when he is in danger. You remember Galosga. These are my twins Marasa and Andanyu, named for Marcia and Antonius, and Adhela, my latest. Hadyu is my fellow clansmen from the Xiongnu. Nathaniel, a Jewish merchant who has thrown in his lot with us. And Decurion Ziri, from Lusius Quietus, who led our escort here."

Decurion Ziri nodded, excusing himself, satisfied that Aulus and Marcus were indeed very well acquainted; he would carry that fact back to Lusius Quietus. The rest of the business appeared to be personal, and Aulus would share of that what he chose to share.

"You have kept the good condition you acquired on our journey," Marcus quipped.

"Aye, that I have, Marcus. I remember that first day on the road out of that of Luoyang. I was puffing and wheezing like a blown nag, afraid that I would be the one to slow us down, have all of us caught. But at the end of the trip, I felt like I was twenty again, and I have never wanted to go back to what I was before. My time in the gymnasium is now as important as my time on the Senate floor." Aulus was clad in a leather musculated corselet, a Roman *gladius* on a belt and baldric about his waist, gray hair cropped short in a very soldierly manner. It fitted his sixty plus years very well. "But this isn't about me. What brought you across thousands of miles of the worst terrain I ever saw in my life? To here, in the middle of a war in Armenia?'

"Well, you do remember lending Marcia and I the use of your official seal?" Aulus nodded, and Marcus continued. "It worked very well for many years."

'It did, and I recall your first letter to Marcia actually beat us to Turfam. It was there waiting for us when we straggled in."

"And so it continued. It took years to exchange information, but that was expected. Then a few years ago, her letters stopped coming. Mei and I got very concerned, and when my mother died, we sold our house and set out with Ibrahim's generous gift to attempt to reach Rome and find her and Antonius. Along the way, we met up with Hina and Galosga and their companions in Turfam, then Nathaniel in Sogdiana, a stranger who has proven himself our most faithful friend and ally."

"I see," said Aulus. He shifted awkwardly in his seat, trying to find a more polite way to phrase his next question. "Hina, you are as beautiful as ever, and your Latin excellent, but Galosga, you and your friend ... you are scarred."

"The killing spots came upon our clan. Most died, some few survived but bore the scars, and even fewer, like Hina and our children, the disease did not touch. It wiped out our clan, and was the reason we were in Turfam when Marcus and Mei arrived. We chose to go with them, to whatever the west has to offer us. Tengri showed us that this was to be our path."

"Well, welcome to the turbulent west. You arrived just in time for one our innumerable wars." Aulus turned his attention back to Marcus. "Hmm, as I said, Marcia is doing very well indeed, as of a just a few months ago. A mother of three children, a boy Colloscius, and a girl Aena, named for you two," he said, nodding toward Galosga and Hina. "As best she could manage your names in Latin. Her latest, Androcles, was born about two years ago.

And Antonius is back under the eagles again, just a few hundred miles from here, prefect of camps under Gaius Lucullus commanding his old legion, the Twelfth Lightning Bolt. The Twelfth will be pacifying the highlands over the winter, then secure the northern borders against the Sarmatians and a Parthian amphibious landing in our rear. And Shmuel is now Samuel, one of his centurions."

"Well, I think I am beginning to understand why Parthia has such great interest in me personally! Before we reached the Parthian border, Nathaniel discovered that they were looking for me specifically, by both my Roman and Hanaean name. Vologases in Ecbatana and Osroës in Ctesiphon are contending for leadership of all Parthia. Vologases had gotten word from Osroës to pick me up and deliver me to Ctesiphon alive. But Vologases was much more curious why I was so important to his rival. It was then I realized there was only one person in Ctesiphon who could know who I was, that was Cyrus Mithridates, our old friend from the Han court, reading our mail. He thought they were coded messages, My very last letter had let Marcia know that I was setting out for Rome, and he had intercepted it."

"Mithridates is the brother of Osroës, and next in line for succession. You pick powerful enemies, Marcus."

"Odd, since I try hard to not pick any at all. Well, Vologases put us up in Ecbatana in style, though we were confined to the palace. Hina even got used to dressing well in silk gowns, she is really quite stunning when she wears something other than riding felts."

Hina came as close to blushing as she was capable.

Marcus continued. "It was Hina's turn to make powerful enemies. She entered a royal horse race, won, and beat up Vologases' nephew Farnavantes in front of the whole hippodrome. He must not have been popular, because they all cheered."

Hina grunted. "He quoited the other men's horses, causing them to stumble or run into each other. Several horses broke their legs, many riders were injured and two killed. Just for sport."

"Sounds like *buzkashi*, polo with a dead goat," said Aulus.

"That's not so different."

"So Farnavantes arranged my kidnapping and delivered me to Mithridates in Ctesiphon, expecting a generous reward, favor in the western court. But snakes recognize snakes, and Mithridates put him under house arrest in the palace. I don't know if he is still alive. Mithridates questioned me extensively about our letters. He is convinced they are some sort of coded correspondence between Rome and China, and just could not believe that innocent family babble would be traveling under Senatorial seal. When war broke out in earnest, he just threw me in jail in the basement. Galosga broke me out, and we all headed north … and here we are."

"Sir, if I may add some insights here." Nathaniel interjected and Aulus nodded his acquiescence. "I was originally in Mithridates' pay. He dispatched me on a three-year trip to the East on a generous stipend to ascertain Hanaean troop movements and intentions. He is absolutely convinced that the Hanaeans could attack his rear in concert with a war with Rome."

"Will they?"

"They put troops as far west as Sogdiana about forty years ago, but mostly to secure a supply of horses from Ferghana. There was a Chinese theoretician who wrote on war three hundred years ago, noting how many bags of rice it took to deliver one bag to the front a thousand miles away. And Sogdiana is a merchant empire, they do not want to be caught up in wars that would disrupt trade. I got as far as Kashgar before turning around, and that was the gist of my report to Mithridates: no military activity aimed westward, no apparent plans, or even a capability or interest."

"And you delivered that report to Mithridates in person?"

"I did. He interrupted a planning session with his son Sanatruces and grandson Vagharsh, two leading young generals, and Ataradates, the senior commander-in-chief of Osroës' armies, to take my report, pretty much as I just told you. He paid me a significant sum of silver, then invited me to stay. Which I did until Farnavantes burst in with Marcus. If Farnavantes had connected me to Marcus, Mithridates would likely have ensured that I spent a long painful time dying. But Marcus' impression was correct, Mithridates was not happy at the interruption, and the shape Marcus was in. Farnavantes was trying to sell out his henchmen, and Mithridates really did not like the man."

"Amazing. You all have had free access, more or less, to the highest levels of politics of both Parthian factions. And Nathaniel, you have not only passed up a chance to enrich yourself with the reward on Marcus' head, but also put your own on a chopping block to protect him. Your trustworthiness is proven. We need to get back to social matters, because afterwards, we are going to convene a meeting with all of the *Princeps'* staff and generals, because you look right now to be our most valuable resource into the enemy's thoughts and designs. More wine, all?"

CHAPTER 67:

A NEW SET OF CARDS TO PLAY

Ctesiphon, September 114AD

Mithridates picked up a scroll, throwing it across the room with such force that its spindle shattered into several pieces. "Nathaniel! That lying Jewish bastard was with them? With Trajan?"

Sanatruces picked up the fragments of the spindle and put them on his father's desk. "Unfortunately, he was. He was with them when they came to Quietus' headquarters around Lake Van, and Quietus gave them a cavalry escort directly to Trajan's headquarters. Trajan apparently interrupted a staff meeting to receive them personally. And the next day, the Armenian leadership surrendered Artaxata, and accepted Severus as the Roman governor. They have annexed Armenia, almost without a fight."

"What about the Parthian garrison there?"

"The Armenian leadership negotiated their safe passage back to Parthia. They are enroute back as we speak. Almost all of the seven thousand men survived the siege."

"Have them publicly executed to a man. Their orders were to hold Artaxata at all costs. They take orders from us, not the Armenians, and they disobeyed those orders without so much as a skirmish with the Romans."

"With Armenia pacified, the Romans will unleash their hordes on us in the spring. We will be needing every man we have, Father."

"We will not need men who have proven themselves cowards in front of the enemy. Execute them all." Mithridates repeated, waving his hand dismissively.

Sanatruces had adopted the Roman-style wax tablet as a means of taking notes. Black wax over white wood tablet sheets, small, waterproof, and easily erased. He made a note of his father's command.

"Despite what Nathaniel said, the East cannot be silent. And the path for the Han armies to us goes through Ecbatana. We will, as we planned, fade away before the Roman onslaught next spring. Let them come on unopposed and stretch their supply lines to the breaking point. We will deal with the real threat from the east, and subdue Ecbatana and the usurper Vologases."

Sanatruces took more notes.

"Ariobarzanes has lined up a new agent in Italy?"

"He has, Father."

"His task is to arrange the kidnapping of two wives, Marcia, and I believe, Livia, Galba's wife, and bring them here. I am not sure how to play this hand, but I am sure that something will present itself when I have those two cards. Get Farnavantes involved, he owes me something to get back into my good graces."

"Yes, Father." More notes.

HAPTER 68:

THE WINTER CAMPAIGN

The Armenian Highlands, October-December 114AD

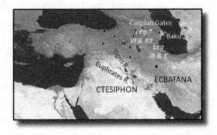

The wind moaned softly through the pine boughs, heavily laden with the first winter snowfall in the foothills of the white-capped Armenian Highlands. Somewhere in the distance, birds called, and an eagle screamed in the cloudless blue sky high above.

Normally, a Roman army camp was a mobile fortress of six thousand men that made no attempt to hide its presence. Its whole purpose was to announce loudly the arrival of the power and might of the Roman Empire, setting itself up, unannounced, overnight on the enemy's doorstep. Precisely organized behind a palisaded ditch excavated to heave up an earthen parapet, its tents laid out in neat rectangular grids, its trumpets announced its arrival with periodic calls for reveille, messing, and watch changes. Nothing hidden.

But this was not a normal Roman camp. This time, there were sounds among the pine boughs that did not quite fit in: an occasional nicker of a restless horse or bray of a mule, muted metallic sounds, human voices speaking to each other in hushed tones, perhaps a large party of hunters or wood-gatherers. If one followed the faint wisp of woodsmoke, one might pick out among the pines part of a rectangular tent where snow had fallen from its roof to reveal an unnatural, rectangular man-made corner. And an especially sharp-eyed observer might notice here and there, white-clad archers, bows drawn, arrows notched, surveying the perimeter from well-chosen places of concealment. But nothing that bespoke the presence of a Roman legion.

Bruttius Praesans, *legatus* of the Sixth Ironclad Legion, made his way into this seemingly jumbled camp, one of the cohorts of the Twelfth Thunderbolt. He and his soldiers gave their horses to a soldier to tend, and wended their way through the maze of campfires and half-hidden tent tie-downs, to find the tent of the Twelfth's commander, Gaius Lucullus. The commander's tent was an eight-man tent like all the others, though shared only by himself and his prefect of camps, Antonius Aristides.

Bruttius scratched on the tent flap, then entered with his two men without waiting to be invited. "By all the gods, Gaius, you have this camp well-hidden! I was afraid I had stumbled into a batch of Armenian rebels, then I heard your men speaking Latin." Gaius was seated at a desk in the middle of the spartan command center, two soldiers' cots on either side of the tent, bedding still tangled from overnight.

"Well, that's what we are trying to do, stay out of sight, even from someone knowing where to look for us. Grab chairs and seat yourselves," said Gaiius, waving in the direction of a number of folding chairs propped up on the walls. "Let me summon Tigran, our Armenian advisor, and Paulus Herrerius, my first lance. Antonius, please? And a servant to provide us something hot to drink. Bruttius, have you and your men had breakfast?" Antonius nodded and left.

"We have, thank you, but something warm would be most welcome." He and his men shed their white hooded coats and gloves, unstrapping their caked snowshoes. They blew on their hands, stamping their feet, their breath cloudy in the very cold morning air. "While no one is here but us, Gaius, can we trust our Armenian advisors?"

Gaius stirred the coals of the brazier and added some charcoal to take the chill off. "About as much as Varrus should have trusted Arminius in the Teutoberger Forest. But we don't have much choice. And what he is advising so far makes sense, small units, cohorts or smaller, which means I keep the bulk of the legion in reserve in the lowlands in case we are ambushed. If I sense anything amiss, I will let you know at once. We can risk two cohorts up here, but we can't risk the rest of our two legions and leave nothing protecting Trajan's rear from the rebels."

"Exactly. Let me introduce Claudius Semperens, my *primus pilus*, and Julius Viragus, my prefect of camps."

Courtesies were exchanged while servants entered to distribute hot mulled wine among the officers. Antonius, Paulus Herrerius and Tigran entered the tent. Tigran was a round-headed lightly-bearded man with piercing eyes, his black hair cut short in Roman fashion.

"So, what brings you here this cold snowy morning, Bruttius?" asked Gaius.

"My scouts have located a rebel camp, almost midway between our two legions, in that little river valley below us. Perhaps two, three hundred men. They seem to have little or no guard set."

"This is where Armenians come to fight off invaders," volunteered Tigran. "We can hit and run with impunity, and no one can follow us into the mountains."

Bruttius fixed Tigran with an intense suspicious gaze, which Tigran returned without blinking. "So, are we the invaders, Tigran? And why are you helping us against your countrymen?"

"The invaders are the Parthians, who have controlled our country for generations. A large number of my people want to see the Parthians gone for good, even if it means we trade them for Roman rule. The Cappadocians and Anatolians do not find your yoke heavy on their shoulders, but we have found the Parthian yoke unbearable. I wish the rebels here in the mountains understood, but no matter." He answered slowly and distinctly in well-spoken Latin, never shifting his eyes away from Bruttius' intense gaze.

Bruttius was the one to shift his eyes away first. "Well answered, Tigran, well answered."

Gaius interjected to end the standoff between the two. "So, just a few miles between our two camps, and three hundred men?"

"Two miles at the most, and downhill. And yes, three hundred men at most, so far unalerted, even though we are practically on top of them."

"Well, that may not last longer than their next hunting party, so I propose we each contribute a century, get them in position overnight, and launch our attack at first light. I'll contribute a third century, so you and I can observe the fight, and commit it as a reserve force if necessary. We can try out the new mountain-fighting tactics Tigran has schooled us in."

The rest of the meeting dealt with terrain, the positioning of the three centuries, and signaling. It was agreed that white signal flags would be used, easily mistaken for small clumps of snow falling from the heavily laden trees if seen. There were to be no escapees, no prisoners.

No Roman century ever advanced as those three had overnight. Two squads of eight sharpshooter archers each, wrapped completely in white hooded robes, minimal armor to disclose their movement by metallic clinks and clanks, scurried on snowshoes to advance a dozen feet in the brilliant light of a full moon. They then took any available shelter, behind trees or bushes or just prone on the ground, scanning the area for any response to their movement. Hearing none, they then gave hand signals for the next squad to come forward. Following the archers were six infantry squads, armed with the traditional *gladii* and *pila*, then two more squads of archers. They moved as animals move, a short distance, checking for predators. As a result, it took most of the night for the Sixth's century to take the high ground a hundred yards behind the camp, blocking its retreat. The Twelfth's century, commanded by Secundus Lucullus and his centurion Samuel Elisarius, had taken the opposite position, while the two commanders looked on from two hundred yards back. Single flicks of white flags indicated that the two centuries were ready to attack.

Gaius had considered holding his son's century back as the reserve unit; but that would be unfair to him, so he committed him to the forward unit, and now faced the possibility of watching his son's death before his eyes in the next few minutes. He shook his head to clear the thought and turned his attention to the Armenian camp below, dozens of conical tents straggled higgledy-piggledy around a mostly frozen creek. A few early risers were out and about, stoking campfires to life. An Armenian elk hung gutted from a tree, ready to be butchered. "Looks like we will have fresh meat tonight, Bruttius. Do you see any guards or sentries?"

"No, none at all. Let's give the signal."

Gaius turned his head and gave Antonius the thumbs up. His signalman flashed the white signal flag twice. One of the fire tenders noticed the flashes of white and briefly looked in their direction. Seeing nothing more, he turned back to the fire. Gaius heard his son make a piercing whistle, and the back two squads of archers in both centuries broke cover to fire high arcing trajectories into the camp below. Although unaimed, some of the arrows found their mark, and the cries of the wounded brought others out of the tent, providing many more targets for the next volley.

The Armenians milled around the camp, unsure of the source of the arrows. The third volley, incendiaries, lit off tents, bedrolls and brush around the campground, as well as finding some human targets who batted, screaming, at the flames around their wounds.

Secundus gave two shrill whistles. The rear echelon archers faded back into cover, and the sharpshooters emerged and fired point-blank into the confused mass, many of whom were still struggling to string their own bows. Dozens of men were down, dead or wounded, when Secundus blew three sharp whistles. The two front squads of archers parted to the left and right, opening a path for the infantry. They charged in formation, with the battle cry 'Varrus', in their white coveralls, their shields covered with white linen. They released a volley of *pila,* then closed to finish the action, sword to sword. The sharpshooters ensured that no one escaped the melee to the left or right. The Sixth's century on the far side charged into the slaughter from the rear, and the battle was soon over.

"I think we can break cover now, Gaius," said Bruttius. Gaius nodded, stood up, and the century straggled into the remains of the camp on snowshoes, no longer attempting to maintain cover. The soldiers were finishing off the wounded, since there were to be no prisoners, but Samuel intervened on the last, an apparently unwounded individual who had attempted to hide himself during the slaughter. He took him to Secundus, who then took him to Gaius. "With all due respect, sir, we have one unwounded. I recommend we take him back to the cohort, we may be able to get some valuable intelligence from him, where their headquarters are, who the leaders are," said Secundus.

Gaius nodded affirmatively. "Good thinking, Tribune. Oh, and a well-executed battle plan."

"Thank you, sir." Secundus saluted and returned to martial his century back into order.

There were two hundred seventy-six Armenians killed, and one captured. There were six Romans with minor injuries, two of them accidental. They left the Armenian camp as it was, for the rebels to wonder how the slaughter might have happened.

The prisoner provided a wealth of intelligence on the other camps, which were all about the size of the first. Over the next several weeks, centuries from the two cohorts slaughtered over a thousand rebels. The word was out that the Romans were raiding at will, so the camps became better guarded and prepared. That made the fights last longer, but the outcomes were invariably the same, a one-sided slaughter. Tigran's training of the cohorts in mountain fighting tactics, though unorthodox by Roman standards, had paid off.

By the time the heavy snows of December came, the mountain cohorts had encountered no more camps for weeks. Hunters informed them that the rebels had dispersed back to the lowlands to avoid further ambushes.

The mountain cohorts rejoined their legions in the lower foothills, and departed the mountains for their rear-guard positions, joining the Tenth Straits and Third Gallic legions further south on the Caspian coast. The Sixth took up position at the Caspian Gates, a narrow strip of land separating the eastern flank of the Greater Caucasus from the Caspian Sea, where they guarded the lowlands from invasion by the Sarmatian barbarians from the steppes north of the mountains. The Twelfth continued south to the windy port city of Baku, where they had operated fifteen years earlier, to guard against an amphibious assault by Parthian troops.

CHAPTER 69:

A LIFE-LONG FRIEND

Aquileia, December 114AD

The carriage rolled up to the entrance to the villa, preceded and followed by two pairs of armed horsemen in an unusual December snowfall, the light flakes powdering the grass and sprinkling the pines with white. Servants rushed out to snare the traces of the horses as the riders dismounted, while another servant opened the door of the carriage to allow the passengers to emerge. Still more clustered about the rear of the carriage, two undoing the straps of the leather baggage-carrier, the rest withdrawing baggage and satchels of personal belongings, quickly bringing them inside the door of the villa.

Desdemona knocked at the door of the study where Marcia was engrossed in reading a scroll and entered, unannounced. "They are here, Marcia."

"Thank you, Desdemona, I will be down immediately." Marcia put away the scroll and hurried to the atrium, where servants stood attentively by the guests, a red-headed woman, a very plump elderly man with balding white hair clad in a brilliant white tunic with a purple Senatorial band on it, and a teen-aged youth. Marcia rushed to embrace the woman, kissing her on both cheeks. "Livia Galba, I am so pleased to see that you and your family arrived safely in this dreadful winter weather."

"Not dreadful, Marcia, and actually quite beautiful. The road to your villa is quite good, far better than the road to Aquileia. in fact. Our servants were out several times to manhandle the carriage out of the drifts on that road."

"I am glad you arrived safely," said Marcia, relinquishing the embrace to take the hand of the youth. "And this is your son, Pontus Servilius, and this gentleman is…?"

"Lucian Septimius Pontus, a senatorial colleague of Aulus. He heard we were visiting and insisted on accompanying us to ensure that all is well."

Marcia extended her hand in a masculine manner, and after a moment's hesitation, Lucian accepted. "Charmed, my dear young Marcia. Livia has told me so much about you."

Marcia accepted his hand in a military grip, hand on wrist, "But not so much about you. You are?"

Lucian fumbled to return the unfamiliar grip properly, ultimately grasping her wrist. "Aulus' colleague, as Livia said, and his lifelong friend."

"Pleased, Lucian Septimius. Welcome to our humble home and school."

"And Antonius? Where might he be?" replied Lucian.

"Following the eagles again, with Gaius Lucullus. Or had Livia not so informed you?"

"She had not. When?"

"Last spring. Gaius said he wished my husband might be available as prefect of the camps. Antonius took that as a directive, and off he went," said Marcia.'

"The abandoned wife?" asked Lucius.

"The other wife. I always knew he was wed to the eagles long before me," she replied with a smile. "Come, let us continue our talk inside by the warm fire."

She led them to the doorway where a brass brazier filled with glowing coals radiated warmth, under an overhang that kept out the snow. Servants, under Desdemona's direction, brought chairs, took their winter wraps, then brought platters of snacks and drinks, departing quietly. The three seated themselves, warming their hands. Seated next to Livia, Marcia heard her whisper to Desdemona that the Senator's wine was not to be watered.

"This is quite the impressive establishment, a villa and a school combined. Who runs this in Antonius' absence?" asked Lucian. The servants brought trays of wine. Lucian emptied his sizable cup in just two swallows, then held it out for a refill.

"I do, of course. We both run it together when he is here. I teach the Hanaean language and manners to those few merchants so interested, though Antonius can also speak the language fairly well. He teaches Greek, his birth language, and the various Greek philosophies, though he prefers Stoicism, his personal following. I speak conversational Greek, but not the language of philosophy, or ancient Homer. The latter I can barely understand. We both also teach Bactrian to those traders going that way overland."

"Interesting enterprise for a retired centurion." Again, Lucian quickly devoured his second cup of wine.

"He was a very well-educated centurion, though he kept it hidden as a common soldier. His father was a Greek tutor to the wealthier families here, and raised Antonius accordingly, before he left to follow the eagles. He read the *Iliad* and the *Odyssey* in the ancient language before he was twelve, and memorized quite a bit of it."

"It must have cost a fortune to set this school up."

"It did. But we had a generous stipend from the *Princeps*, and we procured this villa for a song from a friend of Aulus who had fallen on hard times. We were most lucky."

"How many students do you have here?" Lucian was on his third cup.

"Usually, four or five. They can live here, if they choose, and we prefer they do, as it is easier to learn a language, as we did, by speaking only that language all the time. But this winter is slow, and we have no students at all until January, a gentleman who wishes to learn Hanaean."

"He is planning a trip to the east?"

"Not really. He wants to be able to negotiate directly with Hanaean traders in India, in the hopes of getting better prices without Indian middlemen. Not too many want to duplicate our adventure!" she said with a smile and a knowing wink. "It was quite the trip."

Livia interjected. "Aulus made another trip to the land of the Han a few years ago. But fortunately, it was much less adventurous than the first! And more profitable."

"Livia tells me you left a brother behind in China." After four cups, Lucian's eyes were going glassy, his speech starting to slur.

"I did, and I miss Marcus terribly. We were the rock to each other's pebble. But Aulus found a way for us to keep in touch using his seal. Marcus wanted to stay and take care of our elderly mother. Unfortunately, something has happened. I haven't heard from him in several years. I hope all is well."

"That is sad. What did you talk about in your letters?"

"Just day-to-day stuff, our children, his wife, our mama. Nothing important." Marcia was annoyed with his prying into her personal business, but considered it to be perhaps a case of too much to drink. She wondered why Livia had requested his wine not be watered, as he was going to be very drunk quite soon.

"No politics, of course." Lucian held out his cup for a fifth refill.

"Of course not. I wouldn't know how to talk about those things, and Marcus wouldn't understand if I did. I just hope all is well with him and Mei."

"Mei is his wife?"

"She is."

"And his children?"

"They have none."

"Interesting. I know how the Roman post works. But I am intrigued with using caravans."

"Correspondence is almost as important to the caravans as the goods they carry. It is how the merchants stay in touch, know what each want or need, what they will pay."

"How does it get to Marcus? ... did it get, I am sorry." His head was beginning to sag, his triple chins waggling as he tried to speak very precisely and coherently.

"Our village is very small, but we make a very fine wine, and the caravans all stop there to pick up some. We don't have a caravansary; they just encamp in the fields below us by a river."

"Mmm, interesting. Have to try some of that wine someday." His head sagged further to his chest and his breathing slowed. His question time was obviously over, and he was soon snoring."

Marcia signaled for Desdemona. "Have Alaric and some other of the men help the good Senator to a bed chamber. One on the first floor, I don't think he can handle the steps."

Alaric and Brutus entered the room, and picked up the somnolent Lucian, who awakened enough to walk, with hefty assistance from the two big servants, to one of the students' rooms on the other side of the atrium. They deposited his bulky frame on the bed, then reported back to the mistress. "He is all taken care of, Marcia," reported Alaric. "We left a bucket by the bed in case he becomes ill overnight."

"Thank you, Alaric. Sorry to have disturbed your game of *tria*. I don't think we'll be needing you the rest of the night."

Alaric left, and Marcia turned to Livia. "Aulus' 'life-long friend' is quite the drinker. Why on earth did you order his drinks not be watered?"

"Lucian is as much Aulus' 'life-long friend" as the three-headed Cerberus is a housepet. I ordered them not watered to be rid of him. He spent the entire trip interrogating me, as he started in on you until the wine intervened. I don't trust him, but he is too powerful for me to refuse his company."

"Close to the *Princeps?*"

"Not at all, Trajan despises him. Lucian has been in the Senate fifty years, and although he has accomplished little himself, he knows all of the bribes and little misdeeds of the other Senators, and has little reluctance to expose them if they cross him. During the terrible days of Diometian, several of his victims wound up executed or ordered to commit suicide, their estates forfeited. Fortunately, that is not likely to happen today, but nobody has forgotten that, and they all have their peccadillos."

"Aulus too?" Marcia smiled.

"Nothing serious, none that I know of." Livia laughed softly. "But that doesn't keep Lucian from making things up. Don't tell him too much. I don't know why he has attached himself so firmly to me, but don't let him attach himself to you also. I don't trust him."

Desdemona brought more wine, and Livia changed the subject. "Have you heard from Antonius?"

"He arrived, and Gaius was quite surprised but happy to have him. The man he was relieving died shortly after, so it was well-timed. Did Aulus ever tell you about Shmuel, from our trip? He did not come to Rome with us, so you never met him."

"Yes, he told me a little, a Jewish rebel, he said."

"At one time. He wound up following the eagles and was just made Centurion of the Fifth Cohort of the Twelfth, going by Samuel Elisarius now.

And there is more. Gaius Lucullus' son, Secundus Lucullus, is his tribune. Gaius was not happy about that."

"Why not?"

"He was proud of Secundus' following in his footsteps, but was adamant that he not be in a legion under his command. Secundus was posted to the Twelfth, then Gaius was abruptly assigned to command it before he found his son came with the legion. He found that out on his first inspection. To Secundus' credit, he hid his surprise as well. And Samuel his centurion. What have you heard from Aulus?"

"Nothing, other than he is part of Trajan's inner circle of advisors, and the legions are on the move, another war begun. Of course, no real news about what they are doing."

"That is our men for us. No real important news, like whether they will live to come back to us." Marcia took another sip of wine.

Later that night Pontus' personal servant Publius slipped silently into the atrium heading for the kitchen, his way lit by a single taper and a few well-banked oil lamps on the walls. All were asleep except for a single night watchman, making his boring rounds.

"Good evening," Alaric asked. "What keeps you up so late at night?"

"My master woke up wanting a snack. The kitchen is that way?"

"Yes. As drunk as he was, I thought he would sleep until the day after tomorrow."

"He usually wakes up after midnight when he gets drunk. His stomach bothers him from all the wine."

The two parted, and Publius came to the kitchen. The light from the taper fell on the row of five identical cork-stoppered ceramic jars of *garum* fish sauce, right where he had noticed them in his afternoon tour. Very orderly, which made his job easier. He lit an oil lamp with the taper, then extinguished the small candle to leave his hands free.

One by one, he opened each jar, and sprinkled a fine white powder from a pouch into it, carefully stirring to blend it in until it disappeared. When all five jars were doctored, he relit the taper, extinguished the lamp, grabbed a bit of bread for cover, and returned to his quarters.

At the next day's evening meal, Pontus appeared to have recovered remarkably well from the previous night's planned, and greatly exaggerated, intoxication. Everyone consumed, as was usual, copious amounts of *garum*, spread liberally on the bread, vegetables and meats. It was the one condiment that Romans consumed on virtually all foods. Publius also put a spoonful on his plate, but carefully did not allow it touch his food.

The dinner conversation lagged, as one by one, each complained of drowsiness. First one, then another, lowered their heads to the table, and finally, Pontus. A dinner servant carrying plates of desserts staggered drunkenly, then collapsed on the floor, dropping the plates with an unnoticed crash. Soon many were snoring.

Publius carefully went about the household, verifying that all were out, including the night watch and the doorman. He lifted the bar securing the door and undid the latch. He then returned to the kitchen, carefully disposed of all of the incriminating *garum*, and rinsed the containers with vinegar to neutralize the toxin. He went back to the dining area, sprinkling vinegar over all the remaining plates with uneaten sauce. He ate his allotted portion of *garum* paste and was soon sound asleep with the others.

CHAPTER 70:

AWAKENING TO CONFUSION

Aquileia, December 114AD

Pontus had not expected the sleeping draught to leave such a pounding headache the next morning. The headache was not helped by the chaos throughout the villa, people yelling loudly, apparently searching for someone or something. Pontus screwed his eyes shut and attempted to get more sleep, but the words penetrated his consciousness. "They're not here, not inside or outside, not anywhere. And the door is wide open."

Headache or not, Pontus jerked himself awake. *The door was supposed to be closed! Who was missing?*

The answer came with the next few shouts. "Get Desdemona to take care of Androcles. Marcia is nowhere to be found. And Livia …"

Marcia and Livia missing? This was not how it was planned. His friend's instructions were to leave the door open, some people would search the house for something of value to the peace faction, then leave, closing the door behind him. *Something of value? By all the gods, Justinius never told him what that might be. Marcia and Livia? A kidnapping? What value could either have to the peace faction? And if I were connected to the kidnapping … what had Justinius gotten me into?* Pontus suddenly felt very ill, and not from the wine and the sleeping draught.

Alaric arrived a few minutes later with two armed soldiers, a prefect and a young tribune, and quickly introduced them to Pontus. "Good morning, sir. This is Brutus Agrippa, prefect of the urban cohort in Aquileia, and his tribune Appius Gallus. Gentlemen, this is Senator Lucian Septimius Pontus, now, by these most unfortunate circumstances, the senior citizen in our compound."

"Good morning, sir." Brutus extended his hand.

Pontus accepted the handshake. "As best as it can be under the circumstances. How may I help you?"

"How did you come to be here in the villa?"

"I traveled up here with Livia, at her invitation. She thought I would find the academy here most interesting, the languages and ways of life of the Distant East."

"To be sure. Did you notice anything untoward last night?"

"Well, everyone did fall asleep suddenly, including myself and all my servants. Until then, nothing out of the ordinary. I arose quite late yesterday, before this all happened. I am afraid I consumed far too much the previous night."

"I see." His tribune was scribbling notes on a wax table.

"The door to the villa was left open. Any chance one of your servants might have left it open?"

"No. All my servants were passed out, as was everyone else. Someone in the household?"

"Unlikely. Their servants are exceedingly loyal to Marcia and Antonius. But I will question them. After I question yours. You do not mind, do you, sir?"

"Uh ... no, please feel free." *Would he question them 'under duress'? Publius was not likely to hold up under torture. But he could not refuse the request. To do so would almost be an admission of guilt and complicity.*

Brutus Agrippa interrogated all of Pontus' servants, while Pontus paced nervously. But Publius held to his agreed-on story, that he had passed out, as had the others. Brutus then questioned the villa's household, and even Aulus' teenaged son, Pontus Servilius. He then conferred with his tribune, who informed him that the food had apparently been doctored. One of the servants' plates was fed to him, and the man promptly passed out again within just a few minutes. The tribune did not know, however, which specific item had been tampered with.

"It looks like an inside operation, sir," concluded the tribune. "The food poisoned, then the door opened to admit the kidnappers. With the other two events here two years ago, I suspect someone in the household is guilty."

"I agree it looks like an inside job, but I have a great deal of respect for the loyalty of all the Aristides household, and also for Antonius Aristides himself, who has been adamant about not questioning his *familia* under duress. You remember that there was a connection two years ago to a burglary and a murder here, and another death in Rome involving one of Senator Galba's servants."

The tribune nodded. "One man. Modorus, an Armenian from Rome."

"The same. The prefect of *vigiles* in Rome told me to be alert for further incidents, as Modorus was guilty of all three, and connected to something bigger, though he never let on just what that connection was. Now we have that incident, and a senior senator who attached himself to Senator Galba's wife Livia, at his insistence according to her son, not at her invitation as Pontus claimed. The missing woman did not even like him, nor does Galba. But I am not going to question a senior Roman senator's servants under torture. I am going to send them back to Rome with a report to the commander of the *vigiles*. Let him make that decision. In the meanwhile, put together a detail to sweep the countryside for our missing women ... or their bodies."

CHAPTER 71:

AWAKENING TO A NIGHTMARE

Somewhere in the Adriatic Sea, December 114AD

Marcia awoke with a pounding headache, throbbing in rhythm with her heartbeat. A sense of nausea accompanied it, like a very bad hangover, though she remembered having only a bit of wine the previous night. She lay very still, trying not to open her eyes and stimulate the hammer in her brain. 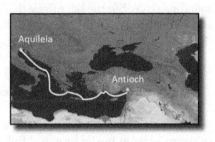 She explored her surroundings with her other senses. She was aware of the sound of rushing water on the other side of the rough wooden wall against which she was lying. A gentle, rhythmic rocking convinced her she was on a boat. Her nose rebelled at the fetid smell of many unwashed bodies, urine and feces.

She felt something hard about her throat. Reaching up slowly to touch it she felt the cold iron of a slave's collar. Opening her eyes, she could see in the dim light that she was linked by chain to the collar of another sleeping woman on her left. Livia, clad in filthy rags, and linked by chain to someone beyond her.

Marcia carefully rolled to her right, but the movement still set off her headache to explosive intensity. Bile rose in her throat, but she forced down the urge to vomit. She found herself chained to another woman on that side, awake and looking back at her. "Time you woke up, sweetie," the woman said.

Where was she? What had happened? The last she remembered was dinner with Livia and Pontus.

Livia stirred and moaned to her left.

"Livia, are you awake?"

"Yes. I think I am going to die, but I am awake. What happened?" Livia struggled to a sitting position.

"I don't know. Something horrible," Marcia answered.

Livia touched the collar about her neck. Anger flashed across her face as she touched it. "Someone has enslaved us. That will be death for them!"

"Maybe," answered Marcia. "Or for us."

Daylight exploded in their eyes as the hatch above them rumbled and opened with a thud. A dark shadow descended the ladder to the hold's deck, a sailor dressed against the cold and wet topside. Someone above passed down a large bucket to him.

"You!" Livia accosted the sailor. "You have placed the wife of Senator Aulus Aemilius Galba, personal friend of the *Princeps* Trajan, in chains. You will pay dearly if you do not release me and my fellow citizen Marcia Lucia Aristida." The woman to Marcia's right gave a harsh laugh.

The sailor held the odoriferous bucket before Livia's face. "You speak well for a slave. But the bill of sale that came with you says you are Aphrodite, and your citizen friend is Diana. So, dump your slop jar in this bucket." Livia shook her head, indicating she had nothing to contribute.

"No matter." The sailor moved on to Marcia.

"Where are you taking us?" asked Marcia.

"Antioch. You got nothin', neither?"

After the sailor completed his rounds of the women in the hold, Marcia spoke to Livia in hushed tones. "Bill of sale? Antioch? What has happened to us?"

"It seems we have been sold into slavery."

Marcia was silent as the impact of this sank in. "By all the gods, what about Androcles, Aena and Colloscius? What has happened to my children?" She burst into tears, harsh choking sobs.

Livia waited until Marcia's crying subsided. "Lucian. It was Lucian Pontus for sure. The bastard poisoned us … but why?"

"Desdemona will see to it my children are taken care of. If she is still alive. If they are still alive." She broke into tears again, overwhelmed by the powerlessness she felt. For the first time in decades, she felt she had no control over the forces that had suddenly buffeted her life. She was, once again, a weak and powerless girl.

The hatch rumbled open again, and a man clambered down the ladder into the stinking hold. He was a well-groomed athletic man clad in a clean white tunic, with a narrow purple stripe of the equestrian order at its hem.

"Oh, thank the mother goddess! You are here to free us. There has been some horrible wrongdoing. I am Livia, the wife of senior senator and advisor to the *Princeps*, Aulus Aemilius Galba, and my friend and fellow citizen Marcia Lucia Aristida."

"Well, my name is Justinius. I am the owner of Aphrodite and Diana, which will be your new names. No matter what your old ones were."

Livia spit a gobbet of saliva in Justinius' direction, staining his tunic.

"Now that is no way for a slave to behave. As you shall learn." He backhanded Livia across the side of her face, knocking her head sideways and drawing blood. "We can do much worse, you know. But behave, and I guarantee that no harm will come to you. I will see to it that the sailors do not come down here to enjoy a little sample of your wares. My job is to deliver you to another customer, in as good a condition as possible. But continue to misbehave …" He shrugged his shoulders.

Livia wiped the trickle of blood from her mouth, her eyes brimming with tears, not of fear but of rage. "In Antioch?" she asked, her eyes flashing.

"Or thereabouts. Now don't go advertising your imagined identities. Your fellow slaves will not believe you anyway. They are used to lying." He turned and went back up the ladder.

As the hatch slammed shut above them, Livia slumped down next to Marcia, drawing shuddering breaths, trying not to sob.

"You two girls really high-class, like you say?" said the woman chained to Marcia's right, clattering her chains to get a look at Livia.

"No, but I thought it might work. We just slaves, like you," Livia replied, using the lowest class accent she could remember.

CHAPTER 72:

UNDER DURESS

Rome, December 114AD

Brutus Agrippa dispatched Senator Pontus and his entourage of servants to Rome under armed escort, with instructions to deliver him directly to the commander of the Urban Cohort there. The party left at daybreak, traveling under imperial orders, changing horses at *mansiones* every twenty to forty miles on the *Via Popilia Venata*. They covered the one-hundred-twenty-mile trip to their first stop at Ravenna on icy, and occasionally snow-packed, roads. The mounted escorts had no problems with the snow and ice, setting a pace that left Lucian Pontus and his servants lurching back and forth inside the Senator's six-person carriage, which occasionally skidded sickeningly sideways on a patch of ice. But the driver slowed expertly as necessary to avoid damage, and the party arrived at midnight for an overnight stay at the Ravenna *mansio*.

Up before first light for a hasty breakfast, the party departed for Rome on a cold clear day, the *Via Flaminia* mercifully free of snow and ice. However, that allowed the escorts to set a faster pace, rattling Pontus and his servants in the carriage like dice in a gaming cup. This made it difficult for Pontus to consider his options. *I am under suspicion, because I was the new person there. But suspicion will not convict me. My servants? Publius knows that I told him to doctor the garum and gave him the powder. But he is loyal ... I think. That's why I picked him. But under duress? No, the City vigiles would never order my slaves to be tortured. Or would they? No, all they have are suspicions. I wish I had never undertaken this for Justinius. What the hell does he have in mind? This is something much bigger than the peace faction, and I don't know what it is!* The carriage careened over rough cobblestones, slamming Pontus' huge bulk into Publius sitting next to him, ending his cogitation.

Just before midnight the party arrived at the Praetorian barracks on the northeast side of Rome, just ahead of the feast of *Saturnalia* on the winter solstice.

Gnaius Petronius, the Prefect of Rome's Urban Cohort, had received the express post from Brutus Agrippa the previous day, outlining both the facts of the case, and Agrippa's strong suspicion that the very senior Senator was somehow connected to it. Agrippa had not wanted to insert himself into what appeared to very high-level Imperial politics from distant Aquileia; Petronius felt that the level of this political affair was far above his station as well: this case linked directly to Senator Galba, the *Princeps'* senior adviser, and potentially to the *Princeps* himself. He had summoned the Prefect of the City, past consul Clodius Crispinus, for an urgent meeting involving the case. He laid out the tenuous Parthian connection to the other three incidents involving the widely separated Galba and Aristides households, a connection he had not shared with Aquileian authorities. He described the mutual connection between the two households to the now-famous mission to China a decade ago, Galba's current status as senior advisor to the *Princeps*, and Antonius Aristides' new status as prefect of camps under yet another veteran of that China mission, Gaius Lucullus, commanding a front-line legion. He made the case that this strongly indicated an attempt to somehow interfere with the prosecution of the war on behalf of the Parthians by Senator Pontus, The Urban Prefect agreed with all of Petronius' concerns, and was with him when the Senator and his servants were brought before him in the Praetorian barracks ... not under guard, but armed Praetorians kept a careful eye on everyone's movements.

"Welcome back to Rome, Lucian Servilius," said Crispinus to the Senator. "I hope you had a comfortable if somewhat rushed return to Rome. How was the weather up north?" He did not extend his hand, nor were there seats to offer the senator.

"I am bruised from being bounced around by every pothole and cobblestone on the *via Flaminia*. And the weather up north was horrible, cold and icy. What is the reason for my so hasty return?"

"We are concerned with the disappearance of Livia, the wife of your colleague Aulus Aemilius, and would like to ask you a few questions."

"Certainly."

"First, why did you accompany Livia Galba to the Aristides household in Aquileia? That is a very long trip in the winter. I don't believe you are acquainted with the Aristides?"

"That household runs an academy dedicated to education in the languages and the cultures of the Distant East, so I was informed by Livia Galba. She thought I would be most interested to learn more of this, and she invited me to accompany her. I am a long-time friend of Aulus Aemilius."

"But her son said you invited yourself, somewhat over her objections. He said she does not care for your company."

"He is a lad, not yet in a man's toga. He is grieving over his mother's strange disappearance. I would not give his statement any credence."

"My second question: in your own words, what happened the night before her disappearance?"

"We sat down to eat, and one by one, everyone became overcome by sleep and passed out. When we awoke the next morning, both Livia Galba and Marcia Lucia Aristida were missing. I hope they have been safely located while I was in transit."

"They have not been. Why did everyone pass out?"

"I presume something in the food was bad, something that everyone ate."

"Brutus Agrippa determined that to be so. A servant was fed the remains of his plate during his investigation, and promptly passed out. Are you aware of the other incidents at the Galba and Aristides households?"

Pontus' heart began to hammer, his face turned beet red. *Other incidents? Justinius had not mentioned other incidents.* "No, sir, I do not … I do not know of other incidents."

Petronius joined in with information of the three cases. "Two years ago, Aulus Aemilius' private secretary, with detailed knowledge of his senatorial, business and personal correspondence, was kidnapped, tortured and killed. Two months later, the gatekeeper of the Aristides household was murdered, then a month later, someone attempted to burglarize that same household but was captured by the *domina* of the household, Marcia Lucia, now missing. The man was an Armenian living in Transtiberian district of Rome, by name Modorus. He was brought here after he was captured in Aquileia, and admitted to all three incidents. He identified the individual who directed him to carry out these tasks. The man was believed to be a Parthian agent, but he fled the City before we could apprehend him, and the Parthian envoy also fled the City shortly after."

Pontus swallowing hard. "I … I had no knowledge of these cases."

"A Parthian connection makes this a potential treason case. I would like to examine your servants that were with you."

"Under duress?"

"If necessary. Appropriate for a treason case." He turned to the Praetorian guards. "Take them below for questioning."

The Praetorian guards led the six servants down three flights of stone stairs to the dark basement, lit by torches fitfully flickering in sconces on the walls. Somewhere in the distance, someone screamed, a long-drawn-out scream that ended in a sob, then a whimper. Then whoever it was screamed again. The six servants were led to separate darkened chambers, each with their own escort. Publius' guard motioned him to sit in a rough chair, fixed rigidly to the floor, from which leather straps dangled. A brazier, in which various iron instruments glowed a dull red, cast a baleful orange glow about the room, enough to see a collection of whips, knives, scissors and other implements, neatly hanging. A dingy rag with dark stains on it, probably blood, lay on the floor at his feet. His guard fastened the leather restraints about his arms and legs.

A pudgy bearded man, clad in a black tunic and leather apron, entered the room. "Are you ready?" he asked the Praetorian.

"Ready. I have my questions to ask." He pulled out a wax tablet.

The pudgy man pulled an iron from the brazier, like a branding iron, blew on its smoking glowing end, and approached Publius.

Publius squirmed in his chair, seized by panic. "Wait! Wait! I will tell you everything just don't ... don't." he began to whimper.

"Go ahead. Tell me what you know," said the guard. "We'll see if they match my questions." The pudgy man looked disappointed, maybe cheated of the chance to do his handiwork.

"I was the one who put a powder into the *garum* sauce. Everyone puts *garum* on everything. *Dominus* Pontus told me to do it and gave me the powder. He said everyone would go to sleep, but I wasn't to eat any of it. When everyone was asleep, I was to unlock and unbar the door, someone would come in and steal something. Then I was to get rid of the sauce, eat my bit, and pass out like everyone else." He burst into tears.

One of his fellow servants in a neighboring chamber gave a bloodcurdling scream.

"Please, don't do that to the others. I was the only one who knew anything about this. They know nothing."

"You did this at Pontus' direction, you say?" asked the Praetorian.

"I did."

"And do you know that if you lie to involve your master in a crime he did not commit, the penalty will be crucifixion?"

"I do."

"Do you know why the senator asked you to do this?"

"No, other than that something important was to be stolen."

"A person?"

"I didn't think so. He didn't seem to think so. Just ... something."

"Was he working with someone?"

"I don't know. He was meeting with someone named Justinius a lot, about a week before we left. I had never met him before." The praetorian scratched a note in his wax tablet, as the screaming resumed in the adjacent cell. "Please, make them stop! They can't tell you anything."

The praetorian nodded to the torturer who stepped outside. The screaming next door died away. The guard undid Publius' bonds. "Let's go."

A grim-faced Crispinus came back to stand before Pontus, flanked by Petronius.

"Where are my servants?" asked Pontus.

"They are being taken care of. Who is Justinius?"

"Justinius Favius. He is a dear friend."

Petronius interjected. "Favius is a man we have our eyes on. He does a lot of business selling Parthian carpets."

"They are very fine carpets, much in demand in the City! That is not a crime," objected Pontus. "I was examining his wares, with an eye to buying several." *Had Publius confessed?*

"To be sure," said Petronius coolly. "Where is he now?"

"I don't know."

"Did you buy any carpets?"

"Not yet. I was just looking, comparing prices. They are very expensive."

"Your friend makes many trips and is very good at being invisible when he leaves the City. We don't know where he is now either, and we had him under surveillance. We believe he is a Parthian agent."

It was Crispinus' turn to take over the conversation. "You directed Publius to poison the food and open the door, as a result of which the wife of the senior advisor to the *Princeps* was kidnapped. If you were acting on behalf of a Parthian agent, your head will be on a spike at the Mamartine Prison before the week is out, and your estates forfeit to the state."

Pontus' face went from florid to pale. He shook his head in the negative, which caused his flabby jowls to swing back and forth. "No! I did not intend to commit treason!"

"Nevertheless, you did, and during a state of war between Rome and Parthia."

"No ... no! I have devoted my life in service to the Senate and the People of Rome!"

"And profited handily by it, as well. However, there is a way out of this by which your life may be spared."

"Please! What is that?"

"Tell us everything you know about this nefarious plot. Your estates will be forfeit, except for a pittance to allow you to get by, living out your life on some faraway island in exile, but you will at least get a chance to die a natural death. And perhaps lose some of that ponderous weight."

Pontus tearfully confessed that Favius had promised that something would be found at the Aristides estate that would favor the peace faction, of which Pontus was a leader. He had never mentioned kidnapping.

But Favius had given them the slip and could not be located. Not even his own household knew where he had gone, or when he would be back.

CHAPTER 73:

BAD NEWS

Elegeia, January 115AD

Trajan read and re-read the urgent dispatch from Crispinus five times, scrutinizing its content. He then rolled two sealed letters back and forth in his hands that had been attached to the Urban Prefect's official report, personal ones to Aulus Galba from his son, and another to Antonius Aristides from his servant Desdemona. He was curious as to their content, but restrained himself from breaking their seals. They were not likely to contain information beyond what Crispinus had given in his report, and they might contain private feelings to which he need not be privy.

Crispinus' report was short on details, but pieced together with what he and his intelligence staff had learned from Marcus, the story was ominous.

Trajan wrapped a wool cloak about himself against the winter chill that pervaded the stone fort that was his winter quarters. It seemed that cold bothered him more than it had when he was younger. Could he be aging? No matter. He summoned a servant to fetch Senator Galba and Marcus Lucius, and sent a runner to summon Antonius Aristides from the Twelfth Lightning Bolt, newly arrived from the highlands in their winter camp nearby.

Aulus and Marcus arrived an hour later as Trajan was himself trying to stir new life into the feeble fire.

"Your Excellency! I'll fetch a servant for you, no need for that," said Aulus.

Marcus was in awe, seeing what had to be the most powerful man in the world being chastised for performing such a mundane task.

"Don't worry about it. When they day comes that I can't stir my own fire, then perhaps it will be time for me to die." He indicated the three chairs before his desk. "Sit down, please. Both of you."

Aulus took a seat, joined by Marcus, attentive to something serious about to be said.

"Please, the serious matter that I must share with you also affects Antonius Aristides. He should be arriving shortly. Please be patient."

In just a few minutes, Antonius entered in military gear, accompanied by Gaius Lucullus. Both saluted, arms across their chests. An alert servant hastily set out a fourth chair for the *legatus*.

"At ease, gentlemen. Gaius, as you are Antonius' commanding *legatus*, you may stay. What I have to say affects you as well. Be seated, please."

The two men took seats on the chairs next to Aulus.

The *Princeps* took a deep breath and led straight into the story. "Livia Galba was visiting Marcia Aristida in Aquileia, when an incident occurred. Both women are missing."

Aulus and Antonius were too stunned to speak.

"Incident? Missing … how? Is she … were they … hurt?" asked Gaius.

"There is no evidence they were hurt. But the authorities have been unable to locate them. The search is continuing."

"How did this happen?"

"I have a report from the Urban Prefect of Rome, Clodius Crispinus, who personally handled this matter. I will read you his report.

> *Vale, Your Excellency.*
>
> *I trust this letter finds you in good health.*
>
> *I must bring to your attention a most disturbing incident. On the Nones of December, the wives of Senator Aulus Aemilius Galba and Antonius Aristides, Prefect of Camps, Leg XII Ful, disappeared from the Aristides household in Aquileia. The disappearance was facilitated by Senator Lucian Septimius Pontus, who had accompanied Galba's wife Livia on the visit to the Aristides household. He confessed to administering a poison to the dinner meal which caused all to become unconscious, during which time the women were taken. He admitted to acting at the direction of Justinius Favius. Favius is a dealer in Parthian carpets, suspected of being a Parthian agent; he is currently unlocated.*
>
> *Acting on your behalf as Urban Prefect, I have removed Lucius Septimius' name from the Senatorial roles and confiscated his extensive estates. He will be exiled to a small island in the northern Black Sea when the inventory of his assets is complete. As he is continuing to cooperate, I have elected not to execute him.*
>
> *There were three other incidents involving these households two years ago, the torture and murder of Aulus Aemilius' personal secretary in Rome, the murder of the doorkeeper at the Aristides household in Aquileia, and subsequent break-in there two months later. The perpetrator, an Armenian living in Rome, was captured and subsequently confessed to all three incidents, and received the extreme penalty. He was acting on behalf of a Parthian agent, who fled before he could be apprehended.*
>
> *The Aquileian authorities are searching for the missing women, or their bodies, but they are as of now unlocated. Those authorities have increased security at the household, which is also an academy; Aulus Aemilius' son Pontus has volunteered to remain and arm himself to help protect the household.*
>
> *I have also included two letters with this official posting, the first from Aulus Aemilius' son to his father, and a second from one of the servants of the Aristides*

household. I wish these letters to be delivered to the recipients with all speed, but via you first.

I am concerned that the Parthian connections indicate that this may be an attempt by Ctesiphon to influence the outcome of the war. I therefore have not delayed in bringing this to your attention, despite the scanty facts available at this writing.

Clodius Crispinus
Urban Prefect
On the Nones of January
868 years from the founding of the City

Trajan paused to let the contents of the letter sink in.

Aulus was the first to respond. He leapt to his feet, uncharacteristically profane. "That bastard Pontus! He should be executed for treason! My wife … if anything has happened to her, I will kill him myself."

Trajan suppressed a chuckle. "He may well wish you had, when he faces his first Crimean winter. It gets quite cold up there, and he will have barely enough money left to buy food, fuel and clothing."

"No matter, he's a gods-cursed traitor!" said Antonius, his face red with anger. He turned to Gaius. "Sir, I request leave to go to Aquileia and search for my Marcia."

Aulus chimed in, still standing, pacing restlessly. "I can arrange transport for you, Antonius. Your Excellency, by your leave, I wish also to return to help search for Livia."

Trajan answered before Gaius could. "Patience, both of you. Marcus has already told us that the cause for this is the code Ctesiphon believes is in your letters, sent under Aulus Aemilius' seal. I expect that the women will be brought east to us. Ctesiphon intends to use them somehow as leverage against you and Aulus to produce the key to that non-existent code. And that is what I believe they were searching for in the other crimes against your household. I believe that the women are on their way east, if they are not already here."

"If they hurt them in any way …" growled Antonius.

"I don't believe they will. Unharmed, they are good bargaining chips. But Ctesiphon has miscalculated gravely. I had misgivings about continuing my campaign beyond Armenia this spring unless they attacked us in Armenia. But Parthia has chosen to launch an attack on our sacred Italian homeland, however small. This has settled it for me. We are going into Mesopotamia this spring, with full force!" Trajan slammed his hand down on his desk.

After composing himself, Trajan recovered the two personal letters "Crispinus forwarded with his report two personal letters for you, Aulus, and you Antonius." He rose to hand them each their letter. "The seals are unbroken."

The room was silent as each read their letters.

Both men were weeping unashamed when they finished the letters. Antonius choked back a sob after finishing his. "My children, they are all right. The infant Androcles is being well cared for. Desdemona, my *domina's* maid servant, has earned her freedom."

Aulus sighed. "My son Pontus Servilius is only fourteen, a few years shy of manhood. But he is a man in his own right. He is staying at the villa to assist in any way."

Marcus spoke up. "The *Princeps* is most correct. My sister and your wife will almost certainly be taken to Mithridates. He will use them against us, as soon as he can figure out a plan. We will no doubt be hearing from him then." He smacked one palm with his other fist noisily in frustration. "Somehow."

CHAPTER 74:

FROM ONE HAND TO ANOTHER

Antioch, March 115AD

The hold of the slave ship had become even more foul after several weeks at sea. Many of the miserable lot had become violently seasick, adding to the fetid miasma. Marcia and Livia had taken to keeping note of their brief glimpses of daylight, tabulating the elapsed days using a small nail they had loosened from a board. After fourteen days, the ship made its first stop, thudding against a dock somewhere. Some of the slaves were taken up, only to be replaced by others, and after a few days the ship lurched away from the mooring and got underway again.

Livia had comforted Marcia that they were the targets, for whatever reason, of this kidnap, and that their children were, in all likelihood, safe and in good hands ... an optimism she could scarcely believe herself. It was necessary that Marcia believed her children safe; after all, Livia's Pontus was near manhood, while Marcia's children were an infant and two toddlers.

They had talked a bit to their fellow slaves. The one on their left, a blond with stringy hair and several missing teeth, was a Briton named Elan. She cackled that she had been a prostitute for as long as she could remember, and hoped that the accommodations at her next brothel would be better than her last. "A stone bed, ladies, ye don't min' me callin' ye that, ye seem nicer 'n' most. A stone bed fer humping me customers, an' a rough blanket ter keep from skinning' me knees. Hope ye get better digs 'n' that." The thought was not promising.

The girl on their right was a red-haired Gaul named Dana, perhaps fourteen or so, terrified at her new circumstances, apparently kidnapped as they had been, and inconsolable. She would say little, just a few words before bursting into tears. It was not a pleasant conversation, but it made the time pass, as the ship continued its implacable rolling and pitching.

Justinius had paid them no more visits, and the sailors were incommunicative. The ship's name, they learned, was the *Bucephalus*, named for the bull-headed warhorse of Alexander. An ostentatious name for such an inauspicious ship. Aside from that they knew only the passage of days, tallied on the deck with sharp edge of the nail.

After thirty-five days and two storms that each lasted a day, drenching the slave hold with seawater and rain through leaking hatches, the rhythm of the ship changed, and it leaned into a hard turn.

"I think we are pulling into port," said Livia.

"I hope it's Antioch. Even a brothel will be better than this." Marcia spat. Her mouth was as foul as the ship's hold, her teeth not having been brushed for over a month.

Shortly after, the thud and cries of the sailors topside, and the clatter of sails coming down and being furled, indicated that they were indeed in another port. And this time, Justinius clattered down the ladder, keys in hand. "You girls get off here. Your next buyer is waiting." He seemed unconcerned at all about their filthy condition, unlocking their chains from the one running along the ship's bulkhead.

The women got to their feet, unsteady from not having walked for more than a month, but they made it up the ladder to the deck, to blink in the brilliant sunlight. A man in a green silk robe and white turban, with a forked black beard, was waiting for them, sizing them up.

Justinius handed him the bills of sale. "Diana and Aphrodite, registered prostitutes. And with that are their licenses, certified free of any disease."

"Which one is which?"

"Does it matter? Give me the money."

The man handed Justinius a velvet sack. Justinius counted out twenty silver *denarii*. "The price was to be two *aurei* for both. You owe me thirty more silvers."

"That is the price, take it, or keep the girls. They are a hot commodity. There is an imperial edict demanding they be turned over immediately when found."

Justinius hesitated, fuming, then decided to go along, signing the bill of sale with an angry flourish. "You are a double-dealing bastard, Farnavantes, but I will go along with it."

The women made no sign of recognition about what he had said about the edict, but it struck some hope in them. Their plight had reached the highest levels.

A swarthy man with him, wearing a tunic, chained the two women, leading them off the ship to a waiting canvas-covered wagon. "In you go, girls," he said, locking their iron tethers to a fitting in the floor.

CHAPTER 75:

CAUSE FOR WAR

Ctesiphon, March 115AD

King Osroës called in his advisors. They individually entered, their heads deeply bowed to prostrate themselves before him, intoning *"Shahanshah,"* then seated themselves on the floor on their haunches. Mithridates entered, followed by Sanatruces, the last to enter. Servants then closed the doors of the king's chamber. Like the others, Mithridates had no cognizance of the purpose of this suddenly called meeting, but surmised that it had something to do with the war with Rome.

King Osroës' face was set like flint behind his beard, his eyes cold. "There has been a development. Scribe, read the letter."

The scribe standing next to the king read a translation of the letter in Aramaic.

King Osroës, the letter began curtly, omitting the honorific 'king of kings' title, and any polite preamble about their long friendship, wishes for peace and concern for his continued good health. Just *King Osroës.*

The unfortunate impasse between our two countries over Armenia had seemed to resolve itself with little bloodshed. I had come to Armenia with considerable forces at my disposal, sufficient to repel any attempt by you to intervene. But I had no intent to expand this minor war beyond my stated purpose of ensuring the security of Armenia. Since you had failed to comply with our treaty, I have since annexed Armenia and set it up as a Roman province under Governor Claudius Severus. At that point, I considered the matter at an end.

However, you have chosen to attack the Senate and the People of Rome, not in Armenia but in our sacred Italian homeland, kidnapping Livia Galba, wife of Senator Aulus Aemilius Galba, my trusted advisor, and Marcia Lucia Aristida, wife of the prefect of camps of Legio XII Fulminata. I assure you, unless these two Roman citizens are handed over unharmed, my forces shall descend upon your country like ravenous wolves, and shall not stop until they reach the sea at Charax.

Marcus Ulpius Traianus,
Imperator Caesar Optimus Maximus, Augustus Germanicus Decius

The scribe rerolled the scroll, stepped back and took a seat on the marble floor. The king scanned the audience. "Does anyone know what he is talking about? He is threatening all-out war and invasion over two women."

Mithridates swallowed hard. He had of course authorized his son to carry out this operation, but this was the first indication that it had been successful. Too successful, as it had reached the ears of Trajan and Osroës before his own. And Galba's wife as well? Kidnapping the wife of a senior Senator, one of Trajan's close advisors … that was almost certain to alert Trajan. But he knew few details of what had been planned. He was about to speak up, but his son spoke first.

"Your most reverend Excellency, I arranged for our agents in Italy to carry out this operation."

Mithridates was proud of his son, but he was certain he was about to see Sanatruces put to death.

"Why?" asked the king sharply.

"Because these two women are linked to coded communications between Rome and China. Trajan's reactions affirm our belief."

A brief flicker of a smile played across the king's narrow lips. "And now you have forced his hand?"

"It appears so, your Excellency."

"And the women are where?"

"They are being brought here. We are not communicating with those delivering them, lest some written correspondence fall into Roman hands, but unless something goes wrong, or has already gone wrong, I expect them here in the palace in the next several weeks."

Mithridates resisted the temptation to heave a sigh of relief. His son was fast on his feet.

"You have done well. Bring them to me when they arrive. I shall dictate now an appropriate response to the Roman king." He stood up abruptly, and all prostrated until he had left the room.

CHAPTER 76:

ANOTHER SNAKE RETURNS

Elegeia, March 115AD

Despite the bitterly cold weather that left the streams rimed with ice, and a continual layer of snow blanketing the ground, the next two months saw considerable preparation for the upcoming war. Legions in the field were continuously on the move, bivouacked in camps hacked out of the frozen ground, training. Though the training was not relevant to the environment in which they would be fighting, it was sufficiently unpleasant that they could look forward to the change that actual combat would bring.

Hina, Galosga, their twins and Hadyu had attached themselves to the cavalry wing of about five hundred horsemen, the Ninth Batavian Cohort under Longinus Clarus, and took an active role in the winter exercises, learning the signals and coordinated tactics so foreign to their native melee fighting style.

The cavalrymen were more than bit reticent at accepting a woman, a pubescent girl and a youth in their fighting ranks, but after a few got a first-hand taste of their fighting abilities, to the uproarious mirth of their comrades, they accepted them, at first grudgingly, then more and more enthusiastically.

On one particularly frigid day, the cavalry was practicing mounted archery. Bales of hay had been set up fifty yards off the icy road, and the horsemen trotted past in succession, dutifully unleashing their arrows in the direction of the targets. Hina and her troop held back, intending to give the mediocre archers a demonstration of proper horse archery. As the last cavalryman completed the perfunctory drill, Hina slipped on her conical felt hat and winked at Galosga, waiting for the field ahead to clear. Then she gave a wild war-scream with arrow and bow clasped in her left hand, goading Devil to a thundering gallop. She stood full off her mount in the stirrups, facing the target coming up on her right. In one fluid motion, she notched the arrow, drew and released the shaft to strike the first bale dead center, then smoothly notching a second for the next bale. Behind her, Galosga, Hadyu, Andanyu and Marasa did likewise, and at the end of the run, ten bales had five arrows each, all within a hands' breadth of each other.

As the five pulled their mounts up to a walk, their flanks steaming in the frigid air, Longinus Clarus, the cavalry wing commander rode up on his horse. "Nice shooting, there, Amazon."

Hina glared at him. "Why are you calling me Amazon?" Everyone by now understood that when her face turned dark, trouble was not far away.

"Amazon. Everybody needs a nickname in this outfit. That's yours. Woman warrior, an Amazon. Haven't you heard of them? You grew up in Scythia, didn't you?"

"I don't know where Scythia is, and I never heard of Amazons." Her face was beginning to lighten, the fire leaving her green eyes, as she gathered she had not been insulted.

"They're legendary women fighters, really fierce. I thought they were a myth, till I met you. I have never seen anyone shoot like that. Even the children."

"Back home, everyone shoots like that. We start teaching them when they are very young."

"Younger than those?" he asked, indicating the twins.

"They started when they were seven. My children," she said, with a little pride. They had done as well as the others.

"My men have a lot to learn. Mounted archery is not a priority for this unit. We do it just enough to say we can, but we can't compare to what you just did. Any chance you could teach my men? Make them better?"

Hina relaxed enough to give a hint of a smile. "I can't teach you everything. You don't have these," she said, lifting her foot in the stirrup. "But I can give you some lessons. She pointed to a bare tree by the road. "Hang a ring about this big from that branch, about eight feet up." She motioned with her hands, indicating it should be about a foot in diameter. "For now, have your men ride past and shoot as many arrows as they can through it starting from fifty yards. Marasa, Andanyu, set a marker for the fifty-yard point. When we are done today, leave the ring hanging, because this is going to take many days of practice."

While the cavalry men attached the target, the twins located a log and set it in the road as a marker.

Hina and Galosga positioned themselves beside the target, well offset, not trusting the archers' accuracy. And one by one, the five hundred men trotted up, getting off two or three arrows at the target, mostly misses. As the short day began to darken, the last man finished. They gathered to hear Hina. "It is a start. We will do this again tomorrow, but tomorrow you gallop. You cannot stroll into a fight. When you are good enough, we will set it to swinging. Your enemy is not going to give you an easy target, he doesn't want to die."

The Roman army always tried to keep a legion's movements in the field close-held. But it was by no means unusual for the legion to arrive at the night's encampment, to be greeted not only by the engineers who had gone ahead to select and survey the site, but also by the suttlers who tagged along, providing the legion with food, clothing, and various other items, often including women. It seemed that the only ones who did not know where the next night's camp would be were the soldiers marching to it. And the bitter cold did not discourage the suttlers, who did a booming business in warm cloaks, woolen leggings and socks to make the chill less miserable.

Therefore, Samuel and Secundus were not surprised to see suttlers greeting them at the Fifth Cohort's spot marked out by the engineers. Samuel needed new socks anyway. But he was surprised to see Manasseh mingling with them.

Ignoring the Jew did not work, as Manasseh sought him out. "How good to see thee again, Shmuel. Thou art well?" he greeted him in Aramaic.

"I am," he answered, omitting the polite counter inquiry. "Thou art a long way from Melitene."

"Not that far for a friend. Can we go somewhere and talk briefly?"

"Not now. I must get my cohort settled in for the night. And we break camp at first light, but then I am sure that you know that."

"Later, perhaps?"

"Not too much later. We will be up before dawn to get on the move again, and my *optio* is duty centurion tonight."

"Promoted, I see. You were the *optio* before."

"So it seems."

Manasseh departed and the centurion and his tribune set about directing the cohort into its proper places, helping to hack the camp's surrounding ditch from the iron-hard frozen soil. It was a drill to which they were well accustomed, having done this every night of the past month. Although they had arrived in late afternoon, it was well after dark before Samuel dismissed the men to pitch their tents and prepare their evening meals. Watch trumpets called away Samuel's *optio* Lucius Ariatus for his night duties, leaving Samuel alone, quite ready to wrap himself in a blanket and sleep the few short hours before a very early rising.

His preparations were interrupted by a scratching at the tent door flap. It was Manasseh.

"Come in, if you must. Close the flap, it's cold out there." Samuel grumbled, as he stirred the charcoals embers in a small brazier, trying to coax more heat from them. "Be seated. You look more like a suttler than a rich banker these days."

Manasseh took one of the folding camp chairs. "On the frontier, it pays not to advertise one's wealth. To all who care, I am a tender of mules." He paused, rubbing his hands together. "I bring you bad news from Petra. Our friend Yakov has fallen on hard times without the generous stipends you sent. He may have to turn his charges back out on the street."

"And you would like me to resume sending my troop's contribution to them."

"If you wish. I am sorry we parted in ill graces the last time we spoke."

"You offered me things that I could not accept, that should not have been offered."

"Do you wish to resume our business relationship?"

"Give me two weeks to get the contributions."

"Where will you be in two weeks?"

"We will be wherever we are. The suttlers will know. I don't. Now I must retire."

CHAPTER 77:

SLAVES AND YET NOT SLAVES

Between Antioch and Ctesiphon, March 115AD

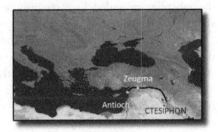

There was nothing better to do than listen and size up the situation, so that is what Marcia did, chained up in the back of the wagon with Livia. In front, Farnavantes, now dressed in rough traveling clothes, sat next to the driver, lurching along the Roman road out of Antioch. There were at least four riders with them. All were speaking Parthian, a language Marcia knew, though not well. She learned from their conversations that they were heading to a place called Zeugma, five days away, where they would cross the Euphrates River into Parthian territory, and on to Ctesiphon. That, she knew, was the western capital of Parthia.

So, that is the connection! The murder of Janus, the break-in, and the murder of Aulus' slave. And now this. They want something from us. I understand them wanting Livia, the wife of a senior advisor to the Princeps. But why me?

About sunset, the wagon pulled off the road to an informal campsite by a small lake. The lake was lined by evergreens, poplar and bull rushes. Farnavantes came into the wagon with a tool in his hand, and unlocked their chains from the fitting on the wagon wall. "You don't need chains anymore," he said, slipping the tool in the next to last link attached to Livia's slave collar. He pried hard and the links opened, allowing it to slip free of the last loop. He repeated the process with Marcia's chain. "Don't get any ideas about running away. There are slave catchers all over, and if they pick you up in these collars without an explanation or master to return you to, they'll take you to the nearest slave market and pocket a nice purse for you. Then you'll be real slaves for life."

He fished two white bundles out of a chest in the wagon and handed one to each of them. "Now, go down by the lake and take about an hour cleaning up. There's oil, fresh clothes, and other things. Now go, you are stinking up the wagon. Throw your old clothes away. My boys will be watching, but they are not to touch you. Our orders are to deliver you, unharmed and unsullied."

"Deliver us to whom?" asked Marcia.

"To the man who wants you. Now go."

The women scurried off to the lake. Two men went with them as guards; while the men didn't touch them, their orders did not forbid them from watching the girls intently as they shed their filthy rags. Audience or not, they slipped naked into the cool waters, and took turns scrubbing off weeks of collected foulness from their bodies until their skin began to emerge, flea-bitten but pink in the setting sun. It took most of an hour for them to get properly clean, at the end of which they were giggling like girls. They emerged from the lake to slip into fresh clean white tunics. Towels had been thoughtfully provided in each bundle, underwear, and even mint chewing sticks to finally clean their teeth and freshen their long-foul mouths.

"Farnavantes, I do not usually thank my kidnappers, but in this case, I will thank you most gratefully for the chance to get clean," said Livia, in as stately a pose as she could assume with a slave collar around her neck.

"You are welcome, *domina*. The slave cover was an unfortunate necessity, but I assure you, I will take good care of you during the rest of trip."

"Where are you taking us?"

"As I said before, to the man who wants your presence."

"Does he have a name?"

Farnavantes paused. "He does," he answered finally.

Dinner had been prepared while they bathed, and they were given a bowl of stew. Simple fare, but after weeks of meagre unpalatable rations, it seemed like a feast, with even a generous leather sack of wine for the two.

Farnavantes returned to his companions by the fire, leaving Marcia and Livia alone.

"Well, this a change for the better," said Livia. "More wine, please."

"To be certain. We seem to be valuable to somebody important." Marcia filled Livia's coarse ceramic cup, also refilling her own. "Don't get tipsy. We need to stay in control at all times."

"Do you see any chance to escape?"

"With these around our necks? He's right, we would be sold as real slaves at some market."

"He said there was an imperial edict of some sort …"

"Nobody looks at slaves. Right now, we just play along, keep our eyes open and say nothing we don't need to say."

Marcia hugged her knees to her chest. The night was beginning to cool quickly, and the cotton tunic offered little warmth. She dropped her voice to a whisper. "I understand their language. They are going to a place called Zeugma, about five days from here, and cross into Parthian territory. From there we go to the capitol Ctesiphon. For now, I suggest we grab one of those blankets and get some sleep, stretched horizontal for a change."

CHAPTER 78:

MARCHING OFF TO WAR

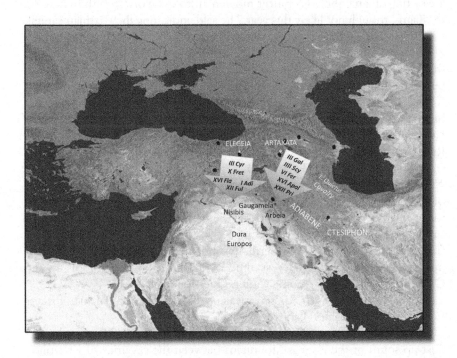

Between Elegeia and Nisibis, April 115AD

While the legions engaged in arduous and unusual winter training, Aulus had spent the season planning the campaign in the south with Trajan. He coordinated meetings with legion commanders to develop the battle plan and assign legions and cavalry to their areas of operation and objectives. By mid-March, the plan was ready, and presented at a meeting of all the legion commanders and Claudius Severus, governor of the new province of Armenia, with Trajan and the other senior advisors to the *Princeps*. The legions, represented by bronze markers, were positioned on a large map of Mesopotamia on a table with the Euphrates and Tigris Rivers highlighted, along with major cities. Aulus, though without military experience, presented the plan before the commanders and Trajan. He had largely developed it based on intelligence and inputs from the legions. Junior officers stood ready to move the legion markers on the map as the plan unfolded. Commanders' aides stood by with wax tablets, ready to take notes. They would all, of course, receive detailed written orders for their own legion's part, but this presentation would be the only opportunity to get a the bird's eye view of the campaign.

Aulus stepped up before the map, and addressed the group in his best senatorial voice, summarizing the battle plan. "So, this is it, gentlemen. We are setting up an enormous pincer movement to close on Ctesiphon here on the Tigris, though not likely this year," he said, indicating the Parthian capital.

"The *III Cyrenaica, X Fretensis, XII Fulminata, XVI Flavia Firma* and *I Adiutrix* will deploy from their winter bases around Elegeia, to break down the door to western Mesopotamia at Nisibis. The Twelfth Lightning Bolt will be point in the advance, with the Sixteenth Steadfast Flavians and First Rescuer covering their flanks. The Tenth Straits will garrison Nisibis, and build a fleet of river craft which will be used next year to advance down the Euphrates. After Nisibis, the remaining legions will follow the Euphrates River to the Parthian fortress at Dura Europos, six hundred miles to the south. In the east, The *III Gallica, IV Scythica, VI Ferrata, XV Apollinaris* and *XXII Primigenia* will deploy from Artaxata through the Taurus Mountains east of Lake Van, along the Tigris River to Adiabene as far as Gaugamela, and to the capital Arbela, if possible before September. Lusius Quietus' Berber cavalry will pacify the area east of the Tigris, then join up with the legionary forces in Adiabene. The northern Mesopotamian area is one of Parthia's major breadbaskets. By harvest time, we will be in control of it, and Ctesiphon will be hungry come winter. Questions?"

Gaius Lucullus was the first to speak up. "Where are the Parthian forces? What kind of opposition can we expect?"

"Surprisingly, there are no Parthian forces at this time. There is a border dust-up south of the Zagros Mountains between the cavalries of Ctesiphon and Ecbatana. For some reason, they seem to be more concerned with their internal rivalry over who should be king of kings, than our invasion. We are aware this may be a trap, but as of now, we expect the opposition to be strictly local. Adiabene is expected to put up the strongest opposition, but most of the rest have already indicated that they are ready to accept Rome's rule."

There were a few other perfunctory questions, about logistics, attitudes of the local kings and satraps. And weather. They would be advancing in the deadly heat of the Mesopotamian summer, in sharp contrast to their winter training.

Trajan closed the meeting with a curt summary. "Aulus Aemilius, you and our *legati* have all put together a most excellent plan. We will be following in the steps of Alexander the Great. Let us pray that we do half as well as he did four centuries ago. Dismissed!" He turned and exited, and commanders milled about shaking hands and discussing points among themselves.

Gaius sought out Aulus. "You have put together a good plan, my friend. I hear that it is mostly your own work. I never knew you to be such a strategist."

"I did not either, Gaius. However, this is my way to get my Livia back, and I will have her back if I have to tear down the palace at Ctesiphon with my bare hands. How is Antonius holding up?" asked Aulus.

"As best as could be expected. He is driving himself to exhaustion to keep from thinking about it."

"He is a good man, Gaius. Take care of him, please."

"Antonius has settled into his duties as camp prefect with a vengeance, tracking every detail of logistics, taking reports from spies, working long past midnight, up long before the sun. Working is the only thing that keeps him sane. I am worried about him. And you?"

"I have been doing as Antonius has," said Aulus, his mouth set grimly. "And now I have to get back to work. Good luck in the campaign."

The Twelfth was moving out the next day, and Samuel and Secundus had spent the day ensuring that the Fifth Cohort was ready in all respects. In the late afternoon, Manasseh showed up at Samuel's tent. "Good day, sir. Do you have contributions for your friend in Petra?"

"I do, in fact." He picked up a purse filled with silver *denarii*. "About sixty *denarii* for you, the men were very generous this time. Superstitious before the war, I think. Your usual percentage?"

"I am afraid with the war on, we have had to raise it to twenty percent, but it will reach your friend Yakov, I assure you." Manasseh handed him a written agreement.

Samuel read the agreement, twice, then signed it and. handed over the purse "You know the war is not going to affect you in any way, it's just an excuse to raise the price. But take it and be gone with you."

The next morning, the legions began their march south. Antonius rode alongside Gaius at the head of the Twelfth. "Well, sir, it seems we're off ter another war," he said.

"So it seems, though an odd one. The spies report no massing Parthian forces ahead of us. Aulus said most of the local rulers are just going to line up with us. Almost like Parthia intends to just stand aside and let us have it all. By the way, are you getting enough sleep? You are no use to me, red-eyed."

"Been sleepin' fine. Just dust in me eyes."

Gaius smiled. "I know you better than that."

"I can't sleep, thinkin' about me *domina*. Work is the only thing ter keep the wolves at bay. Sometimes I imagine that I'm goin' ter find her and rescue her from whoever's got her, and that's the worst. 'Cuz it ain't goin' ter happen."

"Yes, it will. We are going to find her. Ctesiphon kidnapped her and Livia for a reason, and when they play their cards we will know what to do. She is a strong woman, she'll take care of herself and Livia."

"Can we talk about somethin' else? I don't like ter think about it."

"I understand."

They rode on in silence, but liking to think about it or not, it was all that Antonius could do.

CHAPTER 79:

A PAIR OF PLAYING CARDS

Ctesiphon, April 115AD

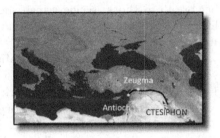

True to his word, Farnavantes ensured that Marcia and Livia were well-treated on the long road trip, and once inside the borders of Parthia, put them up at inns and way stations as they were available. After a week, the white walls of Ctesiphon came into sight.

"We will be there tonight," Farnavantes said simply, removing the women's slave collars, then leaving them in the wagon. The wagon had become their home on the road, isolated from the men outside. It had three comfortable leather seats running the width of the wagon, comfortable enough for sleeping at night, and the men brought them their meals to eat inside. The high canvas top admitted plenty of welcome fresh air, as the weather was already becoming quite warm.

Farnavantes said nothing more about their next custodian, but the women had long ago surmised that it would be someone in the palace, whose high towers rising over the surrounding walls could already be seen.

"He has been pleasant enough, for a kidnapper and slave master, but I will not miss him. There is something very untrustworthy about him," said Marcia.

"I sense that, too," said Livia. "Someone powerful is holding his leash, or I don't think he would be as good as he has been. What happens next?"

"Well, this is where we find out. Certainly, someone in the palace wants us. At least we will find out who that is, and what they want from us."

"Something they have been willing to kill for."

"Yes, that."

That evening, just as the torches in sconces along the palace wall by the street were being lit, Farnavantes dismissed the riders and ushered the women in past the grim blue-clad guards. Their heels clicked on the pavilion's gray marble floor reflecting the light from lamps hanging from the ceiling. Taking the marble stairs at the end, past elaborate tapestries hung on the walls, they climbed to the third floor, past one room whose heavily gilded door was closed. Farnavantes led them to a plainer open door. He knocked at the frame. "Kophasates? Is your master in? I have his long-awaited packages."

"To be sure. He received your letter yesterday and has been eagerly awaiting your arrival, bring them in," Kophasates said from inside the office. He turned to open an interior door. "Your Excellency, Farnavantes is here with your packages."

Marcia silently followed the Parthian dialogue, incensed that she and Livia were just 'packages' to him. The man stepped out, and Marcia drew in her breath in shock, seeing a man she had not seen for over ten years, a lifetime ago. "Koreshi!" she said, calling him by the Hanaean version of his first name, Cyrus.

"I see you recognize me," said Mithridates in Latin. "It is good to see you again. And you," he said, taking Livia's hand. "You must be the beautiful Livia. Aulus Aemilius is certainly a lucky man."

Livia jerked back her hand as though she had touched something foul.

"Come into my office, please. Farnavantes, you have done well. Kophasates will see to your well-earned reward." Mithridates ushered the two women into his office, inviting them to sit on the comfortable sofa opposite his office. "I hope your trip was not too unpleasant."

"Aside from being kidnapped and kept as prostitutes in a stinking slave ship hold for a month?" asked Marcia, with a touch of bitterness.

"I was not aware of how you were brought here. You will understand that we had to ensure that you could neither escape, nor be found by the authorities. I apologize if that was unpleasant. By the way, Marcia, your brother Marcus visited us here a few months ago."

"Marcus? Here? Why?" Marcia was dumbfounded, being struck by too many new and unexpected things.

"Yes. Unfortunately, he had to proceed on his way. He was going to Rome to see you."

"Where is he now?"

"I have no idea, somewhere west, I suppose."

"What do you want with us?" asked Livia.

"We will deal with that later, after you are rested." He handed them each a writing tablet with one sheet of very fine grade papyrus paper, ink and a stylus. "For now, I would like you to write letters to your husbands, assuring them that you are alive and safe. I am sure they are worried about your abrupt removal. You may, if you wish, tell them where you are. We have nothing to hide. If either of you need help with writing, I can summon Kophasates to write it for you."

"We are both quite literate, thank you," said Marcia. She began her letter to Antonius in her exquisite miniscule handwriting. There seemed to be no risk in telling them they were alive and well, and that increased the possibility of a rescue. Livia picked up the clue and began her letter also.

When the letters were finished, they handed them to Mithridates, who scanned each quickly. "I will see that these are taken by courier to your husbands. Even during a war, we have communications with Trajan and his army. Now you must be tired after a long trip. Kophasates will see you to your quarters."

Kophasates led them down the corridor to a room at the back, a luxurious suite with elaborate carpets, plush bedding, and a sitting area with a small desk and chair, and a big sofa. "This will be yours for your stay here. Two maidservants will come to see to your needs momentarily. Have a good night." He left politely.

Mithridates retired to his quarters and poured some excellent red wine and nibbled at a plate of Tigris dates, pondering the situation. When he had ordered the women brought to him, almost a year ago, he had no clear idea just how he would use them, but he was sure that in the months to come, a plan would present itself. None had, and now they were here. What was he to do with them?

The first step was to let their husbands know they were here. That was already done, sure to spur some action, but what? A rescue? Not likely. The head of the last man in charge of palace security had decorated the parapet for months after Marcus' escape, a lesson not lost on his replacement. An attack? Eventually, but the Romans had hundreds of miles yet to cover and several cities to pacify before they would be close to Ctesiphon.

The code, the code, the code! He had teams of the most brilliant code breakers in Parthia, including some of their best mathematicians of the old Babylonian school, going over these letters. Their conclusion? There either was no code, as Marcus had claimed, or it was so cleverly contrived that it appeared invisible. There were several ways the analysts knew how this could be done, but this required a codebook that gave meaning to an individual word or phrase.

One thing was sure, no woman would be capable of using such a sophisticated code. Nothing connected Livia to the code, other than Aulus' seal, though Aulus probably was the final conduit with Trajan.

Marcia had personally written most of the letters to Marcus, Mithridates now knew, by comparing her neat script on her letter to her husband with the scrolls in hand. She probably just populated the key elements encoding Aulus' messages given her by her husband Antonius with idle women's chitchat. Or they may know more, both of them, than they let on. Marcia, in particular, radiated a sense of power and authority totally unlike the meek concubine he had known.

So, the women were pawns in a chess game. He had made his move with them, and the next move would suggest itself when the Romans made their next move. Until then, keep them in comfortable captivity … not much of a plan, but a plan. Then a thought flashed through his mind. What if they were involved in the code? Why not set them to work, deciphering the letters from memory? Better than waiting for the Romans' next move, which might not come for a long while.

Mithridates nibbled another date, washed it down with wine, and retired for the night.

Kophasates went to his own quarters, his duties done after a long day. Except for one more. He lit an oil lamp and pulled writing material and a leather wine sack from under his mattress. *Very interesting. Livia, a Roman lady, and Marcia, an Hanaean lady with a Latin name and regal bearing, despite her short stature. My client will be very interested in these two women and will pay well for this information. Though I do not yet know why Mithridates had them kidnapped and brought to him.*

He jotted some notes on a wax tablet, then consulted his materials and enciphered it. He then copied the enciphered text onto cheap paper, rolled it up into a tube, and inserted it into the neck of the wine sack. He held the wax tablet over the lamp's flame, erasing the plain text beyond any recovery. *It seems I will need to visit the wine merchant tomorrow to exchange this empty wine sack for a full one.*

CHAPTER 80:

INFLEXIBLE PLAYING CARDS

Ctesiphon, April 115AD

As promised, the Parthian-speaking maid servants arrived to attend their needs: luxurious massages, and cutting and styling their hair, something long overdue. They brought the women beautiful silk garments, a green diaphanous dress with a bare shoulder for Livia that went well with her red hair, and a white one in sharp contrast to Marcia's long black hair.

Marcia understood the attendants fairly well, but did not want to let them know that. She spoke only Latin, which they did not understand, using hand gestures. The servants left the women with a plate of dates and sweetmeats, and a flagon of good red wine.

With the maidservants gone, Livia and Marcia indulged in conversation on the sofa in a privacy they had not known for a while, the window curtains billowing gently in the night breeze off the Tigris. "What language were they speaking? I have never heard anything like that before," asked Livia.

"Parthian." Marcia leaned over and almost whispered. "I speak it well enough to understand most. But don't let on. There might come a time when knowing what is said in a side conversation around us in Parthian might be important."

Livia nodded. "So, you knew Mithridates in your past life."

"Only by sight, I never talked to him. He was the Parthian envoy to the Han court when I was there. My brother Marcus got to know him quite well, as did your husband. They thought he was a snake. He tried to set the Han emperor against us and get us executed."

"Yes, Aulus told me about that. Horrible."

"Not so bad. It brought me Antonius." She smiled. "We made love for the first time that night in a nasty cell, with Aulus, Gaius Lucullus and my brother making sure the guards didn't show up."

Livia's eyes twinkled. "Aulus didn't tell me that part of the story."

"We were very discrete. But now we can guess who the snake was behind the murders and break-ins back home."

"Yes, but what does he want from us?"

"I imagine he wants something from Aulus and Antonius, something to do with our old mission, but I haven't any idea what that might be."

"He said your brother had been here?"

"Maybe, or maybe just a play on my feelings. If he was here, I can't imagine Mithridates just letting him go on his way. He is probably here in Ctesiphon in some stinking jail. Or he might have had him put to death." Marcia shivered, though the Ctesiphon night was pleasantly warm.

"I imagine we will see Mithridates tomorrow."

"I imagine so, and tomorrow, and tomorrow, until we are sick of seeing him. We just have to hear what he wants and take it from there. Stall for time, mostly, so we can enjoy the pleasant accommodations. If he delivered our letters, I am sure there will be some attempt to ransom or rescue us."

Sure enough, the maidservants arrived at dawn to help them prepare for breakfast with Mithridates, and escorted them to his private residential chamber, next to his office. It was an expansive chamber with a huge marble living area, with a curtained window the width of it opening onto an esplanade overlooking the gardens below. There were Parthian carpets about the floor, marble and bronze statues, and artwork hanging on the walls.

He greeted them effusively in Latin. "Good morning, good morning, girls. You look absolutely beautiful, both of you." He motioned to a woman wearing a solid green silk shirt and trousers the Marcia recognized as the *salwar kamis* style. "My wife Ariadne. She is Greek, but unfortunately does not speak Latin."

Marcia smiled in Ariadne's direction but chose not to speak to her in Greek. Livia, who also spoke Greek, took her cue from Marcia and remained silent.

"Please join us for breakfast out on the esplanade." He led them through the curtains. A table held a large pan containing steaming, purple-colored chicken thighs and leeks, liberally sprinkled with asafetida, cumin and fennel seeds. Servants stood ready to fill their plates and their silver wine goblets.

It was a rich breakfast for the women, but delicious. They ate with their fingers in silence, then washed them in silver water bowls.

Mithridates broke the silence. "You will meet shortly with my brother *Shananshah* Osroës, the King of all Parthian Kings. You will enter and perform an obeisance to him, prostrate yourself, then rise when commanded. After that, you will find him easy on ceremony, especially around Romans."

Livia's eyes flared. "I bow before no man."

Marcia joined her. "If your brother Osroës wishes to have us forced to our knees, he may do so, if his guards are willing to fight us down, but I will enter standing. I have not prostrated myself before anyone since my time in Luoyang and will not do so again."

"Hmm. Marcia, you seem much more strong-willed than the Si Nuo I remember."

"The woman by that name died in the stinking cell in the palace at Luoyang. If the woman by the name of Marcia Lucia Aristida is to die here at the palace at Ctesiphon, so be it, but she shall die on her feet, and Livia with her."

Livia nodded in assent.

"Very well. I shall communicate this to my brother's staff. He has made exceptions before for Roman sensibilities." Mithridates summoned a servant, whispered in his ears, and waved him off in dispatch. He returned a few moments later and whispered something to Mithridates.

"Very well," he said. "If you were to meet your Roman king Trajan, how would you greet him?"

Livia took the lead. "I have met Marcus Ulpius Trajan on many occasions. He is *Princeps,* 'First among us', not our king, as we find such an institution despicable. I bow my head and address him as 'Your Excellency.' That is all Roman protocol requires."

"Then that is all the protocol we will require of you. Now, to my brother's chambers." Mithridates rose and led them through his office to the hall, to the gilded door of the king's chambers. He knocked discretely, the door opened from the inside, and he led the women in.

The King of Kings' throne room, a showcase of the power and wealth of Parthia, was designed to intimidate through opulence. The floor was white veined marble. Four purple marble pillars surrounded the gilded throne on which sat Osroës, in a gold-filigreed green silk robe, elaborate turban on his head, beard exquisitely coiffed in curls. He held a gold rod in his right hand. Behind him was the wide-winged emblem of Parthia clutching circular olive branches, ridden by a man facing right, all in gold. Bare-chested servants on either side of the throne stoically held braziers for illumination, glancing neither to the right or left.

Mithridates announced, "Greetings, *Shahanshah,*" and prostrated himself, but the women remained standing.

"Rise, brother, and introduce my guests," said the king in flawless Greek.

"This is Livia, wife of Aulus Aemilius Galba, advisor to Emperor Trajan, and Marcia, wife of Antonius Aristides, Prefect of Camps for the Twelfth Lightning Bolt Legion."

"I am pleased to meet you beautiful ladies."

Both gave almost imperceptible head nods. "Your Excellency," responded both, also in Greek.

"My brother Cyrus tells me you have been in communication with China."

"Your Excellency, my brother Marcus remained in China, and we corresponded for several years, until communications stopped," answered Marcia.

"And what did you communicate to each other?"

"I wrote of family events, our children, our academy. He wrote of events in our hometown of Liqian, our mother, and of his wife Mei."

"Did your husband tell you what to put in the letters?"

"No, your Excellency, not usually. Sometimes news of our Academy, but rarely."

"All under the imperial seal of a senior Roman Senator?"

"Given to us by Aulus ... Aulus Aemilius Galba, to speed our letters through Roman territory." She paused, then added, "Your Excellency."

"And Livia, what was your role in these letters?"

"None, Your Excellency. I knew Marcia and her brother corresponded, but I did not know how."

"Though it was your husband's seal they used?"

"I did not know that ... Your Excellency."

"Thank you for your honest answers. We have questions about what might be contained in those letters, so you will remain here as our guests while we resolve those questions. I hope you find your accommodations comfortable. As soon as those questions are resolved, you will be escorted to your husbands. That is all, you may leave."

Mithridates backed out of the king's chamber, but the women had no problem turning their backs on an Eastern potentate to exit, after a polite bow.

Mithridates escorted them to his office. Piled on his desk were a dozen or so scrolls. Marcia recognized the distinctive Galba seal on each, though all were broken. "Sit. These are the letters of concern to me and my brother." He handed one to Marcia, one of her own letters to Marcus from several years ago. "You recognize your own letter?"

"I do."

"Senatorial seals, though they have no authority here, attracted the attention of my staff several years ago. Also, the Hanaean characters on them. They brought your letters to my attention, and I ordered them all intercepted."

"You are the reason his letters stopped coming. And the Hanaean characters just identify the address as Si Nuo, in Liqian, in Gansu province, so the caravanners there knew how to deliver it. Surely you can read that." She pointed to three short rows of chicken-scratch Chinese characters.

"I speak Hanaean but was unable to learn to read or write it. When tensions began to rise with Rome a few years ago, we seized and examined all Roman communications on our side of the border. Spies are everywhere. But I think this is more than simple spying. Much more."

"What more could they be?" asked Marcia, examining the letter.

"A dire threat to our kingdom."

"This just tells him of the birth of my last child. I am sure that Androcles is not now a threat to Parthia, he is only three."

"Idle family business does not warrant an imperial Roman seal. It is up to you two to tell me what threat to Parthia is contained in these letters." He clapped his hands. "Kophasates! Take these scrolls to their room. Make sure they are well-supplied with writing material." He turned back to the women. "You are free to move about as you wish on this floor only. You come to my office by invitation only. Do not visit other offices under any circumstances. Enjoy your stay!" He turned and left without reply.

Kophasates bundled up the letters and put them in a satchel, containing blank scrolls, wax tablets and styli. "Do not mark on the originals. If you need to mark them up, make a copy and mark that up." He escorted them to their room and left.

"Well, now we know what was worth the killing," said Marcia.

"To be sure. What is he talking about?"

"I don't know. A threat to Parthia? How could that be? You understand politics better than I, Livia."

"A threat ... a threat." She rubbed her chin. "Some kind of communication, high level. Maybe between Aulus and the Hanaean court?"

"Hmm, that would be a threat, with a war brewing. And worth killing for, from his perspective. But that's not what they are. We can't give him what doesn't exist."

"I think we need to give him something, make him believe we are working on it. Because if we convince him they are just letters, or when he has what he thinks they are, either way, we are of no further value to him. As long as he thinks we are working on it and will eventually succeed, he will keep us alive. While we think of our next move, shall we go exploring?"

"That sounds like a good idea," Marcia replied.

The third floor had balconies on either side overlooking beautifully pruned and tended gardens. The back section, the servants' area, had a balcony overlooking a working area in the back, untended, and rutted by wagon carts. It was littered with discarded items, and other items in stacked in storage. It was this working area that caught Livia's attention.

"This doesn't seem well guarded. What do you think of our chances for escape?"

"Very little, Livia."

"I thought you were the adventurous one," she laughed.

"Adventurous when there is a chance. We have no money, no idea where to go, and no way to blend in with your flaming red hair and my oriental features. And I speak Parthian with a heavy Roman accent, and you not at all. Getting out might be easy, staying out will not be."

"Well, you are also a realist."

"Let's go over to the other side and admire the garden. It won't smell as bad. And don't worry, something may present itself. But not now."

CHAPTER 81:

AN AGENT NAMED TAURUS

From Elegeia to Nisibis, May 115AD

Marcus had found a niche for himself, Mei and Nathaniel in the *Princep's* intelligence staff, moving with Trajan in the van with the Twelfth. With first-hand knowledge of the palaces at Ctesiphon and Ecbatana, some of the high-level Parthian officials, and even the two contending kings Osroës and Vologases themselves, they were an invaluable source of information. They were also honest enough to admit when they didn't know the answers to questions.

Arrian Atticus, the prefect of intelligence, coordinated orders and reports among the various Roman agents operating in Parthia. Each agent had a nickname that identified the agent. One agent, 'Taurus', was the highest-level agent in Ctesiphon, occasionally giving information about King Osroës himself. Arrian did not know Taurus' real name, nor did he want to, but he knew that Taurus was always accurate. And today, an enciphered message had come in from Taurus, a letter bearing the symbol of a bull. The staff immediately dropped all other work, as Taurus' missives were always important.

Marcus was given the job of decoding the message's cipher. The decoding was simple enough: One wrote down the agent's name, 'Taurus', as the key, then the rest of the letters of the alphabet not used in the key. Underneath that, one wrote down the alphabet in normal order. That way, the encoded letter 't' became 'a', encoded 'a' became 'b' and so forth. The staff looked over Marcus' shoulder as the message emerged from the scrambled text. His hand began to shake as he decoded *Two Latin-speaking women, one of high status named Livia, the other of oriental appearance named Marcia ...*

"That's my sister," he croaked.

Arrian held him by the shoulder. "I'll take over." He decoded the rest of the message, then announced, "We need to get this to the *Princeps* right away."

Trajan examined the message over and over again with Arrian, Nathaniel, Marcus and Mei. It came from a reliable agent. Trajan did not know Taurus' name, what position he held, or what motivated him. Probably some combination of greed, thirst for vengeance, and a sense of higher calling? No matter, he didn't need to know, and Taurus had been reliable in the past. This message vindicated Trajan's instincts. Ctesiphon had in fact kidnapped the girls, keeping them for some purpose. He considered calling Aulus and Antonius, when they, accompanied by Gaius Lucullus, interrupted the meeting.

Lucullus and the two saluted smartly, then he announced: "I apologize for interrupting this meeting, your Excellency, but these men just received letters from their wives this morning. I felt you should know immediately."

"As a matter of fact, we just received intelligence minutes ago that they were in Ctesiphon. Tell me of your letters."

Aulus answered for both. "Yes, sir. Both women report that they are in good health and being well-treated. The handwriting is theirs. Nothing further."

"Consider both the intelligence and their correspondence confirmed. Amazing how fast messages can move when least expected."

"When do we go get 'em?" asked Antonius.

"Nathaniel, what do you think?" asked Trajan.

"I think it will be impossible to repeat what was done to rescue Marcus. A few people probably lost their heads over that. And I doubt they will be kept in prison as he was, but up in the palace proper, not far from Mithridates."

"And his purpose in holding them, again?"

Marcus replied, "He is convinced that, in the family letters Marcia and I were exchanging, there were coded communications between you and the Han empress dowager."

"Ah, yes. I remember. Well, I agree that their rescue will be all but impossible for now. Arrian, can you communicate with Taurus?" asked the *Princeps*.

"We normally do not, for fear of compromising him. But I can."

"Send him a message to tell us exactly where the women are kept, and update us only if it changes. He is far too valuable to compromise."

"Yes, sir!"

Trajan turned to Antonius and Aulus. "A rescue right now has a much greater chance of getting them both killed than any chance of success. I know you and Aulus don't want to wait any longer to see your women, but for now you must. At least you know now that they are alive, and not too far from here. Are they resourceful enough to come up with a way to stall Mithridates?

"I believe Marcia is resourceful enough to do anything she needs to do."

"As is Livia," added Aulus.

"Excellent. Let's hope they do. Marcus, who led your rescue?"

"Nathaniel, and Hina and Galosga of the Xiongnu, and my wife Mei."

"Where are they now?"

"Nathaniel and Mei are in the camp. Hina and Galosga are riding with the Ninth Batavian cavalry."

"Arrian, bring them in, and get every detail of how they got in. We will need to know this."

Hina, Galosga and her companions and children arrived a few hours after Nathaniel and Mei, wearing their sweaty black felt trousers and beige shirts, all dusty from riding, accompanied by their commander Longinus Clarus. Aulus, Gaius, Antonius, Arrian, Marcus and Nathaniel were seated in the anteroom of the *Princeps'* command tent, waiting for them.

Arrian excused himself. "I will get the *Princeps.*" He returned a few minutes later with Trajan.

"Your Excellency," saluted Longinus, as did Hina in proper Roman fashion, her right hand across her chest.

"At ease, Hina. That is a most unusual cavalry uniform."

"It is what my people wear," answered Hina.

"Your Excellency, if they can train my men to shoot like they do, they can wear whatever they like. They are very good," said Longinus.

Trajan smiled. "So I heard. I summoned you here because there have been some developments in Ctesiphon. You were the ones who rescued Marcus from the palace?"

"Yes, sir," answered Hina.

"Aulus' wife Livia, and Antonius' wife Marcia, have been kidnapped and are now being held in the same palace. A rescue now is out of the question, but I need you to share all the information you have on the palace. Nathaniel, you came and went rather freely to the third floor, the king's residence area?"

"Yes, sir, to the office of his brother Mithridates. I was in his employ."

"Excellent. Share what you have with Arrian, we will have need of that eventually." Trajan turned and left, leaving his intelligence man to do his work.

Hina interrupted. "Marcia? Here? Kidnapped? Like her brother?"

Antonius answered. "Aye, so it seems. An' fer the same gods-cursed reason, something about the letters they exchanged."

Hina turned to Longinus. "Release us. We can be in Ctesiphon in a few days, and have them out."

"No, out of the question," answered Aulus. "You were extremely lucky with Marcus, but you can certainly believe their security will not be that sloppy again. And they are probably not in the basement prison, but on the royal floor near the king. Believe me, if I thought there were a chance, Antonius and I would ride with you. But there is none, right now. Let's find out all the details you can remember, we will be able to use them eventually. Let's start with you, Nathaniel, you have the knowledge about the royal floor. Let's hear it."

Arrian took out his wax tablet and stylus, scribbling notes while Nathaniel related what he knew of the guards, how often they changed, how one gained access to the interior: a pass was required, signed by the person who had invited the visitor. Mithridates had the authority to sign such passes, there might be others, but Nathaniel did not know who they might be. The gates closed at sunset, and no one could be admitted until after sunrise. He described the inner pavilion, the marble staircase at the back, and the third floor. "About ten offices up there, but I only ever went to Mithridates'. Odd, once I was inside, I wasn't escorted. I was on my own, to find my own way to where I was going."

"Hmm, interesting," said Arrian, pausing in his scribbling. "I wonder if it is the same now."

"It has always been that way, for all the years I came and went."

"You were given a pass. Any chance you might still have an old one?"

Nathaniel fumbled around in his purse, pulled out a small, tattered scroll. "As luck would have it, my last one." He handed it to Arrian.

Arrian studied it, reading the Aramaic out loud softly. "And that is Mithridates' signature?"

"It is."

"I'd like to keep this. We have some excellent forgers, whose skills might come in handy." Arrian slipped it into a pouch without waiting for permission.

"Mei, how did you get in to see Marcus?"

"The same way Nathaniel said, with a pass. And I also had to find my own way once inside."

"When you visited Marcus, he was on the third floor?"

"Yes, a room at the back, rather nice, a guest room."

"Can you sketch it?" He handed her a parchment sheet and a charcoal stick. While she made her drawing, Arrian continued. "Now, Galosga, you needed no such pass to get in your way."

"No, sir, just a tall date palm, conveniently overlooking the back courtyard. And Hina, with a ladder and some hooks."

"Tell me about that courtyard."

When they were done, Arrian had filled up three tablets with notes. There was no plan yet, but ideas were beginning to percolate.

CHAPTER 82:

LEGIONS ON THE ROLL

Nisibis, May 115AD

The western legions continued their roll to the south. Trajan detached the *XVII Flavia* to take Edessa, the capital of the westernmost satrapy of Osroene under King Abgaros, and the *I Adiutrix* to take neighboring Batnae. Trajan's intent was to secure the westernmost cities of northwestern Mesopotamia before the blazing heat of mid-summer set in.

The *XII Fulminata* led the advance on Nisibis accompanied by the *X Fretensis* and *XII Cyrenaica*. The three legions with their baggage trains stretched out fifteen miles along the road descending out of the Taurus foothills, beside the Mygdonius River leading to Nisibis, Trajan marching at the head of his troops, seemingly tireless for a man in his sixties. Gaius Lucullus and Antonius marched alongside him, though both would have preferred riding. Behind them marched a century of Trajan's Praetorian Guards, his only personal security, and then the Twelfth, singing their marching songs, their boots crunching on the rough unpaved road, the armor jingling, heavy wagons carrying siege engines rumbling between the centuries on their wide wooden wheels.

The days were already hot in the glaring sun, the land turning arid, though fertile alongside the river with fruit trees, vineyards and wheat fields undulating in the breeze. Antonius took a swig of water from his leather sack, then straightened his heavy pack on his shoulders. He removed his helmet long enough to wipe his brow with his forearm, then replaced it. The red *focale* around his neck was dark with sweat.

"Are you all right, Antonius? The day is getting a bit warm," asked Gaius.

"Oh, I be fine, sir. Sweat be getting' in me eyes."

"It is getting warm," acceded the *Princeps,* likewise removing his helmet and wiping his brow. "Still no opposition. Odd"

"I have cavalry out on both flanks. Nothing but sagebrush and vultures," said Gaius. "They are walled up in the city, waiting for us. A siege is to their advantage. If they can hold out to late summer, the heat will be their best ally."

"I am thinking we might dam up and divert that river around Nisibis. Then the summer heat will be our ally, not theirs."

"We can do that."

"Let's see how earnest they are in holding out when we get there."

The legions arrived in the afternoon, deploying their camps on each side of the triangular walled city, the Twelfth on the north straddling the Mygdonius River, the Third Cyrenaican on the east, and the Tenth Straits on the west. The next morning Trajan sent peace envoys to the satrap of the city, King Mannu, allied with Abgarus in Osroene, seeking only his loyalty to Trajan. The envoy was rejected, so the siege began.

The Fifth cohort under Secundus Lucullus and Samuel Elisarius deployed their single *onager* catapult, a stack of sixty-pound stone balls at the ready with a vat of pitch steaming over a fire. The *onager* was flanked on either side by three *carroballista* missile launchers, all about two hundred yards from the wall. The artillery was beyond accurate arrowshot from the defenders, though plunging shots fired at a high angle had already covered the ground before them with spent arrows, growing like weeds out of the gritty soil.

"Pitch is ready, sir. We can fire at your orders," said Samuel.

"On your command, centurion," answered the tribune.

"*Carroballistae!* Let's quiet down those archers on the wall before one of them gets a lucky hit on one of you! *Onager* crew, burning pitch over the wall, high angle. Let's make it hot for them."

The *carroballistae* began their mechanical ratchety-ratchety-thump as their crews cocked and fired them, launching their six-foot bolts with deadly accuracy at the defending archers on the wall. While the Roman artillery was outside of accurate arrowshot range from the wall, the defenders were well within accurate range of the *ballistae*, and after a minute or so, the shower of arrows arcing high in the sky overhead slowed to a few poorly aimed shots, many falling short as the defenders retreated back to avoid being skewered.

The *onager* crew cocked their weapon, loaded one of the heavy stones on the spoon-shaped throwing arm, coated it with black liquid tar, then set it ablaze. The crew checked their aim, stepped back and pulled the firing cord. The tightly wound torsion coil unwound, driving the throwing arm hard into the padded crossbar with a loud thump, causing the back end of the carriage to kick up about a foot off the ground.

"That's why we call it an *onager*, sir. Kicks like a wild ass," said Samuel, watching the flaming payload arc high overhead, streaming black greasy smoke, then plunging to land somewhere behind the wall. "Give the fire crews something to keep them busy."

The crew had already re-cocked, reloaded their second round, and unleashed it. Secundus shaded his eyes to watch its flight, when an arrow seemed to grow from nowhere in his right forearm. "Damn, lucky shot!" He cradled his forearm.

Samuel grabbed Secundus' arm and examined the wound. "*Medicus!* Man down!" he called, but did not wait. He took his dagger, hacked off the arrowhead, and drew the shaft back out. The wound bled but little from the two small holes. "How're you doing, sir?"

"All right, feels more like someone just hit my arm real hard."

"Didn't get much blood, looks like it went right through the muscle."

The *medicus* showed up. Samuel gave him the picture. "Tribune Lucullus here tried to bat at an arrow and stopped it with his arm. I already got the shaft out."

The *medicus* examined the shaft and arrowhead, then the wound, squeezing it to force the blood out. "We need to make it bleed, sir. Sometime they put shit or poison on it, need to get it out."

Secundus stoically endured the rough handling. "Do what you have to do."

After several minutes, the *medicus* doused the wound with vinegar, then wrapped it in a clean white cloth. "That's it, sir. Let me know right away if you feel dizzy, and tomorrow, make sure it does not feel hot. If it does, call me right away. Other than that, you should be fine in a week or so. First wound?"

"First wound." He stood up. "No, not dizzy. Let's get back to fighting."

The barrage continued all day and all night. Secundus remained at his post till well after midnight, when fresh crews relieved the men on artillery. He was up at first light with Samuel, preparing himself for the morning meeting with the *legatus*.

Secundus entered the command tent, a bit late as everyone else had already gathered. "Good morning, tribune," said his father. "What happened to your arm?"

Secundus smiled and undid his helmet. "Lucky arrow shot."

The meeting was uneventful. Gaius, flanked by Antonius and Paulus Herrerius, his *primus pilus,* briefed the tribunes of the ten cohorts. "We are going to keep up the barrage day and night, so make sure your crews work in eight-hour shifts. The *Princeps* does not want the city destroyed, so we are just pounding the buildings immediately inside the walls. Engineers from all three legions will be working about a mile back to dig a new channel for the Mygdanius, to divert it around the city. Fortunately, the city is not big, just a mile on a side, and the river is not, either, so they think they will have that done inside a month. Then July and August will be our allies, not theirs."

Antonius picked up the briefing. "In the meanwhile, until Mannu comes to his senses, take care of yer men during the siege. Good sanitation, I don't want our men getting siege sickness. We have good water, and right now, plenty of supplies, so we don't need to do much foraging. Though yer might want to take advantage of the fruit trees." He picked up a yellow apple from the fruit bowl on the table and took a bite. "They are excellent."

The unrelenting barrage of Nisibis kept up day and night for two weeks, while the course for the new river channel slowly snaked its way south and west around the city. Then the morning meeting brought news that Abgarus had capitulated in Edessa, swearing allegiance to the *Princeps,* and Batnae had also surrendered with no further resistance. The word from the east was equally good, the Sixth Ironclad had occupied Singara, while the rest of the eastern force fell on Gaugamela.

That word apparently had reached Nisibis as well, because Mannu sent out his envoy under a flag of truce, to negotiate an end to the siege before the work on the river bypass could be completed. The artillery fell silent.

The next morning the siege engines were backed off and returned to the supply train. The Fifth Cohort fell out in formation, its six centuries in neat squares. Secundus, his arm fully healed, addressed his men, after first congratulating them first for a job well-done. He then gave them their orders. "We have been tasked to pacify Nisibis, and very specifically we are not, I repeat not, to engage in any looting or abuse of the population. We are to go into the city and assist the population in any way we can with food, medical attention for injuries, shelter, helping to clear rubble. The *Princeps* wants the population to be grateful for our presence, not resentful, and he will ensure that your bonus will more than make up for anything you could loot off the city. Anyone breaking his mandate will find himself severely punished. Now let's march in and introduce them to Roman generosity." With that, the cohort headed in through the open city gate, followed by wagons with food and blankets.

Despite the bombardment that had gone on night and day, little damage had been done to Nisibis; casualties were light. The buildings adjacent to the wall had been pulverized and burned out, but after that, the flaming missiles had fallen on rubble, doing little further damage. The townspeople grudgingly accepted their new occupiers. The Fifth's centuries set up throughout the marketplace, handing out food and blankets, their *medicii* treating the wounded.

Secundus and Samuel decided to wander through the city. "Doesn't feel like we are particularly welcome here," said Secundus.

"No, sir. Folks don't like being conquered much, even if we are not rubbing their faces in the dirt." They passed a building with a window in the shape of two equilateral triangles, and odd square lettering over the door.

"What's that? I don't recognize the writing," asked Secundus.

"It's Hebrew, sir. My Jewish faith. This is a synagogue, the *Beth Shalom,* House of Peace. Do you mind if I go in a minute?"

"I'll come with you."

"No, sir, you can't. It's closed to foreigners, to non-Jews. It would be a great offense for you to come in. Just wait right here, I won't be long."

Samuel opened the heavy wooden door and walked in, smelling the incense, feeling the vague sense of holiness and connectedness that he had not known since childhood. It had been over ten years since he had worshipped, the last time at his mother's funeral. The dark interior was filled with men in prayer shawls, women in veils to the rear. Suddenly, someone noticed him, a man with a skullcap over his long curling black hair, a black and white prayer shawl around his shoulders. His face was dark with anger.

"Out! Out. This is a holy place, not for uncircumcised non-believers! Out!"

"No, I am Shmuel Ben Eliazar, a believer from Galilee, I came to pray …"

"Thou art worse than an unbeliever, thou art an apostate, fighting for the Army of Satan. May thou burn forever in Gehenna! Out, I said."

Samuel backed up, realizing he should not have come in. The crowd had gathered behind the man, evidently their rabbi, all equally angry. "I am sorry, I am leaving," he said, as someone hurled something at him. He backed out into the streets, the crowd's angry curses following him.

Secundus braced him, while putting his hand on his sword, but the door slammed shut.

"I should have remembered. They wouldn't see past my uniform."

"Perhaps you can come here later, without the uniform."

"No, some things you just can't go back to. Let's see how things are in the market."

As they began to walk off, some children had clambered to the roof of the synagogue, pelting them with pebbles. "Go back to Rome!" one of them called out.

The two went back to the marketplace, idly supervising the centuries' efforts, all being well-managed by their own centurions. At one point, an elderly woman, Jewish by dress, gray hair peeking out from under her shawl, approached Samuel. "Thou art the son of an Eliazar in Galilee. Where?" she asked.

"Capernaum by the Sea, mother. You were at the synagogue this morning?" Samuel smiled but was on alert. This could be a distraction, with some *sicarius* lurking behind him with a dagger, ready to strike.

"And thy mother's name?"

"She was Miriam, but she died several years ago."

"I am sorry to hear that. I knew thee when thou wert a child and a young man."

"I was a different person then. Thy name?"

"My name is Ruth. Thou foughtst the Romans then. Now, thou art one?"

He smiled. "No, mother, we robbed innocent travelers and sometimes killed them. My accomplices were not rebels, just bandits. I took to the sea to get away from that."

"How didst thou come to be a Roman?"

"My journeys by sea took me around the world with some Romans. They thought what I did was important, so they forgave me my past misdeeds and gave me citizenship. I went back to Galilee to take care of my mother, but she died. Fighting was what I knew. I joined the Roman army, and here I am."

"If thou wish to worship with us, I will talk to the rabbi. He did not understand."

"No, he was right. I am an apostate. Some things cannot be changed. But thank you." He put a batch of apples into a sack from a merchant's cart, flipped him a silver coin and handed the sack to Ruth. "Please, enjoy them for me."

"God be with you, Shmuel. *Shalom*"

CHAPTER 83:

A GATHERING OF FRIENDS

Nisibis, June 115AD

The victory gave the Twelfth an opportunity to stand down for a few days. Gaius Lucullus called on his prefect Antonius. "A good victory, my friend."

"Aye, that it were. Bein' time for a bit of a reunion, I think," answered Antonius.

"Reunion?' asked the *legatus*.

'Reunion, hell, yes! All us Hanaean veterans have hardly had a chance ter say two words ter each other since the Fates throwed us together. Us an' their kids an' friends. I think we should do it old style, a campfire off by ourselves, plenty ter drink and bedrolls ter sleep out under the stars."

Gaius broke into a big smile. "I think that is a great idea. The Twelfth can do without me for a night, unless the Parthians attack. And I am sure they will be able to find me if that happens. I'll take care of Aulus, my son and Samuel in the Fifth Cohort, and Marcus and Mei, you take care of Hina and her crowd. Tonight after sunset, in the field outside the camp, tell them it is by order of the *legatus*."

Antonius saluted smartly and left. A few hours later, as the sun was setting, he was turning a large goat on a spit over a crackling fire, supervised by Marcus, Mei and Nathaniel. The grease spatters gave off a delightful aroma in the warm night air. Aulus, Gaius, Secundus and Samuel were engaged in an animated conversation, retelling old and new stories, facilitated by Trajan's wine stocks, compliments of the *Princeps*. Everyone was rough-clad, Gaius and Antonius in their old felt riding gear, everyone else in riding tunics.

Venus began to glare through the sunset when Hina and Galosga arrived with their three children and Hadyu, all on horseback. Three-year-old Adhela rode confidently beside them on a small pony. They dismounted, dropped their horses' leads to the ground, and began distributing several sacks of *kumis*, enough for each person. "This is in memory of our many days on the road together," she said, grinning uncharacteristically and taking a big swig from her leather sack.

Aulus accepted his, raising the sack in a toast to Hina. "To the Xiongnu!" He took a swig, wiping his mouth with the back of his hand. "Still tastes like almonds," he said.

"It was not until I got to Parthia that I tasted almonds. You are right. It does taste like that."

"How did you make this stuff, Hina? We have been on the road since leaving Elegeia. Where did you find the time?" asked Gaius.

"It is easy to make on the road. Just milk the mare into the sack, and tie it to the saddle. The sloshing keeps it going." She suddenly got serious. "Have you heard anything from my sister Marcia?"

"No, unfortunately," said Gaius. "Nor of Aulus' wife, Livia, either. We have indications they are being well-treated, but they are, for now, hostage to the Parthian king." The mildly-alcoholic *kumis* was depleted quickly and Aulus played the part of servant, distributing flagons of red wine.

Galosga and Samuel paired off separately to share old stories. "Well, my old friend, I never expected to see you ever again, and certainly not riding with Roman cavalry. I remember the first time you got on a horse. We were betting on how far you would make it before you fell off," said Samuel

"I remember that well. But I have ridden many horses since, and I had a good teacher in Hina. And I never expected to see you in the Roman army, and a centurion now, at that. You were a rebel once."

"Past sins forgiven. How did you come by those scars on your face?"

"A sickness came and wiped out most of our encampment, including *shanyu* Bei. You remember him? Those few who survived, like myself, were scarred. Some very few, like Hina and our children, did not get the disease at all. We were in Turfam when Marcus and Mei found us. It seemed to Hina that Tengri had shown us His way, to follow them. So here we are."

"Well, you speak excellent Latin. I remember when you were with me on the *Orion*, everyone thought you were a deaf-mute."

"I was, really. Everyone's language was just a babble of words. But I learned enough to do what I was told. Thank you for befriending me then. I might well have jumped over side to drown if you hadn't. You know, I wish Yakov and Ibrahim were here. I wonder what became of them?"

"Ibrahim was killed before we got back. But he died a happy man. And I am still in touch with Yakov. He is living to the south of here. I collect money for him. He is running an orphanage for street urchins in a place called Petra. Let's rejoin the group, I think Hina is holding forth."

Hina was indeed holding forth. "I want to go to Ctesiphon, at least to see what we can learn. I and Galosga, Marcus, Mei, and our friend Nathaniel"

Gaius heard her out, then answered her. "Hina, I appreciate your courage, but I think it would be a bad idea now. Marcus, Mei and Nathaniel are well-known to the authorities there now, as are you and Galosga, and very conspicuous also. If you were recognized, your purpose would be instantly known. This might put Marcia and Livia in more danger than they seem to be now."

"How do you know they are safe now?"

"Hina, we have eyes and ears where we need them. Enough said on that, we will need those eyes and ears later to get them out."

"Galosga and I will go alone."

"Hina, as your commander, I could forbid you, but I know that you wouldn't listen. But I can strongly discourage you, because you don't know the customs and language well enough to pass as locals. As soon as word reached the palace that there were strange people in the city asking questions, they would snatch you up. You both are formidable fighters, but they will come for you with ten or twenty men, and they will get you. Then you two will be in danger, beyond our help, and as I said, you may put Marcia and Livia in much more danger as well. So, please, do not do that."

Antonius joined the discussion. "The commander's right, Hina. There is no one that wants 'em out of there as much as Aulus an' me, but now is not the time. An' the goat is done, old friends, let's eat."

The group assembled around the fire, slicing pieces of meat with their daggers, some eating with their hands, some using army-issue metal bowls. Antonius sat down by Hina's children. "So you are Andanyu and Marasa. And already fighters, eh?"

"We are," answered Andanyu. His Latin was heavily accented, but confident and understandable.

"I am the one you are named for. I am Antonius, and Marasa, you are named for my wife Marcia."

"Our mother told us many stories about you. Are they all true?" asked Marasa.

"Probably not all of them. Stories get better over time, you know. And you're little Adhela?" Antonius directed his gaze to the little one, very serious, almost adult in his focus. Antonius noticed that the little boy, just a few months older than his own little Androcles, was armed with a small dagger, bow and quiver. Though small, he knew they were not toys. "Riding already?"

"I have been riding for a long time. I want to fight alongside Marasa and Andanyu, but mother and father say I am not ready." He, too, spoke Latin, though with a childish inflexion.

"There will be time enough for fighting. You grow up fast."

"Not fast enough. This is my fourth summer."

Hina came to sit down cross-legged beside Antonius. "Well, my old friend, it is good to be able to talk with you again."

"It is. Almost enough to make me wish we had a big yurt again."

"We won't need it tonight. It's very warm. How are your children back in … Italia?"

"Italy, right, a place called Aquileia. Aena and Colluscius, like you, we kept our promise, as close as we could get in Latin. And our latest, little Androcles, is just a bit younger than Adhela."

"Are they well?"

"They are well. Our head of household, Desdemona, keeps me informed on that."

"The paper that talks. I am learning my letters and so is Galosga. Such a remarkable thing, that writing can make thousands of miles seem like nothing. Our commander Longinus insists that I read all his orders, and respond in writing. It helps."

"It does."

Gaius beckoned Secundus to join him for a private chat, well away from the fire, both seated on convenient rocks. "Yes, sir, thank you for the invitation" Secundus said.

"Tonight, it's just you and I, father and son, not *legatus* and tribune. We have not been able to be that to each other for more than two years. You have done well. Samuel has a lot of respect for you."

"Thank you ... father."

"That means a lot. My centurions don't report to me on their tribunes, but I make it a point to know what they think of them. Those that don't work out, I reassign to my staff where I can keep an eye on them. Samuel and all of the Fifth Cohort's centurions think well of you. Good job."

"It hasn't always felt like that."

"Your first few years as a tribune are like that. Antonius and I, you know, we go way back, even before he was centurion, just a common soldier, training us tribunes in swordsmanship and basic fighting skills. He has always been a good instructor, he loves doing it."

"I can't picture you as a tribune." Secundus smiled a bit in the dark.

"I was as green as they come. Antonius was there when I killed my first man, actually a horrible accident, in front of his wife and children, in Germany along the Danube. It shook me up something terrible."

"What happened?"

"Some swords came up missing, and we thought the Germans had stolen them, so we went into the village to do a house-to-house search. This man was having none of that, and went for his sword. I should have let Antonius handle it, but I wanted to show off how well I had mastered what he had taught me. I just meant to disarm him, but he lunged and impaled himself. His wife and little children were watching from the door. Turns out the missing swords were just a book-keeping error."

"You never told me about that."

"I haven't told many people about that, and one of them is dead now. Antonius helped me through that time. It was hard."

They sat in silence, watching the stars, the Milky Way tumbling through the stars like a white waterfall in the sky.

"You know, Hina is right, we need to think about what to do about Livia and Marcia," said Secundus.

"I know, son. It is such an impossible problem, that I, and even the *Princeps*, are just ignoring it, hoping a solution will present itself without our having to concoct it. I am concerned that when we get to Ctesiphon, Mithridates will threaten to execute them. Or worse."

"Sometimes it helps to have a picture. Answers present themselves better that way."

"What do you have in mind?"

"I will get with everyone, Nathaniel and Mei, Marcus, Hina and Galosga, and draw as detailed a sketch from what they can tell me of the palace. Arrian also has notes. Nathaniel knows how to get in the front door, Hina knows how to get in the back way. And they probably know about how many paces on each side, how many floors, rooms, parapets, stairs. Where the guards are."

"You always were good at drawing, son."

"Thank you, father. I think if I hadn't decided to follow in your footsteps, I might have been an artist.'

The small talk gave way to reminiscing over days gone by, and the moon was high in the sky when the fire was banked, and Gaius and Secundus, the last ones still awake, crawled into their blankets for the night.

Gaius had not even fallen asleep before a tribune in the darkness was shaking him by the shoulder. "Sir, you must come. Prefect Aristides, Tribune Lucullus and Centurion Eliazar also. It is urgent."

CHAPTER 84:

A DIFFERENT KIND OF WAR

Nisibis, June 115AD

The four soldiers paused to give the nightly password to the sentries on duty, who saluted them smartly and admitted them to the camp. "Well, Tribune, I am glad we talked more and drank less last night," said Gaius as he strode briskly to his command tent in the center.

"Yes, sir. And the conversation was better than any wine," said Secundus.

"And I wish I had drunk less," said Samuel. "But I am ready for whatever."

"As am I," answered Antonius.

A group of tribunes were waiting for them in the anteroom that served as the Gaius' office, standing by his desk. They came to attention and saluted him.

"Well, whatever it is, it must be important for you to summon us before the second night watch has been called out. What's happening?" asked Gaius, taking a seat in his chair, flanked by Secundus and Samuel standing behind him.

"Trouble, sir. Two of our soldiers were killed tonight."

"What happened?"

"Century Two of the Fifth Cohort had the security duty in town today, patrolling in small groups to make sure troublemakers didn't bother the good townsfolk. Two of the men didn't come back as scheduled, and when they went to look for them, they found them murdered."

"How?"

"It was pretty ugly. One had a head injury from a rock thrown from the roof above them. The other had a back injury, from another rock thrown while he was bending over to tend to his mate. But that didn't kill them. They were mutilated."

"Mutilated?"

"Their cocks were cut off and stuck in their mouths, and they were disemboweled. Their guts were just piled up on the street beside them, like gutted hogs."

"Pretty gruesome. Any idea who did that?"

"None. The soldiers started asking people in the area, but they claimed they didn't hear or see anything."

"Continue the questioning tomorrow. Tribune, tell your men to be forceful, but polite, and don't put anyone under duress. This is likely a small group, trying to stir up trouble between us and the townspeople, and we don't need to help the troublemakers do that by roughing up the innocent. And above all, I don't want our soldiers going off on their own to revenge themselves against the people. Anything else?"

"No, sir," the tribunes chorused.

"One last thing. Keep your patrols bigger, at least five men. And the town is off limits for anything not approved by me. Not going to the market or brothels, or drinking in the *tabernae*. Now I have to collect my thoughts so I can tell the *Princeps* of this, so you are all dismissed. And thank you for doing such a thorough investigation in just a few hours. Tribune Secundus, stand fast just a moment, you and your centurion."

The tribunes filed out.

"Sorry this had to be your cohort," said Gaius to the two.

"Aye, an' a damn shame, after such an easy victory," said Antonius.

"I feel like I should have been there," said Secundus.

"And what would you have done to prevent this? No one saw this coming. Not you, and not I. Just help your men understand how important it is that they not take their anger out on the people, or whoever did this will succeed, and this town will tie up our whole legion. Likely, the Parthians themselves are the instigators of this. Make sure they understand that."

"Right, and thank you, sir."

"No problem. I need to get on with this, so go back to your cohort, Try to get a little sleep tonight, both of you."

There was to be little sleep in the tribune's tent, as Secundus had to deal with his most distasteful task, telling the family of the dead soldiers that their sons would not be coming home.

"What were their names, Samuel?" asked Secundus, lighting an oil lamp from a small candle.

"Francius Canastus and Alexander Anander. Canastus was from the Gaulish borderlands with Germania, and Anander was a Greek from one of the islands. I'll get their home information and some stories from the men for your letters, sir." They had lost men before, a few to combat, more to accidents and disease this campaign. "The men really appreciate it, that you take the time to write their families like you do. They've never seen another tribune do that before."

"I learned it from my father. They want to know that if they die, their death will mean something to their leader, and they want their families to know that they died an honorable death."

"Right, sir. I'll leave you to your thoughts. See you at first light ... try to get some sleep. Me, too. *Legatus'* orders," he said with a wink.

First light came too early for both, summoned from their tents before breakfast by two tribune *quaestiones*, investigators from the legion headquarters staff. The two *quaestiones* came with an escort of two eight-man squads from Century Two for protection. They wanted to see where the murders had been committed, to see if there were any clues that might lead them to the villains.

No one was in any mood for small talk on the march into the city. The two tribunes had not given their names, and Secundus and Samuel had not asked. They came to the eastern gate of the city just as the sun came full over the horizon. The city was locked down, with no one allowed to enter or depart without a pass. The older of the two *quaestiones* presented theirs, received a salute from the grizzled veteran who undid the latched door in the main gate, and admitted them. They marched down the unusually quiet morning streets in Nisibis, just the barking here and there of dogs, the crowing of roosters. No screams of children at play, no rumble of carts bringing in food and merchandise, no shouts from vendors. Word had spread fast of the murders, and the residents were expecting the worst.

When they rounded the next corner, Samuel's heart thudded in shock. He had been in this street just two days ago, by the Beth Shalom synagogue, and there, not a hundred paces away, were the ugly bloodstains on the cobbles. The bodies had been removed to the camp, but no one had cleaned the blood, now turning black, still attracting flies.

"Damned Jews! I should have known," said the younger of the two tribune *quaestiones,* recognizing the Hebrew script. "We should have finished them off in my father's time! They're nothing but trouble."

Samuel flushed with anger, then spoke up. "Sir, Jews have a strong prohibition against handling blood or dead bodies. It makes them very unclean by their religion. They may kill someone, but I can't see a Jew mutilating a body like that, or being anywhere around the people doing it. Someone might have killed them here, hoping we would jump to that conclusion, and round on the Jews and slaughter them for something they didn't do."

The older tribune looked disapprovingly at his companion. "The centurion is right, Trebonius. We need to keep our objectivity. Don't jump to conclusions before we have even examined the scene yet."

The two tribunes squatted to examine the bloodstained area, picking up rocks, looking for a dropped broach or some personal object that could connect someone to the murders. Secundus and Samuel searched the streets in either direction. An old woman came to stand by the door of her mud-brick apartment across the street, in a faded blue wool robe with a gray shawl about her head and shoulders. Samuel recognized her immediately, and called out to her in Aramaic. "Ruth, go back inside. There is nothing for thee out here."

Ruth recognized Samuel by his voice, because his helmet hid much of his face. "Shmuel, thou must leave. It is dangerous to be a Roman soldier here."

Samuel wanted to impress on her the urgency of the situation. "Ruth, this is my duty. Those who did this have unleashed a great danger to this community, and they have no power to defend you all against what may come. It is only because of the patience and wisdom of my commander that he has not already unleashed the wolves of war to avenge these men's death. Tell the elders that, should they know who did this, that they must come forward to tell the Romans, or terrible things may come to pass. Now, go inside. *Shalom*,"

She nodded, and went back inside.

"Who was that that old hag?" asked Trebonius.

"A friend from my childhood. She knew my mother in Galilee."

"Oh, you are that Jew-boy centurion. One of them, are you, now?"

Secundus sprang to his centurion's defense. "He is one of us, Trebonius, and if you wish to compare the *phalerae* battle awards on his corselet with yours, you will find he has far more than you, if indeed you have any at all." Secundus glared at the insolent young man, who could not have been twenty yet.

"I want to know what he said to the old hag. It's part of our investigation." Trebonius was not going to give up his insolence easily.

"I told her to tell the elders that they were in great danger if they don't find out who did this, and to tell us at once when they know. Then I told her to go inside."

The four spent an hour examining everything within a hundred yards of the scene, but came up empty-handed. Finally, Claudius, the older tribune, spoke up. "It seems we don't know much more about this than we did before, except this is in the Jewish neighborhood."

"Actually, on the boundary, sir. The Jewish neighborhood begins here and goes inside to the left to their own market," said Samuel, giving Claudius the respect he seemed to deserve.

"So good point, someone could have chosen this spot specifically to cause the Jews to be accused, like you said."

"I am not saying that a Jew couldn't have done this, sir, but not a faithful one."

"Why don't you go around the neighborhood and talk to them? See what they heard or saw? You speak their language very well."

"I will start with my friend Ruth, but I am not a good choice for the others. I tried to join them in the synagogue the other day and they threw me out. To them, I am just a Jew who has given up his Jewishness, and threw in his lot with heathen Romans. I can recommend some good Aramaic speakers for you."

"Good point. If that is where she lives, she must have heard something."

Samuel went across the street and knocked on her door. Ruth opened the door.

"May I ask thee a few questions, Ruth?"

She nodded.

"Yesterday afternoon when these men were killed, you must have seen or heard something."

"I was not here. I was on the other side of the market, with my daughter and grandchildren. When I came back after dark, they were already lying there. It was horrible."

"Did any of thy neighbors see or hear anything?"

"No. Everyone here went to market in the afternoon to buy for the Sabbath weekend. Today."

"Thank you, Ruth. Be safe. *Shalom*."

"Be careful, also. There are bad men about, very bad men. *Shalom*."

"Tell the elders to let us know who those bad men are."

"*Shalom, shalom!*" she impatiently shoved the door shut.

A horrible picture came to Samuel's mind, his short sword at her throat. That could come to pass if Gaius Lucullus gave the order to clean out the neighborhood, slaughter everyone, men, women and children, in revenge for the killing. It was all right for the city to hate us, as long as they feared us. *Could I do it? No, I could not.*

Samuel came back and gave his report to Claudius. "They picked a time when this block would be mostly abandoned. Today is the Jews' holy day, and they aren't allowed to go out and about, everything is closed, so yesterday afternoon everyone was at the market, buying for the weekend."

"Good point, Samuel. Us non-Jews would not have caught that." He cast a dark glance at Trebonius. "Let's head back. We need to give *Legatus* Lucullus a report by noon.

As the troops formed up march out, a bunch of children scampered up the roof, and began laughing, pitching stones at the soldiers, pebbles and roof tiles clanging harmlessly off their armor. Samuel made his first prayer of his adult life. *Oh, Adonai, God of my fathers! Please guide these children in the ways of wisdom. Let them stop with the pebbles, let them not hurl heavy stones, or they may all be dead.*

The troops marched out, stoic under the harmless onslaught, except for Trebonius, who cried out in pain as a pebble hit his hand, as though he had been actually hurt. The jeering laughter of the children rang in their ears.

CHAPTER 85:

A DEAD BENEFACTOR

Petra, June 115AD

Jacobus was reading a scroll at his desk when a slight cough at the doorway. It was the boy Stick. "Welcome, Stick, come on in."

"There is a man at the door, Aharon, the one you did not want admitted. I told him that, but he said he had something important for you," said the nine-year old.

"Thank you. You did well. Let's go see what that snake has to offer now. More trouble, no doubt."

"No doubt."

Jacobus, Stick by his side, opened the door to see the grizzled Jew. "What do you want?" Jacobus asked abruptly, with no intent to be courteous.

Aharon produced a clinking pouch from under his cloak. "A gift from your friend Shmuel with the Twelfth. He got a contribution off to you before the war." He extended the pouch in his bony hand.

Jacobus accepted it, and checked the contents. Several dozen silver *denarii*. It would make a welcome addition to their cash resources. And a wax tablet from Shmuel. "Thank you."

"I thought you might need this, especially since your patron Benjamin's unfortunate accident."

"Accident?"

"Oh, perhaps you have not yet heard. He was found dead in the streets by the temple, stabbed. Robbery, I suppose. Terrible things are happening now."

Jacobus stammered. "Dead? Dead? Of a robbery?"

"Yes, most unfortunate. I understand he has taken good care of your children for the past year. Perhaps Shmuel can continue to make contributions in his place ... for now." He rearranged his robes. "Well, I will be off now." He turned and left without a farewell.

Jacobus closed the door.

"Benjamin is dead?" asked Stick.

"So he said. I will see what I can find out. Robbery is not unusual here, but murder is. Go fetch Miranda for me and have her meet me in my office."

Miranda appeared a few minutes later. "Sorry, I was washing clothes. It is hot today." She tucked her sweaty dark hair back over her head. "Benjamin is dead?"

"That is what Aharon said. But Shmuel sent us more silver, and a note."

"How did he die?"

"Stabbed in a robbery. Unusual, I think. I will talk to the *vigiles* and see what they have to tell us." He spread the coins out on the desk, a total of thirty-two in all.

"That should take care of things for a month, two if we are careful." She scooped them up and put them back in the leather pouch. "I'll put this away. Let's see what Shmuel had to say."

The two examined the letter, written in Latin.

Ave, *Jacobus*.

I hope the letter finds you and Miranda in good health. I accumulated another contribution from my troops in your behalf. It is more difficult now, because we are on campaign and I cannot excuse them from watch duties as generously as I could before. But many are enthusiastic about what you do with your children and contribute anyway.

With the campaign and its uncertainties, I cannot say how often I can send you our gift, but Manasseh seems to have no trouble finding where we are. For now, we are pacifying Nisibis, and expect to be here for some time. I do not trust Manasseh. I gave him fifty-five denarii, you might note how many actually reached you. He claims the cut is due to the dangers of war.

Be well. When this campaign ends, I may find an opportunity to take some leave and come down to visit you and to meet your wife.

Be well, Samuel.

"He kept twenty-three *denarii* for himself! That is almost half!" she snorted in derision.

"When you have the only way to move that, you can charge what you wish. Anyway, over half of it got here."

Jacobus went down the Street of Columns to the basilica carved into the pink sandstone, where the *vigiles* were headquartered. Inside its huge doorway, the coolness was in sharp contrast to the blazing noonday heat outside, and dark in the windowless interior. Large oil lamps hung from the ceiling, and more in sconces along the wall to light the way. The *vigiles*' headquarters was easily identified by the men lounging about outside wearing light-weight soldiers' armor, some squatting on the floor playing dice. Jacobus entered the office and announced to no one in particular, "I am looking for the Prefect."

"I am he. Josephus Farvius. What do you need?" said a portly man in a white tunic with a purple equestrian stripe at its hem. The man did not rise from his desk.

"Good day, sir. My name is Jacobus. I need to make an inquiry."

"Ah, yes. The man who runs the orphanage. Sit. You do good work. What's the inquiry?"

"A friend, Benjamin by name, was murdered yesterday. I was hoping to learn the details of this unfortunate incident."

"As we would also. Murders are unusual. It happened right outside on the Street of Columns by the marketplace, during daylight, not a few hundred paces from our headquarters here. He was stabbed. We believe it was a robbery, his purse was gone."

"Thank you, I am sorry to hear that. I never heard of a robbery ending in a murder."

"Rarely happens. Sometimes if the victim puts up a fight, especially if he is a physically big, strong person, the robber may kill to protect himself. But Benjamin was an elderly man. And rich enough to hand over his purse and not miss it. "

"That is what I thought. Well, thank you, I guess there is not much more to know."

"One of your boys nicked his purse last year, didn't he?"

"He did, and we made him give it back. That is how Benjamin became our benefactor. We had fallen on hard times, and Stick, the boy, thought he would help us out. We were not pleased, but it worked out well. Till now."

"Well, I will keep you posted if we find anything else. The funeral will be Saturday, beginning on the Altar of Sacrifice, then winding down to his mausoleum on the south side past the Siq."

"Thank you, and good day."

CHAPTER 86:

UNRAVELING THE SCROLLS

Ctesiphon, June 115AD

Sanatruces concluded his meeting with Mithridates. "So, the Romans took Nisibis without too much trouble, but they are finding it harder to hold. Two of their soldiers were killed by locals, I understand rather gruesomely. The Romans are on high alert."

"Who killed them?"

"We don't know for sure. It was on the border of the Jewish neighborhood. Our agents have been trying to goad them into attacking the Romans, but the Jews won't claim it."

"That is smart. If that got back to Trajan, he would level the neighborhood and crucify the lot of them. But that won't stop us from claiming they did it. Play that against the Jews of Edessa, and ask them why they haven't the courage to rise up against those who destroyed their Temple and scattered them into exile. If we can get each of the cities in their new province of Mesopotamia to go up in flames, the Romans won't stay long."

"I'll see to it."

Kophasates entered with a tray of iced juices, for the oppressive Ctesiphon summer was setting in and though it was just mid-morning, the air was hot and heavy, with no breeze stirring the silk drapes.

"Thank you, Kophasates. Are the girls ready to tell us what the letters mean? They have been at it for a month. If they are not, it may be time to change their accommodations for less luxurious ones."

"They are, at least a bit. Shall I summon them?"

"Please. My son, you can stay for this. It may be interesting."

Kophasates came back with the two women, who stood respectfully, each holding a single scroll.

"Sit," said Mithridates, indicating they should sit on the carpeted floor. He was running out of patience with them. "What do you have to tell me?"

Livia took the lead. "We apologize for the delay. We did not take a major part in composing these letters, and do not have the codebook necessary to read these in their entirety. We have had to reconstruct as much as we could from memory. I hope that will suffice."

"Fine. Proceed."

"As you guessed, these are communications between Trajan himself, and the Han Emperor He."

"Emperor He is dead. His consort Empress Dowager Deng has been ruling for a decade." He looked disgusted at this first factual inaccuracy.

Livia, unruffled, showed no emotion or hesitancy. "I apologize. That sort of detail is not in the code book. It just said 'Han ruler,' and we assumed it was the Emperor He of Marcia's time. I apologize."

"Go on, then."

"So, this scroll here, describing Marcia's difficult birth and the long time of birthing, speaks of the difficulties of establishing the relationship between Trajan and the Han ruler, and the great distances separating them. 'Wishing you could be here with me' is an indication that he wishes the Hanaeans to begin moving their forces westward." This was easy to remember, since the birth of Marcia's third child was only three years ago.

Mithridates nodded his head, indicating he found this credible.

Marcia spoke up next. "This letter came in reply, though this is the first time I have seen it. It described the death and cremation of our mother, the sale of their house, and the beginning of their westward journey. This is some crisis for the Hans, I am not sure what, but it indicates that it was put to rest, 'cremated,' and they are arranging the finances to comply with the request and begin moving forces. Like the other letter, it was combined with real events, Marcus departing with his wife to come here." She re-rolled the scroll, then sat primly on her haunches, her legs beneath her.

Livia spoke up. "I apologize that it has taken so long to make such small progress. We wanted to make sure we did this as accurately as possible. We hope to make more progress on the details in these two letters, as well as the others. We are reconstructing the codewords from memory, and we were not involved in the coding in most of the letters, so it will take some time."

"Kophasates, take these girls back to their quarters, and give them some of that excellent lemon juice. They have done good work on a hot day.'

After Kophasates left, the two women embraced, their mouths against each other's shoulders to muffle their giggles until they subsided. They released each other, smiling into each other's eyes.

"Livia, I cannot believe you convinced them," said Marcia, her blue eyes wide in amazement.

"It is easiest to make some believe when it fits with what they already believe. The rest was just making it convincing."

"Well, we seem to have bought more time. Shall we concoct another tale over a goblet of lemonade?"

Kophasates encoded another missive for his client that night, carefully worded so that, even if decoded by the Parthians, it would not reveal the full details, implicating him. *The packages are convincing the Gift that the truth is what it thinks it is.* He hoped his client would understand it.

CHAPTER 87:

WORD FROM TAURUS

Nisibis, July 115AD

Arrian came into the intelligence tent with an empty wine sack. A message from Taurus, he was sure, because that was his usual 'envelope' for his missives. He considered giving it to Marcus to decode, as it might contain news of his sister. He quickly reconsidered, as it might contain bad news, maybe very bad news instead. He carried it over to his small desk, opened the top and extracted the carefully rolled missive. As expected, it had the bull symbol, and he quickly deciphered it. The message was cryptic: Taurus was speaking around something, something that would link immediately back to him, if the Parthians were to find out. After all, breaking these codes was not all that difficult, just time-consuming. 'The gift' referred to Mithridates, whose name meant 'The Gift from Mithra." The packages? That could be the two women. And 'the truth is what it thinks it is?' Not clear, not clear at all.

In any event, it was time to bring Marcus in, as the news, whatever it was, was not bad. And Marcus wasted no time filling in the blanks.

"It is easy. They are telling him what he believes, that the letters are coded messages between Trajan and the Han court. They are buying time for themselves, probably making things up, just enough to keep him interested," said Marcus. "I thought of doing that, but I wasn't sure I could pull it off."

"I see," said Arrian. "I'll get this to Aulus Aemilius as fast as possible. You fetch Antonius and bring him to Aulus Aemilius' tent."

A few minutes later, Arrian scratched at Aulus' tent flap. Aulus answered in a robe, obviously freshly-risen from sleep. "Good morning," he yawned, running his hands through his disheveled hair. "What do you have?"

"Sorry to disturb you, sir, A message from Taurus."

"Come in, then. I am sorry, I couldn't sleep last night."

"Thank you. Antonius will be with us shortly. We have news of your wives from Ctesiphon."

"How are they?" He said, agitated. "From that agent in the palace? What was his name?"

"Taurus, sir. And I suppose still all right, but no details."

A servant discretely entered the tent with two cups of hot beverage, offering one to each.

"Thank you," said Aulus, accepting the drink and taking a seat on a folding camp chair by his desk.

Antonius and Marcus entered. "Good mornin'" said Antonius, taking a seat in another chair opposite Aulus. "What do we have here?"

Marcus could not hide his happiness. "Another message from Ctesiphon. Good news, I think. Arrian?"

"The message literally says, 'The packages are convincing the Gift that the truth is what it thinks it is.' He uses a roundabout way like this when, if the information were deciphered, it would otherwise implicate him. Such as, if he were the only other one in the room when the information was disclosed. 'The Gift' is Mithridates, and we believe the packages are the women. They are convincing him that what he believes is true, that the letters contain hidden messages. We presume, by making up such hidden messages, they are buying themselves time, because if they don't give him something, he has no further use for them. Which means that their continued safety is in their skill and ingenuity. They have to give him something, often enough to make him want more."

"That is good news, good news indeed, Arrian," said Aulus. "Sounds like something Livia would think of. She can be very subtle when she wants."

"I guess she and Marcia make a good team."

"Let's hope so."

July was beastly hot in Ctesiphon, not even a whisper of a breeze, and the humidity from the Tigris hung in the air like a hot damp towel. Somewhere in the room, a fly buzzed noisily, but other than that, it was utterly still in the palace. It was little past noon, and everyone, including Marcia and Livia, were down to sleep through the hottest part of the day. Both wore just the lightest of shifts, nevertheless wet with sweat.

Livia stirred. "I can't sleep. I am going for a walk," she said, pulling on light white outer garments.

"See you in a few. Try not to wake me," said Marcia.

Some time later she roused to a sound at the door as it opened. *It must be Livia.* She rolled back to sleep.

But it was not Livia's footfalls. Heavy, masculine padding steps. She rolled over, wrapping some bedclothes around her.

It was Mithridates. "I just wanted to make sure you were resting well. It is a very hot day, even for Ctesiphon. Can I get you a cool drink?" he said smoothly.

"No, thank you."

Mithridates smirked, licking his lips in anticipation. "Why not drop that covering off yourself?" he asked. "I want to see what Wang Ming found so attractive about you."

"I think not. And don't mention that name around me. Ever."

He took a step toward the bed. "Don't order me about like a common servant. I want to see all of you, and I want to see it all now."

Marcia briefly wished she had a dagger, but no matter: Hina had taught her many ways to defend herself without weapons, and she had kept those skills sharp over the years. She unwrapped the confining sheet from about her and stood up. "Then look, all you want."

Mithridates admired her lean taut frame, her well-muscled legs almost fully exposed by the short shift. He took a few more steps toward her. When he got within a few feet, she launched a powerful kick to his crotch with her left foot, recovered, pivoted on her left to launch her right leg in a sweeping kick behind his knees, knocking him to the ground. Marcia was on him like a cat, snarling, forcing him facedown, straddling him, forcing one hand painfully up behind him as she searched for that special nerve in the neck.

She found it, and as he began to cry out in pain, she released the pressure slightly. "Cry out and the guards will have a big laugh at the King's brother subdued by such a slight woman as I am. I don't think your brother Osroës would be impressed if you can't handle me."

"I'll have you killed for this," he said through clenched teeth.

"Not without everyone knowing how I subdued you. And besides, you would not learn what you want me to tell you."

"I'll get it from Livia!"

"I am the one who wrote the letters. You'll get nothing from her."

"Then I'll kill her!"

"And everyone will know that you were beaten by a wisp of a girl. I know you are in the line of succession, but not after news like that. I have what you need, and I will give it to you as fast as I can, but right now, you are going to stand up, walk out that door, and forget all about this. Otherwise, you are going to have to explain the marks I will leave."

Mithridates nodded and Marcia let him up. He rearranged his clothing. He glared at her, but with a bit of respect. "You are certainly right, you are not Si Huar."

"No, I am not."

He left, and Marcia collapsed on the bed. She never had doubts during a fight, it was just like a practice bout, but afterwards they came in droves. She felt chill now, despite the heat. *Did I do the right thing? There was nothing else I could have done, other than submit, and I would never do that. Maybe I bought some time with that threat? Perhaps. But he will find a way to work his revenge.*

Livia came in the door and surveyed the disarray. "Marcia! What happened?"

"Mithridates came by to see if he could sample my wares. I sent him on his way."

"Sent him on his way? You didn't …"

"Of course not. I dissuaded him."

"I see. Dissuaded? You fought him off?"

"He was an easy fight, and he was caught completely by surprise."

"He'll kill you, he'll kill both of us!"

"No, not unless he wants the whole palace laughing at him for losing to a woman. And I reminded him, he won't get what he wants. He'll be a problem later on, but for now, he won't do anything."

CHAPTER 88:

INSURRECTION

Nisibis, August 115AD

Gaius Lucullus studied the detailed city map of Nisibis. Trajan had headed south with the *III Cyrenaica* for Dura Europos, while the Twelfth was left here to finish building the small fleet of boats for the southern campaign. Fortunately, that job was nearly done, the legion could soon march south to join the rest of the force.

And none too soon for Gaius. The occupation of Nisibis had not gone well. After the butchery of two soldiers from the Fifth Cohort, he had ordered the city patrolled by eight-man squads as a show of force. But eight men in narrow streets surrounded by two and three-story mud buildings on either side was not a show of force, it was an invitation to harassment. Each patrol was peppered by rocks thrown by jeering, laughing children from the roofs of those buildings. It had started around the Jewish quarter where the murders occurred, but by now had spread to all the city, as they realized that the patrols could not respond to it. Morale for the troops was at rock bottom, dealing with something they could not fight. Any day, something bigger than a pebble was going to be thrown, and Gaius would have more dead soldiers. He regretted having ordered the patrols. But that was the decision he had made, and backing down now would not look good, not to his troops and not to the rebellious townspeople.

"Sir, the mayor of Nisibis, as you ordered, sir," said his aide, sticking his head through the tent flap.

"Send him in."

Isdris entered, wearing a long white robe and a blue turban. Behind his full salt-and-pepper beard, gold chains and baubles hung around his neck. "You asked for me, Your Excellency?"

"I did. Last week I asked your assistance in dealing with the harassment of my troops on patrol, and yet it has continued."

"It is children. I am sorry sir, but they are hard to control."

"Perhaps it is time to end the patrols, and simply severely curtail the comings and goings to your city. And you should know, many rebellious cities have felt the fury of Roman retaliation. The *Princeps* was hoping to avoid that, but he is gone, and if this does not cease very soon, Nisibis will feel it as well. Do you understand me?"

"Clearly, but sir, this is just children, not a rebellion."

"No matter, end it. You may leave."

Pullus enjoyed the half-pay increase that came with his promotion to squad leader, in charge of the *contubernia* of seven men who shared the tent with him. Several of them were older than his nineteen years by several summers, but because he was able to read and write, he was promoted over them.

What he did not enjoy were the patrols through the city. On this morning, as a hail of small stones rained down from the rooftops, he reminded himself that the best way to deal with the stones that clattered down on his armor was to treat them as rain drops and march on, the mocking laughter of the children ringing in his ears. But it was humiliating.

The squad was turning by the Jewish quarter when there was a loud thump, and a bundle of heavy logs fell across the width of the street, blocking their path. As a crowd started to gather on the other side, someone threw a torch, and the naptha-soaked wood burst into a smoky pyre with a whoosh.

"All right, maintain order. About face, and let's get the hell out of here," he ordered, but as they faced back to where they had come, another bundle fell and burst into flames.

"Pullus, we're trapped!"

"No, break up, we'll go through these houses to the market behind. Shields up!"

The men scrambled, trying each of the doors along either side of the street in the mud-brick walled buildings, but all were barred solidly from the inside, and they had nothing to use to batter them down. The pebbles thrown by children were replaced by large rocks thrown by men and women with angry curses.

Pullus felt terrified. He had known the two men who had been so brutally murdered here last month, and he did not want to end up like them. But he had to lead these men. "Javelins! Throw javelins!" he ordered.

The men responded, hurling their eight-foot *pili* toward the rooftop, but most did not make the thirty feet up the wall, clattering off to land in the streets, their metal points bent and useless. A few cleared the walls but there were no screams. And now they had nothing to reach their tormentors.

"Form the *testudo!*" Pullus ordered, and the eight men huddled behind and underneath their interlocked shields, as large rocks thudded off them.

"Sir, what are we going to do?" asked one, panic tinging his words.

"Wait it out and survive," he answered, not believing what he was saying. No one knew what was happening to them, and their fate was in the hands of the people above.

Boiling water splashed on shields, scalding some of the men, who struggled to break free. "Stay inside! Break free and they'll pick us off one by one."

The next liquid splashing down was not water. Pullus recognized the telltale tang of naptha. He barely had time to curse, before someone dropped a torch into the volatile mix. Shields and men exploded into flame, scattering through the street, batting ineffectually at their flaming uniforms. Pullus felt the agony of being burnt alive, the searing pain in his lungs as he inhaled the flames, the absence of pain as he fell to the ground, then blackness.

The watch posts on the city walls had reported the fire to the Fifth Cohort. When the squad failed to return on schedule, Secundus sent word to the commander, ordered the Second Century to investigate in force with combat packs, half of the ten squads with bows to clear the rooftops, and small hand-held battering rams to knock down any obstacles. Secundus with Samuel led the century, but he was well aware that in the narrow streets, he could barely fit two squads side by side. But fortunately, there was no harassment.

They came by the still-burning barrier by the Jewish quarter. "Get your *dolabra* shovels out and clear that shit out of the street," Samuel ordered.

But on the inside, they found the still-smoldering bodies of their messmates, some still clutching their shields and swords, some charred beyond recognition, all dead. The smell of burnt meat filled the air.

Secundus gave the order he had hoped he never had to give. "Put everyone in these buildings to the sword! No one is to be left alive," he ordered.

The men battered down the doors and poured through the buildings on either side, but there were no ensuing screams. One by one, the men returned with the same report: there was no one inside.

The marketplace behind the buildings was vacant also. Secundus ordered it put to the torch, then all the buildings of the Jewish quarter. They, too, were all empty.

Samuel watched, sick, as the flames leaped from the windows of the Beth Shalom synagogue. He wondered if they had managed to save the Torah in their haste to get out. He pictured his sword at the throat of Ruth, begging for her life. Could he have done it? Was he a centurion or a Jew?

Secundus came up to him. "Are you all right, Samuel?"

"I am fine, sir."

"You lie. I know you are Jewish, and I know you have some feelings about this. It had to be done. They played with fire, and they had to be paid in kind."

"I know, sir. I had just promoted Pullus to squad leader, he was very proud. This was just his second patrol. I feel for that, too."

"On my authority, I am cancelling all city patrols, unless the *legatus* orders otherwise. Patrol on the parapets of the city walls, and double the watch posts there. I can't afford to squander any more men in these city streets."

Gaius Lucullus took the report from Secundus, Samuel by his side. "You did well, Tribune. Do you have any idea where they might have gone?"

"None. As Jews they would have been conspicuous anywhere else in the city. I guess they pre-planned this and got most everyone out of town ahead of time and then themselves. They had to know there would be retaliation," said Secundus

"And we never saw that happening. This was a skillfully-played ambush, not just some angry townspeople who don't like Roman soldiers. Well, the rest of the city will have to pay the price." He turned to his aide. "Send a message to Mayor Isdris, that effective immediately, nothing and no one comes or goes from Nisibis without my personal permission, and that includes food. Tell him I hope he has a good food reserve inside the walls."

CHAPTER 89:

DISTRACTION

Ctesiphon, August 115AD

Sanatruces was puzzled by his father. Mithridates seemed to be focused on something else, paying little attention to his presentation and uncharacteristically, asking no questions.

"So that is the situation. Nisibis, Edessa and Batnae have all had minor uprisings that, although they were small, forced the Romans to commit much larger forces to garrison them, just as we planned. Which means fewer forces to bring to bear on us next year. Any questions, father?"

Mithridates shook his head distractedly. "Uh, no, none at all. You did well. Oh, one question for you. What about the cities in the east, Arbela and Mosila?"

Sanatruces was pleased to note that his father was paying more attention than he thought. "We have had the most luck working with the Jewish populations. Many of them migrated out of Judea a half-century ago during the Jewish rebellion and settled with their co-religionists here. There are elements in those communities that do not take much persuading to poke the Romans in the eye."

"What about our own people? Don't they want to throw the Romans back out also?"

"Unfortunately, not if it involves risking their lives. They just see the Romans as another local satrap, and if the Romans don't weigh too heavily on them, they are willing to just wait them out. My agents haven't had much luck stirring them up to take action, and we don't want to press them too hard, or it may get back to the Romans."

Mithridates nodded, then went back to thinking of something else.

"How goes the interrogation of the girls? Have they produced anything useful?"

"Yes, they have confirmed that the letters are communications between Trajan and the Han court."

"Any specifics?"

"Bits and pieces, nothing significant."

"They could be stalling for time."

"Perhaps. I don't think so. Let's talk more of the insurrections. What else do you have in mind?"

"I have sent agents to the cities of Cyrene and Cyprus to see what they can stir up. They have large Jewish communities, and an uprising on Roman territory in their rear will certainly get Trajan's attention. Back to the girls, I would suggest you set some deadline for them. If they will not, or cannot, produce anything significant by then, I question whether we should waste any more time on them."

"Really, son, I will take care of the girls in my own way. I really don't want to waste any more time talking about them." Mithridates was uncharacteristically angry and short with Sanatruces.

Marcia and Livia leaned on the marble balcony, cool in the August heat, looking out on the park below. Mercifully, a gentle breezed stirred, cooling the sweat on their foreheads.

"Strange that Mithridates hasn't summoned us to give him a report for over a week," said Livia.

"Well, we need to keep putting together snippets for him. I don't want him to feel we have outlived our usefulness," said Marcia.

"Certainly not. Say, do you notice that door in the wall over there?"

"The one by the bushes with the yellow flowers?"

"Yes, that's the one. Notice that people just seem to keep coming and going, without anyone checking?"

"I am sure there is someone outside. They can't leave an entrance to the palace unguarded."

"Yes, but they are guarding an entrance. I wonder if they check on those leaving. Why would they?"

"You are thinking of escape again, aren't you?" said Marcia.

"I am always thinking of escape. We are going to die here if we don't, sooner or later."

Marcia pondered the idea. "You know, I have always felt my accented Parthian would be a disadvantage, but I certainly don't look Roman. There are many people with my features not too far east of here, and I do speak Bactrian. I could pass as that, or as a traveler. And many of the nomads have red hair. My friend Hina from my travels, she has hair like yours, but long and straight. As long as you didn't open your mouth, you might pass."

"I thought you were dead set against trying."

"Not dead set. But there are a lot of things we need that we don't have, and can't get. Money, sleeping rolls, traveling clothes. And horses, unless you want to walk all the way to Roman lines. Wherever they are."

"Always the realist. But I wonder … how do we get them?"

CHAPTER 90:

ESCAPE

Ctesiphon, August 115AD

Mithridates and Sanatruces entered the King of King's chamber and prostrated themselves before Osroës on his golden throne,

At a nod from the king, the two rose to take their seats on pillows on the floor, taking their place beside Ataradates, the commander-in-chief of the Parthian armies, Zacharias the Jew, and several other advisors, all sitting cross-legged.

"What news do you bring from the north, nephew?" asked the king.

"I bring good new, Your Most Excellent Highness. The insurrections have killed dozens of Roman soldiers in Nisibis, Batnae and Edessa, and forced them to commit more troops to garrison the cities. They are limited in their ability to patrol, and some areas are beyond their control. We have agents planning uprisings in their territories in the eastern Mediterranean but that will take some planning, perhaps next year before we can execute them. The Jewish communities have been very supportive of these efforts. The Jews in Nisibis evacuated the city before their latest confrontation, fearing retributions there. Unfortunately, the others in Nisibis are unwilling to provoke the Romans further. One of the Roman legions, the one they call the Cyrenaican, has pushed further south to take our fortress at Dura Europos."

"Very well, Sanatruces. Zacharias, what of the usurper Vologases?"

"Vologases has launched troops to take Susa, Your Most Excellent Highness, ten thousand light horse, as many infantry, and siege engines. His intent is to exploit your distraction by the Romans to move within a hundred miles of you."

"I am not distracted by them, I am amused at the speed of their advance and waiting to see them stumble. Sanatruces, what can you do to forestall this effort?"

"I have already dispatched my son Vargharsh with ten thousand light horse and five thousand heavy cavalry to reinforce Susa and defeat Vologases' forces as they come out of the Zagros Mountains."

"Excellent. Now Mithridates, my brother, what of the threat from Han China?"

"Your Most Excellent Highness, there have been no movements of troops even as far as Bactria or Sogdiana. The Empress Dowager Deng appears unwilling to commit her troops over such a vast distance, and if they were to move now, it would be two years before they arrived. Therefore, there is no threat from the east. We have made some progress in decoding the Roman communications with them. The girls we brought here from Italy have been very helpful. They finally confirmed it was a coded communication, and they have recalled a few of the code words. However, with no evidence of a threat, I feel they are of no further use to us."

"Also most excellent, brother. Dispose of them as you wish."

After returning to Mithridates' office, Kophasates welcomed father and son with cool glasses of wine. They accepted them without so much as a glance in acknowledgment.

"Our presentations went well," said Mithridates.

"Indeed. I am comfortable with our strategy. The Romans cannot resist a chase, as Hannibal demonstrated to them many times. You said something that surprised me, however, and that was that you had no further use for the girls."

"None. The Han are not getting into it, so what is in the letters matters not. I have no reason to keep them living in luxury here."

"What did you have in mind? If you are getting rid of them, I'll take the redhead," he said with a smile.

"I am sure you would. However, I have a friend of mine who runs a high-class brothel, who is willing to pay a huge price to add the redheaded wife of a senior advisor to Trajan to his stable. He is coming by tomorrow to take them. We brought them here as Roman whores, we can send them on their way as that, it seems fitting. However, I am sure he will let you break both of them in for him. Not here, though. The screaming would be unseemly."

"I think I shall." Sanatruces licked his lips in anticipation. "I think I surely shall."

When Sanatruces and Mithridates went down for their mid-day nap in the August heat, Kophasates quietly left. He had developed a bit of affection for the two women. Livia reminded him of his own red-haired daughter, headstrong and confident. He knocked on their door. There was a delay. They too would be napping. Marcia finally answered the door, cracking it a little.

"Kophasates! Come in, please, we are honored."

He entered. Both women had wrapped robes about their sleeping shifts, Livia still adjusting hers. "You are in great danger. I must help you leave."

"That is a terrible risk, Kophasates. You will be killed for doing that," said Marcia.

"Mithridates is getting rid of you, selling you to a whoremaster. He feels you have outlived your usefulness to him."

"And he gets the revenge he wants," said Marcia bitterly.

"I am going to send you to someone I trust, and he will get you both to my contact. But we must leave now, while everyone is asleep." He pressed a sack of silver coins into Marcia's hand. "That's 20 *drachmae*, about the same as Roman *denarii*. Now get dressed. I can't be wandering the halls, so I will stay, but I will respect your modesty." He turned his back.

"Not so fast. Who is your contact, and why should I trust him? Or you, for that matter?" asked Livia

"He is the communications channel to my client, whom I believe is Trajan, or someone close to him. I have kept him informed of your status, and he is concerned for your well-being."

The two women began changing, wriggling into their dresses and slipping their feet into slippers. "We're ready, you can turn around."

"Excellent. I will check the corridor, then we can go. I will get you as far as the Palace gate and see you through, on Mithridates' order. You go down the street five blocks and on the left is a market. Find the wine merchant, his name is Phraates. Give him this." He pressed two notes into Marcia's hand, one plain indicating that he should take care of the two women, the other undecipherable. "The one is for him, the other for my client. He will know what to do."

As expected, the palace was silent, with none but servants about, and only a few of them in the heat. The women glanced nervously back and forth.

"None of that," he said softly. "Act as if this was the most natural thing for you to be doing. Don't skulk."

They crossed the marble pavilion. The young guard at the door was the only one in the entire massive space. Kophasates walked comfortably up to him. "Two to exit, please, young man."

The young man, sweating, grabbed the hefty iron handle and opened the massive ten-foot bronze door. He never asked on whose authority, and Kophasates gave none. He turned to the women. "You know the way. Good luck."

"Thank you, Kophasates. Save yourself as well," said Marcia

Walking down the street, they felt free, the freest they had felt since last December when this nightmare began. There were few people on the street as well. "That was unexpected," said Livia.

"That it was. He is risking his life for us."

"I hope he is not caught."

"I don't see how he cannot be."

Five blocks down they found the market, vacant except for a few stray cats looking for scraps or rats. The wine merchant's stall was distinguished by sacks and amphorae of wine, and behind the counter sat a man, fanning himself. He seemed to be the only one awake during siesta time.

"Are you Phraates?" asked Marcia in Parthian.

"I am. Would you like some wine on this hot day? It is why I remain open when all else is closed."

"Thank you, no. I bring you this from Kophasates." She handed him a note.

"Oh, my. You must come inside quickly. I am sorry, it is a mess back there."

The two followed Phraates into the interior. There was a rough cot, unmade, many wine amphorae much larger than the ones for sale outside, spilled wine and food on the floor. "I am sorry, I live here since my wife died. You speak good Parthian."

"I traveled a lot. Unfortunately, Livia does not, only Latin and Greek."

"I also speak Greek," he said, switching languages easily, though with a heavy accent. "You are in danger. He says I am to get you to our client, along with this other note."

Phraates rolled it up and slipped it into the neck of a wine sack. "Your clothes are beautiful, but not fit for traveling. When the market opens this evening, I will get you some rough clothes. Stay inside, what you are wearing is far too conspicuous for this market. I will summon my courier, and he will get you on your way. Now, you two should make yourself as comfortable as you can in my hovel, and I insist you two have a cup of wine on me."

The two women sipped wine, warm, flies buzzing around it, trying to get to the sweet drink. They drank quickly, then Phraates pulled the wool curtain over the entranceway, and they tried to sleep.

If the palace was hot, at least the huge marble building absorbed much of the heat. The mud brick buildings of the town just re-radiated it inside, after mixing it with the smells of the market, moldering cast-off garbage and excrement. Both women tossed restlessly, but finally dozed, their silken clothes soaked with sweat, clinging to their bodies.

Late in the afternoon, Phraates returned with bundles of beige cotton clothes and a friend. He opened the curtain discretely. "Are you awake?" he asked.

"We are. Come in," said Livia.

"Your clothes. Change and I will dispose of your nice ones."

"They are no longer nice."

The women put on the long, baggy dresses, and headscarves which hid their distinctive hair. They suddenly did not feel so conspicuous, and the rough-knit cotton seemed to handle the heat better than fine silk. They signaled Phraates, who came in with his somewhat pudgy and unkempt middle-aged friend, with a shaggy brown beard and very long mustache.

"Excellent. We must move swiftly. My friend Varaza will get you out of Ctesiphon tonight, and put many miles behind you by morning. As soon as you are missed they will be searching for you. If anyone asks, you are Varaza's wife and sister."

"I don't look too much like you, so I'll be your wife, as long as you don't expect me to act the part," Marcia said, extending her hand with a smile.

"And I'll be your sister," said Livia, likewise taking Varaza's hand. He smiled shyly.

"So, you have more than an empty wine sack to get to our client. Travel fast," said Phraates.

Marcia interrupted, taking the purse Kophasates had given her. "What can I do to repay you?"

"Nothing, that is your traveling money. Now be off with you, before someone comes looking for you and I lose my head."

"Thank you, Phraates. And please tell Kophasates we thank him very much, the next time you see him."

"There may not be a next time for him. Now go."

The two women clambered onto the bench of the rickety wagon, and Varaza clucked the mules into a sluggish trot.

By the time the moon came up, Ctesiphon was a dim glow in the night, miles behind them. Marcia checked the direction using the Great Bear as Antonius had taught her many years ago. They were heading north.

CHAPTER 91:

THE ONLY WAY OUT

Ctesiphon, August 115AD

Kophasates climbed the deserted staircase back to his room on the third floor. There were several things left to be done. First, he collected the codes from under his mattress, and burnt them in a candle flame. There would be no more communications with his client.

Late in the afternoon, as people began to stir in the md-day heat, he went back to the servants' quarters at the end of the floor, and let the maidservants know that Marcia and Livia did not want to be disturbed.

"Shall we bring them breakfast in the morning, sir?" asked one.

"Only if they ask. They are not feeling well."

That done, he returned to his room and opened a jar of wine, pouring it into a fine green Egyptian glass, flecked with gold. He had bought Livia, Marcia and Phraates a good twelve hours, maybe more, to put between them and Ctesiphon. Maybe thirty miles.

As the red wine warmed his stomach, he thought of Livia's fine red hair, so much like his daughter's. He had not seen Farana for ten years, since she married and moved far south to Charax on the Persian Gulf. He had married her off quickly, to keep her from the former king Pacorus. She also looked so much like his wife Adeshta.

He had not thought of Adeshta for a long time. He had put her out of his mind because it was too painful to think of her, like a burning iron in his mind. So happy, so loving, so proud of their daughter, looking forward to giving him a son and Farana a brother. His mind drifted back to that time.

Pacorus, Osroës' predecessor as King, called for her to be brought to him, as was his habit with the wives of his counsellors. She was gone for several days, then one of the king's servants called for him to claim the body. Stunned, he summoned the courage to ask the King what happened, and he had just laughed. "I guess she couldn't handle the excitement," he said.

There was no leaving the palace, no going elsewhere and starting over, just living day to day without his Adeshta. The servants took over raising Farana, while evenings found Kophasates drinking himself to oblivion in the market stall of the wine merchant Phraates.

"It's late, my friend. One more, for I must close soon."

I was the only one left in the stall, and the market was dark, with just a few lamps lit. "One more, yes." I pushed some coins across the rough counter.

Phraates pushed them back and refilled his bowl. "On me. You drink like a troubled man. Sometimes talking is more helpful than drinking."

So, I told him of what had happened. Things that should never leave the palace, I told him, and he just listened sympathetically. I staggered back to the palace that night, but found myself there the next night, looking forward to unburdening myself of the pain, with the only person I could talk to. We became friends, and eventually I needed less alcohol to deaden the pain.

He shared his life. He had been born here, but his father had migrated to Sidon on the Mediterranean Sea, taking his family with him. That was Roman territory, and his father ended up serving in the auxiliaries with the Roman army, thereby earning his citizenship. And in the process, earning citizenship for Phraates as well. Then he returned here when his father died.

I did not know what citizenship meant. Phraates spoke very highly of it. "You have rights, not like here. You can't be imprisoned, beaten or killed without a trial. That doesn't mean that powerful men don't break the law, but the law governs them as well as you. Not like here. Not like what happened to you and your wife."

Reliving the past, he realized he had finished that jar, and opened another. But first, before the wine took him away, one more thing. He took the remaining package from under his bed, a bag of finely-chopped leaves of hemlock. He poured them into the jar of wine, replaced the cap, and shook it vigorously. Letting the leaves do their work, he returned to thoughts of the past.

Day by day, I talked to him, and late at night would share tidbits of palace goings on, sharing laughs at the foibles of those in power. Finally, he thanked me for my insights. "Thank you, your information is very much appreciated by my client."

For a moment I was shocked. His client? Had he just been using me to gain information for someone else? Was I involved in some sort of intrigue with competitors for the throne? Such things could cost my head, or worse. But no, we were friends, and I continued to trust him. He finally told me that his clients were on the Roman side, but their sole concern was to have knowledge of what was going on, so that war could be prevented. He eventually gave me the code sheets and showed me how to use them, just substituting one letter for another. The wine flasks were our dead-drop, a way to get them out of the palace undetected. And I felt like I was avenging my beloved Adeshta.

And I have done so. And now I must die, before the torturers extract all that I know, putting Phraates and the women at risk.

It was growing dark outside. He lit a lamp from a taper, and poured himself more wine. Little flakes of leaves floated in the drink. He took the first glassful in a single swallow, then poured another. The leaves added some bitterness to the drink but not much.

By the third glass, he felt the tell-tale chill begin in his lower legs. *It's working. I have tried to have good thoughts, to speak good words, and do good deeds. This is the best of good deeds, to give my life to save another. Soon, if what Zarathustra has taught us is true, my soul will be reunited with my higher spirit together, and with my Adeshta.*

There was a moment of fear and panic after the fourth glass, when suddenly he could not breathe, his heart pounding. He thrashed a bit, spilling the wine and upending the jar to shatter on the floor. Then he was still.

CHAPTER 92:

ON THE ROAD

The Road to Dura Europos, August 115AD

Varaza was most uncommunicative, rebuffing any attempt by Marcia to engage him in conversation. He remained focused on everything around, as though expecting mounted troops to pull up at any moment and order him over. After a few one-word answers, Marcia gave up. He was intent on driving all night, so she curled up in the wagon bed with Livia and went to sleep.

Dawn found them with the sun to their back, crossing the Tigris River on a little rope-drawn ferry between two jetties at the little village of Baghdad. Varaza seemed tireless, pressing on till late afternoon, when he pulled up next to a canal, near some extensive farmers' fields. "I can go no farther," he said. "I will fix food for you, then we sleep."

"Varaza, you rest. I will make camp for us and prepare dinner," said Marcia.

"What do you know of such things?"

"I lived rough on the road for two years a while back, in far worse places than this. Get some rest," she said with a smile. She was already undoing the mules, tethering them by the canal where they could drink, and brushing them down.

Varaza was too tired to argue, and he watched her long enough to know that she knew what she was doing. Thirty-six hours without sleep had taken its toll. He propped himself against a small tree and was quickly snoring.

"What was that all about?" asked Livia, as that whole exchange, more than anything Varaza had said since they met, had been all in Parthian.

"We are setting up the camp for tonight. He is done. Find some twigs and small sticks for the fire, maybe some dung if you can find any dry. I will see what I can find for food and cooking gear in the wagon."

Livia made a face, but set out and returned with a bundle of sticks and two handfuls of crumbly dung.

When they awoke Varaza, the sun was low on the horizon. The fire flickered brightly and a stewpot bubbled on the fire, suspended by a chain from a tripod of sticks. For the first time, he smiled. "You do seem to know what you are doing. Thank you," he said to Marcia.

"You are most welcome, and thank you for getting us out of Ctesiphon so quickly." She dished up some stew, salt pork, vegetables and barley mush into a bowl, adding a chunk of bread to the mix, and handed it to him. She took her own serving, as did Livia, and the two sat down beside him. The food was delightful, as they had eaten nothing but some hard bread, washed down with water, since leaving Ctesiphon.

"Where are you taking us?" she asked.

"The border at Dura Europos," he answered, in between bites of bread sopped in the soup.

"How far away is that?"

"About a week."

"What will you do with us when we get there?"

"Turn you over to my contact."

"Who is that?"

"Petronius."

"What will he do with us?"

"Pass you on to Phraates' client."

"And who is that?" There was growing frustration in Marcia's voice.

"Look, I have no idea. I deliver wineskins to Petronius, he takes them from me, sometimes gives me some in return, and I take them back to Phraates. Both pay me for my trouble. That's all I know, that's all I need to know. This is the first time I have delivered people to him. Phraates said you were very important to his client, so I'm sure you'll be safe, if that is what is worrying you."

"What's in the wineskins?"

"They are empty, no wine. Something in them, I guess. I never looked. Another thing I don't need to know about."

"Sounds mysterious. Thank you for what you have told us." She took a bit of her stew. "You know, I can spell you driving the mules if you like. A week of driving the mules can get tiresome. And with two, if the mules can handle the heat, maybe we can cover a few more miles each day."

"I would like to hear about your time on the road. You seem to have learned a lot."

"Quite a bit. Maybe later, if you have any wineskins that aren't empty. It's a long story. Right now, I have to talk with my friend, she doesn't speak Parthian."

She turned to face Livia. "We are going to Dura Europos, a border fort about a week from here. Antonius told me a little about it. It seems that whoever is receiving us has a Roman name, and we are very important to him. Other than that, Varaza doesn't know very much. He's a courier, I think for smugglers, and makes it a point to know as little as possible"

"At least they are smuggling us to Rome. Phraates is one of the smugglers?" Livia asked.

"I guess. The client belongs to Phraates, so I guess so." She changed the subject. "I will be taking turns driving. Can you handle a mule team?"

"Not very well, I'm afraid. If they got spooked, I don't think I could get them under control."

"No matter, best not, then. He's going to break out some wine later."

Varaza cleaned up the cooking gear in the canal, put some more wood on the fire, and fetched a very full wineskin from the back of the wagon, opened it, took a swig, and passed it to Marcia, who then passed it on to Livia, and she back to him. And Marcia launched in a long story of caravans, mountains, deserts, bandits, and Hina of the wild Xiongnu.

They were up at first light, snatched some bread for breakfast and were on the road before the sun was fully up, Marcia driving, Varaza sitting beside her.

"You know, I really don't feel safe on the road without a dagger. I usually carry one, but I lost it a while back. You don't have a spare, do you?" she asked.

"I always carry a spare." He reached under the seat and pulled up a leather sheath with a wood-handled blade in it, about ten inches long. He handed it to her. "It's big for a woman."

"No, it's about the right size. Thank you." He had passed the test. If there was anything bad afoot, he certainly would not have given her a weapon. And she felt a lot better armed, without depending on someone else to defend her.

"About noon, we will reach Pallacottas, where a big canal by that name branches off from the river. The locals call it Fallujah, 'division', because that is where the canal divides from the river. There is a small tavern that I always stop at, the woman serves good meals. Beyond Pallacottas, there isn't much until Dura Europos. And it's a good time to change riders."

As the wagon entered the outskirts of the city, a large square of several dozen mudbrick beehive-shaped structures lined the north side of the road. "What are those?" asked Marcia.

"Those are warehouses for the grain from all those fields." He indicated the waving fields of wheat, yellow-green and ready for the harvest. "They store it there waiting for the boats to take it south to Ctesiphon. Here is the tavern, the one with the ram's head on it, pull in here and tie up."

Marcia clucked the mules to the right and edged them up to the hitching rail, Varaza got off and tethered them. A boy came up with a large jug, almost as big as he was. "Water for the mules?" he asked.

Varaza nodded, fishing his pouch from underneath his shirt.

The boy poured the jug into a trough by the hitching rail. When he was done, Varaza pressed a bronze coin into the boy's outstretched hand.

The tavern was a small mudbrick building alongside the canal. A multicolored awning shaded the front, and several tables were set up under it. A matronly woman came out, wiping her hands on a stained apron. "Varaza, good to see you again," she said, then eyed the two women. "Traveling with company this time?"

"Business, Faryane. These women needed to go north, and I was the only respectable traveler they could find."

"You all look hot. Would you like something cool to drink?"

"Of course."

She came back with a wooden platter with three bronze mugs on it, the condensation beading on their sides.

"Beautiful," Marcia said, taking hers. "How do you keep anything so cold in this heat?"

"We have a spring behind the house, the water is very cold. Travelers love it, that is why they always stop at the Ram passing through Pallicotas."

"You girls should try her lamb stew. It is excellent," said Varaza.

"I think so." Marcia turned to Livia and translated. She nodded, and Faryane disappeared into the tavern, to return a few minutes later with three steaming bowls and fresh-baked bread.

"Enjoy. This will be the last meal we don't cook ourselves for the next several days."

When they had finished eating, Varaza leaned back in his chair. "Phraates told me you girls were in very big trouble, and that I should get away from Ctesiphon as fast as possible. I think we have enough distance behind us to relax a bit. The further we go, the more we blend in with all the other travelers coming and going."

"I hope so." Marcia waited for him to ask them what sort of trouble, but he didn't. Varaza, it seemed, never asked questions about things he didn't need to know.

They settled up with Faryane, Marcia insisting on paying from the pouch Kophasates had given her, generously giving her a silver *drachma* for the meal. They then set out again, Varaza driving, Marcia teaching Livia some Parthian words.

As Varaza had said, there were no more big towns on the road north, just small farming villages, interspersed among fields, increasingly smaller and more arid. Although all three were looking over their shoulders for cavalry coming from the south to take them back to Ctesiphon, there were none. The only military formations were from the north, away from the Romans, both light horse archers and heavily armored *catafracti* cavalry. All civilian traffic pulled over to give them passage.

The last four days were mostly desert, except for a narrow band of arid green alongside the river. Then the Parthian fortress city of Dura Europos loomed ahead, guarding the upper approaches to the Euphrates River.

But guarding the approaches to the Parthian fortress was the orderly grid of a Roman army camp, the tents brilliant white in the sunlight.

CHAPTER 93:

PLAYING CARDS LOST

Ctesiphon Palace, August 115AD

It was mid-morning when a pudgy man in a red and gold robe appeared at the door to Mithridates' office. "Good morning, Cyrus. I was surprised not to be greeted by your faithful Kophasates this morning."

Mithridates stood, rounding his desk to embrace the big man in a hug, politely kissing both cheeks in greeting. "And good morning to you, Pharnaces. Kophasates did not come in this morning. So far, I haven't needed his services, so I did not send for him. Perhaps he is ill. You are here for your latest acquisitions?"

"Yes, I am. What are they like?"

"Both beautiful, not young, but experienced and still beautiful. One is the red-haired wife of a Senator, a senior advisor to Trajan, so she will be a worthy addition to your stable of lovelies. The other is very unusual, Chinese but speaks flawless Latin. Wife of the prefect of one of the Roman legions, so also a prize. Petite, but she appears very strong. Both have a bit of spitfire in them, but I am sure you can break them of that."

"Those are rare finds indeed," said Pharnaces. "How did you come by them?"

"We thought they had information of some use, so I had them brought here. We have gotten what we needed, so I have no further use for them. I am sure that you, however, will put them to good work. As a favor, my son would like to help you break them into their new line of work this evening."

"Interesting. To be sure, I will be happy to entertain Sanatruces for you. Let's go see what they look like."

"This way." He led Pharnaces down the hall to their room.

"You put them up in quite the style."

"It helped gain their cooperation." He opened the door to an empty room. "Sorry, they are not here. Perhaps out wandering or bathing. I'll have Kophasates find them for you." He backtracked down the hall to his secretary's room.

Mithridates opened the door to find Kophasates face down on the floor, chair toppled over, a puddle of wine around a broken wine bottle. Mithridates touched the man's face above his gray beard and withdrew his hand in disgust, wiping it on his sleeve. "He is as cold as a stone. Dead," he said, rising. "It happens at his age, people die for no reason. The gods just take them. I will miss him, he was a good secretary. Let's go back to my office, I will summon some servants to find your prizes and take care of the body."

But the servants could not find the women, not on the floor where they were constrained to stay, nor anywhere in the palace. It was late in the afternoon before Mithridates learned from the palace guards that two women matching their description had left the palace in the heat of the day in the company of a gray-bearded man, who had returned alone. It did not appear that Pharnaces would be getting his prizes any time soon.

CHAPTER 94:

DURA EUROPOS

Dura Europos, August 115AD

Varaza shifted on the wagon seat to catch a better view of the city several miles off. "Looks like the Roman army has gotten here first," he said. "Doesn't look like a siege in progress. But I want to know what I am getting into before I am in it."

"The Roman army camp is fine with us, Varaza. We'll vouch for you. They'll take us in as soon as I tell them who I am," said Livia.

"I am to deliver you to Petronius in the city," said Varaza, looking fixedly ahead, clucking the mules into motion to end the conversation. The wagon rumbled on in silence on the road traversing the Euphrates flood plain, a rugged gray sandy escarpment to their left marking the bank separating the fertile plain from the barren desert beyond. The women sat in silence, their fates once again in the hands of someone else.

After about half an hour, the city was just a mile off, the encampment a bit closer, by the southern gate where the road entered the city. There was a contingent of Roman soldiers guarding the gate, but traffic seemed to be coming and going without much trouble. Marcia recognized the shield marking of the *III Cyrenaica*.

"Looks like whatever happened here, it's over. I am going in. Trust me, Petronius will take care of you. I have to trust you, too. If you alert the soldiers, I may be in serious trouble."

Livia gave a silent nod, not promising anything. Marcia followed her lead, and sat silently beside her on the wagon bench, carefully watching everything for any sign of trouble.

The wagon ahead of them was huge, pulled by a team of eight mules, piled high with something under tarps pulled tight. The sentries waved the vehicle over and undid the covers for some sort of inspection, while the traffic backed up behind Varaza's wagon. The soldiers were in no hurry, poking and prodding the bags of grain with their lances to see if anything or anyone was concealed in them. After about fifteen minutes, satisfied, they reattached the tarps and waved the wagon on.

Varaza pulled up. A soldier walked up to question him. "Business in the city?" he asked, in barely passable Parthian.

"Visiting a friend," answered Varaza. "If it is permitted."

"What are you carrying?" asked the soldier, eyeing the women and the nearly empty wagon bed.

"Just traveling supplies."

"Go on in." The soldier waved him on and signaled the next wagon forward.

They passed through the open gate, two gaping doors each perhaps fifteen feet high and ten feet wide, a foot thick, and plated on the outside with bronze. They entered a tunnel ten feet long through the massive base of the wall. This was obviously a place meant to withstand a long siege, yet it seemed to have fallen quickly, without damage. Exiting the tunnel back into the sunlight, the city seemed to be going about its normal business, with no signs of damage.

"Thank you," said Varaza.

"For what?" said Livia.

"For not betraying me to the guards."

"You had best hope you haven't lied to us about Petronius."

"I haven't."

The city was laid out in Greek style, spacious, with orderly streets crossing at right angles. To their right, by the eastern wall next to the river, several white marble colonnaded temples looked over the central area. A smaller temple along the western wall looked back at them. Varaza steered his wagon along a street by the smaller temple toward a caravansary. He pulled up, and a worker came out to take the reins of the mules and led the snorting animals inside after the three dismounted. Varaza snatched his traveling bag off the bed as the wagon lurched off, and led them across the street to a modest-sized white-washed mudbrick house, using the door knocker to summon a servant, who slid open a viewport.

"Varaza to see Petronius," said Varaza, and the door swung open.

The interior was well-appointed with elegant carpets, decorative vases of various colors and finishes, and a small bronze statue of Atlas with the weight of a huge globe on his shoulders. The servant indicated a couch, and the three sat.

Petronius swept into the room. "Varaza, always good to see you. And with friends this time, I see," he said in Parthian, smiling at the two women. Varaza and Petronius exchanged kisses on each other's cheeks. Petronius, despite the Roman name, did not appear to be in any way Roman in appearance, with the bronze complexion and shiny black hair of Asia Minor, his beard carefully barbered to a fine point. He was wearing a green ankle-length robe and blue turban.

"And you, my friend." Varaza fished through his bag to remove a wineskin, and handed it to Petronius, who extracted a rolled-up paper from its neck. "This is unusual, as the contents are for your eyes. You should read it first."

Petronius pried up what appeared to be a decorative insert in the low table in the middle of the room and extracted a piece of paper. He pulled a wax tablet from his robe, and began deciphering the message, his eyebrows raising as the message appeared. "Oh, indeed!" he said, switching to flawless Latin. "And these are the two women. Livia Aemilia, you are certainly a woman of considerable importance. You will both be happy to know that your husbands are both just a few miles from here, with the *XII Fulminata*. Would you like to freshen up after your long trip?"

"Aulus has seen me worse. This has been an ordeal for both of us, and we want it over as soon as possible. We can bathe wherever he is."

"He is in an army camp, with not much in the way of facilities for women. Please, accept my hospitality for a few moments, and I will also provide you some dresses, which you will not find in the army camp, either. I will send word ahead, so they will be expecting you."

The two women acquiesced, and a servant led them to a small bath at the rear of the building, where female attendants waited to tend to them.

"I am glad you changed your mind, Livia. I think I have gotten some fleas on the road," said Marcia, scratching at herself.

"Me, too," said Livia.

An hour later, bathed, perfumed, hair untangled, wearing light white *stolae*, fresh clothes for the first time more than a week, the two women were much more comfortable and presentable as they were led back to rejoin Petronius. He had laid out a small lunch for the two, dates, rolls of meat and cheese, and wine.

"Where is Varaza?" asked Marcia. Lunch, like a bath, seemed to take priority over finally getting back with Antonius.

"His business was done. He will be heading back to Ctesiphon tomorrow."

"And what is your business? Your Latin is excellent."

"I deal in various matters." Another uncommunicative person. "When you are finished, I will see you to *XII Ful*'s camp." He very comfortably used the military slang name for the legion.

"Latin is your first language," said Marcia.

"I have several first languages."

Lunch finished, he led them to the stables through an interior door in the house, where an ornate enclosed wagon awaited, finely polished wood with painted decorations, a winged Pegasus in flight on each door. He held a door open for them to climb in to take their seats on the well-padded leather-clad bench in the rear, then he climbed in take the front seat facing them. The driver clambered up to his seat, servants opened the stable doors and the wagon rolled smoothly out onto the street, heading to the northern gate.

"What happened here? The city seems to have fallen without a fight," asked Marcia, as they passed a patrol of Roman soldiers going the opposite direction.

"That it did. The Parthian soldiers left before the Romans even got here."

"Why? This city looks like it could hold out for months."

"Years, actually. You'll have to ask the Parthians."

Marcia's heart leapt as she saw the familiar banner of *XII Ful* fluttering over the desert to the north of the city. Antonius' legion. Their ordeal was almost over.

CHAPTER 95:

REUNITED

Outside Dura Europos, August 115AD

Arrian was in the intelligence tent, studying various reports, trying to ignore the heat, when a scratching at the flap attracted his attention. He got up to attend to the distraction.

"Messages from Petronius, sir," said the runner, handing him two pieces of papyrus paper. Arrian examined them, both encrypted, one with the bull from Taurus, the other with a jagged polygon, a stylized rock, indicating it was from Petronius. Petronius had never entrusted any of Taurus' missives to runners since their arrival at the city, always bringing them in person. And he had never sent any sort of enciphered message. *Odd.*

Arrian decided to decipher Taurus' message first. It cryptically decoded as "Your packages are enroute. This will be my last message." The 'packages' must mean the women, but how could they be enroute? Had Mithridates released them? And what did Taurus mean about this being his last message? Was he perhaps coming with them? Had he been compromised?

Perhaps the answer was in Petronius' letter. So, he decoded it using the keyword *petrus*, meaning 'rock'. 'The women have arrived. I will bring them to you shortly.' *They are here! No mention of Taurus, but they are here!*

"Marcus, a message from Taurus. You are not going to believe this, but your sister will be here shortly."

Nathaniel looked up from his work, surprised at the exchange.

"Marcia? Here? How?"

"I have no idea. But I have to get Aulus Aemilius. Be ready, if they arrive before I get back."

Arrian ran the short distance to Aulus' tent, where he found the senator deep into his noon-time nap. "Sir, wake up, wake up! Your wife is coming. Wake up."

Aulus snorted and opened his eyes, trying to focus, and understand what he thought he had heard. "Livia is here?" He swung his feet over the cot.

"She will be, sir, probably inside the hour. And Antonius' wife also. At the intelligence tent."

Aulus leaped to his feet, and slithered his tunic on over his head. "Go get Antonius. The *Princeps* will want to be there also, I'll go get him."

Antonius was attempting to read various reports, sweat dripping off his nose. *Damned August heat! I should learn how to sleep through heat of the day, but it seems so lazy. On the other hand, yer can't get much done, so why not?"* He patted at a drop that had spattered on a scroll, trying to get it off without smearing the ink into illegibility.

Scratching at the tent distracted him, and that group of letters dissolved into inky blackness as the bead of sweat engulfed them. *Hope that wasn't an important part of the report.* "Coming! I'm coming. Oh, Arrian, it's you. Come in, what's up?"

"Your wife, sir. She will be in the camp shortly, maybe within the hour."

"Within the hour! How the hell?"

"I don't know. But hurry."

Antonius fastened on his corselet and sword buckler, grabbing his helmet. "Just a bit, lad, I'm going ter bring *Legatus* Lucullus along with us."

Arrian's men in the intelligence tent snapped to attention and saluted at the unexpected arrival of the *Princeps,* his senior advisor, their legion commander and his prefect. Trajan acknowledged their salute. "At ease, gentlemen. We are expecting two very important women to be coming soon, so go about your work till they arrive."

They had barely settled back down to resume their work, when an expensive wagon rolled up outside. A man in a green robe with black pointed beard emerged and held the door open for two women to emerge, and he led them into the tent. They had barely cleared the entrance when they caught sight of their husbands and they flew together in two crushing embraces. After several long and passionate kisses, Marcia and Antonius disentangled themselves, and Marcia stared at her brother Marcus, waiting patiently. Then he, too, was the recipient of a bone-crushing embrace.

Trajan smiled through it all. "You seem very glad to see each other again," he said. "Arrian, can you tell me how this all came about?"

"Petronius here is our man in Dura Europos, the man who helped us deliver the city without a fight. He will tell what he knows. Petronius, the *Princeps* Trajan, and Gaius Lucullus, our commander."

Petronius gave a deep bow. "Your Excellency. I know but what I learned from these two women in the last hour. Our agent in Ctesiphon arranged their escape from the palace, He dispatched them here using our mutual courier."

"That is excellent, excellent indeed. And I have heard how you delivered the city to us. You saved many lives, and much time."

"They thought you were coming with far more legions than this."

"When you are few, appear to be many," said Marcus.

"What is that?" asked Trajan, amused at the interruption.

Marcus explained, "A Chinese philosopher-general from long ago. 'When you are many, appear to be few, when you are few, appear to be many.' On the importance of deception in war."

Trajan nodded. "Oh, I would like to know more of him. But later. Let's allow these to get reacquainted with each other. There will be a reception in my *Praetorium* in their honor tonight after sunset, in the cool of the evening. And you two also, Petronius, Arrian, come along also. You were both essential in bringing these women home."

Gaius Lucullus spoke up. "Your Excellency, they have some close friends with us who are not here. May I extend your invitation to them?"

"You certainly may. And anyone else you think should be there."

CHAPTER 96:

TOGETHER AGAIN

Outside Dura Europos, August 115AD

Marcia shivered as the last delightful spasm of pleasure left her body. "Oh, I have missed that so much," she said, wiping sweat from Antonius' cheek. "Even if it is so damned hot, and this army cot is so damned small."

"The only way fer two ter sleep in it is one atop the other."

"That's fine by me. But next time you get the bottom. The wooden bars in the frame are killing my back."

Antonius grabbed her and rolled her to the top. "Yer wish is my command." The cot creaked as the two giggled. Then Antonius got serious. "I thought I had lost you, *domina*. I don't think I could live without you."

"I know. All I knew was that wherever I was, whatever they forced me to do, I was going to escape and find my way back to wherever you were." She cuddled close to him, twirling the long hairs on his chest, winding them around her finger. "Because I can't live without you, either." She lay thoughtful for a moment. "The children? Are they all right?"

"Desdemona has done a fine job of seeing to their care, she's earned her manumission for that. Alaric has been working with Agrippa to see to everyone's safety."

"She is a good woman."

They lay silently in each other's arms, intoxicated with the warmth, feel and smell of each other's body. Marcia took Antonius' face in both hands and kissed him long and deeply. "You know, we still have a few hours before sunset."

Antonius adjusted the single shoulder strap on Marcia's *stola*. "There, beautiful. I'm so glad yer back, an' unhurt," he said, giving her a peck on her cheek.

"So am I. And Hina and Galosga? Of all people? They are here also? How by the gods did that happen?"

"Their clan was wiped out by sickness, and Marcus found them in Turfam. They decided to follow him west, 'cuz they had nowhere else to go. We have a niece and two nephews, twins Marasa and Andanyu, named for us, just twelve but already riding with the cavalry. Xiongnu children grow up fast. Little Adhela is just four, but he's ridin' on his own."

"I can't wait to see them. I thought she was lost to me forever."

"Gaius sent riders out to the Ninth Batavians. They're riding with them, and hopefully they will be at Trajan's welcome party for you and Livia tonight. They have been showing the Ninth a few tricks from the steppes that aren't in any Roman manual. Their commander Longinus Clarus is very pleased with them."

"Sounds like Hina. She is a natural teacher."

"She has been following your situation. She was sure you would find a way out of that mess."

"The way out found me."

Antonius put finishing touches on his dress armor. As they exited the tent, Livia and Aulus were leaving their nearby tent, one of several big tents for senior people flanking Trajan's and Lucullus' *praetoria* in the center of the camp. The four exchanged pleasantries and walked over to the imperial tent, the men acknowledging salutes from Trajan's contingent of praetorian guardsmen. Inside was a hub of activity, as servants were setting out serving dishes about the *triclinia* sofas.

Gaius Lucullus emerged from the crowd to greet them, accompanied by Marcus, Mei and Nathaniel. "I haven't had a chance to tell you how glad we are to have you both back, safe and unharmed. You two must have a few stories to tell."

"Mostly boring ones. We didn't do anything but wait it out," answered Livia.

Marcia embraced Marcus. "My dearest brother, I never thought I would see you again."

"I was hoping to find you, but the path was complicated," said Marcus. "This is my wife Mei, and our dear friend Nathaniel, without whom I would not be here."

Marcia took Mei's hand. "I had heard about you in Marcus' letters. I never believed I would meet you." She turned toward Nathaniel. "I want to hear your stories. I am sure they are not boring ones."

Gaius continued on. "Marcia, you will be happy to know that everyone has promised to be here tonight. Including Hina and Galosga. Somehow, the gods have reunited everyone from our trip, except for Yakov. And he is not too far away, about a week's ride south of here in Petra."

"It's so hard to believe that we are all together," said Marcia. "Marcus, it took us two years to get back to Rome after we left you in Liqian."

"The *Princeps* wants all of us to dine with him. He finds our reunion very fortuitous. And he will want everyone's story. I am sorry that my son Secundus and his centurion Samuel could not be here. You knew him as Shmuel, but he has Latinized his name. They are guarding Nisibis with the

Fifth Cohort, my son's first independent operation in command," said Gaius, obviously proud of his son.

A voice came from behind Marcia, in accented *han-yu*, a voice she had never expected to hear again. "Hello, sister."

Marcia whirled to find Hina behind her, with Galosga and their three children, and, smiling with amusement, Longinus Clarus, their *decurion,* in dress uniform. They had long *spatha* cavalry sabers crossed behind Roman circular *clipeus* cavalry shields on their backs, but otherwise would have been at home in the steppes in their flannel riding gear and conical hats.

Marcia responded in *han-yu* as well, hugging her, hugging Galosga, and greeting the children.

Gaius returned. "I see you made it, Hina."

Hina switched to Latin, to Marcia's obvious surprise. "I would not miss my sister."

The blare of a trumpet announced the arrival of the *Princeps,* and the crowd inside the tent fell silent. Dressed in his cream-colored uniform and purple cape, Trajan stepped forward onto the dais at the back of the tent with an aide. Trajan announced, "Twelve years ago, I had the honor to welcome back Senator Aulus Aemilius Galba, *Legatus* Gaius Aetius Lucullus, *Praefectus* Antonius Aristides and his wife Marcia to Rome from their trip around the world to the land of the Hanaeans. They were hailed before the Senate as 'the new Argonauts'. There were many others who made their return possible, but did not return with them to Rome. But the gods have seen fit to reunite all of these travelers, setting them in motion on another epic journey. The gods guided their footsteps to rejoin the veterans of their first odyssey here at Dura Europos. And here they are."

An aide read out their names, and Aulus and Livia, Antonius and Marcia, Marcus and Mei, Nathaniel, and Hina, Galosga and their children, took their place beside Trajan.

"These people did not start out together, did not plan to meet here, they did not know their companions were here. Each set out for their own reasons, some by choice, some by foul play, some because the gods destroyed their fellow countrymen, leaving them nowhere to go except this god-chosen route. The hands of the gods clearly shaped their journeys to bring them here, to this momentous moment in the history of Rome, when we finally vanquish the enemy who has threatened Europe since the time when Rome was nothing but mud huts. This is a sign of the gods' approval of what we do today, and these are the unwitting messengers of the gods!"

The tent erupted into loud cheers, continuing until the *Princeps* waved them into silence. "Enough, enough! Let us celebrate the arrival of these auspicious wanderers, and the approval the gods have shown for our mission." He led them off the dais to the angular purple *triclinia* dining couches in front of the dais. The servants began lighting lamps, as darkness was quickly settling in.

"Thank you for the good words, Your Excellency," said Livia.

"Thank you for your courage, both of you. We have been following your plight closely, though we were unable to do much to help. How did you manage to escape?"

"We did not escape, Your Excellency. Mithridates' secretary Kophasates got us out of the palace. Mithridates was done with us, and was going to sell us off to a brothel to be Parthian whores. He got us out of the palace, to a friend in town, who put us on the road," said Livia.

Marcus interrupted. "Kophasates was apparently the agent we called Taurus. He took great risk to do that, and his last message that arrived with Livia and Marcia said we would not be hearing from him again. We presume he is dead."

"He was a Roman agent? In the palace?" asked Marcia.

"Yes, and one of the most valuable ones we had. His information shall be missed, I fear. It was through him we knew you were there, and were being treated as well as could be expected."

Trajan turned toward Hina and Galosga. "I understand you two have taken over the Ninth Batavian and taught them some new rules for cavalry fighting."

"We have taught them some things my people have used on the steppes for ages, Your Excellency. Their mounted archery is getting to be quite good. I had good help from my clansman Hadyu, but he was out on patrol today and could not be here."

"You are molding the Ninth into something like the Parthian horse-archers, which have been our bane every time we fight them. Light, agile, able to make lightning attacks, then retreat out of range, regroup and attack again. It will be interesting to put your horsemen up against theirs. I suspect yours will do quite well."

"If we ever get a chance to see a Parthian army of any sort, Your Excellency," said Gaius. "I am concerned about this string of easy, bloodless victories we have had, like we are being drawn further and further into a trap."

"As am I, Gaius. Dura Europos ought to have been able to withstand a siege indefinitely, as long as they had food. It should not have fallen so quickly, without a fight. We will go no further this year, and I will attend to organizing our new province of Mesopotamia. This talk of war reminds me, Marcus, you said something about an Hanaean philosopher-general this afternoon. Can you tell me more?"

"Yes, sir. His Hanaean name was Sun-Tzu, and he wrote a book on war several centuries ago. It's Chinese warfare, different from how we fight, and it is old, but Arrian thinks it makes a lot of sense. I brought it with me, but it is in Hanaean. If you like, I could translate it for you."

"That would be most useful, Marcus. I would like to see what he has to say. Please do so."

And so, the evening went on, pleasantries with the most powerful man in Europe, talking about their adventures in getting to this most unlikely rendezvous at Dura Europos.

Later that month, in Aquileia, Desdemona accepted the official letter from the prefect Brutus Agrippa with trembling hands. With an official imperial seal, it could not be good news. She broke the seal and unrolled the fine Augustan papyrus to find two letters, one short, one long.

The short one simply certified this to be official correspondence, signed by the *Princeps* himself.

The second was in Marcia's careful hand. Desdemona heart beat fast, her eyes tearing up so much she could not read for a moment. Then, blinking the tears away, she read.

My Dearest Desdemona,

I pray that this letter finds you, our children and all our servants, safe and good health. I am well, reunited with Antonius with his legion in Mesopotamia, and Livia with Aulus. The Princeps is traveling with the legion and most kindly offered me his seal to deliver this message to you by the most expeditious means possible.

As you may guess, Livia and I underwent many adventures getting here, too many to relate now. Suffice it to say, though we were often terrified, nothing bad happened to us.

For the time, we will remain with the legion and our husbands, for it will be difficult for two women to travel alone such a vast distance, as we can well attest. I miss Aena, Colloscius and little Androcles very much. Please hug them for me, and tell them I will be home with them as soon as I can safely make the trip.

Your letter of manumission will arrive shortly, in recognition of your faithfulness and service. With all my love and gratitude,

Marcia Lucia Aristida

CHAPTER 97:

GARRISON UNDONE

Outside Nisibis, September 115AD

Secundus Lucullus felt a bit of pride that his father and commander had entrusted him to garrison Nisibis, especially after the tumultuous events of the summer had left ten soldiers dead, brutally murdered in two carefully orchestrated ambushes. This was his first independent duty, commanding the Fifth Cohort far out of reach of any immediate support, with the rest of the legion now sequestered far south at Dura Europos along with the *III Cyr*. Anything that came up, he would have to deal with it. It both intimidated him and emboldened him.

Early on, he had decided to treat Samuel as though he were *primus pilus*, the 'first lance', which in a sense befitted him, as the senior centurion of the cohort now. And as such, Secundus carefully sought his advice on all decisions, and he introduced along the way a bit of informality to their relationship. Like the evening meals in his tent together. The centurion had been wary of the invitation following the evening reports at first, but it had since become a tradition. Secundus had always prepared his meals himself, not wanting to burden a soldier with the task of waiting on him, something he had learned from his father. But this had evolved into the two alternating this task. And today was Samuel's turn. He had brought a pot of prepared stew, lamb, beans and vegetables, and set it on the hook over the fire.

The two sat around the desk, Samuel giving Secundus his daily reports, while the stew bubbled on the fire, scenting the air.

"The big news is the engineers left to go back to the Twelfth. The boats are finished, prefabricated, and laid out in wagons ready to go south. About a hundred fifty-oared pentecosters, and a trireme for the *Princeps*. Other than that, just six men sick today, nothing serious. The men need to pay more attention to where they site their latrines, and I sent all the centurions out to check on this. Our supplies are holding out well. Mayor Isdris is keeping us well-supplied with grain and livestock, and there have been no incidents in the city since last month. I have given permission for the men to go into the city to purchase items from the markets, but they must go armed, and in squads of eight. It looks like it has quieted down. Passwords are out for the night, it's 'Bacchus' if you want to go wandering about tonight, sir."

"'Bacchus', got it. That's a good one. But not a lot of revelry tonight. I have a letter from the *legatus,* he says we can expect to winter over here, so we need to check on what the weather will be like, and make sure that if we need more winter gear, that we requisition it from the legion. Now let's see how your stew is doing, Samuel."

It was indeed ready and the two sat about the table, sharing small talk with their dinner. After an hour, as the sun was about to set, trumpets blew the call for watch change.

"I need to get back, to take reports from my off-going watches," said Samuel, rising. "You'll excuse me, sir?"

"Excused. And thank you for the delicious stew. My turn tomorrow night," answered Secundus.

Secundus sat up, considering the tasks for tomorrow, which were not many, and then decided to retire early, for a quiet night.

At midnight, the trumpets called out another watch change, but Secundus did not awaken to the familiar night sound. However, a short time later, the trumpets blared the staccato call to action, alerting the camp they were under attack. This was followed by the shouts of men running to their positions. Secundus awoke at once, donned his battle gear, and set out at a run, sword drawn, to see what the disturbance was. Flaming arrows arced over the dirt ramparts in high trajectories, and several tents close to the walls were ablaze.

He found Samuel by the rampart over the main gate to the rectangular camp. "What have we got here?" Secundus asked, surprised at the calmness in his voice.

"Attack in progress, sir, a big one, all four sides."

Secundus peered into the midnight blackness. Firepots flickered surrounding the camp every hundred feet or so, for lighting the incendiaries to be launched against them. Other than those low flames, the enemy used no torches or fires, no indication of how many men were out there. His own soldiers had lit torches along the rampart, but they did not penetrate the inky blackness to reveal the enemy. As Secundus watched, a well-aimed arrow in a very flat trajectory felled a soldier standing near one of the torches.

"Samuel, have them douse those torches. And get some men to put out those burning tents. Now! They are highlighting our men, making them targets."

Samuel nodded and sent runners out along the wall to spread the word. One by one, the torches winked out, leaving the two adversaries straining to see the other in blackness. For a time, the arrows abated, with only the unaimed incendiaries continuing to arc into the camp, hoping for a lucky hit.

"Do we have artillery up here yet?" asked Secundus.

"Working on it. Hard to set up in the dark. Everyone will see better as their eyes adjust. Any idea who they are?"

"Organized, and a lot of them. Somebody who doesn't like us much."

The attack settled into a stalemate for the rest of the night. The camp's rampart was surrounded by a palisaded circumvallation, a ditch, filled with caltrops, spikes and thorny briars, aimed at making an approach to the wall difficult. And the steep outer perimeter wall of the ditch made retreat difficult. The enemy knew not to approach this in the dark.

As the sun came up, Secundus could survey the foe. No uniforms, flags, or any uniform armor, just assorted shields, some with various breastplates, others just wearing robes or trousers. But he estimated that there were about five hundred facing them, with that many more facing each of the other walls. They looked like a mob, but mob or not, it outnumbered them four to one.

"I thought you said this would be a quiet day, Samuel," said Secundus with a smile that concealed his deep concern that this situation was very bad.

"So I did, sir, so I did ," said Samuel, surveying the mass. "They don't look too well-trained, though. Just lots of them."

Just then, someone stepped forward from the mass under a white flag. Some archers bent their bows, targeting him, but Secundus waved them down. "Stand easy. Let's hear what he has to say."

The man, who appeared to be in his forties, came to within a few paces the circumvallation, a dozen paces from the rampart. Secundus stood up, hands on his hips, his red cape lifting in the morning breeze. "Speak your piece."

"Gaius Aetius Secundus Lucullus, son of Gaius Aetius Lucullus! You are in a dire situation. Surrender now. There is no dishonor in surrendering against overwhelming odds. I guarantee the safety of you and your men, back to Cappadocia from whence you came."

"You know a lot about me. What is your name?"

"My name is Sanatruces. Can I have your answer, Secundus? The safety of your men, or certain annihilation?"

Secundus took a *pilum* from a nearby soldier and launched it to land a few feet from Sanatruces, quivering in the ground. "That is my answer, Sanatruces. Nothing is certain. Now get back to your rabble, or I will put the next one through your chest."

The men on the ramparts cheered boisterously. Sanatruces turned on his heel without another word, and headed back to his men. As he got back to the line, a rain of arrows began, and the soldiers, Secundus and Samuel also, squatted under the shelter of their shields over their heads.

"Good show, sir, but what next?" asked Samuel.

"Let's do what they least expect, Samuel. Let's attack. They're not soldiers, they'll scatter like sheep. Get the word out, centuries one and two out this gate, three to north gate, four to the south gate, and five and six to the west gate. Keep some archers back on the walls for cover. When you have them ready and in place, have the *cornicen* blow the ready signal, and mine will blow attack. Charge and cut them down."

Samuel nodded and hurried off. After about a half hour, the soldiers had all disappeared from the wall, and were mustered by their assigned gates when the trumpet blew the wavering ready call. Secundus signaled his *cornicen* to blow the staccato attack call. All four gates flew open and the centuries charged out at the run, Secundus at the head of century one, under covering arrow fire from archers on the wall.

The attack did take the enemy by surprise, but despite their disheveled appearance, they were not an undisciplined mob. What appeared to be soldiers in the back row prevented a rout, stiffening the gaggle into supporting ranks to take the charge head on. It became a slugfest, the Roman having a small advantage with their uniform rectangular shields against the enemy's mismatched, motley collection. However, the advantage slowly shifted to the four-to-one odds. Bodies piled up, more in the motley rags of the foe, but Romans were going down also. Secundus reluctantly signaled recall, the centuries echoed the command, and the centuries began a fighting retreat back to the gates.

Back inside, Secundus noticed that he was covered in blood, though since nothing hurt, it must belong the others, those faces contorted in pain, rage and fear that he had cut down, trying to hack his way to Sanatruces. The first men he had ever killed, how many? Secundus made a tour of the men with Samuel, encouraging the wounded as they were bandaged. The men congratulated Secundus on his daring charge, but the young tribune did not feel the elation.

Samuel recognized the man's feeling. "You did good, sir," he said.

"This was my first real combat, and I called it all wrong. There were real soldiers out there, dressed in rags. I saw what they wanted me to see, and now dozens of my men are dead. Men we can't spare."

"You called it right, and if things had gone just a bit better in the first few minutes, we might be the ones celebrating now. You took them completely off guard."

"But I was wrong."

"It's not wrong when you walk off the field leaving more enemy dead behind than your own. Like you said, it was your first real combat, and you done good. And you called it right again, when you signaled recall. Don't second-guess yourself, you have a lot more tough choices ahead."

"All right. What do you recommend we do next?"

"Hunker down. I don't think they'll try to take the camp. But we have to think about food, and especially about water. We only have what's inside the walls, a few days' at most. We need to start rationing now."

"Do it."

"Yes, sir." Samuel turned to leave, then looked over his shoulder. "Like I said, you done good. Damned good. Like your father."

Secundus managed a smile.

Samuel studied the besiegers' layout throughout the day. Their forces clustered about the four gates, leaving huge gaps between their forces at the four corners of the camp, and there seemed to be only a few horses scattered about their ranks, transportation or pack animals, not pursuit cavalry. A plan began to form in his mind, a way to get word of their plight to Dura Europos. He consulted with Titus Plotius, one of the best riders in the Cohort. They developed a plan, then went to see Secundus.

"We think we can get a message to Dura Europos, sir."

"Let's hear it."

"This is Titus Plotius. Likes to jump obstacles with his horse, always wanted to be in the cavalry. It's going to be a moonless night tonight. We'll darken the camp, like we did last night, and start a distraction on the west wall. Titus here will go out the south gate, then head southeast through the gap in their forces. He'll be long gone before they saddle up something to chase after him in the dark."

"And my horse is fast, sir."

"You realize that if you're captured, they will probably torture you to death," said Secundus, not as a question.

"They won't capture me. The centurion and me, we looked over their camp. They didn't bring much of anything by way of horses. Most look like mules."

"It's two hundred miles to Dura Europos."

"About four days, sir, Bella is good for it, she is a strong lady."

"All right, I'll compose a message for you to take. Samuel, I'll give it to you after the afternoon reports."

That evening, Secundus gave Samuel the wax tablet with the message, but without much encouragement. "Not much help, I am afraid. Four days to get there, then at least a week to move forces up here. We haven't food or water to hold out for two weeks. At least they will know we tried, and that their rear is exposed."

"He'll get through, and we will find a way to break the siege."

"How?"

"I am working on it."

CHAPTER 98:

BETRAYAL

Outside Nisibis, September 115AD

Around midnight, Titus Plotius made his run, counting on most of the besiegers to be asleep. The soldiers opened the gates as quietly as possible, Titus slipped out and made his way through the southeastern gap in the lines.

Secundus and Samuel watched from the wall. There was no challenge, no outcry, until clear of the lines, Titus spurred his horse into a gallop, the tintinnabulation of his horseshoes ringing like bells off the rocky cobbles clearly audible to the fort, as well as to the sentries below. There were shouts, confusion, a few torches flared ineffectively in the darkness, but the hoofbeats continued in the night and until no longer audible.

"Looks like he got through."

"Looks like he did, sir. They don't look like they are going to try to follow him. Let's call it a night, daylight will be here soon enough."

The next day, Samuel continued trying to figure a way to break the siege, but the solution evaded him. Another charge would lack the surprise of yesterday, and they would just lose men. They could all attack just one of the four groups, in even odds, but then they would be flanked by the other three. A night attack was out of the question, as in the darkness and chaos, they would kill as many of their own as that of the enemy.

Staying where they were was the best option for now, though that meant just a handful of beans for breakfast and dinner after the meat ran out. Fortunately, they had just purchased several dozen cattle carcasses and vegetables from the market, so that would last a while, two weeks or so.

Water was a bigger concern. They had been getting their water from the Mygdonius River daily, flowing south out of the city, but they were now cut off from that. They could see the river in the distance, just a half mile away, but they couldn't drink from it. Samuel had inventoried the water, finding they had three hundred amphorae, about two gallons of water per man, a week's worth at most. Not enough.

The cohort had its complement of ten *ballistae* torsion crossbow artillery, now distributed defensively on the walls. They could fire on the camp, and the weapons were accurate enough to kill or disable quite a few of the men below, but they would run out of the three-foot bolts before they ran out of targets. Samuel wanted to reserve them for the assault, which he felt was coming sooner than he wanted. He needed pitch, which he did not have, and boiling water, which he needed for drinking, to help repel the assault.

He had few options to present to Secundus at the evening briefing, and they decided to conserve resources, hoping for the rescue which they knew would come too late. They moved tents back from the wall, to make them harder to hit with incendiaries, and waited.

In the end, it was the besiegers who decided to risk the night attack, slipping up to the ditch in the dark with bridging ladders, then hurling grappling hooks over the wall and scaling it by rope. By the time the Fifth rose to the defense, a large number of the attackers were over the wall, engaging the night watch, while others dropped down to attack the gate guards and open up the fort. Torches were lit, tents were set ablaze, and the interior of the camp was a mass of confused defenders struggling against a barely-seen enemy in the flickering firelight. Despite Secundus' efforts to rally the defense, he saw his men slowly being hewn down by the black-clad night raiders. He leapt into the fight, Samuel at his side, killing several, until a hammer blow to the head put him down, and hands seized Samuel from behind. The first gray light of dawn was tinging the eastern sky.

"Bring him here," said Sanatruces, gesturing toward Samuel. "I want that one alive. Kill the rest." His men brought Samuel to him, then went about from body to body, dispatching the wounded.

"Wait," said Samuel. "Whatever you want from me, you spare my tribune there, or you can just kill me now." He was relieved to see Secundus struggle to his feet, his head streaming blood.

"Gaius Aetius Secundus Lucullus, son of Gaius Aetius Lucullus, your commander. A fair enough trade. Manasseh wants to renew his old offer to you."

Secundus stumbled up to Samuel's side. "Steady. Sir, I need to get you back to your father, so he knows about this treachery," Samuel hissed, hoping he would not be overheard. "Whatever happens, ask him to remember the son of Ibrahim. Got that?"

"The son of Ibrahim. Yes."

Manasseh spoke in Aramaic. "Shmuel, this is your chance to redeem yourself, and take your rightful place as the commander of the Jewish army of liberation. You will lead them against the oppressors, like Joshua and David before you. If you refuse, you both die slowly, you will be last. You will watch your Roman friend scream his life away, before we turn to you."

"First, you will bandage my friend's head, before I answer your question. He is bleeding badly. Otherwise, the answer is no, and you can kill us in whatever order suits you. Your Jewish army can remain leaderless."

Manasseh gave the command, and two of the night raiders came up to tend Secundus' injury.

"And now?" asked Manasseh, an impatient edge to his voice.

"I will answer your question when I see him on his way back to the legion tomorrow."

He took a seat on the ground, and Secundus joined him, the bandage about his head already turning dark with blood in the firelight.

Samuel struggled with his thoughts. *Damn! I would just as soon they kill us now. All my cohort, dead. Some I have been friends with my entire time in the army, ten years, the Dacian wars. I failed them.*

"What is going on?" asked Secundus. "What were you and he talking about?"

"I guess I'm bluffing, but I don't think I have any stakes to play. If I don't, then we both cross the Styx with all our comrades. If I do, you ride out of here in the morning. How is your head?"

As if to answer, Secundus turned aside to retch. When he was finished, he held his head in his hands, not speaking.

I hope he is able to ride out in the morning.

Manasseh and Sanatruces walked off, conferring. Two soldiers came up to guard Samuel and Secundus, tying their hands behind their backs. *I guess we die after sunrise.* Samuel dozed fitfully in the seated position, but each time his head flopped forward in sleep, he snapped awake. With the rope cutting off circulation, his hands lost all feeling. He eventually did fall asleep, and awoke, wishing the previous night had just been a nightmare. The sun was high, well after sunrise.

It had not been just a bad dream. The bodies were still strewn about the camp, the black-clad raiders picking them over for souvenirs, rings, swords, whatever. Samuel felt sick at the sight.

Secundus still slept beside him.

Sanatruces came up with Manasseh, a soldier leading a horse.

"Wake your companion up, then give us your answer. If you agree, then Secundus can ride out of here, if he can. If he can't, you are still bound by your word." Sanatruces was speaking Latin, and Secundus roused sleepily at his words. A soldier released his ropes.

"Remember what I said, Secundus, 'son of Ibrahim.' Remember that."

Secundus rose unsteadily, and the soldier helped him onto a brown mare. He glared blearily about the camp, and slowly trotted off.

The Parthians and Jews had sent Secundus on his way with nothing but a horse, a sack of water, a loaf of bread, and a serious head injury. His head throbbed, his vision blurred, concentrating on keeping his saddle, hoping the horse would stick to the road. At times he halfway passed out. When he was awake, he was aware only of a sense of betrayal by the centurion he had learned to trust so well. *Some deal with Manasseh. I have seen him about the camp with Samuel. Bastard handed us over to them. What did he say, 'son of Ibrahim'? That would be Ibrahim, Father told me about him, but never mentioned a son. Men! I lost all my men! I have shamed my father.*

Late in the afternoon, he could ride no further. He stopped by a copse of trees and bushes by the river, tethered the horse, and went to fitful sleep in the horse blanket.

The next morning, the headache had subsided. He felt refreshed, ready to take a look about to see where he was going. He was pretty sure this was the road the legion had departed on, heading for Dura Europos. The sun indicated it led south, and there weren't many roads in this area. The road had been following the Mygdanius River when he left Nisibis, and it was either the same river, or had joined another. No matter. He stripped off what was left of his armor, the leather cuirass, buckler with empty scabbard, and shoved it deep into the bushes. He would ride in just his tunic, no need to look more conspicuous than necessary.

The activity reminded him that he had not eaten the bread they had given him. He took a few bites, washed it down with water, and refilled the leather sack from the cool, bubbling river. He washed his face and head, surprised at the amount of caked blood.

He then mounted up, but the exertion of getting into the saddle reminded him that he still had a severe head injury. The drums in his head began to pound again.

CHAPTER 99:

RESCUE TOO LATE

Leg XII Ful, **October 115AD**

The soldiers helped the exhausted horseman from his mount, and hurried him into the commander's *praetorium* tent, while others tended to the exhausted, hard-ridden animal. They interrupted Gaius Lucullus, in session with Aulus, Antonius and Paulus Herrerius, his *primus pilus*. "Urgent message from the Fifth Cohort, sir. They are under heavy attack."

"Please, stand easy. The report"

"Sir, I am Titus Plotius. Me and my horse, we rode harder than we ever have to get here as soon as possible." He fished the wax tablet from under his tunic. "Report from Tribune Lucullus, sir."

"My son, is he all right?" asked Gaius, accepting the report.

Titus had, as many had, noticed that their tribune and the commander had the same last name, but he had never suspected that the relationship was that close. "He was when I left, sir."

Gaius studied the tablet. "Antonius, get Arrian in here at once, then send for Longinus Clarus and the First Cohort's tribune. We're going to need cavalry."

"Right away, sir. What's up?"

"The Fifth is under heavy attack, besieged, surrounded and outnumbered four to one. And the leader identifies himself as Sanatruces."

"Sanatruces?"

"None other. Nephew to King Osroës, son of our old friend Mithridates."

Antonius nodded, needing nothing more.

Gaius turned back to Titus. "Casualties?"

"Tribune Secundus ordered an attack the day before I left. The group looked like a ragamuffin mob, no uniforms or battle gear, and it went well for a few minutes, but there were soldiers in the group stiffening the resistance. We lost a bunch of men, I don't know how many, but from where I was, they lost more. We pulled back into the camp. That was when the tribune and Centurion Elisarius sent me out with the message."

"How did you get out, surrounded like that?"

"Lucullus ... beggin' your pardon, sir, Tribune Lucullus ... he ordered the camp be kept dark, so they didn't have something to shoot at, and they didn't see us open the gate. I rode out between their lines, real slow and quiet, and was mostly out before they ever raised the alarm. I don't think they ever tried to chase me."

"Good move. When did you leave?"

"Three days ago, last midnight."

"By Jupiter, you covered more than seventy miles a day!"

"Me and Bella, my horse, we rode hard."

"Go get some rest. Is someone tending to Bella?"

"Yes, but I'll check on her myself, sir. Then I'll rest."

"Dismissed, And good job, Titus."

Titus left, and as he left, Antonius returned with Arrian. Gaius turned his attention to his intelligence officer. "We have an interesting development. Sanatruces is leading an attack on the Fifth up at Nisibis."

"Sanatruces? This could be the start of serious fighting."

"I think so, too. The soldiers tried to pass themselves off as civilians, but when attacked they stiffened like professionals." Gaius turned to Aulus. "Tell the *Princeps* that I am redeploying the Twelfth back to Nisibis. My intention is to relieve my Fifth Cohort, then pacify Nisibis once and for all. Warn him that this may mark the beginning of serious Parthian resistance. I would go myself, but if we are going to aid the Fifth, some of our elements have to be leaving this afternoon."

"On my way, Gaius."

Marcia had enjoyed being back with Hina, riding with the Ninth. It seemed that the decade between the beginning of their sisterhood and now had never existed. Hina came up with a horse, a bow, a *clipeus* shield and a *spatha* sword. The first afternoon, she was riding drills with the Ninth, when the *decurion* Longinus Clarus challenged her presence in the training field. Hina introduced Marcia as her sister: the big Amazon of a woman with long red hair, a barbarian plains rider, with a short, petite but wiry Hanaean woman who inexplicably spoke better Latin than he did. And he noted that she, too, rode with those same peculiar attachments, footrests below the saddle, as Hina did.

He decided to see what she could do. Hina was twice the rider as any of his men, and if her unlikely sister was half as good, she would be better than most of his men. She proved herself to be much better than that. And she was doing it for the sheer fun of it.

So, several days after Marcia had joined the group, a runner called Clarus away to the commander's tent.

"*Decurion* Clarus, sir, you requested my presence?" he said, saluting.

"I did. Your men are ready to ride?" asked Gaius.

"They are, sir."

"We are going back to Nisibis, at a hard pace, short notice. I want to be there in three to four days. Our Fifth Cohort is under siege, and we need to arrive quickly to relieve them. I would like to leave this afternoon, before sundown. We have a quarter moon, and I would like to stay on the move until moonset. I want you reconnoitering out front of the First Cohort. The rest of the legion will decamp at daybreak."

Longinus thought a moment. "It's noon. I need a few hours for my men to break camp, get their gear together. We can ride well before sunset."

"Make it so. I won't keep you from your tasks, decurion, Dismissed."

Marcia got the word for the imminent deployment, along with Hina and her group. She took little Adhela back to the legion to stay with Livia, then went back to Antonius' tent to gather a few things. Antonius was waiting.

"You are riding with the Ninth?" he asked.

His suddenly precise Latin told her he was genuinely concerned, as her husband, not as a tough soldier. "I am. I have been training for several days now, and it seems our *decurion* is getting used to women with swords."

"I figured you would be. Remember, *domina*, you may be riding into a fireball. Don't take any chances you don't have to. You've ridden against bandits, many years ago, but you may be going up against first-class soldiers now. It'll be different. Very different."

She hoisted her pack on her shoulders, and reached up to give him a peck on the cheek. "I love you, Antonius, and I intend to get back to being wife and mother again. I'll be careful"

The Ninth Batavians headed out of camp, with plenty of sunlight left. Marcia rode with Hina and Galosga, Marasa and Andanyu riding flank with Hadyu. "We're going to rescue the Fifth Cohort. Gaius' son is their tribune and Samuel their centurion. They've been under siege for a while, I hope we are in time," she informed them.

Hina's eyes were those of a predatory cat, she sniffed through her nose as though trying to scent out trouble. She was in her element, getting ready to ride into battle. "We will be in time," she said confidently. "Tengri takes care of His own, and we are His."

Galosga, too, seem to look forward to the upcoming action, his teeth bared.

CHAPTER 100:

JUST IN TIME

Leg XII Ful, **October 115AD**

Hina was riding point with Marasa and Andanyu, sweeping back and forth either side of the road looking for signs of trouble. Marasa was the first to spot the brown horse, trotting slowly with a rider wobbling listlessly in the saddle, on the road about a half-mile ahead. "Mother, I am off," she yelled over her shoulder as she spurred her gray pony into a gallop, shield, bow and *spatha* bouncing on her back.

She quickly closed the distance, and checked out the unresponsive rider. She then gave the piercing scream of an eagle, the signal for assistance. Hina and Andanyu quickly pulled up beside her, reigning in their horses, snorting and tossing their heads, to a halt beside Marasa on her mount.

The man's head was bandaged with a dirty blood-soaked rag. His eyes lolled, not appearing to see anything, though he muttered incoherently. "Mother, this one seems Roman, I think he is speaking Latin, but I can't understand him."

"Dismount. Let's get him down. He looks very thirsty." The three levered the limp man off his horse, his inert weight making it awkward. They laid the man on the ground and Hina gave him a drink from her water sack. He coughed and sputtered, water trickling down his unshaven chin, but then indicated he wanted more. Again, he coughed and sputtered and asked for more, but Hina put the sack away. His eyes seemed to be coming into focus.

"Enough for now. You'll get sick if you drink too much now. Do you understand me?" she asked in Latin.

He nodded. He was Roman, or at least spoke Latin.

"What is your name?" He seemed vaguely familiar, but with a bandage covering half his head, she couldn't recognize him either.

"Secundus ... Secundus Lucullus, Fifth Cohort," he croaked.

Secundus! Gaius' son! "What happened to you?"

"Cohort ... massacred. Betrayed. I am ... only one left. I must tell you ... Ibrahim's son."

She gave him a little more water, allowing him only a sip.

"We are going to put you over your horse and tie you in place so you don't fall. We will get you taken care of."

He nodded.

"Marasa, his arms, Andanyu, his feet. Now lift." Together they hoisted Secundus across the saddle on his belly. Andanyu cut a length of rope with his dagger, securing the man in place with a few expertly-fashioned knots.

Hina gently lifted his head. "Are you comfortable?"

He shook his head affirmatively.

"It's only a few miles. We will go gently."

Hina took the inert Secundus back to the main body of the Ninth, leaving the rest to continue as point. She delivered him to Longinus. "He is Secundus Lucullus, the Fifth's Tribune," she said.

Longinus called for the *medici*, who dismounted and came at the run with their kits. "Let's leave them to their work. He looks half-dead. We need to be alert. *Cornicen,* blow the signal for 'enemy about'. Hina, you get back to the point."

In about an hour, with clean fresh bandages and opiated against the pain, the *medici* loaded Secundus into a cart, and headed him off to the First Cohort. Marcia rode with them.

On their arrival, soldiers sent for the commander, who hurried to his unconscious son with Antonius. "He will be out for about a day. It's a bad head injury, he is lucky to be alive," the *medici* reported. "We may have to send him on to the main body behind us. He's near the limit that we can deal with our level."

Gaius studied his son intently, his jaw muscles working. This is what he had secretly dreaded since finding his son under his command. "Did he give any report?"

"He said the Fifth was wiped out, except for him … and the traitor Samuel," Marcia said.

"Samuel? He betrayed them?"

"That was all he said, Gaius. I know it seems hard to believe, but that was what he said."

"Longinus Clarus put the Ninth at full readiness. He did not know where the enemy might have been. They may have followed, using him as bait."

"Good call, I will do the same for the legion."

Marcia and Antonius retired to his tent. Talk about Samuel, and what role he might have played in the massacre dominated the conversation.

"It just doesn't sound like the Shmuel we knew," she said.

"With a head injury, his mind might be playing tricks on him," said Antonius.

"But if it is true, why? For what reason? Samuel had honor, status, respect. Why throw that away? And he said something else, 'son of Ibrahim.' That would be Yakov. But he isn't here."

"Yakov is in Petra, running an orphanage, like he wanted to do. Samuel had been in touch with him. Collected contributions from his men. Hmm ... he sent the money by way of a Jewish moneychanger, I forget his name, but I never liked the sight of the man. Maybe Samuel got sucked into something over his head, but something that would cause him to let five hundred of his men be slaughtered? I'd have to hear that from him."

Gaius visited his son the next evening in the sick tent. Secundus was lying on a cot, his head tightly wrapped in white linen.

The *medicus* was attending him when Gaius entered. "Sir!" he said, standing erect to salute him.

"At ease. He looks better than he did yesterday," said Gaius.

"Aye. A little food and water helped a lot. He took a bad bang to his head. We're going to keep him lying down for a few days, to let the bones heal, but he will be fine in about a week. I'll leave you two to chat." He turned and left the tent.

Secundus spoke before Gaius had a chance to say anything. "Commander, I failed you and I failed my men. They are all dead, and it is my fault. Do with me what you will."

"Son, you lost your first battle. You will lose more. Tell me what happened."

Secundus recounted their being surrounded, his sortie against a ragtag mob that turned out to be backed by soldiers led by Sanatruces, the fatal night attack, and the ensuing massacre. "We were betrayed. Samuel Elisarius and I were the only ones left, and he cut some sort of deal with Sanatruces and one of the leaders, someone he knew, in exchange for my life. It was all in Aramaic, I couldn't understand any of it. I knew the man, some sort of suttler who had been hanging around the cohort for some time, talking with Elisarius. He said one thing, about the son of Ibrahim. Ibrahim you told me about in your stories, but he is dead. And his son?"

"Yakov was his adopted son. He is living south of here, in Petra. Samuel was trying to tell us something, maybe that he would go there if he escaped."

"Good, because I would have him beaten to death by the legion he betrayed! But Petra ... he was collecting money from the men for some orphanage there."

"That would be Yakov's. He was setting up an orphanage there for street urchins the last I heard from him."

"So, *legatus,* do with me what you will. I allowed myself to be betrayed by a traitor, and now my men are dead."

"Call me father, please. There is no one here but you and I. I am going to put you back in command of the Fifth, as soon as I set it back up with the men I can cobble from the other centuries, and from the other legions. You may have only a few under strength centuries, but it will be a cohort."

"*Legatus,* you said you would treat me as any other tribune. Would you do this if I were not your son?"

"I would, because I am not sure you were betrayed. Samuel, from what you said, fought to the end, then cut a deal to save your life. I think the dice on this throw are still in play."

CHAPTER 101:

RELUCTANT LEADER

Nisibis, October 115AD

Samuel saw Secundus set on his way, though he had no part in it. It appeared that they were planning for him to die enroute, but they had kept their deal, sparing him ... for the moment. Manasseh led Samuel into Nisibis, to the Jewish quarter. Evacuated during the last crisis, it was back to normal, the markets thriving, people going about their business. The walls still bore black smoke stains, where they had been torched two months ago after the massacre of Pullus' squad, but the damage to the mudbrick buildings had been minor and quickly repaired.

Samuel followed Manasseh into the marketplace where a hundred sullen men stood. "Samuel, these are your men. Train them, turn them into the Army of the Lord."

Samuel thought they reminded him of himself, a decade past, part of a reluctant deck force on the *Europa* about to receive the ministrations of Antonius. Now it was his turn to establish himself as their leader. *Could I rise to the task? Should I?*

Samuel growled at the would-be soldiers. "All right. If you are the best that can be scraped up to go against Rome, they have nothing to fear. We are going to start with a run, to see what you are made of. Trot to the south gate, then all out until I tell you to turn around, then back to the city."

Some slipped off their robes, others did not. They stood around, waiting. "Let's go! Anyone who doesn't finish will not be a part of the Army of the Lord." He started out, not looking back to see if they were following, hoping they would not. But the sound of footsteps told him at least some had.

It was an easy trot to the gate, but once through the checkpoint, he increased the pace to the point where he expected some to drop out. He led them down the road by the Mygdanius River, past the burnt-out encampment of his cohort. He felt a wave of nausea at the buzzards plucking at his former comrades. They had not buried the dead, leaving them to the scavengers. The stench of death filled his nostrils and he resisted the temptation to vomit. Instead, he increased the pace to a killing one. After another mile, he looked back to see one man drop out to drink from the river. Falling back to the next man behind him, he hissed, "Take the lead and speed it up. I'll kick your ass if I catch back up to find you lagging it." He looped back to the man, now joined by another, drinking at the river. He came up behind them at full run, knocking the one about ten feet into the river. He pulled up the second by his collar, and hurled him into the water. "You want a damned drink? Drink all you want, then walk back. You're done!"

He caught back up, slightly pleased to find that his erstwhile *optio* had kept the pace up. He went another mile, then turned them around. It would be a good five miles, and about half had stayed with him, though a dozen stragglers spread out a hundred yards back, struggling. At the gates, he slowed to a jog back to the Jewish market, pulling up by the fountain.

"Now you lazy sods can get a drink of water." He waited until the last had drunk before he took a few sips.

"Now I bet everyone of you would like to kick my apostate ass. So, now's your chance. Anyone who can put me down can take the afternoon off." And one by one, they came up to try to take him down. Each wound up face down in the dirt. Some tried to take him two at time: they, too, wound up in the dirt.

By now, the sun was getting low. Samuel dismissed them to wherever it was they stayed, with orders to be here at first light. He would need a barracks for them, to give them unit identity. *No, wait. I am not creating soldiers to fight my comrades. I am biding time until I can get out of here. Tomorrow, next week, somehow, I am gone or I am dead, I am not going to be their leader.*

Manasseh came up, smiling with approval. "You worked them hard, Shmuel, that is good."

"Thank you,' he said off-handedly.

"You will do well. I am off to evening prayers. Will you join me?"

Samuel reluctantly followed to the Beth Shalom synagogue, not sure if he remembered any of the prayers from his childhood. As he entered in, there was a bucket drawn from the *mikvah* bath. Manasseh stooped to wash his hands, and Samuel followed.

Samuel did not speak Hebrew, and sat silently through a service he mostly did not understand, but vaguely remembered, until they reached the *Shema.* That one he remembered: *Sh'ma Yisrael Adonai Eloheinu Adonai Eḥad.* 'Hear, O Israel the Lord Our God is One." It sent a frisson of goosebumps over his body, reciting that prayer from his childhood.

After the service, Manasseh led him out, and left him on his own. *I guess I am supposed to find my own damned accommodations.*

A familiar voice behind him made him turn around to find Ruth. "You are back, Shmuel."

"I am, Mother, but it is not a happy time for me."

"Would you break bread with me? You seem alone. The Romans have left, but you are still here."

"As I said, it is not a happy time, but yes, I would be glad to join you." He followed her to her small apartment, near where he remembered it. Inside, it was still blackened from the torch, but the furniture showed no damage.

"Sit at my table. I will prepare us a light meal. My husband has been dead for several years, and my children have moved on, so I am alone here. You may sleep on the couch if you have no place to stay."

She ladled out some stew which had been warming on the fire, and broke some bread, setting it before him. He took a taste.

"Very good. Lamb stew."

"I saw you working with our boys today. Are you with us? Will you train them to repel the Romans now?"

"You don't understand, Mother. My cohort, five hundred men, all my friends, they were all slaughtered by Parthians soldiers who had mixed in a few Jews to make it look like an insurrection. The Romans will be back in overwhelming force in a few days, and there is nothing I could do, or would do, to try to repel them. They will destroy Nisibis and everyone in it. You have to get out, as do I. The Romans think I betrayed them."

"Where would you go?"

"I have a friend south of here. You must come with me. What happened here last summer will be like nothing compared with what the Romans will bring this time."

"I cannot, Shmuel. These are my people, and if they are to die here, I will die with them. But you go, if you must. If you can."

"Can you find me a wagon?"

"No! Manasseh's men are everywhere, watching everyone. They are watching you, too."

"Who is Manasseh? I knew him as a petty moneychanger. When did he become a power here?"

"Several months ago, the Parthian man came from the *Shahanshah*, promising to help us get the Promised Land back, to rebuild the Temple, to restore the glory of Israel. Manasseh saw money in it. Like you said, he is a moneychanger and a greedy lender. If people cannot pay their loans, he takes all they have. Now he has power, and controls everyone. The Parthians back him, and no one dares to go against him, not even Isdris. Manasseh started the trouble against the Romans."

"The Parthian man, he is the one who calls himself Sanatruces?"

"Yes, he is related to the king. Now, Shmuel, this old woman must go to bed. Make yourself comfortable on the couch," she said, handing him a blanket from a box in the corner.

"Good night, Mother. I will take care." He kissed her on the cheek.

If she stays, she may not live. When the Romans see their comrades rotting in the field, they will leave no one alive. Including me, the traitor.

Samuel tried to remember everything he knew about Nisibis. *One gate on each of the walls. Manasseh's men would be watching each, as well as the regular guards. What about at night? Closed and barred. The river? It ran through the city, but they must have dug underground tunnels for its entrance and exit.*

And how would I swim underwater, with weapons and enough gear to get to Petra?

I need to grow a beard. Do I have enough time to do that before Gaius comes storming up here?

Samuel missed all he had lost. *I could have chosen to die today, but then they would have killed Secundus. I at least got him out alive. But if he got back, then Gaius will consider me a traitor, even if the deal I made was to save his son's life.*

With many questions and no answers, Samuel fell into a fitful sleep. At dawn, he would again pretend to train his little mob.

CHAPTER 102:

A PLAN FORMS

Nisibis, October 115AD

It did not take long for Samuel to establish the respect of his erstwhile soldiers. And as they established the habit of obedience, a plan began to form in his mind. He might not have enough time to make it work, or he might have too much time. It depended on whether Titus Plotius or Secundus had made it back. Titus maybe, but he was a single Roman soldier trying to cover two hundred miles in potentially hostile country. Secundus? From the way he sat his horse, Samuel did not think he would have lasted the day. He was badly hurt, barely conscious. But if either made it back, the legion would send forces here, forces that would arrive in a week or so.

On the other hand, if neither made it, the legion would just set up its winter quarters at Dura Europos, blithely unaware that the enemy was gathering in its rear. There would be no opportunity for Samuel to execute his plan. In that case, he would somehow escape. Where to go? To the legion? He was, in their eyes, a deserter and a traitor. Unless he could convince the commander otherwise, he would receive a traitor's death, beaten to death by his own men. To Yakov in Petra? Then what? He would confirm himself as a deserter and traitor, now on Roman soil, and there would be nowhere he could go where he would be safe.

The soldiers backing the rebels were Parthians, led by someone named Sanatruces. They blended in with the civilians, and more were arriving every day. Sanatruces had executed King Mannu for surrendering, putting his head on a pike before his old palace and setting Manasseh up as the minor potentate over the city, sitting on his throne in the ostentatious palace.

Samuel made it a point to play up to Manasseh, because Manasseh's confidence and trust in him were critical. He went daily into the city offices. Mannaseh expected his visitors to bow, and Samuel reluctantly did so as he entered, trying to hide his bitter distaste for the man.

"Good to see thee again, Shmuel ben Eliazar. How are your soldiers doing?" said Manasseh.

"Very well. They are ready to take on duties, and I would like to set them to guarding one of the city gates. They need the responsibilities and the routine."

"Excellent. Sanatruces was observing you training them, and he was very impressed. I will be adding to your tiny legion as you develop it. Yes, take the main gate. Evening watch."

"At once, sir." *I hadn't expected it to be this easy. Does he really trust me, or is this a trap?* "If I may ask, sir, who is Sanatruces?"

"Sanatruces is the nephew of the King of Kings, Osroës. He has just left for Ctesiphon to give the King a personal report on all that goes on here, including your noble efforts. And your request is well-timed. Our agents report that the Romans are on the move north in full force. Remember where your loyalties lie while you are guarding that gate now, Shmuel. To them you are a traitor."

"I fight for the God of Israel now, Manasseh." *But I don't think my God is yours, you spawn of Satan.* He saluted, and left abruptly, discretely surveying the area to see if there were any bodyguards in hiding. He saw none.

The legion on the road north meant he had just a few days to put his plan in action.

Samuel collected his thoughts, on his way to give his men the news. *What is Manasseh thinking? The Twelfth will not relent in their siege this time, the river diversion is almost complete from the last siege, and when they find their unburied comrades outside the city, they will unleash hell, and not stop until everyone in the city is dead or sold off into slavery.*

The answer is, he is not thinking. He is a money changer with a lust for power and more money, not a strategist. This is Sanatruces' plan, and Nisibis is just bait, to make us disperse our legions ahead of next year's offensive. He doesn't care how long Nisibis holds out, as long as it keeps the Twelfth out of position.

Samuel sought out Joshua, who had become his *optio*, his second in command of sorts. Samuel had developed a grudging respect for the young man, strong and determined to become a good leader. He restrained those feelings, knowing that he might have to order him, and all his new little squad into certain death. *There's got a to be a way to keep at least a few alive. They're good kids.*

"We are picking up new duties. Evening guard at the main gate. Divide them up how you wish, we are on till the fourth hour of night. And be sharp, the legion is on its way back to teach you lads a lesson."

"Sir!" said Joshua, and hustled off to do the watch bill.

I have got to do something to save not only these boys, but as many of the townspeople as I can. Ruth, I have to save her. And as many more as I can, even if I am to be beaten to death as a traitor. My life doesn't matter now.

The next day, Samuel experimented with the palace security, and found there was none. He went into Manasseh's chamber, armed with his sword and dagger. No one checked, Manasseh did not notice. And again, there seemed to be no bodyguards around the novice king.

The legion arrived the next day. Samuel nearly cried at the familiar tempestuous noise of a legion's arrival, the blaring trumpets, shouted commands, the cadence of marching feet and the rumble of wagons. As he expected, they immediately saw the remains of the Fifth, now carrion for the buzzards. Samuel watched as men were dispatched to collect the dead and burn them on funeral pyres.

There was no call for the city to surrender and Samuel knew there would be none. After viewing the carnage, *Legatus* Lucullus would be offering no quarter. The city would be destroyed, its inhabitants slaughtered, in revenge for what had been done to the Fifth. Samuel had heard of such revenge attacks, but had never participated in one. Now he was to be the target of one. Tonight would be the time to execute his plan.

CHAPTER 103:

PLAN FOR REVENGE

Leg XII Ful, **October 115AD**

The bodies of the men who had been the Fifth Cohort enraged Gaius like nothing he had ever known. As described by his son, the slaughter had been gratuitous, wounded men butchered along with those who had surrendered. And the bodies, unburied, had been left to the kites and crows, rotting in the sun. Nisibis would not long survive the Fifth.

Antonius, accompanied by Marcia, came respectfully into the tent where Gaius was seated at his campaign desk, the tips of his fingers pressed firmly together by his chin. "One piece of good news, sir. The boats, they never noticed 'em. Still bundled up in the wagons, the way the engineers left 'em. If they'd have burned 'em, we would be starting all over again."

"It's like Secundus described, just wholesale slaughter. Not one person is to be left alive here. We are going to make an example that will not be forgotten."

"And the women and children?" asked Marcia.

"They will be part of the example. The people of Mesopotamia must know that if they slaughter Roman soldiers, they and their families will pay the price."

"You know the women and children had nothing to do with this."

"I know nothing of the sort, and Marcia, I am not going to discuss this with you. My decision is final."

Antonius put hand on her shoulder, indicating she should let this pass for now.

"How is the diversion for the river going?" asked Gaius.

"Mostly where we left it, three-quarters done. Take a few days to finish it, then we block the channel into the city and it's done," responded Antonius.

"Good. I want to start the bombardment tomorrow, incendiaries and sixty-pounders, no restrictions. What we don't level, I want burned out."

"How is Secundus?" asked Marcia.

"Getting better every day. He was up to doing a little walking today. The doctor says back to duty in a few days, but I think he is optimistic. Maybe a week. Antonius, have you reshuffled the men to reform the Fifth?"

"About one-third strength, two centuries. Actually less. You know they don't give up their best men ter go re-form a cohort, they get rid of the malingerers, ne'er-do-wells and malcontents. The Fifth is going ter need strong centurions ter whip them in line."

"I am working with Paulus Herrerius on that. As you said, hard to get them to give up their best." Turning to Marcia, he said, "Now, what brings you here?"

"Antonius, to be honest. And you heard what I came to say. Spare the women and children."

"I will consider what you said, Marcia. But now is not the time for mercy. I am sorry."

CHAPTER 104:

REVENGE TAKEN

Nisibis, October 115AD

It would have to be tonight. Samuel braced himself, considering that this very likely could be the last night of his life. Again, he went to Manasseh in the King's chambers, carrying a canvas sack, and entering without knocking or bowing.

Manasseh was seated at a small table, eating his dinner. "What is the meaning of this interruption, Shmuel? What the ..." He made a gurgling sound as Samuel thrust a dagger deep into Manasseh's ribcage, twisting, searching for heart and vital arteries to make a quick end of the man. Manasseh thrashed spasmodically, Samuel's left hand firmly over his mouth against any outcry, for what seemed far too long a time, then the man went limp. Samuel checked to ensure he was dead, then dragged him into a back room. He was pleased that there had been little blood, that much less to clean up in the king's chamber. And the back room turned out to be Manasseh's bed chamber, so much the better.

The next step was to cut off the man's head, and Samuel set about this grisly task with mechanical efficiency, first carefully opening the carotid arteries to bleed off the remaining blood, then slicing through the tough cartilage of the throat, and the muscle, gristle and bones of the neck. *Not unlike preparing an animal for sacrifice.* In a few minutes, the head came free, blood still dripping from the stump of the neck. Samuel stuffed it into the sack he had brought. He thoroughly washed his face and hands in the washbasin, then inspected himself. He had worn a dark robe, so any bloodstains would not be visible in the night. He closed the bedchamber door, wiped down the few bloodstains around the table, and replaced the dinner plates and their contents which had spilled onto the floor.

He hurried out of the palace and back to his boys at the gate. He summoned Joshua. "Lad, we have a mission from Manasseh. Everyone needs to do exactly as I say, this mission is vital. First, douse the torches and fires. I want you to open the gates, and I don't want the Romans seeing them open, so keep it dark. Half come with me to Roman lines, you and the other half remain behind to keep the gates open. If anyone challenges you, say it is on the orders of Manasseh. Got that?"

"Got it."

"Now get the boys ready, and on my orders, do it."

In a few minutes, the gates creaked open in darkness and the contingent of guards sallied forth into the night, led by Samuel, toward the dirt ramparts of the legion camp. They got within a few hundred feet of the camp guards before they were challenged. "Halt, who goes there? Say the password."

"I am Centurion Samuel Elisarius of the Fifth Cohort, and I have a message for Legate Lucullus from King Manasseh of Nisibis."

"Stand where you are."

In another few minutes, another voice called out in the dark. "I am Tribune Tiberius Petronius of the First Cohort. What are you doing still alive, centurion? I thought all of the Fifth were wiped out."

"They were, I and Tribune Lucullus were the only survivors. Is he well?"

"He is well. What is your message?"

"May we approach?"

"You may approach, sheath your weapons."

Samuel's boys knew no Latin, so the exchange was lost to them. "Sheath your weapons, boys, then follow me. Do not make any sudden moves, no matter what you see."

Samuel approached the tribune and sentries lit by torches in sconces by the gate. "Here is my message." He withdrew the gruesome contents of the sack. "The head of Manasseh, the would-be king of Nisibis and puppet of Parthia who was responsible for the massacre of my men. He died at my hand. And the gates of the city are open, let that be known, before someone discovers the ruse and closes them."

Samuel's shocked guard contingent attempted to draw their weapons, but the Roman sentries were on them at once, disarming them before their swords cleared the scabbards

"Spare these young men, please, they were not part of the massacre. Take me to the legate, please."

"Centurion, pass the word. Get the ready centuries out to seize the gates. Elisarius, come with me."

Gaius was aroused by the trumpets calling away the ready centuries. He had sent runners to find out what was going on, when Tiberius Petronius brought Samuel before him.

"Sir, this man purports to be Samuel Elisarius of the Fifth, with an interesting message."

"He is indeed Samuel, I know him well, Tiberius. Samuel, your message?"

Samuel wordlessly again withdrew the head of Manasseh from the sack. In the lamplight, the face was still twisted in the grimace of fear, pain and fury from the moment of his death, the eyes wide and staring sightlessly. "I present you the head of Manasseh, the cause of all our problems here, and the death of my men, dead at my hand. I will give you the Parthian soldiers that backed the rebels, and the rebel leaders who killed my men. Now you may do with me what you will, give me a traitor's death if you see me as such, but spare the townspeople and the women and children. They had nothing to do with this. This plot came from Ctesiphon, from the King's nephew Sanatruces, to lure you away, to disperse and isolate this legion, and cause you to alienate the people. Kill me if you wish, but do not fall into Sanatruces' trap."

"Sir, he opened the gates of the city. I dispatched the ready centuries to seize them and keep them open."

"Very well." Gaius turned to Paulus Herrerius and Antonius, who had just come to the commander's tent to find out what the signals were about. "Paulus, Samuel has left the Nisibis gates open. Sound the general alert and begin forming up the legion. As soon as the ready centuries have secured the gates, we are going to sortie *en masse* and take the city." He glanced at Samuel. "And do not, I repeat, do not, sack the city, despite what the men have seen in the field today. Make sure that order is understood by every tribune and every centurion before you sound the advance to march out."

"A night attack, sir?" asked Antonius

"A night attack."

"No traitor's death for you tonight, Samuel," said Gaius. "Go to the quartermaster and draw your battle gear. Then come back and tell me how you pulled this off."

CHAPTER 105:

A CITY RETAKEN

Nisibis, October 115AD

Joshua was certainly puzzled at the sudden and strange orders, but just a few days with Shmuel had taught him never to question an order. He could not see what happened to Shmuel and his party, just a few hundred yards away, but he seemed to have caused great deal of confusion in the Roman camp, brightly lit by torches along the rampart. Horns sounded, there was great commotion, a column of men streamed out of the camp, backlit by the torches and fires inside. They disappeared into the inky blackness, but he could hear the approach of many feet and heavy armor advancing at a run.

He hesitated. His orders were to keep the gates open, but what if Shmuel had failed? Should he close them?

He considered this too long, for the lead century of eighty men was less than fifty paces from the gate when he gave the order to close it. His men put their shoulders to the heavy doors, but it was still half-open when a volley of hurled lances slammed through the open space. One lance found one of the sentries, transfixing him, the rest, terrified, buried themselves in the dirt roadway or scampered off, followed by Joshua.

The century gained entry and formed a perimeter around the gate, while the other two ready centuries arrived at the run. Two hundred and fifty men now held that gate, guarding it inside and out, waiting to be joined by the remaining four thousand men. So far, the city had not responded except for some sleepy townspeople who peeked out their doors to see what the noise and shouting was about. Seeing Roman soldiers at the gate, they promptly closed their doors again. All knew what had happened to the Roman garrison, all knew what the Roman legion would now do in revenge.

After an hour, the trumpets blew again, and the gates of the Roman camp disgorged the rest of the rest of the legion, marching, not running. By now, the Parthian guards on the city ramparts were alert, and reinforcements had arrived. They began to fire volleys of flaming arrows at the advancing force, ineffective in the darkness. *Carroballistae* rolled up on wagons and quickly cleared the ramparts of defenders. Incendiary bolts lit fires that illuminated the dark for the artillery. The legion fanned out around the city. The First Cohort entered the open gate a century at a time, each century wheeling in the streets toward its assigned objective, one of the remaining barred gates, to open it and admit the remaining cohorts outside. Some of the rebels and soldiers had thrown together barricades in opposition, but they offered little resistance to the invaders.

By daybreak the entire legion was in the city. Gaius Lucullus entered with his headquarters staff, and headed for the King's palace, with Samuel, now in ill-fitting but functional battle dress, at his side.

He looked with disgust at the moldering head on a pike, flies buzzing around its open mouth. "Whose head is that, Samuel?"

"King Mannu, sir. Sanatruces had him put to death for surrendering to you without a fight, so Manasseh said."

"Have someone take it down, and replace it with Manasseh's. Lead me to the King's chamber."

"Scene of the crime, sir." Samuel smiled.

They entered the door, while centurions posted guards at the door. Samuel led to the way to the top floor, to the king's chambers. There they found some confusion, servants trying to remove Manasseh's body, and a few Parthian soldiers and rebel collaborators trying vainly to plan a defense. Manasseh's death had left them leaderless. The soldiers put everyone on their knees.

"Anyone you recognize, Samuel?" asked Gaius.

"These four are Parthians, those three are collaborators. The rest are just the king's servants."

"Tell the servants to continue disposing of Manasseh's body."

While Samuel gave the direction to the servants, the centurions bundled off the seven leaders.

"I am going to set up my headquarters in this building. In a few hours, I want to meet with the reliable leaders of this city, and sort out who was involved in the insurrection. Samuel, I want you with me."

"Yes, sir. And there is someone I want with me, a woman from the Jewish quarter. She can help me identify some of the rebels."

"Go get her."

CHAPTER 106:

INSURRECTION SPREADS

Petra, October 115AD

Aharon accepted Judah's embrace, though he was not sure that was the man's real name. He also accepted a heavy sack of coins that the man pressed into his hand.

"Sanatruces sends his regards in the form of coins. He regrets he cannot deliver this personally, but the day will come when you and he shall meet."

"You may send him my thanks. Does he have any instructions?"

"None other than the importance of what you are to do. We will drive the Romans out of Mesopotamia by insurrection, and then out of all of Syria, Judea, Egypt and Asia Minor. Yours is to be the first within their boundary."

"I am honored."

"Do not limit yourself to just our people. Enlist the Gentiles who also suffer under the Roman yoke. Smash the Roman idols, smash the temples to their god-emperors. And good luck."

Judah departed, and Aharon counted out the sack's generous contents. A talent of five hundred silver *denarii* weighing sixty pounds, a generous sum, worth twenty gold *aurei*. That would have been a more compact amount, but much more conspicuous to distribute. He separated out two dozen for his 'fee' and slipped them into his purse. The rest would buy a lot of support. Aharon considered his options.

The criminal underclass would be happy to riot and burn for a price, as long as they also got to loot, rape and pillage. But they would have to wait for the word, to do it all at once, and a few of these coins would buy their patience and forbearance.

His people could be more of a problem. The Jews had settled here, as had he, during the Jewish uprising a half-century past. The rabbis knew full well the fierce lash of Roman vengeance for rebellion and had no desire to taste it again. After the Romans had annexed Petra ten years past, the Jewish leaders had worked closely with the new governors to ensure them of their loyalty, in exchange for protection from anti-Jewish mobs, and for some special rights. They did not have to offer sacrifices to Roman gods or to the Roman god-emperor, unless they wished to avail themselves of Roman courts. And even there, many judges would accept their oaths by the Lord

God *Adonai*. The Jews of Petra lived well under the Romans, and most would not join any uprising, the rabbis especially. However, there was a cadre of hotheads and would-be patriots that these coins could entice.

There was the risk, however, of the rabbis' spies. They also knew who the hotheads were, keeping close watch on them to ensure they did not get out of hand.

Then there were the Christians. Most of them, like the Jews, had reached an accommodation with the Romans, and they too kept their more zealous followers on a short leash. As long as the Christians did not challenge the way the Romans lived, or their gods and god-emperors, the Romans pretty much left them alone also. But there were a few Christians who might be enticed. Most were itinerant preachers living in the desert, modeling themselves on a prophet they called John who had been a contemporary of their Christ a century ago. Like him, they preached fiery sermons to a flock that wandered out of the city to hear them. That flock included the most zealous of the Christians, but also included spies, both of the Christian leaders, and also Romans pretending to seek salvation, keeping careful notes. The Christians, too, Aharon would have to approach very judiciously. There were spies everywhere.

Aharon spent a week making his rounds through the red sandstone city, picking up a few dozen supporters. He did not need many, and his cadre would recruit friends they knew and trusted. The legion had been withdrawn for the war with Parthia, and there were just two centuries and a few *vigiles* to keep order. Perhaps by the end of the month? And the sack of *denarii* was by no means depleted. There was one more on his list.

Stick answered the door, directing Aharon to remain outside while he summoned his father. "Father, it is Aharon again. Shall I send him away?"

Jacobus rose from his chair. "No, I will see what he wants. Thank you, go back to your chores."

Jacobus opened the door. "What do you want?" he asked, without a hint of courtesy.

"I bring you silver," he said, jingling a small sack. "May I come in?"

Jacobus stepped aside. "Come in. Another one from Shmuel?" They had plenty of money now, but more was always welcome.

"From me. I know you must be hard-pressed after your benefactor's unfortunate death, and I admire the work you do."

Jacobus did not accept the sack from Aharon's outstretched hand. It hung, suspended between them for several seconds, before Aharon dropped his arm.

"Aharon, as you know, I do not trust you. Please be on your way. I do not need your money"

"Wait, Yakov! Dark days are coming. The trust from your dead benefactor will not be available to you when the disorders come and the banks are overturned. And the disorders are coming soon, the word is out on the streets. Please. Take it. For the children." He lifted his arm up again, proffering the sack of coins.

Jacobus still did not take the bag. *He will want something in exchange. And how did he know about Benjamin's will? That had not been made public, just a private reading in the Roman court in the basilica with those listed in the document. Enough was enough!*

Jacobus was short and thin but very wiry, and years of service as his father Ibrahim's enforcer, and sometimes hit-man, left him with plenty of fighting skills, not overly diminished through lack of recent use. He closed the gap between himself and the Jew, grabbing the surprised man by the throat until he gasped for breath. "You! Out of this house now! If you come here again, it will not go well for you."

He released the man's throat and spun him around, grabbing the sack of coins from his hand, and twisting his arm up behind the man's back until the old man whimpered in pain. He marched him to the door and hurled him outside to land in the dusty street. Jacobus tossed the bag of coins at him.

"Keep your filthy money, dog. Do not think to blackmail me with your false gifts."

He was pleased that some neighbors had opened their doors to watch the strange disturbance at his normally quiet house. *Good. There would be witnesses that I did not accept his money.*

Some of Jacobus' boys worked at the caravansary as loaders and animal handlers when the caravans passed through. The work was hard and long, but paid well. This morning, Miranda had accompanied some of them, hoping to purchase some local goods from the merchants who had set up stalls inside to sell, to the caravanners and also to locals. She wanted fabric and thread for clothes, and maybe some unusual fruits and vegetables. Miranda thought to drop in on Ahmad, the boss of the caravansary, for advice on the best deals. She found him arguing fiercely with a merchant about quantities and prices of some goods. The merchant was either mistaking the amount owed, or was outright lying. She knew Ahmad well enough to intervene.

She scratched gently at the wooden door frame. "Good morning, Ahmad. And to you, sir. May I be of assistance?"

Ahmad, a portly bearded man with a dirty grayish turban, answered politely. "Nothing that a woman could resolve for us. My friend and I are having a discussion about prices and quantities."

"May I wait?"

"If you wish." He turned to the merchant. "Now, Farouk, as you were saying, I think three hundred *sesterces* for forty bolts of cotton cloth, it just seems too much."

"Each one costs five *sesterces*. It's that simple. Ask your bookkeeper," said Farouk.

"Unfortunately, he is dead. But I know when the price is too high."

Miranda interrupted politely. "Five *sesterces* for each bolt? And you are buying forty of them?"

"That's correct, Miranda. It just seems too much."

She smiled and turned to the merchant. "The correct answer is two hundred. Ahmad is right. Three hundred is too much."

"Witch! You don't know what you are talking about. Stay out of men's business."

"Ahmad, may I see your abacus, please?" asked Miranda.

He handed her the counting tool. Her fingers flew over the balls in a blur, ending up with two balls in the last column.

"Two hundred it is, Ahmad." She smiled as she handed it back to him.

"You did that in your head?" asked Farouk.

"I have been doing bookkeeping for a long time." She did not want to reveal that she had been a slave when she mastered that arcane art of figuring numbers in her head, a trick her former owner, a Greek mathematician in Alexandria, had taught her.

Farouk considered challenging her, but he knew she was right. He had been caught, and backed down. "Two hundred then. My men must have made a mistake."

"No matter." Ahmad counted out the required sum in coins from his wooden cash box, then threw in a few more *denarii*. "To soften your embarrassment, my friend."

Farouk accepted the coins, pushed the multicolored bolts of cloth across the table, gave Miranda a look that was half false smile and half snarl, and left.

Ahmad offered her the choice of any one of the bolts. She picked the pale green one. She left the caravansary with the fabric, and a job as the caravansary's new bookkeeper.

And as Jacobus had expected, she was furious when she found he had even admitted the scoundrel into the house.

"You know that man is not to be trusted. And if he believes that trouble is coming, you can be sure that he has something to do with it."

"I think he is more of a cheat and a liar than a man of violence, Miranda."

"If there is money to be made from it, he will indulge in violence, Jacobus. He will pay others to do his dirty work. And among us women, we are hearing the same rumors, that bad things are brewing. I thought it might be gossip, but this makes it more likely. You need to go the *vigiles* and tell them what you know."

"I can't tell them anything factual, just rumors."

"He may try to blackmail you, saying that you accepted money to do some nasty thing, or that you stole it from him. Go now, to protect yourself. He is a scoundrel, and a dangerous one."

Jacobus walked down the Street of Columns to the basilica and the *vigiles'* office. He found Josephus Farvius at his desk. "Sir? May I have a moment?" he asked.

"You are always welcome. Sit. How are the children?"

"They are well, sir. And the boys are mostly young men now. I bring you some information. It is not much, but perhaps it may add to whatever you know."

"I am always willing to take information. What is it?"

"You know the Jewish moneychanger Aharon?"

"I do. A cheat and thief by reputation."

"For several years, I received money via him, from a friend serving with the *Legio XII Fulminata*. Contributions for us from his men. I know that some of that money stuck to his fingers, but it was enough to keep us going. Of course, with the war, that money has been very infrequent, but with Benjamin's generous bequest in his will, we no longer needed that."

"You are accusing him of cheating you?"

"No, sir, something more sinister. Today, he came to my house to give me money, it seemed quite a lot. He said it was for the children. I threw him out, and did not take his money. But he talked about coming disturbances, things that would disrupt the bankers, interrupt Benjamin's legacy to us. He shouldn't have known about that. You were there, that was a private reading here in the court."

"Interesting. And we too are hearing rumbles of some big disturbance coming."

"Miranda said the women are hearing that also."

"I think we should pay Aharon a visit, see what he knows. And keep an eye on whom he visits. At first, I thought this was just market talk, rumors and gossip, but if Aharon is uncharacteristically throwing money around, he may be involved. Thank you for the information."

Jacobus went home and got his old sword, dagger and baldric from under the bed. He began sharpening the blades, something he hadn't felt the need to do for several years. Rust had not gotten to the metal and each weapon took a nice edge.

I need to get daggers for everyone, and swords for the older boys. And teach them how to use them.

CHAPTER 107:

UPRISING

Petra, November 115AD

Jacobus, Vergilius and Simeon were having lunch in the orphanage, along with Josephus Farvius. Vergilius, a retired centurion, and Simeon, similarly retired from the Judaean auxiliaries, both neighbors, were conferring with Jacobus on how best to defend the area. Simeon was rabbi to the small community of Jews who had served in the Judean auxiliaries, often not welcome in the synagogue inside the city.

"There's only two centuries defending the whole city. I have alerted them about the threat, so they have doubled the watch on the basilica. But depending on how big this uprising is, if it happens, that's about all they can defend. The rest of the city will be wide open," said Josephus.

"We are in a pretty good position here, in the mountains west of the Street of Façades. The road is narrow, cliffs on both sides, a few men can hold off dozens," said Vergilius.

"Agreed. We have a lot of veterans up here. This is a nice place to live, and we intend to keep it that way. We've got damned near a full century of volunteers up here, half of them veterans, a lot from the Dacian war. I think we can keep trouble out of this side of the city," said Simeon.

"If the trouble is not inside our neighborhood. Can we trust everyone?" asked Jacobus.

"Good question. As near as I can tell, yes, but we won't know for sure until the trouble starts," said Simeon,

Farvius nodded in agreement. "My *vigiles* will defend the basilica and water supply, and are organizing volunteers from other neighborhoods. But the neighborhoods will have to take care of themselves. The bankers have their own bodyguards. It looks like we are as ready as we can be. How are your young men coming along, Jacobus?"

"I am trying to pack as much into their training as I can. Everybody has a dagger, even Mouse and Miranda, and everyone over twelve has a sword. They are tough and street-smart, but they have never had to fight for their lives before, and they need to be ready. And they need to realize that if they can avoid the fight, they should. We won't know what they will be facing."

Farvius replied, "Hopefully, just toughs and blowhards who won't want to go after anyone who resists them. But we will see. Let us not let this nice lunch that Miranda has prepared for us go to waste."

The uprising, when it came, broke like a violent storm. The two centuries, encamped in the plain about a mile south of the city center, took the first assault. Black smoke curling up from the camps, visible from Jacobus' rooftop, indicated it had not gone well for the legionaries. He sent word to Vergilius to form up his men.

Their neighborhood was perched on the foothills of Jabal ad-Deir, the mountain to the west of the city, connected to the city center by a narrow extension of Facades Street through the city walls, winding through a narrow canyon. If trouble were to come, it would come through that easily-defended canyon, and Vergilius deployed just a dozen men to block the road. On either side of the surrounding canyon were two dozen archers. By the time trouble came to meet the very visible small neighborhood guard, that trouble would be already surrounded by the well-concealed bowmen.

The men deployed, Vergilius and Jacobus returned to their rooftop to watch the events unfolding in the hapless city. Miranda, Stick and Mouse joined them, the older boys now a part of Virgilius' neighborhood defense.

Black smoke was now pouring from the red-roofed basilica, the caravansary and other points in the city, rising vertically until picked up by the winds and spreading out in a hazy layer. The *vigiles* guarding the basilica appeared to have been caught by surprise, as was the army camp. They watched silently, hoping that their friends would be spared.

After about an hour, some stragglers came up the road at a run, bearing swords, occasionally glancing behind themselves to see if they had been followed. They were *vigiles*, led by Josephus Farvius, and some battle-clad soldiers, all blackened from smoke, some blood-stained. Vergilius and Jacobus went to down to meet them, escorting them into the neighborhood to his house.

"Have some water," Jacobus said, indicating the fountain in the center of the atrium. Miranda came with towels. "Wash up, please. Is anyone hurt?"

"Only the ones who splashed their blood on us," joked one of the gorier soldiers.

"It did not seem to go well down there, Josephus," said Jacobus

"It did not. They caught us by surprise. It was a slaughter. Fortunately, the governor was away at Alexandria, or he would be dead, too."

"Aye, and that was not just a mob. There were soldiers in with them, Parthians, I think, trying to look like locals," added the soldier.

Over the next few hours, more soldiers, *vigiles* and civilians straggled in, welcome additions to the thin neighborhood defenses. Fortunately, one of the many reservoirs supplying the desert city was inside their lines, so water would not be a problem, and they had stockpiled two months of dried and preserved foods, and flour for bread. Small farms around them kept goats and chickens. If the neighborhood could withstand the siege, food was not going to be a problem.

By late afternoon, the first band of thirty or so would-be pillagers came up the road, amused at the sight of the small guarding force. The hidden archers stood up from their hiding places, catching them by surprise from the left and the right. The guard force then hacked into the confused mass of raiders, sending them reeling back into the city, several wounded and dead left behind. Simeon took charge of questioning the wounded Jewish captives.

"Who is leading your uprising?" he asked one.

"The Lord God of Israel," the man answered defiantly.

"The Lord God of Israel would not have allowed you to suffer such an ignominious defeat as you just did," Simeon retorted

"We will be back. It has been a glorious day."

"A glorious day of cowardly looting, raping and murdering, all in the name of God." Simeon spat on the ground in disgust.

The prisoner continued his rant. "You, you are worse than the uncircumcised Roman pigs, serving them, doing their bidding, murdering our people in the name of their false idols."

"I have done none of those things. And that makes me more faithful to the Law of Moses than what you have done today. Now who is your leader?"

"His name is Judah."

"And who sends him?"

"Osroës, the King of Kings, who will restore us to our lands and rebuild our Temple. Join us."

"You would exchange a ruler who exercises his power in the name of law, for one who exercises his power at his own whim? That is a fool's bargain. Farvius, Vergilius, this man is yours. I need nothing further from him." Simeon turned away.

That night, three soldiers were sent to alert the Judean governor, in Caesarea Maritima two hundred miles away, of an uprising on his southern border. They went by way of the new Roman road connecting Petra to the west with Gaza, then along the coast road, staging every twenty miles to change horses. The exhausted riders made the trip in two days.

The next day, the rebels reattacked, this time with soldiers embedded in the mob. The archers carefully held their fire until they could identify those soldiers. Once they were taken out, the mob collapsed and retreated back to the city.

Now it was time to wait, and hope for relief.

CHAPTER 108:

COHORT ON THE MOVE

Nisibis, December 115AD

Secundus scrutinized his new cohort. "How are the boys coming, Samuel?" he asked.

"Considering they started out as the sorriest lot of never-do-wells I ever worked with, they've come a long way. We have three functioning centuries now."

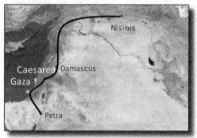

"I wish we had six, but the *legatus* said that was the most he could scrape up. He promised more from other legions, but that takes time. You've done well with them. And I am sorry I doubted you last month."

"No matter, sir, it must have looked pretty strange, but it was the only chance I had to get you out alive. We lost some good men that day, though, a lot of my good friends."

"I know."

Samuel changed the subject. "You know what the boys call themselves now? The 'rat-pack.' Made up a marching song around that. They've got some pride in themselves now, and that is good."

They were interrupted by Gaius Lucullus entering the tent, with just a hint of forewarning. They rose to attention to salute, but he quickly waved them back down. "At ease, gentlemen. How is the training for your new centuries coming?"

"We were just discussing that. Very well, sir, considering what we started with. Any news on when we might get the other three centuries?" asked Secundus.

"Very soon, but not the way we expected. I just got word from Tiberianus, the governor of Judea. There is a rebellion in Petra, and the provincial administration has been overthrown. I am detaching your cohort and the Ninth Batavians to go there and put it down. You'll pick up another century from *III Cyrenaica* in Damascus, and two garrison centuries from Judea south of Lake Tiberias, then on to Petra by way of Gaza. It's seven hundred miles, the sooner you can leave, the better. Governor Tiberianus will keep you updated on the situation from Caesarea. The *Princeps* and Aulus Aemilius will be leaving for Antioch for the winter, but they will be following your progress closely."

"That is unexpected, but aye, sir, we can be ready to move out in a day. I'd like to see us make twenty-five miles per day, if the troops are up to it."

"That is optimistic, but you will be outside of hostile territory. Don't let your guard down, however. These insurrections seem to be spreading. We picked you because Samuel is close to our old friend Yakov. If he is still alive, he will be a source of information we can trust."

"Aye, sir." Secundus turned toward Samuel. "Any comments or reservations? Is the 'Ratpack' ready for real fighting?"

"We'll soon find out. Considering that the road ahead of us is worth a lot less than the road behind us, I am going to try for thirty miles per day, and get there in three weeks."

"Your call."

Gaius readied to leave. "If you have no questions, then, I will leave you two to your preparations. Gods go with you."

"Aye, sir," answered both with a salute.

In the intelligence tent, Arrian Atticus looked over the report from Caesarea that Marcus had just handed him. "Petra is overrun?" he asked.

"Apparently by dissatisfied locals, backed by soldiers believed to be Parthians," answered Marcus.

"Nisibis all over again."

"It seems that way. The *legatus* is detaching the Fifth Cohort and the Ninth Batavian cavalry to retake the city.'

"Are they ready for that? That cohort just got put back together, and is just at half-strength."

"The commander thinks so. They will pick up three more centuries enroute. Arrian, I have a request."

"Certainly."

"Arrian, I want to go with them. I have been training with Samuel's men in their field exercises."

"Marcus, you are forty-five years old. Legionaries your age are looking forward to retiring with the *diploma* to a farm somewhere. I need your language skills here. Why do you want to do this?

"My sister will be riding with the Ninth. I don't want her doing my share of the fighting."

"Hmm. Well, if the tribune will accept your services, I won't stand in your way. I suspect after two days on the road, at the pace they are going to set, you will wish you were back here."

"Thank you, Arrian."

And the next morning, when the Fifth moved out, Marcus Lucius and his wife Mei were with Tribune Secundus Lucullus at the head of the fragmentary *Turba Rattorum* 'Rat Pack' Fifth Cohort.

CHAPTER 109:

RENEWING FRIENDSHIPS

Via Triana Nova, December 115AD

Samuel set a hard pace for the Fifth. He had promised Secundus thirty miles per day, and the 'Ratpack' had covered almost five hundred miles in two weeks, ten hours on the road, plus time to erect, then take down, the earthen ramparts of their marching camp. Samuel had relaxed the size of the earthen ramparts to shorten the day, and compensated by doubling the night watch while in Parthian territory. But once out of Parthian territory, he felt comfortable with relaxing the night watch as well, as long as the 'Rat Pack' maintained their good pace. The cohort even composed their own marching song celebrating their outcast status.

The long trek made an opportunity for renewed friendships. As Marcus and his companions had done on their last trek together ten years back, they frequently congregated together after the evening meal, Marcia, Marcus and Mei, Hina and Galosga, at Samuel's tent. Secundus almost always joined in, enjoying the jokes and stories of his father's exploits and mishaps back then, many that his father had never shared with him.

This evening, Mei came wearing riding felts, with a sword strapped behind the shield on her back, like Marcia, Hina and Galosga. Marcus, Samuel and Secundus wore their battle dress.

"Mei! With a sword tonight. What is the occasion?" asked Secundus.

"The sword is the occasion," said Mei, a smile brightening her Hanaean features, making her eyelids lift. "I have satisfied Hina and Marcia that I can use it well enough to defend myself."

'Well, congratulations, Mei. It seems we now have three fighting women, though I can't understand why."

"I am too old to be a fighter like Marcia and Hina. But if we are in a fight, I do not want soldiers trying to defend me when they should be fighting the enemy," answered Mei.

Tonight was a night of reminiscing. Hina had made *kumis*, passing the sack around for each to take a nip. Adhela sat by Mei. She had become the little boy's adopted aunt, freeing his parents and siblings for their duties, and the two had become quite close.

"This reminds me of our trip together ten years ago, when I would come and share your yurt so I could sleep with Galosga," said Hina, squeezing Galosga's hand

"Those were special times," said Marcus.

"Very special times, but you made it hard on us single guys, all of that shuffling and heavy breathing from your side of the yurt. At least Marcia and Antonius tried to keep it quiet," said Samuel. This elicited laughter from everyone, and about as much of a blush from Hina as she ever allowed.

"How did you and Galosga meet?" asked Secundus. "He is not of your people."

Marcia interjected with a smile. "He was her second choice, after Antonius turned her down."

"Galosga was certainly the better choice." Hina laughed, fingering the little stone arrowhead on a thong about her neck. "Men back then either feared me, or wanted to control me. Galosga did neither. And that made me afraid, wanting to control him. But he did not allow me fear or control, either. He healed me, in a way no one else could, the man who fell into my life. And that time together in the yurt, that was the first time I had felt part of a family in a long time." She interlaced her fingers with those of Galosga, a rare public display of tenderness on her part.

"That is an interesting amulet," said Secundus, eying her amulet. "What is it?"

Hina slipped the thong holding the arrowhead over her head and handed it to Secundus. "It was a gift from Galosga, the day we became lovers, the day we first met. It is a part of his world."

"Interesting, it looks like a worked-stone arrowhead. Sometimes people find things like that when digging, but no one knows who made them or why. What is it made of, Galosga?"

"I don't know the Latin word for it, our word for it was *dawisgala*. A special stone that we could work into knives, arrowheads and other tools."

"Interesting. It looks like flint. Why didn't you use metal?"

"We had no metal."

"Hmm. Where is this place you come from?"

"Far across the sea, to the West."

"Sounds like another world completely," Secundus handed the arrowhead back to Hina

"It is," said Galosga.

Hina accepted the arrowhead back and put it around her neck. "Galosga has told me a lot about the sea that he crossed, such a great expanse of water. I have seen nothing bigger than a lake. I want to see the ocean. Galosga says the water rolls in waves, like the plains of grass wave in the wind in my home."

"What are you going to do when you get to Rome, Hina?" asked Samuel. "You are going to the City, I guess."

"Well, I have heard so much of Rome, that I guess we shall have to go there. Then we will go stay with Marcia and Antonius in ... Aquileia? ... did I say that right?"

"You did. Yes, they will be staying with us, in our villa until they build their own home. There is plenty of pastureland for horses. Who knows, they may want to go back to living in yurts, migrating all over Italy." Marcia said with a smile, eliciting more chuckles.

"I think we will stay in one place. Tengri may have set my destiny to the west, but He told me nothing about how to live in that new world. Marcia wants my help to write a grammar and dictionary for Xiongnu."

"Our world is growing. One never knows when a trader may want to know that language also," said Marcia.

Marcus got up to put another small log on the fire, then sat back down.

Secundus asked, "Marcus, what about you and Mei? Will you also be staying in Aquileia with your sister and Antonius?"

"Yes, we will, also part of their growing staff of teachers. Pass the *kumis*, please."

Mei chimed in. "It will be a new world for us, also. And new worlds are best shared with someone who knows that world."

Hina passed around the sack of *kumis*. "So, Tribune Secundus Lucullus," asked Hina in mock seriousness, "What is our plan for Petra?"

"At Damascus, we will pick up Trajan's new road, the *Via Traiana Nova*. It should be good traveling, though parts of it are still under construction. That road runs south through Petra to the Red Sea at Aela. I have received reports from Caesarea that Samuel's friend Jacobus is holding a neighborhood on the west side of Petra, so we will approach from that direction. Since Jacobus knows you all, I will send you, Samuel, with Marcus, Marcia, Hina, and Galosga to see if you can establish contact with him, if he is still holding the neighborhood. That will certainly verify our *bona fides* with him, one of the reasons we are all in this together. The soldiers who got out said Jacobus has a few *vigiles*, legionaries, and veterans organized as a defense, in a pretty strong position."

Hina passed around the *kumis* one last time and everyone took a sip. "Well, that is done." She thumped the empty sack. "Tomorrow will come early, so let's retire."

CHAPTER 110:

THE EARTH MOVES

Antioch, 13 December 115AD

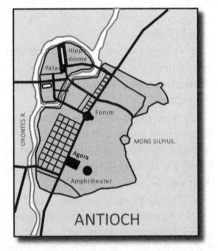

Trajan arrived in Antioch in early December, accompanied by Aulus Galba and his wife Livia, Claudius Severus, and several other senior advisors. Their carriages rolled across the bridge across the Orontes River, to the palace on the island forming the western part of the city, isolated from the main part of the city on the eastern shore.

Publius Hadrian was waiting to greet them with his wife Vibia Sabina and Trajan's wife Pompeia Plotina, wearing wraps about their shoulders against the cool December air. Pompeia beamed at her husband and greeted him with a gentle kiss, then took her place at his side.

"Welcome back, your Excellency. I trust the war goes well?" asked Hadrian.

"Well indeed, Publius. You have met Aulus Aemilius from our last trip. This is his beautiful wife Livia, who came to us via a round-about trip through Ctesiphon, compliments of our friend Cyrus Mithridates."

Hadrian smiled his bright smile, taking Livia's hand in his. "I am pleased to meet you, and I am looking forward to hearing of your adventures."

Livia returned the smile. "There are parts of that story that are shocking, but one of the perpetrators has paid the price."

Trajan indicated Claudius Severus. "Our good friend, Gaius Claudius, is now governor of our newest province Armenia."

"Congratulations, Gaius Claudius. I understand that your old province of Arabia Nabataea has come under some duress," said Livia.

"Sadly so. Bad news travels quickly, it seems. But a cohort is enroute to Petra, and they should be arriving shortly to restore order," said Claudius.

Trajan introduced his other advisors, then Hadrian ushered Trajan's inner circle to his private *triclinium* dining room in the *praetorium* palace. "I thought we might dine here, so I can show off my latest addition," he said, indicating windows of the finest Egyptian glass lining the wall, giving a view of the river and the city while keeping the December chill at bay outside. "Barely a ripple can be seen looking through them."

"Well done, Publius. There is a bit of a breeze up today, so sitting on the patio might be a bit unpleasant" said Trajan, reclining on the *triclinium* dining sofa with Pompeia beside him. Hadrian took the *triclinium* opposite him, flanked by Vibia Sabina. Claudius Severus took his seat at Trajan's left, while Aulus and Livia took their seats to Trajan's right.

Servants brought meals. "So, tell me of your adventures, Lady Livia," asked Hadrian.

"It began when I visited a friend in Aquileia," she began. She related their kidnapping, the horrible trip in a slave ship, their time in Ctesiphon, and their ultimate escape. "I understand that Kophasates gave his life to get us out of the palace."

Trajan interjected. "Kophasates was a Roman agent, highly placed in the king's court there. We received his final message indicating the women were free and enroute, and that it would be his last message. We presume he was killed. He had provided us valuable services, not least of which was arranging their escape."

"Highly placed, indeed," said Hadrian.

Livia continued her story. "And for the last four months, I have been living in the army camp with Aulus. And my friend Marcia, she is riding with the cavalry. She has a barbarian friend from the Distant East, also riding with the cavalry, and between the two, they are quite the pair of Amazons. In fact, she is with the cohort riding to relieve Petra."

"You certainly have interesting friends, Livia," said Hadrian.

"Well, I will allow Marcia and Hina to be the Amazons. I intend to spend some quiet time here enjoying this civilized city, far from all the noise and tumult of the world at war, and then return to Rome, and to my son Pontus Servilius."

"How old is he?" asked Hadrian.

"He is fifteen now. He is staying with Marcia's villa in Aquileia to help manage the place in everyone's absence."

"I sent a letter to him, confirming that he is *sui maneris*, in his own hands as an adult," said Aulus. "A bit early, but he is doing a man's work, and needs the authority to do so. I am very proud of him."

The servants cleared away the lunch, and the women retired to chat privately, while the advisors were brought back in. Trajan had been away from the center of imperial affairs for a year, and many items needed his attention and decision. By late afternoon everyone retired to the hot baths by the palace, then enjoyed a fine dinner in Trajan's honor. However, it had been a long trip, and everyone retired early.

Sometime after midnight, Aulus awoke to the barking of dogs. It seemed that every dog in the city had decided to bark or howl, and some roosters had begun to join in. He went out on the patio, but it was a quiet night, brilliantly illuminated by a full moon, nothing out of the ordinary, no signs of fires anywhere in the dimly-lit sleeping city. He turned to go back to bed with Livia, when he heard, or rather felt, a distant rumble, like thunder. But the sky was clear. The dogs suddenly stopped barking, and the rumble grew till the floor began to shake.

He shook Livia's shoulder. "Wake up, wake up, I think we are having an earthquake."

Livia stirred sleepily, then swung her feet out of bed. Everything in the room was tinkling, vibrating, or creaking. As she stood up, the first wave hit, then the sickening feeling of the solid marble floor rolling like the sea beneath her feet. Somewhere in the room, something fell, shattering.

"Get your sandals on, quickly, we need to get outside. Quickly!" said Aulus, fitting his last sandal on his foot.

The wave of shaking retreated, then came booming back, harder than before. An oil lamp fell from a wall sconce, igniting drapery. In the hallway, everyone was groping in the semi-darkness, trying to find the way out, down the stairs. Overhead, an ornate chandelier swung crazily back and forth, then broke free, its oil lamps scattering their flaming fuel as it fell. Someone screamed as the chandelier hit him, but that was mostly lost in the chaotic shouts and screams of the panic-stricken mob. Someone in front of Aulus stumbled on the stairs, now cracking and fissuring. Aulus helped the man up, then pushed him forcefully down the stairs. "Outside, outside," he shouted, following him.

The earthquake tapered off to a gentle vibration, but then with a roar returned. By now most of the people in the palace were outside. In the moonlight, Aulus watched in horror as one of the marble columns holding up the roof of the bath house next to the palace swayed, then collapsed, scattering its many barrel-shaped elements onto the crowd. Almost in slow motion, the roof began to give way, the other columns giving out.

"To the hippodrome!" Aulus called, beckoning those around him to the racetrack, the largest open area complex on the island, where they would be free from falling debris. Looking east to the city, a flickering red and yellow glow told of innumerable fires that would soon add to the devastation.

Two hundred miles to the south, Caesarea was shaken by the same earthquake, but not so strong as to cause any damage. Fisherman in the harbor, preparing their boats for the morning launch, had paid it little mind.

But about thirty minutes later, their boats settled into the sand as the water receded … and receded … and incredibly, receded even further. Fishermen gestured, pointing at fish and other sea creatures left stranded, flopping helplessly in the moon-lit sand. What was the cause of this mysterious tide? Then, as quickly as the sea had receded, it returned, this time backed by a mountain of water that grew to tower far above their heads. They had only a few seconds to gape at the sight before they drowned in the deluge of water, their bodies and their boats picked up and cast far inland. The wave rampaged through the city, turning ramshackle huts, ornate temples and the elegant Roman governmental buildings alike, into rubble. In just a few seconds, Caesarea Maritima, the capital of the Roman province of Judea, was wiped out, most of the population drowned in their sleep.

Seventy miles east of Caesarea on the *Via Traiana Nova*, Trajan's new highway, the Fifth Cohort, now reinforced to full strength with the three promised centuries, was bedded down for the night in its marching camp, sentries posted. They would be in Petra in just five more days.

Late into the second four-hour watch of the night, there was a minor earthquake, not uncommon in the region. It would be noted in the morning report.

CHAPTER 111:

AFTERMATH

Antioch, December 115AD

Ten thousand people, everyone on the island palace complex, crowded into the hippodrome. The quarter-mile racetrack had seats for eighty thousand spectators, safe from overhanging structures. The rumbling of the earth continued off and on throughout the morning. Though not nearly as violent as the first quake, each aftershock was strong enough to do additional damage, causing panic in the crowd.

South of the palace, smoke poured from the partially-collapsed bath house, in flames from the furnaces that had kept the waters warm.

Bodies were being laid out in the northern turn of the racetrack for loved ones to identify. There were over a hundred, and the number was growing.

Aulus, with Livia's help, had begun organizing his own small area of the racetrack. Fountains scattered throughout the seating areas were still functioning, but ten thousand people use a lot of water for washing injuries and drinking. The racetrack had a good medical station to treat injured charioteers, well-supplied with bandages and medicines. Livia set up a nurses' station there, and dispatched runners to seek out people with medical skills, particularly the racetrack *medici* who would be well-skilled in the more serious injuries coming in, fractures and head injuries. Before too long, her night clothes were stained with blood. Someone draped a shawl around her shoulders.

Two hours after sunrise, Trajan emerged on the imperial box on the western side of the track, accompanied by his Praetorian Guard soldiers blowing trumpets to attract the crowd's attention and silence them. He was followed by the bearded Hadrian.

They survived, thank all the gods and goddesses! Aulus strained to hear the *Princeps* address the crowd.

"People of Antioch! We suffered a great disaster today, but every disaster is a challenge from the gods. You face that challenge today, to help one another, to recover those lost in the rubble, and to begin rebuilding Antioch. You will rise to that challenge to make Antioch the Golden City, Queen of the East, once again. My Praetorian Guardsmen will escort you across the bridges, as soon as the engineers have determined they are safe, to the city parks where you will be given tents and food. I have sent word to surrounding cities, and relief is on its way. The Imperial treasury will spare no expense to expedite your rebuilding. Rejoice that you are alive!"

It was a short address, but it seemed to calm the crowd. Aulus made his way through the crowd to the imperial box, leaving Livia to continue at the nurses' station. When they arrived, a Guardsman blocked his way with drawn sword, but Aulus waved it away. "Stand aside, soldier, I am Aulus Aemilius Galba, senior advisor to the *Princeps*. He needs my services."

The Guardsman sheathed his sword. "Sorry, sir, I did not recognize you."

Aulus was still wearing his night clothes, now filthy. "No matter. Thank you for attending to the *Princep's* security, we can't afford to have anything untoward happen to him now, can we?"

"No, sir," the lad smiled. He might have been twenty years old, and like everyone else, it seemed, he and his uniform were smudged with ash and soot. "Go on in, sir."

Aulus met Trajan in the room immediately behind the open box, with Hadrian and a number of city officials and governors of the surrounding provinces. "Aulus! You made it through all right. And Livia?" asked the *Princeps*.

"She is in the medical station, helping with the wounded. If there are any women's clothing available, she is still in her night clothes."

Trajan's wife Pompeia was in the corner with Vibia. "I have some, I'll take them to her," she said. "Where's the station?"

"Immediately to the right of this box." Aulus indicated the direction. "On the racetrack level."

Trajan took him by the arm. "Hadrian has dispatched his engineers and architects to survey the damage to the city. They are to report back to us by late afternoon. See my aide for some clothing. You, too, are still in your night clothes."

Back in the medical station, Pompeia arrived carrying a bag, having changed her clothing to just a simple cotton shift tied around the waist. She found Livia treating a man, one of about twenty, lying, sitting or standing about the station with various injuries, some more obvious than others.

"Lady Plotina! What are you doing here?" asked Livia

"Bringing you clothes. Aulus said you were still in your night clothes. And Pompeia will do just fine." She handed her the bag. "I decided you would need some help. I brought Trajan's doctor Ascanius." She indicated a slender, gray-haired man to her left.

"Good, someone who knows what they are doing."

The doctor smiled. "This is the man you are working on?" he asked, indicating the man prone on the table, bleeding heavily from his thigh. Livia was pressing firmly on the gash with a blood-soaked rag.

"He is. I can't get the bleeding to stop."

"Go change. I'll take care of him. There is some bread in the bag. You haven't eaten yet, I am sure."

Livia returned, wearing the same simple shift that Pompeia wore, to find the two intently working on the patient. Ascanius had applied a tourniquet, and was in the process of suturing the gaping cut. "You did well," he said. "The cut nicked his femoral artery, but you kept him from bleeding to death."

"I didn't know what I was doing. I just kept pressing on it with a rag, but it wouldn't stop." The floor around the table was littered with bloody rags, discarded during her efforts.

"You saved his life. Take a few minutes off, you've earned it. Lady Plotina and I will deal with these."

Livia went outside to the dirt racetrack, blinking in the sunlight. She devoured the bread standing. No, she had eaten nothing since her rude awakening in the night.

She came back to the station, to find Pompeia quietly taking directions from Ascanius, as he sutured another wound. Her shift was now also stained with blood. Together the three handled the injured, with Livia coordinating among the other women and men who had volunteered to help.

By late afternoon, the last of the survey party had returned. The report was grim. The city, with a population of a half-million people, had suffered severe damage, a quarter of the buildings collapsed or partially collapsed. Many more were obviously damaged, but would require inspection to determine if they should be repaired or torn down. The streets were full of rubble. There was no good count of the dead, but it looked like it would run to the tens of thousands or more. Hundreds of thousands of people were camped in improvised shelters in the park dedicated to Daphne by Apollo's temple southwest of the city. There they were safe from furthers shudders of the earth and falling debris, with plenty of fresh water from the lakes and springs. More people crowded into the Forum and the Amphitheater. The granaries were undamaged, as were the markets in the *Agora* market area, so food was available. None of the five bridges were damaged.

The most serious problem was the damage to the aqueduct supplying the city with water from the springs in Daphne Park southwest of the city. Two of the arches in the northern part of the city had collapsed, leaving that part without water. Firefighters had no water for their hand-pumped carts and bucket brigades, fires left burning uncontrolled throughout that part of the city. Some of the engineers had remained behind, working to rig a make-shift wooden trough, caulked with pitch, to suspend across the breach to restore flow across the damaged span.

The engineer completed his report. "In short, sir, we need heavy construction *machinae*, lifting cranes to clear the rubble, and people to run them. There are probably thousands of people buried in the rubble, but if we hurry, many can be saved. But we need more than the shovels, pickaxes and bare hands that we are using now."

Trajan stood. "Thank you all for your prompt and thorough inspection of the city. Whatever this city has is at your disposal, and I shall solicit as much help as we can from the surrounding cities." Trajan's aide had taken careful notes.

The next day, teams of oxen pulled a dozen treadmill-powered multi-pulley cranes, capable of lifting many tons, and wagons carried the smaller three and five-pulley cranes, to lift the massive stone blocks and beams to expose survivors. Over the next several days, despite the ongoing aftershocks, there were miraculous rescues from the rubble. One woman survived, buried alive for five days with her infant, nursing both her child and herself from her breast milk, and licking water that trickled into her tomb, until one of the heavy cranes lifted the massive stone block from above her.

In all, over two hundred thousand died. But Ascanius, Livia and Lady Plotina saved hundreds, as did many others working throughout the devastated city, treating the wounded, rescuing people from collapsed buildings, and extinguishing fires.

CHAPTER 112:

ARRIVAL

Paran, near Petra, December 115AD

The Fifth 'Ratpack' made good their forced march, arriving in the vicinity of Petra in late December, ahead of even Samuel's optimistic estimates. They camped at the oasis town of Paran, and Secundus called a meeting with the commander of the Ninth Batavians, Longinus Clarus. When Longinus arrived in the evening, Secundus, Samuel and Marcus were consulting a leather map spread on the desk by the light of an oil lamp, stirred by the night breeze, casting flickering shadows. All three were still in battle dress, their sweat-stained leather gritty with sand.

"Welcome, Longinus. I hope your horses didn't have too much trouble keeping up with the brisk pace set by my infantry," said Secundus. "I understand you brought Hina, Galosga and Marcia with you."

"I assumed you wanted to talk about the approach to Petra."

"Right. By our estimates, if the map is any good, and Samuel's estimate of our miles traveled is correct, we are about twenty miles west of Petra. We are going to camp here. I put in full ramparts and doubled the night watch. I don't want any more surprises like we had in Nisibis. Do likewise, Longinus. How are you fixed for fodder for your animals?"

"Yes, sir, will do. The fodder is fine, I requisitioned some in Paran, and the water is good."

"Good. We can only stay here a short time before someone from Paran goes to Petra and lets it drop that there is a cohort with cavalry outside their oasis. Then we lose all surprise. Samuel, you go with Marcus and the women at first light, this road leads to the west side of Petra and Jacobus' neighborhood, if it is still his. It should be the first good village you come upon. Go in traveling clothes, no weapons showing. Just introduce yourselves as travelers. If Jacobus is there, go in and talk to him, find out his situation. If not, find out what else you can. In any event, be back by nightfall, so I can plan our next move."

"Yes, sir," responded Samuel, everyone else nodding.

"Everyone, get a good night's sleep, and good luck tomorrow."

Hina and Galosga, with Marcia, stayed overnight in Marcus' tent. They were already awake when Samuel came to rouse them at the first gray light of dawn. The five trotted down the road toward Petra in silence, the only sound the tip-tipping of the horses' hooves on the rock-paved road, the only light the thin sliver of moon facing the not-yet-risen sun.

The sun was just beginning to peek over the horizon when their horses clambered through the Jabal ad-Deir pass and they saw what seemed to be Jacobus' neighborhood. Three armed men guarded the entrance, behind a barricade of rocks and tree trunks.

"That doesn't look good," said Marcus.

"Depends on who they are. They seem to be standing a professional watch, not lounging around," said Samuel.

"Halt and state your business," said one of the men in the local Aramaic tongue. Aramaic, spoken with a Latin accent, very familiar to Samuel.

"Good morning to thee, sir. I and my friends were hoping to find an old friend. Doth someone named Yakov live here, runs an orphanage or something?"

"If he doth?"

"We'd like to see him, if we can. We have a traveled a long way."

Two of the guards put their heads together, talking quietly. Then the first one spoke again. "What are thy names?"

"I am Shmuel, this is Hina and Galosga, these two are Si Nuo and Si Huar," indicating Marcia and Marcus. It seemed premature to use their Latin names. "Unusual names all, from the Distant East. We made a long trip with Yakov ten years ago, and have thought of him often."

"Art thou armed?"

"We have swords for protection against bandits, rolled up in our bags behind the saddles."

"Go tether thy horses over there by the trees. Then come back here."

The five did as they were told, nervous at being separated from their mounts and weapons.

The third guard was dispatched, apparently as a messenger.

They stood around for a tense half-hour, trying not to show their unease. Finally, Jacobus showed up. He blinked at the crew. "I didn't think it possible, but no one knows enough to make up that story and those names." He turned to the guards and spoke in Latin. "Let them in, I think Samuel has arrived with help." He turned back to his party.

"It seems you still hold your enclave," said Samuel, also switching back to Latin. "Is it safe to talk?"

"Yes, these are my men, veterans of the *X Fretensis* legion. We also have some retired Judean auxiliaries."

"I thought so. The Twelfth detached my cohort to make the trip from Nisibis, as soon as we got word of your predicament. My cohort and the cavalry are camped in Paran. We're here to take back Petra."

"Good. Let's go to my house, and you can also tell me how the hell you gathered all our old friends together."

Jacobus' house was just a few houses into the neighborhood. They led their horses in, putting them in a little stable in his backyard. Miranda greeted them at the door. "My wife, Miranda. These are friends from my old trip, Hina, Galosga, Marcus, Marcia and Samuel. Though how they got here I have no idea. Have you eaten yet?"

"No, just a little bread before we left Paran," said Samuel.

"Miranda, bring some falafel and hummus with pita bread, and some watered wine."

Miranda smiled and left.

"Sit down, sit down. Marcus, you stayed in that little town in China, and Hina and Galosga, you left us in Turfam. And Marcia, you were going to Rome with Antonius. I am sure you have some interesting stories. But you are here on serious business, and we can catch up on those later. What do you need to know, Samuel?"

"Everything you know about Petra. How many men are holding it, how badly damaged is it, what is the best way to take it back?"

"We are not sure how many, but the good news is that they don't seem to have enough to overrun our little stronghold. They made a few unsuccessful attempts to take us after the uprising. After that, they just bottled us up here, like they don't have enough men to lose."

"Are there Parthians with them?"

"Yes, how did you know?"

"We had the same kind of uprising in Nisibis up north, Parthian soldiers dressed up like locals backing a mob that otherwise would have scattered and run. My cohort was garrisoning the place, they caught us by surprise with a night attack and butchered us. We just got reconstituted. How much of the town is damaged?"

"I am able to slip a man in from time to time. He is a hunter, and knows paths through Jabal Ad-Deir that mountain goats haven't found. He goes around their little contingent blocking the road and shows up in town, just another local. The basilica was burnt, but seems intact aside from smoke stains. The rebels are using that as their headquarters. They seem to be governing the town from there, keeping the locals in check. People don't seem to be too happy with situation, especially the Jews, but there are a few heads on pikes around town, so nobody complains too much."

"So, the Jews are not involved here?"

"The hotheads and zealots form the rebel's core group, but most of the Jews want to stay out of it. The rest of the rebels, as near as my friend can tell, are just thugs and criminals, in it for the loot."

"Sounds a lot like Nisibis. This seems to be a part of Ctesiphon's plan, stir up our rear areas and create trouble in our own provinces, make us split our forces, saving their army for when we are scattered all over the place, putting out brushfires. We had more opposition from the Armenians than we have had in Mesopotamia. Do you know who is leading it?"

"Someone named Judah, a Jew from somewhere in Parthia. There was a money changer, Aharon, who was involved in funding it, but he hasn't been seen since before it started. He was the man who got the money to me that you sent here. He tried to recruit me and the Christians to his cause."

"Interesting. The man whom I used to get the money to you followed my legion around as a suttler after we deployed. He also tried to recruit me to lead the Jewish Army. He wound up running things in Nisibis, until I killed him."

Miranda came with breakfast and set it before each.

"Let's eat, then I will send for Josephus Farvius, the local head of the *vigiles*, and some of the survivors of the century that was garrisoned here. And you can tell me your stories while we eat."

Josephus Farvius and his companions showed up around noon. They quickly decided that any kind of massed assault would be a bad idea: the rebels would just fade away into the population, remaining there as a threat for a future time.

Farvius had brought a map of the city, laid out on fine vellum, that showed all the streets and major buildings, neatly labeled. "The Colonnaded Street runs east and west, then curves up this way. You are here. The basilica is on the north, and the temple opposite. I think you can take the basilica with a single century; more would be stepping on each other. We are not sure how many men they have, but I don't it's over two hundred. I think they might not put up much of a fight against even a single century."

Samuel nodded. "You're probably right, but I think the rebels will fight to get it back. We could use that century as bait, to lure the rebels into massing. Then we can respond with force."

"You said you have cavalry. How do you plan to use your cavalry in the city?"

"I'm not. The city is only about a mile in diameter, the cavalry can ride circuits around it, to keep the bad guys from escaping."

"What is at the edge of the city?" asked Hina.

"A sort of a steep sandy slope. Don't let your horses go over it, they probably won't be able to get back up," said Farvius.

"Can a century come in from the west, through your enclave to the east exit?"

"It should not be a problem," said Farvius. "Keep it quiet, there are only about ten men blocking the exit. If you surprise them, they will turn and run, but if they hear you coming, they will call for reinforcements."

After some more discussions, the five returned to the cohort by late afternoon, bringing Farvius' map with them. Secundus and Longinus Clarus was waiting for them. They spent some time talking about the situation.

"Nice map," said Secundus, admiring the neatly-laid out map, lettered in a fine uncial handwritten print.

"Compliments of the *vigiles*. They'll probably want it back," said Samuel.

"So, you think a single century, moving up by surprise and taking the basilica, will make them want to take it back," said Longinus, locating the building on the map.

"I think the rebels will want to lay low for a day or two to see if any more forces show up. Then they will try, but the century should be able to hold out for a day at least," said Secundus.

"How do we get in undetected?" asked Samuel.

"Move up at night, get to the enclave before dawn. The password is 'Nisibis'."

"Use the first century. I want to lead it," said Samuel.

"I'll use the first century, but you are not leading it. Use their centurion. I need you with me for the main attack. Nobody else has your experience."

"Sir, we just promoted that lad from the ranks because we needed a centurion."

"He'll have to rise to the occasion. I can't spare you," said Secundus.

"Yes, sir." Samuel acquiesced. "I recommend we go tonight. The longer we wait, the sooner they will know they are facing a whole cohort."

"I agree," said Secundus. "Looks good. I want a few men to stay behind in the enclave, with horses, to let us know if anything goes awry. I don't want the rest of us marching into a disaster. What do you recommend for the main attack on day three?"

"On the second night, we all move out with the cavalry. Same entrance, same password, arrive before dawn. We'll have to go through the enclave one century at a time. It's narrow through there." Samuel pointed at the map. "Each century will have to form up after they leave. Second century will relieve the first at the basilica here, the third will take the temple opposite it here. The banks are all to the left of the basilica here, the fourth century will take their buildings. The last two centuries will stay in reserve on the western edge of the city. We can put them where we need them."

"What about the cavalry?" asked Longinus.

"Cavalry will go through last, two groups riding in opposite directions around Petra, this way, and that way." Samuel indicated the routes on the map. "Be careful. There is a steep sandy drop off at the edge, you might not get horses back up easily."

"Samuel, good plan. We may make changes to it, but it looks basically good. Go alert the First that they are leading the charge, and make sure their centurion is up for it. If he's not, I'll give you one from another century. He's critical."

CHAPTER 113:

THE POINT OF THE SPEAR

Petra, December 115AD

Sergius Lepidus felt proud to be marching through the night at the head of the First Century, confident for the first time as a centurion. In his early years, he had been a petty thief, joining the army to stay ahead of his dues for that life, and he continued that life as a soldier. He had the scars on his back to show for it from multiple floggings. The only reason he was raised to centurion was that he had been in the army five years, longer than anyone else in the reformed first century of the Fifth Cohort, though he had known little fighting, minor skirmishes where he had tried to avoid the front lines. There had been hard, no-nonsense training under Samuel, then the grueling three-week march from Nisibis.

But through it all, Samuel treated him with the respect due a centurion, something Sergius had never known before. And that afternoon, Samuel let him know that the entire operation to retake Petra depended on his century, and on him. Sergius had told him that he wasn't sure he could do it.

If you had said anything else, said Samuel, *I would have gotten someone else. Of course, you're not sure. So now go and do it. I think you can.*

Around midnight, they had set out on the twenty-mile night march to Petra, in a moonless night, no torches, night vision only. It was amazing what you could see by starlight after a few hours. Someone picked the marching song, his marching song, one that he had made up as a joke:

> *We are the dregs, dregs, dregs,*
> *Dregs of the Fighting Twelfth, the dregs!*
> *That's what we are, the dregs.*
> *But we are rats, rats, rats,*
> *And rats have teeth, teeth, teeth,*
> *And they bite, bite, bite,*
> *That's what they do, they bite,*
> *The fighting Ratpack Fifth!*

The whole cohort had adopted his song as their marching chant.

They arrived at the enclave's checkpoint just as the sun was coming up, gave the password, and broke ranks to straggle through the narrow village.

Josephus Farvius met them at the eastern exit. "You didn't waste any time getting here. Do your men need to eat?"

"We'll eat after we take the basilica, sir. I am Sergius Lepidus, centurion of the First Century, Fifth Cohort." He extended his hand.

"Your men look good, Sergius." He took Sergius' hand in a military grip, each clasping the others' wrist. "No change from what Samuel saw yesterday. Good luck to you."

"Thank you, sir." He turned to his men, "Go out by squads, and once outside, form up far enough ahead that the other squads can fall in behind you. Draw swords!"

Sergius suddenly doubted himself. *I am going into a fight for the first time, and leading these men. Can I really do this? What if I get us all killed?* Then he shook the thoughts off. As Samuel had told him, in one of their many talks, *If you doubt yourself, your men will know it, and they will lose heart. Shake it off!* He was the first one out, sword drawn, the *signifier* with the century's standard and the *cornifer* with his trumpet on either side of him.

The first squad exited, followed in turn by another and another, interrupting the bandit guards a hundred yards off at their breakfast. The *cornifer* blew his trumpet, a shrill blast that could be heard all the way to the city, and sixty men advanced, swords peeking from between their shields, tapping on the shield in rhythm to their steps as they advanced on the rebels.

The rebels fled on the run back to Petra, and the century advanced relentlessly down the Colonnaded Street. As they turned right to enter the city proper, the *cornifer* blew another blast to announce their arrival. People were coming out of the houses to watch. Someone cheered, and soon the all of the people were cheering, pumping their fists in the air.

As the crowd cheered, Sergius noticed something impaled on a stick by the side of the road ... a head, blackened by the sun, its mouth open in a silent scream, its wide eyes staring at the last horror it had seen. *Looks like they have had a rough go of it.* His doubts were evaporating, he was here to set things right.

They came to the basilica government building, and he gave the command for a left flank. The century executed smartly, never losing the rhythm of their tapping swords, and advanced up the steps to the entrance. Some men on the colonnaded porch looked at them wide-eyed, scattering off to the left and right. Inside, Sergius could hears shouts in a language he did not know. It seemed, however, the person shouting was not happy with someone.

The century entered the wide rectangular marble pavilion inside the basilica, offices along the side and back whitewashed sandstone walls, showing signs of extensive smoke damage. Sergius halted the century and dispersed squads to secure each of the four entrances, exactly where Samuel had shown him on the map. The other two squads he dispatched upstairs to root out anyone hiding there.

Whoever had been shouting in here had fled, as well as the people at whom he had been shouting. The first floor was empty.

A soldier brought down a man from upstairs at sword-point. "Found him hiding under a table, sir." The man, wearing a brown robe, had the build of a soldier, defiant eyes and a pointed black beard.

"What's your name, soldier?" asked Sergius.

The man spat on the floor, and tried to jerk his arm away from the soldier's restraint.

"No matter, then. Take him outside and kill him. I can't waste men guarding him."

"Yes, sir." He led the man away.

About half an hour later, Sergius assembled the century. "You've had a hard march, without much sleep. Odd squads, find a place to sleep. Even squads, cover the entrances. Wake your reliefs in six hours, then you get some sleep, too."

Sergius was not planning on sleep, but he knew he was going to have to get some soon. He did not want to be exhausted when things heated up, but now was not the time … there were too many things to think about. Finally, he felt like the centurion he was, responsible for his little 'rats.' They were looking to him to keep them alive. He found an office, where he could just sit and gather his thoughts.

Farvius Josephus came into the basilica about noon. "I sent my man into town this morning, and it seems you have it well in hand, Sergius."

"So far, but it is too easy. I expect trouble any minute."

"Tomorrow or the day after. I think they are waiting to see who else shows up today."

"I hope you are right."

The next day was quiet enough that a few townspeople came around to meet with him and his soldiers. Sergius requested they find the people who could identify the heads on the street, and claim their loved ones. He did not want to take them down, because he would have to dispose of them. By evening, the grisly markers were gone.

The next day dawned peacefully enough. Sergius thought that maybe there would be no attempt to retake the basilica, that the rebels had fled.

But around noon, all hell broke loose. About two hundred men came from out of nowhere to surround the building. Some were slingers, launching walnut-sized sling stones from a hundred yards away, but it was difficult for them to find their targets through the windows and doors. "What are we going to do about the slingers, Sergius?"

"Stay out of sight. They can't hit what they can't see, and they can't retake the building with slingers. When they get ready to rush the doors, we'll deal with them, and the slingers will be afraid of hitting their own men."

Sergius roused the off-duty squads, and everyone stayed beside the doors and windows, some carefully sneaking a cautious peek out to see if anyone was coming.

After about an hour, about a hundred men rushed all four entrances. Sergius' 'rats' took them head on. Although the soldiers guarding the doors were outnumbered four or five to one, no more attackers could get through the door at one time than were defending it. The Romans were armored and had shields, the attackers did not. A few got through some undefended windows, but they were quickly cut down. In fifteen minutes, it was over. The attackers retreated, leaving three or four bodies of their comrades by each door. There were no Roman casualties other than a few minor injuries.

The sling barrage started up again, this time covering another assault team carrying ladders. They set up against the walls, trying to get into the second-floor windows. Sergius dispatched two squads upstairs. There were sounds of fighting, shouts and scuffling, and a scream as one ladder was detached from the window, falling backward with five men on it. But this cost Sergius his first casualty. The soldier lingered too long in the window to admire his handiwork. A sling bullet caught him full in the face, breaking his jaw. He was alive, but out of the fight.

This assault ebbed as the first one had. Sergius took this lull to rally his men. "All right, you bunch of rats. You took the worst they could throw at us, and you didn't give an inch. Hang on, help will arrive tomorrow, we just have to get through the night."

Someone picked up the marching song. They were in good spirits.

A man stepped out of the surrounding mob and stepped forward under a flag of truce. He approached the bottom of the stairs and called out in Latin: "My name is Judah ben Levi. Romans, your situation is hopeless. You are surrounded and outnumbered. I offer you your lives, just leave and go back to where you came."

"Piss off, you bugger. I offer you the chance to claim your dead. Here's one from inside." Sergius tossed the body of one of the window intruders down the stairs. It landed with a wet thump at Judah's feet.

"You'll pay for your insolence, you Roman pig."

"Not until after you finish paying for yours." Sergius turned and went inside.

The attacks resumed, repeating about once an hour. Judah was not a creative strategist. There were about four variations of his assaults, and after seeing each, Sergius' men rapidly learned how best to repel them.

The attempt to retake the basilica had forced Judah to clear the defenses of Jacobus' enclave. In the late afternoon, Farvius and Jacobus with about twenty-five veterans quietly came into town unnoticed, and attacked the rear of Judah's men as they attempted another assault. The surprise was complete, and Judah lost another dozen fighters. Confusion broke out in his ranks, and dozens more left the field. Farvius' men then retreated into the city, disappearing as only a native could.

Judah would have to reckon on Farvius' reappearing if he launched another assault. Between casualties and desertion, he was down to about a hundred men, and now at least twenty would have to defend their rear. He was down to the minimum he needed to hold the city if he were able to dislodge the Romans, so he launched one more half-hearted attack, then settled into a siege. Eventually the Romans would run out of food.

Sergius feared a night attack, as Samuel had related happening at Nisibis, but other than harassment and shouts, none materialized. He spent the evening sitting with his wounded, complementing them on their bravery, assuring them they would soon be well again.

The worst one, however, was the man who had been hit by the sling stone in the jaw. A soldier, a field medic *capsarius* bandager named Valentinian, was treating him as best he could. The man's swollen, purplish jaw was at a crazy angle with respect to his face, and his bloody mouth showed many shattered teeth. He seemed unconscious, and the man was laying a cooling wet cloth on the injury, now blood-stained.

"How's he doing?" asked Sergius.

"Not good, I am afraid. He is in a lot of pain, but I can't give him any opium, he can't swallow easily. Some of those teeth need to come out, but I don't dare move that jaw. Fortunately, he has passed out."

"Good, thank you. What's his name?"

"Varius."

"I'll sit with him a few minutes. Go tend the others."

"Yes."

Sergius sat down beside the man, and took his hand in his own. "Thought I'd sit with you a minute, Varius, let you know you did a great job today. You saved the basilica."

He went on talking about much of nothing, and suddenly the man opened his eyes, looking at him as he talked, groaning a bit.

"Hello, you're awake. Listen, the *medicus* will be here tomorrow with the rest of the cohort. He'll fix you up just fine, you'll be just fine. Better than before. Now go back to sleep, it will take away the pain."

The man animated his eyes, then closed them again. *As much of a smile as he could muster.* Sergius sat by the man for a while, his mind going over the events of the day, anticipating those of tomorrow.

CHAPTER 114:

REINFORCEMENTS

Petra, December 115AD

Sergius was on the floor, leaning against the wall by a window, sleeping lightly at daybreak, when in the distance, he heard the shrill bray of a trumpet. Rousing himself, he went to the top floor, and looked toward the west. He could see a century formed up a half mile away at the bend in the Colonnaded Street, another forming behind it. The rest of the Ratpack had arrived.

The bandits surrounding them also saw them, their attention focused in that direction also. Sergius saw his opportunity and rushed downstairs.

"Wake up! Everyone, wake up! The Fifth is here. And we have a chance to settle the score. Forget guarding the doors and windows, gather around me!" He waved his arms excitedly.

"We all have seen the soldiers that are mixed in with that rabble. It will take half an hour for the Fifth to get here. Let's go on the offensive. Don't try to fight in formation, let's rush out the door and do a mêlée. Each of you pick out a soldier and engage him. Judah is mine, if he is out there. Lots of yelling, adds to the confusion." He drew his sword and picked up his shield. "Let's go! Follow me."

Sergius hadn't looked to see if they were following him, but their cries assured him that they were. And the rabble turned away from the shock of seeing not one, but several centuries advancing down the street a half mile away, to see their attackers coming at them on the run.

The soldiers were easy to identify, they were more sure of themselves, carried themselves differently. His men each singled out one and came at him, while Sergius searched in the early morning light for Judah, taller than most, with a light blue turban the last he had seen him.

Sergius found him trying to direct his people, trying to keep some from running off, his sword drawn. "Judah, come to me!" he called. Judah turned and advanced on him, crouching low in a battle stance. Sergius did likewise, casting away his bulky rectangular shield. It would be in the way for what was to come.

The two circled like cats, sizing each other up, making feints with their swords to gauge each other's reaction. Judah's lips were parted in a feral grin.

One-on-one fighting with swords was not Sergius' strong point, but he had been in many, many fights of various kinds in his past life of crime, so he understood the psychology of fighting. His world narrowed to just the ten-foot circle around him.

He never looked away from Judah's eyes, which betrayed the man's next move. Sergius countered it easily, tapping Judah's sword lightly with his, to let his opponent know he could.

Judah attempted a thrust at Sergius' midriff. He sidestepped it easily, and parried hard, their swords clanging from the impact. He let Judah make several more thrusts, then while sidestepping, instead of parrying, he made his own thrust, extending his sword arm straight forward, like a striking serpent.

Judah sidestepped, but not fast enough to avoid the sword blade ripping through his clothing. First blood? Not much, but yes, he had grazed the man.

And that enraged Judah. The anger showed on his face. Sergius, on the other hand, was cold, unemotional. It almost seemed as if he were watching this dance of death from a safe distance. Judah was becoming a bit more erratic in his movements, and once again he thrust, too aggressively this time. He lost his balance as Sergius sidestepped, kicking the side of Judah's leg, hard. The man almost went down, recovered, but now at a big disadvantage, Sergius beside him, not in front. Sergius swung his sword to the right in a sweeping arc, connecting with Judah's upper arm. He felt his sword bite through muscle and hit bone. Judah cried out and dropped his sword.

Sergius put the point of his sword at Judah's throat. "It seems you are out of the fight."

"Go ahead and finish me," said Judah with disdain, clutching his wound with his left hand. Blood was seeping through his fingers.

Sergius almost did, but quickly reconsidered. "You know some things we might want to know." He poked the skin of Judah's throat with the tip, dimpling it, then dragging it along to draw a few drops of blood. "I'll keep you alive till the rest of the Ratpack gets here. They can deal with you."

The fight over, Sergius' world expanded to take in the struggle still going on around him. Several men were down, only one of them his, and the Fifth was now a few blocks down the street, coming at the double. Farvius' men were in the fight also, having seen what was going on and joining in.

Hina, Marcia and Mei had ridden out with the group covering the road south, while Marasa and Andanyu rode with Hadyu to cover the escape to the north. They could not round the mountain to cover the escape east through the *Siq*, but the desert would ensure that no one got far by that route.

Hina hadn't felt like this since the last time she had let her men into battle a lifetime past, a mixture of elation and tension. She had trained the Ninth Batavians for months, molding them into a unique Roman cavalry unit, mounted archers able to fire at a gallop with a deadly accuracy. Not as good as the Xiongnu, but quite good nevertheless. She was the only one who knew how to wield these new mounted archers in combat, so Longinus had given her command of this *turma*, a squadron of thirty horsemen. More than her *arban* of ten men, less than the *zuun* of a hundred that she had commanded in her homeland, so far away and long ago. But motherhood and a long peace in Dzhungaria had intervened; she had never led the *zuun* into combat. The men, having trained under her for months, had no problems accepting her as commander, and she kept the *decurion* in place as her second.

Marcia was beside her, Mei on the other. She rode close enough to Mei to give her a comforting pat on her thigh. It would be Mei's first fight.

The shouts, screams and clatter of the battle in the city could be clearly heard from a mile away, and it didn't take long for the first of the rebels to struggle out of the fight, seeking escape from the fracas.

She pointed at the stragglers, a few dozen, and turned to her *cornifer*. "Sound the charge. Shoot when I do!" There were some things the Romans did that she had learned to like, and the complex trumpet calls, easily heard over the din of battle, was one of them. She took up her bow, drew a handful of arrows from her quiver, and spurred Devil into fierce charge, while she gave the ululating battle cry of the steppes. The *turma* thundered alongside her, their bows ready, each giving their own battle cries, some guttural, some even musical. At a hundred yards from the first group, she notched an arrow, drew and let fly. Her single arrow was quickly followed by a volley of thirty from the other horsemen, and she noted with pride that Mei was already notching her next shot, as was Marcia. By the time Hina had drawn her bow again, about half the rebels were down or reeling about, wounded. As the horsemen closed, those not yet wounded knelt and put their hands up, hoping for quarter.

The battle heat was on Hina, and she wanted to keep killing until they were all dead, but Longinus wanted captives for questioning. She reluctantly gave the order to cease fire, trembling with the emotions that come after a battle. Her soldiers dismounted with ropes to bind the survivors, others to check the wounded and dead. It had been a short fight.

She pulled up alongside Mei. "How did you do?" she asked.

Mei managed a smile. "I think I got one," she said, then suddenly turned her head to the other side of her horse to retch.

Back in the city, the Fifth came to a halt between the basilica and the temple. The first century broke ranks to join the fight, which was by now almost over. Samuel and Secundus came up to find the grinning Sergius holding Judah at sword point. "I have a present for you. He purports to be their leader, and he is not from here. I kept him alive just for you."

"Well done, Sergius. We'll take him off your hands. Marcus will have some questions for him." Secundus signaled two passing soldiers, who took custody of Judah and led him away.

"How many men did you lose?" asked Samuel.

"None, unless we lost some in this fracas, one man is down. About a dozen wounded, one seriously." As he was speaking, the *capsarius* carried out Varius on a litter. "That's the one, broken jaw from a sling stone. It looks very bad."

"We set the hospital tent up in the enclave. Papirius Aelianus works miracles. If any doctor can fix that jaw, he can."

"I hope so."

"Well, it looks like you lived up to Samuel's faith in you," said Secundus. "It looks like you've earned your first combat *phalera* for your breastplate. We'll have a little award ceremony after things quiet down."

"I didn't do anything, sir. My men did all the fighting," Sergius said. "My men did all the fighting."

"Give me a list of those that deserve awards also."

CHAPTER 115:

TENDING THE WOUNDED

Petra, December 115AD

Sergius desperately needed sleep, but he needed to see to his wounded men first, especially Varius. What might happen to him? If they could not repair that broken jaw, how would he live, disfigured and unable to eat? After tending to essential matters, seeing his men relieved for some much-needed rest and food, he trudged the mile back to the enclave, and found the hospital tent set up in the middle of the main street.

He entered in. The air was thick with the smell of vinegar, and various ointments, potions and medicinal herbs. His father had been an herbalist, and had wanted Sergius to follow in his footsteps. The smells reminded him of his father's shed. *But I ran away. Ran away because he tried to beat discipline into me. And I never looked back. I wonder what became of him?*

The cots were empty, except for the one occupied by Varius. A u-shaped collar behind his neck held his jaw, bound in place to the ends of the collar, wrapping around Varius' head. The surgeon, Papirius Aelinanus, was tending to him as Servius approached, along with Sergius' field medic Valentinian. Noticing Sergius, the surgeon signaled him to approach. "I am just making the last checks on his dressing. Please, you can see your man, though he is unconscious right now. I gave him a generous amount of opium when I reset his jaw. And he won't be able to say much more than grunts for a few weeks."

"Thank you," said Sergius. "His jaw is straight."

"Straight, though very swollen now. That will go down."

"It was amazing," said Valentinian. "A good thing I didn't try to pull any of his teeth. He used them to set the alignment right."

"I pulled the loosest ones. He may lose another, but I can't put the force on his jaw now to pull it," said Papirius. "He will be eating broth and soup for a while."

"How long will that take to heal?"

"A month to six weeks. We have to keep him immobilized for a week while the bones knit. After that, he can be up and around a bit."

"Well, they said you could work miracles, and it looks like you did."

"Thank you. You have a good *capsarius* in Valentinian here." Papirius nodded toward the young medic. "He kept him stable, didn't let the fracture become worse. Did all the right things."

Secundus, accompanied by Samuel, entered the tent. "Checking on your wounded, I see," said the tribune.

"Yes, sir … the only one here."

"The others were all treated back in town and sent to their tents. Minor wounds, all of them," volunteered Valentinian.

"Good to hear. And this is the man who stopped a slingstone with his jaw?"

"It is, sir."

"Well, I hope he did more damage to the stone than it did to his jaw."

"He kept the rebels from occupying the second floor of the basilica. He is one of those I had in mind should earn an award for saving the building. We might have been overrun before you arrived, without what he did."

"It certainly looks like he deserves it." Secundus turned toward the doctor. "Papirius, how long for his recovery?"

"A month to six weeks."

"I just received a letter from the legion. The Twelfth wants us in Dura Europos as soon as we have things settled here. I just sent them a reply that we would leave by the end of January, and arrive by the end of February. Will he be able to travel by then?"

"Maybe. He can travel in the hospital wagon, if he can't march in ranks."

"Very well."

Samuel directed his attention to the bedraggled Sergius. "Go get some rest. You did well."

CHAPTER 116:

A GRAND GATHERING

Petra, December 115AD

It took a few days to put it together, but Jacobus with Farvius planned a massive get-together for their old and new friends. It was also a chance to show off the beauty of Petra to all the newcomers.

In the center of town by the basilica on the Colonnaded Street, there was a huge, well-watered park, with statues, columned domes, and a huge bathing and swimming pool fifty paces in length, with an island pavilion in the middle. Tinkling fountains and waterfalls throughout the garden kept the area green, flowers always in bloom, and they also cooled the dry desert air. It was a bit worse due to lack of care during the recent insurrection, but it was still beautiful, and had not been damaged in the takeover. It did not take much persuasion to convince the new city administration to give the city's liberators, the off-duty centuries of the Fifth Cohort, a special celebration. Throughout the park next to the temple were several firepits, with rotisseries big enough for roasting pigs, goats and small calves. The merchants in town generously contributed the animals, along with plentiful supplies of a good local wine. And all the townspeople were invited to take part in the great celebration.

Jacobus had reserved one firepit for his own particular party, the veterans of the long trip back from Han China years back, a rather significant number of people that Jacobus had never expected to see again: Hina, Galosga, their three children and Hadyu, her commander Longinus, Marcia, Marcus and his wife Mei, Samuel and his tribune Secundus Lucullus, standing in for his father Gaius. And there was his wife Miranda, Stick, Mouse, and several of his older boys. And Farvius brought his *vigiles*. In all, more than thirty gathered around a goat, the sweet aroma of roasting meat filling the air as grease hissed on the embers below it, Stick managing the iron crank.

The newly-installed city fathers had just finished their speeches, thanking the Fifth and the power of the people of Rome for ridding their city of the murderous rebels, praising the soldiers' valor, and making the city open to all of them. The crowd erupted into cheers as the speeches finished, ending with swelling calls of '*Io Triumphe*', the Latin cheer for a conquering army.

As the din subsided, Jacobus took this opportunity to motion his own group to silence. Raising his glass, he said, "I never expected to see any of you, my old friends, ever again, much less to see us all gathered together as we are. Let me propose a toast, to shared adventures, to shared hazards, and to life-long friendships."

Samuel then raised his glass. "And I propose a toast to Jacobus' father, that piratical scourge of the seas, the great Ibrahim, who steered us through a dangerous course out of China. It is sad to say he is not with us today, but I was honored to be asked to offer his funeral prayer. To Ibrahim!"

"Samuel, or I should call you Shmuel as we all did then, I am touched. My father's life was a friendless one filled with associates, co-conspirators, allies for the moment ... but never a friend he could trust. Trust is denied the pirate. He died unexpectedly that night, but he was surrounded by all of you, the most trusted friends a man could ever want. To all of you!"

Hina produced several leather sacks of *kumis,* passing them around, and one of the *vigiles* produced a lyre and began to play some light tunes. The veterans of the grand odyssey gathered together, joined by Longinus and Secundus.

Longinus opened the conversation. "Hina, I knew you and Marcia met on some grand adventure in the past, but Han China? Does the place even exist?"

"It exists, and yes, I made only a short part of that journey. Long enough to meet the man I love, and to find my sister Marcia."

"Marcia, how did you two meet?" Longinus eyed marcia quizzically.

"We had just arrived at the Xiongnu camp for the first time, and she tried to bed my Antonius. Very openly."

"An interesting way to begin your sisterhood. What happened?"

"He turned her down. She had to settle for Galosga instead." Marcia covered her mouth to hide her tittering.

Hina joined in. "I had a habit of taking strange men when they came into our camp, and these were by far the strangest people I had ever seen. Antonius was the first who ever turned me down. And I have been glad ever since. Antonius has been good for Marcia, and Galosga has been good for me."

"We have many stories. We should write them down, as they make as good a tale as Homer's *Odyssey.* When we got back to Rome, the people called us Jason and the New Argonauts." Marcia smiled, her blue eyes twinkling behind their oriental folds. "Jacobus, I have a question. We got here through the worst desert I have ever seen, past a great lake so full of salt it forms on the shoreline. Yet this place is a splendid jewel amidst all of the surrounding barrenness, full of sweet cold water. How do you do it?"

"There is always a little rain in the mountains around us. It is all captured, held and channeled down here to the valley. The Nabataeans have been building their water management here for centuries, every year making it a little better."

"And I have an announcement of interest to us all," offered Secundus. "I received a letter from the legion indicating that they would depart Dura Europos at the end of February, and inquiring on how we were doing recovering Petra. I sent them a reply that it was going well, that I expect to depart here at the end of January to join them at Dura Europos ahead of their departure. So, you will have about a month at this beautiful garden spot in the desert. They also said there was a great earthquake in Antioch, but the *Princeps* was unharmed."

"Aulus and Livia were in Antioch with the *Princeps*. Are they all right?" asked Marcia.

"Unfortunately, they did not mention them. But if they were with the *Princeps* then they too are probably fine."

Over the next several hours, they shared stories of their adventures together while the others joined in songs to the accompaniment of the lyre, some beautiful, some bawdy.

Marcus and Mei paired off with Stick and Mouse, talking animatedly, just the four of them, as the boy turned the crank to turn the goat.

Mouse was intrigued with her oriental features. "Why do your eyes look funny, Aunt Mei?" she asked with childish innocence.

Mei smiled at the little girl. "Where I come from, most everyone's eyes are like this, and it would be your eyes that look funny."

"Where is that?"

"It is far, far away from here, toward the rising sun. It would take you two whole birthdays to walk that far."

"I don't have birthdays. I wasn't born, I just came to live here."

"Everyone was born."

"Not me, I just grew up on the street."

Stick joined in. "We have a special day, the day we came to live with Mother Miranda and Father Jacobus. They take care of us now."

"You both speak good Latin."

"They make us learn it, so we can have a good life. They teach us how to read and write, too."

"I know the whole *abecederium*." Mouse announced proudly, and proceeded to reel off all the letters of the alphabet.

Stick jumped in, as his erstwhile sister was dominating the whole conversation. "How many children do you have, Aunt Mei?" he asked.

"We don't have any," she said, trying to keep her face from darkening.

"Are you going to have some someday?"

"No ... we can't." Her efforts failed, a tear came to her eyes, and Marcus' face darkened as well."

"I'm sorry. I asked something that made you sad."
"It's all right. Let me take a turn with the goat," said Marcus.

CHAPTER 117:

A CITY IN RECOVERY

Antioch, January 116AD

After several days, the more violent aftershocks that followed the immensely destructive earthquake finally subsided to just uncomfortable stirrings in the earth. These minor quakes alarmed the citizens, who rushed outdoors fearing them as harbingers of more death and destruction. But these tremors only lasted a few seconds, and never built in magnitude.

Trajan had set up his temporary headquarters in the imperial box on the hippodrome, opposite the palace, taking daily briefings on the recovery effort. These briefings he insisted be kept short, so that all could concentrate on the recovery, not on keeping him informed of each minor effort. The briefing on the *ides* of January in mid-month, however, came a full month after the earthquake, and it was an opportunity to recap all aspects of the recovery. It ran from two hours after sunrise until noon. Hadrian, as the Syrian governor, Aulus Galba and Trajan's other advisors sat by his side, while the various recovery leaders presented their progress and identified their special needs.

In summary, a month after the quake, the main streets were clear of rubble, though many were cracked and fissured. This gave access to twenty-mule-team wagons that hauled off tons of rubble, much of which was going to reinforce breakwaters at the port of Seleucia. Many side streets remained blocked to wagons by collapsed buildings, but enough rubble had been cleared to give pedestrians and horses access. Battering rams were used to demolish dangerously damaged buildings, which were then picked apart by the giant treadmill cranes.

Workers had completed emergency repairs to the damaged aqueducts, though some still leaked torrential streams of water from cracks; water was restored to the city's fountains, wells and firefighters.

A fleet of ships crowded the harbor at Seleucia Pieria, waiting to offload their cargos of food and mechanical hardware to assist in the recovery.

And the major port at Caesarea Maritima was back in operation, though at reduced capacity, after the devastating tidal wave that came at the same time as the earthquake.

Quintus Sevilius presented the death toll last. "Your Excellency, we have recovered over a hundred thousand bodies, and believe there are that many more waiting to be found. We fear we have lost about a third of the city's population. We have had mass cremations going for weeks, but in many cases, we had to resort to mass burials outside the city. There were simply too many corpses for us properly cremate, and great risk for disease," the briefer concluded with a sigh.

"Do we have any identities for the dead?" asked Trajan.

"In some cases, family members survived and identified them. We have a list of those. But in most cases, no. They are unfortunately just numbers. The people are putting flyers around the Forum and the Agora marketplace to see if anyone knows the whereabouts of a loved one, or in some cases, putting up a notice that they have survived, where they are staying, hoping to reconnect. This is the saddest duty I have ever had to perform."

"Thank you, Quintus. And thank you all for your presentations. I wanted today to have a firm understanding of the recovery, which seems to be well underway. As you all know, there is also a war on, which will soon demand my attention. I will be departing at the end of January, leaving the city in the very capable hands of Governor Publius Aelius Hadrian. You may return to your very important duties." He rose, Hadrian and his advisors with him, and departed.

Trajan, Hadrian and Aulus assembled with their wives in Hadrian's newly-reopened dining room. Servants brought a light lunch, wine, olives, dates, and thinly-sliced meats.

Hadrian indicated the thin wool curtains covering the window, billowing in the wind. They admitted light, but kept the warmth from the braziers in and the chill January breezes out.

"I apologize for the lack of a view, cousin, but it will take some time to replace the expensive Egyptian glass in those windows, and there are other priorities for the *praetorium* at this time."

"No matter," answered Trajan. "We are fortunate that it did not suffer more damage."

Hadrian fancied himself a talented architect, and took the opportunity to show off his knowledge. "The Greeks learned how make earthquake-proof columns. They make the column, then cut it into five-foot sections, put a hollow in the middle of each and a hole to the outside. They bind them together, pour molten lead into the hole and seal it with matching marble. They can sway to motion of the ground, but won't fracture or come apart."

"Interesting," said Trajan. "I wonder what causes earthquakes. Ill will of the gods?"

"Some Greeks believe that there are caverns deep in the earth filled with air. Sometimes they collapse, causing the shaking. Pliny, on the other hand, thought it was particular alignments of the planets and the sun. The truth is, no one knows for sure," said Aulus.

Hadrian returned to the business at hand. "So, you will be leaving for the eastern theater at the end of the month?"

"Yes, I will be going to Nisibis. There are boats stockpiled there for Lusius Quietus, who is wintering in Cizre. He needs the boats to cross the Tigris to finish pacifying Adiabene and taking Mosila. The *XXII Primigenia* is handling the river crossing, since they have the experience of river warfare from their time on the Rhine. I want to be there for the crossing, but once they are across, I am going to Dura Europos. I am leading the assault down the Euphrates, Lusius Quietus down the Tigris."

After a few minutes devoted to eating, Pompeia spoke up. "So, Livia, will you be leaving with Aulus Aemilius?"

"Oh, no! I have had enough camp life to last me a lifetime. There are only three other women in the camp and they have become Amazons, riding with the cavalry, so they were seldom around. That is not for me, I am going to stay here in Antioch and offer frequent sacrifices for no further earthquakes."

"Amazons? Who might those be? Are we recruiting Sarmatians now?" asked Hadrian, smiling.

"One of those women makes the Sarmatians look tame and peaceful, Your Excellency," said Aulus. "That would be the barbarian Hina. She was with us on our trek out of China, when we were traveling with the Xiongnu. Back then, she commanded a squad of ten men, not unusual for those people, and after she left us, was given the command of a hundred men. Sort of a wild centurion. She joined up with Marcus Lucius on his way out of China, and she and her husband actually broke Marcus out of the Ctesiphon palace jail. She showed some Xiongnu tricks to Longinus Clarus' Ninth Batavians, and he was impressed."

"Interesting, and the other two?" asked Hadrian.

"The second is Marcus' Chinese wife Mei. She came under the influence of Hina. The third one is Marcia Lucia, the wife of Antonius Aristides. She is just a slip of a girl, not two talents in weight, but believe me, she can be a wildcat. I have seen her fight, and I would not want to be the one fighting her. She became Hina's protégée when we were with the Xiongnu, and she taught her everything. The two consider themselves sisters."

"A different life for women in the Distant East," observed Hadrian's wife Vibia Sabina.

"Not necessarily better, but different, Lady Vibia," answered Aulus. "Marcia had been a much-abused concubine of a court functionary, and she was falsely accused of infidelity with Antonius and tried before the Han king. As she was a Roman citizen, many generations removed, I put myself at her defense, but alas, my rhetoric was insufficient, and I succeeded only in getting us all condemned to death. So, I think she learned to fight so that she could never be dominated like that again. And she became, as I said, quite good at it."

CHAPTER 118:

SEDUCTION

Antioch, February 116AD

Marcus Ulpius Trajan left abruptly for the front, too abrupt even for his usual passionate farewell to Pompeia. She was disappointed, and a little angry, that he had done so, and the copy of Ovid's *Art of Love* that she was reading did not aid her state of mind. Nevertheless, she was satisfied that he was usually attentive to her needs, and discrete about his outside dalliances.

There was a quiet knock at the entrance to her chambers. A servant spoke quietly. "My Lady, Lady Vibia Sabina to see you."

Pompeia set aside the scroll on her small table. "Please, send her in. I need the company."

Vibia Sabina entered a few minutes later. "Good morning, Aunt Pompeia. Are you well?"

Pompeia smiled. "Considering that Marcus Ulpius, in his rush to get back to the fighting, forgot to give me a proper farewell, yes, I am well, Vibia," she said with a smile.

"At least he does attend to you. Publius and I sleep separately, and he very seldom takes time from chasing boys to come warm my bed. Perhaps I should grow a beard."

"I understand he prefers beardless boys. But what brings you to see me?"

"Publius is angry with Uncle Marcus. He was expecting an adoption ceremony, and that too was forgotten, with the earthquake and Uncle Marcus' haste to get back to the war."

Pompeia considered lying to Hadrian's wife. The adoption ceremony had not been forgotten. He had discussed this with her a few days ago. Trajan wanted to appoint a regent, someone in Rome with no personal imperial ambitions, to rule as caretaker in the event of his death, while the Senate considered a list of candidates. Hadrian headed his draft list, but several others were on it also. Pompeia decided to tell just part of the truth. "Your uncle is going to send Publius' name on to the Senate as his successor," she said

"And that is why he is angry. You are right, Aunt Pompeia, he is sending Publius' name to the Senate, but he is not the only one being recommended. He is also recommending Lusius Quietus, Avidius Negrinus and several others. They also have their own strong followers in the Senate. Publius has been Uncle Marcus' most loyal supporter and campaigner, and now he feels that he is being cast out, just one of many for the Senate to choose."

How did he know that? Marcus Ulpius had no intention of discussing this with Hadrian, and the letter had not even been drafted yet. Was Publius spying on his cousin? "If he has others in mind, he did not discuss that with me," she lied.

"Besides the ones on the list, there are many others who think they should be *princeps*. Publius is concerned that without a clear succession, there will be strife, maybe even civil war. And Uncle Marcus' reputation will be ruined." Vibia paused for a breath. She did not normally engage in politics, and her discomfort showed. "Publius would like to talk to you about this, if you would."

"I will talk to him."

The two women returned to small talk.

Pompeia, accompanied by her maidservant and bodyguard, wandered down the halls of the governor's *praesidium*, which smelled of fresh plaster and paint, though the mosaic floors still bore the scars of the earthquake, cracked and in some places still tilted askew. She reached Hadrian's office and entered unannounced, catching Hadrian attending to a scroll at his desk in the company of a bevy of tunic-clad servants.

"You wished to see me?" she said, her tone of voice indicating that she should not be kept waiting.

"Pompeia, my dear, yes, I do. You have spoken with Vibia?" Hadrian asked, putting aside the scroll, and waving the servants out. Pompeia likewise dismissed hers. This was to be a very private conversation.

"I have."

Hadrian shut the door. "What we discuss must not leave this room. For the good of the Principate."

"The good of the Principate did not prevent Marcus Ulpius' private discussions with me from reaching your ears," she said, her lips tight.

"Marcus Ulpius shared that discussion with other ears than yours, and those ears shared those discussions with me. For the good of the Principate." Hadrian said, returning to his seat.

"And how is it that those ears had a greater concern for the Principate than does my husband, the *Princeps*?"

"My dear cousin has a vision of Rome that ceased to exist centuries ago. He expects the wise old men of the Senate to shrewdly choose his successor from his list of candidates, and choose the one that will be best for Rome. They will not."

"And who might they choose, if not you?"

"There are dozens of men who would be *Princeps*. Some, like Marcus Ulpius, for the good of Rome. Others, for money, power or just plain vanity.

And each of those men have a half-dozen Senators who will put them forth as alternative candidates."

"And you, of course, are one who considers only the good of Rome."

"You are angry with me, Pompeia, for challenging our dear Marcus Ulpius. But he and I have challenged each other throughout our whole lives. If he were here, I would tell him to his face that what he has proposed is stupid, unworkable, and likely to result in a disastrous civil war as the contenders vie for the ultimate prize. But he is not here. You are, so I am happy to share my concerns with you. Those on his list, if it is submitted to the Senate, are not likely to be the next *princeps,* and whoever does fill that role, will see to it that Marcus Ulpius is not remembered for the good he has done, as the *Optimus Princeps,* the best of the best. They will instead attempt to remove his memory from the public, so that its light does not dim their own. As they did with Domitian twenty years ago. *Damnatio memoriae,* the condemnation of all his memories, his statues, monuments, everything, pulled down, destroyed and effaced by lesser men. I don't want that to happen to my beloved cousin, your beloved husband." He fell silent, his chin on his fingers behind his curly bronze beard.

Pompeia was stunned. She was twenty-five when Domitian was assassinated and his body unceremoniously cremated with no public ceremony, and she remembered it well. Domitian had not been a good emperor, and had made many enemies, but he had not been a Nero or Caligula, either. But the Senate wasted no time erasing his name from history. Like her husband, Domitian had no children, and had not adopted a successor to be his heir, so there was no one to defend his name and legacy. The conspirators put up the weak-willed, aging Nerva, who had reigned just long enough to adopt Marcus Ulpius as his successor before dying.

She cleared her throat. "No, I don't want that, either."

"I can't write my cousin to request him to reconsider that course of action, because, officially, I do not know of it. But you can, my dear Pompeia. Please consider it."

"I will be honest, the list you speak of has not even been drafted yet."

"Thank you for being honest. I would appreciate it if you expressed my concerns to him, without hinting that I know of this. He respects your insight. The others are good men also, and I would be glad to stand aside for them, but I don't believe the Senate will make an honest judgment."

"I have to be very careful how I express these thoughts to Marcus Ulpius. Anyone other than him reading the letter must not know that his proper succession may be uncertain."

"You are an astute woman, Pompeia." Hadrian put his fingers back under his chin, and looked at her intently, smiling.

"What are you staring at, Publius?"

"I was admiring your beautiful yellow *stola*. That, and the dark green wrap, go so well with your red hair."

Pompeia smiled, blushing. "Publius, you are flattering me. I am far too old to be attractive, your wife's great aunt. And besides, I am not a boy."

He laughed. "Your mind is what attracts me. If there were more women like you, I would have no need of boys." He kept smiling, discomfiting her still more. He was a strikingly handsome man, very physical in appearance, and that golden-hued beard added to his features. Against her best efforts, she felt her loins stirring.

She knew that Marcus Ulpius had had his dalliances, with women and sometimes with boys. Pompeia had also, during his many long absences, occasionally shared her bed with others. Both had been discrete, careful not to create problems, for each other or for the dignity of the Principate. But with Publius Hadrian? He was too close, far too close, Marcus Ulpius' cousin, his probable successor and the husband of her grandniece. Was he wooing her, with that witty smile and his dancing gray eyes?

She stirred in her seat, trying to calm her emotions, hoping they did not show. "Well, thank you for the compliment, my dear Publius. And thank you for your concerns. I will find a way to express them to Marcus Ulpius in my next letter. I have taken up enough of your time, I must go now." She took her eyes off Hadrian's and stood up. He was quite a handsome, charming man, after all, despite his proclivities.

"There is no need to hurry."

"I must go now." She quickly crossed to the door and exited, hoping he did not notice that she was trembling.

"Come visit me any time, my dearest Pompeia, you are always welcome."

CHAPTER 119:

MISCALCULATION

Ctesiphon, January 116AD

Mithridates stood, his green and gold robe swirling about him. "Come in, come in, my son! It has been a long time. Come in and take a seat," he said, gesturing to the padded sofa.

Sanatruces entered and took his seat. "I bring bad news, father," he said, dejection darkening his face. "We have lost Petra."

"That is by no means bad news, son. We never needed Petra. What you did in Nisibis was to lay waste to a cohort of one of their vaunted legions, then force them to detach another on a seven-hundred-mile jaunt to recover Petra. And they will march back to Nisibis just in time to step out on their spring campaign, without any winter training. This worked exactly as we wanted, and you should be proud of your work."

"Thank you, father. Perhaps I was too connected with what we had done."

"What we wanted to do was to use these insurrections to scatter their forces. The Romans could not ignore an uprising in one of their newest provinces. And they had to send a whole cohort on a very long march to recover it, thanks to what you did."

Sanatruces managed a weak smile. "Still, I wish we could have kept Petra, taking it from the Romans. And unfortunately, Trajan was not killed in the Antioch earthquake. Just one of his consuls."

"Yes, the gods mocked us that day. Not even injured. From the field, what do you make of his plans? It would seem he would consolidate what he has taken this season."

"We believe he will do that. He has taken Armenia and Mesopotamia in short order, but he needs time to firm up the administration of these new provinces. We have demonstrated that his newly-taken rear areas are not secure, and that we can even threaten him on Roman territory. He will not want to over-extend his forces this year. He has built about a hundred or so boats at Nisibis, that we expect he will use to patrol the Tigris, move small units around quickly, as required, messenger duty … that sort of thing."

"Why weren't they destroyed when we held Nisibis?"

"Poor execution. The man we had put in charge missed them, believing the wagons to be loaded with timbers. He thought he could sell them for a tidy profit, so he didn't burn them. The Romans got them back."

"But, no big offensive this year?"

"I do not think so. Some small forays, maybe an attempt to move further south down the Tigris and Euphrates. The big attack will come next year, with his divided forces coming down the Tigris and Euphrates to converge on us here. He will probably start very early, so he can launch the attack before it gets too hot here in the south. In the meanwhile, we want to get our insurrections mounted now. We have organized sympathetic followers among the Jews in Judea, Cyrenaica, Alexandria, and Cyprus. If those areas go up in flames, he will probably have to redeploy some of his legions there to put them down, and will not be able to mount the big offensive when he is ready. We will defeat him without fighting him."

"Interesting. When I was with the Han ten years ago, I learned of a book on warfare by one of their great strategists of five hundred years ago. That strategist said the greatest victories are achieved by not having to fight for them. This looks like you have done well. Tell my brother Osroës what you have told me, it is all good news."

CHAPTER 120:

CROSSING THE TIGRIS

Cizre, February 116AD

Trajan arrived at the headquarters of his eastern forces at Cizre with little fanfare, as there was work to be done. After an obligatory speech to the assembled troops and Lusius Quietus' Berber cavalry, he removed his cream-colored helmet with its purple crest and retired to the command *praetorium*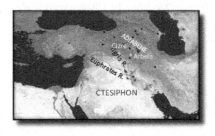
with Aulus and his staff to discuss the upcoming operations. He went straight to the map on the center table, outlining the Tigris river, the Adiabene fortifications on the east bank, and the dispositions of Lusius' cavalry. The legions *XII Primigenia, III Gallicae, III Scythia, VI Ferrata,* and *XV Apollinaris* were marked on the west bank in and around Cizre. Lusius Quietus spoke up first.

"Welcome back, Your Excellency. My apologies for not crossing the river last year. It was a miscalculation on our part. There is almost no wood to be had within a hundred miles on this side of the Tigris. Plenty on the other side, but not for us."

"That is not a problem, Lusius. We have brought you all the boats you need from Nisibis in our wagon train. Aulus, what do we have in that train?" He turned to the Senator.

"We have fifty light thirty-oared *naves lusoriae* patrol boats, and ten *naves actuariae* transports for the assault." Aulus turned toward Lucius Licinius Sura, commanding the Fifteenth Lucky Capricorns. "Your engineers built these boats, Lucius Licinius. Would you tell us about them?"

"Certainly, Aulus Aemilius. They are prefabricated, so it will take about a week to reassemble them. We will use the patrol boats to secure the opposite beachhead with two cohorts, under cover of the larger transports outfitted with *ballista* artillery to cover the landing. After the beachhead is secure, we will use the patrol boats to form a pontoon bridge to get everyone else across. After everyone is over, we will break up the bridge to prevent the Adiabenes from crossing behind us, then return the boats to service. The patrol boats and transports will go south with us to take the Adiabene capital at Arbela, doing whatever needs to be done."

"Very well," said the *Princeps*. "Riverine warfare is what you have done for years on the Rhine, and there is none among us who can do it better than you here on the Tigris. You are in command of this amphibious assault. Your cohorts will be the first to land and take the beachhead, but the rest of your legion will be the last to cross over. Overall command will then revert back to Lusius Quietus." He turned toward the swarthy Berber cavalry commander. "Lusius, take charge of the legions and the cavalry as they cross over, deploy them as Lucius Licinius requires to support the rest of the crossing. Then we unseat King Mahaspes from Arbela and break up his alliance with Singara. With Adiabene out of the way, your way will be clear to Ctesiphon, where you and I will meet up again at the end of summer."

"Yes, sir," said the Berber, rendering a stoic salute.

"Very well. You can work out the rest of the details of the crossing without my interference. I have had a long trip from Antioch, and I am going to retire to my quarters." He departed smartly, his purple cloak swirling.

The boats were assembled on the western shore, opposite a large island separated from the far bank by a narrow branch of the river. Once the Romans gained a foothold on it, the narrow strait separating it from the eastern shore would make it very defensible while the remainder of the force congregated on it. The Adiabenes noted the activity, moving several thousand troops to repel the coming invasion. When the boats appeared to be nearing completion, the Adiabene troops occupied the island, to oppose the initial beachhead.

Unfortunately, the Adiabenes were in the wrong place, at the wrong time. It was all a deception. Overnight, twenty of the boats had quietly sortied without lights, drifting downstream with a thousand men aboard to the real beachhead ten miles south.

It was a dark, moonless night, and the twenty boats were groping blindly in the blackness, drifting silently with the current without lanterns or torches. Only the gurgle of water overside betrayed their presence. All eyes on each hull strained to see another boat, to avoid a collision.

Serianus was at the helm of the boat ignominiously named Thirty-One. There had been no time wasted naming the boats as they were hastily assembled and launched the past week, but Serianus felt like this was an ill omen. Boats and ships should have names, but all Thirty-One had were the Roman numerals 'XXXI' splashed on her bow. But she was a *navis lusoria*, a 'dancing ship', seventy feet of narrow, nimble responsiveness, and Serianus loved commanding these boats, as he had done on the Rhine.

Thirty-One's thirty oars were raised and canted inward vertically, barely visible as they rolled with the boat against the stars, at the ready but protected against collision. In the bow, the leadsman tossed his weight overside, searching for sandbars, retrieving it, and quietly calling out the depth for Serianus. They were an hour underway, with about another hour to go. Serianus watched the wheel of the stars overhead, estimating where they would be an hour from now.

Something in the night noise caught Serianus' attention. At first, he thought it was his nerves, but then it became clear, the gurgle of water around another ship, not his own, and far too close. He located it in the darkness, closing on his port side. He put the tiller hard over, and called out loudly, "Collision! Collision port side! All hands fend off the other ship!"

His shout caught the attention of the other ship, and one could hear shouts, curses and the patter of feet as they, too, prepared to avoid disaster. Soldiers lined the sides of both ships, with boat hooks, poles and oars to push other ship away.

The ships came close enough for the crews to see each other's faces, poles and tillers fiercely straining to reduce the ships' momentum. They did contact, but with all that effort, it was just a solid thump that did no damage. Serianus tried to still his pounding heart.

Trajan, with Aulus by his side, surrounded by Lusius Quietus and the five legion commanders, gathered on a small promontory overlooking the river, well before sunrise on a chilly spring dawn. It was far too dark to see anything on the moonless night, but they knew what was riding on the river: ten patrol boats carrying fifty troops each, and the ten larger transports armed with *ballistae* artillery to cover the landing.

Aulus wrapped his cloak about. "Looks like it worked. No lights on the other side, sir."

"They could be there in force. We will know when we land."

The darkness gave way to the grayness of pre-dawn, and the boats could be made out now as still dark shapes on the drifting mists of the river. There was a brief flash of a lantern from one, covered and uncovered three times in succession.

Lucius Licinius Sura, commanding the amphibious assault, spoke up quietly to Trajan. "That is the signal, Your Excellency. The landing has begun. And the rest of our fleet will sortie from upriver to join us at noon. I don't want to make it easy for the Adiabenes to follow them down the river to find the real landing site." His wry smile was visible in the half-light.

"Good deception, Lucius Licinius."

"I hope it works. I hate making opposed landings."

Despite all efforts, sound carried well in the quiet windless morning: the thumps and bumps of oars being fitted, anchors raised and secured, quiet commands, then the hushed cadences called on each boat to synchronize the rowers. The dark shapes began an almost imperceptible advance from mid-stream to their landing site.

By the time it was bright enough to make out colors, the ten patrol boats were lined up on the opposite shoreline, discharging their cohort, while the transports patrolled close, within artillery range. Once they were ashore, the boats turned around, crossing to pick up the second cohort, returning to discharge them just minutes after sunrise.

"It appears you got our first cohort across, Lucius Licinius," said Aulus.

"It appears so. And unless the Adiabenes are counting men and boats upstream, they won't even know we are already across for some hours. It will take perhaps another day for them to move their soldiers. We will be well on to our way completing the pontoon bridge by the time they arrive."

Satisfied that the crossing had gone well, Trajan turned and the group retired to his command tent to plan the rest of the day.

Two of the boats began the return to the west bank, each paying out a heavy hawser from an anchoring emplacement of the eastern beach. These two ropes would serve to anchor the bow and stern of each of the patrol boats, holding them bows-on into the current, to be covered by planking that would form the bridge deck. Fifty of the ten-foot-wide boats side by side would just span the river.

By the time the remaining boats arrived by mid-afternoon, the ten assault patrol boats were already lashed in place, covered by decking on the western shore. It did not take long for the new arrivals to join their companions, and by the time the sun went down, all boats were in place, and planks across provided a narrow walkway across the stream. This would be widened the next day to sixty feet, reinforced to carry men, horses and wagons.

And the Adiabenes did arrive, too late to prevent the landing, and unprepared to face the full fifty-thousand-man force that would soon pour across the hastily-constructed bridge.

CHAPTER 121:

THE RATPACK RETURNS

Dura Europos, March 116AD

The Fifth Cohort, with the Ninth Batavian cavalry in their rear, rejoined the Twelfth, loudly singing their marching song, to the great amusement of the rest of the legion. They were proudly announcing their status as the legion's dregs, but word of their success in liberating Petra had preceded them. Secundus Lucullus and his centurion Samuel Elisarius had hammered the dregs of the legion, the shiftless ne'er-do-wells, thieves and shirkers that the other cohorts had wanted to purge from their ranks, into a proud, blooded fighting unit. At a word from Secundus, Samuel bawled out the command to halt, and three hundred and fifty pairs of boots slammed to a stop as one before the legion commander and his staff on their podium, raising a little cloud of dust. They stood silently at attention, their *pila* erect on their shoulders, while Gaius Lucullus surveyed his son's handiwork.

"Let me be the first to welcome the Ninth Batavians and the Ratpack Fifth back home to the legion,' said Gaius, pausing to allow a titter of amusement to ripple through the rest of the legion, which had turned out to observe the Fifth's return. "Word of your endeavors in Petra have reached me, and let me tell you how proud we are that you made such short work of a serious threat to our newly-acquired province. You all will be excused from duties for the next three days, to recover from your long and arduous march. But in three days, be prepared to fall out in full dress uniform for your awards. Let's hear it for the Ratpack and the Ninth Batavians! Dismissed, and get some rest!"

The legion cheered, and Samuel gave the order to fall out. A runner came up to Secundus. "The *legatus* wants to see you, sir, and your centurion," said the soldier.

The two headed off to the *praetorium* tent, and were joined by Longinus Clarus of the Ninth, along with Hina, Galosga, Marcia, Marcus and Mei. Secundus gave the password of the day and the two soldiers guarding the entrance snapped erect, saluted and admitted them to the interior.

The inside had no lamps and needed none, illuminated by the yellowish glow of bright sunlight through the white canvas. Gaius Lucullus was seated at his desk, surrounded by Antonius, the camp prefect, and Paulus Herrerius, his *primus pilus*. The group saluted as one, right fists slammed across their chests. "At ease, gentlemen. And ... uh, you ladies, also. Take seats, please." Gaius waved to the waiting campaign seats before his desk. "Welcome back. That was a nice piece of work in Petra, Tribune Lucullus."

"We had a lot of help from the holdouts there. What was left of the *vigiles*, veterans and Jacobus, whom I believe you knew," said Secundus. "Without them, it would have been a lot harder and longer."

"Jacobus, yes. How is he?"

"Very well, and married now. He runs a home for street children there. He was one once, he said."

"Yes, he was adopted by that delightful pirate Ibrahim. But that is another story. What did they do?"

"They had fortified a walled residential area where they lived just west of the main city. We got one century in undetected. They were able to take the basilica by surprise and hold it while we brought up the rest of the cohort and the cavalry the same way. The rebels were trying to overrun them when we arrived on the scene. That ended that, and the cavalry made short work of those trying to escape. Longinus, would you like to discuss the cavalry side of things?" said Secundus, turning to Longinus Clarus.

"As the Tribune said, sir, we rode out, flanking the town to cut off their escape. I have got to say some good things about our Xiongnu. They have been teaching us things I didn't think we could ever do well, like mounted archery. Trying to round up a bunch of stragglers from horseback can usually turn into a lot of confusion, and some always get away. But we just peppered them with arrows from a couple dozen yards out, and those we didn't hit just threw up their hands before we could get off three volleys. I think with what Hina has taught us, we can go one-on-one with the Parthian light cavalry."

"Glad to see the fight is still in you, Hina. And your children?" said Gaius.

"They are fourteen, so they are adults among us," she said with a smile. "They are fine, tending Adhela for me now. And Marcia and Mei did well also."

"Well done on teaching our cavalry new tricks."

"They learned fast."

Gaius turned toward his son. "Well done, Tribune Lucullus. Tell us about the insurrection." He smiled and added, "My son."

"Pretty much as at Nisibis, some Jewish, mostly bandits, with some Parthian soldiers in the mix backing them up. However, unlike at Nisibis, we brought the leader Judah back with us. Somewhat the worse for wear, being in a cage, bouncing around in the back of a cart on our way back." He chuckled. "I thought your people might want to interrogate him."

"That is great news, good thinking to bring him back alive. We'll see what we can get out of him."

"Probably not much. He hasn't lost his sense of defiance, but I think he would rather have been executed than imprisoned so long in such Spartan conditions. He insists that Osroës is going to liberate all the Jewish people and restore the Temple for them, so this is definitely Ctesiphon's doing. He keeps saying there is much more to come, but we haven't gotten him to tell us what that is."

"Arrian has some expert interrogators. He'll put them to work on him." Gaius leaned back in his seat. "I wanted to have you all together for some special news, news that I don't want shared with your troops. The *Princeps* will be arriving tonight, and the awards presentation will be in three days … he will be doing the presentations, and to you three women as well. We want this to be a surprise to the troops. We will form up the entire legion, then call out the Ratpack, and the individuals, for the awards."

Samuel and Marcus delivered the bedraggled Judah, still in his cage, to Arrian at the intelligence tent. "I brought you a surprise. Judah, the leader of the Petra rebellion."

"Welcome to my humble tent, Judah," said Arrian in Aramaic. "You look like you could use a bath."

Judah grunted but said nothing. Samuel said, "We made sure he bathed every few days in Petra so he didn't get sick and die. But on the road, we were having a hard enough time keeping ourselves clean."

Arrian signaled for some soldiers to step forward and provide security as he undid the lock. "These men will escort you to the tub. Don't try to escape, you won't get far." He turned to the soldiers, who escorted him out. "And find him a fresh tunic. Burn the one he is wearing," he called after them.

"No manacles?" asked Marcus.

"Not right now. There are a lot of ways to interrogate people. My preferred approach is to gain their confidence. Befriend them, be sympathetic and very often they will quickly spill everything they know. And most of it will be true. Torture them, and they will tell you what they think you want to hear, just to make it stop. We'll see how this goes." He laid out some bread, cheese and wine on his desk. "I presumed he hasn't had lunch yet?"

The soldiers brought Judah back in half an hour, much cleaner and sweeter-smelling. "Have a seat, Judah, and take lunch with me. What is your full name?"

"Judah bin Daoud," he said, picking up the bread and tearing off a hunk. He was trying to be defiant, but the food was too tempting.

"We will be putting you up in better accommodations here. It's still a prison, you understand, since you are our prisoner, but it is larger, one we use for our own soldiers when they are detained. Do you read?"

"Aramaic and Hebrew."

"We probably have little of that in the camp."

"I have a copy of the Torah," offered Samuel.

"Really? You are a Roman soldier and a practicing Believer?" asked Judah.

"I was born Jewish, grew up in Galilee, and like you, I was once a rebel. But unfortunately, my circumstances as the only Jew in the legion do not allow me to to closely follow the Law. I will get the scroll for you. It will help the time pass more swiftly. Take care of it, it was my father's."

"What will happen to me?" Judah said, with just enough of a quiver to his voice to betray his concern for the future.

Samuel looked to Arrian, who answered, "First, we will settle you into your new accommodations. Tomorrow we can talk again. We want to learn some things you may know, things that might save some lives, both Roman and Jewish. More wine? You seem to have finished that quickly."

"No ... uh, yes, please."

Arrian refilled his glass. "Where were you born, Judah?"

"I was born in Ninu, on the Tigris."

"How did your family come to be here?"

"We have always been here. Not all Jews went back to Israel when Cyrus released them centuries back. Many of us stayed. My family did." He turned to Samuel. "But you were born and raised in Galilee? Did you ever visit Jerusalem?"

Samuel shook his head. "No. We moved to Tyre when the war broke out. When I was growing up, it was not a good place to visit, after the Jewish rebellion."

"So how did you come to be soldier of Rome?"

"That is a long story that I will save for later, a story of ships and the sea, camels ... and my friend Marcus."

Arrian concluded the talk. "Judah, I am sure you would like to get some rest after your grueling trip. My soldiers will escort you to your cell. If you need anything, have one of your guards summon me."

The soldiers escorted him away. When he was gone, Arrian turned to Samuel. "I didn't know you were Jewish. If you don't mind, I would like to have you participate in our talks with Judah. What was the Torah that you offered to bring him?"

"That is the Jewish holy scriptures. And yes, I will help out as my duties allow."

"A very nice touch indeed. He was all set to resist pain and torture, and what he got was a bath, food, and friendly conversation." He turned to Marcus. "Something to note. The trick to this type of interrogation is to get the person used to answering your questions. So, ask them simple things first, things that are of no value." He turned back to Samuel. "Now go fetch that Torah of yours for him."

CHAPTER 122:

AWARDS

Dura Europos, March 116AD

Sergius, decked out in his best parade kit, inspected the soldiers of his century, likewise in their parade dress uniforms, dug out from the bottom of their footlockers, and carefully cleaned, oiled and polished the night before. Sergius stopped before each man, and inquired of him, "Are you complete?" Upon getting the affirmative answer, Sergius punched the man hard enough in the chest to cause any loose armor to betray itself by rattling. Thus far, none had.

He was moderately surprised to see Varius in the ranks. He had heard he had been released from the hospital, but he had not expected him to rejoin the ranks so quickly. But here he was, in his dress gear also. Sergius studied the man's jaw, now correctly aligned, the chin as prominent as before. "Looks like Papirius Aelinanus did a good job repairing your jaw. Try not to use it to beat back slingstones again."

Varius smiled, keeping his eyes front. "Yes, Centurion. I got sick of eating soup for six weeks."

"You look good. Everything is in working order now?"

"I can bite like a mastiff again."

"Very well. Are you ready?"

"For anything."

Sergius hit him solidly in the chest. Nothing rattled, and he moved on to the next man.

His inspection complete, he took his place at the head of the First Century, putting the men at rest. They might be here a while until the *Princeps* showed up.

In fact, it was only a few minutes before the trumpets brayed to announce Trajan's arrival, to bring the legion to attention. The *Princeps* took his place on the dais before the ten cohorts of the Twelfth, two assistants carrying a large wooden box. They set it down beside him, opened and stepped behind it.

Trajan began his speech, extolling the Twelfth for their bravery and fidelity, and warning them of the hard days to come. Sergius was half dozing on his feet, when he heard Trajan say "… the Ratpack Fifth Cohort." He snapped immediately awake.

Trajan continued. "The Ratpack was cobbled together to reestablish the Fifth Cohort, after it was wiped out nearly to man. With little time to train or learn to work together with their new team, they were dispatched on a seven-hundred-mile forced march to relieve the besieged city of Petra from rebels. They covered that distance in just three weeks, a phenomenal march unmatched by any in the Roman Army. Tribune Secundus Lucullus and Centurion Samuel Elisarius, step forward."

The two did so, stopping to salute before him.

"Please remove your helmets," said Trajan. His assistants rifled through the contents of the box and produced two crowns and a banner. They handed the first crown to Trajan, who held it aloft for all to see."

"This is the Crown of the Preserver, awarded to those who have shielded and saved any of Rome's citizens or allies. The Fifth Cohort, under these men's able leadership, did so preserve the citizens of Petra. Bow your head, Secundus Lucullus."

Secundus bowed his head, and Trajan placed the crown on his head. Trajan's assistant passed the second crown to him, and the exercise was repeated with Samuel Elisarius. They then handed Secundus a yellow banner, emblazoned with the crown. "Proudly add this to the Ratpack Fifth Cohort's battle banners on the cohort standards. Well done." He then spoke in his parade ground voice, carrying over the assembled six thousand men. "Let us hear it for the Ratpack Fifth!" The legion roared out their approval, which culminated in chants of "Ratpack, Ratpack, Ratpack." Trajan dismissed the two back to their ranks and waved the legion to silence.

"Now Centurion Sergius Lepidus, of the First Century, Fifth Cohort, step forward."

Sergius, taken completely by surprise, could not feel his feet walking to the dais, his mouth dry at the unexpected calling. He hoped he did not embarrass himself before the entire legion by stumbling. He lurched to a halt and saluted.

Trajan's assistant handed him another crown. The *Princeps* held it aloft. "The *corona muralis*, the Crown of the Walls, is bestowed upon the first soldier to climb the wall of a besieged city and place the standard of the attacking army upon it." He moved it back and forth over his head for the entire legion to see it. "Centurion Lepidus, you led the initial attack on the city of Petra, seizing the basilica from the rebels who had defiled it, with just your single century, and holding it for two days against overwhelming odds until relieved by the rest of the Fifth Cohort. Your valor, courage, determination and leadership were essential to the retaking of the city, and you are truly deserving of this crown. Remove your helmet and bow your head please, Centurion Lepidus."

Sergius did so, and Trajan placed the golden crown on his head, its ring a replica of a wall with ramparts along the top. His aide gave him a green banner, which he held for all to see. "For the First Century, your battle banner for this enormous accomplishment." He handed it to Sergius. Then again in his stentorian tones, he pronounced, "Let us hear it for Centurion Lepidus and First Century, Fifth Cohort of the Twelfth Lightning Bolt!"

The troops erupted in cries of "Lepidus and the First of the Fifth, Lepidus and the First of the Fifth." Trajan let them continue, then waved them to silence. "Centurion Lepidus, you are dismissed."

Sergius saluted, turned on his heel and returned to his place at the head of his century. Had it really been only six months since he had been flogged for theft, denounced as the most useless of soldiers?

"Now I must make a most unusual presentation, to the three women of the Ninth Batavian Cavalry, who contributed so significantly to this great victory, and whose careful preparation of the Ninth have prepared a great surprise for the Parthian cavalry. I call Hina of the Xiongnu, Mei Lucia, and Marcia Lucia Aristida to dismount and approach the dais.

All three wore Roman helmets and corselets, but over unconventional felt riding gear. They approached and saluted.

"It is unheard of for the women of Rome to serve in combat. But it is not unheard of in the far lands to our east for them to so serve. Rumors of such women have given rise to our fabled stories of Amazons. Standing before us is one such Amazon, Hina, a barbarian woman of the Xiongnu people, a centurion in her own right, having commanded in her homeland a cavalry force of one hundred men. She is also a wife devoted to her husband and the mother of three children. She has trained the Ninth in Xiongnu tactics which will take the Parthians by complete surprise when they find that we, too, have mastered the 'Parthian shot'. Her training and leadership in the battle of Petra ensured that all the rebels were quickly rounded up. We have no awards appropriate for this most extraordinary woman, so I have had a special one struck for this occasion." His aide handed him a gold medal, about the size of an *aureus*, on a silk ribbon. He held it up. "*Victoria Victrix* is our female goddess of victory, so it is most appropriate that she appear on one side of this award, with my head on the other. Hina, please accept this award for your service," he said, placing it around her neck.

"Marcia Lucia Aristida is a Roman citizeness, and wife of the Twelfth's prefect of camps Antonius Aristides. She is the descendant of Marcus Lucius of *Legio III Crassiana*, and is part Hanaean and part Roman. She is also the protégé of Hina, with all of Hina's combats skills. Marcia Lucia, you have been in my service for two decades, as translator for the Hanaean mission to Rome, and for the Galba return expedition to Han China, and now with the Ninth Batavian Cavalry. Few men in all history have done all that you have done, so it is my pleasure to award you also the *Victoria Victrix*."

"Finally, I must award the *Victoria Victrix* to Mei, the Hanaean wife of Marcus Lucius Quintus, Marcia's brother. Mei is the latest protégé of Hina, and served admirably at the battle of Petra."

"Dismissed. Return to your mounts."

The legion cheered uproariously.

CHAPTER 123:

A DECISION TO GO HOME

Dura Europos, March 116AD

The awardees were invited to a lunch in Trajan's command tent, to be accompanied by their commanders and select friends. Hina, Marcia and Mei were accompanied by their husbands, and Longinus Clarus as their commander; Secundus, Samuel and Sergius came accompanied by Gaius Lucullus as their commander. The Praetorian Guardsmen saluted smartly as they entered, and servants in white tunics guided the honorees, with Antonius, Marcus and Galosga, to places at one side of a long table in the middle of the tent, and their commanders to the other side.

Everyone remained standing until Trajan, in a purple tunic with geometric shapes in gold along its hems, emerged from his personal quarters on the far side of the tent. He strode to the table, taking his place in the center, between his two commanders. "Seats, gentlemen... and ladies," he said, taking his own seat in a campaign chair.

Servants brought bowls of chilled green vegetable soup. Everyone waited for the *Princeps* to take his first taste before they, too, dipped their spoons into the broth.

"Again, let me congratulate you all on what you have accomplished. You are all writing history by your deeds, and for some of you, this is not the first time you have done so." He turned toward Marcia. "And what are your further plans, Marcia Lucia Aristida?"

Marcia was silent for a moment. She had made her decision a while ago, but she had not discussed it with anyone, not even Antonius. Was this the time to reveal it, unrehearsed? She hesitated, took Antonius' hand in hers under the table, then cleared her throat. "Your Excellency, if it be possible, I would like to return to my home in Aquileia at the earliest opportunity. My children need me, and I need them."

The tent fell silent. Marcia felt like all eyes were upon her. Had she created some great social calamity, insulting the *Princeps* after receiving an unprecedented award for valor?

Hina then spoke up. "Your Excellency, I undertook a great journey to be by my sister's side. Where she goes, I go also."

Marcia felt Antonius squeeze her hand. Had she truly ruined the occasion, perhaps incurred Trajan's ire?

Then Trajan smiled, a smile that illuminated the dimly sunlit tent. "Of course, Marcia Lucia! You were taken from your home and family by force, and while you have served us with the utmost duty and loyalty, I cannot stand in the way of your return. How long have you been gone?"

"For over a year, Your Excellency. December of the previous year. And if I don't leave now, I will miss the sailing season, and not be home until next summer."

"And Marcus, will you and Mei be returning with Marcia?"

"No, Your Excellency, I will be staying to support the Twelfth's intelligence staff. There is still much to be done, and I feel I have some significant skills for them. Mei will be staying with me, but I hope no longer riding in combat with the Ninth," said Marcus.

"Thank you for your dedication to duty, Marcus, and you, Mei for yours," answered Trajan. He turned his attention back to Marcia. "You have certainly waited long enough. You and your companions may ride with my next support and communications cohort to Antioch, and from there take my fast mail packet to Rome. You should be home by the end of September. You shall all be missed, but I suspect not as much as your children are missing you now. How old are they?"

Marcia drew a deep breath and smiled, as Antonius squeezed her hand. "My oldest son Colloscius is almost thirteen, getting close to donning his man's toga, my girl Aena is ten, and my youngest, Androcles, is four"

"Go with my blessing. Antonius, they may draw the ordinary stipend for traveling, no need to expend money for a trip that was never of their choosing. My *librarii* clerks will cut orders authorizing transportation and use of the *cursus publicus*."

Marcia rested her head on Antonius' shoulder in a dream-like state as conversation swirled around her. She was going home! And in style, at best speed. She had feared that if she delayed too long, the sailing season would close with the November gales, and she would have to remain with the legion a whole year longer.

There was a flurry of excitement among the group after the lunch as all compared notes on Marcia's sudden revelation and Trajan's most generous acquiescence.

CHAPTER 124:

BARBARIANS IN THE PALACE

Antioch, April 116AD

Marcia, with Hadyu, Hina and Galosga and their children rode out with a cohort of Praetorian Guards. The Guardsmen were carrying communications from Trajan to Hadrian at Antioch. Adhela, riding his own small pony on his first very long trek, controlled his animal with ease, wearing his very own twelve-inch sword, which he sharpened nightly.

Riding with the guardsmen, they made the three-hundred-and-fifty-mile trek to Antioch in under three weeks, arriving at the city in mid-April. Marcia surveyed the damaged city as the cohort entered the south gate. Rubble had been piled high in the parks to the right of the main road opposite the *agora*, treadmill cranes in operation around them, hoisting that rubble to dump it noisily onto huge carts to be hauled away, pulled by teams of oxen. The *agora* marketplace was open, however, and merchants of every ilk set up under blue and white tents, hawking their wares to women who threaded the maze-like paths between the vendors' tents. She had heard Aulus' description of the horrific damage caused by the earthquake, but seeing its remaining after-effects herself was still shocking.

At the forum, they turned left to cross the bridge across the Orontes. As they passed through the gate, the Praetorian commander rode back to them. "Ladies, you seem to have attracted some attention of the highest sort. There is a coach waiting up front to take all of you to Lady Plotina Augusta."

Marcia gasped. "Lady Plotina, the *Princeps'* wife? That can't be, we are all still in our riding clothes."

"That's what I told the servant. But he said you were to bathe and change at the governor's praesidium. So, dismount, I'll have the soldiers take care of your horses. Give them all your weapons, none are allowed in the praesidium." Adhela gripped his weapon defensively. "Hina, you can disarm him for me," the commander said with a smile. "Enjoy the imperial hospitality. Follow me to your coach."

Everyone dismounted, disarmed, and followed the commander to where a very large coach, pulled by six beautifully-matched white horses, red harnesses with silver trappings, each crowned with a purple horsehair top knot, waited their arrival. It was by far and away the longest, most luxurious coach Marcia had ever seen, twenty feet in length with four rows of purple velvet seats, each pair of facing seats with its own pair of doors swung open to receive the large party. The cart was gilt-trimmed purple, the lacquered black doors emblazoned with eagle, olive branch and 'SPQR' in gold and black.

An attendant, with a carefully trimmed black beard, greeted them, holding the forward door open for them. He was wearing a brilliantly white tunic, with geometric designs in gold at the hem. "Thank you for responding so promptly," he said. "You will be able to bathe at the governor's palace, and there will be a change of clothes for all of you."

Hina motioned Marasa, Andanyu and Adhela into the second pair of seats. Galosga and Hina climbed into the front, with Hadyu and Marcia.

"I think this is the *Princeps'* own coach," said Marcia. "The most powerful man in the world, and Lady Plotina sent us his personal coach."

"It is beautiful beyond anything I have seen," said Galosga, stroking the gold and silver fittings of the interior. "Who is Lady Plotina?"

"Lady Plotina is Trajan's wife. If he is the most powerful man in the world, she is the most powerful woman."

"Why is she interested in us?" asked Hina, a bit unnerved at the social implications, so far above any of her experiences. Galosga took her hand, sensing her unease.

"I wrote Livia of our coming. I presume Livia told her," said Marcia. "And Trajan no doubt sent word of our coming. I have met her once, many years ago, when we returned to Rome with Aulus. She was a very pleasant person, very much like her husband. Hina, you are nervous, chewing on your thumbnail is a dead giveaway. Relax, be yourself, your usual straightforward self. She will like you, as everyone else always does."

"Thank you. Yes, I fear that I might embarrass you as I did at Ecbatana."

"You didn't embarrass us there at all." Marcia said with a laugh. "You won a horse race you weren't supposed to enter, and beat up a man who desperately needed it, to everyone's amusement. You will be fine."

The coach wound its way along the main thoroughfare to the governor's praesidium. On the island where the praesidium was located, most of the debris had been cleared away, reconstruction in progress everywhere. The coach pulled to a halt in front of the steps of the colonnaded praesidium's entrance. Waiting for them there were Livia, Lady Plotina, and a burly bearded man whom Marcia did not recognize, with a bevy of servants behind them.

Marcia had no sooner dismounted the coach than Livia enveloped her in a hug, kissing her cheek, ignoring her dusty riding felts. "My little Amazon! You are going home! You and your friends."

"We are. At last."

Pompeia had been smiling, watching the reunion, then came to stand by Livia's side. Livia indicated her. "This is Lady Pompeia Plotina Augusta, the wife of Marcus Ulpius Trajan." She then turned to Pompeia. "Let me introduce them all. I believe you have met Marcia Lucia Aristida."

"The years have been kind to you, Marcia," said Lady Plotina

After the other introductions were made and hands shaken, Pompeia continued, "I am pleased to meet you all. Marcus Ulpius has said great things about your many deeds. I look forward to hearing your stories firsthand." She indicated the bearded man by her side, clad in a white toga with a very wide purple border. "This is Publius Aelius Hadrian, our cousin and the governor of Syria."

"I, too, look forward to hearing your stories," he said, smiling broadly, his teeth bright white behind his coppery beard, uncommon among Roman aristocracy.

Servants came from behind the governor to take the group's baggage. "Come," said Pompeia. "The servants will bring your baggage to your rooms. I am sure you will want to refresh yourself after the long trip."

Pompeia, Livia and Hadrian led the group up the stairs, then departed, while the servants led them to a very luxurious guest apartment on the west side. It boasted a large common sitting area with an intricate mosaic floor, still cracked from earthquake damage, and six adjoining bedrooms, each with its own balcony overlooking the garden below. They indicated their choice of bedrooms to the servants, who carried the baggage into each. The head servant, the major domo, dismissed the others, then said "You will find all the clothing you need in each room. If you will, please change into robes. The servants will return in a few minutes to claim your riding clothes for cleaning, and escort you to the baths."

Everyone was dazzled and amazed by the elegance, exploring the room, touching the elegant statues, admiring the paintings on the wall.

Marcia took charge of the group. "Go to your rooms, shed your clothes. You will find robes in the closets for the baths."

The servants returned and led them to the baths, a cavernous room at the rear of the first floor. Light entered the room from huge windows high in the wall, augmented by strategically placed lamps, illuminating a room of red walls painted with various frescoes of gods, goddess, heroes and animals. One large pool with a mosaic floor with nautical motifs ran the length of the room, with naked bathers of both sexes cavorting in it. Lamplight from two small rooms at the far corners beyond it showed a small pool in each, one room filled with steam. In rooms off to the side, masseurs worked on naked or barely-clad bodies by the yellow light of oil lamps. There was a hint of woodsmoke in the air, from the hypocausts heating the floors and pools.

Marcia gathered them around. "That room over there is the *caldarium*, the hot pool. Let's begin there. Then we will splash around and swim in this big pool, the *tepidarium*, and finally the *frigidarium* to cool off. After that, I, for one, am going to get a massage." She shrugged off her robe, hung it on hook in the anteroom, took a towel from one of the cubbyholes, and naked, padded on bare feet to the hot bath. Everyone else did likewise.

By the time they got to the *tepidarium*, they were in fine fettle, splashing and dunking each other like children, swimming laps along the length of the big pool. They did not stay long in the *frigidarium*. A quick dip was all that was needed, then the massages, and back to the room for a nap.

A servant awakened them in the late afternoon for dinner with the Lady Plotina, Livia and Hadrian. Marcia selected a green filigreed *stola* with matching green slippers, and came into the sitting room to find everyone well decked out, Mei in red, Hina in yellow. The servant led them to the dining room. One of the glass windows had been repaired, its watery glass giving a view of the Orontes River below, but the remaining windows remained hidden behind white wool curtains. Hadrian reclined on a couch at the center of a long low table, with Lady Plotina to his right, Livia beside her. His wife Vibia Sabina was on his left. Their places were set on the opposite side. As Marcia's entourage approached the table, servants directed them to their couches, Marcia opposite Lady Plotina, with Hina, Galosga, and the children to her left, Hadyu to her right.

Hadrian greeted them. "Welcome to my praesidium, ladies and gentlemen. I apologize, parts of it are still in the process of repair. We had a severe earthquake here a few months ago, and it is a tribute to the architect that it suffered only minor damage. I hope you had a safe and uneventful trip here from the front lines."

"We did, Your Excellency," said Marcia. "And your praesidium is indeed beautiful."

"And Hina, I understand that you are the mentress of Marcia in the way of the warrior."

"I am, but she learned well. As my mentor told me many years ago, I could not make her a fighter, but if she were a fighter, I could make her a better one. She is a very good fighter," said Hina.

"And where are you from?"

"The steppe lands north of China, Your Excellency." Hina went on to relate her life, how she became a warrior, and eventually met Marcia and Galosga, Hadrian occasionally asking questions. She talked for half an hour. Finally, he asked, "And how did you come to be here?"

"It was the hand of Tengri," she said.

"Tengri is …?" asked Hadrian

"The Sky God, who created all things, and shapes the lives of all people. He sent the spotted sickness among my people, wiping them out, sparing just those of us before you, but taking away any reason for us to stay. I had been sent to Turfam to find a cure where I encountered Marcus, on his way west to rejoin Marcia. We had no other direction to go so we joined him, to find my sister Marcia. Tengri sent a shooting star through the sky to the west, to indicate the direction I was to go. So, I am here."

"A truly amazing story, Hina, truly amazing." Hadrian was impressed with the woman. She radiated power, both physical and mental, like no other woman he had ever known. And she was beautiful, long red hair and green eyes, with a tall powerfully-muscled body. He turned to Lady Plotina. "I am sorry, Pompeia, I have dominated our dinner conversation."

In fact, Pompeia and Livia had been following Hina's story so closely that they had scarcely touched their dinners.

"That is no problem, cousin," answered Pompeia. "And thank you for your story, Hina." She turned to the twins and Adhela. "Are you going to be like your mother and father when you grow up?" she asked, with a hint of unintended adult condescension.

"We are already adults, Lady Plotina, but we continue to learn from them," answered Marasa.

Hina interjected. "Among our people, we become adults when one is able to bear or father children, at twelve. Marasa and Andanyu rode with the Ninth Batavian cavalry at Petra and took an active part in the fighting. Both have killed their first man."

"And I am almost grown," said Adhela, with all the pride a five-year-old could muster. "I rode all the way from Dew Ropos by myself."

This brought a bit of laughter from the table. "Your children do grow up most quickly, Hina," Pompeia said.

"The steppes are a harsh and unforgiving place. Our children learn to ride at two, and by their fifth birthday, they ride their own small pony. They learn archery and fighting at that age also. Adhela is good with both."

"The soldier took away my sword," he said, sounding miffed.

"He will give it back later, Adhela, and ours also. These are very important people here, and no one can have weapons around them."

"I want to compliment you on your fine Latin, Hina. A bit of an accent but your grammar is very good," said Hadrian. "Who was your teacher?"

"Marcia, Your Excellency. We both speak Chinese fluently, so she was able to explain everything to me. And Marcus has taught me to read and write. But I have taken your time away from my companions, Your Excellency, and I fear my dinner is getting cold."

Livia picked up the thread. "Marcia, how are you getting back to Rome?"

"There is a fast packet ship leaving Seleucia Pieria next week, and the *Princeps* has most kindly booked us passage as his official guests."

"Is there any chance there is room for one more?" Livia asked, half-joking.

"More than a chance, dear Livia. I can add you to the roster by his authority," said Pompeia.

"Good. It is time that I too go home. I hope the voyage will be much more pleasant than our last one!"

They turned to their dinner of pheasant, then to each others' stories, punctuated by frequent glasses of wine. It was quite late when Pompeia decided it was time to end the party.

And throughout the night, Vibia Sabina, Hadrian's wife, had said not a word.

CHAPTER 125:

NIGHT TALK

Antioch, April 116AD

Though it was quite late, Hadrian went alone to Pompeia's chambers, rather than his own. Her servant admitted him.

Pompeia was letting down her auburn hair, spreading about her shoulders over her night shift.

"What can I do for you at this late hour, Publius?" she asked.

"I was so excited about our guests, I wanted to talk to you, if that is all right. Do you mind?"

"Why not talk to Vibia? You hardly spoke to her at all tonight."

"Vibia would not understand what I have to say. She is a sweet child, but would not understand."

"All right. Girls, bring us some wine and then leave us, I will call for you when I am ready for bed." She motioned to the couch and sat down, Hadrian beside her. She expected he would want to talk about more than their guests, perhaps about the letter, and for that he would want the utmost privacy. And perhaps more. "So, you found our guests interesting?"

"Most interesting indeed. Especially the barbarian woman, Hina, though hardly barbarian in her demeanor. Until tonight, I always regarded you as the most powerful woman I know, with your political acumen. But I hate to disappoint you, you have been displaced. You still excel in political acumen, but Hina radiates sheer physical power. I would not want to fight her. She looks like she would be formidable."

"I agree she is an awesome woman, Publius, but I don't think that is why you came to my chambers so late."

"To be sure. Your political acumen again, Pompeia. I wanted to inquire about the letter to my cousin that we discussed earlier."

"It hasn't been written yet. I actually have started it several time, but as I said, I don't want to reveal too much in the open, in case someone other than Marcus Ulpius should see it."

"To be sure."

Pompeia paused to change the subject. "As you said, you were quite taken by our Amazon. I am surprised you didn't follow her to her bedchamber, rather than mine."

Hadrian's smile behind his gold-flecked beard was bright in the lamplight. "I don't think her very large husband would have approved. He said very little. I wonder where he is from?"

"I guess also from the Distant East."

"Galosga, his name was." Hadrian put his hand affectionately on Pompeia's upper thigh, covered by her thin night shift. He left it there. Pompeia thought about brushing it away, too intimate. But she didn't, feeling its warmth. Hadrian looked her deeply in the eyes, his face very close to hers. "Well, it is late. I think will let you call your maidservants back, and get some sleep. Thank you for considering the letter. Good night, Pompeia." He winked, then left.

Pompeia exhaled a heavy sigh, trembling. She had known Publius for as long as she had been married to Marcus Ulpius. Why was she so suddenly, irrationally, attracted to him? And him, a notorious boy-lover, to her?

CHAPTER 126:

FIRST TIME TO SEA

Seleucia Pieria, April 116AD

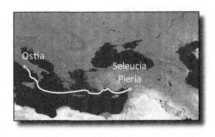

The same elegant coach that had brought Marcia and her friends to the *praesidium* at Antioch delivered them a week later to the docks of Seleucia Pieria, where the *Ajax* rode at her mooring. The coach halted by the ship's gangway, horses snorting and stamping while a servant opened the doors for them. Marcia and Livia stepped out first, followed by everyone else. The servant deposited their baggage on the pier, going aboard to seek out sailors to assist in carrying the luggage on board.

Marcia admired the *Ajax'* fine lines with a knowing eye. The ship was far smaller than the *Europa* on which she had sailed many years ago, perhaps half her size, sitting much lower in the water, and much slimmer. She sported only two masts, the stout main, and a foremast thrusting forward at a jaunty forty-five-degree angle. On the prow could be seen the carved image of her bearded Greek hero namesake, his eyes searching the horizon for their outbound course to home. Aft, the stern ornament curved gracefully forward, ending in a golden eagle in flight. "Well, Livia, I hope the accommodations are better than on our last ship," she said.

"If they are not, I will stay here," Livia said with a laugh.

Marcia, Livia and Galosga had spent time at sea before. However, Hadyu, Hina and her children not only had never been on a ship before, but they had never even seen the ocean, knowing it only through Galosga's stories. They stared in amazement at the vast expanse of blue water extending to the horizon beyond the harbor entrance, rippling with wind-tossed choppy whitecaps. The *Ajax* bobbed in rhythm to the chop, water slapping between her hull and the concrete dock, lines occasionally creaking in tension.

Sailors came down to fetch their luggage, the captain behind them. He was bearded, clad in a white tunic with a red cloak wrapped about him against the spring chill. His salt-and-pepper beard reminded Marcia of the Arab pirate-turned-comrade Ibrahim of so long ago.

"Good morning," he said. "Which one of you is Marcia Lucia Aristida?"

"I am she."

"I am Alexander Phaedon, *navarklos*, master of the *Ajax*. Is this all your party?"

"It is."

"May I see your documents?"

Marcia produced the sealed scroll Pompeia had given her. The *navarklos* broke the seal, scrutinized the list, then did a quick head count to confirm the tally of passengers.

"Very well. The soldiers already brought your horses and riding gear aboard. They are in the stables on the second deck. Please check on them, make sure they are well, and that nothing has been lost."

"We will."

"Our cabins have two bunks each. How would you like to divide up your party?" He pulled out a wax tablet and stylus.

Marcia ticked off the combinations on her fingers. "Livia can stay with me, Hina and Galosga, that's two. Hina, how would you like to divide up the rest of your group?"

"Marasa with Adhela, Andanyu with Hadyu," she answered.

"Very well. That's four cabins. If you will each point out your baggage, I will have my men deliver them."

As sailors lugged the baggage aboard, the captain spoke again. "Follow me, I will escort you to your cabins. Have any of you been to sea before?"

"Livia and I have been passengers before, Galosga is a former deckhand. Everyone else is a first-timer."

"A deckhand? What ship?" he asked.

"The *Europa*, an Indian ocean freighter."

"That is a famous ship, made the run to China, did she?"

"We were on her."

"I will have to hear your stories. She and the *Asia* are very well-known for that trip. The rest of you, you will likely be seasick the first few days. Please eat, no matter if you throw it up, we have dried bread for you. Remember, no matter how bad you feel, you will not die." He opened a hatch on the quarterdeck, and levered himself down a steep ladder to the second deck, illuminated by open port holes, several tables in place. "This is the officers' mess, where you will eat. Aft of us through that hatch are their quarters. Yours are forward amidships." He opened a hatch in the middle of the forward bulkhead. Daylight gave way to lit oil lamps by doors lining either side of the narrow passageway. "These are your cabins. I am giving you the first four on the starboard side, so you can all be together. There is a tub forward on the port side for bathing, a latrine opposite. There is a hatch all the way forward like this one, do not use it. It leads to the crew's quarters, and they may be in various stages of undress."

Marcia nodded.

"We are not taking on any more passengers from here, though we may pick some up enroute. We sail before sunset at high tide, so please stay on board. Ladies Marcia and Livia, your cabin." He opened the door to reveal a cabin with a single port hole, its hatch opened to admit light and air, a bunk on either side, storage drawers beneath them. An unlit oil lamp swung lazily over a small table in the middle, benches for seats. "Always extinguish that oil lamp when you leave. Fire is a great danger at sea. There is a holder for tapers by the small lamp by the door outside to relight it when you enter. The port hole can be opened at sea, depending on weather, for air and light. Any questions?"

"How long will it take us to get to Rome?"

"We will be landing at Portus in Ostia. Your imperial orders will get you passage to Rome via riverboat from there. With our two stops, we will arrive in about three weeks or less, depending on winds and weather, which should be good this time of year."

"Thank you, captain," said Marcia.

"That will be all then, I will let you get settled in. Dinner tonight will be after we get underway, and thereafter at the eleventh hour of the day, an hour before sunset. Enjoy your trip." Alexander excused himself, and exited down the passageway, while Marcia got everyone settled into their respective cabins.

Hina was unsteady at the gentle rocking of the *Ajax* beneath her feet. Galosga explained that she should not fight the motion of the ship, but to ride it, so to speak, like a horse, moving with it, never against it. Hina changed out of her finery, and rummaged through her chest to find a set of her old comfortable riding felts. She changed, attempting to apply Galosga's suggestion. She was not looking forward to dinner. Above their heads, there were shouted commands, the patter of feet running back and forth, heavy rumbles and thumps of things being dragged across the deck, ratcheting noises, all the sounds familiar to Galosga as the sounds of a ship awakening from her slumber. He lay on his bunk, bare-chested, arm behind his head. "*Huldaji,* look out the port hole. Focus on the horizon. Focus your mind on that unmoving object, and let the ship move around you."

Hina tried but she was already tasting bile in her throat. She watched as a large rowboat with eight rowers coasted by. She craned her head out to see where it went. It came to a stop by the bow as the rowers backed water. A rope splashed into the water beside it, the men retrieving it to make it fast to the boat's stern. Then they applied their oars, and ever so slowly, the unmoving horizon began to drift to her left. She lost it, vomiting out the opening.

"Remember, the horizon's not moving, we are." Galosga could tell by the near-imperceptible movements of the ship, that her bow was being swung out by the oarsmen.

Hina wiped her mouth, and took a bit of water from her sack to wash her mouth. She looked out again, focused on the unmoving horizon, and suddenly things fell into place ... *yes, we were moving, not the land.* Her stomach quieted a bit. "I want to go upstairs," she said.

"This is not a good time to be topside, *Huldaji*. It's a busy place up there now, and the crew won't want us in the way. Just keep watching the horizon from here."

The rowboat towed them out, their bow now facing the harbor exit. There was a loud fluttering, then a pop, as the foresail filled, casting its shadow on the water. The ship's head came down and she could feel the ship begin to move, slightly choppy, plowing into the waves, not riding with them but over them. Another flutter and pop, and the mainsail in the middle filled, adding its shadow to the water.

Another shouted command and the tow boat undid the line at its stern, casting it into the water where it snaked its way back to the ship. The crew waved, then steered away from the ship, which began to pound its way through the waves. "Are we sinking?" she asked in horror, feeling the deck no longer level beneath her feet, but tilted slightly to one side.

"No, *Huldajii*. That's normal, she's catching the wind from the side. Relax and enjoy the ride."

Fear was an unusual emotion for Hina, and she worked hard to conquer it. This was a most unusual fear, the fear of the unknown, hard for her to deal with. *Ride it like a horse, Galosga had said.* She ran that thought through her mind, and suddenly, with legs limber, bending under the ship's upthrust, straightening as it settled back down into the waves, she was able to stand without holding onto something. And there was a predictable rhythm to the ship's moving ... she could anticipate the next move before it happened.

"You're getting the idea, Hina. Are you feeling better?"

Hina did a quick inventory of her gut. "Yes, I actually am. Thank you!" She swayed over to where Galosga lay on the bunk. "Move over, I am going to lie down next to you."

A bell clanged topside, and a crewman rapped on each passenger door, announcing dinner. The ship was moving smoothly through the water with a gentle rocking motion, the sound of rushing water outside marking its passage. Hina and Galosga made their way to the officer's mess to find everyone else already there, except for Hadyu. Hina and Galosga took a table with the twins and Adhela. The *navarklos* Alexander Phaedon and some of the officers were at the other table, with Marcia engaged in a lively discussion of her time on the *Europa*.

"Where's Hadyu?" asked Hina.

"He is very sick, mother," answered Andanyu. "Too sick to leave the cabin."

"Throwing up, having a hard time moving?"

"Yes."

"He is seasick. He should get up and move around, it will help it pass. I'll see to him after dinner," said Galosga, taking some bread from one of the bowls set in circular indentations cut in the table. "Your mother had some problems at first, but I think she will be fine until our first storm. How did you three do?"

"We had no trouble," said Marasa. "We went on deck to watch the sailors make the ship move out. It was like when we broke our encampment on the steppes for our migration, everyone had a job to do, working together. And the sea ... when we left the harbor, it was like you said, the grasslands of home, but blue. Like the grass, rippling in the wind."

"I hope you stayed out of the way."

"We did, and we had to hang onto Adhela, he very much wanted to help the men."

"I could have helped," grumped Adhela.

"I am sure you could have, son. Be sure to go topside tonight to see the stars. They are very beautiful at night, with no city lights to dim them, or trees or mountains to block the view, just like on the steppes of home. Go with your brother and sister to make sure you don't fall overboard."

"I can swim."

"You would have to swim a very long way to get back to land."

"So, you did not start out well, mother?" asked Marasa.

"Not well. I am still a bit queasy but I think I am past it. Galosga, what was that about a storm?"

Galosga laughed. "Hopefully not like some I have been in. Let's hope for gentle seas like this for the next few weeks."

The seas were gentle for the next several weeks, though not as gentle as Hina would have liked at times. The *Ajax* made brief one-night layovers at Ephesus and Corinth to exchange imperial correspondence, then reached Ostia in early May. And the stars in the dark sea skies were indeed magnificent.

CHAPTER 127:

THE FINAL PUSH

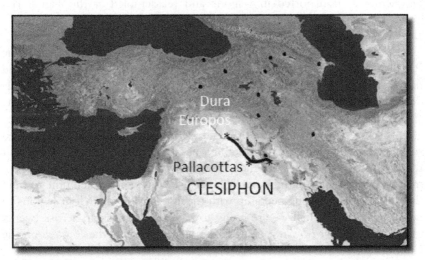

Dura Europos, April 116AD

Gaius Lucullus and Antonius had spent the morning, and part of the afternoon, in the planning session with the *Princeps*, where they and the other four *legati* commanding the western legions had put the finishing touches on the summer campaign strategy. They returned to the Twelfth's command tent to find that *primus pilus* Paulus Herrerius had already assembled the tribunes and selected centurions, awaiting them in the dry heat. They rose as the commander entered.

"At ease, gentlemen," said Gaius. "This won't be a long meeting. There weren't a lot of changes from what we discussed last winter. Trajan will lead the campaign on the Euphrates from his flagship trireme *Romulus*, with a flotilla of fifty *naves lusoriae* patrol boats. These will provide logistic support, rapid communications, and scouting. The boats will carry our heavy equipment, siege engines and artillery, so the legions can move faster on land. As necessary, they will conduct amphibious operations against strong points on the river in advance of our arrival." An orderly set goblets of water on the desk by the two men, and Gaius took a sip. "Our first objective will be the town of Hit, then Pallacottas, where the King's Canal branches off for the Tigris. After that, I have good news and bad news." He paused for effect. "The good news is that your men will not have to dig a canal through the desert. The engineers have determined that the Euphrates is much higher than the Tigris, and the waters in the canal will flow too swiftly for safety."

There was a buzz of conversation, the officers obviously glad to be relieved of that task.

Trajan continued. "The bad news is that we will have to move the fifty ships twenty miles overland at Sippar via road. The patrol boats can be disassembled, transported in wagons and reassembled at the Tigris. But Trajan's trireme will have to be moved across on rollers."

"Why can't we use the Royal Canal at Pallacottas?" asked Secundus.

"You were busy in Petra when we had that discussion last winter. The Parthians know we are coming and have made it unnavigable with rocks and dams." He took another sip. "The scouts report that the two towns are lightly defended, and the Parthians haven't moved forces to oppose us. But stay alert, trouble can come at any time. Antonius?"

Antonius cleared his throat. "Each legion is to provide three hundred rowers for ten of the boats, doubling as an amphibious landing force if required, so each of our cohorts will provide thirty men for our quota. Pick men with experience in these patrol boats, we won't have much time to train them. We'll pair our engineers up with those from the other four legions to figure out how the hell we are going to haul a fifty-ton ship across twenty miles of desert. Or how to persuade the *Princeps* to leave the *Romulus* on the Euphrates."

Gaius took over. "That's about it, gentlemen. We will march out in three days. Sorry to keep you sitting in the heat of the day so long. Let's go to war. Dismissed!"

The men saluted, and after they were gone, Gaius and senior staff stripped off their uniforms down to their tunics. Antonius set his gear down on the floor, its leather now dark with sweat. "We need to talk Trajan out of hauling his damned flagship across the desert. It's unnecessary, just for show. The patrol boats will pack up nicely, but that beast ... I'd rather dig that twenty-mile canal all by myself than try to move that boat. If we even can move it."

"I agree with Antonius, sir," said Paulus. 'We have to change his mind."

"You both are right. It's not like Trajan to do things for show. I hope our success isn't going to his head. In my opinion, we should leave it here on the Euphrates, with about ten patrol boats. I think the other *legati* are thinking the same thing, it's a lot of work for nothing. Right now, though, I am most concerned about the lack of opposition. The Parthians have to know that we are on the move towards their capital, but they are not offering any resistance. Something is up."

There was something up, something very big. But it did not stand between them and Ctesiphon. It stood behind them, far to their rear.

CHAPTER 128:

EVACUATION

Ctesiphon, April 116AD

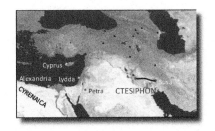

Sanatruces rushed into Mithridate's office with the bad news. "We have miscalculated badly, Father. The Roman armies are on the move. They will be on our doorstep in just a few weeks!"

"Relax, my son. It is Trajan who has miscalculated. I thought he would never make such a rash move as that. I expected him to spend this year consolidating his ill-gotten gains, then move on to us next year, or even the year after. What he has done makes it easier for us, not harder. We have to evacuate my brother Osroës, his family and all the government. We just move our timetable forward. Have you begun standing up the insurrections we discussed last winter?"

"I have. I dispatched a Jewish agent to Alexandria with a respectable sum to foment the rebellion. He organized the uprising in Petra, though it didn't take the Romans long to put it down. I didn't think they could move a cohort that far, that fast after Nisibis, but they did. They arrived before we were ready, and had some extensive inside help that we hadn't expected."

"That is excellent. But where did the inside help come from?"

"Some holdouts fortified a residential area. Remnants of the urban cohort, army veterans mostly. They were in an easily-defended narrow pass west of town, and the leader decided to just besiege them and starve them out. In retrospect a bad call. The cohort arrived from the west, and was able establish a toehold unobserved there and take the rebels by surprise."

"Too bad. I was thinking to use Petra for my approach into Egypt when the time came. No matter. What do you have planned for the new insurrections?"

Sanatruces ticked off his objectives on his finger. "First and foremost, Egypt, and Alexandria in particular, are targets the Romans can't ignore. Not only does the city of Rome itself depend on Egyptian grain, but the tax revenues from their Indian Ocean ventures flow through there, a sizable part of their state budget."

He ticked off his second objective. "We are targeting Cyrenaea, to prevent easy landing spots west of Alexandria for any of Rome's European legions to put down the Alexandrian rebellion."

Another finger. "Third, Judea. The supply and communications for Trajan's Mesopotamian legions goes through there. With Caesarea out of action due to the earthquake, the major port now resupplying his legions is Lydda, and that will be our focus. An insurrection there will disrupt their supply lines and also deny landing spots for their European legions north of Egypt."

Sanatruces raised his fourth finger. "Finally, Cyprus, important for its proximity to Egypt, Cyrenea and Judea. Any legions from Europe will have to preposition themselves there, along with ships and supplies. An insurrection there will force them make opposed assaults on the island, further slowing their efforts to put down the costly insurrection in Alexandria."

Sanatruces put down his hand. "And all of these places, now lightly defended, have large Jewish populations from which we can draw support. These four insurrections will leave them with but one source for legions to put them down in a timely manner ... withdrawing their forces from Mesopotamia, coming overland. And we will have plenty of insurrections here to entertain the remaining forces. We have already begun secretly fortifying Hatra."

Mithridates smiled. "That is a brilliant plan! Simple, but brilliant. Do you have all the resources you need?"

"Yes, and if I need more, I will let you know."

"Excellent. Well, with the Romans on their way here, we are going to evacuate Ctesiphon quickly. My brother will take the army and government to Susa in the Zagros Mountains, leaving the Romans an empty shell to conquer. Let us present this to my brother."

The two went into the Royal Court. Sanatruces repeated his planned insurgency, leaving King Osroës similarly impressed. "You may launch your plan immediately," he said.

Sanatruces bowed, saying softly, "Your Excellency." He saw no reason to reveal that he had already set his plan in motion.

Mithridates turned to the second subject. "Brother, with the Romans on the move, you must evacuate and take the government and army to Susa. The legions will be here in a month or so."

"I am ahead of you. They are already preparing to leave, and we will be gone within the week. My daughter Afrand wants to stay behind, to spit in Trajan's eye."

"Is that wise? They will hold her as hostage to use against you."

"Trajan is a victim of his own civility. He won't do that. And she speaks fluent Latin, so she will be a valuable pair of eyes in his camp. You are not my only source of intelligence, brother." The king smiled. "Dismissed. Put your most excellent plan in motion."

CHAPTER 129:

LANDFALL IN ITALY

Portus in Ostia, May 116AD

The lighthouse on the island guarding the entrance to the harbor of Portus could be seen from ten miles out, a flickering flare on the horizon. It was surrounded by a dim halo from the nightlights of Ostia. Marcia and Livia, too excited about their imminent arrival in Italy to sleep, had lined the rail since midnight, looking for the lighthouse. Its loom emerged just as the sky behind them was turning gray with dawn. Somewhere forward, the lookout had seen the light also, and called out the alert to the night watch on the quarterdeck. The helmsman adjusted the steering oars slightly, and the bow swung ever so slightly, putting the light dead on the bow.

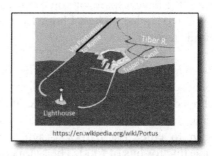

"We are back," said Livia. "It has been almost two years."

"It has," answered Marcia. "I have been away from my children for far too long. How well do you know Ostia?"

"Not at all."

"I came though Portus ten years ago, but everything was done for us, and a lot of construction going on then. I am sure that the captain will assist us."

By the time the ship's bell announced the second hour of the day, time for breakfast, they could clearly make out the structure of the white lighthouse, now billowing dark smoke for the daytime signal. Dozens of other ships around the *Ajax* were all making for the harbor. Marcia and her group returned to the officer's mess to join the rest of their party.

"You looked like you haven't slept," said Hina to Marcia.

"I haven't. Livia and I are so excited to be back. We will be in port in a few hours."

"By noon, to be sure," said the captain. "We will be inside the breakwaters in about an hour, then wait our turn for entrance to the harbor."

"How do we get to Rome from here?" asked Livia.

"You can ride your horses, and rent a cart for your baggage, if you like. Rome is about an hour or so north by the *Via Portuensis* road just outside the port. Or with your orders, you could requisition a river barge on the east side of the harbor. That will take longer than riding, but some of them have nice accommodations for passengers."

"I think we'll ride. Livia, once we get to Rome, how do we get to your home?" Marcia asked.

"Yes, The *Via Portuensis* goes right inside Rome, by the *Pons Probi* bridge to the *Clivus Publicius* then up the Aventine Hill. But I don't have a horse."

"We have a spare, or you can ride in the cart."

Livia smiled. "Then, I hope Ennius is expecting our big crowd. He is our head steward."

Everyone went on deck after breakfast to watch the *Ajax'* entrance between the breakwaters. The lighthouse, a good two hundred feet high, slipped by them on the port side, its black smoke acrid against the sea salt tang. Inside the breakwater, a dozen ships waited, sails brailed up, for their turn to enter the harbor, seagulls wheeling and quarrelling over them, questing for bits of food. The sailors on the *Ajax* chanted, as they too hauled on the brail lines to furl the sails to the yardarms. The ship came dead in the water, the anchor splashing down. The ship was suddenly uncharacteristically quiet for the first time in weeks.

A small boat came alongside, and the crew let down a rope ladder, helping a bearded man onto the deck. He went aft to the quarterdeck, conferred with the captain, and in a few minutes, sailors manned the capstan to hoist the anchor while others let out the sails to about half-unfurled, and *Ajax* made her way to the harbor entrance.

"That was the pilot, I think," said Galosga, knowingly. "I think we should go below, change and get our baggage ready."

About a half-hour later, they were back on deck, everyone in riding gear, Livia in a borrowed set of felts. Inside the harbor, there was a forest of bared masts, hundreds of ships of various sizes moored to quays on the eastern side of the bay. As the *Ajax* slipped by them, Marcia noted that each dock, formed by quays extending out from the perimeter, had an alphanumeric indicator on the wall at its end. When they reached '*C XII*', the skipper ordered the sails furled, and smartly turned the ship to nose in between the quays. The *Ajax* bled off speed, and its bow bumped into the well-padded end of its dock with just a gentle thump. Seamen put over lines, and it was done.

Captain Alexander Phaedon came down to see them off. "I thank you all for the most interesting company I have ever entertained on my vessel," he said, taking Marcia's hand in his. "My sailors will see to your baggage and horses. You can rent a wagon for your baggage at the liveries by the *Via Portuensis,* and drop it off in Rome. Good luck on the rest of your journey."

"I thank you for your hospitality, Captain," said Livia.

The sailors assisted Marcia and Livia in locating the wagon stands, where they negotiated a fair price for a solid wagon. They rode back to the ship, loaded their baggage and were off, Livia driving, the extra horse in tow.

The *Via Portuensis* was a major thoroughfare, a hundred feet wide with white pavestones, crowded with hundreds of riders and pedestrians, wagons and oxcarts, most going north to the City. Hina, Galosga, their children and Hadyu rode in silence, through the beautiful green countryside, in awe of what they saw.

It took two hours to cover the twenty miles to Rome. The *Via Portuensis* joined the *Via Campagna,* entering the City through the thick red-brick Servian walls, overgrown with centuries of ivy, at the Trigeminal Gate. Livia led the group on the road through the cattle market of the *Forum Boarium,* thick with the smell of manure, thousands of cattle in stalls, lowing, awaiting their execution and quartering to feed Rome's masses. They passed between the white circular columns of the temple of Hercules Victor and the rectangular temple of Portuna, then the northwest end of the *Circus Maximus,* Rome's racetrack, with multicolored banners rippling along its perimeter. The Palatine Hill, crowned with the massive Flavian Palace overlooked the racetrack, abutting the Imperial box midway along the racetrack's northern side.

Livia made her way along the *Clivus Publicius* thoroughfare to ascend the Aventine Hill, facing the racetrack from its southern side, finally stopping at the Galba household.

The servants came to inquire about the visitors, and when they saw Livia, they could not contain their joy, shouting back to the doorkeeper. "It's Lady Livia! She's back! With friends!"

Ennius came out to greet her. Age and the cares of the past year had turned his hair gray, but he remained spry. "Welcome back, *domina.* We just got your letter from Antioch saying you would be arriving soon. I hope you had a safe trip?"

"We did, Ennius, we did, and a most interesting one. These are my friends. Marcia, you have met, the wife of Antonius Aristides. Hina and Galosga, the Xiongnu you have heard Aulus tell of in his adventure, their children Marasa, Andanyu and Adhela, and their friend Hadyu. These have come a great way, halfway around the world."

"I am pleased to meet you," said Ennius, bowing politely. "Do they all speak Latin?"

Hina laughed. "We all do. Not as well as we would like, but they tell us we do well." Her voice was deep, with an accent borne in the far-away steppes of China.

"You do indeed. I am Ennius, head of the Galba household. I will see that all your needs are met. And yes, I have heard of you. Hina of the Xiongnu, Galba called you."

"You are right," said Hina. "You pronounced it well."

Livia interjected. "We won't be staying more than a day or two. We must get Marcia up to Aquileia and back to her children and my Pontus. I will go with them, and bring Pontus home."

The servants busied themselves, unloading the baggage and tending the animals, while Ennius escorted his guests into the spacious interior, past the pool and fountain in the atrium to the guest rooms at the rear.

It so happened the following day that there was a race at the *Circus Maximus*. Marcia could not miss the chance to introduce Hina, Galosga, their children, and Hadyu to this event.

"This will be like Ecbatana again," said Hina eagerly.

"Well, not exactly," said Marcia. "The *Circus* seats a quarter-million people. You have too great a chance of getting separated in that crowd, and no way to understand directions back to the Galba household. And there are many who will take advantage of your lack of knowledge."

"What is a quarter million? I don't understand that number," said Hina.

"It is probably more than the population of all Ecbatana. More people than you ever saw in one place, or even imagined seeing. We will have a great view from the park at the edge of the Aventine Hill. There will be many people taking picnics there to watch the races, away from the crowd, with its muggers and pickpockets."

And so they did. The park was by the Temple of Diana on the *Clivus Publicius*, the main road, with a great view overlooking the racetrack less than a half-mile away. Although the race was still hours off, the stadium stands on either side of the racetrack were already full, spectators vigorously waving various red, white, blue and green banners, cheering for their teams. The roar of the packed stadium rose up to the hill. And in the park, here and there, families and friends gathered to watch the race.

"That is a quarter million people?" asked Hina.

"Not quite, they are still filling up," said Marcia. "Maybe half of that today."

"You were right, I like the park."

After lunch, the first race started, ten four-horse *quadrigae* chariots, their drivers wearing their team colors. The murmur of the crowd exploded into the roar of an ocean storm as the cages swung open and the charioteers launched their mounts headlong into the race. Five laps and three dramatic pileups later, a Green driver crossed the finish line two lengths ahead of his nearest Red pursuer, and began his victory lap, the stadium a sea of green flags and cheering fans.

A few knots of disgruntled spectators in the stands began engaging in a violent brawl over the outcome. "Yes, I am definitely glad we chose the park," said Hina.

CHAPTER 130:

A MOST SERIOUS UPRISING

Alexandria, May 116AD

Aharon had left Petra six months ago, before the uprising. He was an instigator and organizer, someone to stir up an insurrection, but not one to lead it when the fighting started. That had been Judah's role, though it hadn't gone well. Word of the Roman retaliation had reached Alexandria well ahead of Aharon. No matter, it had been expected.

Judah had given him detailed instructions, and a sack of money, dispatching him to Alexandria. There he was to meet with the leaders of the Jewish quarter, distributing money and directions from Sanatruces. Petra and Nisibis had been sideshows, tests to measure the Romans' resolve, distractions to their invasion. Alexandria, Cyrene, Lydda and Cyprus were to be the main events, major uprisings that would threaten the entire empire. If Alexandria fell, even the city of Rome itself would be threatened, being dependent for its daily bread on Egyptian wheat, taxes for its budget, all dispatched on massive freighters.

Although the orthodox side of Aharon blanched at the ungodly idolatry, sinfulness and decadence of Alexandria, his esthetic side could not fail to admire its beauty, its gleaming white buildings, the wide central highway of the Canopic Way bisecting the city. The towering lighthouse of Pharos overlooked the city, its top periodically flashing the reflected sunlight brilliantly, guiding the never-ending stream of ships into the city's two harbors.

Aharon entered the city by the eastern Sun Gate, locating an inn with a livery just off the Canopic Way. He dropped his baggage, secured his money, and found a much-needed bathing house. Refreshed, he set off to find the Jewish quarter on foot, carrying a small sack of coins.

The Jewish quarter was on the northeastern quadrant of the city. He was to find the Synagogue of Peace, on the Street of the Fishermen. It was an impressive two-story white building, its single grated window overlaid with a geometric design in black metal. He rang the bell by the door. Eventually, someone inside opened a sliding window in the door.

"Yes?" asked the denizen of the darkened interior.

"I am Aharon bin Yusuf. Judah bin Daoud of Ninu sends me."

"Yes, just a minute." Metallic clanking could be heard as the door was unbolted. The door was opened, revealing the man inside to be a black-bearded rabbi, clad in a dark blue robe with checkered blue and green prayer shawl. "Come in, Aharon bin Yusuf. I am Rabbi Gamaliel. Have you been traveling long?"

"Several months. From Petra."

"Please have a seat." Gamaliel summoned a white-clad servant from the interior. "Water and wine for our guest."

"Are you alone?"

"Yes."

The rabbi fell silent, playing with his thick beard in thought. "Judah is well?"

"I believe he is dead. The Romans retook Petra after I left."

"So I heard." The servant set a carafe of water, another of wine, and two goblets on the table, along with some dates.

Aharon took a sip. "You were to arrange a meeting for me."

"I seem to remember that Judah was sending someone here. But that was six months ago."

"I had to travel carefully to avoid Roman authorities."

"We all have to avoid Roman authorities these days. The ones we know, and the ones we don't." Gamaliel fixed Aharon in his blue-eyed gaze. "And you are, again, please?"

"Aharon bin Yusuf of Ninu. As was Judah."

"Judah I know, or knew, if what you say is true. You, I do not know, nor do I know anyone else from Ninu."

Aharon fished in the pocket of his robe and extracted a small rolled scroll. "Judah said you would want to see this." He handed it to Gamaliel.

Gamaliel unrolled it. It was printed in the neat block squares of the Hebrew alphabet. He read it silently, his lips moving, then handed it back. "Can you read it?"

"Yes, though not well. Judah could both read and speak Hebrew. I can read the scriptures, but I am not conversational in our old tongue."

"Read what you can."

"Greetings to my ... old friend, I think ... Gamaliel. I think ... I wish, no, I hope, that you are well. Please ... I don't know the word ... Aharon bin Yusuf as our ... together, between us, no, our mutual friend. I ..."

"Enough. If you were coming with a false reference, you would certainly be able to read it better. You are right, you are not conversational in Hebrew. But that affirms you. What else do you have for me?"

Aharon produced his small pouch sack filled with silver coins. "From Judah. And our mutual benefactor. There is more, when our meeting is arranged."

"He was generous. You understand, we must always make sure we know with whom we speak. These are dangerous times."

"As Petra showed."

"As it surely did, and Nisibis as well. You are in luck. My friends with whom you are to meet are still in the city, on other tasks. Frankly, we thought you would not be coming after two months passed. Have you accommodations?"

"I am staying at a local inn, the Cormorant."

"I know the place. It has a good reputation. I will leave word for you when things are prepared."

After several days, messengers left word that the meeting was ready. Aharon hurried to the synagogue in a wagon, loaded with the sixty-pound chest of money. He hitched his mule outside. Gamaliel was waiting with four other men, who assisted hefting the cumbersome chest inside.

"Welcome, Aharon. These are our companions Lukuas of Cyrene, Artemio of Cyprus, and the brothers Julian and Pappus of Judea. They are here to listen to what you have to say."

"Is there anyone else in the building?" asked Aharon.

"Only my servants."

"Dismiss them. The fewer ears to hear what we have to say, and tongues to wag about it, the better." Aharon took a seat.

Gamaliel returned a few minutes later. "We are alone."

"That is good. I bring word from Judah bin Daoud of Ninu, and through him, Sanatruces, the nephew of King Osroës of Parthia. We have staged small uprisings in Mesopotamia in the Roman rear, to test their mettle and disperse their forces. Unfortunately, Judah was almost certainly killed in the last insurrection in Petra. However, now is the time to strike in the heart of the eastern empire. Your task is to create so much fire and fury that the Romans will be forced to redeploy their legions from Mesopotamia, leaving the rest vulnerable to the Parthians."

"What are the chances of success?"

"Almost all their soldiers are in Parthia, leaving eastern provinces very vulnerable. If you strike together, it will be two months or more before the Romans legions can reach you. By then you should have a firm grip on your major cities. Alexandria is the priority. Take control of the harbor, and Rome will starve. The second is Judea. The Roman supply lines to Mesopotamia run through our homeland via Lydda, since Caesarea was so badly damaged by the tidal flood. Taking the ports in Cyrenaica and Cyprus will prevent Roman reinforcement with western legions by sea." Aharon unlocked the chest on the table and opened it to reveal it full of silver *denarii*. "Take what you need to buy weapons, support, whatever you need. There is twenty-five thousand sesterces worth of silver in there."

"And when the Roman legions arrive?" asked Lukuas.

"You fight them. We have beaten Roman legions in Judea before, and we can beat them again. Our Lord *Adonai* is on our side."

The discussion devolved to tactics. Lukuas would concentrate on the key port cities of Cyrenaica, Berenice, Ptolemais and Cyrene, while Artemion would select defensible cities in Cyprus. Julian and Pappas would plan the assault on Lydda and other places in Judea.

CHAPTER 131:

AN UNRESISTING FOE

Seleucia on the Tigris, May 116AD

The Twelfth Thunderbolt Legion passed south, leading the other four legions of the western force along the road paralleling the Euphrates, accompanied by the fifty light troop transports and Trajan's trireme on the river. The western force surged unopposed through the bitumen pits of Hit, bypassed the Royal Canal at Pallicotas, finally halting at Sippar, just twenty miles west of Seleucia, sister city to the capital Ctesiphon on the far bank of the Tigris River.

The five legions set up camps a few miles apart. The trireme would remain with the holding force, but the troop transports would be needed to cross the Tigris. Two sixty-foot-high treadmill cranes, each powered by five men, hoisted each seventy-foot boat, dismasted and stripped of oars, onto a pair of wagons to be towed by oxen for the next twenty miles. The boats were distributed, ten to each legion of the western force. In just forty-eight hours, the legions were on the road to Seleucia, the Twelfth in the van, Trajan leading the march on foot, as was his manner.

Samuel and Secundus trudged at the head of the Ratpack Fifth. Although it was just a few hours after daybreak, it was already hot and windless, and the worst of the day was yet to come. Samuel felt the sweat trickle down his face, and inside his leather corselet. The heat had stilled the voices of the men, no longer singing their Ratpack anthem. They concentrated on placing one foot ahead of the other, crunching grittily on the gravelly road, to cover the twenty miles separating them from Seleucia and the next camp.

"Hot day, sir."

"That it is, Samuel." The two had long ago established a mutual respect for each other.

A trumpet ahead blared a command, picked up and echoed in turn by each of the cohorts. "Why the hell are we stopping?" asked Samuel, as much under his breath as to Secundus. He turned his head to bellow to the men behind "Halt! Hold your position."

Five hundred pairs of boots crunched to a stop.

Secundus looked around, trying to determine the cause for the sudden stop, scanning the horizon for evidence of enemy formations. There were none, just the endless green irrigated fields and orchards as far as the eye could see, their farmers in attendance. The wind came up a bit, cooling the sweat on his face. "Well, at last a breeze," he said, using his *focale* neck scarf to wipe his face. Then something caught his eye, a brown line, like a line of distant mountains, on the southern horizon. "Samuel, do you see that?" he asked, pointing.

Samuel scrutinized the sight. "No mountains here, sir. And I swear ... I think it's moving, a bit bigger than it just was."

As they watched, the apparition did indeed grow larger, coming closer. As Samuel watched, a white farmhouse perhaps two miles away disappeared under the swirling mass. "It's moving fast, sir. I don't think we can outrun it."

"What is it?"

"Looks like something from Hades, coming to devour the world." The wind had picked up considerably, airborne sand and grit now stinging his exposed skin. This gave Samuel a clue. "I think it's a sandstorm. I've heard of them, never seen one. Get your *sagum* cloak up around your head, it's going to get hard to breath." He turned to the men behind. "*Tempestas harunae!* Sandstorm! Cover your heads with your cloaks. Sit down and don't move, no matter what, until the wind dies down. Wait it out!"

The sandstorm now towered over them like a mountain, just a few hundred yards away, reddish brown and black, swirling. Some of the men, disobeying orders, had broken out their eight-man tents, intending to shelter inside them, but the wind, now blowing at gale force, snatched the canvas from their hands, whirling it away into the darkening sandy shadow land.

Samuel grabbed Secundus' hand. "Sit, sir, it's on us. I don't think we're going to make Seleucia tonight." That was the end of any conversation, for the wind was now a banshee shriek, and light faded to pitch blackness as the monster enveloped them.

How long would it last? Would it get worse? Could it kill? None knew, and the wind and sand left those questions unanswered. The men would have to wait it out, controlling their fear, until whatever gods had brought this terror upon them finished their punishment. What time was it? Was it even day or night? There was no difference, they were suspended in timelessness. Secundus and Samuel succumbed to fatigue, huddled dozing together as the storm screamed around them.

After an interminable period, Secundus thought the wind had slackened a bit. He looked around, and behind him, he could see the dark shapes of his men, likewise huddled together behind him. After about an hour, the air cleared, and they could see that the entire legion buried in fine, gritty sand. Horses stood up, snorting, shaking themselves to clear the grit, as did the men. As far as the eye could see, the road had disappeared, buried under a foot of sand. Samuel bellowed orders for the men begin digging the road out, and they attacked the sand with their *dolabrae* shovels.

Trajan, with Aulus and his principate staff, had accompanied Gaius Lucullus and his headquarters team, marching, as was his wont, at the head of the column. They had fared no better than the men in ranks, caught in the open without shelter.

Gaius searched for the *Princeps*. Trajan's elegant purple *sagum* made him easy to spot. "Are you all right, Your Excellency?" asked Gaius, assisting Trajan in shedding the sand from his uniform.

"I will be, after I go somewhere to strip down. The sand has penetrated my armor everywhere. I think I have more inside my corselet than outside," he said with a smile. "Be sure to have the men do likewise, before we resume our march. The sand will scratch them raw if they don't."

"Will do, sir. Is the storm over?"

"The locals traveling with my staff say it is, and there is not likely to be another for a few weeks. We have a lot of work to do, to get the legions moving again. Send riders to the other legions. Find out what they need, and when they can get moving again. I expect no one is going anywhere until late tomorrow. You, your prefect of the camps and your *primus pilus* join me in my praetorium tent for evening meal, if you are able."

"Yes, Your Excellency." Gaius saluted and shuffled off through the thick sand.

At sunset, Gaius and Antonius joined Trajan and Aulus in the command tent with the staff. The cooks were still digging out the mess wagons, so the fare was spartan, on a par with that of the troops this evening ... boiled beans and some two-day old bread, washed down with wine.

"How are the troops faring, Gaius? Any injuries?"

"They are well, some irritated hides and eyes, nothing serious. The doctors are putting some ointments on them."

"And the gear?"

"The biggest problem are the ten boats. We had hoisted each of the hulls up and strapped them down on two wagons each. They weren't too heavy, and we able to tow them with ox teams. However, they were uncovered, and the storm filled them with sand. The wagons broke down under the excess weight, wheels and axles broken. The engineers are going to hoist them up, then repair or replace wagons under them. They think they'll be done by tomorrow noon."

"Are you going to need the big cranes?"

"Just one, not two like when we loaded them. Hoist up just the bow, fix the forward wagon, then lift the stern and do the rear one. The fewer of those big cranes to maneuver around, the faster."

"Gaius, be sure to check the hulls thoroughly. The weight of all that sand may have sprung some planking in the hulls, and they'll promptly sink from hidden leaks," said Aulus.

"Well, yes, you are the ship-building expert. Could I prevail on you to assist tomorrow and inspect them? The Ratpack Fifth will be helping the engineers with that, providing the manpower."

"Surely. What time?"

"Right after sunrise. I'll be there to observe how it goes also."

"I'll be there."

Trajan rejoined the conversation. "So, it appears that Parthians are fleeing before us. It has been nothing but a training march since leaving Dura Europos. And now the *speculator* scouts are telling us that Ctesiphon has been evacuated. It seems we will take it all without a single fight."

"Arrian Atticus is very concerned that they are drawing us in, your Excellency. Something is up, but he does not know what. We are in their heartland, and they have not sent so much as a single horseman to engage us," said Gaius

"Perhaps. Or they are caught up with their insurrection at Ecbatana in the east. They may have problems when they get to Susa, if King Vologases wants to keep them out."

"Perhaps. It is certainly hard to hide an army in this flat countryside. And the insurrections we experienced in Nisibis or Petra were nuisances, nothing more. Speaking of insurrections, Arrian said there was rioting in Alexandria."

Aulus laughed. "What else is new? There is always rioting in Alexandria."

The next morning, Aulus and Gaius showed up. The preceding day, the Fifth had cleared the boats of the sand, and assisted the engineers in maneuvering the crane into position by the first boat.

Secundus and Samuel saluted the commander as he approached, accompanied by Aulus. "Good morning, sir," said Secundus.

"Good morning, tribune. I see you have things well in hand. Aulus Aemilus would like to inspect the hulls, to make sure the stress of the sand didn't damage them. He is our expert in all things nautical."

"I think the commander overstates my expertise. There are many I would rather have handy for this inspection than myself, but I guess I shall have to do for now," said Aulus with a smile. "And good morning to you, Samuel. You are both looking well today. Shall we get started?"

"Certainly," said Secundus, leading them to the first hull.

"This is the first boat to be lifted." The boat sat lopsided on its two wagons, some wheels askew or spokes broken on both rigs. "Both wagons need to be fixed or replaced. The rest have only one wagon damaged, we think. But we won't know for sure until we get the weight off them." Secundus shuffled through the calf-high sand. "We only cleared enough sand to get the cranes into position. I wish we had kept the snowshoes from the Armenian campaign a few years ago."

"Yes, they might have come in handy in this stuff."

They approached the first boat, placing a ladder beside it for Aulus to climb up into the long slender hull. He paced back and forth inside, leaning over the side to inspect the exterior, then dismounting to visually check the exterior from below. "It appears sound," he finally said, and repeated the inspection of the other nine craft, while Secundus, Samuel and the Fifth prepared to assist the engineers in hoisting the boat.

The lashing holding the boat to the forward wagon was removed, and reused to encircle the hull near the bow, to engage the iron hook of the crane dangling above. On signal from the engineers, five men, stripped to loincloths, began stepping the treadmill that powered the lift. Ever so slowly, the hull lifted, inch by inch, from the wagon until it was clear by a good five feet. More men began muscling the broken wagon out from beneath the suspended boat.

Suddenly, there was a loud crack, and one of the planks of the hull separated, breaking.

"Get the men out from beneath it! Now!" bellowed Samuel. The men on the treadmill lowered the boat back onto the wagon.

Aulus and Gaius came to see what happened. "Well, by all the gods of sea and land, that boat is done," said Aulus, eying the splintered plank. "With the stern held fast, the lift put too much twisting and bending on the hull. This isn't going to work."

"I am truly sorry, sir, we should have foreseen this." said the Publius Asclepius, the lead engineer.

"No matter, Publius. How did you lift them onto the wagons?"

"We used two cranes, Aulus Aemilius. But that will take another day to get the second set up, and then two days to do all the lifting," said the engineer.

Samuel bent down beside one of the wagons, and peered underneath. Then he rose and returned to the perplexed group.

"I have a crazy idea. Do you remember the sleds we saw the locals using in the winter in Armenia? Runners gliding over the snow instead of wheels?"

"Yes."

"What if we put runners under the wagon? You would only have to lift the boat enough to take the weight off the wheel to remove it. Put some makeshift attachment on it to hold the runners, then do the other side."

"Where do we get the runners?" asked Publius.

Samuel pointed to the damaged boat. "As Aulus said, that boat is done. Those planks are curved, and long enough for one to fit under both wagons. Then we don't clear the road, just let the boat ride on the sand. Probably no more work for the oxen than the wheels."

"You know, I think he has got something, Publius," said Aulus. "I'll stick around to help. Those planks are held together by mortice and tenon joints, so you need to be careful prying them apart so you don't break the planks. Publius, go with Samuel to see what sort of undercarriage he needs, and see if we can rig it up quickly. We will have plenty of material from this hull."

Gaius turned to leave. "I am going to go countermand my order to start clearing the roads this morning. We are going to need them with a good layer of sand if this to work."

About noon, the oxen were hitched to the first of the jury-rigged sleds, and, as expected, they had no problems pulling the boat-laden sleds over the sand, at their uncomplaining walking pace. They arrived on the Tigris at sunset, backed the boats into the river while swimmers released the tethers holding them to the cart/sleds, allowing the boats to float free, ready for re-masting and re-rigging. Meanwhile, the legions prepared for the assault on Seleucia.

There was some desultory resistance the next day, arrows and *ballistae* bolts fired from the western wall of the city at the legions. However, in the late afternoon, the city leaders came out in a flag of truce to discuss terms with Trajan. The city surrendered with no further fighting, advising Trajan that the government and army had evacuated Ctesiphon for Susa, as had most of Seleucia's city government as well.

Expecting no resistance, the troops prepared to cross the Tigris in the troop transports. Secundus and Samuel rode a boat with the First Century crammed aboard, standing room only for the short thousand-yard crossing.

Secundus surveyed the river, shimmering in the heat, looking for fortifications or artillery on the far shore. Seeing none, he turned his attention to the five boats, line abreast to either side of them, equally loaded with the remaining centuries of the Fifth.

"Not sure why the Fifth is first across, sir," said Samuel.

"You weren't present at the tribunes' meeting last night with the commander. We drew straws to see who got to make the first landing. We lost, but no matter, it's an unopposed landing."

Just then there was a dull thud from across the river, and ten or so seconds later a boulder hit the river not fifty feet off their bow, rising a column of greenish-white water.

"Unopposed, sir?" asked Samuel. "Looks like catapults to me."

More plumes erupted from the river. One shot found its mark, and one of their little convoy boats turned down river, its bow smashed, taking on water. They could see the men struggling to strip themselves of their heavy armor before leaping into the river, hopefully before the boat sank.

Secundus shouted orders to the helmsman at the tiller. "Turn left! Now! Hold for a count of fifty, then turn right. Keep changing course!"

The men on the portside oars backed water, pulled a few strokes, then the starboard oarsmen backed, zig-zagging the slender craft through the waters. The other boats followed their guide.

This made targeting more difficult, but since the catapults were not very accurate, even against stationary targets, some of the boats blundered into the trajectory of the rocks falling from the blue sky, or into each other.

Samuel sensed the hissing sound even before he heard it. He looked up, saw the black shape, and yelled, "Incoming!" He and the men in the boat braced for what might be certain impact. The boulder missed by mere feet, impacting just feet off the port side, sending a shower of water into the open craft and shattering two oars, but otherwise doing no damage.

More ominously, the next shots trailed black smoke, indicating incendiaries. A hit by one of these could quickly turn a boat into a conflagration, but the smoke trails made their high arcing trajectories visible and avoidable. Secundus' boat ground onto the beach and the soldiers leaped over the side without orders, swords drawn, even before the boats were ashore. They splashed onto the beach and went quickly inland, in no particular formation, searching for the catapults and their crews. Secundus and Samuel followed at a run behind their century, as the other boats grounded with a crunch.

The catapults had been well-concealed behind a grove of low palm trees, a bunker of logs stacked before them as fortification. Several Parthians were already down in pools of spreading blood when Samuel and Secundus caught up with their men. Sergius Lepidus, the centurion of the First Century, held his sword at the throat of an elderly man with white hair and beard, who glared defiantly at him.

"I couldn't kill him, sir. He's like my grandfather," said Sergius to Samuel.

"Stand easy, all," said Samuel. "Keep them alive, under sword-point. We want to find out what other 'unopposed' forces might be waiting for us." He turned to the elderly man and addressed him in fluent Aramaic.

"Good day to you, grandfather. Art thou not a bit old to be commanding a catapult crew?"

The man, bare-chested and clad in just a loin cloth, turned and spat. "I am never too old to kill Roman dogs."

"And a good morning to thee, also,' said Samuel, undoing his water flask. "Wouldst thou care for a some water on this hot day? That was excellent shooting." He offered the flask.

The man continued to glare, his brown eyes hard underneath his bushy white eyebrows.

Samuel took a sip, to assure the man that the flask contained no poison, then offered it to him again. The man looked down, then grabbed the flask and drank thirstily. He wiped his mouth with his hand and handed it back.

"If thou art going to kill me, please do so quickly. It is a hot day."

"I do not intend to kill thee, grandfather. But why art thou all doing the fighting, rather than the young soldiers?" Samuel asked, indicating the other fighters, all elderly.

Just then an armed woman strode arrogantly through the brush, her sword at the ready. She was clad in padded blue fighting gear, with a yellow belt, a black leather sword belt and sheath, her sword in hand. Her helmet covered her head, but whisps of black hair protruded behind her cheek pieces. She addressed Samuel and Secundus in fluent Latin. "The old men are fighting because my father, the King of Kings, has taken the army and fled to Susa. He left me behind, and I refused to let Ctesiphon fall without a resistance. I organized the veterans."

"May I commend you on a fight well-fought, *domina?*" Samuel glanced at Secundus, sensing that the tribune should continue this conversation.

Secundus picked it up, rendering a brief sword salute to the woman, then sheathing his weapon. "I am Secundus Lucullus, tribune of the Fifth Cohort of the *Legio XII Fulminata*. May I have the honor of your name?"

"I am Afrand, daughter of the King of Kings Osroës." She returned the salute, then also sheathed her weapon. "I presume I am your prisoner, though you haven't disarmed me?"

"You may keep your weapon, for now, Lady Afrand, as you have not yet surrendered yourself. Your men have fought their fight. They will not be harmed, unless they put up more resistance. Might we expect more welcoming parties on our way to Ctesiphon?"

"Perhaps."

"Very well, then. I will escort you to *Legatus* Gaius Lucullus. Samuel, take charge of the century and our captives, form a defensive perimeter, and await orders from the commander. Maintain combat formation when you move out, in the event of more attacks or ambushes. I will take a squad of men with me, to escort Lady Afrand."

"Aye, sir!" said Samuel, organizing the men.

Secundus departed in search of the eagles of the Twelfth's headquarters, lost in the disorganization of the amphibious landing. It took about an hour, the squad meandering along the beach among ships being beached, cargo and horses being unloaded, and centuries forming up as they located their scattered men. The command tent was still being pitched. "Where is the *legatus?*" he asked the men, working in loincloths in the heat, sweat running in rivulets on their bronze torsos.

"That way, fifty paces," said one man, indicating the direction with a head nod, not looking away from the taut tent rope he was securing to a stake.

Secundus found the staff clustered about a table in the open air. He walked up, saluted, arm across chest, and introduced himself, eyes straight ahead. "Secundus Lucullus, Tribune of the Fifth Cohort, with Lady Afrand, daughter of King Osroës, sir."

"Well, this is an unexpected surprise, Secundus. Stand easy," said Gaius, raising one eyebrow in surprise. "*Domina*, I would offer you a seat, but they are still being unloaded. Please accept my apologies. I am Gaius Lucullus, *legatus* of the Twelfth Thunderbolt Legion.

"I am Afrand, daughter of the King of Kings Osroës. He regrets he could not welcome you personally, but he has business in Susa to which he must attend."

"Yes, with his government and entire army. Ctesiphon was supposed to be evacuated," said Gaius.

Samuel interjected. "She organized the resistance, sir, and did a credible job. Her catapults took out some of our boats. Fortunately, no one was drowned or seriously injured."

"Yes, that took us quite by surprise. Let me add my compliment to those of the Tribune."

"You are related, with the same *gens* Lucullus?" said Afrand.

"We are. Your Latin is excellent. Are you the king's representative here?"

"I am," she said.

"Well, as representative of the King, you shall meet with *Princeps* Trajan when he comes ashore this afternoon. You will likely remain with him as his guest."

"Guest … or prisoner?"

"Guest. Though you must relinquish your sword in his presence."

"Then I will be free to come and go as I please?"

"No, not really. You will be his very valuable guest."

"No, I will be his very valuable prisoner. But I accept that."

Arrian, accompanied by Nathaniel and Marcus, arrived. Someone had sensed that the intelligence team would be very interested in this woman, and had summoned them. Gaius introduced them. "These are part of my intelligence team. Arrian Atticus leads the team, Nathaniel knowledgeable in all things Parthian, and Marcus Lucius is a master of languages. If you don't mind, my Lady, I would like them to ask you some questions, until the *Princeps* arrives."

"I shall be happy to hear their questions."

"Please escort Lady Afrand to your tent, Arrian. I will have some lunch and refreshments sent to you. Dismissed."

The intelligence tent was also in the process of being set up. Arrian grabbed chairs from the wagon. "It looks like we will have our discussion in this blazing sun, my lady. The tent is not yet ready. Please be seated. You may remove your helmet if you wish." He fumbled in his uniform pouch for his tablet and stylus.

Afrand removed her helmet, shaking out her long raven locks. Her forehead was sweaty, with a red pressure mark from the steel. "I suspect you men have seen few fighting women in your lives."

Afrand was surprised at the reaction her comment got. Both men smiled broadly.

"Too bad you missed my sister Marcia and Hina. They left a few months ago for Italy. I suspect you would have got on well with them. And my wife Mei. She is still with us, riding with the cavalry. You will meet her later," said Marcus.

"I had not expected that. Are the Romans so short of men that they are recruiting women?"

"No, but those three are very good fighters. Hina, a barbarian from the Distant East, has taught our cavalry some new tricks, and I am sure they are disappointed that once again your vaunted Parthian cavalry has evaded them. They are looking forward to trying their new skills."

"That will come. You will not remain in Mesopotamia long." She eyed Marcus carefully. "You are also from the Distant East. Hanaean, I think, but your name Marcus is Roman and your Latin is excellent. Are your people now allied with Trajan?" she asked.

"Yes to the first question, Lady Afrand, and no to the second. That is a great fear of your uncle Cyrus Mithridates, but totally unfounded."

"You know him?"

"I was an unwilling guest in your palace for a while, until Hina rescued me."

"I remember that incident. My uncle was furious at your escape. And your sister, she and another Roman woman, they were also his guests for a time, but they too escaped."

Arrian interrupted. "I am sure you will have an ample time to hear Marcus' stories, but I would like to ask you some questions first. My first is, where did your father and the army go?"

A servant brought a plate of light snacks and well-watered wine. Everyone helped themselves. The princess answered between bites. "He evacuated the government and army to the fortress at Susa, in the Zagros Mountains. He made no secret of this."

"Hmm. And does the King and his brother still fear an alliance between Rome and China?"

"Very much so. Uncle Cyrus believes that the unrest in Ecbatana under the pretender Vologases may have been instigated somehow by the Hanaeans, to support Trajan's invasion of our homeland."

Marcus smiled. "I am pleased you credit us with so much skill and diplomacy, my lady, but I can assure you that communications between

Rome and China are too difficult, slow and unreliable to support such a complex thing. My sister in Italy and I in China communicated under Senatorial seals for ten years, simply to stay in touch, and in all that time we exchanged just ten letters. Mithridates, whom we knew from his time as your envoy to the Han court, was convinced we were using some sort of code in them. Hence our detention," said Marcus.

Nathaniel added to the conversation. "When Marcus escaped, Mithridates had his sister Marcia kidnapped and brought to him from Italy. He was absolutely convinced that there is a Roman-Chinese connection."

"Were the letters coded communication?" Afrand asked.

"Absolutely not," said Nathaniel.

A braying of trumpets outside interrupted the conversation. "It seems like the *Princeps* has arrived. We have a bath being set up for my wife Mei, which you may wish to use to freshen up. I expect he will summon you shortly."

CHAPTER 132:

TRAJAN AND THE PRINCESS

Ctesiphon, May 116AD

Despite the panoply of trumpets announcing the arrival of the most powerful man of all Rome, preceded by twenty-four lictors, followed by his staff and entourage, the *Princeps* was bedraggled, his legs covered with wet black mud to the knees. The purple cloak was soaking wet, its bottom fringe also covered with clinging mud. It was not his most elegant arrival. Nevertheless, his sardonic grin indicated he took it all in stride.

He had attempted a dramatic landing from his boat, vaulting over the gunwale into the water as the boat was beaching itself, intending to splash ashore. The thick river mud, however, did not cooperate with his intentions. He sank up to his knees in the ooze, and only with great difficulty had been able to extract his legs from the sucking mass, one after the other, until he reached the shore. While he had not lost his footing and fallen face down into the muck, he nevertheless was definitely in need of ablutions and a change of clothes.

The soldiers had cheered and applauded him, however, seeing him as always one of their own, and what was a little mud to a true soldier? He shared their triumphs, challenges, and occasional embarrassments with equal aplomb.

Trajan's staff, led by Aulus, accompanied by Tiberius Maximus commanding the *X Fretensis* Legion, had been far less impatient, waiting until the ship was properly beached and the boarding ladder rigged, before disembarking on dry land to join the *Princeps*.

The entourage proceeded to the Twelfth's command tent where Gaius saluted the *Princeps*. Trajan returned the salute, then shrugged. "The mud was thicker and stickier than I thought. I will need to go around by the bath, before I enter your tent."

Gaius smiled. "Around back. It's not hot yet, but as hot as the day already is, I think you will prefer it that way." Servants were already bringing up a complete change of clothes as Trajan headed to the wooden tub.

Gaius ushered the staff into the tent, out of the hot sun. They joined Arrian, Nathaniel and Marcus, who had returned with Lady Afrand. Antonius, Paulus Herrerius and the tribunes were also in the tent, in readiness to accommodate Trajan. A map of Ctesiphon lay on the table. Half an hour later, once again clean and immaculately clad, Trajan entered the command tent, accompanied by a strange man, bearded in Parthian style, but wearing Roman dress. The legion staff, led by Gaius Lucullus, snapped to attention and rendered salutes, a dozen arms slamming to their chests with nearly simultaneous thuds.

"At ease, gentlemen, and seats, please." Trajan seated himself. "Another inexplicably easy victory, gentlemen." He looked at Afrand, still clad in her armor. "Who is our beautiful guest? Have you recruited more lady warriors from the Parthians to replace the ones that went back to Italy?"

"This is Lady Afrand, the daughter of King Osroës She remained behind at his request to welcome us to the Parthian capital. Lady Afrand organized a party of veterans to work catapults this morning to greet us. She was good enough to take out two of our ships, but fortunately no one was hurt," said Gaius.

"Well, *domina*, at least you put up some resistance. I see you have noticed your brother Parthamaspates in my company."

"I was a child when you left in exile, brother. You look more Roman than Parthian."

"I have lived well there."

"I will be putting him on the throne when we enter the city tomorrow morning. Will you be able to ensure a peaceful welcome for us? I would hate to have to take such a beautiful city by force."

"I will go in to talk to the city fathers, and ensure that your entry is peaceable. I will welcome you to the palace on your entry."

"That will be fine, Lady Afrand. Thank you."

Gaius noted that she had very neatly slipped his verbal leash on her, intending to enter the city unescorted. "According to Lady Afrand, King Osroës is in Susa with the army," he said.

"Well, we shall have to pay him a visit soon, to show our respect for his hospitality."

The following morning, the five thousand men of the Twelfth in parade gear, ten cohorts of six centuries each, formed a checkerboard pattern before the main gate of Ctesiphon. Between the legion's headquarters staff and the gate were arrayed the *Princeps* and his Praetorian Guard, even more polished and gleaming in the rising sun. Afrand stepped forward to the closed gate, called out to the guards in the surrounding towers, and a small door opened in one of the massive doors to admit her. She entered in.

After about a half hour, the massive doors swung open and she emerged, flanked by bearded elderly men in turbans and green robes. The group approached Trajan standing before his Guardsmen, who then gave the command to march. A century at a time, the Twelfth marched through the open gates, to effect a peaceful march through the capitulated city to the palace.

The legion halted before the white palace, gleaming in the sun. Twenty-four lictors of the Praetorian Guard, their *fasces* with ax-heads mounted, preceded Trajan, accompanied by Lady Afrand and the city fathers, followed by his staff, as he strode up the wide marble steps to the cool interior pavilion. The remaining Guardsmen flanked the imperial party, arms to hand to defend against any subterfuge.

The thick stone walls and high windows defended the interior against the blazing sun, keeping it cool. At the end of the marble pavilion a fountain played, adding a cooling mist. There were few persons in the interior, just a few caretaker servants standing respectfully at the far wall, staring at the invaders, wondering perhaps if this was to be the last day of their lives. The party ascended the gray marble stairs to the royal chambers on the third floor. Several of the Guardsmen detached to inspect the throne room, returning to indicate that all was clear. The lictors took station, twelve to either side of the gold-clad door, flanked by the Guardsmen.

"Stand at ease, gentlemen," said Trajan, and the lictors lowered their *fasces* to a respectable uniform angle. "I will not be long."

Trajan entered and stood with Parthamaspates and Lady Afrand before the golden throne of the Parthian *Shananshah,* the King of Kings, facing his party and the city fathers, uncomfortable in the throne room.

"Well, it seems that Roman law has finally arrived in Parthia. Lady Afrand, please inform the city fathers that their lives are safe, and no violence will be inflicted on the city. However, rebellion against Roman authority in the city will not be tolerated."

Lady Afrand translated, the city fathers murmured and nodded in agreement.

"Now, Lady Afrand, would you be so kind as to inform me of the status of the Parthian treasury?"

"The treasury is with my father in Susa. We had plenty of time to evacuate it, along with all things of value here. He left the throne for your temporary use."

"We may have use of it far longer than he expected, my lady." He turned to Parthamaspates. "We will have a more formal ceremony later, but for now, you are installed as king. Please take your seat here as the new King of Parthian Kings."

Parthamaspates awkwardly stepped onto the podium and took his seat.

Trajan turned the grizzled commander of the *X Fretensis.* "Tiberius Julius, I hope you will become comfortable here. You may pick your new office as governor of the newly-formed province of Mesopotamia on this floor, convenient to King Parthamaspates."

Just the hint of a smile flickered over Maximus' face at the unexpected appointment. "I thank you very much for the honor, Your Excellency."

"Aulus Aemilius, you and selected members of my staff must survey our new province. We will depart in a week for my ship at Sippar, and proceed south along the Euphrates to Charax and the Persian Gulf. We will return by way of Babylon on the Tigris. We must dispatch a letter for my signature this afternoon to the Senate informing them that *Parthia Capta Est*... Parthia has been taken without resistance."

Aulus cleared his throat. "Your Excellency, with all due respect, would it not be better to delay a few days, to ensure that all is in order before departing?"

"Nonsense. We have had virtually no resistance to date. King Osroës has ceded his palace and throne to me without a fight. There is nothing to be gained in delaying the demonstration of our control over the rest of the province."

Lady Afrand turned aside, concealing the barest of smiles that she could not suppress.

CHAPTER 133:

ALEXANDRIA BURNING

Alexandria, May 116AD

The day started as usual in Alexandria, with shops, businesses, temples and government basilica offices open for business. Ships nudged past the Pharos lighthouse to dock at the Great Harbor, passing ships outbound for points throughout the Mediterranean, while gulls wheeled overhead. It was a beautiful day, one not to last.

About noon, there was a disturbance near the Sun Gate at the eastern end of the Canopic Way, a small riot. The city was on edge, after horrifying reports of the violent insurrection in neighboring Cyrene. The governor Marcus Rutilius Lupus ordered any violence to be put down quickly. He placed one century of the urban cohort continuously on standby, ready to respond immediately to any troubles.

Riots were nothing unusual in the big city. Rabble-rousing activists of one ilk or another would attract a crowd to hear their harangues, and fighting would soon break out among the listeners, then rioters spreading to attack, loot and burn nearby shops. The urban cohort would arrive and quickly put down the disorganized mob.

Today was different. Multiple speakers arose around the Jewish Quarter in the northeast part of the city, reminding the crowd of the violence they had suffered throughout the past century of Roman rule in Alexandria, the murders, the burning of shops and desecration of synagogues, and the massacre of more thousands of Alexandrian Jews seeking to petition Nero to head off the looming horrific war in their homeland. That war had destroyed their temple and scattered hundreds of thousands of Judeans around the empire as slaves and refugees. And tens of thousands of Jews had fled the increasingly anti-Jewish Alexandria. The speakers reminded them that it was the Persians who had restored them to Judea and helped build that second Temple, and that their successors, the Parthians, would restore them to their homeland again and rebuild their temple. It did not take long for the mood to turn ugly, and instigators throughout the mob quickly silenced dissenting voices.

And the crowds had come armed, most with casual daggers or the wickedly curved *sicarii* assassins' blades, some with swords. Tarpaulins were pulled from wagons to distribute more swords, shields, and torches to the mob.

Aharon watched in satisfaction from the roof of his inn as the mob spilled onto the Canopic Way, smashing shops, looting banks, and setting government buildings and temples ablaze. Rabbi Gamaliel had done his organization well. The riot had become a full-fledged uprising, numbering in the thousands, led by Lukuas the Cyrene.

A trumpet announced the arrival of elements of the standby century of the urban cohort. Such a small force would normally have no problem dispersing a much larger crowd of disorganized rabble. But Lukuas had anticipated this. He had positioned his veteran soldiers, freshly arrived from Cyrene, in the front ranks, forming a shield wall against the advancing century, and behind them, phalanx-style, lancers laid their weapons over their shoulders.

The veterans took the brunt of the century's assault, and the two forces locked into a bloody shoving match the width of the Canopic Way, until more of Lukuas' men emerged from streets behind the Romans to take them from the rear. The century was quickly cut down, soldiers breaking ranks to flee the encirclement. The mob quickly looted the soldiers for weapons and armor, and a thick black cloud began to rise over the city, as the mob advanced on the city center.

The fighting and destruction spread rapidly through the city, now filled with screams of terrified citizens and the roar of flames. The governor committed another two centuries to the battle, but they began the fight surrounded, and quickly fell to the rebels. Ships and boats in the harbor hastily slipped their moorings and set to sea, while civilians poured through the western Moon Gate of the Canopic Way to escape the violence. Night was going to be hell on earth for those unable to escape.

The following morning Rabbi Gamaliel joined Aharon on the roof top, to survey a strangely silent city. Fires everywhere burned unattended. Only the Jewish Quarter was unscathed. "You have done well, Rabbi," said Aharon.

"It was the hand of God," Gamaliel replied.

"And the hand of Lukuas. He has swept the Romans from the city like Joshua against the Canaanites. And from Cyrenaica as well. Word on the street is that the governor has abandoned the city."

"He left on one of the ships last night, with his government and what is left of his soldiers. The city is ours."

"Judah and our mutual benefactor will be pleased. Now let us see to the destruction of the heathens' idols."

CHAPTER 134:

RETURN TO AQUILEIA

Aquileia, June 117AD

Marcia and her party, accompanied by Livia, took the *Via Flaminia* from Rome over the Appenine Mountains, then the *Via Sucinaria*, the "Amber Road" along the coast through Ravenna to Aquileia. Livia's coachman and their bodyguard Andromachus took turns driving the cart, with Livia riding, and occasionally taking the reins herself. The rest rode their steeds. Still traveling on Trajan's imperial orders, they were able to spend their nights at one of the many comfortable *mansiones*, covering the three-hundred-and-fifty-mile trip in ten days.

Marcia was nearly moved to tears at the sight of the watchtowers of the academy and her home, as they rode through a copse of trees leading to the carriageway. They had dispatched a letter to Aulus' freedman Lucius Parvus, informing him of their imminent arrival, but they hadn't waited for the reply. They would be expected. And Marcia had the letters of manumission in her baggage.

As they dismounted, the door burst open, Lucius Parvus and all the servants pouring out, along with Livia's son Pontus Servilius, sporting a Hadrian-style curly beard, and Marcia's children Colloscius, Aena and Androcles. There was a flurry of embraces as the group greeted the long-lost Marcia and Livia. Hina and her entourage looked on with Livia's servants, all smiling at the happy reunion. Various sets of hands snagged their baggage as they were hustled into the first atrium.

Marcia settled in a sofa, surrounded by her children. Colloscius was now a serious self-contained twelve-year-old, while Aena was ten and Androcles almost five. "You have all grown so much while I was gone. I missed so much of your life."

"We took care of things while you were gone," said Colloscius, in a very adult tone.

"And Desdemona made sure we did all the things our tutors told us to do," said Aena.

"Here, I want you to meet someone special. This is your Aunt Hina and Uncle Galosga, I told you so much about them, how you are named for them. They have come from far, far away to live with us."

Hina smiled. "Yes, and these are my twins, Aena and Andanyu, named for your mother and father, and my youngest, Adhela. Your cousins."

The twins were fully-armed, with bows and swords crossed under the shields on their backs, daggers and a quiver of arrows at their belts. This caught the attention of Colluscius, and also Livia' son Pontus, who had joined the group, intrigued by their weapons. Pontus was also intrigued by Marasa's green cat-like eyes, raven-black hair, and her nimble, well-muscled warrior's body. Androcles was intrigued by Adhela, about his age, but also sporting a good-sized dagger.

"You are well-armed. Fighters?" Pontus asked awkwardly.

"Yes," the two answered almost in unison. They undid their fighting gear and set it on the floor in the corner. "We do not need to be wearing this in the house."

The four older ones went off to get better acquainted, the two younger ones following behind.

"I think Pontus has his eyes on my name-sake, Hina," said Marcia, laughing gently.

"I am sure Marasa can handle herself with him."

"I am sure she can, but I am glad she left her heavy weapons behind."

Marcia rose to clap her hands loudly to gain everyone's attention. "Please, I have an announcement of great importance to all you servants who have so faithfully served us in my absence. I have in my hands your manumission papers. You are no longer slaves, but free men and women. You may go or stay as you wish. We cannot afford to pay you much if you stay, but you may continue to use your rooms, with meals as before. We will officially register you as freedmen with the magistrate in Aquileia tomorrow. Please come forward as I call your names."

She called Desdemona first. "You have been as much a mother to my children as I have been, the more so in my absence, their only mother."

Desdemona, tears welling in her eyes, could not speak for the joy of the moment.

She was followed by the gruff German bodyguard Alaric, the major domo Brutus, and the rest of the household servants.

Livia then announced, "I will write my husband, Senator Aulus Aemilus Galba, to inform him of your manumission, and request him to nominate you all for citizenship through the Senate, for honorable service in support of the *Princep's* campaign."

When that was completed, Marcia announced, "If our newly-freed men and women will please be seated, I will serve you wine so we can make a toast to your *libertas*."

CHAPTER 135:

TRAJAN'S VICTORY TOUR

Ctesiphon, June 116AD

Trajan spent about a week in Ctesiphon in his command tent, leaving the palace throne to the new king and governor of Mesopotamia. With necessary paperwork complete, he prepared to depart with Aulus and his staff to embark in the *Romulus*, beginning an inspection tour of his newly-conquered territory on the Euphrates south to Charax on the Persian Gulf, then back upriver on the Tigris to Babylon to join Lusius Quietus' eastern force. There he planned to dispatch some of Quietus' legions to attack King Osroës at his temporary capital in Susa. Impatient to leave, he hurried Arrian through his intelligence report.

"The news from the east is good, sir. King Vologases has dispatched forces to counter what he views as an invasion of his territory by Osroës. With any luck, you may find yourself allied with Vologases in besieging Susa."

"If he is willing to relinquish Mesopotamia. I don't think he will, so we must prepare take them on one at a time. Next?"

"The word from the west is less good. There was some sort of major rioting in Cyrenaica. Details are sketchy, but it appears that many were killed."

"They have plenty of auxiliaries to deal with that sort of thing. Anything else?"

The following day, with Trajan's staff onboard, the *Romulus* slipped her moorings and set out downriver. Aulus stood by the gilded rail, listening to the powerful thump-swish rhythm of one hundred and seventy oars working in unison, the chants of the rowers, and the piercing piping coming from belowdecks that kept the rowers synchronized. There was a feel of ominous power in the ship, a slight acceleration with each sweep of the oars.

Aulus, wearing just a light tunic against the heat, watched the swirling white-foaming water slide aft. But his thoughts were not on the ship. His mind was on this accursed victory tour of Trajan's. *I tried everything I could do to convince him to delay this trip. But he is set to celebrate a victory not yet won. After two days, we will be too far down river for any boat to catch us, to bring word of any change. And any change that is worth sending a boat after us is not going to be good news.*

Aulus went back to watching the oars, shiny-wet and dripping, blades rotating from the vertical to the horizontal as they came out of the water, arcing forward, to rotate again to re-enter the water vertically, least resistance to the air on the forward sweep, maximum thrust against the water on the back sweep. This was a well-trained crew.

The trireme crawled like a centipede on the water for about an hour, then on shouted command, the rowers lifted the oars out of the water, drawing them in through the ports so that only the blades remained exposed. Crewmen unfurled the two sails, the big purple mainsail emblazoned with an eagle, SPQR below, surrounded by a wreath, all in gold. As the sails caught the wind, the oarsmen took a much-needed break. Not yet noon, it was already extremely hot, too hot for high-intensity rowing.

Trajan came up beside Aulus, similarly light clad. "Good morning, Aulus Aemilius. Are you enjoying the trip?"

Aulus chose not to answer the question honestly. "I am, your Excellency," he said.

"Charax on the Persian Gulf will be a major new port for us. How much will that cut the distance to reach India?"

"By half at least, but not the time. The winds will be much less favorable. On the beam, whatever the season."

"How do the winds blow there?" the *Princeps* asked.

"Southwest to northeast, very strong, from June to September, then reversing in the fall, just as strong. The wind is on the stern going out in the summer from Eudaemon Arabia, and on the stern coming back from India. From Charax, it will be strong on the beam both seasons."

"You don't sound enthusiastic."

"It will be difficult sailing. And the overland connections to the Mediterranean will be much longer and more expensive. I think the shipping masters will prefer the routes they know, and the short road connection to the Nile and the Mediterranean. They will likely be cheaper."

"And would you prefer that route also?"

"I will try the new route, to see the difference," Aulus answered diplomatically, knowing that the *Princeps* thought that Charax would be a major addition to the Indian trade.

"I am sure you will. I will leave you to your thoughts."

"Thank you, your Excellency."

In the Ctesiphon palace, Governor Tiberius Maximus had set himself up in Mithridates' old office, adjacent to the throne room. Gaius Lucullus, as senior commander of the legions garrisoning the city, had set his headquarters up on the third floor close to the governor. Arrian had set up his intelligence operation in one of the offices clustered around the headquarters complex.

Arrian's interrogation of Afrand had turned into friendly chats. He enjoyed their sparring matches, developing a respect for her charm and wit, as she tried to gain information from him, while carefully avoiding giving away too much information to him.

"Well, I have enjoyed our talk this morning, Afrand."

His aide arrived with a basket of sealed scrolls. "Your morning correspondence, sir."

"Thank you, Servius," said Arrian, taking the basket. "Some more tea for both us, please." He turned to Afrand. "You may stay, but I must attend to business."

Arrian reviewed the scrolls. The first two were reports from the cohorts garrisoning Nisibis and Edessa. A low growl emerged from Arrian's throat.

He rolled that scroll and broke the seal on the second, from the governor of Alexandria. *Not Alexandria! This is serious!*

His hands were shaking as he broke the seal on the last, from the governor of Judea,

The aide returned with a pot of hot herb tea. "Sorry, Servius, this is not going to be a time for tea. Afrand, something has come up. I am afraid you must go to your quarters."

"What is up?" she asked.

"Nothing serious, but I must talk to the commander. Please leave."

Making sure she left, posting Servius to keep her and everyone else out, he gathered up the basket of scrolls and made his way to the commander's office. He entered without knocking. "*Legatus!*" He managed a salute with his right arm across his chest. "I apologize for interrupting you, but I have most urgent news."

Gaius waved to a seat before his desk, the plain well-worn desk he used in his command tent. "Sit. What's the news, Arrian?" He wore his characteristic smile, a smile Arrian knew would soon fade.

"Sir, first, the cohorts garrisoning Nisibis and Edessa reported major insurrections in those cities. The reports are two days old."

"They are holding?"

"As of the time the messages were sent, yes."

"Good. What else?"

"Much more serious, sir. A major insurrection in Cyrene has left that city in flames, and the insurrection has spread to Alexandria. That city is also burning and the governor was forced to flee. The governor of Judea also reports another uprising in Lydda, threatening our supply lines. Both governors are requesting legions to put them down."

Gaius smile had been replaced by a scowl. "Any details on the insurrections?"

"The one in Alexandria broke out in the Jewish quarter, aided by militants newly-arrived from Cyrene. They both broke out about a week ago."

Gaius struck his desk with his hand. "Damn! I knew this victory was too easy. There is a Parthian hand in all this. And the *Princeps* now three days down river! We are going to have to deal with this on our own. Come with me, we need to let the governor know this!"

They briefed Governor Maximus, who was equally concerned. "Get a message to the *Princeps*, by the fastest boat and crew in our inventory. Lusius Quietus just arrived from the eastern campaign. I am going to dispatch him to put down the troubles in Edessa and Nisibis, by whatever means he feels necessary. And another message to Hadrian in Antioch, though he probably already knows this. I need his permission as the eastern military commander-in-chief, in the absence of the *Princeps*, to dispatch troops out of theater to recover Alexandria and Lydda."

The governor paused to consider his next move. "I think we need to strike the head of the snake. I want my old legion *X Fretensis* to move on Susa."

Gaius Lucullus spoke up. "Sir, is it a good idea to disperse our forces at this time? We are spreading ourselves thin."

"So we are. But Osroës has threatened us, and we must threaten him where he hides. And I am going with my old legion."

"Yes, sir."

Tiberius Maximus rose and left.

Antonius hissed quietly to Gaius. "A bad idea, speadin' the forces thin and takin' off on his own campaign. He's the guv'ner, not commander of the Tenth anymore."

"Unfortunately, I think the commander of the Tenth will probably feel the same way. But like you said, he's the governor, and there isn't anything we can do about it, except keep the other legions on task. Hopefully, the *Princeps* will be back soon."

CHAPTER 136:

HADRIAN'S ALARM

Antioch, June 116AD

Pompeia proffered the small scroll to Hadrian. "Publius, I believe this will solve the succession problem."

Hadrian accepted the scroll, unrolling it in the lamplight. It was indeed the solution to that most pressing problem. He read the neatly printed block characters in the precise hand of an accomplished scribe.

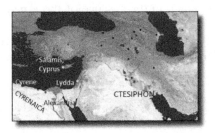

> *I, Marcus Ulpius Trajan, Princeps Optimus Senatu Consulto, do hereby declare my adoption of Publius Aelius Hadrianus as my son, with my strongest desire for him as my successor, in the event of my death.*

Some legal text followed that did not alter the gist of the first sentence. It was signed in Trajan's name, but in Pompeia Plotina's delicate script.

"Pompeia, this could be dangerous. What if my cousin does not agree?"

"Marcus will never see this, Publius. I am going to seal this and put it away. Only in the event of his death without a designated successor will this ever see the light of day."

"But with your signature?"

"I have been signing much of his correspondence this year in his absence. This is only one more item." She took the scroll from Hadrian's hand. "He has ignored all my queries on this matter, most unlike him. Either he has another plan in place, or he is refusing to make this decision." She smiled and laughed softly, a bell-like resonance. "And I don't expect this to be needed anytime soon. He has many years left, and by then, this will, I hope, be more properly resolved. Still, with the war and all the unpredictable events that could happen, this is your insurance, and Rome's as well, for an orderly succession."

"I thank you, Pompeia." He took her delicate hand in his hand and led her to the sofa. "I have excused the servants."

She smiled, following willingly, her pale green *stola* swirling like mist behind her.

A bit later, sated, Hadrian watched her dozing on the sofa. He was surprised at the physical turn in their relationship, and how much he too enjoyed it, given his proclivity toward men. Perhaps it was her acute wit, wisdom, and forcefulness that appealed to him, unlike his wife Vibia. His musings were interrupted by a knock on the door.

Hadrian quickly awakened Pompeia, assisted her in rearranging her *stola*, then straightened his own tunic, before answering the door. Outside stood Virgilius, his aide, obviously in a state of distress.

"Did I not leave word that I was not to be disturbed?" answered Hadrian, annoyed.

"Begging your Excellency's pardon, but we have received news of serious disturbances in the provinces that demand your immediate attention."

Hadrian stepped into the hallway, closing the door behind him, hoping Virgilius had not observed Pompeia's presence. The man was nothing if not discrete, still if tongues were to wag, it would be a major problem. "I'll deal with this matter in my office." He headed down the hall with a firm military gate, Virgilius trailing him like a chastened puppy.

They reached his private office at the end of the hall by the governor's chamber. The guard came to attention, saluting, and Hadrian entered without acknowledging the man. Hadrian took a seat at his desk but did not invite his aide to sit. "Now, what is going on that is so important as to interrupt my afternoon nap?"

Virgilius apprised Hadrian of the dire situation in Alexandria, Crete and Cyrenaica. "Judea reports that the port of Lydda is in flames, many ships sunk, and again many dead," he said, concluding his report.

Hadrian pressed his fingertips together, staring at them intently in silence. Then he spoke, without looking up. "What is behind these riots?"

"They did not say, sir. But all four appear to have begun in the Jewish quarters."

"Four near simultaneous riots, all beginning in the Jewish quarter. This does not appear to be a coincidence. Do they need help?"

"All said it is beyond their urban cohorts' ability to deal with it. They want legions."

"And all our legions are in Mesopotamia!" He slammed his fist on the desk, startling his aide. "Forward these to the *Princeps*. He is in Ctesiphon. Send it by the fastest post, he needs to see this in three or four days. I will send a message to him also, but that can go on the next post."

"Yes, sir."

"Our nearest legions are in Dacia. Send a message to Governor Quintus Marcius Turbo there that I need two legions, as fast he can get them here. It will take six weeks, but I expect this will go on for that long."

"Yes, sir."

"That is all, Virgilius, you were right to awaken me."

"Thank you, sir." He saluted, turned and left. Hadrian put his head in his hands, the pleasant memories of the afternoon's interlude fading fast.

CHAPTER 137:

TRAJAN AT CHARAX

Charax, June 116AD

The *Romulus'* oarsmen expertly glided the big trireme alongside the river pier, shipping their oars inboard. The ship collided with the pilings with just the gentlest of thumps, as line handlers leaped overside to secure the heavy lines to wooden bollards, all aware with some pride that the *Princeps* was observing their precise actions.

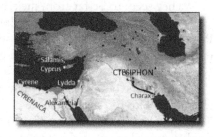

"Well, Aulus Aemilius, we appear to have made it to Charax," said the *Princeps* to the senator at his side.

"We have indeed, your Excellency. And in good time, just four days," said Aulus

"I will dispatch some runners to King Attambelos to arrange our meeting."

King Attambelos was indeed expecting them, Trajan's runners reported, and he had inquired if they might meet for dinner at his palace. Trajan dispatched them back to tell the king that he would arrive the last hour of the day.

"Well, Aulus, we have an hour or so to freshen up. I, for one, could use a cool bath," said Trajan. "My clothes are sticking to my skin in this damp heat."

"As could I."

"Please, join me."

Aulus, along with some members of Trajan's staff and other advisors, made their way aft to where a pool faced with glazed ceramic tiles and intricate mosaics awaited them. The brick-lined firepit beneath the pool, to provide heat with no hazard to the wooden hull, was unlit. The heat and humidity made that most undesirable.

They shed their clothes and in the informality of their nakedness, slipped into the sun-warmed water. The men easily filled it, some water sloshing over the edge.

"So what are your intentions toward King Attambelos, your Excellency?"

"We have been in communications with him for several months. He feels that the best way to preserve his independence is to ally with Rome. We are going to simply affirm that alliance."

"Charax is not large. How have they managed to maintain their independence so far?"

"Mostly through distance. As long as Attambelos took just a reasonable cut on the sea trade coming through them, Ctesiphon saw no reason to annex them."

"They seem to be far from the sea to be such an important port."

"They didn't used to be. A hundred years ago they were at the tip of the Persian Gulf. But the Tigris and Euphrates silted up their bay, and they are now about a hundred miles from the coast."

Two hours before sunset, they set off to the palace, a magnificent gleaming white turreted structure about two miles away. As was his wont, Trajan made the trip on foot, his strong military gait belying his sixty years. As they neared the gate, the king emerged, clad in red and green silk robes.

"Ah, Marcus Ulpius," he said, addressing Trajan by his personal name, in very excellent Greek. "I am so glad to see you. We have quite a feast arranged for you. And your companions?"

"Senator Aulus Aemilius Galba, my senior advisor." Galba nodded, taking the king's proffered hand, as Trajan introduced his remaining entourage.

The king led them inside. Despite the oppressive summer, the white-walled palace was cool inside, the thick masonry absorbing the heat. At various locations servants waved what appeared to be ostrich feathers, to stir the air. The floor was of blue marble, white-veined. Servants and staff joined the king, leading them through polished dark oak doors with gilded fittings into a dining area, reclining Roman-style dining couches around a table laden with roasted pig, goat, fish and fowl, and a plethora of vegetables.

"Please, recline yourself, your Excellency," said the king beckoning Trajan to the purple couch by the center of the table. The king took the single couch on the opposite side facing the *Princeps*, leaving Trajan's entourage to select their own couches to the left and right of him.

"Did you have a pleasant enough journey down here? My outposts spotted your ship two days ago. They reported that it is a truly fine vessel."

"It is. My legion carpenters built her in Nisibis, and she is truly magnificent."

The dinner conversation continued with small talk. Trajan ate sparingly, as was his want, as did Aulus. When everyone had finished, servants cleared the dishes and remaining food from the low table and wiped it down.

The king got down to business. "Marcus Ulpius, we should discuss our future relationship."

"We should, indeed," said Trajan. "I wish to bring the Characene kingdom under Roman protection, to prevent the Parthians from once again imposing their rule over you."

"And at what cost, this protection?"

"No more than what the Parthians imposed on you. Perhaps less. We have a standard tax for all imports of twenty-five percent for goods entering the Empire, of which you would get a part. Due to distance, and your need to provide much of your own defense, you can keep ten percent, and our customs officials will keep the remaining fifteen percent."

"That is generous, indeed, Marcus Ulpius. The Parthians also taxed goods at twenty-five percent, but we had to extract our own levies on what was left. This sounds better financially, but what do you expect us to do in return?"

"Your army will be under Roman command. We will send a cohort to train you in our tactics and signaling, but unless needed by us, it is your force to do with as you see fit. Be judicious in your employment, as we do not want to be brought into a military confrontation with your neighbors."

"Understood."

The rest of the conversation revolved around legalities, and in the end, Trajan produced a scroll for the king's seal of approval.

"Marcus Ulpius, I would like to show you about Charax tomorrow," announced the king to Trajan, as he signed it. "And you are welcome to stay in our guest quarters."

"My regrets, good king Attambelos. My ship departs at first light for the coast, and I must be aboard tonight. Perhaps on my return?"

"I would be most honored," relied the king.

At dawn, with Trajan aboard, the *Romulus* set sail for the Persian Gulf, a day's sail to the south. And at sunset, a fast Roman packet arrived in Charax with word from Ctesiphon, to find themselves still a day behind the *Princeps*.

Trajan's ship reached the coastal port city of Teredon at daybreak, and did not linger to tie up, but nosed cautiously out into the Persian Gulf, pitching as the ocean rollers caught the hull. The sails barely filled, the winds almost calm, making the thick heat even more unbearable, but that same heat also made it impossible for the oarsmen to row the trireme. Aulus and Trajan eyed one of the big freighters nosing out to sea, its sails also almost slack.

"She is bound for India," said Aulus.

"Ah, I wish I were twenty years younger. I would love to see what Alexander saw in that great land. But you have seen it. What was it like?"

"Hot and humid, like this, but it rains a lot. Jungles, elephants, terrible roads. I, for one, look forward to going back north to Ctesiphon. There it is as hot as this, but at least dry." Aulus was feeling testy, not inclined to politeness, dabbing at the sweat on his forehead.

"Well, I agree with that. Perhaps we have done enough sight-seeing for today. Let's head back to Charax, then on to Ctesiphon."

The *Romulus* edged back into the Tigris, and quickly encountered the light *lusoria* packet. The sailors lowered a rope ladder to the small craft, and a man clambered aboard to be greeted by the captain. "Welcome aboard," said the bearded skipper. "You must have news of importance to have come so far in such a small boat."

"It's most urgent news I have for Trajan. He must return to Ctesiphon at once."

"He's in his cabin." The captain summoned a sailor. "Escort this man to *Princeps'* cabin at once."

An hour later, a shift of oarsmen rowing despite the heat, the *Romulus* headed north. There would be no return visit with King Attambelos.

CHAPTER 138:

TRAJAN TO HATRA

Hatra, August, 117AD

Gaius batted at the swarm of flies buzzing around his food. Of all the campaigns of his life, this had to be the worst, besieging an unassailable fortress in the stifling heat of Mesopotamia in the summer. Sweat poured down the back of his corselet in rivulets.

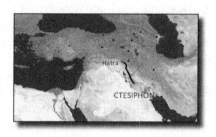

A shadow in the tent entrance announced the arrival of Antonius. "The girls made it back ter Aquileia all right, sir. Just got the letter. Nice of the *Princeps* ter let them use the imperial post."

"Good news. How many men are down with camp sickness?"

"Another two dozen this morning, plus those that aren't reporting to the *medici*. Probably another two dozen."

"We are down nearly a full cohort. I don't see how we can keep this up. I have never seen such putrid water. Even boiling it doesn't make it fit to drink. And the damned flies!" Gaius batted at another, which easily evaded him.

"Word is the *Princeps* is down with it, too. Missed his morning walk-around."

"I'll check with Aulus. If Trajan is down, hopefully we can call this misbegotten siege off. Any word on the other fronts from Arrian?"

"Lusius Quietus has rounded on Edessa, pretty mercilessly, and is heading toward Lydda to reopen our supply lines. The *X Fretensis* is pounding on Susa, but no word on how it is going." Antonius paused, himself batting at one of the myriads of flies in the tent. "I'll let you get back to your dinner, sir."

Gaius pushed his plate away. "I think I will give up and let the flies have it. Half of what I am trying to eat is a fly, anyway. See if you can find a spring somewhere that is not polluted."

"I think the Parthians have contaminated every source of water around here. But I'll send some scouts around ter look again, see if they missed one."

The evening briefing with the *Princeps* was cancelled, confirming the rumor that he, too, had contracted the camp sickness that was decimating the Twelfth's soldiers. And over it all, the stone fortress of Hatra stared down on the legion's orderly rows of tents, its rugged ramparts and deep circumvallation daring the Twelfth to assault its strengths.

The next day came welcome word that Trajan had called off the ill-begotten siege. By afternoon, they were on the march back to Nisibis, a tenth their number riding in medical wagons, unable to march, debilitated by diarrhea and vomiting, dehydrated by the heat and limited foul water. And Trajan was not at his usual place, marching at their lead. He, too, rode in a medical wagon, as debilitated as any of the soldiers. Fortunately, the swarming flies did not follow them.

The Twelfth made a slow pace, and by nightfall had covered just fifteen miles. However, it was far enough to find an oasis whose waters were pure and clean. They dumped their contaminated supplies into the sand, and for once, water was better than fine wine.

Aulus interrupted Gaius, Paulus Herrerius and Antonius at evening meal. "May I join you gentlemen?"

"That depends. Do you bring good news or bad?"

"Mostly bad. Trajan is very ill, and the doctors want to send him back to Antioch as quickly as possible. Lusius Quietus is the new commander-in-chief of all Mesopotamian forces. And he gave the Twelfth a new task. To bypass Nisibis and continue to Alexandria via Petra to put down that insurrection."

"What is left holding Mesopotamia and Babylonia?" asked Antonius.

"Nothing much. The Tenth got routed at Susa and Tiberius Maximus was killed. The *Princeps* client king Parthamaspates is trying to hold it all together with what he has, but it doesn't look good," said Aulus.

"Looks like we are losing three years of effort. I was afraid the Parthians were luring us into a gigantic trap," said Gaius.

"Just like Hannibal. Present the Romans a weak center, and they will pursue it every time, until the wings fall in around them."

"What are you going to do?" asked Antonius.

"I am going with the *Princeps* to Antioch. I am still his senior advisor."

"You'll be missed."

CHAPTER 139:

TRAJAN ILL, HEADING HOME

Dura Europos, July 117AD

The imperial party, with Trajan's Praetorian Guard and the Fifth Cohort of the Twelfth, withdrew to the fort of Dura Europos. Most uncharacteristically, the *Princeps* was not at the head of the marching column.

During a break, Aulus clambered into the hospital wagon in which Trajan was riding. The doctor excused himself to give them privacy. The smell assaulted Aulus' nostrils, the smells of body fluids, and the general odor of sickness. Aulus looked at Trajan's worn features. The *Princeps* was not only ill, he looked weak. Aulus put his hand on the man's shoulder, feeling its frailty. Trajan awakened, and greeted him with a thin, reedy voice.

"Good morning, my friend Aulus." He said, patting the hand resting on his shoulder. "I have missed seeing you. Where have you been?"

"I have been here. You have been asleep. The doctors say you need your rest to fight the sickness." And when he had not been asleep, he had been incoherent, unaware of his surroundings.

"Where are we?"

"We are at the last stop before Dura Europos, just a few more hours. Then on to Antioch. The doctors say you are making good progress."

"Doctors lie. All they are doing is purging me and bleeding me, and feeding me foul medicines. Is my cousin Publius Aelius coming to see me today? I have something important to discuss with him. It was ... it was ... something important, but I don't remember."

"Your cousin Publius is in Antioch, where we are going, your Excellency. He has been attending to the matters of the east while you've been ill. You will see him in a few days."

Trajan was silent, then his eyes fluttered and his head turned to one side, with the susurrations of gentle snoring. Aulus patted his shoulder and left the wagon.

They arrived at the fort in the afternoon. Trajan was taken out of the wagon on a litter, into the fort's hospital.

Secundus checked in with Aulus, knocking politely on the wooden door of his quarters.

"Come in," said Aulus.

"Thank you. How is the *Princeps*? There are rumors, even among the Praetorians, that he is very ill."

"What I say is for you as the *vexillatio* commander, please do not share with the troops, the Guards, or anyone. Not yet."

"Yes, sir."

"He is very sick. As sick as I have ever seen him. We all had camp sickness at Hatra due to the awful water and heat, but we have all pretty much recovered. He has not."

"That is not good."

"He is still violently ill, unable to get out of bed without assistance, barely able to eat, and the doctors are at a loss how to heal him. They are down to daily blood-lettings and purgatives to help get his humors in balance again, but nothing seems to be working. And his faithful secretary Phaedimus seems to have the same illness. And we still have hundreds of miles ahead of us to Antioch."

Secundus nodded, saying nothing.

Aulus continued. "This is strictly between you and me, not to leave this room. I am worried that he may die. Worse yet, he may die without a clearly designated successor, something he has postponed doing for too long. Now it may be too late."

"I thought it was to be his cousin Hadrian."

"Without a clear statement from his Excellency, or an adoption, it will be any ambitious man who can fight his way to the top of the Roman anthill. Civil war among the contenders."

"I have read about that, when Nero was overthrown. 'That most singular year,' as Tacitus called it."

"That it was, Romans fighting Romans. And before that, the Augustan wars, and Caesar's war."

"I don't want to take a side in such a civil war," said Secundus.

"You won't get that choice, if it comes. The choice will pick you."

CHAPTER 140:

DEATH AND SUCCESSION CRISIS

Antioch, August 117AD

Trajan's health improved enroute from Dura Europos, to the point where he was able to get out of bed, and even ride the last few days at the head of the imperial column. Upon his arrival in Antioch, he dismounted and walked unaided to greet Hadrian and his wife Pompeia.

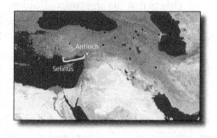

"Welcome back, cousin," said Hadrian, grasping Trajan's hand and noting its limpness. "I see you are back in good health."

"I am in better health, but not yet good, Publius" the *Princeps* said thinly. "I cannot stay long. When will the ship be ready to depart for Rome?"

"It could leave tomorrow if you desire."

"I think I shall do so. I do not desire to be unsociable, but I think I shall take a light dinner in my quarters alone. I am not fit for formal dining yet."

"As you wish, cousin. I shall have preparations made. Rest well."

Aulus joined Hadrian for dinner, along with Pompeia Plotina, Cornelius Palma, the newly-appointed governor of Syria, and Hadrian's senior advisors. They ate in silence, broken by small talk, until Aulus brought up the unmentionable thought that all were avoiding. "The *Princeps* does not appear at all well. If the unthinkable should happen and he dies, I fear there may be a succession crisis," he said.

"There will be no succession crisis," said Pompeia firmly.

"How is that to be avoided, Lady Pompeia? I have discussed this with his Excellency many times, and he has a vague notion of sending a letter to the Senate providing a list of names, including yours, Publius. But he has not done anything in that regard."

"He has designated Publius Aelius as his adopted son and successor," said Pompeia.

"That is good, but when did that happen?"

"Two months ago, he told me this in correspondence. I had it written up for him."

Hadrian reached inside his toga to produce a scroll. "You have stolen my thunder, Aulus Aemilius," said Hadrian. "I was going to announce the happy news after dinner, but now that you brought it up, there will indeed be no succession crisis." He handed the scroll to Aulus.

Aulus unrolled it, scrutinizing the document. It was written in the precise block capitals of a professional scribe, with Trajan's signature at the bottom. But it was not Trajan's signature. Aulus had seen Trajan's scrawling signature many times on many documents. This was a precise and delicate signature.

"This is not his signature, Publius," said Aulus suspiciously. It would not be the first time that a document had been forged to advance someone's future in Roman politics.

"It is mine," said Pompeia. "I have been signing many documents over the past several months on his behalf, with his permission to do so."

The next morning, Trajan again walked unsteadily, Pompeia's hand on his arm, from the carriage to the massive ship *Victoria Victrix,* her sails brailed up, with Trajan's banner, and the red Roman banner emblazoned with the eagle and SPQR, standing out in the morning breeze. Before noon, the ship cast off her lines, and aided by multi-oared tugboats, stood out to sea, her unfurled purple sails billowing in the wind.

A day into the trip, however, it became clear that Trajan was not going to make Rome. Pompeia awoke to find him immobile, mumbling incoherently, his eyes wide with the fear that he could not express. The left side of his face was frozen, twisting his mouth into an effigy of smirk. She summoned Titus Statilius Criton, his doctor, who found him conscious but paralyzed, a victim of apoplexy.

"We must put into the nearest port," said Criton. "I can do nothing for him on the ship. I will tell the captain." He left the imperial cabin quickly.

The ship put into Selinus, and the *Princeps* was whisked into an inconspicuous carriage, concealed to hide his affliction, bound for the hospital there. There was little that could be done for him there, either, more purging and blood-letting. Lady Pompeia stayed by his side through the night. But by morning, she felt the life slip from his hand, and his chest rose, fell, and did not rise again. The *Princeps Optimus Maximus*, the first among equals, the best and the greatest, was with the gods.

CHAPTER 141:

THE IMPERIAL FUNERAL

Antioch, August 117AD

The imperial funeral party processed through Cilicia to Antioch, the Praetorian Guard slow-marching with the wagon carrying the remains of Trajan, their trumpets blowing a mournful dirge. Secundus' Fifth Cohort accompanied them.

It took several days to reach Antioch, which was draped in black for mourning. Hadrian, in a black toga, greeted the funerary entourage in the city park, where a mountain of wood had been stacked in preparation for the cremation, a dais erected for Hadrian, the priests and those who were to speak, in front of hundreds of chairs for the listening audience. The body was placed on the cremation pile in readiness for the coming conflagration. The audience took their seats, while thousands of city residents crowded the park, hoping to hear a bit of the ceremony, or at least to see the event.

Aulus, too, took his seat in the audience. Despite being among the former *Princeps'* senior advisors, Hadrian had not invited him to speak, an ominous sign. Aulus had survived the tumultuous bloody years under Domitian, and he knew how imperial disfavor could suddenly lead to fines, seizure of all property, even proscription and death. *Had I spoken too freely the other day, hinting that Hadrian's adoption might have been forged?*

At noon, the Praetorian Guard blew the imperial salute, the last for the departed *Princeps,* the first for Publius Aelius Hadrian. The priest stepped onto the dais from behind. He alone was clad in the white robes of his order, a white shawl over his head.

"Citizens!" he began. "Citizens, the gods have shown their favor for Publius Aelius Hadrian. The omens are good. Let us praise the gods, let us say farewell to Marcus Ulpius Trajan and let us welcome Publius Aelius as our *Princeps*, the first among equals." The priest stood aside to let Hadrian take the center of the dais, his bronze beard radiant in the sunlight.

"Citizens, we are gathered together to send my cousin Marcus Ulpius to the hands of the gods. He is the son of the divine Nerva, the hero of Dacia and Parthia, and certainly he has been our *Princeps Optimus Maximus*, the best and greatest to serve Rome."

The listeners moaned a droning dirge of farewell to Trajan.

"As I most humbly take up the mantle he so graciously bequeathed to me, I pray that I shall have the fortitude, rectitude and dignity to be his worthy successor."

Hadrian went on for a few more minutes, while Aulus shifted uncomfortably in his seat. *Surely I am not the only one to notice that the signature of his adoption was not Trajan's? There must be dozens seeing it. But perhaps I am the only one to have commented upon it. I think I shall take leave of this place after the funeral.*

At last, Hadrian's acceptance speech reached its conclusion. The crowd, along with Aulus, rose in applause, while the torch bearers by the funeral pyre set it ablaze, slowly and smokey at first, the black smoke whipped by the wind. Then, fueled by naphtha, it roared to life, and the white-shrouded remains of Trajan disappeared behind a wall of flame.

CHAPTER 142:

LEAVING WITHOUT FAREWELL

Antioch, August 117AD

There was, of course, a celebratory feast in honor of Hadrian's accession. Aulus was again not invited to join Hadrian's close inner circle of dining companions around his couch, nor was Pompeia. She seated herself on a couch alone. Aulus came up to her, smiling. "May I join you, Lady Pompeia?"

"I would be pleased. And you may call me Pompeia, please. I am longer the Caesar's wife." She smiled sadly.

"I am sorry for your loss, Pompeia."

"Thank you. We had a wonderful life. He never let his position and power go to his head. He always wanted to return to Hispania and live the life of a farmer, but the gods had other plans for us."

"He was the same with the men in the field. He ate what they ate, slept where they slept, marched where they went. They loved him." Aulus paused. "May I ask a sensitive question of you?"

"Certainly, though depending on what it is, I may not give you an answer." She leaned forward, smiling gently.

"The other day ... I challenged the signature on an important document." Aulus chose his words carefully, as there may be servants whose role it was to monitor and remember private conversations at such an important event.

"You did. And it was of no importance. I have in fact been signing much of his correspondence as he was, as you were, heavily engaged in battles and unable to attend to such things in detail. Publius Aelius ... or should I say now, his Excellency? ... advised me on them. So my signature, or his, was no matter. It received his official seal."

There were other legal issues with such an important adoption, but Aulus let the matter drop. "I hope I did not imply anything that might be offensive to Publius ... his Excellency."

"He was a bit miffed at the time, but I think he has forgotten it all by now."

The conversation returned to the subject of her late husband, Marcus Ulpius, and as she reminisced, her new widowhood came to the fore, and more than once she blinked away tears. After an hour, Aulus excused himself, retiring to his quarters.

The next morning, Aulus quietly packed his own bags, not wanting servants inquiring where he might be going. He did summon the house servants to carry them to one of the many waiting carriages available for residents, as a senior senator carrying his own bags might be conspicuous indeed and the subject of considerable gossip. He had the driver deliver him and his baggage to the camp of the Fifth Cohort, where he sought out Secundus.

"May I join you on your march back to the Twelfth?"

"By all means, sir," replied the tribune.

Aulus noted how very much this young man was beginning to resemble Gaius. "Good. I have news of some importance for your father."

"The crisis you mentioned?"

"Not yet." Aulus hesitated before continuing, ensuring there were no listening ear. "There is a letter. But there are problems."

"What kind?"

"Legal ones, if someone wants to make a case."

"Does anyone want to make that case?"

"Not yet. And the more time passes, the less likely someone will. It will be difficult to risk a civil war over a legal nuance. The problem is my own"

"How is that?" asked Secundus, puzzled.

"Let's go inside. There are too many ears around us."

The two slipped into the command tent, Secundus dismissing the soldier on guard outside and closing the flap behind him.

Aulus seated himself and continued. "When we returned to Antioch, while Trajan appeared on the mend, I expressed my concern over the matter of succession to Hadrian and Lady Plotina, though I didn't then consider it imminent. Hadrian happily produced an adoption letter designating him as Trajan's successor."

"So there is no succession problem," said Secundus, smiling.

"No, but the problem was that the signature on the letter was not Trajan's. I made the mistake of mentioning that. Lady Plotina said she signed it in Trajan's absence on his direction, as she had been doing with much of his correspondence. Hadrian appeared to believe that I had challenged the letter's authenticity. With Trajan's demise following so closely afterward, I believe he may consider me a threat to his legitimacy. I feel that I will be safer with your father's legion, and Hadrian may be less likely to alienate the Twelfth over a threat to his succession that has not yet materialized."

"Then what?"

"I don't know. Hadrian does not have a reputation for killing off his enemies, and if that holds, then I can probably return to Rome. If not, I can always take ship to India for a time."

"Well, you are certainly welcome to travel with us. Though I don't think the Fifth Cohort can offer you much protection if the Praetorian Guards come calling."

A month later, the Ratpack Fifth rejoined the Twelfth at Dura Europos and Aulus reunited with Gaius. He quickly related his story.

Gaius rubbed his chin. "Well, cousin, you have always had a reputation for speaking your mind, but you may have outdone yourself this time," he said with a sly grin. "No matter. Hadrian hasn't come hunting you down, so that is a good sign. No one else is challenging him, and everyone seems pretty pleased with the succession, so it is unlikely you could make a case against his legitimacy, even if you were so inclined."

He leaned back, hands on his desk. "The legion seems to have acquired some new personal guests for a time. Do you remember Afrand?"

"King Osroës' daughter? Why, yes. Why is she still with you after leaving Ctesiphon?" asked Aulus.

"Same reason as you, different threat. Trajan, hard to call him by name now and not *princeps* anymore … Trajan imposed Parthamaspates as client king of the new kingdom of Babylonia, and Afrand felt that he would kill her under some pretext after we left, maybe accuse her of working with her father in Susa to overthrow him. So, she requested our protection, and as we are leaving this hell hole as soon as possible, any information she could provide her father is of little threat to us, and might be outweighed by what she can tell us about him. Anyway, she and Arrian seem to have hit it off well. And Judah, the Jewish revolutionary from Petra … he and Arrian seem to have become friends as well. He makes friends easily. Judah has provided Arrian a lot of information on the organization behind the uprising."

"You are leaving the fight?"

"The fight is over; it has all fallen apart. Hadrian has ordered the legions out. We are bound to Alexandria to assist in recovering that vital city. Join me in my tent for dinner tonight."

It was a bit of crowded tent. Besides Aulus, Gaius' other guests were Afrand and Arrian, Marcus and Mei, Antonius, Paulus Herrerius, and the ten tribune cohort commanders, including Secundus.

"I want to welcome our latest traveling companion, whom you know already as Aulus Aemilius Galba, the former senior advisor to our late Marcus Ulpius Trajan. Trajan's unfortunate passage has left Aulus Aemilius out of a job, and he will be traveling with us enroute to checking out his shipping operations in Alexandria and Myos Hormos. And the Lady Afrand will be traveling as our guest, until she can safely rejoin her father, our former enemy the good King Osroës. Lusius Quietus and his cavalry are making short work of the insurrection in Lydda and the rest of Judea, so our task is to get out of his way as quickly as possible, and head south to assist Marcius Turbo and my old legion, *II Traiana*, in recovering Alexandria. Our next stop will be in Gaza, where we will receive our specific orders from Turbo. Any comments or questions?"

"If I may, your excellency?" asked the Lady Afrand.

Gaius nodded in assent.

"I want to thank you and the men of the Twelfth for your hospitality and concern for my well-being. I fully expected, when I was taken at Ctesiphon, that I would have to die to preserve my dignity, rather than live as a captive slave. But you and your men have treated me with respect, and for that I thank you."

"You are most welcome, my Lady. And we in turn have found you to be an honorable guest, and a good representative of your father, with whom I hope you can be reunited soon. If there are no more questions, let us enjoy our last good meal before it is back to beans, bread and salt pork."

The Twelfth had just returned from putting down the second insurrection at Nisibis in company with a detachment of Lusius Quietus' cavalry, this time with great brutality. Samuel sought out information as to how the fight had gone while his tribune dined with the commander, but learned only that this time it had been indiscriminate slaughter. His inquiries about an old woman named Ruth were returned with replies that a lot of old women, men and children had died that day, no one stood out in particular. Samuel's heart fell, because she had treated him kindly.

The next morning, the legion stood out for Gaza, its eagle glistening in the sunlight, its red banner with the golden crossed lightning bolts fluttering in the breeze. They were leaving this war behind, enroute to yet another.

It took thirty days of hard marching to make Gaza, but when they arrived, they learned that Marcius Turbo's *II Traiana* had already pacified Alexandria, and that Gaius Lucullus' relief had arrived, their new *legatus* Publius Tullius Varro. Gaius, too, was now out of work.

CHAPTER 143:

ADOPTION

Petra, September 117AD

The turnover between Gaius and Publius Tullius Varro took a week, and did not go smoothly. Gaius was smarting from the unexpected and unexplained relief, and Varro was out to prove that he was new and in charge.

"Of course, I am keeping the *praefectus castrorum* Aristides. Where am I going to get another prefect of the camps?" said Varro.

"Antonius is long past fighting age. The only reason he is here is that he voluntarily came to join me when he learned my prefect was very ill at the outset of the war, and in fact Marius died the day after Antonius arrived. Antonius came to help me, and he is leaving with me. Promote Paulus Herrerius to the post, he is qualified and he himself is past retirement age."

"Not an option, you are trading the prefect for the First Lance centurion. With whom do I replace Paulus?"

"Samuel Elisarius of the Fifth Cohort. He is a bit young for the job, but the best centurion in the legion. A good leader, a good fighter."

The arguments got acrimonious, but in the end, Varro acquiesced.

At the end of the week, Gaius, Antonius, Marcus and Mei got together for their last night in camp in Aulus' tent, with several flagons of wine to celebrate the event.

"So, we are finally on our way back to Italy," announced Gaius.

"Not so fast," said Aulus. "It's very late in the sailing season, and the storms are brewing up already. If we leave now, we will probably wind up wintering over somewhere, if we don't get shipwrecked."

"I hadn't thought of that. But you are ever the prudent mariner. Where then should we go?" asked Gaius.

Marcus offered a suggestion. "I would like to go back to Petra, to see Yakov – Jacobus – one more time. And you three haven't seen him. It's only a few days from here. We can winter over there and come back to the coast to take ship in the spring."

"That sounds like a good idea, and I will be tucked away in a faraway place, well away from any of Hadrian's schemes. As will you, too, Gaius. Who knows why Hadrian relieved you?" said Aulus.

"Probably just putting his pets in charge, paying off past favors, but who knows? My head could be on the chopping block with yours. Petra sounds like a good idea," said Gaius.

Antonius opened another flagon of wine. "So, Petra it is."

The five rode leisurely, one or two taking turns with the wagon carrying their possessions, camping rough like in the old days, avoiding the various *mansio* way stations along the way, looking for all the world like common travelers conserving money. Nightly, they reminisced over their long trip fifteen years past, how much all things had changed for them. Aulus and Gaius were more than happy to be free of the politics of their positions, for a while at least, while Marcus and Mei brought them up to date on Yakov, his wife Miranda, and their charges.

"Most of them are young men, but two of them are younger," said Mei. "They have odd names they picked up on the street. Stick is about eleven or twelve, and Mouse is a girl, maybe seven. Yakov and Miranda have saved them from a life on the streets, and have taught all of them how to read, write and figure. It is a beautiful thing they have done."

"He was a street kid hisself there," said Antonius. "Ibrahim took him in, I guess when he was about seven or eight, after he tried ter pinch Ibrahim's purse. So, he is returning the favor now."

In about four days, they reached Jabal ad-Deir, the mountain to the west of the city, and the winding road that led to the residential area to the east of the mountains where Jacobus lived. Marcus took the lead, guiding his horse through the narrow streets until they reached Jacobus' house. They dismounted, tethered their horses to hitching posts by a watering trough out front, and Marcus and Mei knocked on the door.

Jacobus answered. "Marcus, Mei! What are you doing here again?" He looked out the door at the other three. "And Gaius, Antonius and Aulus! Come in, come in." He ushered them into small atrium in the middle of the house where a small fountain bubbled in the middle of a pool. "Here, wash the road dust off. I will get Miranda."

Stick and Mouse came into the atrium, attracted by the sudden commotion. "Aunt Mei, Uncle Marcus!" said Mouse, running to hug Mei. "You came back!"

"Hello, Mouse. And you too, Stick," she replied.

Jacobus returned with Miranda. "These are more of my friends, Aulus Aemilius Galba, Gaius Lucullus, and Antonius Aristides. They are very important people, though they don't look the part right now."

Miranda nodded. "I have heard so much about you. And it is a pleasure to see you and your wife again, Marcus."

Mouse clung possessively to Mei, while Stick hovered protectively around her.

The group took seats around the pool, and Mouse climbed into Mei's lap. "Please, sit down and tell me how you got here. You aren't ... on the run from something, are you?" asked Jacobus.

Aulus took the lead. "In a way, yes. I may have inadvertently insulted the new *Princeps* Hadrian, and Gaius was abruptly replaced as commander of the Twelfth for no reason. With a new *Princeps*, one has no idea how he will use his new power, so it appeared best to stay out of sight. Traveling like we did is about as invisible as one can get. It is too late in the season for taking ship back to Rome, and we decided to come here to see you while we wait out the winter in Petra. By spring, we should know how the new *Princeps* plans to handle his power."

"Well, you are certainly free to stay here. Anyway, I don't think Mouse will let you leave."

And Mouse was certainly not letting Mei leave. "Where is your sword, Aunt Mei?", she asked.

"Packed away." Mei answered.

"Can I see it?"

"Maybe later," she answered, giving the girl an affectionate pat on the head.

Stick showed great interest in Marcus' role in the war.

"Did you do a lot of fighting?" the boy asked.

"Some, not much," Marcus answered.

"Did you kill anyone?"

Marcus nodded.

"What was it like?"

"I don't want to talk about it."

"What else did you do?"

Marcus paused to gather his thoughts, wondering how to describe his intelligence work with Arrian to an eleven-year-old. "I mostly fought the war with words. Looking for information about what the enemy would do next, so we would be ready and not surprised."

"Fighting with words? Do you want to talk about that?"

"Yes, I do."

The two headed off to a corner of the atrium.

About a month after they arrived, the five travelers decided to refresh their fighting skills in the courtyard, with two wooden swords that Antonius produced from his trunk. They each took turns sparring, swapping off one with the other. Stick and Mouse enjoyed watching the bout.

Mei drew the aging but extremely experienced and powerfully built Antonius as her partner. She applied all the rules that Hina had taught her, hoping not to embarrass herself. She was careful to maintain eye contact, to not betray her next move, and perhaps detect Antonius' next. They exchanged several powerful parries, then Antonius lunged. Mei sidestepped to the left, leaving Antonius off balance, his sword arm outstretched, meeting only air where Mei had been. She brought her sword down hard across Antonius' exposed back, a blow that would have been fatal had the sword been real steel. The wooden sword evinced only a pained grunt from him.

Antonius let his sword down and rubbed his back. "Looks like yer won that one, Mei," he said with a pained smile. "Marcia teach yer that move?"

Mei returned the smile. She had not only not embarrassed herself, she had actually beaten Antonius. "She did."

"Yer learned it well. It's one of her best moves. Yer small, like her."

Mouse came up to Mei, smiling. "You beat him, Aunt Mei."

"He was a tough fighter, Mouse," she said, ruffling the girl's fine black hair.

"Would you teach me how to fight?"

"You will have to learn to do a lot of hard things before you can fight, like enduring pain. The fight won't stop just because you're hurt."

"I can do that."

"We'll start small. Run to that wall, as fast as you can, then back."

Mouse darted across the atrium, touched the wall, and came back.

"Now, again, but faster. Put your whole heart into it, and don't slow down coming back."

The drill went on for several minutes, until Mouse returned from a lap panting, her little chest heaving, sweat beading her forehead. She pulled up to a halt and put hand on her slender midriff. "My side hurts."

"You must run through the pain. Again."

Mouse rolled her eyes, but took off on another lap. On her return, Mei waved her to a halt.

"Enough for today. In a fight, your worst enemy is yourself, wanting to quit when it gets hard, not believing you can do it. You have to learn to beat that enemy inside yourself before you can beat anyone else." Mei handed the little girl a towel. "Enough for today. Dry off, let's get some water."

Mei remembered the lessons Hina had given her just a few years ago. Could she give this wisp of a girl those lessons? Should she?

Over the winter, the bonding grew between Marcus and Stick, Mei and Mouse. Stick was reading quite literary Latin now, and going by the Latinized version of his name, Baculus, while Mouse, whom he called Muscula, was now sparring credibly with Mei and some of the younger boys in the household. Mouse was also learning to read Latin under Me's tutelage. Jacobus and Miranda looked on approvingly.

"You too have done well with your little charges," he told Marcus and Mei one afternoon in late winter.

"We are going to miss them when we leave," said Marcus.

"And they you."

"They are like the children we could not have," said Mei, wistfully.

"I have always wanted to be a father, but that was taken from me."

Jacobus thought for a moment. "Marcus, there is more to being a father than simply conception, and none of that was taken from you. They want to go with you …" Jacobus started the sentence, leaving it unfinished.

"We … that would be wonderful. But I know nothing about raising children. And we could not take them from you and Miranda," said Mei.

"Miranda and I have discussed this. We dearly love Stick and Mouse, but we have to share their time with the others. We have never adopted anyone out of our group, but you look like you could be a good family for them."

When they broke the good news to Stick and Mouse, their exuberance could be heard through the house.

CHAPTER 144:

A WINTER WIND

Aquileia, December 117AD

Livia was concerned at the uncharacteristic silence from Aulus, following the death of Trajan and the accession of Hadrian to the purple. Before this, he had written monthly, using the *cursus publicus* to speed the correspondence to his wife. But that had ended with the death of Trajan, and Livia worried that something might have befallen him at the same time. Finally, on a cloudy cold day in November, a traveler brought a letter, a sealed wax tablet, to the household. Not unusual, that was the way common letters were delivered, from hand to hand, to the next traveler going in that direction. Sometimes, they reached their destination; most did not. This one had. Ennius delivered it to Livia. "From Aulus Aemilius, lady."

"Thank you, Ennius ... but what? A common letter? On a wax tablet, not expensive papyrus? That is most unlike him." Livia opened the wax tablet and read the brief letter. It contained few clues for the long silence, or the unusual delivery.

> Ave, *my dearest Livia,*
> *I am at last released from my duties as adviser to the* Princeps, *and look forward to returning home to you and Pontus, to see him don his man's toga. However, weather and other matters delay my return still more. I cannot take ship home until the sailing season reopens in March, and there are matters with the business in Myos Hormos that may occupy me further still. Rest assured, I will return.*
> *With love and affection,*
> *Aulus Aemilius*

She turned to Ennius. "He says he may be delayed in his return to Rome by the sailing season until next year, but other factors may require him to check on the shipping business in Myos Hormos. Bring me Lucius Parvus, please."

"Yes, *domina.*"

Lucius came into her chamber a few minutes later, after a discrete knock on the door.

"Take a look at this, please." Livia handed him the scroll.

Lucius screwed up his eyes, reading. "That is odd," he finally said. "I have been managing his business throughout the war, and other than a few cursory notes from me to him that all was well, we have not discussed this at all. And there is nothing to check on."

"He didn't use the *cursus publicus* and his seal to send this, just a common hand-to-hand letter," Livia continued.

"That is more than odd. It appears that he may be trying to stay out of sight. Perhaps he is in trouble?"

"That is what I thought. Tell Ennius I need to go to Aquileia, to see what Marcia may have heard from Antonius. Have him send her a letter of our coming, though I may get there before it does."

She did not. Traveling in December is not pleasant, with snow over the Apennines requiring the carriage to be dug out several times, Livia bundled up against the cold damp blowing through the wool curtains covering the windows. Nevertheless, they arrived before the *Saturnalia* at the end of December.

The carriage pulled up in the evening to the torch-lit academy villa, the lantern flames flickering in a rising wind. Marcia and Hina, both clad in warm felts, appeared simultaneously with the servants assisting Livia in decamping from the carriage. "Welcome, Livia, I got your letter two days ago. What brings you on this unexpected visit?"

"I hope not bad news. Inside, please, I need to get out of this weather." The wind tugged at Livia's garments.

"Come in, the servants will take care of your baggage."

Marcia led them to a cozy corner of the atrium, with several flaming braziers providing heat. The flames flickered crazily in the wind, swirling around inside the walls through the open *impluvium* overhead. "Sit," she said. "It looks like the *bora* wind is beginning to rise. That can get strong enough to blow down big trees once it gets going. You are lucky you got here when you did. In a few days, nobody may be traveling."

Desdemona brought around some hot spiced wine, then quietly exited.

"Now, what brings you out in such foul weather?"

"I got an unusual letter from Aulus," answered Livia. "Not under his seal via the *cursus publicus*, just a hand-to-hand letter, saying he had to attend to something in Myos Hormos. But Lucius Parvus has been handling the business for him, and he says there is nothing going on that needs his attention. I was wondering what you might have heard from Marcus or Antonius?"

"Well, Antonius said Gaius was unexpectedly relieved of command. He, Gaius and Marcus had mustered out in Gaza, and Aulus was with them. They were all heading home but it was too late in the season to take ship, so they would lay over in Petra with our friend Jacobus until spring. Nothing untoward about anything."

"Nothing too out of the ordinary with that."

"Are you hearing any political rumblings in Rome?" Marcia asked.

"There was a big celebration when Trajan's ashes were brought home, and the Senate deified him. Hadrian stayed back east, dealing with the insurrections, and overseeing the withdrawal of troops. But I am not connected with the political gossip. I leave that political business to my husband." Livia paused, then continued, "I think Aulus wants to become invisible for some reason."

"How did he get along with Hadrian? You saw them in Antioch, didn't you?"

"They seemed to get along well enough, though Aulus was much closer to Trajan than to Hadrian."

"There doesn't seem to be any explanation, but at least everyone is alive, well, and coming home eventually. You are here in time for *Saturnalia*, and thanks to the weather, you are going to stay whether you like it or not. Alaric has just put up a nice big pine tree, and the servants are looking forward to all of us serving them for a change."

"And I guess, mine as well," said Livia, chuckling. "So, Hina, you are living here with Marcia?"

"No, we are not," replied the big woman. "Marcia helped us to buy a horse farm just a few miles from here. The owner died and the family wanted to sell it off to pay his debts. She helped with the paperwork and legal business, which is totally foreign to me, of course. We got several head of horses, all mares, which makes Eagle most happy. And several servants came with the place. Galosga is tending it tonight with Marasa and Andanyu, because of the coming storm, but I had more things to sign, so I came to see Marcia. And it looks like I will be staying over. The family will be up tomorrow to join us for the Saturnalia, weather permitting."

"How much land?" asked Livia.

"About a hundred *jugera*," offered Marcia. "It is a pretty good spread for them."

"We have some fast horses," said Hina. "I may enter the hippodrome races this spring. Hopefully, I won't have to punch someone."

"If you do, I am sure he won't be getting up quickly," said Marcia, laughing.

Galosga did arrive around noon the next day after the wind had abated a bit, with their three offspring, all on horseback, for the grand celebration. Many gifts were exchanged, and the house was ablaze with lights, making the otherwise longest night of the year seem cheery and bright. The servants, though all were freedmen now, took their places on the *triclinia* dining couches, while Marcia, Livia, Hina and Galosga busied themselves in the kitchen, preparing the feast for them. It was the annual day of appreciation for their yearlong service to the household.

The morning after, over a late breakfast, Marcia offered a suggestion. "Livia, you said you were not connected with the political gossip in Rome."

"Yes. Most of it is boring, some are outright lies, either by accident or intent, and offering one's opinion of one story or another can lead to big trouble. I avoid it."

"Brutus Agrippa is the prefect of the urban cohort in Aquileia. Although we are some distance from Rome, he stays connected to political matters. It is his job. Why don't we go into town? I'll introduce you, and the two of you can talk. He may be able to shed light on what is going on with the new *Princeps*."

The next day dawned frosty and cold, but the wind had diminished to nothing. Livia and Marcia, bundled in robes, rode the short distance to the seacoast town, plumed in white steam and smoke rising in the still air from the fires in each building. The horses' hooves crunched through the layer of icy snow on the stone roadway. They reached the headquarters of the urban prefect and located Brutus Agrippa. "Good day, Marcia," he said, smiling. "Chopped someone's arm off again?"

"Not lately," said Marcia, returning his smile. "This is my friend Livia Luculla Galbae. Her husband, Aulus Aemilius Galba, is a senior senator and former close advisor to the former *Princeps* Marcus Ulpius Trajan. She has some concerns she would like to share with you, to see if you can shed some light on those matters for her."

"Well, that is far above my station, *domina* Livia Luculla. But come into my office, I will see what I can do"

Livia seated herself opposite Brutus' desk, littered with scrolls and wax tablets. "My husband has been released from his service to the previous *Princeps*, and not taken up by his successor. But rather than returning home, he wrote me, by regular post rather than his usual *cursus publicus*, a letter hinting that he may be concerned for his safety. Are you aware of anything that might substantiate this?"

"There is word of an assassination plot against the new *Princeps,* involving … let's see." Brutus rummaged through the scrolls on his desk, selecting one of high-quality papyrus with an official seal. "… here it is. Involving Cornelius Palma, Gaius Avidius Nigrinus, Lucius Publilius Celsus and Lusius Quietus. All easterners, no one that I know. Your husband's name is not on the list."

"That is reassuring."

"Plots like this can expand. Perhaps if he stays out of sight, he feels he won't get included."

"Perhaps."

"If I hear anything official against your husband. I will let you know, through Marcia."

"Thank you."

She left and rejoined Marcia in the atrium to leave.

On the way back, Livia shared the gist of their conversation. "Were those four close friends of Aulus?" asked Marcia.

"I don't know any of them. If Aulus knew them, I don't know. But Aulus survived the Domitian principate with his life and property intact when many senators did not. That was before my time, so I have only heard Aulus' stories of his rule, but I certainly hope we will not go back to that sort of thing again."

CHAPTER 145:

DEATH OF A SON

Ctesiphon, January 118AD

Mithridates returned victorious to the palace at Ctesiphon, seating himself on the golden throne as *Shahanshah*, the King of Kings. It was only temporary, until his brother Osroës returned from the fighting in the east with Vologases. Or didn't return, in which case Mithridates would be the permanent *Shahanshah*. In either event, temporary or permanent, it felt good.

Ataradates, his senior general, entered the room, prostrating himself face-down on the floor with a fluidity that belied his sixty years, hands outstretched in obeisance.

"Rise, my good commander. What news do you have for me?" asked Mithridates.

Ataradates rose, as fluidly as he had gone down, a look of concern on his face. "Your son ... I am sorry ... he is dead."

Mithridates sat on the throne in silence, his knuckles on the golden arm rests turning white from the intensity of his grip. He was determined to show no emotion at the horrible news. Finally, in a rasping voice, he asked, "How did he die?"

"He was killed last month, leading our first assault on Ctesiphon. He approached Trajan's troops under a flag of truce, to negotiate their peaceful withdrawal from the city. He wanted to spare Ctesiphon the fate of Seleucia, which the Romans had burned to the ground. Trajan's royal guard approached him, took him captive, and killed him. The Romans displayed his body, but rather than striking fear into our forces, it enraged them. There was to be no mercy to such an enemy."

Mithridates cleared his throat. "He died well." He blinked his eyes, hoping that the tears welling up could be contained, at least until after Ataradates' audience was complete. "Hadrian can now deal with the flames my son lit in their eastern provinces. I have no intent to extinguish them." Mithridates paused, struggling to keep his emotions in check. "There is more news?"

"Certainly, *Shahanshah*. Parthamaspates' commanders have all pledged their allegiance to you. Parthamaspates himself has fled, dressed as a peasant riding an oxcart. He is chasing after the Roman dogs who set him up as king.

His Roman friends departed in considerable haste. My intelligence people are going over the scrolls and records they left behind. It appears that one Hadrian is now their new king, and he has ordered a total withdrawal of all legions from Mesopotamia. We appear to have won. Shall I send a force to hunt down Parthamaspates?"

"No. Let him flee to his Roman friends. He is my brother's son, though he has the Roman stink all over him. How is my brother doing in the east?"

"He is heavily engaged in a fight with Vologases for Susa. It is mountainous terrain, better known to the rebels than to our forces, so it may take a while."

"Will he prevail?"

"Probably. But war is unknowable."

"Any more news?"

"Nothing more, *Shahanshah*."

"You may depart."

The general bowed low at the waist, and face down, backed out of the throne room. Only when he had left did Mithridates allow himself to burst into harsh choking sobs. "My son, my son!"

CHAPTER 146:

ONE STAYS BEHIND

Petra, February 118AD

February did not bring good news. Aulus had been regularly visiting Josephus Farvius, the head of the *vigiles* in Petra, for word of events in Rome. On this latest visit, he was accompanied by Gaius and Antonius.

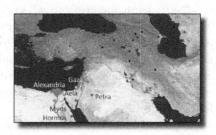

"The word from Rome is disturbing, Aulus Aemilius," said Josephus, tapping a rolled-up scroll on his desk. "Cornelius Palma, our former governor of Nabataea, was elevated to governor of Syria to replace Hadrian on his accession. Now Hadrian has accused him of plotting his assassination, along with Gaius Avidius Nigrinus, the governor of Dacia, and Lucius Publilius Celsus."

"That is indeed not good news, Josephus. Lucius Publilius was a close advisor to Trajan during the war, and a good friend of mine. I feel I could be next."

"There is more. Rumor has it that Lusius Quietus also may have been involved. It seems that the new *Princeps* is indeed cleaning house of potential rivals."

"I think it is about time for me to pay a visit to Myos Hormos and check out one of my ships for a trip to India. I don't think his agents will find a trip like that worthwhile just to do away with an aging Senator. Unfortunately, I won't be able to tell my wife about these plans until right before the ship sails. We'll see how things settle out next year before deciding to go home."

"That's prudent, Aulus Aemilius."

"Thanks you for your time," said Aulus, rising. The three left the office together.

"That is not good news. I hope he will not turn out like the blood-sucker Domitian," said Gaius.

"I certainly hope not. You are welcome to come with me, Gaius."

"I don't think I had enough visibility with Hadrian for him to consider me a threat. I have been away from my Camilla for four years now. I've been following the eagles for thirty years now. I think it is time for me to settle down in Neapolis and stay out of the army and out of politics for the rest of my life."

"And I don't think he's ever heard of me, or Marcus. So, it's back to Aquileia, to Marcia and the Academy for me," said Antonius. "And drop my soldier's talk."

Gaius clapped him on his shoulder. "Well, good luck to you, Aulus. How are you going to travel?"

"There's a caravan heading south to Aela next week, and from there I'll find a ship to Myos Hormos. I'll travel with them."

"Sufficiently inconspicuous," said Gaius.

"Like the good old days. Then maybe ride *Europa* again to India. That will keep me far out of the way. I told Livia that this might happen in a carefully worded common letter. Would you let her know of my plans when you get home? Such letters are unreliable."

"To be sure. I will also write Marcia to advise her of your plans. She will let Livia know."

"Excellent. Would you please stand in for me for my son Pontus' adult toga ceremony? I put him in his own hands by letter last year when he turned fifteen, and he has been wearing it to conduct business since. But a ceremony would be nice, anyway."

"Certainly."

Antonius interjected himself. "Marcia said he certainly did a man's work, caring for the household after she and Livia were kidnapped. We'll see that he gets a great ceremony. Maybe find an artist to paint it, so you can see it on your return. But we are going to miss you. Take care on that trip, and avoid those big storms."

"I certainly will. Let's get back and let Marcus and Mei know."

Marcus, Mei and Jacobus received the news quietly. "I am sorry that you are not returning with us, but I think you a making a good decision, Aulus," said Marcus, little Mouse, now proud of her new name Muscula, on his lap. "You should be far enough out of Hadrian's reach to avoid getting sucked into any trouble."

"And should he confiscate your property, we'll take care of Livia, Pontus and your servants," said Antonius. "They won't want for anything."

"I appreciate that," said Aulus.

The next day, Aulus, Gaius and Antonius made the trip to Gaza on horseback to check on shipping, all in non-descript traveling clothes. Aulus located a reputable coastal trader named Abdael who owned a small fleet of medium-sized freighters that seemed to be in good condition, to get his four friends and two children to Alexandria as soon as possible, for further shipping to Rome. Abdael took them on a tour of one, which had comfortable accommodations.

"I expect to be starting the sailing season by early March," said Abdael. "I have connections in Alexandria. Can I assist you in transferring to a ship going to Rome from there?"

"That won't be necessary, Abdael. I have a friend in Alexandria who has promised them berths on the *Aeneas*." Aulus felt no need to add that he owned the big freighter, and that his friend worked for him. And in his very casual dress, he would not have been believed.

"That ship has a fine reputation. So, let's see, for four adults and two children, the trip will be five days, with a stop at Pelusium, I have some deliveries to make there. That will be one hundred and twenty *sesterces*."

"Seventy-five," said Aulus. "The going rate is fifteen *sesterces* per person, and half for the children."

"Eighty-five," said Abdael.

"You are overcharging my friends, but all right, get us on your schedule." He pulled out his purse and counted out twenty silver *denarii* and five bronze *sestercii* on the table, pushing them to Abdael. "Paid in full."

Abdael raked in the coins. "We will sail on the first day of March, winds and weather permitting. Be here at least the day before, my ships sometimes leave early." He wrote out a small scroll confirming their reservation. "Bring this with you. You can't get on without it. Don't lose it, or you will have to buy another."

"Thank you. We will see you in a few weeks." Aulus pocketed the scroll. The group rose and left.

A few days later, they arrived back in Petra. Aulus made the announcement to Marcus and Mei, "We have booked a ship for you, the *Larus* out of Gaza, leaving on the first of March. You leave the last week of the month with Gaius and Antonius."

"That's great news," said Marcus. "Are you still continuing on to Myos Hormos? Or did you change your mind?"

"Still continuing on. I will give you a letter to my shipping master in Alexandria. His name is Apollonius. He will you put up on the *Aeneas*, if she is available, for the trip to Rome. That will take two or three weeks, depending on weather and other stops she may have. He used to be her skipper."

"What if she's not available?" asked Marcus.

"He will find another. But the big ships don't start sailing till April, so I am sure she will be available."

CHAPTER 147:

AN UNWANTED SURPRISE

Myos Hormos, April 118AD

Preparations were quickly made, and Gaius, Antonius, Marcus and Mei, with Stick and Mouse in tow, made their farewells to Jacobus and Miranda. Stick was a bit saddened to be leaving the only home and family he had ever known, but was looking forward to new adventures, learning to ride a horse, and then a ship on the ocean, something he had never seen. Mouse, on the other hand, clung to Mei, looking forward to being the center of her undivided attention. Aulus bid them farewell, then departed to join the caravan south to the port city of Aela by rented wagon, his belongings packed away in two big footlockers.

Aulus made himself inconspicuous on the caravan, aiding with the daily loading and unloading of the animals, but otherwise keeping to himself. It took only a few days to reach the port city of Aela, where he found a small freighter leaving for Myos Hormos the very next day. The trip took only three days, with the weather sunny, the seas calm and winds favorable.

The freighter found its mooring, and Aulus noted the sleek lines and riggings of the *Asia, Africa* and *Europa,* all still in port. At least one of them should have started the trek south down the Red Sea enroute to India by now.

He rented another wagon to make his way to the residence of Aelia Isadora and Aelia Olympias, sisters, shipping magnates and the best shipbuilders in the city, despite their gender. The weather was already becoming oppressively hot and humid, something that Aulus hated about the port city, along with the stink of uncollected trash and animal droppings. He reached the tan sandstone *domus* that was the women's home and office, dismounted from the wagon, to be greeted by her head servant Salawi, his ebony skin showing signs of age, and his curly hair now white beneath his cap.

"Welcome, *dominus* Aulus Aemilius. We have been expecting you."

The greeting disturbed Aulus. He had not told the Aelia sisters of his plans, expecting they would assist him when he showed up. How did they know he was coming? Aulus kept his composure. "It is an unexpected trip, Salawi."

A figure emerged from the shadow of the doorway. He was clad in the glittering parade ground armor of the Praetorian Guard. His steel red-plumed helmet shone like silver, with brass fittings and band gleaming like gold. Aulus recognized him as one of the tribunes of the Praetorian Guards that had accompanied Trajan. "May I welcome you also, Aulus Aemilius? We have been hoping you would show up here. My name is Tribune Cornelius Attianus."

Aulus' heart skipped several beats. He had gone out of his way to keep his plans secret, but somehow, he had been discovered. He straightened himself to a fully erect posture and took a deep breath to still his nerves. "I presume you have come to execute me, on the *Princeps'* orders." He saw no reason to extend his hand.

"No, at least not yet. Our orders are to escort you to Antioch to meet with the *Princeps*. Anything after that will be his decision. He was very specific that you not be harmed." He gave another signal and two more Praetorians soldiers emerged from the shadows. "Take the senator's baggage to the room arranged for him."

"You knew I was coming here."

"Yes. There are few other places you might go. Home to Rome, your villa in Alexandria, or here at the start of the sailing season. You were not expected to go elsewhere for very long."

Would they have expected me to visit Petra? Perhaps I could have stayed with Jacobus indefinitely. No matter now. "You surmised well. The Aelia sisters, are they well?"

Attianus gave another signal, and quickly the two women appeared. "Isidora and Olympias! Are you well? I hope I haven't brought trouble to your house," said Aulus.

"No trouble," said Isidora. "Cornelius Attianus arrived with his small troop, and said he was to escort you to meet with the *Princeps* when you arrived. They have been good guests during their stay. Are you well?"

"I am well. You were not expecting me?"

"It was a surprise to us that Cornelius said you were due here," said Olympias. "Come in and get a nice bath and out of those traveling clothes. You look like a beggar. Have you a fresh tunic and toga in your luggage?"

"I do."

"Salawi will escort you to the bath, and see that your clothes are cleaned or discarded, as you wish. Come in. Dinner will be at sunset."

Aulus came to dinner, unpleasantly surprised to find Cornelius and his four soldiers, Scipio, Alexis, Frontus and Lucianus, also reclining in the *triclinium* alongside Isidora and Olympias.

"So why the surprise visit by you and your friends, Aulus?" asked Olympia, toying with a bit of fish on her plate. "And no letter warning us."

"I sent one two months ago," Aulus lied. "It must have gotten lost enroute. I just wanted to check on the business here."

"All is well. Your friend Cornelius put an imperial hold on your ships' departures, however, until you arrived."

"They can leave at any convenient time, now that Aulus has arrived, Olympia," said Cornelius. "We just wanted to ensure that he did not go directly to one of the ships and depart, as the *Princeps* very much wants to see him."

"That must be exciting, Aulus, to meet the new *Princeps*," said Isidora.

"We have met before."

"Why does he want to see you?"

"You'll have to ask Cornelius. This is all news to me also. How is the Indian trade this year? You expanded your warehouse in Musiris last year. Did that pay for itself?" asked Aulus, hoping to steer the conversation in a different direction.

He succeeded. The remainder of the dinner discussion revolved around rates, insurance, what was high, what was low, ships and crews, topics totally lost on Cornelius and his men. They focused their attention on the wine, soon becoming a bit inebriated. Cornelius stretched and yawned, "We have an early morning tomorrow. Don't unpack more than what's needed, we are leaving right away." He rose, his men rising with him. "Thank you for your hospitality, *dominae*."

After they left, Isidora turned to Aulus. "Now tell me what is going on, really, Aulus Aemilius. Are you in some sort of trouble with the *Princeps*?"

"Why do you ask?"

"Traveling rough, like a commoner, trying to be very inconspicuous, no announcement of your coming, and some Praetorian guardsmen coming just to catch your arrival. Again, are you in some sort of trouble?"

"I'll know when I see Publius Aelius ... the *Princeps*, rather ... when I see him in Antioch. Right now, I don't want to speculate. And ladies, if you'll excuse me, I think I will also retire early. Thank you for putting up with my unannounced arrival and my uninvited guests."

True to his word, Cornelius was ready to go by early morning with an elegant imperial carriage and two civilian drivers, though Aulus noted that the two doors were fitted with padlocks. At least he would be riding in style and comfort on the long trip to Antioch.

In the course of the trek, he formed a bit of a reluctant friendship with Cornelius, who often rode with him inside to avoid the hot sun. The tribune was fascinated to hear about the Senator's expedition to Han China ten years back, and their wild adventures. Aulus spun some good tales which needed little in the way of embellishment, the pirate Ibrahim, the treacherous Hasdrubal, the Han Court and their death sentence. He did not mention that he and those unlikely companions had just had an equally unlikely reunion during the war, just past.

CHAPTER 148:

THE NEW PRINCEPS

Antioch, May 118AD

Aulus and his escort Cornelius Attianus, with his troops, stayed at the various *mansions,* and their imperial orders ensured that they got the most luxurious of accommodations, the finest meals, and the best horses. And in three weeks, they reached Antioch. Aulus was pleased to see that the rubble from the earthquake two years past had all been cleared away. Newly completed buildings had sprung up from the wreckage in many places. Construction was ongoing everywhere, scaffolded buildings with tall treadmill cranes slowly swinging heavy blocks and columns into place, the air filled with shouts of workers, and grunts of oxen teams leading trundling carts overflowing with building material. It was a good sight. Aulus recalled the terrible sight of the city in the awful aftermath, fire and smoke everywhere, collapsed buildings, the moans of people injured or trapped.

The carriage rolled smoothly over the Orontes River bridge connecting the governmental palaces and buildings on the island to the mainland. Aulus was not surprised to see that here all construction had been completed, all damaged buildings repaired or rebuilt, not a trace or a scar remaining. The carriage rolled to a halt before the *praetorium* palace. White-clad servants stood by while Cornelius unlocked the carriage, then assisted Aulus in dismounting.

"Come, let's go, Aulus Aemilius," said Cornelius. "They will take care of your baggage." They walked up the wide steps to the entrance of the building. Cornelius identified himself to the guards at the huge bronze door inside the colonnade, who snapped to attention, spears erect. One turned, and opened a small door built into the bigger structure.

The guardsmen escorted Aulus through the familiar marble interior. Aulus remembered cracked and tilted floor marbles, mosaics thrown askew, columns knocked over. All had been repaired. They climbed the stairs to the third floor, and stopped at an ornately carved wooden door, highly polished brass fitting glowing like gold. "This is the *Princeps'* temporary imperial court, for as long as he remains here. Stay with my boys for moment," said Cornelius. He identified himself to another pair of guards. One snapped to attention, the other opened the door.

He returned after a few minutes. "The *Princeps* will see you immediately." He held the door for the Senator. "Good luck. Seriously. I have come to really like you."

A servant escorted Aulus into the *Princeps'* personal chamber. Hadrian sat at his desk, clad in a gold-filigreed purple tunic, his bronze beard and hair finely coiffed, studying a long scroll. He looked up. "Aulus Aemilius, this is a pleasant surprise. I am glad that Cornelius was able to catch you before your departure to India." He waved at one of the many chairs before the desk. "Here, sit, please. You have had a long trip."

"No, thank you, your Excellency. I prefer to stand."

Aulus caught a hint of irritation pass over Hadrian's face.

"As you wish." He went back to studying the scroll. Aulus wished he had taken Hadrian up on his offer, for the man was taking his time with the scroll. After fifteen minutes or so, he set it aside, and looked up. "You thought my accession to the principate was irregular."

Aulus looked him in the eyes. "I noted that the signature on the adoption was not that of Marcus Ulpius. Lady Plotina assured me that it was hers, that she had been signing document for him for several months with his permission."

"Nevertheless, such information could create serious problems, were it to get out."

"It did not, and it will not get out. I have no desire to see another year of contending emperors."

"Yet you know this to be true."

Aulus grew impatient. "Publius Aelius, if you wish me to be permanently silenced, please ensure that your headsman uses a sharp sword. I don't care for him to have to strike twice to take my head." He had intentionally used the man's formal name, rather than "your Excellency'.

"You don't seem to be in fear of your life. I could take your life, with or without a sharp sword."

"I have had a good life, a loving wife, and a good son. If my life is to come to an end, now and not later, I won't demean it by groveling just to earn another few years. And I don't wish to disappoint you, but this is not the first time I chose honor rather than life before another emperor. And you will not be the first emperor to condemn me to death." Aulus thought he saw a bit of a twinkle light up in Hadrian's eyes.

"You are not like the others. More like Lusius Quietus you are. He didn't beg, either."

"Lusius Quietus was a good man."

"Perhaps a bit too good. The others all thought they might be emperor. I thought he might be."

"You are afraid of competition."

"No, of a civil war. They were plotting my assassination."

"I have heard that. Is there proof?"

"Yes. We intercepted several letters between them. Vaguely worded, but their meaning was clear. 'Cutting off the head of the serpent while it is small' leaves little doubt, and Nigrinus finally admitted to the plot, implicating Palma, Celsus and Quietus. Lusius' participation surprised me, as like you I considered him to be a good man. Palma, Celsus and Nigrinus were just ambitious politicians with no strong military connections, and they needed Lusius' reputation with the eastern legions to keep any military challenges at bay. I deeply regretted signing his death warrant, though not the others."

Aulus pondered what the *Princeps* had laid out. It was plausible, and there did appear to be proof.

Hadrian continued. "But the rumor of my adoption being invalid is out. Who have you told of this?"

Aulus considered this. *Should I lie and say no one? Or speak the truth, and put Gaius Lucullus and Secundus at risk?*

"Besides Lady Pompeia, who confirmed that she had signed it for him as she had been doing with his permission for some time, I told two very close friends. This was in the context that my comment might have put me at risk of your severe disfavor, and I needed to move very quietly elsewhere. They both understood that my life could be at risk if the story got out. They told no one."

"How might it have gotten out then?"

"Palma was at the dinner that night also. And it would have served him and the plotters' interest to have it publicly known that your accession was invalid, as a pretext for your assassination."

"Of course!" Hadrian slapped his head with his hand. "Of course. He was there as the new governor. He heard what you said, and perhaps set himself to thinking about my overthrow. Aulus Aemilius, you have a well-deserved reputation for honesty and courage. I have nothing to fear from an honest man. Would you join me for dinner tonight? You will find the fare a bit simple, as I was intent on dining alone this evening."

"Simple is fine with me, as long as we stay away from awkward conversations that could get me in trouble … your Excellency," said Aulus, finally allowing himself a smile.

"Attianus will find you accommodations."

Dinner was indeed simple, quail stuffed with a fresh fig, barded with bacon and wrapped in grape leaves, with more figs on the side. And plenty of wine, served by white-clad servants who otherwise remained quietly in the background.

"I don't like to overeat at feasts every night. It is bad for the health," said Hadrian.

"I understand. On my trip back from China, I lost much of my girth, and I never felt better in my life. I have tried to continue eating like that ever since." Aulus paused, then continued. "What are your dreams for your Principate, your Excellency?"

"Call me Publius Aelius, please, in private. The pretentiousness of this office is a burden to me. My dreams? Well, I want to see all this vast realm of ours. My cousin Marcus Ulpius traveled considerably, but he only went to where there were wars. I want to see the places that are at peace, know the people, find out what they need from Rome. We Romans have an awesome responsibility given to us by the gods, and we haven't always done a good job of managing it. We need to stabilize our borders. Expansion beyond what we now have is not sustainable, as we learned in Mesopotamia."

"Those are worthy goals. Anything else?"

"The laws are a mess. Almost a thousand years of mishmash, contradictions, using ancient words no one understands anymore. I want to put a team of jurists together to set this right. And I want to build! I want to fill the Principate with buildings that the world will admire for all time. I fancy myself a bit of an architect, you know." He took a sip of wine, then continued. "What are your goals, now that you are not running from my wrath? Would you like a position here in the east? I could use someone I could trust."

"I am honored, your Excellency. But I want to return to Rome, and my wife and son. I have been gone five years now. Pontus needs a belated ceremony for the donning of his adult toga."

"I am sure you will give him a most memorable ceremony," said Hadrian. "I will miss your good counsel then, Aulus Aemilius. But I have a fast mail packet ship leaving in a few days from the port of Seleucia Pieria. Going to Rome with my correspondence, with no stops enroute. Nothing can get you there faster."

"I thank you, your Excellency. I look forward to the trip."

The rest of the meal consisted of quiet pleasantries, until both adjourned early.

CHAPTER 149:

HOME AT LAST

Rome, September 118AD

The fast packet ship was just that – fast. Long and slender, an overly large imperial purple mainsail and a jaunty foresail, she cut through the blue Mediterranean like a knife. And with no stops, she skirted Crete, threading the narrow needle between Italy and Sicily, to arrive in Ostia less than two weeks after leaving Seleucia Pieria. Aulus disembarked to ride the imperial carriage to the Flavian Palace on the Palatine. Nubian servants there gave him a final ride on a litter to his home on the Aventine. His bags were loaded on a following cart.

He made quite an unexpected entrance. Ennius stepped out to see who the most official visitor might be, and did not wait for Aulus to disentangle himself from the litter before embracing him in a most unservantlike embrace. "Aulus Aemilius! You are back! I thought you were some high-ranking diplomat, arriving unexpected or by accident."

"It is just me, Ennius. You are looking good, but you have grown a few more grey hairs in the past four years. Is Livia home? And Pontus?"

"They are, *dominus*. And you have more unexpected visitors. Gaius Lucullus, Antonius Aristides, one Marcus Lucius and his wife Mei, with two children. They just arrived a few hours ago themselves."

"Well, let's see them then." Ennius directed the other servants to gather up Aulus' baggage, then followed him inside.

Everyone was in the atrium to greet the unexpected dignitary, standing on the far side of the *impluvium* rain pool. Gaius was the first to respond, striding around the pond to slap Aulus on the back. "Aulus, you old scoundrel. You talked Hadrian out of taking your head! And arrived by imperial litter, no less."

He was followed by Livia, who said nothing but gave him a long wet kiss. His son Pontus remained standing, not sure how to react.

"Come over here, son, I have heard great things about you."

"I was just telling him of my plans for his togate ceremony, but it looks like you might be able to handle it after all," Gaius said, smiling.

Finally, Antonius, Marcus, Mei and their two children joined in the reunion. Aulus immediately noticed Stick and Mouse, who introduced themselves by their Latin names, Baculus and Muscula. "They followed you back from Petra, did they?" he said.

"We adopted them. They are our son and daughter now," said Marcus.

"Fatherhood agrees with you, Marcus."

"It completes my life. A completion I thought I would never know."

Livia found her voice at last. "Aulus, Gaius was just explaining this morning that you might be in serious trouble with the new *Princeps*, and on your way to India to lay low. But here you are arriving on an imperial litter. Is it resolved?"

"It is. Hadrian put me on his personal mail packet. It was fast, with no stops, but Gaius, I was expecting that you would get here weeks ago. What happened?"

"Nothing, really. All the ships were still loading grain for the season's first sailing, and the *Aeneas* had to wait for her turn to be filled."

"Leaving us with nothing to do but enjoy the sights of Alexandria," said Antonius, grinning.

"With our pockets full of back pay," said Gaius. "We didn't spend much in Mesopotamia. Listen, why don't you and Livia get reacquainted, and we can continue this conversation later this afternoon?"

Livia did not wait for Aulus to answer. She took his hand and led him out of the atrium to their private quarters, where they did get reacquainted, several times in fact. Afterwards she lay in his arms, half-dozing, her head on his chest. "You don't show your age in bed, *carus meus*," she said.

"Four years without you energized me."

"Mmmh. But I think we should go attend to our guests. I am sure they would like to know what happened, and in fact, so would I."

"In a bit, my dearest, in a bit," Aulus said, rolling on top of her.

Aulus and Livia rejoined the group late in the afternoon. By the pool, Aulus related his story. "I won't share what I said in the presence of Hadrian just before Trajan died, as it is very sensitive. Suffice to say, it might have cast doubt on his legitimacy as Trajan's heir. I spoke without thinking, and by his reaction, I decided it best to disappear, as best as any of Trajan's senior advisors can ever disappear. Then came word of the assassination plot, and the imminent execution of the plotters. So, as you can imagine, when I arrived at Myos Hormos in rough traveling clothes, I was not happy to be greeted by a tribune of the Praetorian Guard, who took me back to Antioch, where I was certain that I, too, was going to face certain execution."

"I am surprised you were not executed on the spot," said Gaius.

"I was, also, but his orders were to take me to Antioch unharmed. And Hadrian saw me at once. Apparently, the question I had inadvertently raised to him about his legitimacy had gotten out, and he wanted to know if I was one of the plotters, or if I were spreading it around myself for my own purposes."

"Was there any proof of the plot or was he just eliminating the competition?" asked Gaius.

"Apparently there was correspondence among them, Cornelius Palma, Gaius Avidius Nigrinus, Lucius Publilius Celsus. and Lusius Quietus. And Palma confessed. So, it appears the plot was legitimate."

"How did you get out of that alive?"

"I spat in his eye, so to speak. I said that if he wanted to execute me, to please make sure his headsman had a sharp blade, I didn't want to be hacked twice."

"Reminds me of Luoyang and the Han emperor, what was his name, Emperor He?"

"He preferred Son of Heaven. But this worked out better. I assured him that I had not told anyone but you and Secundus the details of the question, and that you both understood that my life was at risk if the question were shared. And I reminded him that Cornelius Palma was also at that dinner. Palma was the one who apparently did start spreading the rumor, using it as a justification for Hadrian's overthrow."

"I am surprised that Quietus was in on the plot. He did not seem the political sort."

"He was not, and Hadrian was reluctant to execute him. The other three were the politicians, and they needed someone with unquestioned military muscle to fend off all the other usurpers who would come crawling out from under rocks after they assassinated Hadrian."

"It would indeed have provoked bloody civil war. There are more people who want to be the *Princeps* than can bear the burden."

"True enough. But that is, for now, behind me. What are your plans, Gaius?"

"I am off to Neapolis in the morning to give my wife Camilla, back from Byzantium, my undivided attention for the rest of her life. No more years away from home following the eagles. Or more often the case, walking through eagle shit. I'll leave that to my son and Samuel to sort that out from now on."

"Most disrespectful, quite like you. And Antonius, you all are off in the morning also?"

"We are. We want to get out of Rome before the summer heat sets in. It is nice this time of year in Aquileia. I'm done with eagle shit, too," said Antonius.

"And we want to introduce Marcia to her new niece and nephew Muscula and Baculus," said Mei.

Aulus signaled Chloë for wine all around. "Then let us feast all our homecomings. I am certain we can make sure you leave in the morning with hangovers."

And the eagles that the gods had gathered, against all odds, in Mesopotamia, dispersed in the morning to their homes with the promised hangovers.

HISTORICAL NOTES

The major historical events of this book are accurate, although how they might have happened are fiction on my part. Those details are lost to us. My primary references were *Trajan Optimus Princeps* by Julian Bennett, and contemporary historians Dio Cassius' *Roman History* and Lucius Flavius Arrianus' *Parthica*. The Roman order of battle is pretty accurate, including the surprising two-thousand-mile redeployment of *Legio XXII Primigenia* from Germany, although their actual employment in the course of the war is uncertain. Therefore, I created a credible, though fictional, battle plan.

The *VI Ferrata* did in fact fight in the Armenian highlands on snowshoes. I took the liberty of including the *XII Fulminata* in this effort. I am certain that they did not fight with traditional tactics, and it is credible that they would have operated more as special operations teams, as described. Again, the details are lost to us.

Hadrian's adoption was in fact quite irregular, signed by Trajan's wife Pompeia Plotina and therefore potentially invalid by Roman law, had it been challenged.

The war with Parthia ended with the massive uprisings in the eastern provinces as described, leading Hadrian to withdraw troops from Mesopotamia. It is quite plausible that Ctesiphon induced the Jewish elements in those provinces to take the lead in these insurrections.

Mithridates, who began his literary life as a fictional character in *The Eagle and the Dragon*, turned out to be the historical brother of King Osroës, later taking the throne as Mithridates IV.

Made in United States
Orlando, FL
26 December 2024